WAR'S END SERIES

WAR'S END

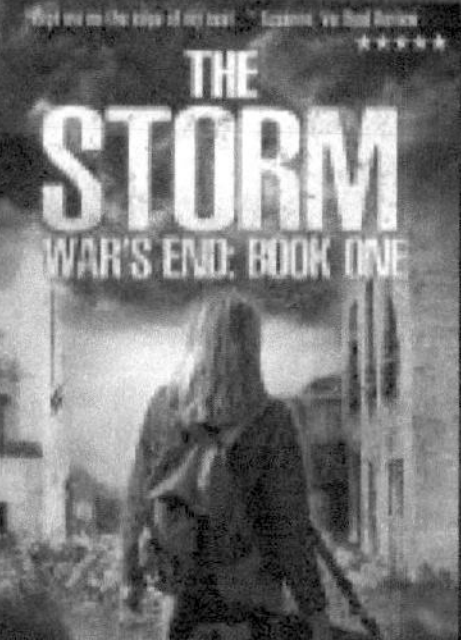

A BRAVE NEW WORLD

WAR'S END: BOOK TWO

CHRISTINE D. SHUCK

TALES OF THE COLLAPSE

WAR'S END: BOOK THREE

CHRISTINE D. SHUCK

CHRISTINE D. SHUCK

War's End Omnibus

Books 1-3

By Christine D. Shuck

Dori, Rachel, and Kate - the teachers at Independent Learning School who acceded to my whiny requests and allowed me to write instead of slog through the boring old Warriner's grammar books. Learning through doing has always been my style, and you helped plant the seeds for the writer that I became. I remain eternally grateful.

Dave, the dog to my cheetah. You really are the best of all of my husbands. Or, as you like to remind me, my final husband!

My children - two born to me, three through a former marriage, and three more through fostering. I've learned from each and every one of you.

Those I have loved and lost - Mum, Nana, Baby Bean, Briall

Everyone else - you know who you are - thank you for being a part of this grand adventure called life!

"Kept me on the edge of my seat..." Susanne, Verified Review

★★★★★

THE STORM

WAR'S END: BOOK ONE

CHRISTINE D. SHUCK

And So It Ends

"We overstayed our welcome. We bullied, we pushed, we invaded... and when we were done, when the world had felt our presence in every corner, felt our hands on their backs, shoving our way into every aspect of their lives, faiths, even their very existence... we were hated. God, they hated us. In retrospect, I can summon no actual surprise for what happened next. Our time had come. For our hypocrisy, for our crimes, we each paid such a terribly high price. The world we had known, the nation that our parents were told to be proud of, a place of fast food and 'freedom fries,' home of the consumer, center of capitalism, world leader, it all ceased to exist. It was a slow, painful end, an extended death rattle, as we slowly tore ourselves apart, and then allowed others to finish what remained.

What was left in the wreckage of the world that was? We were. And this is our story, my story, and the story of us all. We have survived. We have lived on... in a world where ghosts haunt us and memories whisper in our ears. Life continues, one day at a time, and by the skin of our teeth and the force of our will, we will continue. What else can we do?" - Jess's Journal

On "Black Monday" - the long-faltering United States economy collapsed into complete chaos. In the past few years, state after state had found themselves out of money and out of options. The federal government stopped promising bailouts and instead preached "state independence" and "more autonomy." Road projects and other public works halted, and it left hundreds of thousands of state and federal employees holding worthless checks.

Abroad, things moved quickly as well. Quietly, without fanfare or publicity, American troops withdrew from the Middle East and Asian conflicts. In some places they left under cover of night, a stark gaping hole left in their absence. Iraq and Afghanistan dissolved into civil war within days of being abandoned, while their neighbors looked on and tried to decide how to fortify their borders and contain the violence while also profiting from the conflicts.

Where had it all begun? Some said it began with OPEC no longer honoring the decades-long agreement to set prices and sell their oil based on American currency. Others claimed the beginning of the end came with China demanding payment in yen, not United States currency, on the billions in debt the United States owed it. Still others pointed far back to the strategies put into place after World War II that transformed the United States into an economic and political world power and consumer nation.

However, it began, it was now crashing down in ruin. The United States had overextended itself and the future of its citizens, financially and politically, in the hearts and minds of people throughout the world. From the not-so-benign foreign policy, to the endless wars waged in the Middle East, our country, once hailed as a world leader, became a mindless bully. We were the tyrant, the monster at the door. Where there had once been handfuls of money to seemingly any country that asked, now there was only debt and abandonment.

The militias that disappeared underground or forcibly disbanded in the mid-1990s came back with ferocious fervor. Perhaps they had never really left. But everyone from the Luddites to the Neo-Nazi to small bands of survivalists was forming, each seeking to put their own unique vision of how the world should work into action. And with those thousands of voices clamoring for different methods, different approaches—combined with the financial collapse from within, abandonment by the rest of the world and foreign banks screaming for payment — these things brought one of the most powerful nations in the world to its knees. It heaved a great sigh and quickly came apart at the seams. The federal system collapsed first, then the states, breaking into chunks of territories, areas full of in-fighting and instability. Among the military factions, abandoned by their government, rose a dangerous and powerful network of former soldiers in the West. They called themselves the Western Front.

Consisting of units from Fort Pendleton and Fort Irwin and picking up odd assortments of the militaristic militias along the way, the Western Front tore its way through Nevada and Colorado. Their numbers ebbed and flowed, but as more and more of the basic infrastructure of the country broke down, their power in numbers and weaponry increased.

They looked to the east and rumors spread that they would soon be on the move.

Jess was twelve years old on Black Monday, and Christopher was fifteen. But they both remembered that day, just as their parents before them remembered the fall of the Twin Towers or the day they shot President Reagan. Mom lost her job two months before after the latest layoffs, and Dad headed home after sitting around for half the day. No business, no customers, no one out on the streets. As if a death knell sounded, those still employed, those who still had jobs and places to go to, suddenly found themselves at home, wondering what would happen next. That evening they watched the television in dull shock as the President held a press conference to announce that all debts, foreign and private, were to be held void. The British, heavily invested in American banks, were already threatening embargoes. The Chinese had been rioting for weeks over the trade/import issues, and their government was making threats that continued to grow in clarity and intensity.

The world fell apart. Jess's parents said little, and in the months and years that followed, they simply tightened their belts, planted gardens, began raising chickens for eggs and meat, and got by on less. As the infrastructure continued to collapse, utilities and out of area supplies faltered. First there were the brownouts, just a lull in the electrical flow that rarely even caused the computers to reboot. Later there were blackouts, first for a few minutes and finally hours and even days at a time. The price of natural gas spiked so high that Jess's father, Michael, installed a wood-burning stove in the living room against the west wall. It was a prized antique, but it was also an honest-to-goodness working stove and Jess's mother Tess experimented with it regularly, churning out loaves of bread that slowly transformed from inedible black carbon, to uneven half black half browned to beautiful, perfect loaves over a course of a few months. "The pioneers did it," she said proudly, "and I can too!"

But the real Black Monday, the one that came on November 4th, was the one that tore apart Jess' world. And when it was over, when the Western Front troops tore through the small town of Belton, with barely a hiccup of resistance from its terrified residents, destroying any who even dared fight back, Jess learned what actual loss felt like.

In the camps, miles to the South, weeks of marching later, and hours of standing in line at gunpoint, she found herself thrust into a tent. There was a long folding table, three men seated behind it, with several checklists on the battered folding table in front of them.

"Name?" one of them asked, barely looking up.

"Jessica Aaronson." She replied. The second man ran his finger down the lists. "Age?" he asked, bored.

"15."

"Parents?" he asked.

"Daniel and Julie Aaronson." He scanned further, finding nothing. "Any other relatives?"

"My brother, Christopher Aaronson." She tried to stay calm. There were so many people here, so many places they might be. She had been just a few miles away at the store, buying flour and haggling with the store owner, Michael Banks, over the price of apples when the troops came barreling in. Hearing the shots and the tank, Banks pulled a weapon from a hidden place behind the counter. The invaders shot him the second they saw the rifle in his hands. His blood still stained her shirt. For three days she searched desperately for her family as armed men kept the bedraggled, exhausted groups of prisoners under close watch.

The second man found nothing in his lists. He shook his head at the third, who was eyeing Jess in a way that made her skin crawl.

She shivered. It had rained earlier while she stood in line, and she was wet and cold, filthy, and scared. Far too terrified to even care that she had eaten little more than a handful of food in the past few days. Where were Mom and Dad? And Chris? Where the hell was everyone? Belton was not a big town, but not that small either. Jess saw only one neighbor she recognized, Mrs. Dillon, from down the street.

The third man smiled widely at her discomfort. It was an evil smile, full of malice, and Jess shivered in her damp shirt. "Well, she's available for assignment then." He wrote her name down on his list, and checked the Troop Entertainment box and turned to the guard, "Take her to Tent Five." As the trooper took her by the arm and led her away, she could hear him call to her, "I'll be by later to see how you've settled in." He laughed then, and it wasn't a pleasant sound. She heard him snap out "Next!" for the man next in line to step forward.

Her feet slipped in the mud and the trooper kept a firm grip on her arm, practically dragging her along. Mrs. Dillon was there in line. "Did you find your parents, dear?"

Jess was in near tears. "No, Mrs. Dillon. They're taking me to Tent 5; please see if you can find Chris or my mom or dad, please!" She broke into tears then, partially from the painful grip the soldier had on her arm, partly from absolute terror. What the hell was Tent 5?

Behind her, Mrs. Dillon stood stock still, her usually impeccably groomed gray hair in disarray. Strands of gray stuck out from her bun wildly, waving in the late fall wind. A young boy, clad in an oversized, stained blue and red Western Front uniform, stood nearby. He smirked as he watched the girl being dragged away. The old woman turned to him and took a hold of his sleeve. He was barely fifteen, if even that. She shook his arm and demanded, "Where are they taking her?"

"Lemme go, lady!" he wiggled, and the guard stationed nearby leveled his rifle and yelled at her to get back in line.

"Where are they taking her?" she persisted. "What's Tent 5?"

"That's the whores' tent, lady. She's gonna be 'tainment for the men."

Her grip loosened and her eyes widened in horror. He grinned at her maliciously, showing a mouth full of tobacco-stained and twisted teeth.

His tongue darted out to lick his chapped lips. "She gonna 'git it good too." He pulled free of her hand and gave the shocked old woman a hard shove. "Now 'git back in line."

Then the boy spit a long brown stain in the dirt, marking the old woman's shoe with tobacco juice as he walked away. She just stood there, trembling, tears of pity trickling down her lined face. A small, thin, ugly girl behind her in line leaned close and whispered,

"Welcome to hell."

Mrs. Dillon didn't have long to wait. A mere ten minutes later and it was her turn before the three seated men.

"Name?"

"Esther Dillon."

"Age?"

Her lip quivered, "I'm sixty-eight years old."

"Family?"

"Only my husband, Murray, and he died last year."

The second man didn't even bother to look up, but the third man did. And with a cold smile, he simply scribbled her name, checked the Range Disposal box and nodded to the guard. "Take her to the range."

The old woman went quietly. Most of them did. If anyone was paying attention, which they weren't, they would have heard the single shot ring out a few minutes later. She was the tenth one that morning.

Welcome to Hell

"There are those who prey on fear. It isn't war that makes them evil; they are already brutal and sadistic by nature. War simply gives them some level of freedom to do as they will, to act on their deepest, darkest desires."—Jess's Journal

Tent Five was large—larger than any of the other tents in this muddy hell. It sat apart from the others and the only way in or out was ringed with wire. They pulled the main entrance flap to one side. It was dark inside of the tent, and men were entering and leaving. A handful turned to assess the new piece of ass being hauled in.

Jess had tripped twice, slipping in the mud and it caked the front of her jeans, her free arm, and part of her shirt since the soldier had not even paused, just dragged her along until she regained her footing enough to trot unevenly next to him. Her arm was on fire where the soldier gripped it and she felt certain there would be bruises from his relentless iron grip.

Abruptly, just inside the tent flap, they came to a halt. The tent appeared to be a rabbit warren of halls and partitioned rooms. Jess heard a woman screaming, no, at least two, and the unmistakable sounds of sex. Oh God. Oh God, oh God, oh God. Her heart pounded faster. She stood stock still, listening to the sounds and realizing... knowing what kind of place Tent 5 was.

The soldier holding her arm felt her stiffen beside him, looked over at her and likely read the spark of fear on her face, the understanding in her eyes. He waited a moment, even loosened his grip slightly... the half-smile on his lips betrayed his dark amusement.

Seconds ticked by, three, four, and on the fifth second, she pulled hard and jabbed left with her elbow, backpedaling to make a run for it. Her elbow jab missed. He expected it. The soldier kicked her legs out from under her with one ruthlessly efficient maneuver. He sneered down at her; and Jess felt stupid. He had known she would try, and he had even let her try to escape, just so this very thing could happen. The mud was cold and slid up her shirt. She tried to hit him and that earned her a powerful punch, which he delivered to her nose before her body had even hit the ground. Her head thudded on the ground and Jess fell limp.

What the soldier had not prepared for was the knife that had mysteriously appeared in her hand. She had grabbed it from the sheath as she fell. Her eyes snapped open, and she slashed the back of his right knee, cutting deep as he fell to the ground. Bitch! She turned onto her belly, scrambling from him, stumbling to her feet, blood streaming from her nose from his punch, and ran... straight into the arms of two soldiers heading into the tent.

This time, when they knocked her to the ground, she stayed there. The wounded soldier levered himself close enough and attempted to choke her with his hands.

The other men laughed as they pulled him off of her, "You'll get your chance to get her back, Robbie, you dumb bastard, just as soon as you get patched up!"

And with that, the medics arrived and helped him limp away, and Jess lay on the ground, afraid to get up, bleeding from her nose and mouth now, and listening to his furious howls as they headed for the hospital tent. The soldier kicked her in the ribs, hard, and she gasped in pain.

"That's for Robbie. Now you stay there until we say you can move, bitch." She only had a view of his boots, but Jess was sure he was grinning.

A third set of feet approached from deep inside the tent. "Who do we have here, Cooper dear?" the voice was neither male nor female, it defied placement. Jess was tempted to turn and look up at who had spoken but she feared the sadistic bastard standing over her would give her another kick.

Cooper was tall with jet black hair and pale blue eyes. "A new whore for you Carmen," he replied, "And she's a feisty one." He reached down and hauled her to her feet effortlessly. Her head pounded in pain as saw that Carmen still defied description. Man, woman—the creature defied identification. And their expression was utterly heartless as well.

"Hm... rather dirty, aren't you? Didn't your mummy and daddy teach you not to roll around in the mud?" Carmen looked down his/her nose, vaguely amused. "Strip her clothes off, Cooper."

The soldier holding her grinned and pulled her closer against him, groping her breast, squeezing it painfully. The second man unsheathed a long hunting knife. Jess accepted the hopelessness of her situation. If she struggled, she doubted they would stop from cutting her with the vicious thing. As it was, they made quick work of it; Lieutenant Cooper looked disappointed at her lack of struggle. They took it all off, and Jess stood there shivering in the cold air. Without clothes, she couldn't leave the tent. If she provoked them, they would rape her right here, maybe even beat her some more, even kill her.

Stay alive. Wait for the moment. All this, ALL THIS will pass—she counseled herself silently—she held back the tears, and endured their taunts. They would grow bored, want someone more entertaining. Wait. Wait. Wait for the moment. And before she knew it, the Carmen creature dragged her towards crude showers.

Her composure was brittle. It survived the ice-cold water being dunked over her head; the brush scraped roughly against her rapidly bruising skin. Carmen's long nails cut into her skin as she dragged Jess dripping down a short hall, through a curtain, and into a room with a filthy bed in it. It did not survive, however, what happened next.

Carmen was strong. They shoved Jess to the bed and before she could fight back or jump up, Carmen grabbed one wrist and secured Jess to the bed frame with a pair of handcuffs. Lieutenant Cooper was the first one through the door, brushing past and already pulling off his belt as Carmen exited and announced, "She's all yours, boys!"

And hours later, when the men had used her violently, laughed at her tears, and came inside her with satisfied grunts, one after another after another—she lay there in shock. She had blood on her thighs, bruises on her arms and legs. She ached from deep inside in her bones and wondered if Hell could be worse.

Time to Go

"There are moments when all of it is too much, too painful to remember. Yet then I look around at those who I love and realize I would not be here, with these people who I love and who love me, if those awful things had not happened to me. How do you reconcile that?"—Jess's Journal

It was time to go.

Mom and Dad weren't there. Chris wasn't either. No kind words from any familiar face, only the soldiers, young, old, smelling like they'd never showered, hairy, smooth-skinned—all of them on her, using her.

After a while, her body had grown used to it, even if her soul could not. The soldiers, those who laughed at her fear and pain, they now bored with her lack of response and chose other girls. The same men who sought out the newly caught girls or ones who never learned to deal with the abuse—these men were the worst. They took an evil joy out of it; while many of the others came only for the simple release of sex. Some of the men might even have been nice. One or two she even caught herself thinking that she would have dated them, been interested... but never in these circumstances.

She'd tried to be brave, but the first days had hurt so damn much. Some of them laughed at her tears or, like that awful Lieutenant Cooper, found a perverse pleasure in her fear and pain. He visited her day after day, taking his time to hurt her in new and unimaginable ways. Cooper was a regular at Tent 5. He seemed to prefer blue-eyed blond girls and Carmen, the gravel-voiced, angular, androgynous director of Tent 5, seemed eager to give him whatever he wanted.

After all, he was moving up in the ranks. Cooper recently came to Granger's attention and been made second lieutenant. Giving him what he wanted meant he would keep Carmen well supplied with coke, meth, whatever the Western Front troops managed to turn up on their raids.

Jess submitted to all of them. She did not resist, not at all, not after those first few days. Getting punched or kicked hurt like hell, so she did her best to avoid it. She let her eyes go dead and her body limp. As the days passed, most of her bruises faded and disappeared. They watched her close at first, especially that awful creature, Carmen, waiting for her to try to escape again.

"Keep myself fed, so I'm strong. Find clothing. Find a weapon."

She ate everything they gave her, but slowly, so it would seem as if she did not have much of an appetite. That wasn't hard to fake. The food was terrible and, on many days, she felt sure she would die in this awful place. Many girls did, some due to abuse, but usually by their own hand. Twice in the last month she had seen the soldiers pull girls out in the morning, past the others, their bodies stiff and eyes fixed and staring, having figured out how to escape the camp by some ingenious method of suicide.

In a way, she envied them. It seemed easier somehow, instead of dealing with each day's new horrors. A month ago, as the camp moved through a new area, devastating some new town and rounding up the residents. They sorted through them much as the residents of Belton, Jess's hometown, were sorted through.

One of them, a young teenage girl, fought back. She had actually managed to kill one of her rapists, her hidden knife sinking home high in his leg, the femoral artery, and he bled out in seconds. They spent the next five days raping her. Afterward, they cut her throat and left her naked body lying there on the icy ground as the camp moved on.

Twice the camp moved, marched for days on end. Twice Jess watched carefully for an opportunity for escape. Two other girls had tried; bullets tore through them before they made it fifty yards. It was a good lesson - fail to escape, and you did not get another chance.

Jess stared with dead eyes at the landscape of the encampment as she slowly ate her food. Each day, she would sit at the table from a different angle, studying the details without moving. She did this with little movement and no obvious curiosity. To anyone watching her, it would appear as if she did not really notice her surroundings. Tent 5 was close to the center of the camp. The mess tent just a short walk away. The men's showers sat to the north, but they saw little use since it was been far too cold. The latrines sat to the south this time. Thank goodness for that. In the last camp, a couple of idiots by the name of Easter and Burton had dug them to the west of camp and the wind had blown their foul stench over the entire camp for several miserable weeks until the camp moved on.

Jess knew what she needed to do. She didn't question it, didn't mull over it, one way or the other. She was going to live... or kill as many of the soldiers as she could before dying.

After weeks had become months, they had stopped watching her as closely. One of her 'visitors' had dropped a knife, a tiny Muela still in its sheath. He had never visited again, nor reported the loss, most likely because he had died in a raid two days later. The knife was small, and fit in Jess's hand as if it were made for it.

As she lay on the bed, listening to the stirrings of the surrounding camp in the pre-dawn darkness, Jess resolved that it would have to be at night, and soon. The moon was new and the darkness would help hide them.

Them... it was no longer just her that needed to escape. Her friend Erin was in Tent 5 as well. She knew which room Erin was in and how to get to her. She had almost let her composure slip when she saw her best friend hauled in two months ago. Erin had been with her family, visiting friends in Clinton, when the Western Front blasted through Belton. Jess thought of her best friend often, hoped that she was safe, and wished she had gone with her on the trip.

She showed no reaction to Erin's calls to her, not even turned and looked in her direction. Instead, Jess sat at one of the battered tables with several of the other girls, and continued to chew on the half burned, half raw meat, and Jess's long blond hair falling down in a tangled curtain around her face. She felt several sets of eyes on her as Erin screamed her name.

Let them think she was catatonic. Let them think her so messed up inside that nothing affected her anymore. Let them think of her as a piece of furniture. Furniture does not think, it does not scheme, and it sure as hell does not even try to escape. Furniture is there to be used and then ignored until it comes in handy again. How she hoped that is what they thought of her now. Because if they did, then they would not know what was happening until it was too late.

Her lack of response seemed to satisfy the guard. He was tasked with watching the handful of girls eat their meal. The other girls looked over at her, barely interested, several of them glassy-eyed from drugs begged off of the men. Jess saw what the drugs did and alternated between coveting them and hating seeing what they did to the others. It took some of the pain away, made them not care about being violated every day. It also slowly transformed the girls. From what Jess saw, they were the walking dead, not her.

It had killed her to listen to Erin's screams later that morning. She would have given anything not to hear her friend's pain. She even prayed to an indifferent God to strike her deaf. It made no difference, and somehow, she felt responsible. Somehow, she would get them out of there, both of them.

The weather remained cold, sometimes bitterly so. The nights remained below freezing and Carmen forced to dole out clothing to keep the girls warm during the cold nights and days. Socks, but not shoes, were allotted. Jess contrived to steal an extra sock here or somehow 'lose' a shirt. She slowly worked at the hole in the bottom of her mattress until it was open just enough to hide the extra clothing. Without shoes to protect their feet, they would need as many layers of socks as they could squirrel away. The extra clothing would help keep them warm on the chilly nights.

Fortunately, the clothing was the same as the Western Front uniforms, an oversight on the part of Jess's captors that might help her to be less conspicuous when she and Erin made a break for it. There was no way she would leave without her best friend. They would escape or die together. It was the least she could do.

The handcuffs had stopped Jess from escaping long ago. She had tried everything, bent paperclips, a nail, but nothing would budge the locking mechanism. The solution to that problem came in the form of a visit from Allen Banks.

Last evening, just before the camp settled in for the night, Allen had come to her room. Allen was a few years older, also from Belton; he had been in her brother's grade. He used to visit their house often since his grandparents lived just a few blocks away. During the long summer months, he made a regular appearance every four or five days.

He would arrive at the house, red and sweaty from pushing his grandpa's old-fashioned lawnmower over his grandparent's large lawn. Allen had always been a bit on the chunky side, and she barely recognized the slim brown-haired man who pushed aside the curtain flap and advanced toward the bed.

He came in, said nothing and neither had she, neither of their faces betraying any recognition. He climbed on top of her, and leaned in as if he were kissing her neck as he whispered in her ear, "Jessie, a big storm's rolling in tomorrow, next day at the latest," he pressed something into her hand, "Get the hell out of here. Head west. Chris is alive. We will join you if we can, but they watch us even closer than they watch you. When the time comes, you leave, and don't you dare look back or wait for us. Got it?"

She gave a small shudder in response, and he knew she had heard him. His lips brushed her cheek, hesitated for a long second, then pressed fiercely against hers for a moment. It startled her, just as much as the change in his tone did when he sat up and slapped her thigh. "This little bitch is the most boring piece of shit I've had in a long time. Carmen! Get me something that doesn't lie here like some damn log!"

Two other men passing by the open flap laughed as Allen strode out to join them. Jess snuck a peek at the piece of metal in her hand—an honest to God handcuff key! She quickly shoved it out of sight. Later, she hid the handcuff key in the hole in her mattress.

Chris was alive! She composed herself before her face gave her away. For the first time in months, she began to hope. Allen's kiss still burned on her lips. The key would set them free.

Each night, before Carmen went to sleep, she made the rounds and made sure each girl's handcuff was tight around one wrist and secured to the bed frame. By that time, the camp was dark and quiet, with guards posted and the rest asleep. Jess waited in the dark, eyes wide open and staring, body tensed, until she was sure anyone nearby was sound asleep. She fit the key into the lock, released her sore, scabbed wrist from its captivity and crept quietly through a hallway to reconnoiter.

Two guards and a shift change every four hours. The entrance was the only way in or out of the tent. Unless... Jess thought of the knife she had squirreled away in her mattress. Would it be able to cut the tent fabric?

The hardest part of it all was putting the handcuffs back on that night and then lying down to face another day. If she were not ready, completely ready, it would mean failure. Failure meant death, and Jess was not ready to die, not just yet.

It was now late March. Spring and warmer weather were just around the corner. The camp was settling in for the night. No electricity combined with cold nights meant that, after sundown, activity slowed to a crawl. Jess had heard Carmen comment to one of the guards that there was bad weather headed their way. "Looks like there's a hell of a storm brewing. It's coming in from the West fast and hard. We'd best get all the girls secure now before it hits." They turned away two soldiers who complained loudly until one soldier's hat blew off his head and he ran after it. The lone soldier, with no companion to back him up, sulked away.

Night came early, with black storm clouds leading the way, blocking the weak afternoon sun. The wind was beginning to howl, tearing at the tents, forcing the soldiers to damp the campfires for fear of sparks. There was little visibility, and thunder boomed in the distance.

Jess closed her eyes, waiting for the sound of footsteps to die away and darkness to descend. If only they could get out and away before the light show rolled in. She waited long moments, her ears straining for any man-made sound above the wind and patter of rain on the tents. The canvas buckled and shook. It was noisy. That was good, better to hide any sounds she and Erin might make.

At last, when she had satisfied her fears that Carmen and the guards had settled for the night, she slipped the tiny key out of the hole in the mattress and it into the handcuffs. "One... two... three" [click]

The handcuff came loose from her wrist. She sat up quietly, heart pounding, turned and reached for the other handcuff in the dark and quickly opened and removed it from the bed frame. It didn't seem like much of a weapon, but who knew when it might come in handy. She slipped it into the pocket of the shirt she had 'liberated', reached again into the hole in the mattress, pulled out the three pairs of socks and slipped them over her feet. Three tiny, stale rolls of bread followed the handcuffs into her pocket. Food was food, and this bit was better than nothing.

Finally, she pulled the thin blanket off of the bed, taking a moment to fold and roll it into as small and easily transportable bundle as she could. As she stepped into the long corridor, Jess's heart was beating so hard that it pulsed in her ears. Outside the tent, the rain had increased its tempo, the wind howling mournfully. She trembled as she stood in the narrow corridor. She had watched, listened, and she knew exactly where Erin was. She had counted the steps herself when they escorted her to the showers and back. "Just eighteen steps," she counseled, "just eighteen steps, you can do this." She forced herself to move forward, counting each step and knowing, even in the pitch blackness of the corridor, that if she reached out, her hand now extended directly into Erin's room.

Her eyes were straining for any light, but there was none, so Jess closed them and envisioned the cot and its placement and moved towards it from memory. "Just one more step," and she felt the side of the bed against her left hip. Now for the tricky part—how to wake Erin without causing her to scream or make any noise that would wake the others?

She reached out with her left hand and felt for her friend in the dark. She touched hair and felt Erin rouse and begin to tense as she shook off the sleep and realized there was someone standing over her. Jess bent close, "Erie, it's me," she whispered, using her childhood nickname and hoping to God the storm was loud enough to ensure her voice didn't carry to any others.

Her friend began to shake and sob quietly, found Jess's hand and grabbed it tightly. They hugged each other, both crying. It had been so hard for her to ignore her friend, to pretend to not see her. Erin released a small sob, "Shh, it's okay, we're getting out of here tonight," Jess whispered in her friend's ear and patted her friend's back with her free arm. Once Erin had calmed down enough to let go of her hand, Jess quickly undid the handcuffs and freed her.

She sat on the edge of the bed and carefully removed a pair of socks, pushed them into Erin's hands to put on and stripped the bed of its two thin blankets. Then she crept over to the outer wall of the tent and waited for a loud gust of wind and accompanying thunder to begin stabbing the canvas with the little knife. It took a long time to tear a hole in the thick fabric despite the sharp blade, but the girls took turns as Jess explained in a whisper about Allen's visit and the idea of using the storm as cover for their escape.

The rain was now drumming down on the tent, causing various drips where there were holes or thin, worn areas in the thick canvas roof. The girls worked as quickly as they could, their wrists aching from the effort and their knees sore and cold from kneeling on the floor. They had to get out and as far away as possible so that their tracks were washed away by the rain.

Finally, the hole in the canvas was big enough to fit through. It would be a tight squeeze. Jess grabbed Erin's hand and pulled her close, gave her another quick hug. "You ready?" she could barely hear her friend whisper yes over the now near-constant thunder, "Okay. Here is what we're going to do. Climb through the hole and then head towards the right. That's the closest cover, in the trees a few hundred yards away. Whatever happens, don't stop and don't let them take you, no matter what, okay?"

Erin simply hugged her back in response, and Jess could feel her head nod in agreement. She grabbed the blankets, gave one to Erin, and kept one for herself. She also handed Erin one of the sets of handcuffs, "Just in case," and then pushed her way through the hole.

The rain instantly drenched them both. It was intense now, and the lightning wasn't too far off in the distance. They needed to hurry. Erin followed; her blanket clutched tightly in her hands. A quick survey around them showed nothing in the blackness. For all that either of them knew, a sentry could be standing next to them. Jess had a firm mental map of the camp; she had taken surreptitious glances each time the girls were marched to the mess tent for their two meager meals a day.

She looked around, squinting through the water that poured from the sky, heavier than a shower, and ice cold. Where would they find Chris and Allen, which tent were they in?

Allen's words rang in her ears. "When the time comes, you leave, and don't look back or wait for us." Tears joined the rain on her face. "Oh God, Chris, what should I do?" Even Erin did not hear her words; they were lost in the violent downpour. She clutched at Jess's arm, too frightened and disoriented to leave without her. Jess had to make a decision.

She grabbed Erin with her free hand and pulled her close, pointing to the line of trees. At that moment, the lightning came closer and lit up the sky to the west, showing the line of forest, the outlines of the tents and no one else in sight. They walked quickly. Jess fought the urge to run. They didn't have much time, but she feared falling on the uneven ground and twisting an ankle. If they hurt themselves now, they would be able to manage a full-out run later.

Every part of them was soaked by the heavy rain and they shook, adrenaline coursing through them. They neared the edge of the camp and Jess caught a flicker of light as a tent flap opened and a sentry stepped out, holding a small penlight. She pulled Erin with her into the shadow of the tent, her heart beating fast and painful in her chest. The man was only a few steps away. He stood there in the rain, facing away from them, his head tilted to one side as if listening for something.

The rain pelted him, rivulets running down his raincoat, and still he stood there. The pale yellow of the flashlight flicked lazily around, dimly lighting various dark corners of the camp.

The girls clutched one another, hearts hammering in their chests, terrified the soldier might turn around. The lightning was now lighting up the sky above the camp. Finally, after what seemed like hours, instead of mere seconds, he grunted, turned the flashlight off, and slipped back into the tent.

They crept past his tent and began to run towards the trees. Their focus was on safety, the cover of the trees, and they moved as fast as the thin socks on their feet would allow towards the line of forest in the distance. Once they reached the forest, their progress slowed, the dense, twisting floor of the forest slowing them considerably. At least they were out of sight of the camp now. Above, lightning flashed, striking a tree at one point just a few yards from them. Jess could feel her hair stand on end and her body thrum painfully as the current passed through the tree and into the surrounding ground. The simultaneous crack of thunder was ear-splitting.

If they hadn't been so busy trying to put as much distance between themselves and the camp, the girls would have laughed at the irony. Running straight into a storm, a lightning storm, and nothing around them but trees! But at least they could see their way through the darkness and rain. The light show ensured that.

Jess would look later at her feet, bruised and scraped and swollen, and wonder how she had not felt a thing as they sprinted through the twists of the forests, falling, getting back up, and simply running with no clear goal except to put as much distance between them and the soldiers' camp as possible.

The storm passed over them and moved east, and they continued to head west. Slowly, the rain relented. Hours later, dawn lit the tops of the trees, slowly filtering down into the damp forest below. By now, both of them were exhausted, filthy, scratched and bleeding. Fear had spurred them through the forest, deep into its core, but the light of the new day, cloudless and barely above freezing, seemed to leach all energy from them. Their run had slowed to a walk and finally to a slow stumble.

"I gotta stop Jess," Erin panted raggedly. "Do you think it's safe to stop for a little while?" Her hair was a mass of tangles, burrs, and twigs. Her face was scratched and there were countless scratches and even gashes on her legs, the blood smeared and dried, where she had fallen when running. Jess thought her friend looked like hell. But then again, she probably did too; she just didn't have a mirror to gaze into.

In front of them was a stream, high and rushing from the night's rain, willow trees on the opposite bank, and solid ledges of limestone lining the east bank. A fallen tree had created a bridge across and there was a nook on the opposite bank, covered with leaves and moss. It looked as appealing as the softest satin covered bed the girls could imagine sleeping in. They both noticed it at the same time and nodded silently, too exhausted to waste their breath or energy on words—yes, it would suffice. They crossed over the stream to the soft, mossy nook.

They gulped fresh water, which had pooled in a crook of a bowl-shaped rock near their feet. Jess marveled at the realization that they had somehow managed to keep hold of the blankets during their panicked escape. Jess pulled one blanket into a semblance of a large pillow and they both sank down against it, lying close to each other and shivering in their damp clothes. The other blanket barely covered them. Minutes ticked by.

"Jessie? They killed my mom and dad." Erin began to shudder, "And then they shot Toby 'cause he tried to stop them from taking me." Jess put her arms around her friend and held her close as the tears fell.

"They're all gone, Jessie, they just killed them and then they took me... and I saw you..." her voice broke, "and I called to you and you didn't look at me, Jessie... not once."

Jess was crying now as well. "Oh Erie, I wanted to! I wanted to stop them, to run then, but I was scared to. I'm so sorry Erie, I'm so sorry!"

And they said no more; just hugged each other close and cried until they were too exhausted to cry anymore. And then the two girls slept. It would be late afternoon before either of them stirred.

The Story of Allen

"*It is the question, the unknown ending, which bothers me the most. When I reflect on the luck of our escape that night from the Western Front camp, that no one saw us or stopped us, I wonder how we did it when so many others failed. I marvel at how lucky Erin and I were, but the questions always haunt me. What happened to Chris? What about Allen? Did they manage to escape? Did they die trying? I hate not knowing. I keep thinking that somewhere out there, my parents might still be alive. That Chris and Allen might still alive. Some part of me is scared too. I'm scared to stop thinking about them. I guess I'm afraid that if I don't keep them alive in my memories, it will be as if they never existed. And that consequently, a part of me will cease to exist as well. —Jess's Journal*

Allen was an only child, on the plump side for most of his eighteen years, with brown hair and kind brown eyes. He had never been outstanding in much of anything, but he was kind and considerate to family, friends, and strangers alike. His favorite person in the world was his grandfather, Thurman Banks, a soft-spoken man with a shock of white hair and brown eyes the same color as Allen's. After old Thurman hurt his knee one spring, Allen had made it a habit to walk over to his grandparent's house and mow the yard with Grandpa's antique push mower. It took a while, but then he would cool off with a tall glass of blueberry lemonade, courtesy of Gram. Later, he incorporated stopping by at Chris's house for a video game or a game of catch.

He would never be as good as Chris at either activity, but his friend was always happy to see him and Mrs. Aaronson would hug him hello and usher him in the front door. She would give him a gentle push towards the basement where Chris and his friend Toby McGowen were usually hanging out. Chris was good-looking, blond and blue eyed. He was the star quarterback on the team and there was talk of a football scholarship, even in these bad times. Sometimes it seemed to Allen that Chris was everything that Allen was not - good looking, athletic, and popular. But Chris was also down to earth and personable. He looked out for everyone, and he had stuck up for Allen, defended him against snipes about his pudgy waist and poorly defined biceps. He had been an honest and true friend since grade school.

Allen would stay for hours, sometimes for dinner, sometimes the night if it was a Saturday. Eventually the phone would ring and it would be Gramps calling to give him a ride home. On the nights he stayed for dinner, he avoided looking at Chris's little sister Jess. Her blond hair fell in waves around her shoulders. Her eyes were straight-out-of-the-Crayola-box blue and, like her brother, she was unfailingly kind. She never played the bratty little sister and would often join them in the basement with her best friend Erin, Toby's sister. They would play endless video games or, in later years, when the power had failed, they would go for hikes and picnics in the nearby woods and parks.

In a way, Allen had always been in love with Jess. She was cute, sweet, and didn't seem to notice that he wasn't as good-looking or athletic as the other guys. She gave him her friendship, and thanks to the sobering fact that she was too darned pretty for him to even dare to ask out, he nurtured his little crush quietly and didn't seek to make it any more than that. He didn't have the nerve to risk rejection, and she was Chris's little sister, after all. He was certain she was oblivious to his feelings, anyway.

Those endless summer nights in Belton seemed so impossibly far away. What he didn't want to remember were the last few hours he had spent in the town of his birth. The soldiers and guns, the fires set to homes, and everywhere people screaming. He still had nightmares of Mrs. Brown crying in the street over the lifeless body of her husband and one of the kids from a block up wailing for his parents.

He had seen his 10th grade Honors English teacher, Mrs. Grady, with half her face burned. She had run from her house as the flames licked up the walls and consumed her roof, only to be cut down in the street by a bullet. She had stood there after the shot rang out with a startled expression on her face. The red stain widened on her white blouse, and she had slowly crumpled to the ground.

Others had been shot when they tried to return to rescue pets, other family members, or possessions. Half of the town had seemed to be on fire, and he didn't argue with the soldiers as they aimed their weapons at him. He put his arms up, submitted to them as they shoved him to the ground and did a rough search of his pockets for weapons. The soldier searching Allen found his wallet, pulled out the cash inside and punched him, hard, when he raised his head to object.

The wallet, now empty of cash, was thrown to one side. His hands were bound in front of him with zip-tie and he was shoved into a large group of terrified residents.

It was the stuff of nightmares, watching your home destroyed, not knowing whether your parents were alive or dead, and that most of what you loved, what you understood of the world, had been changed irredeemably. Jess's parents were among the same group of prisoners as Allen was. Mr. Aaronson stayed relatively calm, struggling to ease his wife's fears, and Mrs. Aaronson was nearly hysterical, worrying about Jess and Chris. She had sent Jess to the store and Chris had taken off early in the day to visit a friend. She didn't know where. The three of them had huddled together as they were marched from town, south on Y, for miles. There were other groups of prisoners, mainly young men and women. The children were sometimes left behind if they caused trouble for the soldiers. This included moving too slowly or crying too loud. By the end of the second day, most of the adults had exhausted themselves trying to carry the children along and avoid a confrontation with the soldiers.

Already, several older men and women had been shot when they fell behind. Rumors flew thick and fast. Someone reported that they had seen the soldiers set fire to the old folk's home and laugh as its aged residents tried to escape, taking potshots at them and those who ran to help. It was brutal, unbelievable, and Allen wondered at what had happened to the soldiers' humanity. They weren't in a foreign land, where the people looked different or spoke a different language. The soldiers were shooting people who looked like their mothers and fathers, their grandparents.

Allen was witness to both of the Aaronson's end on the third day. One of the soldiers, obviously in command of the others, had had enough of the stragglers. When the man pushed his jet-black hair away from his ice-blue eyes, Allen couldn't see a trace of humanity within. Lieutenant Cooper ordered the adults holding the children to put them down and for everyone to start marching. The children were exhausted. They literally couldn't walk any further, and as they fell behind Julie and then Michael both tried to break ranks and help them. The gap between the group of prisoners and the children was widening and the smaller ones began to wail in fear. Allen watched helplessly as the raven-haired, blue-eyed devil shot Jess and Chris's parents. He felt frozen in time and space and the world felt hollow. A skinny, foul-smelling soldier gave him a good shove with his rifle. To help them meant to join them in their fate and try as he might, he wasn't ready to die. He turned away from the bodies, away from the small children grouped there on the road, and allowed the soldiers to herd him away with the other prisoners.

As he marched away, Allen thought to himself, "This is what war does to us. War takes the best part of us away and makes us into something else." He watched those with some speck of humanity left in them turn away as innocents were slaughtered.

The desire for survival is a strong one. And in the end, even kind-hearted Allen valued life more than the moral high ground. What Allen did in the next few days and weeks and months, what he did to survive, would haunt his dreams every night for the rest of his life.

How ironic that, in the months since the invasion of Belton and his own conscription, his weight had melted off, revealing a strikingly handsome profile beneath. Between the marches, the beatings and threats, and his conscription into this bastardized excuse for a company he had lost the baby fat that had followed him so doggedly into adolescence and young adulthood. His arms and legs were now lean and muscled, his stomach tight and flat. The first time he saw his reflection, he pulled back in surprise. A different man, a stranger with haunted and hollow eyes, stared back at him.

The army that he had been forced to join was no army, no company at all. They weren't soldiers, they were terrorists, thieves and thugs, all rolled into one. To save his own pitiful life, he had convinced them he wanted to join. Allen had kicked and beat the other conscripts. He had visited the women in the tents. He had shouted, "Yes, sir!" with the rest of them. He had done all of this in order to live another day.

He had located Chris and carefully found a way for them to meet and plan an escape. They were both still watched, Chris more than Allen, because he had resisted. Allen had found a way to get near him and talk. He picked a fight and lost and got latrine duty. He knew Chris was already there. Then he had punched Chris, yelled at him, talked trash, and after the initial shock, his friend wised up to the act and played along.

They kept getting themselves in just enough trouble to be assigned the dirty jobs no one else wanted. Then they called insults at each other so that everyone was sure they hated one another. He found ways to communicate important troop movements and other news to his friend. Allen was able to update Chris that Jess and her friend Erin were both in Tent 5.

When Chris first heard about it, he nearly screwed it up for both of them. He lost it so badly. The thought of Jess in that awful place had stopped him in his tracks, and he'd grabbed Allen's shoulder in a painful grip. Allen had punched him hard, hard enough to knock his friend down on the ground with a thump. He hadn't said anything for a long time after that, just stared into the distance. Then he'd got up, dusted himself off, and pulled himself together.

Over time, through the bitter cold of winter, they found ways to meet. Sometimes they would find a way to speak while in line for slop, near the showers, or by picking a fight and getting latrine duty again.

Whatever it took, they had to escape and take the girls with them. It was Chris who had managed to get the handcuff key. He passed it to Allen reluctantly. They had argued about this over and over. He wanted to go to Tent 5 and see Jess. Allen knew what would happen. Chris would lose it again and make a scene. He would fight to get her out, and they'd both end up dead. Jess needed out and Allen was going to move heaven and earth to make sure that happened.

Winter was ending and the weather would soon turn from chilly winds to wet, tumultuous rainstorms. He had seen the first green weeds and spring flowers emerging. There had been a patch of jonquils and tulips in the ruins of an old farm just half a day's walk from here. He was sent out as part of a raiding party mid-March and recognized that winter would be over soon, early even, if the increase in vegetation and greenery were any indication. It was his willing participation in that particular raid which relieved any lingering concerns about where his loyalties lay. This freed him to roam freely through camp, which was the next to final step needed towards putting their escape into motion.

The raid, which had included actions that plagued him with nightmares; was a success and he and the other soldiers were rewarded with a visit to Tent 5. He'd been there twice before, once after he'd kicked the crap out of Chris, punching him in the face while slipping the note he'd written to his friend into his front pocket while he lay stunned and bleeding on the ground. The other time was when he kept some poor newbie recruit in line and stopped him from trying a very poorly planned escape attempt. He'd made it look like the kid had been stealing extra rations instead of getting ready to run. He'd saved the kid's life, but doubted the kid even realized it. In any case, it hadn't really helped him that much. A few days later, the boy had made another attempt, and this time no one had bothered to try to stop him. He was shot dead less than ten yards from the tree line.

Allen knew exactly where Jess was being kept, although before this, he hadn't been to her room. Her screams, coming from the opposite end of the tent the first time he had visited the tent, had given him nightmares. The thought of her being used in such a way twisted his guts in knots and he had restrained himself with difficulty from running in, killing that monster Cooper and attempting some stupid and doomed escape. It had been a solid month before he could return and even then, he wasn't sure he could see her like that, so he stayed on the other side and did not attempt contact. Now that spring was coming, with the possible cover of thunderstorms, they could all escape. Footprints couldn't be as easily tracked without snow and ice on the ground.

Allen took a deep breath as he entered the tent, his guts twisting at the sounds that came from this awful, soul-killing place. It had been nearly four months since he had seen her. He steeled himself for it and pushed aside her room flap and walked in. She was lying there, not handcuffed, thank God; they only did that at night now. She wore a faded red Western Front uniform shirt, and she had a thin blanket covering the rest of her. Someone had just finished with her. Allen's bile rose in his throat as the soldier had swaggered past, zipping up his pants. Allen ignored him and held himself back from doing great violence at that moment. It was all he could do not to turn around and grab the guy from behind in a sleeper hold. It would be righteous and satisfying to choke the life out of him.

She didn't recognize him until he had climbed on top of her and leaned in close. In that moment, she stiffened. It had certainly happened before with some of the boys she had known in high school.

They were conscripts, here under the same circumstances as Allen. But as the months stretched out and the distance between Belton and this place grew, they slowly changed. The tent had seen a slow uptick in visits from conscripts. They avoided each other's gaze if they met in the corridors, but shame didn't stop them from coming back.

Her body was warm and soft underneath him. She smelled, damn, she smelled like vanilla and musk. He whispered in her ear about the plan and slipped her the handcuff key. He was embarrassed to realize he had a hard-on, although who would have blamed him? It was natural; she was beautiful and sweet, even now in this terrible place. She was everything he had ever wanted. Maybe after this was all over, when they escaped, with effort he banished the thought and hope of it from his mind. Back to business. It was time to act tough, like he did with Chris in front of the others. He kissed her lightly on the cheek and took one great liberty—kissing her on the lips. Then he had slapped her thigh hard, talked shit, and got up and walked out of the room. It was the grand and dramatic exit, and it had its effect. Carmen, that monstrous and sexless creature, laughed and pointed him down the hall towards another open room.

As he walked away, his hand strayed to his lips, still feeling the softness of hers against his and he realized that the only thing that had stopped him from grabbing her and running like hell for the door was the image of Chris trying to do it and how it would look when he failed. He had done what he could. Now Jess would have to get her and Erin out at the right time. Cross their fingers, cross the toes, and a truckload of luck, and they all might make it out of there alive.

His pretty fantasy of them escaping hand in hand together was shot to hell when Chris refused to head west that fateful night. Instead, he insisted on heading towards Tennessee. "The girls will need a head start, and plenty of time. I'm heading southeast, so hopefully the trackers will follow my trail. There are three others who know we are planning something and want in on it."

Allen did not like the sound of this. Together, they had a better chance of survival. But three new guys he hadn't met and didn't know if he even trusted?

Alone, what would the girls do in the wilderness? How would they cover their tracks or survive? He asked all of these questions and more of Chris.

"Erin knows plenty of survival skills. Her parents were some kind of survival nuts and Toby knew so much he could practically teach the rest of us how to live off the land and survive during any season. The family went camping all the time. Jess has the key. So, she will get them out of there and Erin will keep them fed. Besides," he said, sounding far more confident than he felt, "we just need to do big circles and then get everyone back to Belton. Not everything burned, not everyone is dead."

Allen just shook his head. This was not what they had planned. "I'll head northwest, get back up to Highway 60; hopefully I'll meet them along the way to Springfield. Don't go far into Tennessee, double back, and we'll all join up again."

It was wishful thinking, this plan of theirs. Its success was contingent on so many variables, and each of them had to go just right for success to occur. Despite the horrors of the past few months, Allen and Chris were still young and idealistic. They had no idea just how badly the plan would go wrong.

In the violent storm that followed, the three other men were shot in the back before they ran past the outermost tent on the north. The girls made it out and took off west, straight into the storm. Allen watched as they disappeared into the trees. Their escape was successful. No one raised an alarm until one of the guards had gone looking for something sweet at three in the morning. When he realized Erin's bed was empty of anything but a strategically placed pillow, he had woken the entire camp.

Chris had also run into the night without incident, heading southeast towards Tennessee. Allen had delayed leaving until he was sure no one was following the girls. He was caught the following day as he lay wrapped in a sodden blanket, having passed out under a fallen tree, exhausted from running.

The memory of Jess's body beneath his kept him focused when they interrogated him. He had said nothing when their fists smashed his nose and knocked out two of his teeth. But he had screamed, oh god how he had screamed, as Cooper's knife cut deep into his ankles, ensuring he would never, ever manage to escape again. Or ever really walk. But Allen knew his time was up. They had thrown the dice and while some had won to play another day, he was a dead man. He said as little as possible, grinding his teeth as Cooper cut on him, and finally screaming when the pain got to be too much. He told them nothing, nothing more than they already knew. They knew that Jess, Erin, Allen and Chris had all come from the same small town. In his heart, he nourished the hope that their escape was certain now. It had been three days and no word.

Cooper leaned close, shoved the knife in all the way to the hilt and twisted it back and forth in the deserter's gut. He smiled as Allen's eyes glazed in agony. He figured he had about twenty minutes, maybe thirty, before the little crap died. He took his time, described how he had screwed the little whores, both of them, but especially the little blond one, every possible way, again and again. He promised the boy he would do it again, when he found them, over and over and over, until they were both dead. He was pissed off and frustrated. Kipling would have a cow when he found out that he had knifed this little weasel, but at the moment he didn't care.

Allen knew he was dying. He felt removed from it all, as the pain seemed to fade away. He could smell her still. That sweet, fresh scent as he had laid against her in Tent 5 stayed with him. He cherished that memory, held it close, and ignored the man standing over him.

It pissed Cooper off that the kid took almost 40 minutes to die. He'd never seen anyone hang on that long. But what pissed him off the most is that when the damn fool finally did die, he was smiling.

Forest Refuge

"*I don't know what I thought. I guess it was that, somehow, Chris and Allen would magically appear. As we walked, hiked, and limped in the days that followed, I looked for them, sure they would be just around the next tree. Every creak from a tree, every rustle of leaves, I would jump and look. In my mind, there were only two outcomes—it would be my brother and friend, or it would be soldiers from the camp. In some ways, that feeling followed me all the way home and stayed with me there for years. If I could only turn quickly enough, there they would be."—Jess's Journal*

A high-pitched whine in Jess's ear woke her with a start. Her body ached, burned in places, and her feet were throbbing. Again, she heard the whine in her ear. It was a mosquito, damned early in the season and hungry for what little blood it could find. Jess slapped at it and then stared at the masses of scratches on her arms and legs. What a night it had been—they had been too busy running for their lives to even feel their injuries until now. Erin's eyes flickered open, pupils dilated in fear, her body tensed. She sat up, disoriented and looking around her wildly, "Wh—what? Where?"

"It's okay, Erie, everything is okay. It's just a mosquito come to finish us off." Jess joked to her friend and was delighted to see her manage a weak smile in return. It felt so damn good to have her best friend in the world back. She hadn't had any bad dreams, and despite their bruises and scratches and swollen feet, she felt as if she and Erin were the two luckiest people in the world right now. And then her thoughts flashed to Allen and Chris. Had they gotten out? She imagined a reunion, and then all four of them setting off together and heading home to Belton. She scanned the trees and fear and bitterness re-surged inside her—how could they possibly find each other when Jess had no idea where they were?

It was at this point that her stomach rumbled painfully, making its presence and its yawning emptiness known. Jess looked around, nothing but trees and more trees and the now quiet, gurgling stream at their feet. Her heart plummeted. What in the hell could you eat in a forest?

The sun was slipping down, casting long shadows around them. They wouldn't get far in the dark, not without moonlight, and Jess had timed her escape with just that, and a convenient thunderstorm, in mind. She turned back to Erin, who was now crouched by the stream, digging her long fingers into the mud near the base of a plant that was growing in the shallow waters. A bulrush-like appendage at the top of the stem waved in protest as Erin tugged at the entire plant, pulling it out, roots and all. In a few months, the spear that was just now beginning to emerge would turn to a dark brown. For now, it was a creamy color, barely yellow, new growth responding to the slowly warming temperatures.

Jess just gaped at her friend and wondered if she had gone absolutely insane. "Uh, Erie? What are you..."

Erin turned and shoved the entire plant into Jess's arms. "Clean all the mud off, will you? Take special care getting it off the roots and the inside of the plant. I'll be back."

And with no further explanation, she walked off, headed away from the stream, towards a thick clump of trees. A few minutes later she was back, one pocket bulging, and her shirt held like an apron in front of her, various leaves and flowers sticking out.

"I saw some ferns, but no fiddleheads; I can't wait until we can pick them." Erin looked over at Jess, who was standing there, looking confused, the cattail dripping mud down her arms. "You haven't washed that off yet. What are you waiting for? Aren't you hungry?" she laughed at Jess's confused expression, "You're holding part of our dinner there, and I'm starving." She gave her friend a small shove, "Rinse it off and I'll explain."

If her friend was losing her mind, she was acting particularly calm while doing it. Jess complied, mystified at the thought of eating some mucky old weed. As she rubbed away mud and waited until the water ran clean, Erin reminisced about camping with her family over the years.

"You remember how my dad was, always into the survival stuff." She laughed as the tears sparkled in her eyes, "He used to put on some silly old movie, Red Dawn, and tell us to pay attention 'cause that's how the world would end." She shook her head at the thought, "I just thought he was full of it."

She finished rinsing off the cattail and was silent for a moment, reliving their loss before she shook off the memory and brought her thoughts back to the present.

"We can't eat the fiddleheads till they emerge in about two weeks, and that's a damn shame. They're the best. We usually pick 'em, cook 'em and smother 'em in Cheez Whiz, dee-lish!" She rinsed the rest of the leaves and flowers free of any insects or clinging dirt.

Jess wasn't as sure about their dinner plans. "You sure this stuff won't make us sick? I mean, if it were food, wouldn't everyone eat it?" This earned a giggle from Erin, who handed her a handful of something resembling giant clover leaves.

"It's wild, silly, not like a crop that there are tons and tons of. Eat this, it's sorrel, high in Vitamin C." She stifled another giggle as Jess put the leaves into her mouth and bit down and made a face.

"It's sour!"

"Yeah, well, it's good for you, so eat it." Erin handed her some other leaves. "And I actually found a small patch of dandelion."

"I'm not eating some old weed!"

Erin's smile vanished. "If you want to survive, you will. This is food, Jess, and it's all we've got. I picked up some acorns, but we need to roast them, and I don't think we should risk a fire yet. We need energy to keep moving and get out of this forest and as far away from those bastards as possible." Her face took on a haunted look. "You got us out of that awful place, now I'll keep us alive. Okay?"

Jess nodded. Her friend really seemed to know her stuff. Really, when she thought about it, she was too hungry to care what it was. "Okay, Erie" and stuffed the leaves in her mouth. They weren't bad. They reminded her of the peppery taste of arugula. Her stomach seemed to growl a little less, so whether it was 'food' or not, at least one part of her didn't seem to know the difference.

Later, her hand fell to a lump in her pocket and she retrieved the three stale biscuits. They helped provide some substance to the greens they had eaten, and she and Erin tore into them gratefully.

As they ate, the sun dipped below the trees and darkness fell swiftly. The girls finished their sparse meal and took the last few threads of light to wash their arms, legs and feet in the clear, bracing cold water.

As the darkness enveloped them, they curled into their nest, wrapped their arms around each other, and pulled the blanket close. Within moments, they were both sound asleep.

Soldier Running

"*Courage is not the absence of fear, but rather the judgment that something else is more important than fear.*"*—Ambrose Redmoon*

Chris had run through the night, through the onslaught of rain and lightning. He kept running, heading south. He figured he'd made it at least ten miles. He'd stuck to the roads and figured he could dive out of sight in time if he saw lights. The roads had all been empty. The signs for Route VV had given way to Highway U and Chris saw that he was still heading south when the sun began to clear the clouds in the east. It was cold out and his jacket was still damp, despite the rain having ended hours ago. His pants were damp too, but the rest of him was dry and warm from running. After months of being run from one place to the next, along with all the latrine digging duty he'd been assigned, his body was in perfect condition. But even he had his limits. It was time to stop, rest, and eat some of the food he'd managed to squirrel away in the past few days.

A stand of trees a few hundred yards from the road looked promising. Chris could see several evergreens. All the deciduous trees were still bare, but he could create a nest at the base of the evergreens and be out of sight. He turned off the road, avoided patches of mud that would betray his presence, and climbed over a bent section of wire fencing. He could see a house in the far distance. It had smoke curling from the chimney, so it was occupied, but with only a Western Front uniform on him, he figured his chances of getting shot were far more likely than an offer of food. Perhaps after he'd had some sleep, and it was closer to dusk, he would re-consider his options.

He moved the lower branches of the largest evergreen, hacking at one or two in order to lay a bed of pine needles beneath him as cushion and for some relief from the cold, damp ground. The last few months had prepared him for making do with little. He remembered the first few weeks after the troops had stormed Belton. From the stress and fear as they were herded south, to the hard cold ground he had shivered on each night, he had nearly been broken by sheer exhaustion. Eventually he had learned to sleep whenever he was given the chance, whatever the time of day, and in pretty much any conditions short of a firefight. He knew it would be ten minutes, tops, before he would be sound asleep. Around him, birds were waking up and cheeping at each other. He pulled his pack closer to him, double-checked that his little nest was well hidden, and closed his eyes.

He wondered where Jess and Erin were. God, he hoped they had escaped. Were soldiers looking for them? Tracking them? His family had never been what you would call religious; and their parents had never taken them to church on Sunday. But he figured he would dot his i's and cross his t's and pray, anyway. He closed his eyes, "Please God, let Jess and Erin have made it out of there." Considering what they had escaped from, they needed divine intercession just to survive and not be re-captured. He kept his eyes closed and thought about all of them—him, Allen, Jess, Erin—all of them making it back home. How wonderful that would be. The daydream pulled him in and he succumbed to sleep.

It was the dog that woke him. It sniffed him cautiously, wagging its tail slowly. The sun was slipping down behind another bank of clouds and he could hear rumbling in the distance. More rain on its way. Chris figured that was good, it would keep the signs of his passing to a minimum. The dog sniffing him was a mutt, but she had a collar, so... Oh no, this old mutt was definitely a male. Chris wondered if he belonged to the occupants of the nearby house. He hadn't barked or given away his position, a fact for which Chris was profoundly grateful.

A moment later someone called out, far away, too far to hear a name, and the dog bounded away. Chris lay there, unmoving, certain it would lead its master back to his hiding place at any moment. The minutes ticked by and no one came and darkness fell early as the cloud cover moved in and the thunder rumbled louder.

He slowly emerged from his hiding spot as the last of the light faded. The house in the distance looked old, and he hoped they had a root cellar or a smokehouse. Those were typically separate from the property and often had food stored in them. This late in spring, there wouldn't be much left, but he needed something besides the hard biscuits he had in his pack. Some part of him winced at the thought of stealing. That's what it was. But what would he do after the biscuits were gone? He needed clean water too and wondered if the rainfall had washed things clean enough to risk drinking from puddles. There had been no creeks in sight that morning.

The wind had picked up and he could feel a few remaining damp spots on his pants. It wouldn't matter, if the thunder and the black clouds on the horizon were any indication, he would be soaked again in a few hours, anyway. He walked slowly through the thigh high grass until he reached the edge of a large cornfield. Only stubble remained from last year's harvest. Soon it would be filled with green again. Planting would begin in earnest in less than two weeks.

His thoughts flashed to his family's garden in Belton. By late winter, his mother would be busy setting down detailed instructions for the rest of the family on where to plant and what. He could see her sitting at the kitchen table, gardening books scattered around her for reference. She would have numbered all the raised planters in the yard and marked them clearly. When Dad finished tilling up the dirt and removing the weeds, Chris and Jess were always tasked with planting the seeds according to the diagrams Mom had painstakingly drawn during the last months. He smiled at the thought. She was forever muttering about companion planting and 'crop rotation' as she marked, scratched out, and adjusted for new plants each year.

Before he had found Allen, he had held out hope they were still alive. But Allen had said nothing when asked, just looked at the ground and shook his head. If Jess and Erin hadn't made it out... Chris's stomach roiled at the thought... then there would really be nothing left to return to.

Lost in thought, he had walked the entire length of the field and was now nearly at the house. He could see it in flashes of lightning. It was old, as he had hoped, probably late 1800s. The windows on the first floor were boarded up, and it looked as if one of the outbuildings had burned. The work of the Western Front soldiers, no doubt. He could see pale light from one of the upper windows. It flickered, so it had to be a candle or an oil lamp. Maybe even a fireplace. He remembered seeing smoke curling from a chimney this morning. Dangerous to do so, but the occupants were probably armed, and the troops looked for better pickings in the cities or larger towns when possible, which is probably why whoever lived there had survived for this long without having their home burned with them still inside.

He scouted around carefully, hoping the dog wouldn't bark, and found the root cellar a few yards away from the back of the house. It was unlocked, and he carefully eased the door up and slid in. It was dark as a tomb and he tripped on the uneven stone steps and nearly fell, rapping his shin sharply. It was dry, well kept, and only a little musty, despite having dirt walls. He reached into his pocket, pulled out a lighter, and shook it. It was low, but he needed some light. The tiny flame revealed a surprisingly large room and several shelves were still stocked with food. He saw a variety of home canned goods and grabbed for the first green thing he could find. Green beans by the look of it. He also pocketed three apples, a jar of pickled eggs, and two potatoes. His finger began to burn painfully, and he dropped the lighter and lost the light for a few panicked seconds.

The rain had begun to drum down on the wooden cellar door as he rediscovered the lighter and took one more look around. On the lower shelf was a line of what looked like canned meat. He grabbed one and put it in his rucksack, and headed for the door. It was enough to last him several meals and miles of walking. Survival was survival, but he didn't like the thought of taking from others. He hoped that he could repay them some day.

He held himself back from running as he headed back toward the road. It was stupid and dangerous to run on uneven ground. As it was, he twisted his ankles twice on the way back to the road and soaked one of his shoes completely through when he slipped into a puddle.

As soon as his feet hit blacktop, he turned right and headed south at a slow jog. He had miles to go before he would feel safe about heading back east and finally north towards Belton and the girls. Again, he prayed for their escape. After a short break to eat, Chris followed the road, away from Belton, away from the camp, and into the storm.

Shoes Worn Through

"Without Erin, my God, I don't know how I would have survived. No matter what happened, we knew we had each other, and it kept us going those first few months. Somehow, knowing someone else had been through it, knowing each other as we had all of our lives, it somehow gave us both the drive to wake up each morning and try. You can't imagine how hard it was. Some days I wanted to just lie there and not move, not eat, just hide from myself and the world and avoid life. Everything I knew had been taken from me - except for Erie - oh God, Erie, how I miss you so. Even now, all these years later - I think I will miss you forever."—Jess's Journal

Jess woke to cold. Erin had managed to pull all of one blanket and most of the other completely off of her and as Jess awoke in the cold dawn, her stomach wrenched and heaved. She stumbled to the stream, which had slowed to a sedate pace, and the meager contents of her stomach splashed out onto the rocks. "Jessie?" Erin's sleepy voice broke through the stomach-twisting heaves, "Are you okay?"

"Yeah... yeah... just... peachy," she managed between heaves. Her stomach stopped its awful twisting, and she stood back up, dizzy and still a little nauseous. "I've had this damn stomach flu for the last couple of weeks." She groaned as her stomach twisted again and she didn't notice Erin's narrowed eyes and pinched gaze.

"How long have you been sick, Jess?" Erin's voice was clear of any sleepiness now. She sounded frightened.

"About... oh!" Jess listed back towards the stream and heaved again, "Oh man, this sucks! Um... going on," she bent and retched, "about three weeks now. Why?"

"When was your last period?" Erin persisted.

Jess looked at her oddly. "I dunno, a month, maybe two."

"When exactly?"

"How the hell should I know?"

"Well, do you think it's possible that..."

The fear clicked on inside of her. The pieces fell into place. Worse than the twisting of her stomach or how bad her feet ached. Just the thought of...

"NO! Damn it! I told you I've got the stomach flu. Jesus, Erie, lay off the twenty-questions already!" Jess nearly shouted it, her whole being in chaos. She couldn't be pregnant, not that way. Oh god, oh god, oh god. The panic rose up inside her and she bent nearly in half and retched again. Nothing but bile now. Surreptitiously, her hand reached for her belly, seeking a telltale bulge. Nothing.

Jess looked at Erin, who was staring back at her, concern and fear evident in her green eyes. That they both knew the truth was obvious, but Jess wasn't ready to accept it and Erin saw no point in pushing it.

In the end, it would be evident soon, one way or the other. A long, awkward silence passed between them.

Erin finally broke it by saying, "I'll try to find some food, okay?" She glanced over at her friend—Jess was hunched over on a large rock, staring at the burbling stream. "Even if you need to wait for a while to eat it, you know, let your stomach settle down, it'll be good to have it on hand." She reached out and squeezed Jess's shoulder and walked away quietly, up the hill towards the west, looking for a good north-facing slope to find some fresh greens for them to eat.

Yesterday had been unseasonably warm, which had allowed them to sleep comfortably with little cover or shelter, but today was on target for early spring, chilly morning and cool temperatures. The lingering cold of the night made every body part feel stiff and each bruise and cut was magnified. Her feet were throbbing in pain, and Jess noticed the multitude of sticks and burrs wrapped in the dried mud encasing the thick socks. They needed shoes, and blankets, food and somewhere they could safely hide until the camp was struck and the troops moved farther south into Arkansas. She pulled at the mud on her sock and watched pieces crumble away.

She tried to remember when her last period had been and couldn't. It wasn't as if they had ever been regular. She couldn't think of one since, well, since before they had been taken. Shit. Again, her hand reached for her belly. Wait, it wasn't flat, there was a little bump, firm, not soft. Shit, shit, shit!

And then Jess realized it didn't matter. They would die out here, in the middle of the woods, and the awful thing would die inside her. And that was good. It was nothing more than a parasite, an invader, like the soldiers. She almost smiled in satisfaction at the thought of it dying with her. But she sat there, her ass sore from the ground, body aching, her bruised and swollen feet on fire, and her smile turned down. It was replaced with an almost feral snarl. She felt the anger build inside of her. She wasn't ready to die. Not quite yet. Whatever tomorrow would bring; she was going to live, and to hell with them all.

A quiet voice interrupted her thoughts. "Jess? You okay?" Erin had returned while Jess had sat there deep in thought. Jess could see that her friend had more of that friggin' wood sorrel in her hands that had tasted so bitter, plus other green crap that looked just as unappetizing. Erin looked down at Jess with concern and fear.

"Huh? Oh, hey Erie. Yeah," her body sagged a little, and she relaxed, the snarl vanishing from her face. It was replaced by a satisfied smile. "You know, I better learn more about some of those survival skills you learned from your family. And we have got to find some shoes to wear, these socks won't last long."

Before Erin could respond, she continued, "And I've been thinking about those lakes we passed with the camp. You know the ones to the north? They'd have fish and we might be able to find a boat to help move us along and stay off the highway. If we get just a little more north, we could have a fire, maybe catch and cook something. And you know, I've been thinking..."

Erin laughed and hugged her. Come what may, they had each other and relief at their newfound freedom washed over both girls. Some of the plants slipped from Erin's hands. Jess was okay, she was okay, and the rest would sort itself out in time. They would head north towards the lakes. It was a plan.

They ate the greens Erin had picked, and tried to choke down some more of the tuberous roots, but they tasted and smelled like the muck they had been pulled from. Both girls spat out the roots rather than lose what little food they had in their stomachs. The air was warming considerably, and the sun was steadily rising in the sky. It was time to get moving.

They had come from the east, and now they headed due north, following the creek as it steadily grew in width from the few feet in width where they had camped to over ten, even twenty feet wide, in some places. They gathered plants as they walked, nibbling on them to keep their hunger at bay. There was plenty of wild onion. It grew everywhere, and the girls figured it was a favorite of the deer, since they saw tracks wherever they saw onion and the tops of the green plant had obviously been nibbled.

The way wasn't easy, especially since their bruised feet felt every rock, and branch and bramble. There were no mile markers to tell them how far they traveled that day, but the amount of swearing seemed to increase steadily as the day wore on. Already the sun was beginning to sink in the sky. It wouldn't be long until sunset, and Erin stopped for the umpteenth time to pull a particularly painful twig from her now bedraggled and hole-ridden sock.

Jess was slightly ahead of her, stumbling along, exhausted and swearing, "Godawful trees and forest and freaking nature. What I would give for..." She stopped and stared ahead and across the creek to the east. "Oh my god... Oh my god... Erie! There's a house over there!" Her voice fell to a sharp whisper, suddenly associating a house with people, and the fear that it could be occupied.

It wasn't really a house, more of a hunting cabin. The girls could see it clearly as they made their way over the creek and through the ice-cold water, which soaked their socks and numbed their legs all the way to their knees. Teeth chattering, they edged through the trees, looking around for signs of life. Their ears strained for any sound, but there was nothing but the wildlife.

Down a steep incline, and onto the creaky front porch, it took the girls a moment to find the courage to get past the simple doorknob lock with a few well-placed shoves. The door frame splintered, and the girls peered into the sparsely furnished, one-room cabin. There was a kitchenette on the west wall with a tiny window that looked out onto the creek, and a small curtained-off section in the northwest corner turned out to be a crude bathroom. On the south wall to their left was a twin bed built into the wall, cupboards above and below it, and a small table & chair next to it. On the same wall as the door was a couch that had seen better days and a curtained window above it.

Everything was covered with a thick layer of dust. After days of nothing but hard, cold dirt to sleep on, both Jess and Erin figured they had died and gone to heaven.

Some scouting outside in the rapidly fading light upstream revealed a scattered group of cabins, mostly hidden from view in the trees. The silence was overwhelming; none of the other cabins appeared occupied. Erin noticed that the cabin could have running water once the connecting pipe was lowered into the creek. The sharp decline from the creek to the cabin brought a solid stream of water directly through to the sink. Of course, there wasn't any electricity, but there was a propane stove, an oil lamp with a full bottle of oil, a generous supply of propane, and a treasure trove of canned foods in the cabinets. They also found two fishing poles, a .22 Rimfire rifle, and four boxes of ammunition. Erin closed her eyes in silent thanks for that find.

To their delight, they also found a raincoat that was lined and warm, blankets, and even a pair of shoes. "Here Jess, you try these. They're definitely too small for me," Erin passed the shoes to her friend. The shoes were made of canvas and had several holes. "These shoes are damn near worn through," Jess observed, but she tried them on anyway. "Hey, they fit!"

Erin smiled at her. "Better than socks, even if they are full of holes! So does this mean I get dibs on the bed tonight?"

Jess just nodded, poked her big left toe through a hole in the shoe, and grinned. They shook out the blankets outside and used a worn-out dishtowel to dust most of the thick film of dust away. Judging by the expiration dates on the food and the thickness of the dust, whoever owned this cabin hadn't been there in a long time.

There was nothing to identify who had stayed in this place. The girls both wondered, was the owner still alive? Why had this cabin, as remote as it was, been abandoned?

If this cabin could talk, it would have told the girls about a writer and critic by the name of M.G. Wood, who had owned the cabin and two hundred and fifty acres of land that lay to the north and west. Wood had bought the large property shortly after the first real estate crash of 2008 and had great plans for it. There was plenty of room for a main lodge and a succession of small, simple cabins—a quiet and peaceful writing retreat.

The old man who had owned the property before Wood had built the series of cabins and rented them out during the warm months to hunt and fish. After his death of cancer in 2008, his distant relatives in Brooklyn, New York, were all too happy to unload the property for a fraction of what it was worth. Any money, they decided, was better than no money and an ungodly number of trees and dirt. People actually lived in flyover country? Why?

The real estate slump had been followed by the Great Recession. In late 2012, the real estate 'bubble' become a gargantuan sinkhole as the Alte and Option Arm loans shot up to higher rates. And as the new owner struggled with their own financial troubles, dreams of artist's retreats faded and years passed as the cabin stood alone in the woods, a good fifteen miles from the nearest two-lane road.

That night, Jess and Erin feasted on tuna and a large can of hominy. They ignored the expiration dates. Most of the cans showed dates that were a year or more past, and the food tasted just fine to the girls, whose palates were no longer that discerning. After all, they had eaten next to nothing for the past three days. They drank flat, boiled water by lamplight. Erin had insisted on firing up the stove and boiling all the water before they drank it.

"Giardia, it'll give us the runs, among other things," she said by way of explanation, "so it's a good idea to boil the water before we drink it." After the tiny scraps of wild plants they had eaten over the past two days, and the army rations they had been eating for months before that, their dinner was almost too rich to eat. The light outside had completely faded as they licked the remains of the tuna juice from their fingers, sitting on the floor with the lamp turned down low between them.

It wasn't long before they turned it off completely, partly out of fear that someone would see the light, and partly out of the need to conserve their resources. And the night found them curled together on the narrow bed for both warmth and reassurance. The girls slept, barely stirring, when the wind kicked up a notch and the rain moved in.

A Flight Interrupted

"*Memory is a way of holding on to the things you love, the things you are, the things you never want to lose."—Kevin Arnold*

He was home. It was nippy inside, as if the stove's warmth could not push back the chill of the spring morning. Chris could smell the bread baking, but the house was empty, and no one responded when he called out. The only noise was a truck rumbling by outside and men's voices talking quietly in the distance. Jess's room looked as if she had just jumped out of bed. The bed was unmade and there was a pair of dirty socks beside it. A note on the floor in their mother's handwriting read, "Jess honey, please go to town, take that load of apples and see what you can get of flour and sugar." Reading it, he knew then he was in a dream. Jess had gone to the store that day, the last day any of them had been together as a family. The last day that any of them had been free.

He moved on to his room. It looked just as he had left it and was far more of a mess than Jess's room could ever be. Dirty laundry, unmade bed, and his belongings were scattered about, a maze of clutter on the floor. He was surprised by it somehow.

"I was such a complete slob," Chris muttered to himself. He closed the door and headed for his parents' room. It was empty. The bed was made and his mother's pajamas were neatly folded near the pillow on her side of the bed.

"Perhaps everyone is outside," he thought and headed back through the kitchen to go into the backyard. The bread was baking in the oven and he could tell it was nearly time to pull it out. Over the years, they had all developed a nose for it. Flour was short, so they ate every bit that came out of that oven. If they didn't want burned bread, it was in everyone's interest to keep an eye (or nose) out.

He opened the sliding glass door, and the sun blinded his eyes. He had little time to wonder how morning had turned to late afternoon and a pulsing ball of fire that hung in the west. Dreams held by no standards, they knew no scientific laws or rules of physics. His gaze was drawn to his parents standing there, arms raised in the air. His father looked sad. His mother was scared and crying. Michael Aaronson spoke softly, "Please Chris, don't shoot your mother. Shoot me." Chris looked down and realized the rifle in his hands pointed directly at Julie Aaronson's chest.

"It'll be okay, son. I know they told you to do it. Just shoot me and let your mother go." But the rifle barked out one shot and he watched his mother fall to the ground, blood staining the front of her shirt. His father turned away from Chris, his face set in sorrow, and knelt by Julie Aaronson's body, hands to her chest. Her eyes were wide and staring, and there was a single teardrop on her left cheek. Chris's father didn't seem to notice the blood bubbling over his hands and soaking his clothes. He kissed his wife, then turned back to look at his son, "Oh son, what have you done?"

It was his scream that gave him away and brought the two soldiers to his hideaway. The dream faded and Chris opened his eyes to the sight of a rifle barrel and booted foot. He followed the boot up to a leg, up further to the chest and the scraggly beard and gap-toothed grin of Tim Easter. The bastard looked delighted to find him, "Hey there shit-head, where'd you think you were headin'?" He twirled his rifle around and smashed the butt end hard into Chris's forehead. His head bounced once on the ground and before he blacked out, he heard Easter and another soldier laughing.

Pain. A slow drip making its way from his forehead, down the left side of his head and falling slowly, one drop at a time, from his cheek. It was dark out. But he could smell beans and feel a smidgen of warmth from the campfire. Chris tried to move and couldn't. No surprise there. His arms and wrists were bound behind him. He could feel the bark of the tree rough against his back. Easter was practically growling at the other soldier, one Chris didn't recognize, "You best give me that jar, asshole," he snarled at the other man, "I found it and I'll be damned you gonna eat it all." From the looks of it, the two soldiers were about to come to blows over the jar of pickled eggs they had found in Chris's pack.

Tim Easter was a small man, no more than five foot six, if that. He was skinny, although recently he'd put on a little weight after his stash of meth had dried up. He was still stringy, though, and he smelled bad.

Not just body odor, but that tooth rotting in your head kind of thing. He fingered the holster that held his knife, trying to decide if it was worth cutting the other soldier to get his share of the food back. Chris tried to get a better look at the other man, but when he moved his head, pain lanced through him and he let out a small groan. This earned him the attention of both men. Through the haze of pain, he could see they were both grinning with sadistic delight. He didn't recognize the second soldier at all.

"All right! Our little runaway's waking up!" Easter crowed, looking ready to do more damage. He stood up, the pickled eggs forgotten, and unsheathed his knife. "Y'know, Lieutenant Cooper said to bring you back, but he sure didn't say I had to do it all in one piece."

Chris sneered back at the little man, "Lieutenant Cooper is a psychopath, and you're just his sad little suck-up, Easter." It was stupid to trade insults when he was at such a clear disadvantage. The fist that smashed into his face loosened a tooth and broke his nose.

The second blow knocked him out for the second time that day.

As he slowly regained consciousness, he noted that the jar of pickled eggs was empty. So were the beans. His stomach roiled and his head throbbed. Now he was bleeding from a cut below his right eye, copiously from his broken nose and the earlier cut on his forehead. Chris looked as bad as his head felt.

He spit a small glob of blood out of his mouth and focused his eyes on his two captors. Easter turned back at him, eager to hit him again.

He didn't like fair fights 'cause he never won them. This advantage was more his style. "Wake up and ready for more, you little fuck-wad?" he sneered. When Chris didn't respond, he just smiled more, "Your little sis, now she was always ready for more."

Chris tried to still his response, but his pulse quickened and he stiffened. It wasn't just his blood that was making him see red. Easter grinned over to the other soldier, "Burton, you ever have any of that sweet ass? The bitch was in the second room on the left, she was good at fucking."

Burton spoke up, "Oh, yeah, nice sweet ass. You could tell she liked every minute of it. Shame Coop killed her." Chris's fury at the two had been building to a frenzy until the last remark. He stiffened against the bindings; unsure he had heard right. Easter was watching closely, and he nodded.

"Yep, he strangled those stupid whores, both of 'em. Caught up to 'em the same night as the storm and made both of 'em pay for all the trouble they'd caused. Shame too, 'bout your sister, shit; she was good for at least a few more weeks of screwin'."

Chris lunged against his bindings and felt one of the bindings give just a little. He could hear a hoarse scream of pain, and then recognized that it had come from his throat. Not Jess, oh God, not Jess. He shouldn't have listened to Allen, he should have gone in there, died fighting, anything but let them try to escape on their own.

He howled in grief, "You're lying!" If Jess was dead, then he was all alone, no family, no one to go home to.

Much to Easter's and Burton's disappointment, the news that his baby sister was dead quickly turned Chris's initial anger and denial into shock and unresponsiveness. All of their taunts were met with silence.

He did not move when they kicked him or hit him and he said nothing at all.

Easter and Burton left him tied to the tree all that night, and didn't bother offering food or water.

They had also taken a great deal of pleasure recounting Allen Banks' fate to Chris. He had no idea that Allen was the only truth they told that night. All that Chris knew was that no one who had escaped that night had gotten very far. He was the only one left. Eventually, they stopped talking trash and grew bored. As the fire settled into deep orange coals, the two soldiers wrapped themselves up in their blankets and fell asleep. They were undisciplined, good only for simple missions like fetch and retrieve or securing food and weapons; they didn't think to take turns staying awake to keep an eye on their prisoner.

As the two soldiers slept, Chris worked on a section of the rope, sliding it up and down, up and down over the rough bark of the tree. It was close to dawn when the rope finally broke. He didn't run. He retrieved a knife discarded from dinner on the ground near the campfire. Then he quietly arranged the bindings so that they appeared intact.

Easter and Burton had been tasked with bringing him back to the camp. They would be heading back today. If he ran, they would chase him, and likely bring even more men with them. He couldn't risk it.

Some dark part of him wanted them dead, anyway. That dark part relished the idea of spilling their blood and ridding the world of their filthy, stinking presence. So, he waited, eyes closed to slits, until Burton roused first. The man stretched and yawned and staggered off to the woods to piss, kicking at Easter when he passed him.

Easter cursed and sat up, looked over at Chris and decided to have himself even more fun. He threw his blanket off, stood up and swaggered over to the tree where Chris hunched and feigned sleep. He unzipped his pants and aimed the stream of urine straight at Chris's head. What happened next was so quick, so brutally final, that Easter didn't even have time to scream. As he fell to the ground, blood gushing from his genitals and then, a second later from his neck, he just looked confused. He died that way, on the ground, his simple little mind unable to understand how a man could move so fast when he was tied up.

A few minutes later, Burton's body joined Easter's. Chris stood there for a moment, looking down at the two lifeless bodies at his feet and feeling nothing but a red haze of pain inside and out. Monsters like these had killed Jess. Monsters like these had killed his parents, his friends, and everyone he loved. He dragged their bodies into the thicker forest, as far from the road as he could stand to drag them. He pulled brush, dead tree limbs and leaves over the bodies, returned to the campsite and tamped out the last of the smoldering coals. With luck, no one would find the bodies or the campsite for a long time, perhaps never.

He rinsed his hands and face as best he could in a small stream nearby. He had collected the revolver from Burton, and another knife from Easter. He gathered up all the food that was left, which wasn't much, and stuffed it into a rucksack with a blanket. Burton's blanket had smelled slightly less rank than Easter's, but they were both wretched, stinking things. He picked the lesser of the two evils, hitched the rucksack onto his shoulder, stuck the revolver in his jacket pocket and headed for the small pickup truck they had been driving.

He'd drive it out of gas and then ditch it, it was limited to roads and he wanted to disappear. That meant going on foot and probably cross-country. But for now, he wanted some distance between the bodies and him. If they caught up to him again, they wouldn't bother trying to take him back. After what he'd done to the other two, they'd shoot him on sight and apologize to Cooper later.

The needle on the gas tank showed it was half full. That was good luck, the first in days. Chris figured he could get a hundred, maybe even 150 miles from the truck before it ran out of fuel. As he steered the truck onto the road, Chris took a long look up the road he had come from before he turned and headed south. Home wasn't home anymore. Not without Mom or Dad or Jess. Home was gone, and so was the life he had known. He didn't know where he would end up, but he couldn't go back, not ever.

The faded green pickup headed south, all alone on the road, as the rain started up again.

The Cabin in the Woods

"The cabin we found. It came at a moment when I think we were both just ready to sit down and call it quits. We were hungry, exhausted, and so tired of running. I can still see the sagging, moss-covered roof in my mind's eye. In that moment, and in the days that followed, it was nothing less than paradise. It was a place of quiet and of refuge. Our bodies slowly began to heal; our nightmares and fears quieted some. And in some ways, our hearts began to heal there too."—Jess's Journal

Jess began her day by stretching and, as Erin kicked out in her sleep, falling with a solid, painful thump onto the worn-out wood-planked floor. "Ow!" She inhaled dust and sneezed violently.

Erin shot up out of bed at the noise and cracked her head against a small shelf on the wall above. Dust and books rained down on her. "Ow! Aw, crap!"

Both girls glared at each other, Jess clutching her sore hip, and Erin her injured head, before they began to laugh. It was funny, in a 'Three Stooges' kind of way. They laughed, swore as their body parts hurt even more, and took a good look around. The daylight from the two small windows was weak; outside, the rain had continued through the night. It was now morning, and it showed no signs of stopping. It made a quiet thrum against the roof of the cabin. The trees, which were still barren of leaves, shook back and forth with the strong gusts of wind that rattled the windows. Jess could feel drafts each time it did. It was obvious that the cabin was meant only for summer use.

Without a fireplace or insulation, it was barely livable in the nippy spring nights. It certainly wouldn't be warm enough during a harsh winter. But for the moment, it was shelter, and that was exactly what both girls needed.

There was one sizable leak above the kitchen sink and another directly above the toilet. The one above the toilet had managed to soak the floor all around, and a small rivulet of water angled across the uneven floor and pooled in the center of the cabin near the oil lamp and the remains of their dinner from the night before.

Erin eyed the wet toilet, grimaced, "Damn it, I really need to go!"

She grabbed a bowl from the cabinet near the sink and pulled the curtain closed after her and cursed even more when she realized there was no toilet paper and that the toilet was bone-dry. Her bright idea of catching the drips with the bowl didn't work very well. The water simply splashed out of the bowl and showered her with small droplets, which sprayed in every direction like a fine mist. She set it aside and let the roof drip onto her head, cussing and laughing simultaneously.

"You know, we might as well leave the lid open." She called out to Jess, "It's dripping right over the toilet. At least that way there'll be water in the bowl!" They ended up doing just that.

The small stove generated a little heat, but both girls were worried about making it last, so they turned it off as soon as the water had boiled and split a large can of stew between them. With breakfast out of the way, and the rain still coming down at a good clip, they had little they could do except explore the inside of the cabin. Erin didn't have any shoes to go mucking about in the rain with, and Jess had no desire to explore outside by herself.

They went through all the food—canned, dried and powdered, and estimated how much they had. They were lucky, whoever owned this cabin had stocked it very well. With both of them eating three meals apiece, they had about three weeks' supply of food on hand, all the water they needed thanks to the creek, a rifle and ammunition, the ability to fish, and relatively dry shelter. For the moment, they were safer than they had been in a long time. Jess took note of the dates on the labels. All the food had expired within the past eighteen months, but none of the cans were bulging or damaged. It was probably safe to eat and the previous evening's meal had been edible enough. She wondered what had happened to the owners of this little cabin and why they had never returned to it.

"Erie, you know how to shoot, right?" Jess asked her friend after they finished planning out their meals for the rest of the day.

"Yeah, sort of." Erin replied, "I took this handgun shooting course when I was thirteen. My dad and Toby usually went hunting while I stayed home with Mom or came and saw you, so I don't know much about rifles." She pulled the rifle out of its box and began inspecting it.

"It can't be too much different. Let's see..." Erin began to mutter to herself. She found a tattered manual in the box and began to reference back and forth with it. Soon she was busy assembling components and digging into one of the boxes of ammunition.

While Erin lost herself in the task at hand, Jess kept busy by putting all the food back away and then started up the stove. She boiled more water to make hot cocoa. The yearning for some hot, creamy chocolate running over her tongue was almost painful. The water was running clear and cold from the sink spigot. It was slow and had very little pressure. The fact that it was running at all meant that she didn't have to go out into the rain for it, and that sounded more than okay to her.

The rain subsided and the bright rays of the sun were peeking through the clouds. When the water came to a boil, Jess carefully dissolved the contents of the packets into two freshly rinsed mugs. Erin had disassembled, reassembled, loaded and was now peering through the sights of the rifle as she aimed it towards a wall. "I've got it all figured out," she announced, and then sighed in pleasure as Jess handed her a steaming mug. "So, it's pretty straightforward," she paused and took a cautious sip of the hot chocolate, "Oh, damn, this is good." Her eyes rolled, and she grinned at Jess over the rim of her cup and then noticed the sun for the first time. "Hey, the rain has stopped! Right on, we can go out and take a look around—maybe even do some target practice!"

"We aren't shooting that thing off until we are sure there isn't anyone around for miles." Jess interrupted firmly. "Sound like that carries, you know." Erin looked deflated. "But you can show me what you were doing and hell, maybe we can try hunting something if the coast is clear."

The girls savored every last drop of their hot chocolate and then Erin pointed out and named each part of the rifle, referencing the manual every so often as she disassembled and reassembled it again for Jess's benefit. She took care to show her the safety and explained how to load the rifle and how to aim and then let Jess dry-fire it. Jess paid sharp attention. If anyone came near them, she figured she would fill them full of holes and then ask questions. At one point, she swiveled the gun around, crossing in front of Erin. Her friend ducked, grabbed the rifle, and barked, "Don't ever point a firearm at anyone unless you mean to kill them."

Jess rolled her eyes at her friend, "Erie, ease up, it isn't even loaded!"

Erin just stared back and said, "Jess, always assume a gun is loaded. Always treat it like it is. Otherwise, you'll end up shooting yourself or someone else. My dad knew someone who had owned guns for years. He screwed up one day, thought his gun was empty, and shot himself in the foot. Dad always said his friend was lucky that all he ended up with was a hole in the foot and not the head for being so stupid. So, I mean it, treat it like it's always loaded."

Jess sobered and promised to be more careful and pulled on the raincoat. Erin grabbed a blanket for a little additional warmth and they both headed outside. The temperature was already rising as the skies continued to clear, and considering the sun was nearly overhead, it was also close to lunchtime. Neither of them was particularly hungry thanks to the hot chocolate, which gave the girls time to explore their surroundings.

To the west was a small shed, more of a lean-to really, and it was locked with a sturdy padlock that resisted their efforts to open it. They left it for another time when they could find some solid rock or lever to force it open with and then spotted the overgrown remains of a road. From the look of it, you couldn't even call it a road, merely two ruts carved out of the grass and underbrush and certainly not used anytime recent. Near the lean-to there was a ringed fire pit with two enormous stones situated near it, obviously used as seating. Green blades of grass were growing in the middle of the pit, and it looked as though an old bird's nest had fallen down into it from the trees above.

As far as the eye could see, there were trees and underbrush, slowly turning from dead winter brown to green in the wet coolness of spring. None of the other cabins had anything stocked inside them, just bare furniture as thickly dust-covered as their cabin had been.

Neither of the girls had any interest in exploring too far. Erin didn't have shoes, and both girls' feet were still sore and swollen. They stopped often and listened for any sounds, anything that indicated the presence of other people, soldiers or otherwise, but all they heard were the birds, the wind and water rushing in the creek. They were utterly alone.

In the end, they spent six weeks at the cabin recuperating, growing strong, and improving their survival skills. Jess discovered she was a pretty fair shot, and Erin became adept at fishing. They managed to supplement and extend the stock of food at the cabin with fresh, wild plants, and a good deal of fresh-caught fish and squirrel, rabbit, and even the lone wild turkey.

At first, the idea of dressing game that they killed was disgusting and off-putting. Jess found she was more nauseous than ever and Erin had to take over all the gutting and dressing so that her friend could keep most of their hard-earned food down. It was now obvious that Jess was pregnant, but it was something that neither of them spoke of.

They didn't talk about Tent 5 or about their families or friends, and they rarely spoke of the future. But as their bodies healed, they fell into a quiet rhythm of survival—it was what they both needed, time to heal mentally and physically.

The days lengthened and grew warm. It was now mid-May and Jess's belly was well-rounded, quite pronounced due to her thin frame, and her breasts were full. She had begun to help with field dressing their kills after her nausea eased up, but now she could feel the thing inside her kick. God, how she hated it, this parasite that made her sick, shaped her body into something that was alien and awkward, and brought back memories she dearly wished to never re-visit. Each time they tried some new food, some wild plant or mushroom that Erin assured her was safe, Jess secretly hoped it would make her just sick enough for it to let go and disappear from her. That's how she pictured it too, simply dissolving away some evening like a bad dream. She said nothing to Erin of her feelings in this matter, although she was aware of her friend staring at her from time to time, on the verge of speaking of the taboo subject. She could barely stand to think of it herself. Better instead to survive and take one day at a time.

They had managed to break into the small lean-to and found it had served as a smokehouse at one time. Later use seemed to indicate that it was a catch-all for hunting and camping supplies. A gold mine for the girls who knew they would need to move on soon. They found a large tarp, miraculously whole despite the obvious signs of mice, an ax, rope, and a set of knives that Erin immediately claimed would be far better suited to cleaning game than the knives stocked in the cabin.

They cleared everything out of the smokehouse and decided to fire it up and smoke something. This resulted in some hilarious attempts at smoking and preserving the meat first from the turkey they killed (a pitifully scrawny specimen) to more successful forays in smoked rabbit and squirrel. Erin became so good at it that Jess had a hard time keeping up the supply of fresh game until they turned to also smoking the fresh-caught fish.

It was after a particularly large haul from the smokehouse that they found themselves dining on the last of the green beans. The propane stove would be too cumbersome to carry with them, and they were nearly out of propane anyway, despite their careful conservation, so Erin didn't object when Jess started it up and used it to heat not just the water, but the lone can of sweetened condensed milk.

"It's time to move on, isn't it?" Jess said it aloud, even though she knew the answer already. Erin had been on a smoking and preserving kick, and with the supplies dwindling, it was time to leave. They had both known they couldn't stay here forever.

"We've got a long way to go," Erin said as way of an answer, "So I guess it's time we got started." There really wasn't anything more to say. The next day, they packed everything they could comfortably carry, rigging it on a length of tarp between two sturdy poles with leather straps lined with fur at either end. The straps fit over their shoulders, one girl in front, the other in the back to balance the load. The fur lining would be warm in the hot weather, but soft against their skin.

Their supply of dried meat and fish would last for a while, a week or better, before they needed more food. And it was in this way that they started off, both barefoot, their feet hardened by walking without socks or shoes for many weeks now. Jess refused to take the worn-out sneakers—it wasn't fair that Erin had nothing, and she did.

They stripped the cabin of nearly anything that they could use and reasonably transport with them. As they left, the girls closed the door behind them, silently grateful to the unknown owner who had helped them to survive. The woods closed in around them. They followed the ruts in the overgrown path and then turned back towards the creek. It was time to go home.

Welcome to Tennessee

"*Hell is yourself and the only redemption is when a person puts himself aside to feel deeply for another person." – Tennessee Williams*

The dark, unwelcoming barrel of the shotgun was the first thing his eyes focused on. The voice was the second. "Welcome to Tennessee, boy. Now get the heck out." The owner of the voice was male, with a thick drawl. He didn't sound particularly welcoming, but it was the shotgun that brought home the point with crystal clarity. Chris hurt all over, and he was completely disoriented. For a moment, he could not remember where he was or how he had gotten to be on the ground, covered by a filthy blanket. He blinked and tried to focus on the man behind the gun. The rising sun flared behind him and all that Chris could make out was the man's outline.

"I know you can hear me, boy. So's you best cotton to what I just said. Get the heck back whence you came. Now. Before others less kindly than me find you."

Someone who was less kindly than pointing a shotgun at him and telling him to get out? With a statement like that, Chris had no interest in meeting any others. The old man jerked his blanket away, exposing the uniform below. "We don't take kindly to the West telling us how we should live. 'Sides, I've heard some damn messed up stuff coming' in whispers on the wind. You're lucky I don't shoot you right now, boy."

Chris shook his head. He showed his hands were empty of weapons and tried not to look at the shotgun barrel, because it was making him damn nervous.

"Sir, I was a conscript. They took our town, burned it to the ground, and killed most of us. I escaped and they are probably hunting me as we speak." He tried to meet the man's eyes, but the sun was so damned bright. "I've got a broken ankle and no gun at all; I lost it when I nearly drowned in this damned swamp."

As if on cue, the broken ankle began to throb mercilessly. He had hobbled for nearly a mile on it, practically screaming in pain each time he had to put pressure on it. The bones inside had scraped against each other in a way that would have made his skin crawl if he wasn't busy trying to not pass out.

"Lake."

"What?"

"It's a lake, boy. Reelfoot Lake. Formed when the New Madrid went ape crap 'bout 200 years ago. Don'tcha pay attention to your history, boy?"

Chris thought that it wasn't his history, he wasn't from Tennessee. Instead, he simply replied, "Uh, I guess not, sir."

The man just let out a harrumph and stood there, not moving, just staring. Chris shifted uncomfortably, and the bones grated together. He ground his teeth together, aborting a shriek of agony. He tried to sit up but was pushed to the ground by the dark snout of the shotgun barrel. Rough hands went through his pockets, found the spare ammunition clip he hadn't managed to lose, and relieved him of his knife as well. Once that was done, the stranger held out his hand to Chris and slowly pulled him to a sitting position.

"Let me see that ankle, boy." Chris could see that the man was old, seventies maybe, his hair was white through and through. "I was a medic a long-assed time ago now, but I ain't forgotten everything, just my granddaughters' names occasionally, and they usually forgive me for that." He pulled off Chris's boot, which did earn a scream of pain. Chris was desperately trying to clear the black spots in front of his vision as the old man ran his calloused hands lightly over the swollen ankle. "Yep, that's broken and sure, that is." He looked thoughtfully at Chris, looked him over, and looked him up and down.

"Okay, this is what I'm a'gonna do. I'm going to get you out of the open," he gestured to a stand of trees about 100 feet away. "And I'm a'gonna go back and get my girls out here to help get you to our place. Ain't no way you can walk that far and ain't no way an old fart like me is going to be carrying a fine strapping lad like you over my shoulder."

With that, he pulled Chris into a standing position and looped the boy's arm over his shoulders. A hundred feet felt like a hundred miles.

The swelling and throbbing of his broken ankle had him sobbing in pain by the time they reached the break of trees.

The old man settled him slowly down against a tree. Chris's vision darkened and his head swam. "Don't you make a sound there, boy, not a peep. Like I said, there're others won't give you the time of day, just shoot you when they see those colors. I'll bring back a shirt and jeans for you to wear. I'll be back in two licks." Chris barely registered the man's departure through the haze of pain. Eventually, he relaxed enough to doze lightly. It was a welcome respite from the throbbing fire that consumed his foot.

The murmur of voices snapped him back to consciousness. Two teenage girls walked with the old man. The old man had exchanged his shotgun for two long poles and a rucksack. The girls were both armed; their slim hips bulged, each wore a tiny revolver on one side and a sharp, long hunting knife on the other. They looked openly skeptical as they caught their first glimpse of Chris.

The older one, she had to be close to Jess's age, eyed his clothes, "Gramps, you said he was hurt, y'didn't mention he was the enemy."

"He ain't the enemy, girl."

"But he's wearing a Western Front uniform."

The old man looked irritated, "And he's explained why so's you better never mind." He bobbed his head towards Chris. "Boy, I brought you a change of clothes. You to take off those you got on and let us get 'em gone where no one else will go a'looking. Folks round here'd just as soon shoot you if they see those colors. After you're good and dead, they might think of askin' questions. So skivvy on outta them and put on these." He tossed the rucksack and Chris caught it. He pulled off his shirt quickly and then looked distinctly uncomfortable.

The taller girl rolled her eyes, "Oh for Christ's sake, ain't nothing we ain't seen before."

"Carrie Lynn Perdue!" Her grandfather barked, "Don't you use the name of the Lord in vain!"

She was instantly meek. "Yes, Gramps, sorry." Her grandfather harrumphed and gestured for both the girls to turn away while Chris took off his pants. They rolled their eyes and grinned mischievously as they turned their backs.

It took him a fair bit of time to maneuver with his swollen ankle, which had doubled in size from the night before. By the time he had put on the pants and buttoned his shirt, his head was swimming and he felt sick to his stomach. He closed his eyes and willed his stomach to settle. He was startled by the soft, warm hand that gently touched his forehead.

Both of the girls were tall, slender, and had long blond hair. The taller one, who the old man called Carrie, had emerald green eyes and her younger sister had that half blue, half brown, half something else that people usually just called hazel. Right now, a pair of the most amazing green eyes were staring into his and looking concerned. "Gramps, he's got a fever too."

"I ain't surprised about that. Let's get him on the gurney and get him back to the house. Liza, you take these and burn them down at the pits. Make sure no one sees and make sure they're burned to nothing. Then you hustle yourself back to the house right quick, y'hear?"

"Yessir," the girl chirped and disappeared into the woods with the bundle of clothes.

Chris slowly stood up, with Carrie on one side and the old man on the other. They helped him hop to the stretcher; a sturdy piece of canvas attached to the two poles, and laid him down on it.

"I could try to walk," Chris said, his voice sounded embarrassingly feeble to his own ears. Carrie snorted, crouched down at one end, and gripped the poles.

"One, two, and three!" Carrie and her grandfather heaved him into the air and began to walk steadily.

It wasn't long before they were huffing and puffing from the exertion. It took several sets of walking and then sitting down and resting before they reached their destination. What Chris could see of it from his limited view was a decent sized farmhouse and several outbuildings. Several trees on the outskirts of the property had been felled recently and Chris noticed that the view from the house was clear in all directions. It was a well-situated, defensible property. Anyone who tried to take the house would have zero cover for a good 100 yards in any direction.

Unless you were suicidal or had a true hard-on for trouble, it would be advisable to find a better target.

Liza caught up to them, materializing at Chris's right shoulder and grabbing half of her grandfather's side of the stretcher. "Y'didn't blindfold him, Gramps. Y'shoulda."

The old man's breathing was labored. "When I need yer opinion, girl, I'll tell you what it is. You let me do the worryin' 'bout this fella. You burn those clothes down to ash?"

"Uh... yessir." She tripped over a rock and lurched to the left, and the three of them all stumbled and nearly dropped him. Chris's damaged left ankle rapped hard against the undamaged right and he passed out.

Plaids and Paneling

"O*ther things may change us, but we start and end with family"—Anthony Brandt*

Chris opened his eyes and frowned. The deer standing over him was still. It didn't move, it didn't blink, —and it didn't seem to even breathe. It took him several moments to realize it was only a head, a hunting trophy, mounted on the wall.

The past couple of days had been a blur of pain. They had set his ankle. He certainly remembered that. He wished he didn't. He distinctly remembered cursing and screaming, which was surely offensive to the old man and his scream had been embarrassingly effeminate. The pretty girl with the green eyes must have been greatly impressed with that.

After that had come waves of heat, then cold, and the ache from the damaged ankle, all in succession, as they battled the fever that had beset him. His fall into the swamp, the exposure to wet and cold, as well as the stress of the escape and no food in days had opened the door to a bad cold, complete with a racking cough, which had then turned to pneumonia. Today was his first lucid day in what seemed like forever.

He took a moment and looked around him at the room. Paneled walls all covered with furred trophies or pictures of hunters. He was lying on a worn, lumpy couch with a handmade quilt covering him snugly.

He could see it was made of plaid flannels, most likely old cast-off shirts. His stomach growled loudly. How long had it been since he had eaten? He dimly recalled Green Eyes, what was her name, spooning broth into his mouth. When had that been? Last night?

A lively young face appeared in his field of vision. Hazel eyes and pixie nose and damned if he could remember this one's name either. "You're awake!" She grinned at him and then turned and yelled over her shoulder, "Hey Carrie, tell Gramps that he's awake!"

It was Gramps that answered, "Stop your bellowing child, I'm right out here." From his position on the couch, Chris could see that this den opened into a short hall and a kitchen beyond. The old man set down the basket of eggs he had just brought in from outside and made his way slowly into the room. "So, you finally lucid, boy? You've been near to dead for six days."

Six days! Six days he could barely remember. His brain was still fuzzy from sleep as he tried to figure out how far he'd come and how long it had taken. Weeks? Months? He would later map it out and discover that he had traveled for nearly three hundred miles. He'd just kept going, kept running. It hadn't made sense, not then, and certainly not now. Who the hell ran towards Tennessee, anyway? Yet here he was.

The old man was standing there, waiting for Chris to open his mouth and say something, anything, "Thank you sir, for not shooting me." What else could he say?

The old man laughed. He laughed until he choked and then bent double to recover. He grabbed Chris's shoulder for support and managed to wheeze. "Boy, you are something, you truly are. You've been gabbling on for days about Jess and Erin and Allen and I figure I know more 'bout you than you know yourself." He took Chris's hand in his and firmly shook it. "I'm Fenton Perdue, by the way. And I'd like to think I made the right choice in saving your sorry ass. But I'd sure like to hear how a Missouri boy ended up in this neck of the woods, sure and how I would."

The older girl, Carrie, had slid into the room. On her heels was a young boy, maybe five, maybe younger. His hair was blond, and he had the same emerald green eyes. Carrie didn't look old enough to be his mother, but he leaned against her, eyes locked on Chris. Fenton followed Chris's gaze, "That's my grandson, Joseph, and a'course you already met Liza and Carrie. You remember that, right?"

"Yes sir, I remember." His stomach groaned loudly, and Liza giggled.

"Well, shoot, boy, I plumb forgot my manners." Fenton looked embarrassed. "You need to eat. You ain't had nothin' but broth for days." He motioned to the girls, "Help him on into the living room and we'll get some breakfast cooked up."

Chris sat up slowly, amazed at how weak he felt. As soon as he did, another part of his body made itself known. Damn, but he needed to piss.

"I, uh, I think I can make it on my own," he said as the girls tried to take his arms and lift him up. "I uh, could I, uh, use the facilities?" Liza snickered, and Carrie just rolled her eyes at her sister. She smiled at him, a nice smile, and held his arm firmly as he slowly stood up.

A wave of dizziness washed over him and black spots appeared before his eyes. As his vision cleared, he realized he was leaning heavily against the girl. His head had settled against hers and she was desperately trying to hold his weight. Her hair smelled of wood smoke and sage. He had never been near a woman that smelled so wonderful. No perfume in the world could compare.

He closed his eyes and sniffed again. "Um..." The uneasy tone in Carrie's voice snapped him out of it, as did the now screaming urgency to pee. He muttered an apology and took some of his weight back, battling the dizziness and the sharp protest from his damaged ankle and allowed her to guide him down a dark hall to the bathroom. There was a bucket of water inside, sitting next to the toilet. "We lost water pressure a few months ago, so just do what you need to, and then I'll come in and flush it out with the bucket. Okay?"

"Yeah, okay. Thanks, Carrie." She vanished from the open door. The bathroom was very dim. It didn't have any exterior windows, and what light there was came from a bedroom off of the hall. The old man had mentioned breakfast, so it must be morning. He pulled the pants down and sat on the toilet, too exhausted to stand, and closed his eyes in relief. A few moments later, she came in as he was wrestling with the bucket while trying to balance on one leg.

"I said I'd do it."

"I know. I just..." his voice trailed off. He could barely stand, barely walk, felt as weak as a kitten and all he wanted to do was sniff her hair again. She just smelled, so... his vision blurred again. He needed food, and he really needed to sit the hell back down.

"Liza! Gramps! Help!" he could hear Carrie's voice calling from far away and he came to with a start as he crashed to the ground, rapping his broken ankle sharply against the bathroom cabinet. Hands grabbed him on all sides, pulling and pushing him to a standing position. They shuffled awkwardly back down the hall with Carrie directing, "No Gramps, not back in the den. Let's get him out to the living room. We can prop him up and feed him easier there."

Before long, he was settled in what he was sure was the most comfortable recliner, he had ever had the luxury of sitting in. "I don't see why he's gotta sit in my chair," Fenton grumbled.

"It'll be easier to set a table up for him here."

"But he's in my chair!"

"Oh Gramps, you'll live." And with that, Carrie walked into the kitchen and began cracking eggs and turning the oven on to heat. "I'm fixing biscuits and gravy with eggs on the side." She announced, her hands busy, "Joseph, go grab us a jar of peaches and dish some up for... for..." "We don't even know your name."

"It's Chris. Chris Aaronson." He fell in love at that next moment. The moment the girl turned and smiled at him. Her teeth were perfect and her smile dazzled him. "Hi Chris," she turned back to her brother, "Get some of those peaches in a cup for Chris, Joseph. And stop gawping at him, he don't bite."

The little boy filled the bowl and Chris attacked the offered food, trembling weakly, as he tried to hold himself back from inhaling the peaches. Eggs replaced the peaches along with a cup of steaming black coffee. After that followed the biscuits and the gravy and Chris ate everything they placed in front of him. He even ran a finger along the plate to catch the last bits of gravy and crumbs.

He looked up to see the entire family watching him. The old man was smiling. The little boy, Joseph, was staring; he'd never seen anyone eat so much so quickly. And the girls looked pleased, especially Carrie, when he licked his finger clean of gravy and thanked her.

"Now, boy," Fenton said.

"His name is Chris," Liza inserted.

"I know what the boy's name is, girl!" Fenton snapped, "Now, boy... I mean, Chris," He rolled his eyes at Liza, "We'd sure like to hear 'bout how you ended up in Tennessee."

Chris started at the beginning and told them how the Western Front had invaded Belton, shooting anyone who fought back, burning houses, taking the young and able. He explained how his sister and two of their friends had also been held in the camp, how they had planned an escape. He told them he had run southeast of the camp for more than twenty miles and thought he had escaped successfully and planned to turn north and circle around Springfield and head back towards Belton when two soldiers had caught him, beaten him, and tied him up.

"I found out that my sister and everyone who had escaped that night had already been captured and that I was the last one left. They said Cooper was in charge now and that he had... he had..." He broke down then, unable to repeat the terrible soul-killing things the men reported that Cooper had done to Jess before he killed her and Erin and the rest.

"Everyone I know is dead. My parents, my sister, my friends." His eyes were dark holes of pain. "They were planning on taking me back to camp, but I managed to kill both of them. If I hadn't, they would have never stopped hunting me." He looked at them then. The girls had tears in their eyes. "After that I took the truck, drove it until it was out of gas and then I just started walking. I don't know what I expected to find, or where I was planning on going. I just... couldn't stay there. And I kept going until I fell into that swamp and lost my gun."

"Lake," Fenton corrected.

"Huh? Oh yeah, right. Lake. And that's when you found me."

Carrie asked softly, "And where would you go once you're healed?"

Chris tried to imagine what tomorrow would bring and simply shrugged. "I've got nowhere in particular to go. My family is gone. I don't want to fight in another man's army, especially not one that killed everyone I loved. I just..." his voice trailed off. He hadn't really thought about what he wanted to do or where he would go.

He'd just kept walking and tried not to think about anything more than food, shelter and basic survival. A wave of exhaustion hit him then. The moving around for the first time in days, the massive amount of food he had just eaten, all of it hit him at once and he drooped.

"Boy, you are all done in. Close your eyes and get some shut-eye. We'll talk later." As Chris closed his eyes gratefully, the old man sighed and shook his head, "And a'course, he's in my chair."

The last thing Chris heard before he succumbed to sleep was Carrie, "Oh Gramps, you'll live."

A Long Walk

"When Quincy found us, I knew he was gone. I knew it, and I mourned, for he was a good and kind man. At the time, there seemed to be so few of them left.

She showed up alone, no mama and no brother. I can only guess at what happened after we left. Maybe we were tracked, maybe it was just bad luck. I'll never know. But my heart jumped when I saw her. I named her Quincy right there on that bridge, moments after we recognized her loping along, her nose to the ground, sussing out where we had trekked in the two weeks since we'd last seen her. I suppose I could have been more original, but I saw the sign on the bridge leading into the town of Quincy and figured it was fate. I am thankful she found us. She ended up saving my life more times than I can remember."—Jess's Journal

"Clinton? Shee-it. You girls got one hell of a long walk ahead of you," the grizzled old man laughed, "sure you don't wanna stay here with me?" He winked at them.

It was a tense few hours since first meeting, but Arno Cooper, "Ever'one 'round here just calls me Coop," appeared relatively harmless. It helped that he hadn't been armed with a gun and they were both ready to draw blood rather than pass the time of day. Being back on the road nearly three weeks now hadn't dulled them at all. They were jumpy and scared, so they knew he was there long before he was aware of them. He had been muttering to himself, picking burrs off of his shirt, slapping at the occasional mosquito and inspecting some traps along the same creek the girls had been following for the past three days.

Jess had seen him first and wanted to avoid him. She suggested tracking around in a broad circle, but the woods were thick with black locust trees. These nightmarish trees were loaded with sharp spines on their branches. They had stumbled into a dense thicket of the trees a week or so ago and been rewarded by several painful bloody wounds before they had managed to escape to open ground. Erin was far braver; she wanted to know where they were, and how far they had to go to get to Clinton.

Without a map, the next best thing was asking someone. They had both agreed to tell no one of their ultimate destination. If anyone was looking for them, or if the soldiers took a turn back northwest, they reasoned that it would be better for them to be heading for Clinton. After all, that was familiar enough country to get them the rest of the way home to Belton. And right at the moment they came to an agreement, the dog lying on the ground near the old man had woken up, let out a short bark and 'pointed' right at them.

It was early June, and the day was already uncomfortably warm. If you looked a distance away, you could see the waves of heat pulsing through the air. Old Coop, who turned out to be an experienced trapper, had managed to snare a skunk, two squirrels, and a large groundhog in his traps. The skunk's smell was overwhelming at first; the girls' eyes watered from their vantage point only a few yards away.

He had offered to share his bounty and their store of smoked fish had run out two days ago—by now their growling, empty stomachs were stronger and no doubt louder than their fear. They stood back and watched as he field-dressed the catch, started a small campfire, and talked endlessly. In a way, it was a comfort to hear another voice. He spoke of troop movements and then turned autobiographical.

"My Alice, she passed away a few months after Black Monday and my boy Scott joined up with uh, with the Army not long after." Blood dripped from his fingers as he skinned the skunk, "Haven't heard nuthin' in over two years from him, but we was never what you'd call close."

He waved a gore-covered finger at Erin, "Fetch us some water from the creek there, would ya' Missie?" A streak of blood smeared across his cheek as he wiped the sweat away. Erin warily took the indicated bucket and headed for the stream, never looking away from the old man.

He slowed in his constant patter, took a long look at Jess and asked, "Them soldiers knock you up, girl?" Jess bristled and said nothing. He took her silence for confirmation and said, "My Alice, she had herself an affair, got herself knocked up. The man was worthless, wouldn't stand by her and took the next Greyhound outta town after I came and, err... talked to 'im. I coulda divorced her, but I didn't. I stuck by her and she birthed that child," he stopped and smiled crookedly at Jess, "We named her Tiffany and I swear to you I never loved a child more than I loved that little girl. Now my boy Scott, he was some five years older than his little sister. He was my own flesh and blood. But he and me, we was always strangers living in the same house."

Erin had returned and was listening quietly, the pail of water sloshing in her hands. He turned and gestured for her to put it near the campfire and Jess spoke for the first time, her finger slowly easing off of the large hunting knife near her side, "So what happened to her?"

The old man's hands stopped for a moment at their work. He stopped and looked up at Jess and said, "Same as what happened to you girls, except my girl ain't never gonna come back." His grizzled and lined face twisted in pain and he looked down at the small bloody creature in his hands, "I heard she gave 'em hell. Got one of 'ems knives from 'em, sneaky-like and cut up one of the bastards nice and good. They killed her for it, after they were done using her, then dumped her like she was a piece of trash."

He took a deep breath, swatted at a hovering mosquito and continued, "I'd been tracking 'em since she went missing. See, she'd been in town visiting a friend of hers the day they blew through. Three days later I found her body, and I found one of 'em who was too shot up to fight.

They'd left him behind, too. Damn, when I was in the Service you didn't run off and leave your men, and y'sure didn't rape innocent young girls. Anyway, he told me everythin' afore he died." Cooper's eyes were red and bloodshot when he looked back up. "I'm just an old man. I wanted to kill 'em all, but a'stead I took her back home and buried her next to her mama. Thank God my Alice weren't alive to see what they did to her baby." He shook his head, bent back to skinning and repeated, "I'm just an old man. God forgive me, I'm just an old man."

Erin and Jess exchanged glances. It was a beautiful summer day, hot, even in the shade. Both the girls' skins were tanned and brown. In another space and time, you would think summer break from school, swimming pools, guys and even a party or two. Above them, the clouds were white and fluffy with just a hint of gray. The rain would come tonight, like it had each evening before, and when it did, it would sink blissfully into the earth and add to the humidity the following day.

How could it be so beautiful out when there was so much loss and heartache? The sun shone overhead and the birds sang. Life went on, and it seemed so impudent, as if life was laughing at their traumas and dismissing them as irrelevant. In the shade of the trees near the creek, with only the mosquitoes to harass them, they felt relatively safe. Here was a man who had lost someone. He hurt just as they hurt, and what was to be done? What measure of justice would he ever receive? Cooper was just another lonely old man, his world crushed by events beyond his control in a world gone mad.

The old man led the way back up the creek to a small double-wide and a handful of outbuildings in various stages of disrepair. Several chickens clucked and scuttled about in a fenced section of the yard with a small chicken coop attached. The mobile home had seen better days. Two of the windows had been smashed, and Coop had simply nailed plywood over them. He shrugged, "Ain't much in the way of supplies for fixin' the windows around here no more. I just did what I could. It leaks a little when it rains."

He had a solid patch of garden, filled with green beans, peas, and a multitude of other plants. "What I don't like, I just barter." He grinned, "I ain't terribly fond of watermelon, for instance, but my Alice always growed it and so I just kept it up. I got a neighbor up the way who is particularly skilled at bagging turkeys. I make sure he's got plenty of watermelons in the summer and he takes care to see I got me a turkey or two each winter. It all works out."

It was a quiet place. It wasn't fancy, but it was peaceful, and they reveled in the comfort of sleeping in an honest-to-God, full-sized bed that had room enough for both of them.

In the end, they would spend two weeks with old Coop in his small ramshackle mobile home a mile to the north of the creek where they had found him. They stayed in Tiffany's room, not willing to be separated, still not willing to trust even a beaten-down, grizzled old man. With his hospitality came changes of clothes and shoes in both girls' sizes. Scott's shoes had fit Erin and Tiffany's had fit Jess. Finally, they were able to have something different from the ragged remains of those hated Western Front uniforms. The uniforms were stained and dirty anyway, stiff from being worn day in and day out and only hand-washed and hung to dry when the days were warm enough to go without while they dried. They burned them at the first opportunity.

Tiffany had been both girls' size, but certainly not their taste—hers ran to sparkly, sequined tops and lots of pink. She must have been a real girly girl in her clothing and decor. Perhaps that was what made it rather shocking for the girls to imagine her actually taking a knife and killing a man.

Jess found that Scott's spare clothes were more accommodating of her swelling belly, and old Cooper assured her that they were welcome to any of the clothing they wanted from his children's rooms. They fished and stocked up on meat from Cooper's traps and ate fresh peas and strawberries, which seemed to grow overnight in the raised beds behind the old man's trailer.

As the sun dipped down below the horizon on the twelfth day, both girls found themselves at ease with Cooper. Erin sat cross-legged on the ground in a pink crop top with Princess emblazoned upon it in sequins, while Jess relaxed in a lawn chair in camouflage fatigues and a giant black Insane Clown Posse t-shirt. She winced as the baby rolled and kicked inside her, pressing sharply on her full (it always seemed full these days) bladder. She turned to her left, reached down and scratched behind the girl pup's ears. Cooper had just two of them left. The puppies were ten weeks old. They frolicked around the property, long legs and lean bodies, still awkward as they ran.

They cried out with piteous yaps when the old man would tie them up and take their mother away with him to go trapping. One of them, the girl pup, had taken a shine to Jess and kept seeking her out, butting her head against Jess's hand and insisted on following her everywhere. Her liquid brown eyes stared up at Jess and her tongue would frantically lick the air as Jess bent close and stroked the puppy's soft fur.

The pup's fur was brown with patches of white and she had huge, floppy ears that perked up with interest at the smallest sound from Jess. Each morning, the little pup was the first to greet Jess, and she howled at night when Old Coop locked her up with the others in the dog run. How Jess wished she could take the pup with her, but it was impossible. They barely had enough food for themselves, much less a growing puppy.

She met Erin's gaze and nodded to her friend. They had talked about it the night before. It was time to move on. Cooper had just finished telling a funny joke and Erin's smile dropped. Her face grew serious and her laughter was cut short. She cleared her throat, "We, uh, we need to get back on the road again, Coop." The old man fell silent, looked at the ground, and said nothing. Erin continued, "We've got to go home. We need to find out if anyone of our friends or family managed to stay alive."

Cooper looked like he was about to object, or try to talk them out of it. He opened his mouth to speak, but the words never came out of his throat. He struggled silently for a moment and tried to collect his thoughts before speaking. It was obvious to both of them how much he had enjoyed having them there and how desperately lonely the old man was.

When the words did come, his voice sounded rough and strained, "Well, a 'course y'all gotta go. I knew you'd be headin' on once y'got some rest in. Y'headin' out tomorra'?"

Jess's throat felt tight. Cooper was a decent man, the first either of them had seen in a long time. He was a little rough around the edges, but deep inside, there rested a good, kind soul. "Yeah, tomorrow."

The old man nodded, "Well, y'all need somethin' better 'n that rifle and one lonely box of ammo."

He got up and ducked into the trailer, rummaged inside a cabinet and returned with several boxes under his arm and sat back down in his weather-beaten wood chair. He tossed a box of shells to Erin. They were 22s, a full box of them. Erin grinned like she'd been handed gold. But Cooper wasn't done yet.

"Y'all need somethin' small and easy to conceal like this little lady." He reached into the box and pulled out a revolver, with inlaid wood in the handle and black steel. He handed it to Jess.

She ran her hands over it. It wasn't a new gun, but it had been well cared for. It smelled sharply of cleaning fluid and the wood felt as smooth as silk. He showed her how to pull it apart and pointed out the grip safety on the back strap. She looked up and saw Coop's eyes steady on her. "Smith and Wesson, Model 40 Centennial. She's small, easy to hide in your pocket, but I found a holster for her. I used to take my Tiffany target shooting with this little lady. She takes five rounds, and ya got 'bout 30 rounds of .38s left in that there box. You keep her with you at all times. Keep her loaded. Will ya do that, Missie?"

Jess nodded, unable to speak, reminded suddenly of her dad. This man looked nothing like her dad, but he was a father through and through. You can tell that about some people. They are the people who change irrevocably when parenthood visits them. They never stop caring; never stop seeing their own children in stranger's faces. She struggled up from the lawn chair, leaned over and hugged the old man, and went inside the trailer. She suddenly felt exhausted, and she didn't trust herself not to cry. She lay down in Tiffany's frilly pink bed and closed her eyes. Outside, she could hear Erin and Coop talking, too quiet to be heard. By the time Erin joined her in bed, Jess was sound asleep.

Jess and Erin were both up with the dawn. They weren't surprised to see Old Coop awake as well. And he had already brewed up a large pot of his dwindling stash of coffee and baked some biscuits for them to eat and take on the road. They had packed extra changes of clothes and Erin was sporting hot pants and a crop top with 'Spoiled Rotten' spelled out in a rainbow of shiny letters across the front. She had the rifle slung across her back, and Jess had her shiny revolver in a holster strapped to her fatigues. The pups were tied up, the little female crying and lunging at her lead, trying to escape and join the girls. Jess knelt down and hugged the pup close, felt her warm body writhe against her and the dog's tiny tongue lick her desperately. Somehow, the pup knew she was leaving.

The sun was out, and it was time to go. Coop reached out and hugged Erin. "You stay safe now, y'hear me, girlie?" Erin smiled and thanked him, and then it was Jess's turn. He hugged her, then reached out and put a rough, gnarled hand firmly on her rounded belly. She nearly jerked away, but the sad look in his eyes stopped her. "Jessie girl, listen to me now and humor an old man."

She stilled and looked back into his eyes. "This baby in you, it ain't done nothin'. It ain't asked to be here, and it's as innocent as one of God's lambs." Even now, with it so obvious what was happening, she hated to think about it and tried to pull away, but Coop persisted, "I know you think this ain't what you want. An' I can't blame you girl if y'think you hate this creature inside you, but it's a blessin' and someday you'll see it that way."

He held her gaze with his and said, "Children are blessin's. They are the gift God gives us to tell us the world ain't all pain and death and loneliness." His eyes blurred with tears. "I hold my children in my heart and think of them each day. You remember what I said when this child comes outta you. Will you remember that, Jessie?"

His features blurred as the tears leaked from her eyes and ran down her face. For that moment, she let them fall. She was so damned scared, and he knew it, he understood it somehow, and she felt like curling up in his arms and never leaving this quiet place.

Instead, she nodded tearfully and hugged him, and managed to croak out, "Thanks." Tears blurring both of their vision, the girls set out along the creek, large new backpacks full of food and supplies slung to their backs. The old man stood there for a long time, long after they had disappeared from sight, before slowly turning away and returning to his lonely, empty home.

A Good Fit

"I *long, as does every human being, to be at home wherever I find myself."—Maya Angelou*

Chris pulled the weeds from the raised beds of the kitchen garden and threw them towards the enclosure where the chickens clucked and jockeyed for position. They angled for the larger bits, pecked and squabbled over the choicer pieces. It reminded him painfully of home. Jess had done this for Mom in the family garden back in Belton.

They might have had a smaller plot of land, not a full-fledged farm with a pond and fields, but chickens are pretty much the same wherever you go. He closed his eyes, remembered her voice as she talked to the chickens, her wavy blond hair tied back in a ponytail and the chickens clucked back at her, bobbing their heads in time as she spoke. What she would say to them, he didn't know, but the sound of her voice, and the memory of it now, was bittersweet.

The sun was barely up, the house behind him was quiet, and he savored this moment of solitude. It would be another scorcher today. Already the air was uncomfortably hot and humid. His ankle still ached, but it had been set straight and he hoped it would heal completely, given time. He had come down the back stairs too quickly, and it had twinged a painful warning until he slowed down. He didn't have far to go. The raised beds were, after all, right off of the kitchen. Here the curled leaves of lettuce sprang in a dramatic show of greens and reds. The pole beans and green beans were growing well and there was room for more in a half-used bed. The soil was rich and loose, well-composted.

He thought of his mother, Julie, digging her hands deep into the soil. She would smile and dig, weed, plant, and talk about the gardens for hours. How she had loved her gardens! The memory of her smiling face hurt him deep inside. He imagined his parents' last moments, as they tried desperately to stop the enemy soldiers from abandoning a group of small children on the road so many miles from home. It was just like her to speak up, to try to stop such a thing from happening, and for Dad to stand beside her no matter the personal cost.

He had wrung the details out of Allen. It had been hard to hear, yet harder still to not know. His friend had looked haunted as he had recounted the Aaronson's end. As if he thought Chris would hold him responsible somehow or blame him for not interceding. If only he hadn't had taken that hike and gotten caught up in the first wave, he would have been with them when it all came down. Chris didn't blame Allen, not at all. Instead, he blamed himself. He hadn't been there when they needed him most. And they had died there, miles from home, alone. They had deserved better than that.

He sat on the edge of a raised planter and looked over the greenery. Everywhere there was green and life growing. The beans snaked their way up the poles and the peas were fat and heavy, ready for picking. Plump, red strawberries hid under leaves and he picked a few and ate them. They were warm and juicy, the sweet tang bursting on his tongue when he bit into them. The plants were growing fast, but he would need to water today. He'd do that and ask the old man if there were any more of the bean and squash seeds left to plant since there was still time to get them in and growing.

As he shifted, his ankle twinged again. He still favored it, but it was getting stronger by the day, and his limp was barely noticeable.

He nearly jumped out of his skin when Carrie's voice sounded at his ear. It would be a long time before he would be able to react normally. He was still in combat mode, ready to run or fight at the drop of a hat. She patted his shoulder and smiled. "How's your ankle today?"

The wonderful scent of her, this combination of sage and wood smoke, washed over him, "I... uh... it's fine. Damn, but you scared the hell out of me."

"I'm sorry." her emerald-green eyes stared into his, twinkling in amusement. "I didn't mean to." She was close, way too close, and Fenton would damn near kill him if he so much as touched her. Of that, he was sure. Carrie laid her hand on his cheek.

Chris was handsome, there was no denying it. Carrie stared at his deep blue eyes. The only imperfections were the scar on his forehead and a slightly bent nose. Both of the wounds had come from those soldiers.

In a way, it made him more handsome in her eyes. He had a way of looking at her that made her want to get closer. She was used to guys taking the lead with her. She'd done her share of making out, but nothing more. Going all the way was supposed to mean something, and she figured she knew who that guy was. Chris liked her, but he still pulled away and she didn't know quite how to handle it. It sometimes felt as if he was avoiding being alone with her.

Chris had to stop this. Carrie was only sixteen, and Fenton was protective of both girls. The old man was very, very protective. The two of them had been dancing around each other for weeks. She flirted with him constantly and he struggled with keeping the image of Fenton and his shotgun in the forefront of his memory. The old man wasn't going to cotton to Chris, cozying up to his precious granddaughter. There were limits to a man's hospitality, after all.

He shook his head at her and gently removed her hand from his cheek. Carrie looked hurt and a little put out, but then she smiled and told hold of his hand, pulling him to his feet. "Come on, I want to show you something. If you think you could handle a bit of a hike." His ankle twinged again in protest at the thought of going anywhere. And worse, he wasn't sure he should be alone with her. It was getting harder and harder to resist the impulse to kiss her. Against his better judgment, he let her pull him along. They walked out past the perimeter of the property, into the trees, which quickly became thick woods.

The going was difficult and several times they stopped so that he could rest for a moment. The heat of the morning was radically altered underneath the leafy canopy of trees and there was a cool breeze. "It's just a little way further." Carrie pulled him up, and they walked again, slowly edging their way down an embankment and crossing a lively creek. He could see tiny fish darting between the rocks and several dragonflies buzzed by with iridescent green and blue-hued wings. They crossed the creek, squeezed through a stand of trees, and stopped in a small clearing. Wildflowers bloomed everywhere and he could see a chimney and the remains, mostly intact, of a small stone house. The roof sagged, and it looked as if it had been deserted for a long time.

The clearing was a paradise of flowers, birds chirping, and the gurgle of the creek behind them. Carrie smiled at Chris and stepped closer. "Do you like what you see?"

The scenery melted away, and all Chris could see were beautiful eyes and perfect skin and soft lips. He slipped his hand behind her head, ran his hands through her hair, and kissed her softly. The kiss went on and on, intensifying as her mouth opened to him and their tongues entwined. She pressed herself against him and his other hand slid slowly down her back, finding her shapely buttocks and pulling her up closer. His breathing had quickened and, in his mind, a war was being fought. Part of him wanted to stop this; because he was sure Fenton would come around the corner at any minute with the shotgun and shoot him dead for touching his precious granddaughter. The other part of him wanted to pull her to the ground, slip off her tight, sexy jeans and drive into her.

A few hot moments later and they had ended up on the ground, her shirt unbuttoned and a white, lacy bra covered her perky young breasts. He took a deep breath and sat up. Carrie looked hurt. "What's wrong?"

"Besides the fact that you are beautiful and sexy and I want to do far more than just kiss you?" Chris smiled, "I'm thinking that Fenton has got one damned scary shotgun."

Carrie's eyes lit up at hearing "beautiful and sexy," and looked disappointed at the mention of her grandfather. "Gramps is just being protective. Since our parents died, he's taken care of us. He doesn't think of me as a woman."

"You're not a woman, you're only sixteen," Chris reminded her gently, "And I'm nearly twenty."

"I'll be seventeen in less than a month, and your nineteen, not twenty," she retorted, bristling at his comment. "I know my mind and I'm not some silly little girl."

"No, no you're not." He kissed her again, long and slow. It was full of promise of things to come. "But I cannot have sex with you, Carrie. Not now. I like you. I like you a lot, damn it. I like your whole family, for that matter. I don't want to piss off Fenton and I don't want to rush things with you." He took her hand, looked down at the ground, "I've been thinking. I've been doing a lot of thinking and I want to stay. Here. With all of you Perdue's."

Her eyes sparkled at the next words, "And I'm thinking that I've never met anyone I thought smelled as wonderful as you, or who was as smart and funny and beautiful as you. I think that here is a good fit for me. I can help with the stuff Fenton is getting too old to do. We could make this farm work, and not just survive, but be okay here. Better than okay. But if I stay, then I gotta do this right between you and me. I gotta do it like Fenton expects me to and damn well court you and not have sex the first time we go off alone together."

She laughed at that. And she knew he was right, even if she didn't like it. "You really want to stay?"

"Yeah, I really do."

"Okay."

They returned to the house with a load of blueberries. The abandoned stone house was the original homestead on the property. The blueberry bushes were bountiful there and had grown wild after they had been left behind. They wrapped the blueberries in Chris's shirt since they didn't have a basket. When they returned, Fenton was sitting in a chair on the wide front porch, thoroughly cleaning his shotgun. He looked pissed. Carrie started to say something to her grandfather, but Chris handed her the shirt full of blueberries and gave her a small shove towards the house. He limped over to Fenton and sat down, very aware of his own bare chest and the set look on the old man's face.

"Mr. Perdue." The old man harrumphed and said nothing. "My ankle is healing and, if you want, I can be on my way in a few more days with my thanks for your help and hospitality."

Chris took a deep breath. "But I'd like to stay, sir. I think I could be of use here. For one, I could get some of those blueberry bushes dug up and transplanted closer to the house. I know how to take care of chickens; raise vegetables and I can learn the rest. I've helped my dad with roofing and construction, and once my ankle is healed, I could fix that leak in the barn. If you'd want to keep me on, that is."

There was a long silence as the old man digested the offer and oiled the barrel of the shotgun. "I ain't blind y'know. I seen you two looking at each other. Whatcha plannin' on doin' 'bout that?"

The shotgun was currently in pieces. Chris figured he was relatively safe. "Sir, I'd like permission to court your granddaughter."

If he could have read Fenton Perdue's mind at the moment, he would have known instantly that his words and his attitude were perfect. Fenton was old-fashioned. He'd been raised by his grandparents after his father died in the war and his mother lost her life in childbirth. His grandfather had instilled in him a sense of honor and chivalry that was long dead in the modern world.

The old man loved his grandchildren more than life itself. When their father had died in the Amtrak bombings just months before Joseph was born, Fenton had insisted the kids and their mother Amy move back to the family farm. She had been a tiny wisp of a woman who had given birth to Joseph three months to the day after they buried her husband. Just a few months later, Fenton had insisted she see a doctor.

She had been losing weight and was listless and slept round the clock. They'd had to put baby Joseph on formula because Amy just didn't have enough milk to sustain him. The doctor gave her a battery of tests, looked grim, and sent her to a specialist in Nashville. She was diagnosed with pancreatic cancer. She had died less than three months later. It had been just Fenton and the children ever since.

He stopped polishing the shotgun and looked over at Chris, met his eyes, searched them for deceit. He thought about how happy Carrie had looked in the last few weeks and how gentle Chris was with Joseph.

Even Liza seemed to appreciate his company, especially when she had discovered that they shared a love for science fiction. Chris had done a lot of reading those first two weeks while his ankle healed. There was no denying it; the boy was a good fit for their family.

Young love. I wonder if it will actually take. He thought about Molly, who had passed away over thirty years ago now. They'd met at a square dance when she was fifteen and he was eighteen, going on nineteen.

Her daddy had been a doctor and her mama a nurse in the war. They wanted something more for their daughter than a life as a farmer's wife. But as the years had passed, they had seen how much the two were in love. Fenton had ended up being drafted and sent off to Vietnam as a medic. Thousands of miles from home, he had watched men bleed out, spending the last moments of their lives in alien jungles, so far from their homes. So many lives lost, so many dreams dead with them, before he had returned home to his grandparent's farm, safe. After three years of courting, he had asked Molly's daddy for his blessing and the man had given it. They had married, built this enormous house after his grandparents died, and began practicing at making babies. Oh, how they had practiced! Both of them were only children, and they wanted a big family. They dreamed of a passel of kids to fill the house's five large bedrooms and tumble through the gardens.

Fenton looked out over the land. It had been in his family for more than a century. And for the last five years, he had wondered who would take it on next. Joseph? Carrie? Liza? Who would stay and work this land? The dreams he and Molly had had of a passel of little Perdues died the day of Isaac's birth. The birthing had been hard, and the doctors said if they hadn't of taken everything out, she would've bled to death. They loved their son and loved each other for the rest of their time together. That time hadn't been nearly as long as Fenton would have liked. Molly had gotten breast cancer during Isaac's freshman year in high school and passed away less than a year later.

He looked again at Chris and realized the boy had been sitting there patiently, waiting for an answer. "Yes, son, you can court my granddaughter. And heal up quick, 'cause I think the southwest corner of the house roof is needin' some repairs."

"Thank you, sir."

"Gramps."

"Sir?"

"Y' can call me Gramps. Everyone else does."

"Right... Gramps."

Fenton closed his eyes and listened as Chris got up slowly and limped inside the house. He heard the boy whisper to Carrie. She let out a happy squeal and gave him a loud kiss. Fenton smiled sadly. I miss you, Molly.

Coop's End

"A *damn smart man that I cain't 'member the name of right now said, 'There comes a time when you have to make a decision. Y'either lie down and get busy dying, or y'haul yer ass up and gits to fightin.'"—Arno Cooper*

It had been a week and still the pup moped, barely touched her food, and refused to play with her brother. At present, she was lying near Coop's feet, staring at the bend in the road where she had seen the girls disappear from sight. Her brother was pulling on her ear with his sharp teeth and trying like hell to get her to play—but the girl pup wouldn't budge.

Coop saw the writing on the wall. The pup had given her heart to that Jessie, and there wasn't anything to be done about it except send her on her way. He smiled as he thought of it. This one was worth a lot. She had the right instincts to be one of the best hunting dogs he had ever bred. Lord knows he had been breeding them long enough to know. She was young, but damned smart.

Annie, the pups' dam, was the only one of Coop's dogs to survive when the troops blew through town. She had been out with Coop, checking lines and rooting out pheasants. Annie and the old man had returned to chaos—the rest of the dogs dead, Tiffany missing, the trailer a jumbled mess and their entire stash of canned food gone. Except the beets, seems no one wanted the beets. Damn fools. Coop smiled at the thought. He liked beets.

A couple of months later, Annie disappeared for a few days. Several weeks after she returned, it became obvious she was knocked up. Coop chuckled at the irony that for all his careful breeding, Annie had apparently found just the right mix of wild seed. All three of the pups she had borne in this litter were exceptional. One boy pup had been snatched up by the Walkers and Faen Brooks was coming for the last boy pup today.

Coop reached down and petted the little girl's ears. "I shoulda sent y'with her when they left." The pup whined sadly. "Hands down, girl, you're the best I got." The pup did not respond, just continued to stare down the road.

His rough hands slowly undid the collar from the pup's neck. Dozens of pups had worn this old leather collar, but none of them had been quite like this one. It seemed fitting somehow, considering what he was planning on doing. The pup looked up at him, tail slowly thumping. "Go on with yeh," he pointed towards the road, "You got a long road ahead of you if you're gonna catch up with 'em. So's you best get started." Annie gave her daughter one sharp bark of encouragement.

For the first time in over a week, the girl pup looked excited and alive. She looked up at Coop and back at her dam, then turned and ran towards the road. She stopped for a moment, stared back at the trailer and its inhabitants, wagged her tail, put her nose to the ground and then disappeared round the bend and on into the trees.

About an hour later, Faen Brooks showed up. He was a small man, with dark hair, pale blue eyes and sunburned skin. He was Coop's cousin three times removed. Around these parts, if your family stayed around for long, and most did, eventually everyone was related to everyone else.

"Hey Coop, whatcha know?" The old man just grunted and pointed to Annie. She was lying on the ground a few yards away, not so patiently enduring her son's industrious attempts to get her to play. The boy pup tugged on one of her ears, which earned him a short growl and quick snapping of teeth to show her displeasure.

"I need a full pack of jerky, any dried fruit you got," Coop replied, staring at his prize hounds, "and every box of ammo you can spare."

Faen looked pissed, "Now look here Coop, y'know we ain't got much, that's askin' an awful damn lot for one little pup that ain't even proven himself."

The old man didn't even look up. "That's for everythin', not just the pup."

"What the hell you talkin' bout, old timer, what everything?"

Coop looked over at the younger man, "The dogs, both of 'em. The trailer, the land, most of my traps, and whatever else you want."

The silence stretched on as Faen tried to stare Coop down.

One minute...

Two minutes...

Three...

He finally broke, "Godamnit Coop, no. This won't bring her back. Scott is still out there. What's he gonna do when he comes back from the Army? Find y'all gone with no one left?" Faen shook his head. "Think about how he'd feel, old man, with his whole family gone. He'd..."

The old man interrupted, "Scott didn't join the Army," he looked down at the ground, "That boy ain't got a home to come back to after what he done."

The younger man gaped at Coop in shock. No matter how bad Scott had acted up in years past, the old man had always shown him a patience and understanding that belied the crusty old-timer image that Coop had cultivated so well over the years.

Coop continued, "He joined 'em, the Western Front, he joined 'em willingly, and he was one of the bastards that tried to," his voice broke, "tried to... Tiffany was his sister, his own blood!" He sat for a moment, body shaking.

"I thought I could set it to rest, but I can't. I'm going to that camp, and I'm gonna finish him, and as many more as I can. That's just the way it is, Faen, so's you take Annie and that pup and you take good care of 'em, y'hear?"

Faen just stood there in shock, unable to form words; finally, he nodded, reached out a hand and grasped the old man's shoulder. "I'll take the dogs now. Come back with a full pack for ya. Y'leaving first thing in the mornin'?"

"Yep."

"I'll bring it by at first light."

Faen's wife, Connie, went ballistic when she heard about Coop's plans the next day at breakfast. Faen had gone out at first light with a full pack of food and three boxes of shells that they really couldn't spare.

He gave it all to Coop and watched the old man take U.S. 13, turn a bend and disappear from sight. Annie had gone crazy, pulling at the lead and trying like hell to break free. Faen calmed her down as best he could. She was a fine hound, but her heart belonged to Coop.

As he fought to keep the dog in line, his thoughts turned to his kids. Mick was turning twelve soon. Emmy was just six years old. Faen's stomach clenched at the thought of what this war could do to them in the years to come and wished the old man well.

He didn't tell her the truth about Coop's boy. That was something he just couldn't fathom. How could that boy join the Western Front? He'd always seemed a bit cold. The girls thought he was devilishly handsome, and Faen had to agree on the devilish part of it. Still, the idea that he had joined the Western Front—it was like suggesting you join the Union when you lived in the South, or like joining Al Qaeda after losing your family in the Twin Towers bombing. It was crazy!

Some part of him feared that if he said it aloud, it would make it real. He may never have liked the boy, but damn, he wouldn't have expected this out of him. Besides, Connie had babysat Scott when she was a teenager and she'd always had a soft spot for the kid.

Faen just sat and stared at his scrambled eggs and let Connie rant about the stupidity of old men. When that didn't work, she pleaded with Faen to get on the road, catch up to Coop, and talk some sense into the old man, but her husband was unmoved. "He's got a right, Connie, he's gotta do this and I expect he'll be back. 'Member, he was some badass in 'Nam. I hear tell he had something like a hundred and fifty-eight kills. Shit, but that old man was legend back in the day."

Swearing earned him a small, annoyed smack on the back of his head from his wife. Only five feet tall, Connie was a spitfire, and she didn't like swearing. God help Mick and Emmy if they let loose anything they had picked up in the schoolyard. She had thrashed Mick but good after he had uttered "Jesus Christ" within earshot. Connie was a deeply religious woman, and she did not cotton to profanity of any kind.

Faen knew the chances of the old man coming back weren't good, not at all, but if it calmed down Connie, well, she'd come around to an understanding of it later. That night she was so angry at Faen she made him sleep on the couch. Despite the fact that he could feel every spring and every lump in the aged thing, he slept well, feeling safe, well away from his angry little wife.

By nightfall on the first day, Coop made it almost seven miles before he stopped and pitched a tent. By his reckoning, it would take two, maybe three, days of hard walking before he reached the camp. In the end, it took him nearly a week and a half. He twisted his ankle crossing a river. Two of the bridges had been torn out and his arthritis slowed him down considerably.

The last night of Coop's life found him camped without a fire. He didn't even set up the tent. He was so close that could hear men calling to each other in the enemy camp as he oiled hinges and sharpened the teeth of his snares and traps, all of them.

Coop's traps, snares and guns killed and maimed a lot of men early that morning. He had been a sniper in Vietnam, brought in on the tail end of the Tet Offensive. He had lost his cherry (in more ways than one) near Khe Sanh. Arno Cooper had been one of the best snipers the Army had ever had.

But time catches up to us all. Thirty-four minutes after the first shot had been fired; twenty-eight men lay dead. One of those twenty-eight was a good and honest man.

Captain Scott Cooper stood over Old Coop's lifeless body, the Glock 40s barrel still smoking. There was not a trace of emotion in his handsome face, no recognition or acknowledgment of the man he had once called Pops in his pale blue eyes.

He ran a hand through his coal-black hair, removed a stray leaf, and walked away from the old man's body without a backward glance.

Rise to Power

"War is the perfect excuse for all of my most beautiful dreams to come true. I've been waiting my whole life for this."—Scott Cooper

When the two girls had escaped into the storm, he had heard talk there were others connected to them. He asked the right questions, got a hold of one who hadn't managed to run fast enough, and got to use his favorite knife.

In the end, that sniveling little deserter had told him little he didn't already know and begged for death. Five men had tried to desert the same night as the girls escaped under the cover of a violent thunderstorm. Three were shot, the fourth, one Allen Banks, had made it almost to Highway 60 before they caught up with him and hamstrung him. The fifth had run southeast, towards Tennessee, and gotten away. That one was the blond girl's brother.

Scott seethed as he walked past the bodies of the men his father had killed and kicked one furiously. He was still pissed all these months later that he hadn't found the deserter or the two little whores right away. He had lost valuable time; there was no word from Easter or Burton, the two fools he had sent south after the brother. He had just sent another pair of men in search of the two whores after the last pair disappeared or deserted. He spat a fine stream of tobacco juice on the ground and walked back to his nice tent. It was the largest, and it had an actual honest-to-God bed in it. Right about now, one of the new whores would be waiting there for him.

He liked breaking the new ones in; they were more interesting when they fought. He likened it to breaking a horse—you had to break their spirit, break them to the point that the stupid whores knew you were the one with the power.

The camp had just blown through another Podunk town and picked up some new girls to replace those fool enough not to root out the bastards growing in them. He didn't waste time—when he heard of any whores who started showing he didn't even bother wasting a bullet. The knife worked just as well and it felt better.

The other men kept their distance now. They followed his orders and kept their mouths shut. No more Captain Kipling to give them orders, no more arguments about whether Tent 5 was within guidelines – Cooper had used that favorite knife of his and taken care of the CO nearly two months ago. That damn politically correct little twit would not be rattling on about human rights anymore.

Kipling had been field-promoted after Granger had been taken out in a skirmish near Bolivar. Scott shook his head at the loss. Granger had been a mean S.O.B. who didn't give a crap about the Geneva Convention or what any other fool political monkeys thought.

He had set up Tent 5, coordinated the sorting of prisoners, and arranged for the range disposal of the old and weak. Under Granger's command, this rattletrap group of fighters, once saddled with some stupid official military designation Cooper couldn't even remember now, had become a terrifying future for any unfortunate towns that lay in its path. Few survived the onslaught, and those that did were either conscripted or put to use in other ways.

Those too old or young to fight, work or whore were ended quickly and efficiently. No need to let survivors loose to warn others of troop movements or to get some stupid ideas to fight back later.

Granger had been a great man and Cooper had been his apt pupil. Then he had to up and die and that fool Kipling had taken over. Nearly shut things down around here. He was old school; he'd been with the regiment from when it still was a regiment and still in contact with the Western Front.

The long silence from HQ had rankled at Kipling. He'd complained to Granger that they needed to follow commands and find out what the hell had happened. But since the entire cell phone array had been destroyed, along with most of the power stations and other networks, they were back to the frigging Dark Ages. "We might as well be fighting in the Civil fucking War." Cooper had listened to the two go at it and wondered why Granger didn't just shoot the uppity little twerp.

The night Kipling ordered Cooper into his tent to tell him how things were going to change now that Granger was dead and that orders would be coming soon to stand down... that was when Cooper had had enough. He waited until the camp was quiet and then he put to use some of those skills his dad had so foolishly taught him. He snuck in and cut Captain Kipling's throat from ear to ear. There hadn't been any voices saying "nay" when he told the men the next day that Kipling had put him in charge. He'd sent two men on the southern routes that night, and two on the road towards Belton, those runaway whores' hometown. "No one deserts and no whores get to leave," he said, surveying the mass of faces he had called to the camp meeting. "You leave here and it better damn well be in a body bag."

The following weeks would see several tests of that edict—in the end, no one survived stepping away from camp, unless they were under orders to go.

He was almost to his tent, and he pulled on his belt, unbuckling it in anticipation. Inside of the dark tent he removed his ammo belt, placing it well within range. Most of his men were idiots, just begging to be told what to do and where to march. The fact that he kept them fed, clothed, and well-laid did wonders, but he was no fool. There were some who still thought they were in the Army, and he knew that the way he had taken the reins of power in this crappy little corner of the world could be the same way they got rid of him. He was taking no chances. He kept a knife close by as well.

The girl was there, tied securely to the bed, her wrists and ankles already bleeding and raw from trying to free herself. Excellent, a fighter, he'd have himself a nice little ride. As it was, she started screaming and even attempted to bite him the minute he removed her gag. A solid punch to the mouth slowed her down and the second punch knocked her unconscious for a few precious seconds. He straddled her and waited patiently for her eyes to flicker open. "You can scream all you like," he said, smiling down at her. "In fact, I like it."

His beautiful face turned hard and cruel and his hand lazily traced its way down her from her collarbone, past her breasts and towards her groin, "But if you try to bite me again, I'll break every bone in your face and make sure you choke to death on your own teeth." He smiled again, and the girl began to sob. The devil himself couldn't have been more handsome or more evil. "Great... let's get started then."

The girl's screams weren't the only ones in the camp that night, but they were certainly the loudest. Even heartless Carmen had paled slightly when she saw the girl delivered to Tent 5 the following morning. She had put her in a sectioned off area, an infirmary of sorts, to heal. No other man would have wanted her in the state she was in.

Little good that small kindness did. The ungrateful wretch managed to hang herself with a section of the shower curtain two days later when one of the fool guards had turned away for what he swore was just a moment. Her name was Lucinda Abernathy. She had turned fourteen years old one week earlier.

New in Town

"W*ar does not determine who is right - only who is left." - Bertrand Russell*

Easter stood in front of Chris, blood seeping from a scarf around his neck. In the past few months, Easter had gone from a deathly white to a pale gray, then slowly darkening as he decayed further with each new dream. His skin had turned almost black now. "Your sister is dead because you failed, Aaronson," the corpse sneered. "You couldn't even pull off an escape. Banks, your sister, your parents, it's all on you. You couldn't even kill me right, 'cause here I am hauntin' your dreams all these months later."

Chris twisted away from Easter's grasping hands. The stench of the corpse filled his nose and made him want to retch. "You're just a dream. You're dead and you're just a dream, Easter." He shoved the corpse away from him and ran, trying to put distance between this remnant and himself, tried in vain to escape the dream.

He ran for what seemed like forever, but when he turned around, there was Easter and behind him, Burton too. "Everything you touch will rot and die, Aaronson, just like me. You can't protect 'em, you'll only get that sweet little piece of ass raped and murdered, just like the rest. I could use a taste of that sweet little thing," the corpse taunted him. Chris screamed then, consumed with horror at the thought of Carrie at the hands of Easter or the likes of Cooper and all the rest.

"Chris! Chris! Wake up!" He came to in the dark, someone standing over him, a light in the doorway.

"Carrie girl, you stand back, child." He heard Fenton's voice from the doorway.

"But Gramps, I..." Chris realized the person standing over him was Carrie.

"No buts, girl, stand back," Fenton's gruff voice admonished. "The boy's havin' more than just a bad dream. You give him space now." He had pulled Carrie out of range. "Son, can you hear me?"

Chris was still shaking from the dream. The smell of rot and decay lingered in his nose. "Yessir." The old man came nearer and an oil lamp lit his way. He extended a hand to Chris, pulling him up from his huddle at the foot of the bed. How had he gotten there? He didn't even remember. He put a hand on Chris's shoulder, motioned to the others to leave, and closed the bedroom door, giving the two men some privacy. He pushed Chris down onto the edge of the bed and settled into a chair close by.

Fenton's voice was uncharacteristically kind. "Son, what were you dreaming about?"

Chris shuddered and told him about the nightmares. "I keep having them. They aren't going away. And now... now they always bring up Carrie... I just... I'd do anything to protect her and Liza and Joseph and you."

"Son, I know that. I let you stay here and I feel that in you." Fenton reached over and clasped Chris's shoulder. "You did what you could for your family and their deaths are not your fault, son. They just aren't." The man's eyes welled with tears at the thought of the losses he had seen in the past few years. "We are your family now, Chris, and don't you forget that. I know you'll do right by us, too."

"But sir, what if..." His guts were still twisting over the thought of Carrie ever being hurt, "What if I'm bad luck? What if being near me gets people... hurt?"

Fenton grasped Chris's shoulder harder. "You are not to blame for the evils of war, son. God only knows why we have to suffer so, mebbe it'll make us all better men, but you gotta believe that the world can be better." He smiled crookedly, "Believin' is half the battle to makin' it happen." He let go of Chris and sat back in the chair. "Besides, you crap out on me and who's gonna get the back field plowed for the winter crops? Go back to sleep, son. And don't let me catch my granddaughter visitin' you after hours. I reckon I can tell when two's been sharin' a bed or not."

With that he stood up and stretched, limbs creaking, and ambled to the door and on out of the room where the others were huddled in the hallway. "Back to bed, all of you. And that'd best be your own beds if you know what's good for you!" The old man was mellowing a bit; he had chosen not to make too fine a point on the fact that Chris's bed had shown signs of two people, not one, recently sleeping in it.

A few minutes later, a slight creak at the door had announced Carrie's presence. "Chris?" her voice sounded worried. "You okay?" He smiled in the darkness in her direction.

"Yeah babe, I'm okay." She slid onto the bed next to him. Despite the unrelenting, muggy nights, Carrie would sneak into his bedroom each night and they would sleep spooned against each other. He felt her now, just inches away from him, and felt his body respond to her presence as it did each night. He'd managed to keep himself under control, despite the ever-increasing desire to consummate what they had only danced and teased around for months now. "You'd best go back to bed."

He could feel her disappointment and the hint of a pout. "Why can't I stay here with you? I'll make sure and be gone before Gramps wakes up."

"I think we've pushed our luck enough for tonight. 'Sides, we're going into town tomorrow. Let me get a shred of sleep and if I have any more of these damned nightmares, I'm not gonna be waking you up too." He found her lips and kissed them. Sure enough, they were pouting.

She returned his kiss enthusiastically, and Chris pulled her onto his lap and lifted her easily as he stood up, felt her long legs wrap around his waist. He walked to the doorway in this manner, which elicited a frustrated growl from Carrie as she realized he was putting her out of his room for the night. He was learning just how willful the Perdue women could be. One last long kiss and he set her down and slowly shut the door as she grumbled her way down the hall.

The nightmares stayed away, and he managed five blissful hours of sleep before being pounced on by a ball of energy just after dawn. "It's wake up time, Chris!" Joseph Perdue was bubbling over with excitement, "We're goin' to town today!" The three-year-old bounced on him over and over. He was a cute kid, which was the only reason Chris didn't strangle him after Joseph kneed him accidentally in the groin.

Liza appeared in the doorway. A smirk spread over her face as she took in the scene of Chris bent double and Joseph jumping on the bed blissfully unaware of the pain he had just inflicted. Joseph kept jumping, "Mornin' Liza!"

"Mornin' Joseph. Go get yourself dressed so we can go to town right after breakfast." She tried not to laugh at Chris's pained expression.

"Mornin' Chris, you coming into town with us? Or do you think you need to... um... rest some more?" Her lip was twitching.

"I'll be fine, thanks so much, Liza." Chris gave her a look that spoke volumes, and she ran off to the kitchen, laughing merrily. He slid gingerly out of bed, concentrating on carefully easing his aching gonads into a pair of jeans. Fenton had kept him busy fixing everything from fencing to roofs and his skin had darkened to a light bronze in the hot summer sun. His chest was well developed after months of hard work and he grinned as Carrie stopped by his doorway and let out a low, appreciative whistle.

Fenton came walking by then and harrumphed at his granddaughter, "Mind yourself, girl."

She winked and her face assumed an innocent expression. "I am Gramps!" The old man moved down the hall, calling for his coffee. From the smell wafting from the kitchen, Liza had brewed it already and was now working on the rest of breakfast. The girls took turns prepping breakfast for the family, and Chris often lent a hand with lunch and dinner. Every meal they sat down as a family and ate together, no matter what project was underway. Fenton insisted on it.

Chris's family hadn't been much different, so it felt normal, reassuring.

The Perdues would say grace, talk about their plans or projects for the day and enjoy the bounty of their hard work. Running the farm was full of challenges and the work seemed unending, but Chris had eaten better in the last few months than he had when he'd been conscripted.

Overall, the time spent with the Perdues had been one of healing, physically and emotionally. He had been laid up until mid-April, but by mid-May he was working hard each day in the fields. By summer, he had been agile enough to begin repairing the barn and re-shingling the roof of the farmhouse.

The girls had convinced Fenton to take down the various trophies and removed the worn sofa from the den. A full-size mattress and box springs which had belonged to their parents had been retrieved from the basement and the small closet held all of their father Isaac's old clothes. Chris was nearly the same size and the jeans and shirts fit relatively well, although his growing muscles made the shirts rather tight. Fenton had told Chris he was welcome to any of Isaac's clothes that could fit, and it helped that they didn't have to explain purchases of men's clothing in town until they were good and ready.

He was nervous about the trip to town. Tiptonville wasn't a large place by any means. Chris hadn't thought his hometown was much of anything, but it had held tenfold the number of residents that Tiptonville boasted. Of course, that was before everything had gone to hell. Who knew how many lived there now or in Tiptonville for that matter. He wasn't sure he was ready to meet the townfolk or that they would buy the story he and the Perdues had cooked up of him being a friend of the family.

Fenton had made it clear that Chris wasn't to ever speak of his participation, unwilling or not, with the Western Front. "There's some'd rather string you up from the nearest tree than get your story. They find that out, boyo." Fenton had warned him gruffly, "You keep your mouth shut and follow our lead."

They had had a near miss a week or so back when a couple of boys Carrie's age had stopped by the farm looking for work. Fenton hadn't told them "no" but instead said they should check back around harvest time. Chris had been off at the old farmstead, digging up the smaller starts of blueberry bushes to transplant nearer the farmhouse.

Carrie hadn't been in favor of that, mainly because having the bushes closer to the house meant they couldn't run off with the excuse of picking blueberries. She had stalked away from him in a snit and been at the farmhouse and able to help Fenton run the boys off after basic pleasantries had been exchanged, along with a promise to come to town soon.

Lost in his thoughts, Chris picked at his food. Liza looked offended. "What? Is there somethin' wrong with the eggs?"

"Wha... huh? The eggs? No, no, the eggs are fine." Chris looked down at his plate, still filled with food and shoveled a large bite in his mouth, chewed and swallowed. "I just, Gramps, you sure me coming into town is a good idea?"

"Son, it'll be fine." The old man reached over and squeezed Chris's shoulder. "You're a friend of the family and you visited us here 'bout five years back. Your family is gone, but you found our address in some papers, remembered us, and headed our way. You been here since late spring and been earnin' your keep working on our farm." He winked then, "No one's gonna believe an old codger like me would put up with you or take you in 'less you was who I said you was."

He turned towards little Joseph. "Now mind you, Joseph. Anyone asks you who young Chris here is and you just say he's a friend of the family. You remember that, right Joseph?" The boy nodded solemnly.

Fenton looked over at Carrie, "And you, girl, don't you be hangin' on him or making them damn googly eyes. You made a list of what we need, right?"

Carrie looked offended and muttered under her breath before responding, "I got the list right here, Gramps." She read it aloud, and he had her add three items—buckshot, a 1982 Chevy pickup truck repair manual and propane.

"Don't know what we can get or what'll be available, but we'll ask 'bout 'em. Okay, let's get going! We got a long trip ahead of us." The truck had refused to start the previous day and Chris had wished for the hundredth time that he had taken the basic automotive classes at school like his buddy Allen did. He had been the one to ask Fenton if he had a truck repair manual and the old man had looked embarrassed and shook his head no. Apparently, Chris wasn't the only one who had skipped automotive class. "Football." The old man gruffly commented, "I was busy with football. That is until I mashed my left knee the last game of the season. Still pains me."

They would do it the old-fashioned way and take a horse and buggy the three plus miles into town. The last time they had gone into town, while Chris was still laid up with his broken ankle, they had walked, and Fenton's left knee had swollen to twice its size. He couldn't walk without grunting in pain for weeks.

With Ichabod hitched and ready, they had climbed into the buggy and started off. The road was clear, except several abandoned vehicles that had been pulled off of the road. Chris thought that it looked as if there had been a conflict of some kind, but not recently. Two of the trucks were not only turned over, they had been set on fire. Fenton followed Chris's gaze as it lingered on the skeletons hanging from the burned-out trucks.

"Western Front," he said gruffly, "I told you we don't much cotton to the West trying to tell us how to live. Those boys are a warnin' to anyone else foolhardy enough to bother with us." Chris realized how dangerous admitting he had any association with the Western Front, unwilling or not, would be to all of them.

Two tall lookout posts sat on each side of the road right before they reached town. They were similar to the 'high hides' that deer hunters use, but were larger and probably better insulated for winter use. The rough wood was covered in corrugated metal sheets. Chris figured it was hotter than hell in those things. He could see the outline of a man inside and noticed the cold, dark snub of a rifle in the other lookout post. They had a great view from up there, and could sound the alarm long before anyone came within striking distance of town.

Fenton followed his gaze and waved towards the outposts. Chris did his best to look as unarmed and helpless as possible. Anyone with a decent set of binoculars would see that both the girls and the old man were armed, so he figured the snipers manning the outposts wouldn't shoot him or think he was holding them hostage. He was nervous nonetheless.

His focus on the high lookouts provided an excellent opportunity for the men stationed in the waist high grass to approach without his notice. He couldn't help flinching in response to the rifle that appeared to his right. "Hold up!" The man that held it eyed him suspiciously, "Ho there, Fenton."

The old man smiled down at the armed man, "Ho there, John. Like you to meet a friend of the family. This here's Chris Aaronson, hails from a ways from here." The armed man looked them over carefully, noting the relaxed looks on the rest of the family.

"Friend of the family?"

"Yup," Fenton nodded coolly, "The son of friends of Amy's. He came out here, what, five years ago a'visitin.'" He pursed his lips. "Nothin' left for him so's he sought us out, due t' his family bein' gone. He's been helping out on the farm these past two months. Came just in the nick of time for plantin' season."

John nodded, letting the barrel slide away from the group and backing away. He let out a shrill whistle to the sentries above and their guns disappeared. "Take care Fenton." He nodded at Chris. "Nice to meet you, Chris. You all go on through."

The buggy pulled away, passing the outposts and continued towards town. Chris heaved a sigh of relief, and Carrie squeezed his arm. "That was John Carter, he's Carl's stepdad." She leaned close, and whispered, "Liza and Carl like each other."

Fenton grunted, "I heard that."

"Oh Gramps!"

The first of the town buildings appeared at the crest of the hill. Chris looked around. Most of the buildings were intact, and there wasn't much to see. It was a tiny town, a fraction of the size of Belton.

Chris had thought Belton was small compared to the sprawling streets in Kansas City, just a twenty-minute drive to the north, but this was like having a Main Street and nothing else. How had they made out so much better than Belton? Dumb luck?

The first sign of damage that Chris noticed was the crumpled water tower. Carrie followed his gaze. "They took out the water right away. I haven't had a decent shower since, thanks to those bastards."

Fenton growled at her choice of words, "Mind your tongue, girl." He didn't say much more. After all, he missed regular showers too.

There was a café, but it looked deserted, most of the windows had boards over them. There was a large two-story brick building with white columns on the left side of the street. "That's the old bank," Fenton noted as they passed by, "Least it was until they built that fool building next to it." He cocked his thumb at the Regions bank sign, which was broken, and the building the sign belonged to was gutted.

Directly following the stately brick building was a narrow alley and then another fairly plain two-story brown brick building. At first glance, it seemed to be nothing more than a dump for miscellaneous junk. But the buggy turned and headed towards it and Chris could see a rough hand-lettered sign in the window that read, "Tiptonville Trade Mart." Just inside the door was a tough-looking man with a rifle tucked against his shoulder. The guy looked him over suspiciously and rested a large hand on the Bowie strapped on his thigh.

Fenton handed Joseph down to Chris and carefully eased out of the buggy with a low groan. Riding in the buggy had been easier than walking, but the old man wasn't as flexible as he used to be. He handed the reins to Carrie and pointed to a bike rack twenty feet away.

There was a dappled pony already strapped there. She nodded and walked the horse and buggy over to it while the others headed towards the Trade Mart. At the entrance, Fenton put his arm across Chris's shoulders and nodded to the man. "Morning Wes, this here is Chris, a friend of the family. He's been with us these past two months, working the farm."

Wes's gaze never left Chris. His nod was brusque. "Where you hail from?"

"Northwest of here, sir."

"You've been in the forces, seen action, haven't you?"

Chris had been unprepared for such a direct question. "I, uh..."

Fenton interceded, "The boy has seen loss. He lost his family and then headed here because he had nowhere else to go. I think Wes that we can leave it at that."

Wes's eyes narrowed as he shifted his focus to Fenton. "Been reports of Western Front troops deserting, coming this way. Also been raids, south in Dyersburg. Bastards came into the outskirts and were forced back west." His eyes moved back to Chris, coldly assessing him. "Them soldiers been doing more than just shooting men, Perdue, they've been killing kids and older people, raping the women. I hear tell they ripped up parts of Missouri bad, and I also hear they ain't 'zactly following orders from the chain of command no more." He said all of this while trying to stare Chris down.

Chris just stared back, feeling more pissed by the minute. This guy figured he was from the west and was coming to all the wrong conclusions. Carrie broke the impasse by returning from hitching the horse and grabbed Chris's and Fenton's sleeves. "Come on, I've got a list a mile long and we need to figure out what crops we brought in can be traded for. And it's gonna be hotter than he..." She gave a quick glance over at her grandfather, "heck... soon. We need to get unloaded and reloaded, and I want to check out the local news before we have to head back home. You were going to look for the Chilton's manual, remember?" She said all of this in one quick tirade and then stood staring at Chris expectantly while ignoring Wes's glare.

After they moved past and away from Wes, Chris relaxed and let out a deep breath. Something told him that guy was going to be trouble. For the rest of the time, they were there, Chris felt like every move he made was being watched. Anytime he looked up and towards the direction of the entrance, he could see Wes staring at him.

They spent nearly an hour at the Trade Mart and Chris watched Liza and Carrie go to work, negotiating the best trade they could for what crops they had brought in. He smiled as he watched the girls at work.

They were naturals, born to haggle and seemed to be experts at negotiating the best trade possible. His smile turned down when he thought of Jess, and how good she had been at it. He had turned his back to Wes and could feel the man's stare, right in the middle of his back. It made him wish he had a gun, or at the least a knife, but Fenton had worried that if he were armed, he would be shot by the sentries on the approach. After seeing the burned-out trucks, bodies and the sentry towers, he understood the old man's concerns. The citizens of Tiptonville were determined to keep the rest of their people alive and well... and keep the rest of the world at gunpoint.

They finished up at the Trade Mart and headed for another small store down the block. Inside it was filled with an eclectic mix of hardware, automotive, and farm equipment parts. This store didn't have any armed guard at the front, only one ancient, white-haired old man at the back counter. "Mr. Liles!" Fenton called out loudly, smiling like a kid.

The old man peered, squinting at them through thick glasses. Chris thought he must be the oldest man he had ever seen.

They moved closer, Fenton in the lead, and the old man grinned, showing nothing but toothless gums. "Young Fenton! How are you, boy?" Hearing a man that he called Gramps referred to as a 'boy' was rather disconcerting.

"I'm fine, sir, just fine." Fenton took the old man's hand gently and gave it a firm shake. At one time, the man may have been larger, but now he seemed a frail wisp, with papery thin skin and several large dark bruises on his face and hands. He was alert, and looked over the group before him, quickly singling out Chris for his attention. "Hello, young man, and who might you be?"

Fenton pulled Chris over to him. "Chris, this here is Mr. Otis Liles. Mr. Liles taught us Biology in high school and he was the team's football coach as well. Mr. Liles kept me in line but good." Good sweet lord, the old man had to be ancient! "Mr. Liles, this young man is a friend of the family and he's been helping out on the farm for the past couple of months." Chris nodded and shook the old man's cool, bony hand carefully.

"Hello, Mr. Liles."

The old man beamed. "My boys never seem to forget me, though they are getting fewer and fewer each year." His smile dropped. "Especially with the troubles we've had lately. It's good to meet you, young man."

His attention turned to Carrie and Liza and down to little Joseph. "It's so good to see the three of you children growing up so well!" They all nodded and smiled at Mr. Liles. "What can I do for you, Fenton, my boy?"

"Well, Mr. Liles, I guess I should have taken that Auto class from Mr. Elias." Fenton looked sheepish, "The truck has broken down and I need a Chilton's manual to see if I can fix it."

The next half hour involved a flurry of questions on the problem, including a lecture on how carburetors worked. Eventually the entire group was involved in finding the appropriate book, stashed in a dark corner with liberal amounts of dust and dirt, and then directed to various parts of the store for parts needed to fix the problem. In return, the old man accepted a small basket of eggs, a loaf of freshly baked bread, and the promise of a future dinner at the farm. In spite of his fragile appearance, Otis Liles moved more spryly than Fenton did, despite Fenton being decades younger.

Their mission complete, Chris and the Perdues said their goodbyes and headed for the door. Mr. Liles would be visiting them for dinner in three days, and Chris was eager to find out just how old the old man really was. As they made their way out of Mr. Liles' store, waving goodbye and thanks, Chris glanced over and saw that Wes was standing there at the corner, watching and waiting for them. Chris could feel the tension building. This guy meant trouble, bad trouble.

Carrie whispered next to him, "Ignore him, Chris. He's a jerk." But Chris kept eye contact, he couldn't help it, this guy got his innards to jangling.

Fenton eyed Wes, nodded curtly at him, and gripped Chris's shoulder firmly. "Time we got back to the farm, son. Liza, go unhitch that horse." Wes was advancing toward them, his eyes drilling into Chris.

Chris stood his ground, returning the gaze steadily. Fenton's grip tightened. "Son, you go help Liza with Ichabod. That damn horse has been skittish since he smelled those burnt bodies outside of town. Go on with you now." He pushed Chris in the other direction and stepped toward Wes.

Wes stopped short of simply walking around the old man, but his gaze never left Chris, who had turned his back to Wes, Liza sidling up to him on one side, Joseph's hand firmly in his, as he walked towards the horse and buggy a few yards away.

He could hear Wes speaking to Fenton, sounding angry, and Fenton's calm and clear reply, "Wes Perkins, you may have served in the Gulf and know your way 'round a rifle, but you don't know nothin' 'bout people. That boy is nothing you need to worry about and he is what I've said he is, a friend of the family. You leave it at that, and don't make me raise my voice. I still remember your punk ass trying to bully the others in preschool and it looks as if you haven't changed a bit in thirty-five years of living."

Wes looked pissed, especially over being reminded of the fact that Fenton had known him when he was barely out of diapers. "You'd best get back to your post and worry about keeping this town safe, 'stead of worrying about things that aren't any of your business."

As he turned and marched away with Carrie towards the buggy, Wes called after him, "Well, don't expect none of us to be coming down as far as your farm, old man. You're on your own way out there."

"That's the way I like it!" Fenton grumbled, muttering further comments that were neither friendly nor repeatable in mixed company.

Carrie would have smiled if she wasn't so scared for Chris. Wes was bad news. He'd come back from Iraq in 2006, rumors of a dishonorable discharge on the wind, and slapped around his young wife so badly that one day she'd left town with their two kids and never come back.

When the fighting had broken out, he'd taken lead, and showed some of the other younger men in town some rather effective, lethal fighting strategies. It had kept most of the residents of Tiptonville and the surrounding area free of the death and destruction other small towns had suffered, but something about Wes Perkins wasn't quite right. No one spoke of it much now, but Wes wasn't someone you wanted near you in times of peace and only questionably in times of war.

They loaded up the buggy, climbed in, and drove past Wes's hard stare.

"I'll be keeping an eye on you," he said, staring at Chris as the buggy drove away, back out of town. They passed the outposts silently and breathed a collective sigh of relief after they had passed the burned-out trucks and cleared the town limits.

As the farm came into view, Carrie leaned over and hugged Chris tightly. "You're new in town. It will get better, I promise." Her touch was reassuring, and Chris relaxed into it, even if he didn't believe her words for one second.

The Hidey-Hole

"The first time we heard gunfire, my parents told me that it was nothing. We read by lamplight in the basement and pretended to be pioneers. It would have worked if they weren't so scared. But I remember the fear even though their features have faded from my memory. I pretended right along with them for Tina's sake, she was only three and I; I was the big brother, after all.

By the third night of gunfire had gotten closer. The sirens, normally used to warn us of dangerous weather, were going off, warning all citizens of Clinton of an imminent invasion.

No one was pretending to be pioneers anymore. We were all just scared and edgy, and Mom and Dad insisted we sleep inside the cupboard nook behind the false front. There was a shelter in the basement that we had made for all four of us, with another hiding spot within the cupboard built inside and a false back inside of that. It was so small that only Tina and I could fit, and it led into a crawlspace that smelled of mildew and dust. We were able to drag blankets and pillows through with us, and Tina was terrified and cried herself to sleep huddled against me. With the cement walls of the basement above and all around us, we could hear very little from outside our little nest. And that night, as Tina and I slept, the troops moved into the town, and quickly began smashing through the houses, street by street.

I think they knew what would happen. I have such a hard time forgiving them that they would die and we should live. What kind of world was left for two small children to exist in all alone?" - David's Journal

David woke first. His eyes snapped open. He had been dreaming it was Christmas morning, with presents all around the tree. The dream had frayed away, disrupted by screams. Now he heard nothing. There were no screams, no murmurs, no guns or explosions—not even the crunch of the gravel road outside. Tina slept curled against him, her breath warm and moist. His shirt was damp at the spot where her face pressed against his chest. Normally he would have shoved her away, called her a little baby. But at the moment, he wasn't feeling so big himself. He felt small and alone. It was light out. He could see that much, but nothing else. He strained his ears to hear anything but the soft rhythm of Tina's breaths, in, out, occasionally sighing as she slept, whining to herself. A bad dream?

After several minutes, he could hear the faint twittering of a bird, the crackle of gunfire far, far away. Were Mom and Dad still sleeping? Tina's breathing barely changed as he carefully shifted her off of him, covering her with a warm blanket like Mom always did before he slipped away, back through the hidey-hole into the hidden room. The room was empty, the door was open and, and he could see... sky?

David blinked, confused, and rubbed his eyes. Perhaps this was a dream.

He stepped through the wreckage of fallen timbers, small mountains of furniture mixed with plaster and wood and clothing. Open pipes dribbled water, and he realized his feet were wet. He stumbled forward, earning a great painful gash on his leg from a protruding board. The silence was terrifying, but hearing the noises he made reverberate through the mess of what had been his home was even more awful. His mind was devoid of any words to describe what he saw or name the overwhelming dread he felt. Mom and Dad weren't in the room. His home was destroyed. He was completely alone.

The boy stood and stared. His leg bled freely from the wound, but he took no notice, standing there immobile until he heard a high wail of fear behind him. He turned to see Tina's small tousled head peering from the false-front cupboard. Her eyes were black holes of terror. She looked just as confused and shell-shocked as he must have, and her lower lip quivered.

"Mommy!" she wailed, ignoring David as he waded back to her and tried to help her out and up. "I want Mommy!" she wailed again before he could shush her. He slapped a hand over her mouth.

"Shh! We'll find Mom and Dad, but you gotta be quiet! The bad guys might still be here!" he warned her. Although it seemed impossible that things could get worse, her eyes grew bigger at the thought. She quieted, screwing up her face at the dark mess of water and clinging to her brother, wrapping her arms and legs around him.

He lifted her up and tried to carry her, but the way was too cluttered and he tripped, spilling them both into the dirty water and plaster that lay throughout the basement.

To her credit, Tina made very little noise, despite her skinned knees. Her world had changed far too much, and she was in the same state of shock that he was. By the time they managed to crawl and shove their way out of the debris to the other end of the basement, they were both filthy and wet. The stairs leading up were broken in several places, but enough of the staircase was intact for them to climb up and out.

Tina clung to her brother's back like a monkey, and then silently followed him after he set her down and pushed through the remnants of their home. Slowly, both children exited through what had been the living room and into the back yard.

It took just moments for the two children to find the lifeless bodies of their parents. They lay crumpled in the grass within feet of each other. Dad looked as if he had been trying to reach Mom. His arm was stretched out towards her. Their mother lay face up, eyes staring wide open and clouded, and Dad was just an arm's length away on his stomach.

David sat down abruptly on the grass next to his mother. He reached forward hesitantly and touched her. Her skin was cold, rubbery, and he felt his stomach flop and his hands shook as he reached over and closed her lifeless, staring eyes.

Tina said nothing, just held his free hand and pressed her face into his shoulder. Her little body was shaking uncontrollably. He thought briefly that he should say something, tell her Mom and Dad were in heaven or something, but he couldn't make the words come. Not any words. What can a ten-year-old child say to his baby sister of three? Neither of them had words for the horror before them.

It would be hours before they left the bodies of their parents. And then it was only because of the gnawing pain in their stomachs. Life rudely continues on in the face of death, and bodies still need nourishment.

David dug through the wreckage until he found a snack pack of fruit cocktail, the kind with the pull-top lids. They both ate ravenously, silently, avoiding the sharp rim as they dipped their fingers in for the last little specks of syrup.

Tina stared up at him, absently licking a dribble of fruit cocktail syrup from the corner of her mouth. "I'll find us more food in a little while," he told her and walked over to the shed in the corner of the property.

It was still intact, rather incongruous when you looked at all the devastated houses around it. On the inside of the door hung a shovel, and David took it down from its hook and walked back to where his parents lay.

Digging a hole deep enough for both of them was amazingly hard.

David dug and dug and the patch widened, deepened until it was a few feet across and maybe half a foot in depth. His hands, back and shoulders hurt, and he was dirty and horribly hungry. Tina had refused to leave his side and sat clinging to his leg, slowing his movements and exhausting him further. He stopped, rubbed his hands, and straightened his back. Behind him, Tina sucked on her thumb noisily and whimpered for food.

"C'mon, Teen," he took her hand in his, "I'll find you somethin' to eat." They trudged past the remains of their home and on to the Connor's who lived down the street. The Connors had left a week ago, headed east towards family in Illinois, and Mr. Connor had come by and told Mom and Dad to help themselves to whatever they left behind. Most of it was probably still there in the hand-dug bomb shelter hidden behind shelves of books. It was a survival cache that they didn't have room to take with them when they ran, when news of the advancing troops had spread.

The bomb shelter had been raided. The shelves of books that Mrs. Connor loved so much had been tossed willy-nilly to the ground, but no one had discovered the cache of foods concealed behind the bookshelves. David found canned meats, vegetables, ready-to-eat soups, even canned milk. A trip through the Connor's ruined house also yielded a hand-operated can opener. David wrestled with it, opening a can of milk and one of the soups, and greedily sucked down his share of both before his sister could have a chance to eat. The look on her face made him feel awful. Her lip trembled, and he patted her hair clumsily and made sure she ate the rest of the soup and milk.

"Sorry 'Teen, I was awful hungry. Hey look, there's some of Miz Connor's homemade strawberry jam, ya want some?"

Tina perked up and minutes later was happily sucking strawberry jam off her fingers as David led her to a broken and dripping water pipe to wash up.

Tina's fine blond hair would soon become matted beyond all hope of redemption. David did his best to keep his sister's hands and face clean, but the rest of her took on a grayish grimy appearance in the days, weeks and finally months that followed.

In the end, it had taken two full days to dig the single grave deep enough to bury their parents' bodies in and a full week for the blisters to heal. The stock of canned food at the Connor's had eventually run out. David expanded his searches to the other ruined houses around them. Twice they had hidden from troops marching through the area.

The uniforms were different, but a stranger was a stranger and the children were too frightened to test the foreign soldier's kindness. The men strode through the ruined stretches of houses, their machine guns hanging from their shoulders, searching for loot, for food or clean water, or anything else they took a fancy to. They robbed the dead, shot at any stray animal unfortunate enough to cross their paths, and drank bottles of alcohol (David had read the labels of the empty bottles discarded at their camp sites) before finally moving south towards more populated areas.

Spring had turned to high summer, but their hidey-hole stayed relatively cool. David made sure that they both drank from the broken water pipes and not the pond or the brackish water that collected in the drainage ditches. Only once had they made that mistake, and Tina had gotten so sick he was afraid she would die. She had run a fever, hot to the touch and glassy eyes for two days before slowly getting better. When the water pipes slowed to a trickle and finally petered out, David searched for new ones, with Tina following silently behind wherever he went.

There was a pattern to the days now. Each morning, he would wake first and then shake his sister awake. He would turn his back while she used the overflowing, stinking toilet in the house down the street, and take her to the nearest water source and make sure she washed her face and hands. They would eat canned food for breakfast, wash again, and scout for supplies. They took it street by street, fanning out in ever-widening circles. The walks were taking longer and longer, and often they would stop at a familiar shelter and sleep for a while with the sun burning hot overhead. Tina was still little, so she needed more sleep. And David found it easy to nod off with his sister cuddled against him, even on the hottest day, her little body moist and heavy.

Later, they would take what they had found and head back to the hidey-hole for dinner and to sleep. Sleep came with the setting sun. The few candles they had found were precious and the flashlights and batteries even more so. By the time the darkness fell completely, the two children were already well snuggled into their nest, lying close to each other for comfort. If their parents could see them now, David mused one night, they would both be smiling in surprise and pride at how good he was being with Tina. The only time they argued had been over what to eat, pickles or olives, for dinner one night. Other than that, he had been the best big brother he could be; better than his parents would have ever dreamed. Tina whimpered suddenly in her sleep and he pulled her closer and patted her matted hair until her breathing evened and her body relaxed once again.

Two More Makes Four

"I *'ve learned so many things in the past ten years. Things they didn't teach in school or even in the Boy Scouts. If the me that was ever met the me that is—would I even recognize myself? I know how to take a life. And I have done it to save me and mine. I know how to butcher game and livestock, raise food to eat, track deer, and break through ice in the winter to make sure I've got water to drink. I know lots of things—but most importantly, I know that you don't have to be blood to be family. Jess, little Erin, Becka, Jacob—they're all my family, just as much as Tina is. Even Q2 is family. Even Lord Flea. I can't imagine life without them. I don't think I would want to."—David's Journal*

Jess and Erin moved steadily north, following first the Luc River, then Clinton Lake, and now some other unknown body of water. Their progress was far slower now that Jess's belly had swelled, pushing against the oversized shirt and forcing her pants to swoop in under it.

They were held with a safety pin now that the button had popped off. She was so damned tired of walking. Worse yet, the awful thing inside kept kicking her. It kept her awake during the nights when they lay on the hard ground, exhausted from another long day of walking.

Erin still insisted on boiling any of the water they found. There was usually dirt or sand in it now that the rains were less frequent and the water levels low in the creeks. The flat dull taste it had after being boiled tasted putrid to Jess, but she drank it anyway, despite the way her stomach roiled in protest. At least she could keep food down. That was an improvement over the spring, but now backaches and heartburn had set in.

The sun wasn't even beginning to dip down over the horizon when they reached the outskirts of Clinton, and Erin insisted they stop at the ruins of a church. Quincy had been whining and nuzzling at Jess's hand for the past hour. She was only a few months old, but the young dog knew when her mistress tired.

"You've got circles under your eyes so bad it looks like you've been punched," Erin observed, giving Jess a gentle shove down on a nearby pew after lining it with a tattered and filthy blanket. "For crying out loud, just lay down for a little while. I'll scout for some food and water and make sure the area is safe. Quincy, you watch her close and make sure she rests." The dog whined softly in response.

Jess didn't argue, she was too exhausted. She sunk down on the pew and closed her eyes. Quincy licked her hand softly, whined again, and settled down on the ground, keeping contact with Jess at all times. The pup was acting weird and had been all day. Jess's back hurt, her feet hurt. Hell, just about everything hurt today. Last night had been sleepless; they had both listened to the gunfire in the distance, wondering if it was headed their way.

So now, when Jess closed her eyes, sleep came quickly, stealing across her and propelling her instantly into a dream. A nightmare really, it was always the same—men surrounding her and reaching for her. She pushed herself against the far wall, trying to escape, always trying to push them away as they crushed her beneath their sweating bodies.

It was the crunch of feet on broken glass and Quincy's short, quick bark that woke her instantly, her heart pounding in fear. Half her mind was still in the nightmare. Instantly her hand found Lady, as she liked to call her gift from old Coop. She kept her eyes closed as she listened for the next step. She would die before she went back, of that she was determined. Another quiet crunch, this one only a few feet away, and she launched herself upward despite her awkward, protruding belly.

Brandishing the revolver, she screamed wordlessly. The tiny child cowered before her, mouth open and stock still, a terrified expression on its grimy face. Quincy's body pressed firmly against Jess's legs, and her tail thumped against the ground as she whined in excitement.

It was just a child. A little slip of a thing, no older than four years and maybe not even that. It had matted, filthy hair that might have been a light ash brown if it were clean. To guess, Jess would have to say it was a girl, but with all the grime, it was difficult to tell. The child's eyes flicked away from Jess and focused on someone behind her and she spun to find a young boy, older, equally filthy, looking terrified and armed with a brick. He held it defensively, eyeing her with a wary, frightened stare.

Just then, Erin's voice rang out, "Whoa kid, drop the rock! We come in peace!" She had returned from scavenging and was standing in the broken doorway of the church with several cans tucked under one arm and a blessedly rare, unopened bottle of spring water in her hand.

Both children shifted on their feet, their attention turned to her and they prepared to bolt. Erin smiled winningly. "I found beef stew and green beans and even some sweet, condensed milk. Is anyone hungry?" The little one licked her lips at the mention of the milk and looked over at the older boy for direction. It was obvious to both of the girls that, except for each other, these two children were completely alone.

Jess took advantage of the girl's interest and spoke. "My name is Jess, and that's my friend Erin. What's your name?"

A grimy thumb had found its way into the girl's mouth and it muffled her words, "Deena."

The boy spoke up, "She's Tina, and I'm David."

Jess smiled at them and sat back down. They were only kids. She would be less threatening if she were sitting. Besides, she was still tired.

She put the revolver away and gave the older boy a steady, reassuring look. He eyed her back warily. "We'll share what we've got with you if you're hungry."

The boy nodded and relaxed his hold on the brick, finally setting it down as Erin pulled a prized can opener out of their pack and opened the cans. Both children said nothing, just stared intently at the cans of food until they were opened and offered to them. And even after that, there were only quiet smacks of satisfaction intermixed with loud gulps.

The little one, Tina, giggled as Quincy placed her paws on the girl's shoulders and licked her face ecstatically. The pup was unable to control her enthusiasm at meeting new friends, especially one of such a small size. Jess was amused to note see the dog's industrious tongue had cleared away a great deal of the grime.

Erin teased details from the boy, learning that he and his sister were alone, and had been for months now. Recently, they had heard gunfire again and hidden from the soldiers moving through the area. "They shot the Tubman's dog Reggie," David noted solemnly, "we hid from everyone after seeing that."

Jess and Erin told the children an edited version of how they had been captured by soldiers and had finally managed to escape. "You did the right thing to hide," Jess assured them. "Those men are very dangerous."

Tina had finished licking the last of the condensed milk from the can and boldly climbed into Erin's lap, tucking herself against the teenager and playing with the collar of her shirt before slowly slipping into a light doze. David offered to show the girls the hidey-hole and Erin stood up, shifting the sleeping child to her shoulder. Tina was still young and used to regular naps. She wrapped her legs around Erin's waist and whined. Both the girls found themselves smiling; the tiny girl was adorable despite her grimy, tattered appearance.

It was only a few blocks to the hidey-hole, but Jess felt nauseous and dizzy by the time they arrived. Quincy was close to her side, so close that twice she nearly tripped over the pup.

"What is up with you, Quincy?" the dog merely whined and licked at her hand while trying to move closer.

Every day that passed, she had moved slower and slower, and her belly grew bigger and bigger. It had made for miserably slow travel as well.

It disgusted her, the thing kicking and rolling inside her and the way her body felt like it didn't belong to her anymore. Had it ever? Since the soldiers had taken them, since that moment she had been dragged into Tent 5, her body had no longer been her own. She was tired of running, and tired of the thing inside her. Her stomach twisted again, cramping painfully, "Great, not only am I friggin' tired, but now I'm going to be sick."

By her side, Quincy whined softly and licked at Jess's hand. The pup had been glued to her side all day, quietly whining and butting Jess's hand with her wet nose. David pointed to a tiny, dirty hole in the middle of the ruins of a house and announced, "That's where Tina and I sleep."

There was no way to get down the staircase, unless you weighed less than 50 pounds, and the tiny hole he was pointing to was far too small for Jess or even Erin to fit through. A few yards away from the ruined house was an uneven mound of dirt. Erin followed Jess's gaze and took in the crude marker and heaps of dead flowers scattered over the hard earth. It had to be the kids' parents.

The sun dipped lower in the sky and the ominous beginnings of thunder rumbled in the distance. Jess stared at the dark gray storm clouds gathering. There wasn't any shelter to speak of; even the ruined church behind them had been missing its roof. Jess felt like screaming, crying, and just plain collapsing on the ground in frustration and exhaustion. Things couldn't possibly get worse.

Or could they?

Jess felt a gush of fluid rush out of her, flowing down her pant legs and soaking her tattered pants and shoes. It wasn't a stomachache; it wasn't bad food... it was coming.

Jacob's Birth

"Jacob asked me today about his father. I didn't know what to say. I haven't told him the truth. I love him so much, so very, very much. I look at him and I know exactly who his father is. His face was so distinctive, and Jacob looks just like him except for the eyes. My sweet Jacob has my blue eyes, not his father's ice blue. Sometimes I tell myself I can't know for sure; it could have been any one of them. And it could have been... but it's not. Jacob got angry last Saturday. He was so angry I thought he was going to hit David, who had been teasing him relentlessly. But the look on his face brought back awful memories. David said I turned as white as a ghost. How do I tell my son, who I love more than life itself, that his father is a monster? How do I tell him that if I ever see that bastard again, I'm going to kill him? Instead, I lied. I told him his daddy died before I got to know him very well."—Jess's Journal

There was very little in the way of shelter with the roof of the house gone and rain fast approaching. Neither Erin nor Jess could fit through the small hidey-hole in the basement. But shelter here they must, there was too much activity to the south. Troops were moving through. In addition to the thunder, they could now hear gunfire coming from the south.

Had they known that Clinton had become a battleground between several warring factions of groups with names they had not even heard of, the girls would have avoided the ruined town. But there had been no way of knowing and now they were in the thick of it, with the baby coming, and soldiers to the south heading their way.

The storm was barreling in from the West, clouds black and menacing, lightning dancing through them and the accompanying thunder was growing in frequency. If they went east, it would only follow them, and there was no known shelter that direction, anyway. A few hours at most, and they would be caught in the heart of what was promising to be a violent summer storm.

Jess was relieved when Erin came back from checking out the shed, which she said would do in a pinch. The roof was intact, and she smiled encouragingly at Jess who was sitting on the ground, pinch-faced and white-knuckled, clutching a clump of grass as another contraction hit, "Come on, I'll get the packs and the kids can bring blankets and pillows."

Jess just nodded. The pain was getting bad, and she was scared. God, she was so damned scared. What if something went wrong? What if she started hemorrhaging? Or what if the thing got stuck inside her? More than anything, though, she just wanted it out.

This thing had been growing inside her body, taking her food for its own, slowing her down, and making her vulnerable. She wished for the hundredth time she had been brave enough to kill it early on.

When her water had burst, she had looked at her wet pants and shoes and the small pool of fluid forming around her feet in numb shock.

This nightmare that was her life, with the desperation of day-to-day survival, she had found it surprisingly easy to ignore the expanding belly. Even the incessant kicks of the unwelcome creature that was inside her; how many times had she shrugged it off, worrying instead about how much further they could walk in a day, or how long the smoked meat would last before they needed more?

A shed it was, full of lawn equipment that Erin and David hastily pulled out and threw to one side. There was a momentary surprise as a family of rabbits burst from a hole beneath the structure and ran pell-mell into the brush. Quincy left Jess's side for the first time that day and dove after them. "Quincy!" Erin called in exasperation, but the pup ignored her, then disappeared from view, eager to catch a rabbit for her mistress.

The grass was overgrown, high, and thick, low-branched trees surrounded the shed. If they were lucky, the roof would have no leaks and with evening coming it was a relatively safe place to hide from enemy eyes.

They quickly set about making a nest of sorts. They needed two, actually, one for the children in the far corner and one for Jess to have her baby in. Blankets, old clothes, and an armful of stained couch cushions were put to use.

Erin turned to David, "I'll need water, lots of it. Take the bucket and fill it as full as you can." He left silently, Tina a step behind him, holding on to his shirttail with one grubby fist. They headed for the pipeline. When the water had stopped running months back after a particularly fierce firefight, he had searched for days and finally found a broken pipe one block of demolished houses over. At first it had gushed water, but now it was down to a small, but steady trickle. It would take a while to fill the bucket.

Thunder rolled ominously, and Tina trotted to keep up until they reached the pipe. In the distance they could hear the chatter of machine guns. The troops were close, too close, and David wished he could just run back to the hidey-hole and forget about getting water or waiting for the baby to be born. He wondered if Jess would die, didn't having a baby sometimes kill the moms?

Back in the old days, back when there were covered wagons and no cars, women and babies died in childbirth. He'd read about it in a book, so it had to be true. It didn't seem right, having a baby here without a doctor. You were supposed to go to hospitals for things like that. He remembered when Mom had Tina just over three years ago. She was gone for days to the hospital; he had visited with his dad every day. His mom had looked so tired, but smiling and happy too. He had even held the squalling red bundle that was his sister. But the hospital was gone, nothing but a bombed-out shell. Besides, even if it hadn't been bombed, there weren't any doctors there. They had run away, died, or been captured long ago.

Tina tugged on his shirt, and David jumped in surprise. He'd been standing there staring off into space while the bucket filled to the top, dribbled over and trickled onto his shoe. He hadn't even noticed he was so lost in thought. He hoisted the bucket, making his way back to Erin and Jess, slower now, the bucket heavy and sloshing from side to side.

As they neared the old shed, the rain began to fall, fat large drops that turned into a downpour the last twenty feet to the shed door. They could hear Jess's groans of pain as they pulled the door open. David hoped no one would come close enough to the shed to hear or find them, and again he wished he and Tina were in their hidey-hole.

Hours passed. The night had long since descended along with the storm. The branches of the trees whipped in the wind outside the small structure, flailing themselves on the roof like grief-stricken mourners, despairing at what the world had become. A small leak was dripping in one corner, and the door rattled with each gust of wind.

Lightning flashed, lighting up the two small windows of the shed, and the accompanying thunder shook the small building in tandem with Jess's screams. David and Tina were huddled in a corner, terrified, eyes big as saucers. The children were torn between wanting desperately to be back in their hidey-hole and staying with these two girls who had fed them and befriended them. And the screams were ear-splitting. If it weren't for the furious storm outside, David would have pulled his sister to her feet and fled back to the only home he had known.

Instead, he and Tina watched in horrified fascination, his sister rocking herself back and forth in his lap, sucking on her thumb and fully attached to his shirt like a small monkey to its mother. It wouldn't be long now.

"Oh God! Erin! It hurts, it hurts! Oh god, get this thing out of me!" Jess was sobbing in fear between the screams.

The baby was almost there, and the pressure and pain were unbearable. Surely, she was being ripped apart. She felt mind-numbing terror at the thought of bleeding to death and could only envision this creature inside her as some awful alien clawing its way out of her. Jess was losing her grip while Erin tried to make wordless sounds of support as she held Jess's hand and peered down between her friend's legs. A lightning flash lit up the shed, and she saw... she saw...

"Jess! I can see it! I can see its head! Hold on sweetie! It's almost here!"

She reached for the cleanest sheet she could find; ready to catch the damn thing when it shot out. She imagined it would be rocket-powered by the sheer force of Jess's pushes. Jess hunched forward, her face screwed up, and her mouth opened to let out the loudest scream yet.

Her body convulsed and the baby's head pushed out, hesitated for a short moment at the shoulders and then slowly slid out. It was all rather boneless and anticlimactic as Erin lifted it with shaking hands.

Blood and amniotic fluid had gushed out with it, and there was this weird white paste all over the thing. It didn't move, not a twitch. What was this nasty white shit all over the kid? It was... wait... she looked at the naked infant closely in the darkness... and aided by another flash of lightning, she saw... a boy... it was a boy!

"It's a boy, Jess, you had a boy," she grinned, "Told ya you were carrying him low."

"Is it, is it... dead?" Jess asked, with an almost hopeful tone to her voice.

It seemed for a moment to be the epitome of how awful life was, this creature who had occupied her, a product of the horror she and Erin had endured at the hands of the soldiers.

The noise of the storm seemed to subside, and there were several long seconds of silence. The baby didn't move. The door to the shed swung open and all four of the occupants looked up to see the deadly black nose of an AK-47 pointed directly at them.

The soldier swung his rifle at each in turn. The baby, who had been so silent, so surely dead, let out a liquid gurgle, a burbling cough, and then... a thin wail of dissatisfaction. But no one looked at the baby; their eyes were riveted on this creature of death, with his deadly weapon pointed at them, standing stock-still in the doorway. Tall, blond, and, as the lightning lit his face, rather good-looking. He stood for a moment, taking in the scene before him.

There were two young children huddled in a corner and two teenage girls frozen in fear at his feet. In the red-haired girl's arms was a tiny, squirming newborn. Another flash of lightning showed he was a boy.

The baby had obviously been born mere seconds ago; his umbilical cord was still attached. They all looked at him with undisguised terror.

Corporal Jacob Daniels Sr. turned his gun to each in turn. A rifle was propped in the far corner of the shed. He stared at the newborn and remembered the day his son had been born. The nurse had handed him his tiny son, wiped clean and wrapped in a soft blanket, and he had stood there in the Army hospital in Fort Hood, stunned at how tiny and fragile the child was.

Jacob Junior, in that happier time and place they had named him, later they called him JJ for short. A thousand images of his smiling face flickered through the Corporal's memories like a home movie. He had grown so quickly from a tiny infant to smiling toddler and finally into that precocious four-year-old who insisted he was going to grow up and be just like Daddy.

But Nancy hadn't wanted to be a military wife. She'd wanted more. She'd wanted to finish her Master's in Art History, and who was he to hold her back? When the end had come, she had already moved to Austin and served him papers. He'd managed to come and visit and see them as often as he could on furlough. But it wasn't enough for little Jacob, who would cry and beg his father not to leave at the end of the visit.

No one had ever been able to tell him exactly what happened to Nancy and JJ, but they had been too close, probably still asleep on that beautiful Saturday morning, when a small tactical nuke blew a crater into the northeast section of the city and annihilated anything within a twelve-block radius of the Arts District and the University of Texas where Nancy was a student. He wanted to believe it had been quick, that his boy hadn't suffered, and that he hadn't died screaming like the scores of others they had showed on the enormous viewscreens in the Fort Hood Commons.

The children at his feet were holding their breaths, eyes wide, terrified.

They were all children, even the older two, who couldn't be out of their teens yet. What in the hell was he doing here? As if losing JJ wasn't enough. This war, it was killing them all, taking apart families and destroying lives. He could hear his men moving closer, calling over the radio for his status. Soon, they would be close enough to see the shed and its occupants.

Inexplicably, almost unbelievably, he lowered his gun. His body sagged slightly, revealed exhaustion and... pain?

In a voice that was surprisingly soft, barely heard above the thunder and wind, he said, "I had a son once. It seems... so... long ago. His name was Jacob." Then, without another word, he turned away, softly shutting the door behind him and disappeared into the raging storm.

The baby was still crying softly, as if he were politely asking to be put back in the warm world, and next to the steady heartbeat that he had been evicted so rudely from. Erin sat numbly, as the baby wiggled, his umbilical cord still attached, looking at this alien creature in her arms that had somehow just saved them from certain death.

Tears began to stream from Jess's eyes and she held out her arms, "I want to see him."

Suddenly this thing was a child, a boy, something that was a part of her, not a piece of the monster who had raped her and put his seed in her. And as Erin gently passed the baby to her, she felt her heart stretch, as if the holes of so much loss were knitting together. Mom was gone. Dad was gone. Christopher was gone. Their memories, the loss she felt at their absence in her life, were overwhelming. Gone, so many people she had loved and needed.

But this one, this small little crying, naked boy child, somehow, he filled those gaping holes, and she felt her heart expanding in her chest.

She pulled him up closer to her, softly touching the baby beneath all the sticky paste and blood. His heart beat was strong; his face wrinkled and red. She barely noticed Erin pull out the small knife and sever the umbilical cord, or take a soft piece of cloth, dip it in water and begin to clean off the sticky paste and the blood that covered them both. When they were relatively clean, she set a blanket around Jess's shoulders and covered the infant with another.

Jess just looked into the baby's bright blue eyes and smiled. "Hi," she hesitated for a moment, "I guess I'm your mommy."

The baby's soft cries stilled, as he blinked once at her. His small hand fisted and waved as if to say hello back. They stared into each other's eyes for a long moment. Jess's mind raced with images of those long dead. Mom, Dad, Chris, Allen, people she had depended on and been devastated when they were torn from her. This child, this little baby, needed her, he needed her.

And then, as if it were the most natural thing in the world, she pulled open her shirt and offered one breast to the tiny little mouth. And all four of them stared in fascination as the baby began to nurse.

Outside, the storm raged on as a corporal called to his men, "Move north. There's nothing here but the dead."

And the troops marched on, with Corporal Jacob Daniels, Sr. leading them. He marched through the mud, past a row of bombed-out houses. He barely noticed the crude grave markers, or the bodies lying in ditches far north of the small town. Instead, he remembered the laughter of a blond-haired little boy who had died far too young.

After the Storm

"I only knew Erin for a short time. She seemed so much older, I guess I thought of her as an adult. Looking back, I realize that both Erin and Jess were barely five years older than me, still teenagers, essentially still kids themselves. War and loss took away so much of our childhood. Yet, somehow, Jess and Erin didn't just save Tina and me, they saved our childhood too. We still had to take on responsibilities and tasks that many adults hadn't had just a decade earlier, but they were both young and they knew how important it was to have fun. I remember smiling more in just a few weeks than I had in nearly a year."—David's Journal

Erin closed the tattered, water-stained book with a thump; she had found it in the remains of the town's library. "Says here he's got jaundice, that's why he's all yellow."

Jess rubbed her eyes, yawned until her jaw cracked and jiggled the baby against her. He was asleep, and had been asleep for well over five hours now, but she was so worried about his lack of appetite and the further yellowing of his skin that she had not been able to sleep.

"Great," she could hear herself snapping, "So what the hell do we do?"

Erin's satisfied grin turned down at the edges. "Well, it says here he needs ultraviolet light. Some kind of incubator thingie that they have in hospitals... but the hospital is in ruins. And it probably needs electricity to run it, which we also don't have."

Jess felt a wave of despair wash over her. It felt like the whole world was aligned against her. Quincy whined and laid her head on Jess's leg.

She had come back before daybreak the morning after the storm, a long scratch on her muzzle, a tiny limp, dead rabbit in her mouth. She seemed abjectly apologetic for running off the day before. She had barely left Jess's side in the two days since and was fascinated by the tiny human her mistress held so close.

Jess jiggled Jacob a little more forcefully; desperate to wake him and be sure he ate. It seemed he hadn't eaten much at all since he was born, and she was beginning to be afraid he would just fade away. The sun was out, and it was a beautiful day outside the shed. Tina had fallen asleep in the sun, her half-eaten peach in one hand, and David had returned a few minutes before with fresh water to wash their dishes in.

"Great, just great! What do we do now?" The lack of sleep was making her nuts, so was the heat, and the kids and the...

"Just put him in the sun." David stood behind them, a bucket of water rested on the ground near his left foot, water still sloshing over one side. Somewhere in the wreckage of his house, he had found shorts, and they were ripped on one side of the waistband. He had also taken off his shoes and his bare feet were caked with mud.

Both of the girls turned and looked at the boy. They looked so confused, he thought maybe they hadn't heard him the first time. "Just put him in the sun. Not for long, just a little while, a few minutes." They still stared at him and said nothing. "You said he needed ultraviolet light, right?"

Erin nodded slowly, "Yes... but..."

"But what? The sun has ultraviolet light. I read it in a book." He looked at them with the disdainful expression only an eleven-year-old child can pull off successfully. Erin and Jess continued to gape at him as he shrugged and took the tiny baby from Jess carefully. "Like this," he said, speaking to the baby, "out here in the sun where it's nice and warm."

He gently laid the sleeping baby down and pulled the covers away from the baby's skin. The infant squirmed slightly in his sleep and was still again.

"But won't he get sunburned?" Jess felt stupid asking this of David, who was little more than a small boy in her eyes.

David rolled his eyes at her, "Of course he will... if you leave him out too long! Just a few minutes at a time. Thataways he won't get too much sun, but at least he'll be less yellow."

Jess and Erin both looked at each other and then Erin shrugged, "Aw hell, what can it hurt?"

They tried it. Jess placed him in the sun for five minutes at a time, wrapped him back up, and did it again and again throughout the day. By the end of the next day, he seemed a little more alert, a lot hungrier and far less yellow. Sunlight seemed to have done the trick nicely.

But now they found themselves faced with another problem—diapers.

Every house they searched came up empty of them. They all felt far from safe in the town, so a fire was out of the question. No fire meant no hot water and no way to clean themselves or their clothes.

Currently, the infant was swaddled in strips of a sheet that had been relatively clean. Erin knew they would need to move on soon—and that meant supplies and diapers if they could find them.

She took David and headed back to the ruined library on the other side of town. It was located in a strip mall near some stores. It looked like Ground Zero for the firefight they had heard several days ago.

The bodies had been left to rot in the hot summer sun. The stench was overpowering as they approached the Big Lots' store. Fifty yards from that was the collapsed west wall of the library. Erin pointed David towards the library. "I'll meet you there, but I need to check this out first, okay?"

David just nodded and backed away to the safety of the ruined books. Whenever a breeze blew over the bodies, his stomach roiled in protest. He tried to breathe through his mouth so he didn't lose his breakfast.

Erin wrapped a cloth around her mouth and nose, took a few deep breaths and then entered the Big Lots. She avoided looking down as she stepped over one, two, and then a third body near the entrance. She brushed away the flies that swarmed around her and managed to make it down a main aisle before retching into a bin of throw rugs.

"Baby section, baby section," she murmured to herself, trying desperately to not think about the smell or the bodies. She turned right and passed through the clothing and accessories section and took a sharp left.

Success! Many of the hooks were empty, but there were layette sets, onesies, tiny socks and hats, a lone pink blanket, and... diapers. Holy cow, actual diapers! Erin forgot about the awful smell from the corpses, ran back to the previous aisle and grabbed large bags to stuff the diapers into. She grabbed every package of diapers. They were all different sizes, but who cared? At least they were better than rags!

It took two trips to retrieve all the baby-related items, and she and David lugged the mess back to Jess with triumphant grins. At least now they had something to dress Jacob in. He was tiny, even the newborn sizes hung off of him with room to spare.

The next morning, Erin and David returned to the ruined library. There they rummaged through the collapsed building, tossing books into two piles—ones that would help and ones that wouldn't. The system seemed to work pretty well. Many of the books were water-damaged and unusable, others had no bearing on their hopes for survival. Danielle Steel was definitely on the larger not helpful pile.

Erin was at one end of the building, looking through what remained of home and garden topics, such as vegetable gardening and a book on how to raise chickens. David had burrowed into one corner and found some books on trails and wilderness camping and survival skills.

When the sun was directly overhead, they stopped, exhausted by the heat, found a tree and sat in the shade of it and Erin opened a can of beets she had been avoiding eating until she absolutely had to. David didn't look too impressed with the lunch menu, but he reached in and took a slice of the reddish-purple vegetable. A moment of silence passed and their hands connected as they both reached into the can at the same moment.

David grinned up at her, his lips and teeth stained red, and juice dribbling down his chin, "It isn't too bad, y'know?" She found herself agreeing. Who would have known that canned beets could taste so good?

"What's that you've got?" He asked, pointing to a plain white book she had on the top of her stack of books.

Erin looked over at the book and held it up so the boy could read the title—" Wild Edibles of Missouri," Erin shrugged, "This canned food is catch as catch can. Who knows when we'll have it or when we won't? I figure we'll supplement with wild plants along the way. Jess and I ate plenty on the way here. Some of it isn't bad tasting at all. But I only know of some plants, not all of them, so this'll help."

David looked stunned at the idea and began to look suspiciously at the greenery surrounding the ruined building. The grass was patchy, mostly weeds and high growth now that summer had come and there was no one left to even care about mowing.

"Like what? Do you mean like... weeds?" he asked, looking hard at the landscape, as if expecting them to tell him their secrets.

Erin smiled and obliged him by opening up and thumbing through the book. She murmured to herself for a moment and then said, "Dandelion. You can make tea with it, and you can put the leaves into a salad or cook them. And it says that dandelion leaves are very nutritious and it is a liver cleanser. We ate them on the way here, but I didn't know about the liver cleansing part of it." She paged to the front of the book, scanned some of the pages and raised her eyebrows.

"Huh. Amaranth. Well, I'll be... I'm sure I've seen that along the way." She turned the book so that David could see a picture of the plant; the blooms were heavy with seed. "It says here that you can eat the seeds, shoots and leaves of the plant."

David looked around. Over in one corner, there was a huge clump of dandelions and plenty of other unfamiliar plants he would have previously dismissed as simply being worthless weeds. He smiled, "That's cool. Can I read that book too?" She grinned back and passed him the book.

By the end of the day, they had a decent stack of books on a variety of subjects. It would have taken several trips to bring all the books they had set aside back, but David led the older girl to a trailer buried in the high grass down the street. It was small, the kind you hitch to the back of a car.

"It's kinda like a big wheelbarrow," he commented as he dumped an armful of books into it. It had sidewalls, about one foot high, that held the books with plenty of room to spare. Once they had loaded it up, they each grabbed a part of the chain looped around the handle and headed back towards the hidey-hole and shed.

Twice on their way back, they saw other people rummaging through the rubble of houses. Erin looked over at David each time and asked, "Do you know them?" He just shook his head. "Best we keep going then." And they walked on, ignored by the survivors who seemed intent on salvaging any remnant of their lives that they could.

Erin and Jess knew they had to move on, and discussed it the fifth night following Jacob's birth as they lay under the bright full moon. David and Tina had retreated to their hidey-hole for the night, burrowing underground where they felt safest. "We need to move on," Erin began, "it isn't safe here."

Jess had been dozing with Jacob nestled in the crook of her left arm, steadily nursing at her breast. "Hm," she murmured sleepily, "it isn't safe anywhere." At the moment, here in their little bed of blankets, under the stars and moon, it felt safe enough, but she lay there and thought about home and became more alert. "We could try to go home. Maybe some managed to escape or hide out."

"Maybe."

The pause lengthened into minutes as they both lay there, staring at the sky. Neither one of them wanted to voice the hope out loud—the persistent niggle in both of their brains that suggested that perhaps some of their family or friends had survived the enemy assault. What if in just saying it out loud, they jinxed it? Hope was almost a painful weight, a yawning need for normalcy. This past week had been so beautiful, so peaceful after the fierce storm.

The sun had shone bright and full each day, the air thick and hot and full of the earthy smells of plants growing and blooming. The earth had continued to turn, despite the chaos in the land, and now the dog days of summer were at their peak. It was hard to believe that it was late August already. If it weren't for the shattered remains of houses all around them, it would have been a normal summer day.

Jess spoke first, "We used to camp out in your backyard on nights like this."

Erin smiled in the moonlight. "Remember how Chris and Toby came over and scared us one night? I swear I peed my pants, I was so scared!"

Jess giggled. They had been about eight years old and their older brothers had snuck into the backyard wearing hockey masks. This after they had watched a horror flick in the basement that night starring some bad guy named Jason who wore a hockey mask. "Remember how loud

I screamed? Your mom and dad thought we were being murdered! And then we were all in trouble for watching that awful movie!"

They both giggled like little girls at the memory and fell silent, lost in the memories of those that they had lost. Across the night sky a satellite moved steadily. The Big Dipper was clear and easy to see. Moments passed, and then they both spoke at once.

"I miss them so much."

"Let's go home."

A sigh and a deep breath, and Jess spoke again in the silence, "Yeah, let's go home."

Come With Us

"I asked Jess once why they didn't leave me and Tina there in Clinton. We were a liability, as was proved just a few short days later. I asked her why, and she just looked at me and said, 'We were family, even then, and family doesn't leave family.' I'd like to say that was the moment I fell in love with her. But truth be told, I'd been a goner for a lot longer than that. She never blamed me for what happened to Erin, not once. I wonder if I would have felt the same."—David's Journal

The morning dawned, the temperature rising quickly, making each of the small group wish desperately for the good old days of electricity and air-conditioning. Except Tina, perhaps, who had no real memory of such luxuries. The sun wasn't even up above their heads and it was already miserably hot. The cicadas thrummed noisily, filling the air with rasping waves of sound.

Jacob whined fretfully at Jess's breast, suckling half-heartedly, his skin moist and slightly flushed. Erin had found a can of evaporated milk and handed it to the children to drink. Tina drank a lion's share of it before handing it to David, who drained his portion in two huge gulps. A can of pears disappeared almost as quickly.

Erin had foisted Spam on Jess, along with a handful of dandelion greens. "I found out we can make tea out of the flowers if we find a safe place to have a fire." Jess simply raised an eyebrow and grimaced at the bitter taste of the leaves in her mouth. She balanced Jacob with one hand and tried rolling Spam inside of the leaves—that seemed to cut the bitterness substantially. Their eyes met over David and Tina's heads.

Erin spoke first, "We used to live north of here, you know." Tina was busy licking the inside of the pear can, but David looked up and nodded. "And we've been talking about heading back there."

David froze, looked scared. "You're going to leave?" Tina had been oblivious to the conversation until the word 'leave' was uttered and she began to whimper, her eyes big and fearful.

"Well, Belton, that's the town we used to live in, has lots of houses and they aren't all bombed out like here," Erin said. She said it, hoping it was true, hoping she wouldn't return and be proved a liar.

"We want you to come with us," added Jess. "You can't stay here. There's not much food left, and the house is in pieces, no roof. What would you do when winter comes?" From the startled look on David's face, it was obvious he hadn't thought that far ahead. "If my house is still there, my family might even still be alive, and we'd be safe," she went on.

For a moment she allowed herself to imagine the shock and surprise on her parent's and brother's faces when they saw Jacob. It would be a hard thing for them to accept—to know how he came to be. But they would look at him and see he was a baby, innocent, and besides, he had her eyes. In the end, they would love him! She let the daydream carry her away for a moment before returning to reality and the work of convincing the two children to accompany them.

"Come with us."

Tina had stopped whimpering and now had a grubby, syrup-covered thumb stuck in her mouth. Her eyes were fastened on David, waiting for reassurance and direction. Erin and Jess watched as he looked back over his shoulder at the mounded grave of their parents. Grass had begun to grow on it, poking out of the piles of drying, limp flowers that Tina heaped on the mound each morning and night. The crude cross David had fastened out sticks and twine, listed to one side. It seemed wrong somehow to leave them here, but he knew the older girls were right.

He nodded. Jess smiled at him and hugged Tina close to her with her free arm. It was settled.

They didn't leave that day or the next—it would be five days before they were ready. It was still very soon after Jacob's birth and Jess was slow and tired easily. Belton was nearly sixty miles away. That wasn't much when you considered how far they had already come, but there were five of them now, not two, and the going would be slow.

"We need a plan on what to do if we run into any troops," Erin said later that day. They had stopped to rest in the shade after scouting nearby houses for rope and backpacks. The jackpot, a tent big enough to sleep all of them, had been discovered in Mr. Pierson's shed. The Pierson's had a son close to David's age. Joey was a year younger, but they had played together regularly.

The Pierson's hadn't run like so many others did. The main house had burned, and David poked through the ruins a couple of weeks later and found skeletons. He didn't stop to puzzle it out, or figure out who had died there. It was just a jumble of horror in his memory. He'd run like the devil himself was after him and not returned.

David had pulled out the now tattered and worn book, "Wild Edibles of Missouri." He had been reading it obsessively since Erin showed it to him at the ruined library. The once pristine white cover was now grubby with dirt, beet juice, and God knows what else. The pages had been dog-eared and little slips of ragged paper tucked into the special sections. She gazed at him a moment and then shrugged and turned back to Jess. At this rate, the kid was going to be an expert on edible plants.

Jess had leaned back against the tree; Jacob was sleeping contentedly against her side in a sling they had rigged from the remains of an old sheet. Her eyes were closed, sweat trickling down her face. "We could take Highway 7, then Highway 49, after we reach Harrisonville. That's the only way I know."

Her friend sighed in exasperation. Jess wasn't good for much these days. She was still weak and sore, and the baby woke up every couple of hours wanting food. Asking her for advice was rather pointless. If Jess had been any more exhausted, she would have probably volunteered to return to the enemy camp some 200 miles or more behind them. Erin rubbed her eyes. She wasn't getting much more sleep than Jess was.

Each time the baby cried at night, she too was instantly awake, terrified someone would hear him. Now that they had thought of the sling, he cried far less, especially during the day when the sling rocked him to and fro. He seemed comforted by that. She rubbed her eyes and desperately tried to think about crossing miles of grassy fields out in the open for anyone to see. She closed her eyes, stretched back in the grass and tried to will a solution into being.

David's words took her by surprise. "We need camouflage so we can't be seen."

"Huh?"

"You know, we need to look like the ground we're walking through and we should only travel at night or early in the morning when no one is out and around." Erin sat bolt upright and stared at the kid. For only being eleven years old, the kid was damn smart. He continued, ignoring her stare, "I read this book where it said that if you were goin' through forests than you wear green, and in the desert, you wear tan, 'cause it makes ya blend in. I can see pretty well in the dark, y'know, I could lead." He looked up then and studied her. "What? Did I say something wrong?"

Erin couldn't speak. She just stared at him and shook her head, "Damn kid, you are something else. C'mon, we sure have some work to do."

She turned to Jess who had fallen asleep, the baby cuddled against her chest and Tina's tangled head of hair resting against one leg. Quincy lay at her feet, tiny puppy paws twitching in time to some doggy dream. They looked kind of cute, in a ragged, half-starved, and filthy sort of way. For the tenth time that day, she wished for a hot shower and handfuls of scented shampoo and conditioner.

"Come on, they won't be going anywhere soon." And the two of them headed off to find spray paint.

Leaving Clinton

"Can you put a price on family? Can you put one on sacrifice? Tonight, my thoughts are on all the ones who are gone... Mom... Dad... Chris... Erin. They say that, when someone dies, they don't truly die if you keep them in your heart. Those words seem so trite, so small and insignificant. War, death, knowing what gunfire sounds like and how it feels to be so damned hungry you think you're gonna die. Those things seem real to me. They aren't some stupid platitude that no one really understands. Not anymore, at least."—Jess's Journal

When Jess opened her eyes, the sun was sinking. A red-orange ball of heat occupying the horizon to the west. She was disoriented, her mind still foggy with sleep and the heat of the day. A handful of wilted dandelions thrust in her face did not help matters.

She jerked back and focused on Tina's grubby face, smiling proudly, "I found dinna." She waved the dandelions, still sporting a clump of dirt and several terrified ants which were running pell-mell back and forth across the leaves trying to escape their doom. "See Yess, I found dinna.'"

Jess couldn't help but smile at the child. Grubby face and hopelessly tangled hair notwithstanding, she was an adorable child. "Oh sweetie, you did. You found dinner! Thank you, Tina!" She took the wilted greens from the tiny, nearly black fist and looked around for the others.

On a level patch of land, Erin and David had erected the big tent they had found and were at one edge of it, obviously exchanging heated words. "What are they doing?" She asked it aloud, but hadn't really directed it towards the little girl.

"Dey's arguing," the little girl replied apprehensively, "Brother wants big stripes and Erin made small stripes and den dey started yellin.'" Her face took on a knowing expression, "Dey's need a nap."

As she finished, David walked away from Erin, huffing and mad. He stomped over and sat down nearby, practically shaking with anger. His face was red, and he looked close to tears.

Before Jess could utter a word, Jacob woke with a wail of hunger. She busied herself with adjusting layers. She shifted the infant so that his tiny mouth could reach her breast and he greedily began to nurse. She winced. Her breasts were sore and painful still—when would her boobs get used to feeding this little guy?

Erin came over and flopped onto the ground near Jess and the baby. "Good lord, strip me naked and tie me to a friggin' anthill. I give up."

She snuck a peek at David, who was looking the other way, shoulders stiff and back hunched, desperately trying not to let the tears show. "I think that we are all hungry and need to eat. And as for you, kid, I'm sorry I didn't listen, 'cause you're probably right about the damn stripes too. You're right about damn near everything else these days."

David let out a small but audible sniffle, "Kid, I'm sorry, okay? We'll do it your way, all right?"

"My name's not kid, it's David. I'm named after my dad," the boy's voice cracked with emotion despite his best efforts to sound dignified. He was tired, exhausted and hungry, and worn out from the late summer heat. He was, after all, only eleven.

Tina cuddled up to him and patted his hand, "So-kay, brother, s'okay." She looked over at Erin reproachfully, "You was swearin', that's not nice."

Jess grinned at Erin. "She's right, you know. Be nice or we will strip you naked and tie you to an anthill!" Her smile belied the threat, and it seemed contagious. Before long, even David was smiling tentatively through his tears.

Erin looked defensive, and then apologized again. "I am sorry, David. Let's stop for now and rustle up some grub for everyone, okay?"

The boy wiped his eyes and nose with the back of his hand and just nodded, still unable to speak. He reached for their small stash of canned goods and located a can opener. The group dined on cold pork and beans, some surprisingly tasty Vienna sausages, one for each of them, and a large jar of spiced peaches. Out of politeness, they each tried a wilted dandelion flower, after removing the ants, and praised Tina loudly for her efforts. The little girl beamed with pride.

As the last of the light died, Erin and David went back to the tent and finished the painting. The tent was now camouflaged for the forest and the two returned speculating on how they could camouflage it for the plains that they would also be crossing through.

Their plans were interrupted by the sounds of sporadic gunfire. Both Erin and Jess's eyes turned to the distance—the shots were coming from the southeast. Shit! Their eyes turned to the tent and recognized it would be akin to a flashing beacon that someone was around. They needed to be hidden... now. In what seemed like seconds, the tent was down. While the girls disassembled, David and Tina ran and gathered personal items, hiding them and doing their best to erase the evidence of their presence from the grassy lawn. The basement of the children's ruined house seemed more than attractive at the moment, despite the dangerous descent over the broken stairs. Jess and Erin had learned the trick of it in the last two weeks—hug the wall and hope to God the supports didn't break loose. With little words and black terror in Jess and Erin's eyes, they made their way into the dark, cluttered basement. It was dark outside by now, thank God, and that would hide them better than anything else.

Jacob had woken and began to wail as Jess made her way to the bottom of the stairs.

"Jesus Jess, shut him the hell up!" Erin hissed. "They're almost on top of us!"

She shoved her friend into a dark corner and pulled the remains of a bookcase over as a cover of sorts, then ran to the opposite end of the basement looking for another dark spot to hide. Tina had already crawled into the depths of the hidey-hole and David's feet disappeared behind her. The gunfire was loud now, and they heard the men yelling at one another as they moved down the deserted street.

Jess patted him, made soft shushing noises, and tried to get him to nurse. The baby would have none of it. Jacob began to wail louder, picking up on her fear and broadcasting it. It was as if she were standing with a megaphone advertising their position. She was terrified of being discovered. It didn't matter that these men couldn't possibly be from the camp that she and Erin had escaped from. They had guns, and they were soldiers. None of the kids needed to know anything more than that. Their survival was dependent on their adeptness at hiding and scrounging. In this, all four were clearly on the same page.

Jess would later learn of the absolute chaos the Western Front had devolved into. There were no organized attacks, no common enemy to fight against, there were simply the ones with guns and the ones without and a lot of hungry, desperate people on both sides. The 'troops' the children hid from that night were nothing more than a leaderless group of thugs who, after losing their commander and three-quarters of their complement in a skirmish five miles to the southeast were trying to make their way around a larger group of equally starving and desperate men to the north. None of it really mattered, because in two weeks' time every one of the men currently terrifying the kids would be dead... after they made the error of engaging a group far larger.

Jess knew none of this. She only knew that Jacob was picking up on her terror and that his cries would end them all if she didn't do something fast. Despite her pounding heart and the fear that shot through her like knives, urging her to run in blind panic, she took one deep calming breath and then another and another. Slowly, she willed her body to relax and allowed a sense of peace to envelope her.

One hand cupped Jacob's head, and she hummed silently and steadily. She closed her eyes and remembered the weeks spent healing in that quiet cabin in the woods. She pictured that peaceful week spent with old Coop and the days of the journey along the way to Clinton. The other hand gently held Quincy's muzzle closed. Life wasn't all pain and fear and death. She knew that. She thought of her parents, of Chris and Erin and her childhood and smiled at the memories they still brought her.

She hummed softly to the infant in her arms, whispering in his ear. "I love you Jacob, I love you so much."

The infant stilled, turned his head and rooted for her breast, whimpering softly now, responding to her change in mood. The pup whined softly; her little body occasionally flinched at the loud explosions of sound. Jess wondered what the little mutt thought of it all.

The men passed, exchanging calls, rummaging in the ruined house above, shooting at shadows. They moved on. When it was quiet, Erin gathered up a blanket and found her way back to Jess, who was half asleep. Jacob snored gently, moist and warm against her. Erin caressed his tiny head, which was silky soft. She murmured apologies to her friend.

"Sorry Jessie, I didn't mean it; I know he couldn't help being scared."

"S'okay, Erie. It all came out all right." Jess replied, "But I think we better head east for a bit. Those guys went north and we don't want to run into them anytime soon."

The children didn't emerge from their hidey-hole, except for David poking his head out and whispering good night to Erin, who bedded down close by. A night on a cement floor was a small price to pay for their narrow escape.

The Sacrifice

"*It was my fault. I still remember it. When I'm alone with my thoughts, I think about how I was the one responsible for what happened that awful day. It was the first time I've killed anyone. The first time I had held a gun in my hands, pointed it at any living creature and pulled the trigger. It didn't look like it does in the movies. There is this anticlimactic moment when the body falls and you wonder if they are really dead. You walk up, the sound of the gunshot still ringing in your ears and you see it. There is that look in someone's eyes as they lie there dying and there's nothing you can do. You just stand and watch what was a person become empty, as if someone walked out and left the house, door hanging open, with all the familiar furnishings, but no one inside to greet you."—David's Journal*

The day dawned hot and muggy. Jess woke first, and smelled, then felt the wet coming from the bundled baby. The diaper had leaked, soaked through his wrap and into her clothes. "Ugh!" He'd crapped too, by the smell of it. The sun was barely brightening the sky and as she moved, he woke and began to fuss.

Her movements woke Erin, who blearily made her way up the half-smashed stairs. As Erin emerged to ground level, she looked around for any signs of the soldiers. The area looked clear. Quincy followed, nimbly climbing the rickety stairs and squatting to relieve herself before returning down the stairs to Jess's side.

Jacob's thin wail of distress began to build as Jess set him down and searched for clean clothing in the packs a few feet away. She had just pulled on a relatively clean shirt when David, followed by his little sister, emerged from their hidey-hole.

Erin called down, "Looks all clear. I think they headed north. Let's get some food and eat it quick. I think we should head east, and soon. Who knows who might come up the road next."

Jess couldn't help but agree. She started to strap Lady to her waist and hesitated, looking over at David. He had been eyeing firearms with more interest in the past few days. They made eye contact. "Would you like to carry it?" she asked him. His eyes widened, and he grinned.

"This isn't a toy, you know. The second you don't respect it, you're dead. This is a machine made for killing." He stared up at her and nodded silently. "I'm just loaning it to you. It's hard to handle with the baby and all."

She showed him how to carry it, even found a way to attach the holster to a piece of rope he could use as a belt, and gave him a push up the stairs to Erin. "Ask her to show you how to use it."

They took care of their basic needs, ate a little breakfast and were ready to go by mid-morning. The tent they had taken such pains with the day before had been torn in their haste to dismantle and hide it before the soldiers discovered them. A large hole in it made it useless at keeping out rain or wind and it was at the worst of spots. Part of the support structure for the tent stuck through. It had been rendered useless.

Instead, they would pull the little trailer Erin and David had found. It had good solid tires on it, but it wouldn't be good for extreme terrain and neither of the girls liked the idea of it leaving tracks as they went through muddy areas. It was useful for now, and they decided that if it became impractical, they could always carry their belongings on their backs.

Jess and Erin exchanged looks above the heads of the younger ones.

The looks were solemn—if they brought these kids with them, they were responsible for them. It meant they had to be cared for, fed, and sheltered. Once they left, they were committed to protecting David and Tina's lives just as much as they would their own. They wouldn't back out now, but it suddenly dawned on them just how much responsibility they were taking on. A few weeks ago, they had been responsible for each other—just two lives. Now, with the birth of Jacob, and meeting David and Tina, the task of surviving had become far more complicated. There was an unspoken question and challenge hovering there in the air between them for a moment, then a sort of release. They were committed, and it was time to go.

Tina cried for the first few blocks and then stopped. She was young, in a few years she would have few, if any, memories of her parents to cherish. David said nothing, but he cried silently all the way out of town and well into the empty fields.

He silently mourned his parents, and the battered home they had left behind until the flowers and plants they were walking through distracted him. As they moved through the fields, he began to pay attention to everything growing around him.

Here was chicory. The leaves could be added to soup and salad and the roots ground into coffee. He wrinkled his nose at that. His dad had always drunk coffee black and with no sugar. Here was a wild carrot. It didn't taste good raw, the book said, but it would be okay if cooked in a soup. A while ago, they had passed several clumps of wild onions and he had stopped long enough to pick them. The tall plants with yellow sunflowers were everywhere.

David recognized them from a sketch in the book as Jerusalem artichoke. Their tubers, whatever those were, were edible. He paused for a moment and Tina stumbled to a halt behind him as he realized that he was surrounded by food. After months of fearing the canned food would run out and that he and Tina would starve to death, this was a revelation of epic proportions.

They quickly abandoned the little trailer. It had been fantastic on paved roads, the surface it was designed for, but when it came to heaving it over fences, it was too much. Jess couldn't handle much with the baby and if she handed him to one of the children, he immediately began to wail. That left Erin to wrestle it over a fence with two vertically challenged, and noticeably weaker, children helping her. The first day was spent making little progress in terms of distance. Finally, they stopped, divided and reduced their belongings into a transportable system between the four.

The only incident came on the second afternoon as they passed by a small stream. David casually reached out and uprooted some plant with an umbel of white flowers and began to clean off the root. Erin looked over, did a double-take, and snatched it from his hand before he could take a bite.

Before he could think to say anything more than a startled, "Hey" she had examined it intensely, thrown it to one side and pulled him over to the stream.

"Wash. Now. Anywhere you touched that plant." She instructed, tight-lipped and frightened.

"Why? It was wild carrot, Queen-somethin' lace. That's food. I know it isn't supposed to be good raw, but I figured I'd try a bite, anyway." He argued, confused and angry.

"No. That was water hemlock. Look closer." She pulled him over to the discarded plant, jabbing her finger fiercely at the areas of the plant. "See? Smooth stem, not hairy like wild carrot. And see how it is mottled? And almost purple-colored, not green?" The boy stopped looking defensive and his face assumed a look of terrified wonder.

"The leaves are lance-shaped, not feathery. This plant would have killed you if you had eaten any of it. Horribly and painfully, I might add." Her fierce look gave Jess a full-body shiver.

David washed thoroughly in the muddy, shallow stream. He did it silently, and no one said anything. Jess and Tina were somewhat afraid to, and Erin tried to calm down. How close that had been! If he had eaten just a bite, just one bite. She looked down and realized her hands were shaking. Erin closed her eyes and tried to breathe calmly.

When she opened them, David was standing there, hands still moist from the stream, with a determined look on his face. "Show me again, Erin. So, I'll know and remember."

Knowledge would keep them alive, nourish them, and protect them from harm. He would learn this and never forget. She showed him again the characteristics, and he watched and listened with an intensity that impressed both girls. Even Tina watched and learned. The rest of the day was spent identifying plants as they walked. They found lamb's quarters and gathered it for adding to soup later on, as well as plenty of wild carrot that reappeared in the meadows they walked through and were easy to pull up and gnaw as they walked. The book was right, raw wild carrot didn't taste good at all.

"We need a shovel," David pointed at the tall Jerusalem Artichokes, "A little one that we can use to dig up the tubers." He liked that word.

When David had broken down and asked what tubers were, Erin had not laughed as he expected her to. Instead, she had explained that they were the thick underground parts of a plant that were edible.

"Like potatoes or, well, Jerusalem Artichoke looks more like ginger root, actually. Have you ever seen fresh ginger root?" He shook his head, absorbed her explanation, looked again at the tall plants and wished he could start digging.

Two days of walking did not get them far. Not with a newborn and a small child. David could handle the day-long walks, but Tina stumbled behind, moving slower and slower until they were forced to stop every hour or so. Jacob was even more demanding. The gentle rocking motion of the sling helped him to sleep, but still woke every two to three hours for feedings. She learned to nurse as she walked, but his constant waking at night exhausted her. Each time Tina slowed down, Jess stopped and sat down, too. Their progress was agonizingly slow.

It was a testament to how long all of them had survived that they did not complain or argue. They simply did what they could and took every opportunity they could to rest. Late in the afternoon on the fourth day Tina simply sat down on the ground and refused to move an inch farther. There wasn't much argument from anyone except Erin, who was worried about camping out in the open. It helped ease her mind to see that the grass and weeds were tall; she even hiked a way back and said that from her vantage point, she couldn't even see the small group once she got very far.

"Unless anyone saw us stop here, we should be fine." They munched on the last of a box of crackers. David and Erin took turns peering through binoculars at an old farmhouse in the far distance.

David said, "I just want to hike over there and see if there is anything we could use. Like a shovel." He was still obsessed with the tubers and was eager to get a chance to dig them up.

Tina was already fast asleep, curled up in a dirty little bundle near Jess's feet, and Erin and Jess were finishing off a can of green beans. It wasn't much, but it was enough to quiet their stomachs.

Quincy nuzzled Jess and whined softly, as if asking permission, "Oh, go on with you. Catch us a rabbit or a squirrel, okay?"

The little dog was fast, damned fast, and she managed to keep herself well fed on birds and rodents. Every couple of days, she would flush a rabbit and bring it back to the girls, her tail wagging madly. She would lay it at their feet, neck neatly broken, not a mark on its fur. They didn't feel bad for the soft little bunny—food was food and rabbit turned into pretty good rabbit stew. Quincy wagged her tail and disappeared into the tall grass.

Jess waved a hand at him. "Go ahead kid. Sorry, I mean, David. Just keep your eyes open, all right?"

David jumped up, adjusted the cord around his waist that held the revolver, and dashed into the field, eager to explore the farmhouse. He quickly disappeared from view. Erin pulled her lank hair out of the ponytail holder and grimaced over the twigs and knots running through it. "God, what I would give for a shower. Think that place has got any running water?"

Jess just shrugged. She was too tired to think. Jacob fussed at her breast and she patted his back rhythmically until he settled down and began to nurse steadily. In the months and years that would follow this day, Jess would wake screaming. She would wonder over and over why she didn't stop Erin or David. Her exhaustion, coupled with lack of preparedness from Erin and the curiosity of youth from David, would be their undoing on that hot, fall day. Jess didn't see what was coming, didn't recognize that they had all cheated death for far too long. She said nothing as Erin stretched, grimaced over her grimy state, and set the .22 Rimfire on the ground next to Jess. "I'm going to go with him and just see what's over there. I'll be back soon."

She disappeared into the overgrown field of grass and the tattered remnants of last year's corn. Tina turned over, rubbed her face against Jess's leg, and burrowed closer. The heavy curtain of sleep began to steal over Jess as Jacob's lips fell from her breast and his breathing deepened into sleep. Moments ticked by.

It was still light when Jess heard the scream. The sun had slipped below the horizon, and there was little light left in the sky. From this distance it was wordless, impossible to be sure what she had heard, but she was sure it was Erin. Quincy had just returned with a large rabbit in her jaws. Its furry legs were still kicking. The dog turned in the direction of the farmhouse, dropped the rabbit onto the ground and began to growl steadily.

It was enough to wake Tina as well, and she jerked to a sitting position and looked around in confusion for her brother.

"Tina, listen to me. Take the baby and be very quiet." Jess pointed to a tree in the distance. "Go to that tree and wait for us to find you. I'm going to go find your brother and Erin."

The little girl nodded, and Jess quickly wrapped her son in a sling around Tina, praying the little girl wouldn't trip and fall. "Take it slow, okay? And be very quiet!"

"Quincy," she turned to the dog, "Stay with Tina. Stay, girl!" The dog let out a mournful whine and looked agitated, but she obeyed.

She grabbed the rifle, gave the little girl a small push in the right direction and then turned and ran, keeping as low as she could, towards the old farmhouse. Whatever the trouble was, she was headed straight for it.

She was within thirty feet of the farmhouse when the first shot rang out. Another ten feet out when the second shot came and then she was inside, no hesitation, bullet in the chamber, finger on the trigger and the adrenaline pumping through her.

There were four people in the main room—two soldiers, Erin and David. One man was already dead on the ground. Erin was down and clutching at her chest. A stain of red quickly spread from beneath her hands. The second man was aiming his pistol at David, but he was distracted by Jess bursting in. She took it in quickly, aimed at the man and pulled the trigger, chambered another round and shot again. Two dark holes appeared in his chest and he stared down at them in surprise. The soldier stood there unmoving for one long moment, then collapsed to the ground and did not move.

Jess skidded on her knees to her friend's side. She grabbed Erin's free hand, her mind racing with thoughts of bandages and stopping the massive flow of blood. Oh God, there was so much blood.

Her friend attempted to speak. Erin's mouth opened, choked on the blood now surging through her esophagus. Blood sprayed from her mouth, spattering Jess. She tried again to speak, gasped, and then breathed no more. She died there, her eyes wide open and staring, her hand limp in Jess's grasp.

Jess began to scream.

A Good Harvest

"Remember to be gentle with yourself and others. We are all children of chance and none can say why some fields will blossom while others lay brown beneath the August sun. Care for those around you. Look past your differences. Their dreams are no less than yours, their choices no more easily made. And give, give in any way you can, of whatever you possess. To give is to love. To withhold is to wither. Care less for your harvest than for how it is shared and your life will have meaning and your heart will have peace."—Kent Nerburn

Fine-boned fingers covered his eyes, the smell of freshly turned dirt and the mint she had been picking filled his nose. "Guess who?"

Chris smiled, "Hey Liza. Making mint tea?"

Carrie's sister let out a disappointed sniff. "You knew it was me!"

"Of course, I did. You smell different from Carrie." He didn't tell her that Carrie had this indescribable scent, this earthy combination of sage and wood smoke that was almost drug like. It pulled him in and made him want to get closer, wrap his arms around her, and never let go. Liza smelled good too, but she smelled of childhood and cinnamon. He couldn't explain it any better than that.

In the past few weeks Liza's attitude toward him, and towards her sister, had begun to alter. She kept seeking him out when the others were busy with tasks. And whenever Carrie and he were together, she picked fights and argued with her sister endlessly.

It had taken him a while, but he had come to suspect that Liza had a crush. She would be fourteen in just a few months, and she was acting as if Carrie was more a rival than a sister. Carrie was confused by the behavior, commenting to Chris in private that they had always been close and rarely fought like other siblings. "I just don't know what's with Liza these days. Everything I say or do is wrong," Carrie nibbled her thumbnail, "It's almost as if she is dying to pick a fight with me. But why?"

Chris had caught Liza spying on them twice now. They still hadn't gone all the way, but they were getting close, and he was worried that things were coming to a head. He had to deal with it, somehow. He looked up at Liza, who was staring down at him with a confused, half-hopeful smile. Crap. He set down the basket of tomatoes he had been picking. It was nearly full, the red and orange fruits firm and beautiful, promising to explode with juice the instant they were cut into. He figured he had three more baskets to pick before he would be done for the day.

"Liza, we need to talk."

She grinned happily, "Did you finish Voyage from Yesteryear already? I just left it by your door two days ago."

He shook his head and her expression turned from excited to guarded. "No, I haven't finished reading it yet. But it's good," he smiled at her, "I had a hard time putting it down this morning and getting to work."

He pointed to the raised planters and the tomato cages. "Help me pick more?"

"Sure."

As they fell into a rhythm, he got up the courage to say what was on his mind. "You know Liza, you are a very pretty girl." He saw her hand pause; almost drop the tomato she was holding. "I know you like me. And really, I'm flattered, I am." He met her eyes then, she looked afraid, "But I..."

"You're in love with Carrie."

"Yeah, I am. I want to marry her." Her chin dropped to her chest, and he thought he saw a small tear fall to the ground. "Liza, I'm sorry. I know that doesn't make it any better, but I really am. 'Cause you are a really cool chick, and you love sci-fi, which totally kicks ass," that elicited a small wet giggle, "I want us to be friends and, if your granddad doesn't shoot me first, someday I'd like to be your brother."

Liza looked up at him, her eyes wet with tears, "I... oh... why do you have to be so damn nice, Chris? Couldn't you just say, buzz off kid, your sister's way hotter than you?"

It was his turn to look away. He hated to see the kid cry. "Sorry Liza, that's just how I'm wired, I guess. And besides, you aren't a kid anymore, and you are hot. Or did you miss the way Carl Owens stared at you all last week?"

He didn't dare tell her how much she reminded him of Jess when she was a high school freshman. It was painful to look at her sometimes.

Just thinking about Jess now, imagining how she had died, made him want to scream. He hadn't protected her, but he would protect Carrie and Liza, Joseph and Fenton with his dying breath. He couldn't bring back what he had lost, but he could make sure he didn't lose anything more. Lost in his thoughts, he was surprised when Liza wrapped her arms around him. He hugged her back, hoping he was doing the right thing, and she kissed him lightly on the cheek. Before he could react, she had bounded away, heading for some quiet corner to compose herself.

He visibly jumped when Carrie's voice spoke from behind him. "So, that was what was going on these past few weeks?" Chris whirled around to face her. "That's why she's been so pissy! She likes you?" She seemed blown away by this fact.

He smiled at her. "Is it so hard to believe?"

"Well, no." She stood there with a peculiar smile on her face.

"Well, then what are you smiling about?" He was feeling a bit defensive. After all, he'd tried to be nice about it and the kid had still run off crying.

"I'm thinking that you are really, really sweet." Carrie stepped forward, put a hand on each side of his face, and kissed him softly. "You saw it when I didn't. You made her feel cared for, even if she couldn't have you. Thank you for that."

"You aren't pissed because I hugged her and she kissed me?"

He couldn't believe his good luck. A beautiful, sexy girl who wasn't crazy with jealousy? She shook her head wordlessly and kissed him again, this time with promise and intent. He kissed her back, ran his hands down her back and slid his hands over her short shorts. The kiss was intense, passionate.

Unfortunately, it was cut short by a shout for help from Fenton. The shout came from the barn where Fenton had been tinkering with the truck for the past week now. The carburetor had been a relatively easy fix, but the huge dent that Liza had put into the front fender when she ran it into a fence while learning to drive had caused significant damage. The Chilton's manual they had found in town was getting its fair share of use as Fenton paged through it, uttering long-winded complaints about the dangers of teenage drivers.

His yell brought everyone running. This was a good thing, since he seemed determined to bleed to death from a large gash on his forehead. Blood streaked down his face and Liza beat the rest of them to the barn, arriving at her grandfather's side first. Her face still showed signs of tears, but no one noticed. Chris pulled off his shirt and used it to apply pressure to the wound.

"Jesus, Gramps," Carrie helped her grandfather to a seated position on an old tire, "what happened?"

Fenton gave her an irritated look. "Young lady, you keep using the Lord's name in vain and I'll wash your mouth out with soap. By damn, I can't even see out of this eye!"

His right eye was covered in blood, which had alarmed Chris until he realized it was merely flowing from the wound above.

"I managed to walk into the shelf over there."

He gestured at a shelf that had been mounted on the wall and stacked with boxes of screws. It was now hanging precariously from one end and all the screws were in a jumble of broken boxes on the floor.

Liza examined the wound. "Head wounds bleed a lot, but this is a deep gash. Good one, Gramps." He grimaced at her.

"We had better clean it up and put in some stitches." Liza spent time studying medical texts when she wasn't reading science fiction. It made sense for at least one person to know medicine, especially in these times, and Fenton and Carrie had both encouraged her studies by trading eggs and live chicks for two medical textbooks. Liza had begun studying in earnest the year after her mother's death. She had helped Fenton set Chris's ankle when he had first arrived and even corrected his technique when they wrapped and then splinted it. Currently, she was working her way through a thick manual on obstetrics. Chris had seen one of the pictures and felt his stomach roil. Definitely not his cup of tea.

"Can you make Gramps better, Sis?" Joseph asked. The kid looked scared.

Liz paused in her examination to smile at her little brother. "I sure can, Joseph. Gramps is going to be just fine. Let's get him back to the house and then we'll fix him up better than ever." She turned back to Fenton and the three of them hoisted him to his feet.

In the end, the couple of stitches had been ten perfect little sutures. Fenton insisted on several healthy swigs from a full bottle of Jack Daniels hidden deep on a high shelf. Chris retrieved it and smiled. He could see ten other bottles of hard liquor, all unopened. He figured old Fenton had put them up there about three years ago, about the time the girls and their mother had arrived, and hadn't touched them since.

"That there needle is gonna hurt," Fenton had given as way of explanation, "I plan on making it hurt less." He had still had a few choice things to say during the procedure.

Carrie started canning the tomatoes Chris already picked. He picked the rest while she worked over the stove blanching, peeling, and preparing the tomatoes. This task lasted late into the night. They lit a gas lamp to see by and kept working on the pile of tomatoes.

As they worked, they listened to Fenton sing, quite drunkenly now that nearly half the bottle of whiskey was gone. When in his cups, Fenton seemed overly fond of Elvis Presley. The tomatoes were all canned; jars lined every piece of available countertop.

Joseph was curled in a small ball on the couch and Fenton was launching into the fifth rendition of "You Ain't Nothing but a Hound Dog" when Liza took the bottle out of his hand and handed it to Chris.

She rolled her eyes at him, suppressing a smile, and nodded to the high shelf. She and Carrie each took a side and gently pulled Fenton to his feet. They guided him slowly up the stairs to his room.

Chris returned the bottle to the shelf and took a moment to look over what else was up there. The old man had quite a selection.

The warm hand that ran up his leg quickly changed his focus. The thought that came next was shocking in its simplicity. "What are you waiting for?"

He climbed down from the counter and turned to face Carrie. The moon had risen in the sky and the light from it poured in the kitchen window. He leaned over, blew out the lamp, and pulled her close. She felt the change in him and responded in kind; shivering slightly as his lips found her neck and worked their way up to her right ear. He whispered in it, “Let’s go for a walk.” He felt rather than saw her nod.

He grabbed several blankets, spread one over little Joseph and the other two he tucked under his arm. Quietly they slipped out of the door, closing it quietly behind them.

Hand in hand, they walked. They didn’t discuss it, and their feet carried them unerringly to the old farmstead. It was their special place. They had been slipping away for make-out sessions there as often as possible in the last few months. He carefully spread the blanket out and they lay down side by side. The stars were incredibly bright and beautiful. It was warm and all around them the night pulsed with life, thousands of tiny creatures attending to their nocturnal activities. They took notice of the two humans in their midst and shied away, creating a bubble of space around the couple.

As they watched a satellite slowly make its way across the sky, Chris wondered if the space station was still up there, and if there were any astronauts inside. If there were, and if the rest of the world was in as bad of shape as the U.S. was, they were nothing but frozen skeletons by now.

He pushed those thoughts out of his mind and thought instead of how amazing Carrie smelled, even with the scent of tomatoes clinging to her. He reached down and took her hand in his. It felt tiny and fragile in comparison with his, but he knew that was an illusion. Carrie was a strong woman, in mind and spirit. She knew her mind, and she fought for what she wanted. Here he had a future, a family and love.

He pulled her close and leaned in for a kiss. It heated and went on and on as their pulses quickened. Their clothing fell in a heap, and the lovemaking was as gentle as he could make it for her. In the end, he collapsed beside her, burrowed his face into her neck and kissed her moist skin.

All of these months of playing, of dancing about and teasing, and they had finally gone and done it. At least he knew Fenton wasn’t busy cleaning his shotgun right now. The minutes ticked by and Chris pulled part of the thin blanket over them. He could hear Carrie’s breathing settle and even out.

"Carrie?"

"Mm?"

He jostled her, "Wake up."

"I'm awake."

He pulled himself to one elbow and looked into her face. He could see it clearly in the moonlight. Her eyes were open, and she had a satisfied, almost smug smile. He reached out and smoothed a lock of hair back behind her left ear. "I love you Carrie Lynn Perdue. Will you marry me?"

She smiled even wider, put her hands on both sides of his face. "I love you too, Christopher Michael Aaronson. And yes, I will marry you."

What followed was a good deal more of what had just occurred. It continued, with little sleep through most of that night. The sun was just beginning to peek over the horizon as the two lovers slipped back inside the house.

The Silence of Screams

"Seeing her there, I knew she was gone. The blood pooled from her back, mixing with the blood of those two animals. Even in death, they contaminated and sickened everything they touched. David was shaking and crying and still he tried to do right by her, reaching forward, closing her staring eyes. He said that I screamed over and over and over until he brought me Jacob and thrust him into my arms. But I don't remember screaming at all. I only remember thinking how deafening the silence was. We buried her the next morning, out back, in a small, overgrown garden, near a clump of iris. I remember there was a creek nearby. David found a large limestone slab and shoved it at the head of the mound. We didn't bury the others. To hell with them."—Jess's Journal

The first sound that David heard through his tortured and ringing eardrums was Jess's screams. They were wordless, horrifying keens of despair as she clutched Erin's hand and rocked back and forth. Blood covered both of them and pooled on the floor. He dropped the revolver he had been clutching, watched it slide from nerveless fingers.

Oh God, he had actually killed one of them. But he'd been too late. The second one, the dark-haired greasy one, had gotten a shot off, straight into Erin before Jess had come running and dropped him with two quick shots. Erin's eyes were open still, staring, and she had a slightly bewildered look on her face.

For a moment he had wondered if there was a chance she would be okay, that she would recover, and then he saw the wound and the blood that poured from it, and from her mouth and nose. Tears came then, as he stared at her, watched her try to speak, choke and weakly spit out a mouthful of blood. Her head fell back against the wood floor, her eyes glazed, and he knew she was gone.

That's when Jess had begun to scream, and it seemed as if the screams grew louder with each passing moment. He reached over, his fingers trembling, and closed Erin's eyes. Mom's had been like that, but clouded, and he could still picture their faces. On the ground, bodies cold and stiff, life gone. He was too shell-shocked, terrified by what he had done and how this had gone so wrong to think any longer. He just sat and cried while Jess screamed over and over and over.

Minutes, what seemed like hours, went by and the shadows had darkened. Night was almost upon them. He came to his senses, got up, and walked out of the farmhouse and into the field to find Tina and the baby. He didn't have to go far.

Jacob's shrieks of hunger and fear were like a beacon. He found Jacob and Tina huddled near a fallen tree. The baby howled for milk and Tina just shook in complete terror. He hugged her to him and took Jacob into his arms. The baby's face was bright red from screaming. No amount of shushing or cooing would help. He could still hear Jess keening in the farmhouse. Erin was dead. Why had he wanted to explore the shed and farmhouse? Why?

Quincy had stayed with them all the way back to the farmhouse. She whined in response to the sounds of Jess's obvious distress. But her mistress had told her to stay with Tina, and young as she was, the pup followed orders. Tina kept a death grip on his shirttail as he trudged back to the house with Jacob shrieking the entire way. Maybe if he could get the baby in Jess's arms, she'd calm down and feed him.

Anything but that awful sound she kept making. Tina stopped in her tracks at the sight of the bodies and refused to enter the front door. Her tiny body shivered with fear. He had to pull loose from her grasp in order to get to Jess and thrust Jacob into her arms.

The baby's screams triggered the mothering instinct and she could feel her breasts fill painfully in response. Somehow, Jess let go of her friend's limp and lifeless hand and stood up. She couldn't stay in this room. She made her way to the front porch, her shrieks turned to deep, racking sobs and finally to a half-hearted humming as she tried to calm her screaming son.

Out of the room, it didn't seem real. Erin couldn't be gone. Not after all they had been through. They had survived the troops taking their town. They had survived Tent 5 and the months after in the cabin in the woods. They had made the long trek to Clinton and avoided the soldiers and the gunfire. And now, on their way home, to die like this? It couldn't be. Night had descended and there were few stars, just inky shadows.

David reappeared with Tina, dragging most of their supplies and equipment, and his voice was cracked, wounded, when he spoke. "There's a big tree, not too far away. We could stay there for tonight, Jess. It's away from the house, in case others come. What do you think?"

When Jess answered, she could barely manage a whisper from her raw throat, "Yeah. Okay, lead the way."

It wasn't far to walk. They stumbled in the dark to the tree, pulled their blankets close to each other and lay down on the hard ground. Jess felt the boy snuggle his back into hers, Tina wrapped in his arms and Jacob in hers. There was some comfort to feeling him wedged against her and needing reassurance. Quincy curled against her legs, whining softly.

"We'll bury her in the morning and move on, in case there's more of 'em."

Out of the dark came his response, "'Kay."

The Peace of Earth

"I love the warm months. When the memories come, when my heart breaks just thinking of those I have lost, I go out into the garden. I pull up grass and weeds and train the vines. I dig deep in the rich earth. It brings me comfort and soothes the hurt. Each year is a miracle, each day and week and month that passes is a song of triumph. We rise again, we survive, and I can feel life in each handful of dirt I move."—Jess's Journal

Jess lay on a pad from the porch swing, a thin blanket over her. Jacob was cuddled close. He was asleep, having fussed and cried a good part of the night. She wasn't much better off. Her dreams had been bloody and violent.

The world seemed full of death and despair, despite the sun and the birds chirping. Signs of life and growth surrounded her. It felt like a slap in the face. How dare the world be so beautiful, right here, when only a few hundred feet away Erin's lifeless body lay? She had managed to dig down several feet before the sun climbed high in the sky. She collapsed on the ground to rest and nursed Jacob.

David had scrounged a late breakfast, discovering several woody radishes and asparagus stalks in the old garden and supplementing them with a precious can of beef stew. Jess hadn't been hungry, but she sat up and ate what David handed her. The food tasted like sawdust. Erin was gone, but no matter how much that hurt, she wasn't, and three young lives depended on her now. They needed her to stay strong.

She swallowed mechanically and sipped again from the cup of tea David had passed to her. It was hot and he must have used the farmhouse stove. It probably ran on propane, this far out in the country. The kitchen was accessible without going through the front entry and living room where the soldier's bodies lay, flies buzzing around them. There were mint leaves floating in the tea.

As she peered down into the cup, David said, "I found some plants out in the garden. A big patch of mint, so I put 'em in a cup and boiled some water." Jess raised her eyebrows and sipped again. "It's just those leaves and nothin' else, but I like it. I picked a lot and put 'em in one of the packs."

He looked away, back at the partially dug hole and the sheet-draped body nearby. "I'll dig for a while."

He didn't want to tell her yet, but he knew he would have to soon. Before he had heated up the water in the kitchen, he had gone through both soldier's pockets. It had taken every bit of nerve he could manage. Hands shaking, he had collected weapons, gone through their packs and found extra ammunition and some cans of food. He had also found something else, something that changed everything and made him want to run screaming back to Clinton with Tina's hand clutched in his. As much as he wished for the safe comfort of his hidey-hole, he knew Erin and Jess had been right. They couldn't survive the winter there. So instead of running, he held his tongue and dug deeply into the earth.

The grave was dug by the time the sun was directly overhead in the sky. Jess had done two more stints, with David helping. She dug into the earth and cried, stopped, and then dug some more. Eventually it was deep enough, and she hugged her friend to her, pulled her body into the open grave and then slowly climbed out. After that came the hardest part. She shoveled the dirt over Erin and slowly buried her friend deep in the ground. Quincy had let out a long, sad howl when the dirt began to cover Erin's body. Then the pup had sunk down on the ground, tail curled up underneath her and ears flat and whined. By the time they had finished shoveling the dirt into place; Jess was shaking with exhaustion and grief. She had no more tears left in her, and her head pounded in agony. A few feet away, Tina fanned Jacob as he slept and watched the process without speaking. She hadn't spoken a word all day.

Tears streaked and mingled with the dirt on David's face as he pulled over a large rock. Despite his young age, the boy was strong. He shrugged off an offer of help from Jess. "I got it." He heaved again and managed to set it upright at the head of the grave. Jess felt a wave of pain and loss crash over her. After all, they had been through; to lose Erin now seemed to be more than she could bear.

Jess searched for the words to a familiar prayer. Her parents hadn't been religious, they had never gone to church, but it seemed like there were special words you were supposed to say during moments like that. David and Tina both looked up at her expectantly. She dug in her memories and finally remembered the Lord's Prayer.

"Our father who art in heaven," the words were reassuring somehow, although she couldn't have explained why. Perhaps certain words, when said in the right sequence, had power.

"Hallowed be thy name. Thy kingdom come; thy will be done..."

Could it be that they had power to bring peace, heal wounds, or renew hope? David's voice chimed in and Tina tried as well, but it was clear she didn't know the words. "On earth as it is in heaven," When they finished, the silence stretched for several long moments. Jess cleared her throat.

"Erie, it doesn't seem right leaving you here. I promise I'll come back and put a better marker here as soon as I can." She stopped, took a deep breath, "You saved my life too many times to count and I will miss you forever. Please forgive me for not being quicker. I love you so much. I'm so sorry."

It didn't seem enough. It felt unfinished somehow. She searched her memories and smiled as the tears slipped down her cheeks. The words flowed as she spoke to the memory of her friend and their childhood adventures. She recalled all the good memories, all the beauty and laughter they had shared. It took a while for Jess to say goodbye to a friend she had grown up with.

When she was done, she placed her son in his sling, picked up what she could carry of their packs, turned toward the east and began to walk. David and Tina followed close behind, and Quincy ran ahead. None of them said anything for a long time.

A Lake Retreat

"*When David showed me the paper he had found, I panicked. What if there were more men out there looking for us? I'll never know how many they sent, or why they felt it was so important to get us back. All I knew was that the note listed descriptions of Erin and me, along with the names of our family and friends. They knew where we came from. And months after we escaped, they were still looking for us. Going home was suddenly a walk in the wrong direction."—Jess's Journal*

David hesitated for several hours, then finally, when they stopped to rest and eat a bit of food, he got up the courage to show Jess the note he had discovered on one of the bodies. The paper had been folded several times and was well worn. But Jess and Erin's names had both been on it, along with a physical description of each girl and the town of Belton as their expected destination. The soldiers had been looking for them. He didn't know why, and that scared him.

"I found this on one of the soldiers," he handed the paper to her and watched her read it. The color drained from her face. "Do you think there might be others?"

Jess said nothing in response. She stared at the paper for a long time, reading and rereading the few words until she had the note, even the shape of the letter formations firmly fixed in her mind.

They finished eating and Jacob fussed inside his wrap. Jess changed his diaper, wrapped him back against her, and began walking without a word to David or Tina. Soon after, east turned to due south as they discovered the first of scores of bodies. There had been fighting here recently, a few days at most, and the smell from the corpses was sickening. Tina whimpered in fear and hid her face in her brother's shirt as they skirted around the dead. Quincy's tail stayed permanently tucked between her legs and she walked as close as possible to Jess, her ears flattened, her body tense.

Jess wondered if the bodies belonged to some of the troops who had passed through Clinton recently. It seemed safer to head south for now. As they turned south, the northwestern edge of Harry Truman Lake appeared and, due to the inability to head east unless they wanted to swim, they hugged the lake edge and continued south, away from Belton, yet again.

It was sunset when they made camp on a bluff overlooking the reservoir. Decades ago, the U.S. Corps of Engineers had purposely flooded sections of the low-lying valley, creating Truman Lake. In the distance, tips of dead, drowned trees poked up from the middle of the water. Even the top of a chimney could be seen. It was an old homestead that had long been abandoned and then submerged when the waters flooded the valley.

They didn't dare build a fire. The highway, probably Highway 7 from Jess's quick review of the map they had found in a broken-down truck, was also within view. What they could see of the highway, someone on the highway could likely also see of them. No reason to take chances.

Again, Jess forced herself to eat. There wasn't much, and because they couldn't build a fire, she let Quincy eat the rabbit she had flushed out and caught shortly before they stopped for the night. The young dog eagerly tore into her meal.

They slept huddled close that night. It was warm, not oppressively so, but warm enough. Still, they needed to feel safe, needed to hear the breath of another living person and feel their presence close. Life was so fleeting, so painfully short at times; they needed each other more than ever before. They slept deeply, without dreams or nightmares on that bluff, legs and arms intertwined, bodies curled close.

Keeping the small band together and safe overrode Jess's desire to head home. They continued south the next day, keeping the water's edge within sight at all times. It was late and almost time to stop for dinner and camp for the night when David commented on the strange tree. It was bent, twice, at nearly perfect right angles. "This tree is weird."

Weird or not, it was a reasonable place to stop. The sun would soon be setting and it was time to scrounge for food. Quincy had disappeared into the brush to the west, probably hunting for a rabbit or squirrel. They heard her give one short, quick bark. David had been picking from bushes and digging up little plants all along the way. All of his studies of the now filthy, dog-eared and ragged book were paying off. He could easily identify plantain, cattail, wild onion, fiddlehead ferns, oxalis and a host of other edible plants. As they walked, he would suddenly stop and dig something up and stick it into his pack.

The long-bladed shovel he found at the farmhouse had become his walking stick and was never far from his reach. Tina had begun to help as well, and when they stopped for any length of time, both children would forage a little, always within sight, and pick up what plants they could to supplement the dwindling supply of canned food.

As Jess began to search through the cans for dinner, David continued to study the strangely formed tree with interest. It was such a specific deformity. And there was nothing in sight that indicated why it would be shaped that way. "It's like it's pointing to something," David commented, unable to stop staring at the tree.

An unexpected voice answered, "It is pointing at something. That, young man, is what the Osage call a thong tree."

The owner of the voice was a bright-eyed old woman, who leaned on a walking stick and blended seamlessly into the trees twenty feet away. A rifle was strapped to her back and her dark eyes sparkled beneath a crown of white hair pulled into a loose bun. Wisps of her hair hung freely. She was slim, dressed in a simple t-shirt and jeans with solid, no-nonsense hiking boots on her feet. Quincy squirmed in excitement at her feet; apparently, she had found a person instead of the usual rabbit or squirrel.

David jumped in response, and the rest of them froze in place. But it was hard to be afraid of one little old woman, especially with Quincy's relaxed canine confidence in the stranger. Jess scanned the rest of the woods surrounding them and saw no one. When her gaze returned to the old woman, she saw long, deep lines etched in her face. It was hard to keep her guard up; the old woman looked friendly and had reached down to scratch Quincy behind the ears. The dog leaned a floppy-eared head against the woman's jeans.

Jess spoke first, "Uh, hi."

David spoke as well, "Why's it called a thong tree and who're the Oh Sage?"

The old woman laughed then and the lines in her face deepened as she did. The children relaxed for the first time in a long time. Here was someone who was not a threat.

"Well, I'm Osage, Little One, and the rest is better explained a short walk from here." She glanced up at the sky, "Rain is coming." She turned and began walking west, away from the lake's edge, stopping only briefly to glance back and crook a bony finger at the group. "Come this way then."

Quincy bounded after her, and a moment later, so did Jess and the kids, lugging the packs they had recently shed from their backs. It was odd. She hadn't even introduced herself, yet the little group followed her wordlessly.

Through the clearing and into the deep woods, they walked. A winding path, with several sharp zigs and zags, was barely visible unless you knew what to look for. It eventually led to the base of a wide-mouthed, low-ceilinged cave. Seconds after they followed the old woman inside of the cave, the skies outside darkened, rumbled ominously, and then opened up and began to pour rain.

Thanks to the rain and clouds, the inside of the cave appeared dim. After bending slightly to pass under an overhanging rock, the ceiling raised above Jess's head. It was about twelve feet high in this main outer chamber. Ahead of them it closed down again to a dimly lit opening in the back. There appeared to be some kind of light source on the other side. They kept to the path on the left and avoided the deep holes dug on the right-hand side. It appeared to be an archaeological dig site in process. Pickets and string sectioned off areas in meter squares, delineating one section from the next. Signs labeled each square and in some of the sections there were spearheads or pot shards laid out in the exact position they had been discovered and excavated.

Jess and the children followed the old woman back through this outer chamber, through the small man-height opening. Jess could see that the light source, judging from the water dripping down on one edge, was a natural skylight that reached all the way up through the cave ceiling. This inner chamber was immense, and there were several other smaller dig sites at regular intervals throughout. It was obvious that the old woman lived here as well. There was a section with a table, several chairs and some stacks of boxes and containers all situated away from the falling water, but close to the 'skylight.' The rain came in and pooled in a lagoon the size of the front chamber, then flowed away along a small rocky stream toward the pitch-black rear of the cave.

The old woman stopped near the campfire located across from her living area. She stirred the embers and gently placed another log on to burn. A spit held three blackened lumps above the crackling fire. It was difficult to tell, but Jess guessed it was probably a squirrel.

She spoke then, as she moved from the fire to the supplies nearby, "Not much meat for all of you, but I wasn't really expecting company. I can cook up some ramen and I'm sure I've got some other goodies in here to add to it." She opened boxes and handed a saucepan to David, "Fill it up with rainwater there and put it on the fire, Min'-dse." She smiled and her teeth were white and perfect. "My name is Dr. Madeleine Falling Water, but you can call me Madge. Let's get some dinner and then we'll have story time."

Jess wasn't sure what to think of the old woman or of story time, but at that moment Jacob signaled he was awake, hungry, and ready for a change by wailing loud and long. She pulled him out of her wrap, where he had been hidden from sight, and Madge moved faster than it seemed possible for a woman her age.

Before Jess could object, Jacob was lifted from her arms with a cry of joy and a barrage of words in a strange, guttural language. Oddly, the baby stopped crying immediately and stared at the old woman intensely, watching and listening to everything she said.

She unwrapped his coverings, clucked over his wet and bulging diaper, and immediately set him on a coat on the cave floor and changed him, reaching impatiently for the clean diaper which Jess found and handed to her after a bit of scrambling. Madge then swept him up in her arms and spoke rapidly in the foreign language to the infant, cooing and kissing, and then handing him back to Jess to nurse.

She pointed a slender, bony finger at Tina. "Little one, Ni'-da-wi, go out to the front of the cave and pick as many dandelions as you can find." She gave the little girl a soft push back towards the entrance to the cave and pulled Jess by her free hand to a chair set apart from the others in one corner. "Here child, sit here and give your son his dinner."

Jess sat in the chair and let out a small groan of pleasure. It was a canvas sling, suspended on a wooden frame, and then lined with soft furs. It felt delicious. She arranged her wraps, offered Jacob her breast and settled back blissfully content in the most comfortable seat she had sat in since the week at old Cooper's place. Her eyes closed, and she slowly drifted towards sleep as the others moved about the cave, preparing dinner.

Jess was startled awake by a steaming cup of tea thrust under her nose a half hour later. The tea was followed by a hearty bowl of ramen noodles, thick with dandelion greens, and small bits of savory squirrel meat floating in it. They ate in shifts, for there were only two bowls. The light from the natural skylight had dimmed and disappeared as night fell. The fire was built up, and they made little niches of blankets or backpacks to curl up against and stare at the old woman. She had promised them a story, after all. She reached over and plucked Jacob from Jess's arms, cuddling and cooing at him, and began to speak.

"One day, the chief of the Quiet Earth people was hunting in the forest. He was looking for a symbol to give life to his people. He came upon the tracks of a giant deer and he became very excited.

'Grandfather Deer,' he said, 'surely you will show yourself to me. You will be the symbol of my people.'

He followed the tracks. His eyes were on nothing else as he followed those tracks, and he ran fast through the forest. Suddenly, he ran right into a huge spider web that stretched between the trees, across the trail. When he got up, he was terribly angry. He struck at the spider who was sitting at the edge of the web. But the spider jumped out of reach. Then the spider spoke.

'Grandson,' the spider said, 'why do you run through the woods looking at nothing but the ground?'

The chief felt foolish, but he answered. 'I was following the tracks of a great deer,' the chief said. 'I am seeking a symbol of strength for my people.'

'I can be such a symbol,' said the spider.

'How can you be a symbol of strength?' said the chief. 'You are small and weak, and I didn't even see you as I followed the great Deer.'

'Grandson,' said the spider, 'look upon me. I am patient. I watch and I wait. Then all things come to me. If your people learn this, they will be strong indeed.'

The chief saw that this was so. And so, the spider became one of the symbols of the people."

Madge looked around. Tina was nearly asleep, curled in a ball near the old woman's feet. David was staring attentively and Jess was nearly asleep herself. She smiled at David. "What did you think of the story?"

He didn't smile, instead he looked sad. David thought of the old farmhouse and the blood and of Erin. In his memory, so fresh and raw, he could still hear Jess's screams as she held her friend's hand.

"I should have watched and waited more, but I didn't and then Erin died." The old woman nodded slowly. Jess opened her eyes, stared at David and Madge, but said nothing. She wondered where this was going.

The old woman's voice was kind and matter of fact. "This happens. Many have died this past year and even more will die in the months and years to come. You are young, you are Min'-dse, the bow. You bend, and you learn and grow strong. You stay alive, someday you will be Ku'-rux, the bear," she smiled at him, then made a fierce face and growled playfully, her wrinkled hands imitating the claws of the bear.

"You will be a fierce warrior. But you must first learn patience, to watch and wait for the right moment; this will make you a strong man someday."

Madge nodded then at Jess and stroked Jacob's sleeping cheek, "You too are young, but you and your family have seen much hardship. Will you tell me your story?"

David interjected, "We aren't family. Jess and Erin found Tina and me in Clinton. Our parents are dead. And Erin is dead now too. The soldiers killed her."

The old woman stared at David for a moment. "Min'-dse, you are all family now. In the past, my people warred with other tribes. When too many of the warriors died, my tribe would go out and take people from other tribes to adopt and bring into the tribe so that our numbers did not dwindle and be gone forever from this world. You have found each other, bonded together in a common need, and this means that you are family."

She reached down and stroked Tina's hair.

"But it is late and you are all tired. Let us share more stories tomorrow, when our bodies are well-rested."

She pulled herself upright and brought Jacob back to Jess, watching approvingly as Jess carefully folded the infant back into the sling without waking him. She showed them a sleeping chamber that branched off to the left of the large inner chamber. They were surprised to see that the sleeping chamber had six cots in it.

Only one cot had blankets, and it was obviously Madge's cot. Jess and David looked at each other in the flickering lantern light. It felt as if they had hit the jackpot. First, they had eaten a hot, satisfying dinner and now they each had an actual bed to sleep in. They smiled for the first time in days.

Madge bustled about and reached into a box, and pulled out blankets for each of them. David went back and woke up Tina and held her hand as she stumbled sleepily into the small, dark chamber. Madge had lain down on her cot, and hummed some wordless song for a few minutes, lulling them into sleep. All that could be heard after that was the occasional pop or spit from the fire and the soft splashing of rain.

Sanctuary

"There was something about Madge that spoke about security, knowledge, and peace. She knew so much, instantly cared for us, and pulled us into her world. We were safe, loved, and protected. I learned more about the ancient people who had occupied this land, and how relevant their lives and knowledge were to us right now, than I ever imagined possible. Somehow, too, she helped me find some peace with Erin's death and my part in it. She was a mother, favorite aunt, and revered grandmother, all rolled into one. Madge reminded me that family is not always who we are born with, but who we choose to love. She helped me to see how much we all belonged together."—David's Journal

The fire crackled merrily, flames licking over the newly added wood. The skylight in the cave showed that dawn had barely arrived. The light was still gray and indistinct when Jess awoke to the sounds of Madge bustling about. She was muttering to herself and had a list and pen in hand. When she looked over and saw Jess's eyes open, she smiled at her, "There is much to do today, child, so much to do. We must make this place into a refuge for you and yours. Winter will be coming soon."

Jess wasn't sure what to say in response. Winter? Stay in a cave for a full winter? A nice meal and a night's stay. That was fine, but a full winter? She wondered if the old woman was stable. Perhaps she was suffering from dementia or was just old and crazy. With all that had happened, it was a wonder they weren't all crazy. The memory of Erin's empty staring eyes flashed through her mind. And the bodies, so many bodies to the north. How would they ever survive to get past the fighting?

Were there others out there looking for them? As her mind tumbled through its fears and concerns, she began to waver. Perhaps a winter here wasn't such a bad idea. Her thoughts were interrupted by David yawning and stretching at her feet. His eyes widened in momentary fear as he looked around, his sleep-fogged brain not remembering the night before for one short moment.

As the others woke, Jacob kicked and grumbled a moment before letting out a wail of hunger and discomfort. He was wet again, and Jess realized they were almost out of diapers.

Madge eyed the dwindling stack of diapers her and added to her list, "We'll need grass and rabbit skin for Mi'-da-in-ga, wood for bowls, at least two deer." David had already made his way to her side, reading over the list.

"Who's Meedah, Meedah..." He stumbled over the word.

"Mi'-da-in-ga," Madge replied, stressing each syllable, "It means Playful Sun."

"Okay," David looked confused, "Who is that?"

"The little one, the boy. You call him Jacob, yes?" Jess nodded. "Well, he needs diapers, and there's no Pampers factory around here. We must get sweet grass and rabbit skin for his wraps."

David and Jess exchanged raised eyebrows. In the coming months, they would find Madge to be an enormous wealth of information, support, and love. Throughout their stay, however, she would insist on calling them by strange names they had difficulty pronouncing. No matter how often they referred to each other by their given names, she would always respond with a correction. It was her one idiosyncrasy and one that they soon came to accept.

When Tina crossed her legs and looked nervously about, Madge led the children out of the cave and made a sharp turn to the left. The path through the trees was narrow and less than a hundred feet away, there was a small opening in the trees. An outhouse sat squarely in the middle of it. Despite its function, it did not emit a smell. Inside the rough-hewn walls was a toilet seat mounted over a bucket filled with sawdust. Beside it was a barrel piled high with clean sawdust. Madge instructed Tina to throw a handful of sawdust down when she had finished and cover any waste.

A few yards from the outhouse, there was an outdoor shower. The shower could be used by first pumping water through a small pump from the local stream to a water tower nestled high in the trees. They would do this first thing in the morning and the black walls of the water tower pulled in heat and warmed the water quite efficiently during the warm months. It was usually enough for two showers if they took short ones.

After everyone had had a chance to use the outhouse, Madge directed them back to the cave, stopping only to cut down several swaths of milk thistle along the way. She carried them gingerly, her worn hands encased in thick gloves to avoid being pierced by the thorns.

Breakfast was dandelion tea and thick oatmeal sweetened with some wild berries that David had collected the day before. Madge had stripped the leaves and flowers off of the milk thistle and set them to boiling in a pot over the fire. As they sipped the last of their tea and handed the bowls around, Madge told them about her work as an anthropologist and explained that the cave site was an archaeological dig from the Middle Woodland era (200 B.C. to 450 A.D.).

"I headed a team of five up until a year and a half ago. Things just went from bad to worse in Kansas City, where I was based, and when everything fell apart, I headed up here after the first big thaw in the spring. I was hoping that some of the team might make it back here, but so far, no one has. My children are long grown and gone overseas. I haven't heard from any of them for more than a year." Her dark eyes shimmered, "I've been alone here until you children came along."

Quincy quietly gnawed on a small pile of rabbit bones at Jess's feet and then licked the bowls clean after everyone had finished eating.

The next hour was spent sharing their histories with Madge, including the loss of Erin just a few days past. Jess passed Madge the note describing Jess and Erin and listing Belton as their hometown and probably destination.

"We were planning on heading for Belton but with all the fighting... and this note David found on one of the soldiers... I just don't know what to do." Jess confessed, tears in her eyes, "I want to go home, but I'm trying to keep us out of danger."

Madge read the note and said nothing for a few minutes. "I haven't seen hide nor hair of another living soul in over four months until you children showed up. And I'm pretty sure that's likely to continue. This cave is not on any of the common maps; it isn't obvious or noticeable from the water line. And the nearest road is a hard-going seven-mile hike from here. It was most certainly used in the past for shelter by my ancestors. That was a long time ago, but I think we could do so again and make it work, even through the winter. In the spring you could move on if you liked."

She paused and smiled at them each in turn. "I'm not saying it won't be hard. But if my people lived on this land for centuries, I know we can manage to do it for a few months. I've been fine here all summer, and I had packed enough for a team of six, so there are plenty of food stores plus the natural resources nearby. I've been a student of the old ways since I was as young as Min'-dse here."

She nodded towards David. "Some hard work and preparation and we will be fine. In the spring, once your trail has grown cold and your pursuers have given up, then you will be free to return to your home in Belton."

Jess was conflicted. Should they try to survive the winter in a cave? Could they actually do that? Or should they take their chances heading north again, knowing they could be heading straight into danger? A part of her was exhausted and heartsick. She missed home dreadfully, even though she knew that home might not even be there anymore.

Another part of her simply wanted to stop running and rest for a while. It was exhausting, constantly being afraid of every movement in front of you, behind you, and all around you. To stop and breathe, to sleep in one place each night sounded like heaven to her.

She made eye contact with David and even Tina. Tina was young, but she still had a vote. Both seemed eager to stay in the cave. The thought of heading north and encountering bodies, being caught in a firefight or encountering more like those at the farmhouse, was terrifying to them both. Although they said nothing out loud, the answer on their faces was clear. Jess asked, "So... what will we need to do to prepare for winter?"

Old Madge's face lit up, and she pulled the small notebook out of her pocket and began to list off what they would need. It was an odd and varied list, and she explained each item in detail. The next few weeks would be filled with frenzied activity, and a great deal of learning.

Memories of Ancestors

"*You look around you and you see something from long ago. I look at the bones and the history and think of yesterday and tomorrow. What my people knew then, we must know now. Without that knowledge, we cannot survive. The memories of ancestors—how they lived, what they hunted with, even their rituals and legends hold great meaning to us, here and now. Never forget that. It may mean the difference between life and death."—From the Journal of Dr. Madeleine Falling Water*

By mid-October, the nights were quite chilly, but Jess had managed to bag a large buck with one clean shot with Madge's deer rifle, a 94 Winchester model. It was easy once she had thought about their habits. They were active at twilight and at first light.

Conveniently, Jacob was now sleeping a good portion of the night. He woke around 2 a.m. for a feeding and then slept until 8 a.m., sometimes even at 9 a.m. Jess had fully recovered from his birth now, and the extra time he was sleeping meant she wasn't as sleep-deprived as she had been. Thanks to better living conditions and nutritious food, she felt energized, especially in this quiet, peaceful place.

Each morning she would get up carefully, nestle Jacob against Madge, and slip out of the cave and down to a stand of trees downwind from the water's edge. She had studied the deer tracks, and it appeared that several of them always came to the same place to drink from the lake.

The first day she headed out too late and met a surprised buck heading back. The second day, she moved at the wrong time, startling the small group of deer before they were in full range of her scope. The third day was a success. One shot, into the shoulder as the young buck stood broadside 20 yards away, killed the great animal instantly.

She stood over its body, thankful for the magnificent creature's quick death. No suffering, and the animal was dead before it hit the ground. The hunting she and Erin had done at the cabin had not included deer. Not because they weren't around, and Erin had certainly wanted to try, but the .22 Rimfire was far too small of a caliber to be an effective and humane kill. Jess smiled sadly at the thought of her friend. Erin would have been so proud of her right now.

They had all quickly become familiar with the area and moved about the surrounding woods with assurance once Madge showed them other signs that would indicate the location of the cave if any of them got turned around or confused. There were notches on trees, rock piles, and rags tied to branches to help point them back to the rock shelter.

The cave was extensive. The back of the sleeping chamber led to three additional chambers. There was a section used to store dried foods was on the left and then the passage emptied onto a second small chamber which contained another dig site. Madge explained that it was a sacred burial site and asked them not to go any further than the food storage chamber. Beyond the burial chamber, there was another chamber that had collapsed.

"The burial site and beyond are not only sacred but also in danger of collapse," Madge explained, "We had to abandon efforts in that area until we could get it shored up better." She looked sad, "And, of course, I couldn't do it on my own."

The thought of the cave collapsing was frightening until Madge explained the architecture of the cave and showed them the supports that had already been put into place.

"As long as we don't get a major earthquake, like the New Madrid earthquake in 1811-1812, we'll be just fine here."

She smiled crookedly, "If an earthquake that size hits, well, let's just say it's the last thing any of us will have to worry about. Even outside wouldn't be safe. That 1811-1812 series toppled millions of acres of forest."

The rest of the cave traveled for miles. There was another large passage leading west from the back of the large inner chamber. David followed the stream with a lantern in hand for several hundred yards until it disappeared into a rock wall. The cave continued for miles, Madge informed them, but warned them of the dangers of becoming lost in the different passages and sub-chambers that branched off in different directions.

One night, not long after they had decided to stay for the winter, David had dreamed of Erin. It had been more of a memory, really. He had never spoken of what had happened in the farmhouse, and Jess had never asked. He awoke with a shout and it had startled Jacob enough that the baby began to wail.

It was early. The sun was barely peeking over the horizon and he slipped out past the campfires and through the small entrance to the outer chamber. He knelt near one of the pits and stared into it. The sections were neatly marked, and he could see that one of the pits held a small skeleton. Next to it was a spear and what appeared to be the remains of woven grass moccasins. He stared at the hole and tried to forget the dream.

A few minutes later, Madge's bony hand on his shoulder caused him to flinch. Jacob had stopped crying; perhaps he had been lulled back to sleep.

"Mind'se, you are troubled by your dreams. A burden shared can be a burden halved. Will you share with me what yours is?"

David fought the tears welling up inside him. "It was just a dream." He wiped at his eyes with the back of his shirt. It smelled and was stiff with dirt. He needed to wash it soon.

"It was more than a dream, Mind'se. It was about what happened at the farmhouse and how Erin died, wasn't it?"

The old woman was persistent. She had watched David for weeks and knew that whatever had happened in that farmhouse was eating at him. He pushed himself so hard, helping out wherever needed and sinking into his cot each night exhausted from work that would have tired a full-grown man. It was as if he were trying to atone for something.

"I... yes... I." He couldn't even put the words to it. "It was my fault. Erin died, and it was my fault."

Madge sighed and tugged at him until he turned and faced her. She met his eyes with her soft brown, liquid ones. "Do you trust me?"

"Uh, yeah, I mean, I guess so."

Her face was solemn. "Tell me what happened and I will tell you the truth of it. If you were responsible, then you must unburden yourself

Mind'se. Do you trust me to be objective, to tell you honestly what I think?"

He had held it in his heart for far too long and it came spilling out then, the memory of that afternoon tearing from him in great gasps of pain and guilt.

"I wanted to explore the farmhouse. I had done it dozens of times in town, there in Clinton. I'd seen bodies, even found some houses where people were living and they'd just told me to go away or given me a can of food and told me to not come back. We were in the middle of nowhere, so I figured, why not? right?"

The boy's tears poured forth as fast as his words. "Erin wasn't far behind me, but she headed for the farmhouse and I headed for the barn. I had wanted to find a small shovel. I saw one, but it was mounted high and I was trying to find something to climb on. Before I could do that, I heard Erin scream."

David gulped; his cheeks wet with tears and wiped his nose on his shirt. Madge reached out and patted his shoulder. "Go on."

"I went in through the back, as quiet as I could and I was scared, real scared. I wanted to run, but I knew she didn't have a gun, nothing to fight back with. And I know those soldiers, the ones Jess and Erin got away from. They did bad things... they," he looked down at the ground, unable to even speak it out loud.

"They did terrible things. Yes." Madge's answer was soft and forthright. "You were brave to go in, Mind'se."

"I killed one of them." He looked scared then, his eyes darting to her face and searching for any recrimination, but there was none. "I'm not sorry I killed him. But it didn't matter 'cause Erin still died. She saw him aiming at me and ran towards him."

His voice rose in pitch. "She died trying to save me. What if all they were gonna do was take her back with them? If I had run back to Jess, warned her, we could have stopped them together."

"Oh, Mind'se... David, you are..." the old woman's eyes filled with tears, "You are not to blame, my brave one. You did what was right and what was brave. You did what a warrior would do."

She placed her thin, bony hands on each side of his head, stroking his tangled unkempt hair. How long had this child been without parents to love and protect him? And how had he risen to the occasion, willing to take so much on and expect so much from himself?

"You are not to blame," she repeated firmly. "They would have taken her to a place far worse. They would have done unspeakable things to her and they would have killed her in the end. Never blame yourself again for this."

Behind her, Jess had appeared at the rock entrance. She had heard it all, the details she had dreaded asking about and yet wished she had known. To hear how it had all played out was as much of a relief as it was painful. She knew she had blamed him, in some small corner of her heart, and been afraid to ask for fear she would truly hate him if she knew the truth of it. Instead, she found she was relieved. He had tried to protect Erin, just as she had given her life to protect him in return. Madge had said they were a family, and she was right. They were. She placed her hand on David's shoulder, startling him. Madge looked up at her, her old face lined with wrinkles, a question in her eyes.

"Madge is right, David." She said, tears in her own eyes, her voice unsteady. "Family protects family. That's what you did for Erin, and that is what she chose to do for you. We are a family. And I wouldn't have it any other way."

It was a healing moment for all of them. The days and weeks that followed slowly became happy ones as the odd, mismatched band grew to know each other better and make new, gentler memories.

One of the other anthropologists had been an avid bow hunter, and Madge had his bow and arrows. They were composed of an ultra-modern, lightweight substance, and she encouraged Jess and David to practice with targets daily.

After watching him practice, she clucked in approval to Jess, "Min'-dse is grown beyond his years. He knows when to be quiet and listen and watch. His aim improves each day."

By the end of their second week at the cave, the boy insisted on carrying the bow and arrows with him everywhere. As Jess and Madge fished on the edge of the lake early one morning, he moved quietly along the southern edge and disappeared into the forest. Quincy followed silently behind.

Tina watched him go, "He been practicin' walking so he don't make any sound at all." Madge just smiled and patted Tina's head, running her bony hands through the little girl's short brown curls. The months the two children had spent alone had left the small child with a mane of filthy, matted, dreadlocked hair. They had finally given up on getting the worst of the mats out and cut it short the week before. Tina had cried during the entire ordeal. But at least now they could keep it under control.

Madge kept the little girl busy pulling grass and collecting plants while Jess fished. She had fashioned her own fur-lined sling for Jacob and cooed and sang to him. This gave Jess a relief from the constant care.

She was surprised, since up to this point, Jacob would tolerate no one holding him but Jess. He still screamed if David or Tina tried to pick him up, but with Madge, he was content unless he needed to nurse.

Madge pointed at different plants and explained their uses to Tina, who, despite her young age, listened and watched intently. Jess pulled out three good-sized, small-mouthed bass and dumped them into a bucket of water. They kept a lid on it to prevent the fish from jumping back out. Jacob squawked in hunger and Madge had just handed him to Jess when they heard a loud 'whoop' and Quincy let out one sharp double-bark.

"I got one! I got one! Oh wow! I got one!" they could hear David's voice in the distance; he couldn't have been more than a hundred yards away. Jacob squalled in frustration as Jess paused and looked into the woods. A deer? With only a bow and arrow? No way. She looked at Madge, who smiled smugly, and waved her fingers at Jess to feed the baby.

"Three is enough fish for now," she said, reeling in the line. "Besides, it's around ten. They'll be moving towards deeper waters now. You sit and feed Mi'-da-in-ga and I'll go help Min'-dse, who is living up to his name so well." She beckoned to Tina, "Ni'-da-wi, come, we will help your brother dress his first kill." She took the little girl's hand, and they quickly disappeared into the trees.

It was past noon when all three of them re-appeared, Quincy leading the way. The little dog's tail wagged furiously, and from the blood on her muzzle, she had already had a fresh treat. David was strutting. His small chest jutted forward, his shoulders were high and his back straight, his eyes shining with pride. Madge was grinning too, proud as a mother hen. They had rigged a bower of sorts and they dragged the deer carcass behind them. It was partially dressed, and Jess blinked at the surreal scene. Before her were one old woman, two little kids, one dead deer, and one hell of a lot of blood caking them and the mutt running circles around their feet. The corners of her mouth curled up. Damned if he hadn't gotten that deer after all. And with only a bow and arrow!

Lunch was an abbreviated observance. They ate quickly and got to work skinning and butchering the enormous buck. Jess's stomach roiled a bit, and David actually looked as if he were about to be sick.

He gulped hard and got back to work. That seemed to impress Madge even more than the kill. They set up the meat in a smoke hut just ten yards south of the cave. Madge's team member had built it two years ago and had supplemented their packaged food with fresh out of season deer during the past two dig seasons.

Little of the deer went to waste, and Madge even knew how to preserve the hide, which Jess paid special attention to. Later that winter, it would come in handy during the cold nights. They were finally finished by late afternoon and David and Madge prepared the bass, stuffed with wood sorrel, wild carrot, and other fresh edibles that Madge and Tina had gathered. They feasted on the succulent fish and as they finished, Madge turned to David and made a small bow in his direction, with great formality, "Min'-dse, you have lived up to your name truly this day. The spirit of this great deer was sacrificed so that we might all live. Will you tell us now of how you accomplished this great deed?"

Story time, as Madge called it, had become a daily theme for the little group. Usually, Madge would tell them a story about her ancestors, other times she encouraged Jess or David to tell a story that they knew. Jess soon found herself remembering the tales from the Grimm's Brothers and Hans Christian Andersen. David would often share a portion of Harry Potter, especially the first three books. His mother had grown up with the series, attending the movies into her teens, and been excited to share them with him. The nightly story time had begun to include props and theatrics, and everyone looked forward to what performance the evening would bring.

He grinned, "Okay, sure." He looked around, thought for a minute, and then stood before beginning, "I walked into the dark forest, quietly, without making a sound. I had seen the deer before and I had followed his tracks a few days ago. I knew if I walked quietly, he wouldn't know I was there and I'd have the best chance at a good, clean shot." He looked around at the small group, and Jess nodded to him encouragingly. "I walked about a hundred yards in and found a good place to keep a lookout. Somewhere I knew the deer would come by if he wanted to go drink from the lake. I sat for a long time. I was about to give up when Quincy whined quietly. I looked down at her and she was pointing with her foot, and when I looked at where she was pointing it was the deer! I had the bow and arrow ready in my hands and I raised it up, took aim, made sure, and then let the arrow fly!" He yelled then, "And THWACK! It hit him in his chest!"

Jacob woke with a fitful cry from the yell, nuzzled at Jess's breast, and fell back asleep. David looked sheepish until Jess grinned at him, "You did great, David, really, and you were amazing. I never thought an arrow could kill a big deer like that."

The boy lit up, glowing with pride. He went on to describe how Madge helped him send a prayer of thanks to the deer's spirit for giving its life to them. Night had fallen by now and the fire was a lone light in thick darkness. As they settled down for the night, dampening the fire and snuggling under blankets, Jess heard David yawn and comment, "I really think we need at least one more deer to get us through winter, though." The fire crackled quietly. Tina burrowed under the blanket in a small ball against her big brother. They were safe, well-fed, and happy.

Far, far away, guns cracked off shots and bullets tore through flesh and bone. But the little band heard none of this, only the crackle of the fire and the occasional hoot of a nearby owl.

Christmas Presents and Shotguns

"*All weddings, except those with shotguns in evidence, are wonderful."—Liz Smith*

"Oh! Brr!" Carrie closed the door to the house behind her and handed Joseph the basket of eggs. "I hate the cold!" She rubbed her arms vigorously and pushed past Chris to get near the stove. Chris kept his distance. The last few weeks, Carrie had been a bit off. It felt as if she had drawn a perimeter, which included a warning alarm in case anyone got too close. Snappy and tense, she had projected a clear warning to stay away.

The instant he let it slip, he knew there would be trouble. It was just one small, tiny little snort. But out it came, and he immediately regretted it. She turned on him. "Oh, and what are you laughing about?"

Man, oh man, women should come with early warning systems. Or a manual at least. How would it read?

The human female, as she enters the beginning of her monthly menstrual cycle, is a dangerous and unpredictable creature. The utmost care and concern must be shown at this time towards the female. The employment of calming methods, such as the introduction of chocolate at moments of extreme duress, coupled with a shift in attitude toward a more submissive posture from the male of the species, will avoid conflict. Under no circumstances should you engage in an argument with a pre-menstrual female. Avoidance and flight are perfectly acceptable solutions, enabling one to escape with all reproductive parts intact.

Chris saw that Carrie was now glaring... at him... and tapping her foot, expecting an answer. He realized two things at once. One, he had just stood there like an idiot for about a minute, fantasizing about a manual that unfortunately did not exist. And two, he had some stupid shit-eating grin on his face, which looked as if it was further adding to her anger.

"I... uh..."

"Yes?" The yes sounded like a hiss and he knew he was in deep kimchee. Hm, maybe the truth would be best.

"I just thought it was funny because you and Liza and Joseph are from New York and it gets really cold there. Winter down here is a walk in the park, right?"

His brain tuned out the words, but not the vision of her angry face yelling at him. He just stood there, let her yell, and waited until she had stalked off. It was the same response you might see from a deer that freezes, dead in the sights of a hunter, hoping beyond all hope that the hunter will somehow not see him, or perhaps take pity on him and let him go. No such luck, at least, not for this human animal. God, how he wished there was a manual.

"Boy," Fenton snorted close by his ear, "Haven't you got a lick of sense?"

"Sir?"

"Never say what's on your mind to a woman in that state of mind. Might as well commit, what's that word... mahi mahi?"

Liza chimed in, "Mahi-mahi is a fish, Gramps. You mean hara-kiri, or seppuku, which was the ritual disembowelment reserved only for samurai..."

"Got it, Liz. Thanks." Chris interrupted, head hurting from another female voice. No matter that it was a friendly one. "Gramps, if this is PMS, she's been having it for weeks. It's like everything I say or do irritates her."

"Give it time, son, give it time. Only God knows the minds of women, and I gotta wonder if even he doesn't get confused off and on." Fenton thought of Molly, dead for more than thirty years, and smiled wryly, "I can remember bein' in hot water a time or two, myself." Seemed like after they took out all her reproductive parts, it wasn't regular at all. She'd get mad anytime anywhere, or be preternaturally calm, you never could tell.

They cooked lunch and sat down at the table together, even Carrie, who just sat and simmered at one end. Not much was said as they passed sandwich fixings around the table and enjoyed the rich flavor of the pulled pork. One of the largest pigs, Butt Roast, had been slaughtered, cleaned and cured a few weeks ago when the temperatures dipped down into the 40s.

It had been a toss-up between who would be slaughtered, Butt Roast or Applewood Bacon, until they weighed them. Butt Roast tipped the scales at 225 pounds and Applewood Bacon had only weighed 202. He was slated for an early spring slaughter. Chris had been amused to discover that they named the pigs after food. It made sense, though.

One of the other pigs' names was Pork Chop and another Ham Hock. It kept the endgame in plain sight. These creatures weren't pets, they were food.

Chris kept stealing glances at Carrie and looking at just the wrong times. After the third glance, she startled everyone by shouting, "What?!"

"Nothing!" Chris snapped back. God, he felt like an idiot. What in the hell was he doing wrong, anyway? Why was she so pissed at him?

Fenton cleared his throat, scowled at his eldest grandchild, and asked Chris, "You said something about going into town today?"

"Yes sir. I mean... Gramps." He usually got it right, but in moments of high stress, like he'd been having for the past three weeks, he fell back on the crisp and forceful "Sir!" he'd learned as a conscript. "I was planning on a little Christmas shopping and figured I'd get in some bartering with that hog."

Liza chimed in, "I'll go with you, Chris. I've got books to trade." She tried not to look too eager, but Chris knew she was hoping to visit Carl Owens, a friend from school and fellow book geek. They would trade books all right, and some gropes and kisses as well, if he wasn't mistaken. Carl was two years older, and he had been visiting often in the last few months. He had helped out on the farm during harvest. He was a nice kid.

"It's settled then," Chris said. "Liza and I will go, and..."

"What about me?" Carrie looked resentful. "Did you even think of asking what I want? I mean, I..."

"Carrie Lynn Perdue," Fenton stopped the beginning tirade dead in its tracks, "You have been a right large pain in the patoot recently. If you were Joseph's age, I'd send you to your room and tell you to come out when you had a new attitude. As it is, I don't know what to say to you, 'ceptin to shut it and get yourself away 'til you got a civil tongue in your mouth."

Carrie sat there, tears forming in her eyes, opened and shut her mouth like she was about to say something, then stood up, knocking her chair back with a crash, and bolted from the room down the hall to her bedroom. Everyone sat in shock for a moment, Joseph wide-eyed, and they stared down the now-empty hall.

"Gramps!" Liza looked devastated. "You made her cry!" Chris held himself back from pointing out that everything nowadays made her cry. She'd cried the last time they made love; she'd cried over burning bread, and she'd cried a river when they'd slaughtered Butt Roast even though that damned pig had bitten her twice just the month before.

Fenton looked a bit chagrined, but said nothing as he finished his pork sandwich and licked the barbecue sauce off his fingers. He stood up, leaned over and picked up Carrie's chair, and then took hold of her plate.

"I'll go talk to her. Joseph, you get the rest of the dishes to the sink. Liza, Chris, you best get on your way. Take the buggy. It will be quicker and it gets dark 'bout five these days. Y'all want to get back before it's too dark to see anything."

Liza had a stack of books ready to go by the door. She pulled on a coat and shoved half of the stack into Chris's arms once he had finished zipping his coat. Outside, they quickly loaded up the wrapped pieces of pork haunch they wanted to use for trade. They didn't need much in the way of staples right now, but Chris had a very specific present in mind for this visit.

He had seen the ring at the Trade Mart two weeks ago when they were there stocking up for the winter. It wasn't your typical wedding ring of diamonds and gold. Instead, what had struck him and drawn him in was the amazing color of green of the emerald set in the center. It was a square-cut emerald, with four fair-sized diamonds, two on each side, set in a white gold band.

The emerald's color was a rich, forest green. He had gazed at it and felt as if he were staring into Carrie's eyes. Her eye color changed, depending on her mood, from an almost lime green when she was mad to the deep forest green of the emerald right after they made love.

It seemed that lately, all he had seen was the lime green, which snapped with lightning and fire.

When Liza broke the silence, he realized they had already left the farm far behind. "You're getting the ring today, right?" She was the only one he had confided in, mainly because she had seen him talking with the woman who owned it while Carrie was deep in bargaining for flour and sugar with one of the other townsfolk. The old woman had elicited the promise from him to build a new chicken coop and bring her ten pounds of pork and five laying hens in the spring in exchange for the ring. The coop would be easy, and she had agreed to wait for another month for that. But the deposit on the ring was the pork, and he aimed to deliver it in time to pick up the ring and give it to Carrie for Christmas.

"Yeah, I'm getting the ring."

He paused, thinking about Carrie's incredible mood swings lately. Well, mainly they had swung between depressed to irritable, and sometimes plain insane.

"Liza, do you think something's wrong with Carrie? I mean, do you think she still wants to marry me?"

The teenager snorted. "Are you kidding? Carrie loves you. And you love her. If anything, I'll bet she's just wondering why you haven't gotten around to asking her yet."

"But I did. At the end of September. I asked her and she said yes." Liza's neck snapped towards him so quickly he was afraid she had whiplash.

"You asked Carrie to marry you?" Her hands had gone slack on the reins, but the horse plodded on. They were almost to the site of the burned out Western Front trucks and not too far from town. Ichabod knew the way by heart.

"Well yeah. And she said yes, but I didn't have a ring then. I've been looking for one, and..." His voice faded weakly away in the face of yet another angry Perdue woman.

"Have you two, you know, done it?" Liza asked, looking angry and a tiny bit scared.

"Well... umm... yeah."

"When? How often? Did you use protection?" The questions came hard and fast and Chris felt like he was talking to his mother, not a fourteen-year-old girl. This was crazy. Why had he even said anything?

Now she was going to be mad at him too and he didn't know what the hell he had done wrong this time, either.

"Liza... I'm not... I shouldn't be talking about this with you."

"Christopher Michael Aaronson," now she sounded like Fenton, "Just answer the damned question."

Jesus, he seemed to be in for it again. "September, around harvest time. When your Gramps got hurt in the barn. And well, a couple times since," that was a terrible understatement, "and do you see any protection around here?"

He had even checked with the Trade Mart, carefully, of course, to see if he could trade for condoms. No such luck and the pharmacy, what was left of the burned-out shell, was laughable.

"Shit."

"What?!" He was getting frustrated and pissed. Both of them on his ass, ripping his head off and shitting down his neck. Damn but...

"Carrie is pregnant." Chris's mind went blank. They passed the lookouts and Liza collected herself enough to wave at them and jostled Chris to do the same. He put up a hand and waved woodenly, his mind completely and totally overwhelmed. Pregnant? Pregnant! Oh God, pregnant.

Liza spoke again, "And worse yet, Gramps is talking to her right now. Sure as anything, it will come out and he'll just shoot you before he bothers askin' questions." She shook her head, "Damn Chris, I thought you were smarter than that." She patted his leg. "Been nice knowing you."

"Oh, thanks so much for the vote of confidence," he replied sarcastically, and his bowels twisted.

She grinned at him then, "Now when you see the shotgun, run, I'll try to buy you some time, maybe a few hundred yards, enough to make it to the tree line. And remember, avoid the lake, we know you don't do well out there." She was grinning now, obviously remembering how they had found him, laid up with a broken ankle after taking a fall in the bog they still insisted on calling a lake.

"Ha, ha, ha, geez Liza, you are just so damn funny." He glared at her, his mind still reeling. He sobered. "Do you really think she's pregnant?"

They were nearly in town and he said it quietly, under his breath, in case anyone heard their conversation. There were a few folks walking, wrapped up like it was an arctic winter, rather than a cool thirty degrees out.

Liza nodded, with a smirk, "Oh yeah. I remember Mom getting that way when she got pregnant with Joseph. Had Dad running scared until they both figured out what the hell was going on. Dad had a vasectomy after I was born, so it didn't even dawn on them what was happening until she was a few months along. So much for a vasectomy being foolproof. Did you know that shit can grow back? Anyway, Carrie's never been what you'd call regular with her periods, so if she knows, she's just now figured it out."

"Why wouldn't she tell me, though?" Chris protested. "I mean, we love each other. I'm not going anywhere, I want to marry her, and I figured eventually that also meant having babies with her." He stopped then, imagining Carrie's stomach swelling full and round, thought of the child growing inside and months from now, the feel of a tiny baby nestled in his arms. Blond hair, and would her eyes be blue like his or green like Carrie's? For some reason, he couldn't imagine a boy, only a girl. A girl who could wrap his heart around her little finger, and...

"Hell Chris, I don't know why she wouldn't tell you. Maybe she's scared. There aren't any hospitals nearby. I mean, I know I've been studying, but I'm not a full-on doctor. Hell, I'm not even a midwife. And maybe she's afraid you don't want kids, that you won't love her if she goes and gets fat."

"Pregnant isn't fat. Pregnant is beautiful." He said it forcefully, and a bit louder than he intended. One woman looked at them curiously as they passed.

"Oh Chris," Liza sighed. Chris made Carl look like such an idiot, and she liked Carl a lot. Chris had a way of making everyone feel special, loved, and accepted. She smiled up at him.

"Just get the ring. We'll go back home and it will all work out, you'll see. She loves you and you love her. Despite all of Gramps' tough words, he approves of you. He knows you love Carrie as much as he does."

She pulled on the reins and stopped the horse. They were a block from the Trade Mart. "I'm going to Carl's. I'll meet you in an hour at the Trade Mart." She slipped down out of the seat after handing Chris the reins.

As the buggy pulled away, Liza called after him, "Don't get into trouble!" He just waved at her in dismissal. For only being fourteen years old, the girl was already a mother hen. It seemed to run in the family.

The Trade Mart was busy, and the street was full of town folk. There was barely room for Ichabod to be strapped to the bike rack, but he managed to find a spot that required a bit of a squeeze. The horse wasn't going anywhere until he was done.

Chris stopped by the hardware store and dropped off half of a sweet potato pie that Carrie and Liza had made the night before for Mr. Liles. The ancient man was close to entering his 106th year, which blew Chris's mind. Most of the old man's teeth were gone, so sweet potato pie was right up his alley.

The bent and fragile old man had visited the farm twice in the summer, but the onset of winter slowed him down and confined him to town. He was a bit of a celebrity, considering his advanced age, and the rest of the town folk pitched in to keep him fed and warm in his little apartment above the hardware store. He spent a few minutes talking with the old man, relayed Fenton and the rest of the family's greetings and promised to bring chicken soup on his next visit. One of the chickens wasn't producing eggs as much as she used to. It was time to make way for other younger layers. Old Otis loved Carrie's homemade chicken noodle soup and asked about it whenever they visited, no matter the weather. He said his goodbyes and headed toward the Trade Mart.

As he walked in the door, he saw a familiar, unwelcome face—Wes Perkins. The man had added another knife to his collection, he was practically his own armory with two long hunting knives, a short tiny curved knife in a sheath, and today he was sporting what looked like a .44 Magnum and the ubiquitous rifle he carried with him everywhere.

At least this time Chris didn't feel so under-dressed for the occasion. Carrie had given him a ruggedly wicked hunting knife the month of their 'anniversary.' He had been embarrassed that he hadn't remembered and didn't have something to give her in return. It was probably the lack of gift or remembering that it had been exactly one month since they made love for the first time that had started the emotional roller coaster they had been on ever since. He also had begun carrying a M1911, a .45 caliber, well-maintained pistol that Fenton had used in Vietnam.

There had been reports of isolated attacks by deserters or small bands of men. They were usually in search of food or ammunition. They would sneak in, take what they wanted and usually leave without engaging the locals, but one girl had been raped and another older couple had been killed. Both attacks had occurred within the last month. Fenton had made sure everyone, except for Joseph, was armed at all times, around the farm or off the property. Chris met Wes's unfriendly stare with an equally calm one. He would stand his ground, and fuck Wes if he didn't like it.

Wes began to move forward and intercept Chris. He probably wanted to stop him from entering the Trade Mart. But Mrs. Jennings had spied him at that moment and called across the store, gesturing for him to come and see her. She smiled at him and he ignored Wes and strode over.

"Christopher! How are you?"

Not everyone in the town was an asshole like Perkins. Alice Jennings was a widower, with no children. She was also Tiptonville's librarian.

She looked around, "Where's Liza? I have a book for her."

"She'll be here soon, Miz Jennings." He gave her a gentle hug. "She's visiting a friend."

Alice sighed, "I imagine it's that Owens boy. Ah, young love. A bit of a nerd, but then, so is Liza, bless that child. I found a book for her that will fill in her education nicely."

She reached back to a shelf and pulled out the book. "Here it is, 'Epidemiology: Beyond the Basics.'" She started to hand it to him.

"She'll be here soon, Miz Jennings. Would you like to give it to her yourself?"

"Oh yes, dear, that will be fine. In fact," she nodded, shelving the book, "I really need to check if she is ready to move away from obstetrics or if she was interested in advanced surgical procedures next."

She stared at him for a moment, and he waited patiently. "Oh dear, I'm sorry, you want the ring, don't you dear?"

"Yes ma'am, I brought the piece you asked for," he handed the neatly wrapped pork section over to her. "And I can come by after Christmas and start on the coop."

Her eyes lit up, "Oh Christopher, it's far more meat than I had asked for! Are you sure?" She was thin, and Chris wondered if she ate much meat at all these days.

"Fenton wrapped it and sends his regards. He sure appreciates all you've been doing for Liza." The old man had been impressed with the large tomes of medical information that Liza was slowly absorbing and discussing. His forehead wound had been sutured so neatly that there was only a tiny reddish scar that remained.

"Oh, it is nice to have such an apt pupil. Liza is quite a brilliant young woman, you know." At that moment, Liza appeared at his elbow.

"Well thanks, Miz Jennings!" She immediately spied the book on epidemiology. Alice had partially shelved it, but it was sticking out prominently from the rest. "Oh my, you found the epidemiology book!"

Her eyes sparkled. Most girls would look like that over a new dress or shoes, but Liza was not like most girls. Alice handed her the book, and the girl thumbed through the table of contents with intense interest. "Ooh, multiple regression techniques... and it has an appendix for the test of homogeneity of stratified estimates!" She looked up and grinned at Chris and Alice. "This is perfect! Thank you!"

"Careful there, Liza, your inner geek is showing."

Her grin turned to a glare. Alice, finally remembering what Chris had been so patiently waiting for, reached into her pockets and pulled out a small box.

"Christopher dear, I shined it up for you." She handed the box over. It was brown leather, worn in spots. "I tried to find a box to put it in, dear, and I'm sorry, this is the best I could find."

Liza gasped as he opened the box. The emerald and diamonds were blindingly brilliant. "A little toothpaste and water are all it took." Alice's voice sounded a bit misty. Chris was too distracted by the ring to notice the woman's tears, but Liza did, and put her hand on the old woman's arm. Larry Jennings had died nearly two years ago, and Alice still missed him terribly.

Chris stared at the ring, everything inside of him churning. God, he hoped she liked it. What if she didn't? What if she wanted something more traditional? Liza's voice reassured his fears. "Chris, it's beautiful. It matches her eyes exactly!" He looked over at the girl and relaxed. If Liza, a geeky, sci-fi and epidemiology textbook-loving, non-girly girl, thought it was beautiful, then it had to be special.

Chris knew a lot of things. He knew about war and fighting, he knew about hard work and how to fix leaks and raise crops. He knew football. But he was absolutely sure of his own ignorance when it came to women's jewelry. He also had no idea that, if this part of the world had still run on cold hard cash, he would have had to fork over a lot of it. He was holding a ring worth over $7,000.

He didn't know that Alice Jennings had been given the ring by her mother. He didn't realize how special the ring was to the old woman or even that the emerald that was mounted in the ring was her birthstone.

Chris only knew that it had spoken to him, reminded him of Carrie's eyes after they made love or kissed or laughed. He desperately hoped Carrie would like it and that Fenton wouldn't shoot him before he had a chance to give it to her. He smiled at Alice Jennings, "Thank you ma'am, thank you so much."

She smiled in return and patted his cheek softly. "You are welcome, young Christopher. Do bring her in after you've given it to her. I would so like to see it on her hand."

"Yes, ma'am, I will." They said their goodbyes and headed towards the exit. Chris had snapped the box shut and put it away carefully in his jacket. He was in the process of zipping the coat when Wes Perkins stepped into his path.

"Maybe you should watch where you're going, soldier." Wes stood a good half of a head taller and smelled dangerous. It was a sharp gunpowder and oil scent. He was close, purposely so, he stood inside Chris's personal space and it was an obvious challenge. Chris felt Liza's hand settle on his sleeve.

"We need to be getting back home now, Mr. Perkins." She said it with a level voice, but there was a slight tremor in her hand. She was afraid for Chris. Around them, there was a lull in conversation. Chris could feel a dozen sets of eyes, watching and saying nothing.

Wes ignored Liza. He glared at Chris, tried to stare him down. Liza tugged on Chris's arm, "Come on, Chris. Let's go." She tugged on his sleeve firmly. Chris allowed her to pull him to the right and around Perkins, keeping eye contact until Liza jerked him insistently through the door and down the street.

"All right, all right, you can stop walking me like a dog on a leash, now." He snapped at her irritably as she attempted to shove him up into the buggy. "I'm going already." Liza's face was pale.

"Let's just get out of here. Now." She was shaking.

"Okay, okay. Chill out. We're going, we're going." His good mood had vanished. What the fuck was up with that guy, anyway? It was like Perkins knew he had been in the Western Front. And that wasn't possible. No one knew but the Perdues and they sure as hell weren't going to say anything.

The ride out of town was uneventful, but it was tense and silent. They passed the lookouts, and the awful burned-out wrecks of trucks. The burned and blackened skeletons still hung from the windows or lay crushed underneath. Chris's stomach turned every time he saw it. The town had left them there on purpose, as a warning, but it made him sick to see it. No matter what those men had done, they were people. They had been alive and breathing. It didn't seem right to leave their bodies out there, exposed to the elements and not given a proper burial. Then again, he had heard some of the stories, whispered to him by the girls when Fenton wasn't around. The Western Front had done terrible things to the citizens of Tiptonville. They had more than earned the hatred the townspeople felt towards them.

He glanced over at Liza and saw a tear trickle down her nose, then another and another. They were still over a mile from the farm. He pulled Ichabod to a stop, turned and looked at her. The girl was hunched over, arms crossed in front of her protectively, and as she noticed his gaze, she began to sob hysterically.

"What the..." Chris sighed and closed his eyes. This was definitely not his day to deal with the Perdue women. "Look Liza, everything's fine, the guy is an asshole, don't worry about it."

"He knows."

"What? What does he know?"

"That you were in the Western Front."

He started to scoff, then stopped and tried to meet her eyes. They flicked up, met his, and dropped to the buggy floor and she began to cry even harder. "Liza... what did you do?"

"It's what I didn't do. I mean, I tried to burn the clothes. Oh God! Gramps is gonna kill me!"

"Liza..." he grabbed her shoulders, turned her towards him and forced her to meet his eyes, "I'm gonna kill you if you don't tell me what the heck you are talking about."

It rushed out in one large torrent, "I didn't burn the clothes! Your uniform. I mean, I tried, and they were burning and I heard someone coming, so I ran away quick. They must have seen the fire, put it out and found the clothes. "

He gave her a small shake. "Must have?"

She cried harder, "When I went back the next day to check, the clothes were gone."

Chris closed his eyes. "Crap, crap, crap. Double crap. Triple crap... shit!"

"You hate me, don't you?" Liza sounded so tiny, so childlike and fearful. He opened his eyes and saw her wincing in his grasp.

"No Liza, I don't hate you." He struggled to explain his emotions. "I'm worried. I'm scared I've brought trouble to your door, to all of you, and I don't know what to do."

"I'll tell Gramps."

"We will tell Fenton together. Right after I propose to Carrie and right before he shoots me for knocking up his eldest grandchild." He managed a small smile, "Like you said earlier, it will all work out." That earned him a weak laugh in return.

He set Ichabod to a nice trot, and the last twenty minutes were spent with cracks about shotguns and ducking for cover. As they entered the private road that led straight through to the farmhouse, Chris could see he wasn't too far from being right. Fenton had had enough time to not only clean the shotgun, but reassemble it. It was resting across his folded arms and the old man looked pissed.

Liza took it all in and summed it up in one succinct word, which she muttered under her breath, "Shit."

"Elizabeth Molly Ann Perdue," Fenton barked, "you know I can read lips." Liza winced in response. "Boy, you have got some explaining to do." He caressed the barrel of the shotgun and adjusted it so that it aimed, ever so slightly, in Chris's direction.

"You better show him what you got, Chris, now." Liza whispered.

But Chris had a different idea about how this was all going to play out.

"No." He climbed down from the buggy, unbuckled the knife and pistol, and set them up on the seat next to Liza. "Sir, I would like to speak with Carrie, please."

Fenton pursed his lips, reached over and yanked the door to the farmhouse open and bellowed for her. A moment later she appeared, her eyes puffy and red. They widened when they saw Fenton's shotgun.

Chris wasted no time. He strode to the porch, knelt on his knee at the top step, and looked up into Carrie's eyes. "I'm sorry it took me this long to find it. I love you, Carrie Lynn Perdue. So... please," he fished the box out of his pocket and held it up to her, "Will you marry me before your grandfather goes and put me out of his misery?" This earned a choked laugh from Liza and Carrie and an angry grunt from Fenton.

Carrie reached out and took the box from his hand, opening it slowly, and gasping when she did. "Oh my God, it's beautiful!"

Chris sighed, partially in relief, and then in exasperation, as she began to cry. Why did they always have to cry? She pulled him up to her and hugged him violently.

He could feel her tears soaking his neck and he struggled to breathe as she clung to him and cried harder, "Yes, yes, yes! I'll marry you!"

"Young woman, don't you have some news of your own?" Fenton still sounded pissed. Carrie jumped a little at his voice and pulled away from Chris, looking a little scared.

"I'm uh," she struggled to utter the words, "I'm pretty sure I'm pregnant."

Her eyes searched his eyes for rejection or anger. She had been afraid to tell him; afraid he would leave or maybe not want to have kids. They had never talked about it and they were both so young, something that Gramps had repeated over and over until she had dissolved into tears and he had stomped away.

Chris reached down and placed a hand on her stomach. There was the tiniest of bulges there. It was firm, not soft or mushy, and he wondered at the miracle growing inside. His child... their child. He looked into her eyes, watched them turn that emerald green he loved to see.

"We need to get married soon, then. How does January sound to you?"

She laughed and hugged him again. Fenton snorted, but this time it was with less anger. He stomped down the stairs, grabbed Ichabod's reins and began to lead the buggy and Liza away to the barn.

"I'm bringing my shotgun to the wedding." Fenton said as he strode away.

You Reap What You Sow

"Your intelligence is measured by those around you; if you spend your days with idiots, you seal your own fate."—Author Unknown

"The greater the loyalty of a group toward the group, the greater is the motivation among the members to achieve the goals of the group, and the greater the probability that the group will achieve its goals."—Rensis Likert

Captain Scott Cooper seethed as his second in command brought him the numbers. Three more missing. They had slipped away in the night. Two of them had been from the ragged remnants of Tent Five, the pretty blond he'd broken in a couple of months ago and a recent tasty morsel that he hadn't quite finished with.

Of all the whores he'd had, the newest one had reminded him the most of Tiffany. Or at least a young version of his sister before she'd filled out and started knowing her own mind and ran to Daddy to complain about him touching her. He'd gotten the beating of his life after that. Old Coop would have thrown his ass out then and there, but Mama was already sick and had begged her husband to show mercy on Scott. She always had been particularly fond of her son. She had ignored or explained away his dark deeds, saying only "boys will be boys." When Tiffany had gone to her mother first, she had been ignored and then punished for making up such awful lies.

By the time that pathetic, stupid woman had gotten around to dying, he'd left. The uneasy truce between him and Arno collapsed the moment his mother's body had cooled. He'd heard of the Western Front, listened to the whispers that they were now in Colorado and marching east and he'd set out to join up. It was his bravado in walking right up to the troops on those grass-filled plains of Kansas outside of Fort Riley and asking to join that had caught Granger's attention. And later, after their unit had been left as an outpost outside of Springfield, it was his intel that had provided the rewarding raids on nearby towns, including his own hometown.

His mind strayed for a moment as he remembered the girl's body under his, no real woman breasts on the new one, not even the beginnings of pubes. The rest had worked out just fine, though. Sex was what whores were for; no matter how old or young, that was all they were really good for, anyway. His Mama had made that clear when she went tramping around, spreading her legs for that fool in town and getting knocked up with Tiffany.

An awkward cough brought his thoughts back to the present. He blinked, realized he'd been standing there lost in thought for far too long.

Evers looked nervous standing there, waiting for Cooper to either explode or start barking orders. He hadn't wanted this promotion, but the last guy who'd had this job had tried to leave three weeks ago. Tried being the operative word, for he hadn't gotten far at all. It still turned Evers' bowels into jello to think about how that guy had looked when Cooper had finished with him. He had wiped off his blade, ignoring the piece of dead meat at his feet that had screamed for mercy just moments before, and returned the blade to its sheath. He had turned to Tom Evers and said, "Your 2nd Lieutenant now, Evers. Don't let me down."

It had been all Evers could do not to empty his bladder on the spot. Who wanted to be a second to a psychopath? The memory of it was still sharp as he cleared his throat, "There is one more thing, sir."

"Yes?"

"They sliced the tires on the last seven trucks. And we got no spares left."

"We had eight trucks yesterday." Cooper's eyes smoldered with fury, anticipating the next sentence that would come out of Evers mouth.

"Yes sir. They took that last one. They must've pushed it out a few hundred yards before starting it up and driving away 'cause the sentries didn't hear a peep. Well, except for Private Angelo, who they knocked out and tied up. We found him this morning and sounded the alarm."

"Yes," Cooper's voice was dry and cold, "I heard the alarm." It had woken him with a start, pulling him from a dream filled with blood and sex. He felt frustrated, sleep-deprived, and the darkness in him threatened to boil over. He fought to contain it, and then smiled as he focused on a positive outlet for his frustration. "Bring Angelo to see me after I've had some coffee."

Tom Evers saluted, Cooper barely bothered to return it, and the man hastened away. He winced as he imagined what would happen to Private Angelo. The poor kid would probably be better off dead after Cooper took out his frustration on him.

Cooper fought to control his fury. No more trucks. How would they move out without the vehicles? The areas surrounding had been picked clean and anyone still living was deep in hiding. They had crossed into what amounted to a no-man's-land a few days before inside the Mississippi side of border between Arkansas and Mississippi. The closest town was that of Lobdell, Mississippi, and it was dead quiet. Any inhabitants who remained were deep in hiding.

The last two months had been one disaster after another. The unit had moved south into Arkansas and hadn't gotten far, only to a tiny town in the hinter boonies called Mountain Home, and promptly gotten their asses kicked. The small towns were wising up and either fleeing or, in odd cases such as this, arming themselves and fighting. He'd lost nearly five dozen men before they took the town. When Granger had been in charge, they'd had nearly two hundred and fifty men. Now the complement was down to a hundred, maybe less. Especially after a second ass-whipping in Forrest City, miles to the southeast.

The men were losing a taste for war and conquest and more deserted each day. Cooper couldn't understand it. This was his perfect world. It was all he had ever dreamed of after those years of being smothered by his fool whore of a mother and ignored by an indifferent father.

Old Coop had spent more of his time kowtowing to Tiffany. That little slut had the old man wrapped around her finger. What kind of man preferred the company of another man's child, a man who had cuckolded him no less, to his own son?

No matter, each and every day of the past six months, he had gotten to have whatever woman he wanted, take what he wanted and go where he wanted. It wasn't just the power that got his rocks off, it was the freedom to say and do whatever he pleased. He liked to see the fear in the men's eyes. He'd earned every ounce of it and more.

Still, now they were without transportation of any kind. He sipped the steaming cup of atomic waste the cook had prepared. They had managed to grab several pounds of coffee when they blew through the border and into Scott, Mississippi. That had been what he called a grab and stab. Scope out the town from a distance, find the weakest point, hit them at sunrise and grab what you could and kill anyone who tried to stop you. It was better than a frontal assault, especially now that the people who were left were the tougher ones, determined to survive, with the weapons to back themselves up. His thoughts spun like they were stuck in mud up to the axles. How in the devil were they going to keep moving?

The flap of the tent moved aside, and a soldier walked in with Angelo, who was bleeding from a cut on his forehead. No one had bothered to patch him up. Ever since their medic team had up and disappeared halfway through Arkansas, first aid services were a tad scarce nowadays. The man looked terrified. His back was ramrod straight, and he saluted Cooper, a slight tremor in his hand as he did so. Scott nodded to the other soldier, excusing him from the tent, and he left quickly.

A half hour later and Cooper stepped out of his tent. He calmly walked to a creek that ran by the edge of the camp and washed the blood and gore from his hands. His first in command, First Lieutenant Riley, stood a few feet away impassively.

"I'll be taking over your tent, Riley."

"Yes, sir. I'll clear that out for you, sir." Riley then motioned to two of the grunts standing nearby and looking rather pale and pointed them towards Cooper's tent. It would take them several hours, and two panicked runs outside to vomit before they finally managed to clean up the mess. The stains on the canvas walls of the tent, however, were permanent. Riley didn't much care one way or the other. Bloodstains notwithstanding, he liked having a bigger tent.

A unit that had once been nearly 200 men strong was now a very dangerous, violent gang of raiders. Cooper had many more moments of fury and frustration in the next two weeks. By the end of them, only twenty-five men remained of the one hundred plus who had crossed into Mississippi with him. Of that number, six were too terrified and cowed to leave, and twelve of the men were far too stupid to know when to cut and run. Another three were biding their time, hoping for a better opportunity that might include a set of wheels, and the last four, which included Riley and Cooper, were complete psychopaths bent on murder and mayhem. They had managed to hold on to three of the women. The rest of the women had escaped or died while trying to escape.

Some simple-minded redneck named Brad Osterman, and the woman and girl he had taken with him, had broken the back of Western Front outpost while making their timely escape in late October. Disabling the vehicles had dealt a heavy and rather unrecoverable blow to the unit. In time, Cooper and his remaining men managed to scrounge enough useable tires from abandoned vehicles and surrounding terrain to return three vehicles to service. They headed up Highway 1 in mid-November and drove until the road dumped them on Highway 49. This they followed southeast until the road crossed the state line into Tennessee and moved towards Memphis. There were plenty of small towns to loot and burn along the way. The trucks moved inexorably north.

A White Wedding

"Grow old along with me, the best is yet to be."—Robert Browning

Chris pulled the edge of his jacket out of Mutton Chop's curious mouth. Tomorrow was Christmas, and the week had flown by. It had been tense; Fenton was still perturbed that the natural order of things had not been observed.

He finally confronted Chris in the barn after breakfast. Chris had just finished feeding the goats and was mucking out Ichabod's stall when Fenton came in.

"There's courtin', then askin' the father for the girl's hand in marriage," he glared at Chris, "Which would be me since her daddy is gone, marriage, the lovin' and eventually," he stressed the word and glared, "lil 'uns." His vernacular degenerated when his emotions ran high. "You seem to have your priorities ass backwards, young man."

He had said this after three long days of silence and brooding. Chris felt ashamed. The shock of realizing that Carrie was pregnant combined with his concern about her young age and his lack of control had lessened him in the old man's eyes. In the last few months, Fenton had become a unique combination of father, grandfather and mentor. He felt Fenton's disappointment keenly and wished he could change how it had all played out. He studied the ground, searched for the right words, and felt the old man's gaze steady and unrelenting.

"Sir... I," What could he say to make this better? He had agonized over it, but if he couldn't make it better, at least he could apologize and ask forgiveness. "I'm sorry. I know I screwed up."

He looked up and met Fenton's eyes, struck by how old and sad the man looked. "You're right, there's an order to it all and I should've exercised control and waited."

Fenton pursed his lips and sighed. "Christopher, I know you love my granddaughter. I know you'll marry her and I know it coulda played out a lot worse than it did." He shook his head. "You disappointed me, son. But I'll get over it...'cause tomorrow you're gonna make this right."

"Sir?" Chris was confused. Tomorrow was Christmas.

Fenton's eyes had lost their disappointment and sadness, and now they twinkled with mischief. He reached over and clapped Chris hard on the shoulder. "You're getting married tomorrow, son." And with that, he sauntered out of the barn, Chris staring after him, stunned.

In a daze, he finished his chores, not sure what to think about Fenton's statement. It was as if his brain could simply not process what the old man had said. They were getting married tomorrow? On Christmas day? Did people actually do that? Wasn't there a rule or something against it? He shook his head, finished his chores, and headed for the house. It was almost noon and usually there would be lunch in process, but when he opened the front door and walked in, he took in an amazing scene. Boxes of ornaments... everywhere. And an old trunk sat in the middle of the living room, lid open, and Carrie stood on a small stool beside it wearing the most amazing...

"Oh!" Liza ran from Carrie's side, neatly avoiding Joseph, who was sprawled on the floor attaching hooks to tree decorations, "Get out! You aren't allowed to see her dress before the wedding!" She flipped Chris around and shoved him back towards the door, "Out, out, OUT!"

"But... I..." Chris was propelled out the door, which slammed closed behind him. To add insult to injury, the deadbolt turned in the lock. He was locked out of the house! Liza giggled and called through the door, "Hitch up the horse and go to town, you need to bring Mr. Liles back with you and ask Reverend Thomas, Carl and his family, and Mrs. Jennings to be here tomorrow morning for a wedding and then lunch." There was a pause, "Oh! And be sure to get a pound of sugar if you can." Chris started to walk away from the door, "Oh and..."

"For crying out loud, girl, give the boy a list." Fenton interceded.

"Wait there, son, I'll get you a sandwich for the road and Liza will get you a list." And a few minutes later, the door opened wide enough to shove a small lunch sack through.

Liza grinned at Chris as he took the bag. "The list is inside. Don't come back until dark."

Chris just shook his head and took the bag, headed for the barn, and hitched up the horse. The day was turning rather surreal, and he didn't know what to make of it. As Ichabod moved briskly towards the town, his state of shock persisted. Sure, they had talked about marriage and getting married for months. Now that it was here, now that it was apparently just a day away, it felt unreal and frightening and exciting all at once. He couldn't believe it was actually happening. He smiled suddenly. By this time next year, he would be holding their baby in his arms. He could see her now, a little girl, with blond hair and her mama's gorgeous green eyes. The vision of it moved him past the burned-out trucks and skeletons, past the lookouts with barely a thought to wave, and on into town.

He visited Mrs. Jennings first. Liza had written directions on the note on how to find the house and he figured it was right that she should hear the news of the wedding and get the first invitation, since she had been so kind to give him the ring. She lived in a tiny little cottage. It was an exquisite little Victorian with carefully turned spindles and latticework. It would have been immaculate, inside and out, except for the huge piles of books. She seemed to having nothing but stacks of books in one of the bedrooms. No furniture, except for one lone chair, and a lamp surrounded by leaning stacks of books.

"You must stay for lunch, my dear," she said, bustling away to the kitchen despite his protests that he had already eaten. After she filled Chris with soup and bread, they sat in the living room, surrounded by books, and she served him hot mint tea. Liza visited Alice often after the library had been destroyed by fire. They had salvaged all the books they could and set up shop in Alice's tiny house.

She laughed as he described the talk with Fenton and then being thrown out of the house and sent on errands. Her blue eyes sparkled, "Oh my dear, truly, I am happy for you. You and Carrie make a lovely couple." She wagged her finger at him, "And as for the baby, don't you be too hard on yourself, I know for a fact that Fenton may wish for things a certain way, but he knows the world doesn't always work that way." She smiled and sipped her tea.

"Did you know that his wife Molly, and I were best friends?" Chris shook his head, "Well, we were completely inseparable from kindergarten until our senior dance in high school." Her mouth turned down, her lips trembled, and "I wasn't as good of a friend as I should have been. We both saw him at the same moment, and he looked so handsome. An older man, you understand, three years older than Molly and me, Fenton was. He walked in, we both saw him at the same time and she called dibs." Chris laughed.

Alice smiled, "Laugh all you want, but remember, we were young once too, and silly girls do that. She had called dibs, and we were best friends. She got him and I didn't. Oh, how jealous I was!" She took another sip of tea. "Here, have a cookie." She pushed the plate of cookies over and he took one out of politeness, despite his desperately full stomach.

"I met my Larry a year later. We married before Molly and Fenton, and we were all so close in those early years. But Molly had Isaac. As for me... well, the babies just never came. I was so jealous, Christopher, so sad I could never have one."

Her eyes misted, her lip trembled, and "I wasn't a good friend. After all, she went through having Isaac and I couldn't even stand to see that child, wondering year after year why she had had a baby and I didn't. And the years passed, and we didn't speak and then she was gone, before I even knew she was sick." She looked at the carpet, looked back up at Chris, "I'm so sorry dear, I don't know why I told you all of this."

What was it with women? Chris was beginning to wonder if they were just filled with tears. And what was it with the subject of babies and marriage that set them off so? Sitting in the wing-backed chair, trying not to knock off the dainty doilies on each arm, he struggled to think of something to say.

"Mrs. Jennings, you uh, you seem very nice to me." He said it awkwardly, "I, uh, I really had better get going. I have to visit Carl's family and the reverend, and pick up Mr. Liles. If I don't, I doubt I'll get let back into the house tonight."

Alice laughed, wiped at her moist eyes and patted his hand, "You are a dear, young Christopher, listening to an old woman so patiently. Pass word, if you will, to the Carters. I would like to share a ride with them if they wouldn't mind."

The Carters, Carl Owens' mom and his stepdad John, had converted their van to run on biofuel. It ran on a diesel made of corn. The van had plenty of seats and room to spare.

He promised that he would and set off to visit the different houses on his list. He lucked out at the Carter's and promised a dozen eggs in return for the pound of sugar. The Trade Mart was closed for the day, which was a relief. He didn't care to run into Wes Perkins and said as much to Abby. Abigail Carter was a tiny woman, and at age six, her daughter, Tabitha, had already grown past Abigail's shoulder. Her son, Carl, who was sixteen, towered over her and he was still a good head shorter than Chris. Abby gave a wry smile. "Wes has always been a bit of a jerk. Family or no, I don't much associate with him these days now that both our parents have passed."

Chris gave a start. "You're related?" Oh God, he'd put his foot in it this time. His face must have shown his dismay because Abby laughed then. She looked far too young to have a teenage son.

John, Abby's husband, laughed too. "They're first cousins, on Abby's mother's side. Wes's mother was the oldest of five, and Abby's mother was the youngest."

"Mama had me when she was nearly forty. I was quite a surprise, even more so since I was the first to give her a grandbaby." Abby grinned wryly, "Wes always was a jerk," she looked around and saw that Tabitha had gone back to her room and then leaned forward conspiratorially, "A real bastard, actually. Shoulda seen what he did to his wife after he came back from Iraq. Blackened both her eyes. PTSD, be damned, he's always been a prick." Abby shook her head, her short curls dancing, "Those kids were so damned cute. They played with Carl almost every day. Course that was over ten years ago.

He beat her up; she packed up the kids and left the next day. Can't blame her a bit for it, but I sure have wondered where they are now, especially now, with all that's happened out there in the world."

"Abby," John gently interrupted, "Chris needs to be heading home. It's getting late. And the man's getting hitched tomorrow."

Abby apologized and hugged Chris. "We'll be there tomorrow! Give my love to everyone and tell them we'll see them soon!"

And with that, his list of chores complete, Chris headed for home. John and Abby had assured him that there was room for Mrs. Jennings and Mr. Liles in their van and even offered to give Reverend Thomas a lift if he didn't mind a cozy ride. He had the sugar Liza had demanded and everything was a go for a Christmas wedding.

It was pitch black out by the time he returned, and Fenton had left a lantern out on the porch to guide his way. He unhitched Ichabod, set him to eating dinner and closed the barn up tight. The lantern shone brightly, and he could see specks of snow beginning to fall. Just spits of snow, really, nothing exceptional. This was Tennessee after all. He took the steps two at a time and was at the front door before he remembered his reception earlier that day, and decided to knock.

He could hear Joseph's voice and running feet. "Chris is home! Chris is home!" The door opened and the little boy hugged him and peered around behind Chris. "Where's Mr. Liles?"

"He'll be here tomorrow, Joseph, riding in style with the Carter's."

"Oh." The little boy looked disappointed then perked up, "Come see! Come see!" He tugged on Chris's arm and pulled him into the house. Chris shut the door behind him, turned, and took in the beautifully decorated rooms. Liza and Fenton were sitting on the sofa, looking exhausted. Carrie was nowhere in sight. The old trunk was gone, as was the wedding dress that Chris had had only the smallest of glimpses of. In place of the boxes was a tree decorated with all the trimmings, a few wrapped presents underneath, and a fire crackled merrily in the fireplace. Wreaths and garland adorned the walls, and a hand-carved Nativity scene was center-stage on the coffee table. The bookshelf, every one of the shelves normally filled with books, had one shelf cleared for a Christmas village.

Joseph bounded through the living room, skidding to a stop in front of the bookshelf. "Look Chris, look! I did the Christmas village. 'Ceptin we couldn't make the houses light up 'cause they run on 'tricity." His mouth turned down at the corners, mournfully. The little boy had no idea what television was like, and didn't miss it, but he missed making the village light up.

"You did great, Joseph." Chris smiled at the little boy. "Wow," he said, feigning surprise and wonder, "Is that real snow?" Chris pointed to the white folds of fabric the buildings rested on.

"No, silly, it's pretend snow!" the boy bounced up and down, pleased with Chris's response.

The sofa and Fenton's favorite chair had been moved back against one wall and there was now a large empty space in the middle of the living room. Liza didn't move, but she smiled and asked, "What do you think?"

"It looks beautiful," Chris answered honestly. He pointed to the open floor space, "Is that where..."

"Yup," Fenton looked exhausted, "That's where Liza and Carrie say the 'best spot' is for gettin' hitched. Good lord, I'm beat."

"Gramps slaughtered Drumstick today." Liza waved a tired finger towards the oven, which was beginning to emit the most luscious smell. Drumstick had been the largest of their eight turkeys and already slated for Christmas dinner. Chris had noticed the pile of feathers in the corner of the barn. His stomach gave a slow, audible growl. It had been a few hours since he had eaten at Mrs. Jennings. Liza snickered and pointed again towards the kitchen, "There's soup there on the stove." He didn't bother pouring it into a bowl. There was enough left in the pot for him and not much more. It was still warm, too. He grabbed a spoon, an oven mitt and sat on the sofa and ate.

"Where's Carrie?" he asked, trying not to slurp. The soup was full of carrots and potatoes as well as cubes of pork, yum... Butt Roast sure had turned out to be one fine-tasting beast.

"Asleep," Fenton yawned, "in her own bed where she belongs until tomorrow."

"Remember, it's bad luck to see your bride before the wedding," Liza grinned playfully, and wagged her finger. "Don't go sneaking a peek before tomorrow." The evening ended quietly. Chris excused himself at the same time as Fenton and lay down in his room, alone in the bed.

He stared into the dark, unable to sleep as the hours ticked by. He thought of Jess and his parents, all dead, their bodies' cold in the ground. If they had been lucky enough to be buried. He thought about Allen and Toby, even Easter and Burton, and all the nameless others. Chris wished that Carrie was tucked close beside him and he thought of the child growing inside her. So much death, and yet right now, in the face of that death and pain, the promise of new life. How he missed Mom and Dad and Jess. How they would have loved Carrie and all the rest of the Perdue's. How he wished things had been different!

Without the war, and the Western Front, and all the evil and pain he had seen, he would not be here. He would never have run into Fenton, met Carrie, or be getting married or expecting a child. To wish his parents, sister and friends to life would mean the loss of all he had now. He wrestled with this, stuck in a loop of would have's and should have's. The clock chimed four a.m. before he finally drifted off to sleep.

Joseph pile-driving into his stomach was his early morning wake up call. As he struggled to recover from the assault of an overly excited four-year-old, Liza materialized, holding a huge mug of chicory coffee. It was an acquired taste, meaning that they hadn't been able to acquire coffee and had been extending the stash by mixing it half and half with ground chicory, which grew on the roadsides and wild in fields. It didn't have quite the same kick as coffee, but it was hot, and who needed the full caffeine boost, anyway? He muttered his thanks and tried not to spill it on his bare chest as he sipped and Joseph bounced.

Liza took pity on him and grabbed Joseph in mid-bounce. "Come on Joseph, we have to get ready for the wedding." The boy protested he wanted to open presents. "No Joseph, we talked about this. Tonight, we'll open presents."

Before the little boy could begin wailing in earnest, Chris reached over and pulled out a small box from the bedside table. Mr. Liles had given it to him yesterday, instructing that it was a present for Joseph from Chris.

He'd winked at Chris. "Young man, you have enough on your plate with a little one on the way and a wedding tomorrow. Little Joseph will love these. And it'll keep him quiet 'til the ceremony is over." The box was handmade, crafted out of a soft wood. The top slid off to reveal tiny, hand-carved wooden cars with tiny button wheels that turned on tiny spokes held in place with cotter pins.

When Chris had looked over at Mr. Liles' gnarled and twisted hands in surprise, the old man had laughed. "Oh my, no! My grandson made these years back when he still could manage to see all those details. He's blind as a bat nowadays, worse eyesight than me!"

Chris handed the box to Joseph, "Here Joseph, 'cause today's going to be crazy. I want to be sure and give this to you now." The boy looked, took the box, and Chris helped him with the lid. He squealed then and ran off to show the rest of the family his prize.

"Good one, big brother." Liza grinned.

"I'm not your brother yet."

"All in good time." She jabbed her finger in the direction of the closet. "Gramps found you a suit to wear. It belonged to Dad. But you'd best wash first. And hurry up about it, 'cause Carrie's gotta get ready and that takes time."

"Say no more." He headed to the garage, which shared a wall with the kitchen. No water pressure meant that all of their water was from the old well. Thankfully, this was close to the house and could be pumped directly into the kitchen via an old-fashioned pump. However, it did not extend to the bathroom.

Earlier that year, Chris and Fenton had figured a way to run a mount a small sink high up on the shared wall and then run a pipe through the wall to the garage which then emptied into a barrel mounted on concrete blocks five feet off of the ground. By slightly crouching under the spigot, a person could take a rather Spartan shower.

To be able to shower, one would load up the rain barrel by pouring buckets of cold water into the sink straight from the tap and alternating with water boiled in a pan. It took about a half hour to prepare all the water needed for one short shower, and at this time of year, it was freezing cold in the garage. The summer wasn't so bad, but winter sucked and it meant that everyone, except for Joseph, who still got to bathe in the large kitchen sink, usually waited a week or so before bathing. In between full baths, they would just wash their hair in the sink. It worked out well enough. Chris stepped into the frigid garage, washed down quickly and, teeth chattering, wrapped the towel around his waist and sprinted back in.

"Now go in your room and stay there until we tell you to come out," Liza ordered. Chris rolled his eyes at this. He'd seen Carrie every day and night since he'd arrived here. It seemed like a silly ritual. But he let Liza push him into the room and promised he wouldn't peek. The room was dimly lit, and it looked as if it was beginning to snow in earnest. Big fat flakes were drifting down steadily.

Carrie's dad must have been slightly smaller than Chris. The pants fit fine, but the shirt was tight, especially around his shoulders and biceps. Outside of his room, he could hear Liza and Carrie run past his door giggling like giddy schoolgirls. He combed his hair back and looked in dismay at the tie. How in the heck do you tie one of these things?

He settled it around his collar, flipping it this way and that way while peering at his reflection in the mirror. The last time he had worn a tie was senior graduation. That had been silly when you realize that his suit and tie were both covered by his graduation gown. His mother had put it on him, her hands moving with calm assurance as she made a perfect knot. He could see her face now, eyes shining with pride. College had been out of the question, what with the instability of the entire country and the dominoes of the collapse already beginning to fall. She had cried though, and then whooped and hollered with the rest of them as the caps had flown into the air.

He yanked at the tie. It was no use. He was hopeless at this. A soft knock at the door and Fenton's voice, "Boy? You decent?"

"Yes, sir." The door opened and Fenton sidled in, closing the door as one or both of the girls ran past again, giggling madly. He sighed and shook his head.

"Well son, the food is cookin' and the girls are primpin' and," he took in Chris's suit, looked it up and down slowly, "Oh son... oh." He stopped and looked down at his shoes. Chris was alarmed.

"Sir? Is something wrong? Does the shirt look too small? I can't figure out this tie to save my life." His words tumbled out, climbing over each other, revealing his growing panic. Oh God, he was getting married today.

The old man looked up and smiled, his eyes turned misty. "You look fine, son. You do. I was just..." he inhaled, let it out slow, "I was just remembering when I bought that suit for Isaac for his first job interview in the big city. Straight out of college and he was going all the way to the Big Apple."

He shook his head. "Shouldn't be sad about it. My boy landed that job. Workin' there, he met the sweetest girl in the world to marry." He smiled wistfully. "And those two lovebirds made three fine grandchildren to comfort me when he was gone. I just miss him, even now."

He reached out and took the tie from Chris, looped it around his neck, and tied it with practiced hands. "There," he smoothed the tie and turned Chris towards the mirror, thumping him firmly on the back. They stood there silent for a moment, examining Chris's reflection.

Outside, the snow fell harder and the two men could hear Joseph running down the hall shouting that the van was there. "It's nearly time. You take a moment, then come on out and greet our guests. Will you be all right, son?"

Chris gulped, "Yes sir." One final thump, and the old man took his leave to go and greet the reverend and the wedding guests. Chris realized he hadn't eaten anything for breakfast, which was probably a good thing. Right now, he felt downright nauseous. He closed his eyes, thought of his parents and Jess. Deep breath. Then he turned and walked out to greet everyone.

Days later, he would swear that Christmas morning had moved at the speed of light. Looking back on it, he remembered waking up, washing, dressing, greeting guests and the ceremony all flashing past in a blur.

The only true clarity to the memory was the beautiful stranger he had found kissing him back that morning. Carrie's straight blond hair had been a mass of curls that ran from twists on the top of her head to ribbons of gold that danced on her shoulders. Her dress had been an ivory satin, a family heirloom, and it had clung to her hips and cascaded down to the floor. Peeking out from the hem were a pair of Liza's hand-knitted rainbow socks and blue Converse tennis shoes.

"Something borrowed and something blue," she had whispered to him, eyes twinkling.

Until she had spoken, he had wondered if he were dreaming. She was beyond beautiful, beyond his ability to describe in words, a sweet promise of the years to come. The butterflies in his stomach were gone, and he stood and they exchanged vows. He slipped the brilliant emerald and diamond ring onto her finger and kissed his bride.

Everyone applauded. Joseph and Tabitha bounced in and around them, and the snow fell thick and heavy.

It was Christmas Day. It was snowing. It was a white wedding. And Fenton even put his shotgun down long enough to give away the bride.

Home Sweet Cave

"You must plan for every contingency—enough greens, meat, grains, blankets, wood, even access to clean water. Without all of these, and more, you will find yourself in deep trouble mid-winter. Assume nothing, prepare for everything to go wrong, and you just might survive to see spring."—Author Unknown

They packaged the smoked deer meat in waterproof baggies and submerged them in the water. The stream was fed by an underground aquifer which produced ice-cold, clean water for drinking. This eliminated the need for boiling and kept the stored meat at an acceptably cold level. David had been right; they would need at least one more buck to ensure their survival through the winter.

Jess and Tina had gathered large amounts of grass and bulrush for sleep mats as well as absorbent material for Jacob. The supply of diapers had long since run out. Jess watched her son closely, observed his habits, and quickly recognized a pattern of elimination. This allowed her to fashion a handful of strips of deer hide for the outer layer of the diaper, with plenty of grass lining the inside and absorbing any waste at the times he was most likely to need it.

Throughout the weeks, Madge urged cup after cup of milk thistle tea on Jess until she finally asked the old woman why. "It promotes lactation. You need all the milk you can make for Mi'-da-in-ga." She cupped the baby's head and cooed at him lovingly as she explained this. The infant stared back; his deep blue eyes intent on watching the old woman speak. "It also increases your circulation and builds your strength. He is growing well, Mi'-na, a healthy and strong boy child. He will make a brave warrior one day."

Tina watched the old woman intently. She asked Madge about every plant they encountered outside of the cave until she could recite as many as David could. "Why you call her Meena, Grandmother? Her name Yess, not Meena."

Madge smiled at the girl. "For the same reason I call you, Ni'-da-wi, my little fairy child. You with your pretty brown hair. When I see you,

I think of a garden fairy. I call Jess Mi'-na, which means the oldest daughter, for she reminds me of my oldest girl when she was young." For the old woman, naming the children made them family, showed her love for them. For a long time, Tina insisted her name was Ni'-da-wi and would stubbornly refuse to answer to any other.

By the end of October, they had accumulated a large store of fish, which they smoked and then stored in the back of the cave. A small mountain of grass had been gathered, washed, and dried. They used it to stuff bedding and also for absorbing Jacob's waste. David had whittled several bowls out of a fallen log and they no longer had to share bowls. Jess and Tina had learned to weave baskets out of the reeds they had collected from the lake shore. Madge showed them where wild onions grew and they harvested bucketsful of nuts and armfuls of sump weed and plantain.

The first week of November, David bagged another deer with his bow, and he sent a prayer of thanks to its dead spirit. He wasn't Osage, but if Grandmother Madge thought it was a good idea, then he was all for it. It seemed respectful, somehow, to give thanks to this enormous creature. Its meat and hide would help keep them alive through the winter.

Quincy had been with him again on this hunt, although she typically preferred to stay by Jess or Jacob's side. In the evenings or during the day when Jess had to help climb a nut tree and shake the limbs for more nuts, the dog would stay glued to the infant's side, whining softly moments before he stirred. At night, Quincy's soft whine helped Jess to wake and put a breast to little Jacob's mouth before he was even fully awake. That way, there was far less wailing to disturb the small group's slumber.

Quincy was young, but she was an intelligent pup. David looked at the carcass of the giant deer and knew he needed help. He turned back to Quincy, busy sniffing the ground around the deer and said, "Go Quincy, go find Jess and Madge." The pup looked up at him, gave one short bark, and plunged into the forest in the direction of the cave. He began the process of field-dressing the buck. He had just begun on the guts when the rest of their band arrived, Quincy leading the way. Their help made short work of it and soon the deer had joined the newest batch of fish in the smoke hut. "I said the words you taught me, Grandmother." David said as they laid out the last deer haunch in the hut, "I talked to the deer's spirit and thanked him for giving his life so we can eat this winter."

The old woman stopped. It was the first time David had ever called her that, and hugged him close. "Thank you Min'-dse," she turned and looked at the others, misty-eyed, "I am proud to call each of you, my family. You honor the old ways and make me so happy." She hugged each of them in turn and kissed Jacob's forehead gently. "Come, come, we have dinner to prepare for our mighty hunter!"

In November, the temperatures fell dramatically. Madge taught the children how to weave screens of saplings and evergreens to act as a shield across the opening of the cave and reduce the chilly drafts. They built and maintained several fires to deter rodent invaders and increase heat in the living portion of the cave, and kept large stacks of firewood near the cave entrance. If anyone wandered close, they would instantly see that the cave was occupied, but in the long winter months no one ever did. Madge reminded them that the cave was far from any established trails and it wasn't marked on any public maps. The chances of discovery were unlikely. "Only members of my team know of this location." her expression turned grim. "I fear that none of them survived to return."

For the children, it felt as if the world outside their cave had ceased to exist. A new world, full of family, simple food, learning, stories and laughter filled their days. The snow fell deep that year, further insulating their tiny cave beneath the drifts. Jacob rolled over for the first time around Thanksgiving, and David improved his whittling skills. Soon they had wooden bowls, spoons of their own and even several two-tined forks. Jess learned how to sew deerskin hides, and Madge taught Tina her letters and told the ancient stories of her people.

They celebrated Christmas with a feast and an exchange of presents. Jess and Madge had collaborated to create a small doll for Tina. Madge fashioned the body out of stiff cattail reed and Jess sewed on a tiny dress out of buckskin and then pierced tiny berries on a string to drape around the doll's neck for a necklace. Tina was enchanted with it and created a sling for her doll similar to Jess's and Madge's so that she too could carry her 'baby' around.

David had whittled a small piece of wood into a round disk, engraved a rough 'J' onto it, and pierced a hole near the top that he threaded cord through, turning it into a necklace and giving it to Jess. She hugged the boy and immediately put it around her neck.

Madge received a fur muff made of rabbit pelts (mainly from Quincy's kills) and roughly sewn together by Jess. "To keep your hands warm, Grandmother," Jess said, and hugged the old woman. Madge ran her hands over the fur, commenting on its softness, and managed a weak smile. She hadn't been sleeping or eating well in the past week. Jess worried that the old woman was falling ill.

The old woman slowly stood, walked to the back of the cave and retrieved a hide-wrapped bundle and handed it with great ceremony to David. "Min'dse, you have proven yourself an able hunter. My people valued this ability highly. A hunter ensured his people's survival in the darkest of times. Someday you will be a fierce warrior as well and protect your family from harm. Listen, learn, and grow strong. Protect the ones you love at all cost."

The boy's spine straightened, and he opened the bundle, examined each of the objects inside with awe. Madge had given him several of the dig artifacts—a spear tip, a stone knife, and an atlatl. The last object brought a gasp from Jess, for she knew how valuable these artifacts, especially the atlatl, were to Madge and the archaeological world. This was her work, part of the ancient history of her people, and she would not give these things away without long contemplation and deep regard for the boy.

It seemed strange, though, the thought that the old woman would give such valuable artifacts to a child. It bothered Jess a little, as if there were some parts of the story she didn't know. For all Jess knew, the old woman might have the beginnings of dementia or Alzheimer's. She said nothing; however, because she was distracted by the last gift to be handed out.

It was a field journal. Unlined paper, soft tan leather binding, and Jess saw that Madge had carefully written "Jacob" and then Misae was written under it and accompanied by a pictograph of a sun. Jess opened and recognized that the first few pages of the journal were filled with tiny writing. They were journal entries. The first one was dated September 19th, 2016, the day they had met Madge.

Jess looked up and locked eyes with Madge, who said, "I had a dream one day. In it, I saw a group of people walking west. There were adults, some children, even a small baby. Leading them was a handsome young warrior, smooth-chested, barely a man. When I looked upon his face, it was like looking at the sun, blinding, hot. The rays reached out and lit the land before them with a blinding white light. I was not with this group, but I could see them and move among them."

She paused. "I saw you, Mi'-na, but you were older than you are now, fully a woman. You cradled a tiny baby in your arms and a tall young man walked by your side. There were others, a handful of others, all of you walking through the plains. All of you connected by blood, by commitment, by love. A voice came then and said, 'Old woman, stop your dreaming, go to the shore of the lake.' And so, I did."

She smiled at Jess and the others. "And I met you that day. I had just begun this journal, and I have written in it as often as I could in the days since. Someday, you will give it to Mi'-da-in-ga, when he becomes a man. He is the white sun that I saw in my dream, Mi'-na. You will know the right time to give it to him."

Jess took the journal silently. The leather was butter-soft, the papers rough and irregular. She realized that it had to have been made by hand. Madge added, "My daughter Penelope made that and gave it to me two years ago. It was the last time I saw her."

Such a gift! She did the only thing she could think to do. Jess reached out and hugged the old woman close, tears leaking down her cheeks, and said in a whisper, "Thank you Grandmother, I will treasure it always." Their embrace was interrupted by a squirming inside of Jess's sling and temperamental wail from the youngest member of their group.

While Jess fed Jacob, Madge and Tina prepared the food for their long-anticipated Christmas feast. Venison stew, brimming with the greens they had gathered, and the corms of a cattail filled their bellies.

Before the weather had turned too cold, the entire group had hiked southwest several miles from the cave to a grove of hickory trees.

They had spent a day trekking there, gathering as many nuts as they could carry, and then trekking back. Jess marveled at the old woman's cooking skills as they ate not just roasted hickory nuts, but also a type of bread, heavy and dense, made from the nuts and some kind of sweet/tart berries. A prized jar of wild violet jam, which Madge had made in her home in Kansas City and then brought with her to the cave, topped the bread. The sweet finish came in the form of hot chocolate, one cup for each of them, the last of the instant hot chocolate packets that Madge had squirreled away for a 'special' day.

"Grandmother, tell us a story." Tina asked, drowsily nestled against her brother.

Madge smiled, closed her eyes for a minute to think, and then said, "I will tell you the story of the first moccasins." She reached for Jacob, and Jess handed him to her carefully. He was asleep and his eyes didn't even flutter as he was passed from one set of arms to the next.

"There was a great Chief of the Plains who had tender, sensitive feet. Other chiefs laughed at him; the people of the tribe also laughed at the chief's discomfort. The medicine man, an advisor to Chief-of-the-Tender-Feet was afraid and troubled. Each time he was called before the chief, he was asked, 'What are you going to do about it?' The 'it' meant the chief's tender feet."

"Forced by fear, the medicine man at last hit upon a plan. Though he knew that it was not the real answer to the chief's foot problem, it would work. The medicine man had the women weave a long, narrow mat of reeds, and when the chief had to go anywhere, four braves unrolled the mat in front of him. One day, the braves were worn out. They carelessly unrolled the mat over a place where flint arrowheads had been chipped. The arrowheads had long ago taken flight, but the needle-sharp chips remained. When the big chief's tender feet were wounded by these chips, he uttered a series of whoops, which made the nearby aspen tree leaves shake so hard that they have been trembling ever since."

"That night the medicine man was given an impossible task by the angry chief: 'Cover the whole earth with mats so thick that my feet will not suffer. If you fail, you will die when the moon is round.'"

"The frightened medicine man crept back to his lodge. He didn't want to die on the night of the full moon, but he could think of no way to avoid it. Looking down, he saw the hide of an elk pegged to the ground, with two women busily scraping the hair from the hide, and an idea flashed into his head. He sent out many hunters. Many women were busy for many days. The braves cut with hunting knives, and women sewed with bone needles."

"On the day before the moon was round, the medicine man went to the chief and told him that he had covered as much of the earth as possible. When the chief looked from the door of his lodge, he saw many paths of skin stretching as far as he could see. Long strips which could be moved from place to place connected the main leather paths. Even the chief thought that this time the magic of the medicine man had solved tenderfoot transportation for all time."

"One day, as the big chief was walking along one of his smooth, tough leather paths, he saw a pretty maiden of the tribe gliding ahead of him, walking on the hard earth on one side of the chief's pathway. She glanced back when she heard his feet on the elk-hide pathway and smiled. The chief set off at a run to catch up with her, his eyes fixed on the back of She-Who-Smiled, and so his feet strayed from the narrow path and landed in a bunch of needle-sharp thorns! The girl ran for her life when she heard the hideous howls of the chief."

"Two suns later, when the chief was calm enough to speak, he had his medicine man brought before him. He told the man that the next day, when the sun was high in the sky, he would be killed for his failures."

"That night, the medicine man climbed to the top of a high hill in search of advice from friendly spirits on how to cover the entire earth with leather. He slept. In a dream vision, he was shown the answer to his problem. Amid flashes of lightning, he tore down the steep hillside, howling louder than the big chief at times, as jagged rocks wounded his bare feet and legs. He did not stop until he was safely inside his lodge. He worked all night. The warriors who were to send him on the shadow trail came for him just before noon the next day. He was surrounded by the war-club armed guards and he was clutching something rolled in a piece of deerskin tightly to his heart. His cheerful smile surprised those who saw him pass. 'He is brave!' said the men. 'Yes, he is very brave!' said the women."

"The chief was waiting just outside his lodge. Before the medicine man could be led away, he asked if he could say a few words to the chief. 'Speak!' said the chief, sorry to lose a clever medicine man that was very good at most kinds of magic."

"The medicine man quickly knelt beside the chief. He unrolled two strange objects and slipped one of them on each foot of the chief. The chief seemed to be wearing a pair of bear's hairless feet instead of bare feet. He was puzzled at first as he looked at the elk-hide handcraft of his medicine man. 'Great chief,' the medicine man exclaimed joyfully, 'I have found a way to cover the earth with leather! For you, O chief, from now on the earth will always be covered with leather.' And so, it was."

"The cave was quiet. From the dark, David said sleepily, "I like that story." No one said anything more, and the fire burned low as they all slipped into dreams of moccasins and Christmas. Outside, a light snow began to fall.

The Death of Falling Water

"To say goodbye to her was almost more than I could bear. She taught us so much, gave us such hope and loved us so deeply in those few short months. She renewed my trust in others and imbued a sense of joy in the simple act of living. After all that we had seen, life was a challenge. Enjoying the process seemed impossible, but Madge saw things differently. She lived her life on her terms. She was kind, down to earth, and loved us well. If I live to be a hundred, I doubt I could be as special and as wonderful as that old woman was to us. In the end, I can say only this, she became Grandmother Falling Water, and we honor her memory to this day. She reminded us that the world was not all death and hate and violence. She taught us, she loved us, and we will carry her stories and lessons with us forever."—Jess's Journal

One evening, in late January, they gathered around for a story and Madge sat silent for several moments. She had been tired that day, sleeping longer into the morning than usual in the past few weeks and eating less each day. As she sat there silently, Jess was struck by how old Madge looked. When they had arrived, she had not wanted to ask the old woman's age. It would be rude, so she held her tongue. Tina had not been held to the same social norm and had asked her loudly one day if she was a hundred years old. Madge had laughed and shook her head, never answering the little girl. As they sat, there waiting for Madge to begin her story, Jess thought that Madge looked older that evening than she had ever seen her look before. The moment passed, and the old woman looked around, smiled at the children surrounding her and the tiny baby in her arms, cleared her throat and began to speak...

"What is the meaning of life? Why is it that people grow old and die?

"Although he was young, those questions troubled the mind of Little One. He asked the elders about them, but their answers did not satisfy him. Eventually, after asking and asking, he knew there was only one thing to do. He would have to seek the answers in his dreams."

"Little One rose early in the morning and prayed to Wah-Kon-Tah for help. Then he walked away from the village, across the prairie and toward

the hills. He took nothing with him, no food and no water. He was looking for a place where none of his people would see him, a place where a vision could come to him."

"Little One walked a long way. Each night, he camped in a different place, hoping that it would be the right one to give him a dream that could answer his questions. But no such dream came to him."

"At last, he came to a hill that rose above the land like the breast of a young maiden. A spring burst from the rocks near the base of a great elm tree. It was a beautiful place that seemed to be filled with the power of Wah-Kon-Tah. Little One sat down by the base of that elm tree and waited as the sun set. But though he slept, again no sign was given to him."

"When he woke the next morning, he was weak with hunger. 'I must go back home,' he thought. He was filled with despair, but his thoughts were of his parents. He had been gone a long time. Even though it was expected that a young man would seek guidance alone in this fashion, Little One knew they would be worried. 'If I do not return while I still have the strength to walk,' he said, 'I will die here and my family may never find my body.'"

"Little One began to follow a small stream that was fed by a spring. It flowed out of the hills in the direction of his village, and he trusted it to lead him home. He walked and walked until he was not far from his village. But as he walked along that stream, he stumbled and fell among the roots of an old willow tree. Little One clung to the roots of the willow tree. Although he tried to rise, his legs were too weak."

"'Grandfather,' he said to the willow tree, 'It is not possible for me to go on.'"

"Then the ancient willow spoke to him. 'Little One,' it said, 'all the Little Ones always cling to me for support as they walk along the great path of life. See the base of my trunk, which sends forth roots that hold me firm in the earth. They are the sign of my old age. They are darkened and wrinkled with age, but they are still strong. Their strength comes from relying on the earth. When the Little Ones use me as a symbol, they will not fail to see old age as they travel along the path of life.'"

"Those words gave strength to Little One's spirit. He stood again and began to walk. Soon his own village was in sight, and as he sat down to rest for a moment in the grass of the prairie, looking at his village, another vision

came to him. He saw before him the figure of an old man. The old man was strangely familiar, even though Little One had never seen him before."

"'Look upon me,' the old man said. 'What do you see?'"

"'I see an old man whose face is wrinkled with age,' Little One said."

"'Look upon me again,' the old man said."

"Then Little One looked, and as he looked, the lesson shown him by the willow tree filled his heart. 'I see an aged man in sacred clothing,' Little One said. 'The white down of the eagle adorns his head. I see an aged man with the stem of the pipe between his lips. You are firm and rooted to the earth like the ancient willow. I see you standing among the days that are peaceful and beautiful. I see you standing as you will stand in your lodge, my grandfather.'"

"The ancient man smiled. Little One had seen truly. 'My young brother,' the old man said, 'your mind is fixed upon the days that are peaceful and beautiful.' And then he was gone."

"Now Little One's heart was filled with peace, and as he walked into the village, his mind was troubled no longer with those questions about the meaning of life. For he knew that the old man he had seen was himself. The ancient man was Little One as he would be when he became an elder, filled with that great peace and wisdom which would give strength to all the people."

"From that day on, Little One began to spend more time listening to the words his elders spoke, and of all the young men in the village, he was the happiest and the most content."

This was one of the longest stories Madge had ever shared, and she looked exhausted at the end. Usually, her stories were short or often funny. As she finished, she looked down at the ground and tears formed in her eyes. "I have not been entirely honest with you, Little Ones. I told you I came back here to this cave to continue my work, but that isn't the full truth." She paused and stroked Jacob's sleeping face as he lay cuddled in her arms. "In the weeks before fighting broke out in the city, I was not feeling well. I'd lost a lot of weight. No matter how much I tried, I could barely bring myself to eat."

"I underwent a series of tests and the doctors found cancer. They said it was just a matter of time. They told me it was too advanced, and that it had metastasized throughout my organs and they could do nothing for me. They gave me six months and told me to call my children. Then things turned bad in the world, and," she shrugged, "I came here. I tried several herbal remedies and things improved. I felt better, my appetite returned, and I felt younger than I had in years."

She smiled at them, taking in the young, worried faces looking at her in the crackling firelight. "I came out here to die, not to continue my work. Then all of you came, and you made me feel so alive. You have made these past few months a joy and a gift at the end of an old woman's life."

Jess's voice broke as she choked the words out, "You're dying?"

Madge laughed, clear and clean, and the sound bounced and rolled through the cave, magnifying and expanding, "Oh Mi'-na, from the moment we are born we begin to die. My moment will come soon, far sooner than yours, and it will be on my terms and through my choice. I could have stayed there, gotten the treatments that would have robbed me of my hair, turned the food I ate to dust in my mouth. I could have survived with a few less organs than I currently have. But I have lived a long time, and I am satisfied with how I have lived it. I have loved and been loved. Given birth and raised my children. Taught and learned much about my people and my history."

She smiled at them again, tears flowing freely down her lined cheeks, "I thought I had seen everything and done everything I wanted to do, and then you came. And these weeks and months have been a beautiful finish to a well-lived life." Tina crept close, nestled against her right arm, and Madge hugged her close. "But I can feel it in my body, eating away at me, killing me with each day that passes. I don't think it will be much longer, a month, maybe two. Forgive me children, for I asked you to stay not just for your safety, but for my own selfish needs. I did not want to die alone, even here, in the home of my ancestors. I wanted someone to be here in the end. You have seen far too much death, and I ask too much of you, I know I do."

They were all in tears, and Jess reached out and held the old woman's hand. "We won't leave you, Grandmother. We won't leave you alone, I promise." She said it with conviction and David nodded nearby, looking at the ground as he tried to hide his tears.

Madge had not been far off when she said the end would come soon. After that night in January, her condition worsened quickly. They had all made such progress in storing food and supplies in the months before winter that one less hand in chores was not missed. However, Jacob had grown used to hours in Madge's wizened arms. He looked for her, even from the wraps of Jess's sling, and whimpered fretfully.

He was teething, and this did not help his mood. Jess solved this by moving her cot right next to Madge's, so the baby lay between them at night and close to Madge during the day. This brightened his mood and Madge's as well. She would smile with joy when she opened her eyes and saw him there, just inches from her.

Madge would sleep all night, wake for breakfast, then nap again until lunch, and often again until dinner. She touched very little of the food and only smiled and shook her head when Jess or David attempted to feed her more. Slowly, she shrank in size until her bones jutted prominently. She now looked every inch of her Osage heritage with the hawkish nose, high cheekbones and long limbs. David stayed by her side constantly, as did Tina, and they listened to her stories now told in a mere whisper. It was as if she was attempting to fill their heads with every piece of knowledge she had, and they were just as intent on memorizing it.

Jess sat by her side one day and wrote down the names of Madge's children, along with birth dates (as well as Madge's failing memory could remember them), last known locations, and promised to do her best to contact them. They deserved to know what had happened to their mother and the good that she had done for others in the last months of her life.

January slipped into February and as that month drew to a close, it became obvious that the old woman would soon be gone. Her skin was pale and mottled, clammy to the touch. Her breath came in short gasps, and no food or water had passed her lips in over two days. The children had seen heartache and pain and the ugliness of death. Far too much for their short lives, but somehow, this ending was different.

Madge had said she wanted to die on her terms, and she did, surrounded by people who had come to love her and care for her deeply. They stayed awake through the long night and as the rays of the sun pierced through the woven hangings at the front of the cave, Dr. Madeleine Falling Water gave one last, soft gasp and left the world, with all of them by her side, their hands holding hers, tears streaking their faces. Quincy howled mournfully.

That afternoon, Jess and David wrapped the old woman's body in deerskin, sewed it shut, and laid her on the ground a few feet away from the thong tree. The ground was still frozen, and there was no way they could dig a deep enough hole, so they gathered stones and made a cairn. When it was done and the sun was slipping down through the trees, the group gathered and stood at the heap of stones, silent for a few moments. Jess spoke first, reciting a poem Madge had taught her just days before.

"The Track of the sun
across the Sky
leaves its shining message,
Illuminating,
Strengthening,
Warming,
us who are here,
showing us we are not alone,
we are yet alive*!*
And this fire......
Our fire.....
Shall never die"

Tina had discovered some tiny yellow flowers poking up from the snow and she solemnly placed them on the pile of stones. David cleared his throat and began to recite the last story Madge had ever told him...

"A young man wanted to become a respected elder, so he went to an elder and the elder told him, 'You must learn to count to 100.' Simple enough, the young man thought."

"One day, a homeless and dirty old woman limped into town. Some people looked at her and turned away. Others stared and whispered behind their hands."

"The young man felt sorry for the old woman. He approached her and said, 'Grandmother, come in, rest.' He put his arm around her shoulders and took her into his home. He welcomed her, offered her water, and when she had rested and drank some water, he gave her soup."

"He called to his mother and sisters, 'Help Grandmother wash and change. Put her in one of your buckskin dresses and give her those new moccasins.' The mother and sisters bathed the old woman, washed her hair and braided it, dressed her in new clothes."

"Then the family invited her to live with them, to join the family."

"Later, the young man brought her to the elder and introduced her, saying, 'Grandmother has a new family.'"

"The elder asked, 'Is that the old homeless woman? You did this?' When the young man nodded, the elder said, 'That is one.'"

"Thank you, Grandmother, for the lesson and the reminder that there is good in this world." David said clearly, despite the tears slipping down his face, "Look for the day that I learn to count to one hundred."

They could think of nothing more to say. Returning to the cave felt surreal. The heart of this place was gone without old Madge. They ate dinner quietly and Tina fell asleep huddled in David's lap. She had cried off and on all day and was worn out. Jess had wrapped Jacob up and laid him on her cot where he would probably stay until the sun rose. She looked over at David. His face was morose and he stared off in the direction of the cave entrance. It struck Jess that he looked older, more grown up. "When's your birthday?"

"Huh?" He seemed startled to hear her speak.

"When's your birthday?"

"April 4th, I'll be twelve." He seemed a little surprised at the thought. His thoughts drifted to his parents, dead for nearly a year now. He had turned eleven and not even really thought about it. They hadn't exactly been paying attention to calendars at the time it had rolled by last year.

He thought a minute more. "Tina turned four in January. The 11th, I think." He looked embarrassed and somewhat guilty. "I didn't remember her birthday."

Jess stirred the coals of the fire. "I guess I never really asked or thought about it before, myself. I turned sixteen exactly two weeks after Jacob was born. I was so damn tired those first few weeks it's entirely possible that I slept right through it."

She paused, let the silence deepen and then said, "Adults would say you and I are both still kids, you know. But we aren't. We've seen too much awful shit to be kids anymore." She spoke to him as an equal, more than she ever had before.

David nodded slowly, watching her; he wondered where this was heading. Then it dawned on him, and he knew. "You think it might be safe now."

"Huh?" Jess looked confused for a moment. "Oh. Hell, I don't know. It's been nearly six months. That's one heck of a cold trail. They've probably forgotten all about us by now. Besides," she gave a smoldering log a sharp, angry shove, "It isn't two teenage girls anymore, so we don't fit the description on that paper."

"You still do." It was a fact. Her hair was beautiful. Long, deep curls and golden blond, —it was hard to forget hair like that.

"I could cut it short. And then I'll dye it with some of those damn walnut shells that made our fingers black for a week." She grinned, "Can't do much about my eyes, but lots of people have blue eyes."

David grinned back, "Can I help cut it?" The look of horror in her eyes at the thought of him cutting her hair made him laugh for the first time in days.

The Tennessee Four

"T*he battle line between good and evil runs through the heart of every man."- Alexander Solzhenitsyn*

Scott Cooper stretched out on the comfortable bed. At the corner of the bed on the floor, handcuffed to the bedpost, was a girl.

Occasionally, he would hear her sniffle or sob. For the moment, he simply ignored her. They had been traveling for days, hitting farms, but not staying long due to the local militias. Damn, but he was tired. He hadn't been sleeping well, and they'd been on the road too long.

Most of the area seemed to have wised up and organized themselves. Memphis had a particularly strong militia in place, which would have been effective except they were also dealing with a nasty case of cholera.

Just north of Dyersburg, they had managed to get a truck. It was a broken-down rust bucket. The engine ran rough, and none of the men knew much about maintenance, so they kept nursing it along, hoping for something better.

After they had pushed their way into Tennessee, in late November, two men left under the cover of night, while on sentry duty. Two more had died in skirmishes with locals as they navigated through a warren of tiny towns and backwoods hillbillies who were armed to the teeth.

By the time Cooper's band entered Memphis, he was down to nineteen men. At that point, the women they had had with them in Mississippi were all dead and six of the men who had been too scared to leave now realized they would die no matter what. Four of them managed to escape into the sprawling ruins of the city; and the other two were shot in the back as they ran. Four more men, a buddy of Riley's and three more grunts were shot by the Memphis militia. This left him with nine men. He turned and hightailed it out of Memphis, heading northeast up Highway 70. Arlington and Stanton, that took two more of his men, and another, lost on the outskirts of Brownsville. They turned northwest and passed through Ripley without incident before losing one more on the outskirts to Dyersburg. This left Cooper with Riley, Kimmel and Eckhardt. All of them were bad, all of them tough as nails.

They weren't an army any longer. But that was okay in several ways. None of the remaining men were stupid. They were all experienced fighters. And with only four men, there wasn't much advertisement for their presence. Try moving 200+ people through an area and see if someone doesn't notice. Four men, however, were easily hidden. And it was just the right amount for hitting the isolated farms along the way.

The girl gave another hiccupping sob. That annoying sound and the accompanying rumble from his stomach made him sit up. He stood up and pulled his pants on and reached over to the girl. She cowered from him. Her shirt was ripped and bloody, her mouth cut, and the rest of her clothes were gone. Bruises ran up and down her legs. Cooper unlocked the handcuff attached to the bedpost and yanked the girl to her feet.

"Come on, you're going to fix us something to eat."

He dragged her past the other bedrooms, where Riley and Kimmel were still busy with the girl's mother, and down the stairs and into the kitchen. The kitchen was all done up in red and white checked curtains, red cabinets, and matching accessories. Above a small table in the kitchen was a plaque that read Home Sweet Home and under that, Welcome to the Austins.

They had taken the house in the evening, shortly after dinner that evening. Under cover of darkness, they had stormed both doors, two through the front and two in through the back, and the family had been taken unawares, without a shot fired, while sitting in the living room. The blood of the menfolk had splashed the floor and the walls and left dark, rust-colored drag marks out the front door and down the steps. They had put all the bodies in the old farmhouse, out of sight.

Eckhardt didn't seem to mind the blood and gore at all. He was snoring contentedly on the couch, his pants off. Apparently, he'd gotten first dibs on the mother. Cooper hadn't bothered asking. The others knew the girl was his and his alone until such time as he tired of her. This time might come soon if she didn't stop her damned whining.

He kicked Eckhardt as he passed him and the man jumped awake, a sharp hunting knife materializing in his hand. Disconcerted and still in the throes of his dream, he snarled at Cooper.

Scott just laughed. "Find me a chain for her."

He ordered, pointing to the girl. Eckhardt sheathed his knife and walked away, muttering under his breath. A few minutes later, a cold, rusty chain had been attached to the handcuff. The other end of the chain had been wrapped around a column that stood between the kitchen and dining room and locked in place with a padlock. Cooper slid the key into his khakis and sat down in the living room. Morning was dawning, he had worked up an appetite, and after he ate, he wanted to sleep.

The area was remote. They were two miles or so out of town and there was plenty of cover of trees. He set his feet up on the couch, motioned to Eckhardt to keep an eye on the girl in the kitchen, and settled back. Cooper closed his eyes and smiled. They could afford to take a break for a few days, maybe even a couple of weeks. By now, they had learned the trick of it. It had actually become rather easy to take the locals by surprise. Just hit them at dusk when their defenses were down and it's too dark to go running through the woods when you couldn't see where you were going.

From the kitchen, he could hear the girl cry out as Eckhardt moved in and pressed her against the countertop. His hands groped her.

"Leave her be, Saul," Scott called out without opening his eyes, "I want some good old Southern cooking in me. You'll get a turn at that before too long, anyway."

He ignored the man's mutterings as the sounds in the kitchen turned back to cooking.

An hour later, as he gulped down the biscuits and gravy the girl had served up, he smiled. Maybe they'd stay for a while.

Something's Wrong

"*Because I could not stop for Death—*
He kindly stopped for me—
The Carriage held but just Ourselves—
And Immortality." – Emily Dickinson

Liza pulled her prized stethoscope down to her neck and stared thoughtfully at Carrie's stomach. "I wish we had Doppler to listen to the baby's heartbeat. You just don't seem to be gaining much weight."

Carrie rolled her eyes at her little sister. "I've only been able to keep down food for the past month, sis. Give it time."

Liza sighed. "I just wish I had more sophisticated equipment. At least we got some prenatal vitamins for you to take. Try eating just a little more at meals for a while, okay?"

She stared at her sister's belly speculatively and Carrie grew impatient, pulled her shirt down and sat up. It was true, she was barely showing anything at all, and she figured it had to have been four months by now, or near enough. As skinny as she was, it was weird that she didn't have much of a baby bump.

"All right, all right, I'll try and eat more. You're such a worry-wort! Come on, I promised Chris this would be quick and then we could ride the buggy into town and look for parts for the windmill he's hoping to build."

Liza snorted and headed for the door. "What the heck do we need a windmill for, anyway?"

"Electricity!"

Liza scoffed, "No way!"

"Yeah way."

"Whatever."

"Also, he can build one that pumps water straight into the house... including the toilet and bathtub. Maybe we could even get the regulator on the hot water heater going if there's electricity."

"Really?" Liza closed her eyes and imagined the luxury of a long hot bath. Sponge baths and scrubbing their hair in the sink were the norm, despite the jury-rigged shower in the garage.

"Really. I'm taking him to Dorian's Junkyard to see if we can rustle up some parts."

Liza looked starry-eyed at the thought of having running water in the hall bathroom. Not having to hunch under the spigot in the freezing cold garage would be such an unbelievable luxury... and no more flushing the toilet with a bucket each time? Sweet!

Then her thoughts turned to town and visiting Carl, "Wait, let me get some books, and I'll take them in to...uh...trade."

Carrie smirked at her little sister. "Trade, huh? Trade kisses, maybe trade some gropes," she would have said more, but Fenton limped down the hall headed for the bathroom.

His right knee had been bothering him for weeks and their grandfather was a wretched old grump when in pain. He fluttered his fingers in front of him in a shooing motion.

"Carrie-girl, take that sister and brother of yours away to town with you. Joseph keeps wantin' to dive into my lap sayin' he's Superman and Liza's bout to drive me up the wall with all her wantin' to poke and prod on me. And this damn leg is aching till I'm fit to be tied. You all go and get out of my hair for a while. I want me a nice, peaceful nap in my easy chair."

He shuffled past them and closed the bathroom door firmly.

Carrie winked at Liza. "Well, it looks like we're all going into town. Best get those books to trade and I'll round up Joseph." Liza grinned and dashed towards her room to put on a touch of makeup and run a brush through her tangled hair. She pulled it up in a ponytail, shrugged into her warmest coat and was at the front door waiting, books in hand, before Carrie could corral 'Superman' and shove him in a coat. Carrie eyed her sister sternly, "But you have to take him with you."

At Liza's horrified expression, Carrie amended it. "He can play with Tabitha."

"Jeez, sis, and I thought you were cool!" Liza complained. Carrie just laughed.

It was early February and Christmas had been the one and only snowfall that year. It wasn't too cold. The thermometer on the side of the barn registered in the mid-40s, but everything around them was barren and dead except for the random patch of green grass. Winter had them in its grip for at least one more month, possibly two.

The girls and Joseph pitched in and helped Chris finish with the morning chores. They hitched up the wagon, snuggled Joseph and Liza in the back under a thick lap quilt, and Chris and Carrie shared another on the front seat of the wagon. Carrie had pieced the quilts together in the past few weeks, using her great-great-grandmother's treadle-operated sewing machine to finish each quilt. It had been a surprising find. The sewing cabinet had sat in the guest room, served as a table covered with knickknacks. The sewing machine was intact and usable inside, and it had only taken some oil and a new belt to put it back into service. The quilts kept them toasty warm on the drive into town.

Chris had never been to the junkyard. Jim Dorian was a collector, mainly of junk, but if you were looking for the odd or the innovative, then Dorian Junkyard was the place to go. When school had still been in session, the Tiptonville high school kids were taken on an annual trip to the junkyard. Here they learned to re-purpose old items into art, or cobble together eclectic furniture, and more. You never knew what you might find. After they dropped off Liza and Joseph, and made sure it was okay for them to visit, Chris and Carrie headed for the junkyard. Jim Dorian peered out of his double-wide, which was parked at the entrance of the fenced-in junkyard, and grinned at Carrie.

"Well, I'll be. If it ain't Miss Carrie Lynn Perdue." He grinned at Carrie, "You made a lovely little charm bracelet, as I recall. Wore a sparkly blue tank top." Carrie had tried to prepare Chris as they drove over.

"Gramps says that Jim Dorian is some kind of savant. But he's odd. I'm warning you of that right now. He's got this amazing memory. Once he has been introduced to someone, he never forgets their names and he remembers the strangest details. It usually weirds people out, but Gramps says he's harmless."

"Morning, Mr. Dorian. This is my husband, Chris." Carrie still loved saying that, "My last name is Aaronson now." The disheveled man did not tell them congratulations as others had; he simply turned his attention to Chris.

"Chris Aaronson, husband of Carrie Lynn Aaronson. Yes. I've heard of you. Wes says you were with the Western Front. He says you should go and not come back to these here parts." Carrie gasped and Chris bristled. Dorian did not pause at their reactions. "One, two, three names, four if you count the old one, Carrie." His hands fluttered, creating shapes, first a triangle, then a square and finally a ball-shape. He looked down at the ground for a long moment.

"Sixteen, seventeen, eighteen, nineteen, twenty. Grandma always said don't let more than twenty seconds go by without making polite conversation." He looked up and smiled pleasantly. "The weather is nice today, don't you think?"

Chris didn't know how to react, but Carrie recovered quickly. "Lovely weather, Mr. Dorian. The sun is shining. And it feels warmer than yesterday. We're here to see if we can find the parts to make a windmill."

Jim Dorian's eyes lit up. "A windmill! Yes. For water or for electricity. A majority of windmills have four sails, but really six or eight is best."

He began walking rapidly into the heart of the junkyard, "Come this way, twenty-three paces straight, then five paces to the left."

He strode away, counting out loud and snapping his fingers at each step. They quickly followed him, exchanging glances, with Carrie shrugging her shoulders in an "I told you" fashion. Dorian was one odd bird.

An hour later, they had filled the back of the buggy with metal sheets, poles, struts, and what seemed like a million little components. "What can I give in trade, Mr. Dorian?" Carrie asked.

Dorian's eyes fell on her gleaming emerald and diamond wedding ring. "Five stones. One, two, three, four round ones, one square, that makes five. Em-er-ald and di-a-mond. Pretty."

Carrie smiled. "It is very pretty, Mr. Dorian, but I can't offer it in trade. It was a gift and it's my wedding ring."

She said it gently but firmly, making sure there was no misunderstanding. His face was blank in response.

"Perhaps some food to trade, Mr. Dorian? Eggs through until spring? Two of our goats will be birthing soon. Would you like a goat in the spring?"

Dorian looked thin and a tad malnourished. His hair was dull, and his eyes were sunken with dark circles underneath. Not particularly surprising.

His grandmother had died five years ago. In good times, everyone pitched in to help keep him fed. In a small town like this, everyone knew everyone else's business. But it was winter now, and the good times were certainly absent. Most people were struggling to make it through the winter. The residents of Tiptonville weren't bad people, maybe a tad neglectful, but Dorian never asked for help.

Nelda Dorian, Jim's grandmother, had raised him since his parents died in a car accident when he wasn't yet out of diapers. A hard-working, proud woman, she had instilled in him the basics – politeness, hard work, and an independent spirit despite his disabilities.

Jim Dorian smiled in his peculiar way, one side of his mouth curled up, while the other stayed level. He always looked decidedly lopsided. "Pickled eggs, Miz Carrie?"

Carrie grinned back. "Mr. Dorian, I will bring you all the pickled eggs you care to eat!" She was determined to add a few jars of green beans and some fresh potatoes. They still had plenty of the russets left.

A haunch of meat would do him good as well. She promised that one of them would bring it to him next visit into town, which was sure to be soon, what with Liza liking to visit Carl. A sharp cramping in her abdomen halted her step up into the buggy.

Chris had been helping her up when she doubled over in agony.

"What is it? What's wrong?" he asked, panicked. In the past few months, their relationship had changed as her pregnancy progressed. Despite the fact she was barely showing, their lovemaking, once so frequent (as evidenced by the child growing inside of her) had vanished. He insisted that he was just too tired and treated her like a fragile little China doll, handling all of the chores that required any lifting and bending. All of the chores, really, except for feeding the chickens and goats which Joseph was able to do.

"I'm fine, I...ooh!" It felt like she was being stabbed. "Let's just get Liza and Joseph and get out of here, okay? Help me up in the buggy and we'll get on our way." But before he could even help her up, trouble arrived.

"What the hell are you doing here, soldier?" Chris felt his anger rise. It was, of course, Wes Perkins. He stood there, his hands on Ichabod's reins. The horse shifted slightly, uneasy. Even Ichabod could tell Wes was bad news.

"Good day, Wesley Perkins," Dorian piped up, "Two names, no middle name, no middle name, none. Went to Iraq in oh-three and returned in oh-five. Two years gone; eleven years returned. Eleven is a good number. Very good, will be twelve soon." He nodded, examining the ground. "They're gonna make a windmill. Electricity, water, windmill, yes. Six blades, not four."

Wes took this in. He might have been a prick to everyone else, but for some reason, he was always kind to Jim Dorian.

"That's good Jim, very good." He handed the man a small sack. "I brought you some of that food I promised you last week. Why don't you go put it away?"

Dorian nodded to Carrie and Chris and walked away, peering into the bag and muttering as he did. He climbed the steps to the front door of his decrepit double-wide and went inside without another word.

Wes's eyes narrowed. "Building you a communications array there, soldier?"

Carrie gripped her husband's shoulder, trying not to scream as another horrible twisting pain hit.

"Give me a hand into the buggy, Chris." He helped her up, keeping eye contact with Wes the entire time.

Chris sounded calmer than he felt. "I've told you. I'm a friend of the family, well more than that, now that Carrie and I are married. And you heard yourself what we need the parts for, so why don't you just back the hell off, Wes? What is your beef with me, exactly?"

That was all the challenge Wes needed. The man closed the space between them with one fluid stride. His face was inches away from Chris's.

His words were low and menacing. "I know a soldier when I see one. You've seen action. I know about that uniform you tried to burn and I am watching you, every day." His breath stank and he obviously didn't bathe often.

"Chris," Carrie tried to keep the fear and the pain out of her voice as another horrible, twisting pain hit. What was this? Could she be having contractions? "We need to go... now."

The men did not move or speak. It looked as if they were locked in a staring contest, daring the other to move first. It was Carrie's moan of pain that ended it. Chris looked up and realized how white she was. Her lips were thin and her entire body was hunched. He jumped up into the buggy, pulled hard on the reins and turned Ichabod and the buggy towards the Carters' house. He didn't bother to look back at Wes Perkins, who wisely didn't try to stop them. In the two blocks to the Carter's, Carrie's pain seemed to subside. When Chris pulled her close and asked her if she was okay, she nodded.

"I think I'm getting that stomach flu that's going around." She looked up at his concerned face and smiled, "I'm sure I'm fine."

She insisted on waiting in the buggy as Chris jumped down, made room for Liza and Joseph to sit in the back and everyone loaded up.

She said little on the drive home while Joseph and Liza chattered on and on about how Abigail was pretty sure she was pregnant. "She might be about two months along," Liza chattered, "So Little Christopher," she was sure Carrie and Chris were having a boy, "will have someone to play with."

Carrie didn't respond, just leaned in closer to Chris. He pulled the buggy to a stop directly at the steps of the farmhouse. The fact that Carrie had been so quiet scared him more than anything.

Liza jumped out, making a comment about valet service and turned to go inside. "Liza," Chris called to her, "Could you please have a look at Carrie? I'll be there as soon as I get Ichabod settled in." He helped

Carrie down from the buggy gently and smiled at her with concern. "Go lay down, I'll be there in a minute."

It was in the barn that he saw the blood. Why hadn't he noticed it before? He had to have been blind. It was bright red. A large circle of it spread on the quilt, drips of blood down the side of the buggy where he had helped Carrie down. How had he not seen it? He ran then, leaving the horse still hitched to the buggy. He ran full out, despite the sharp pain from his weak ankle. He ran through the open barn doors, across the wide yard and up the stairs, barely touching them as he barreled through the door.

Fenton had barely opened one eye, still half asleep in his favorite recliner, when Chris flew through the door. He passed Joseph, who was sitting at the counter in the kitchen sipping from a cup of hot chocolate left over from breakfast, "What in Hades is going on?"

Fenton bellowed as he stood up, wincing visibly as he put his weight on his bad leg. Chris did not answer. He was too busy flinging open the door as Carrie began to scream and Liza called out frantically for towels.

No one ate dinner that night and Ichabod spent most of the afternoon and evening standing in the barn without being unhitched from the buggy or fed.

At nearly ten o'clock that evening, Fenton and Joseph went out and cared for the horse, which had stood patiently waiting while tears and loss unfolded within the farmhouse walls. The old man moved slowly, as if he could feel the entire weight of the world on his shoulders.

"Gramps?"

"Yes, Joseph?"

"Will Carrie be okay?"

The little boy looked up at his grandfather. He didn't remember either of his parents. His father Isaac had died before he was born and his mother when he was still an infant. Carrie and Liza were his mothers, and Gramps and Chris were his dads. The fear of losing any of them had suddenly been made very real.

Fenton didn't bother to wipe away the tears that still fell all these hours later.

"Yes, Joseph, Carrie will be okay... in time. But she's awful sad right now."

"And the baby? Is the baby, okay?"

"No Joseph." The old man couldn't bear to say anything more. He sat down on the rough plank bench, pulled his grandson close, and cried.

Inside their bedroom, sheets changed and the small body wrapped, Carrie sobbed, her heart breaking. Amy Lynn Aaronson had lived for five brief minutes, each breath a struggle, before her chest had risen no more and her body had stilled and then cooled in their arms. She had been tiny, not a single hair on her head, her skin bright red.

Chris held his wife and cried with her long into the night.

Stones and Trailblazers

"Funny to think of a cave as home, but it was, for just that little while. Despite the drafts and the invading rodents, we healed there again. It seems that, up to that point, our lives had been a cycle of trauma and recovery. I think it was the tipping point, the path to something better. Where the next few weeks would take us would eventually be a place I have come to think of as home. Each step, from Clinton, to the cave, to the moment we stepped into that house in Belton...no matter how terrible some of those memories are... I think I would not be who I am now if not for the steps I took to get here."—David's Journal

Madge's passing had changed everything. The cave was different, less full of life. Jacob whined constantly, looking at each of them in turn as if he were searching for the old woman.

Two days later, Jess reluctantly asked David to help her cut her hair. There were no mirrors, other than a tiny handheld one. Without his help, it would have been by feel. It was a rough job, but her long, wavy hair turned into tight little curls which hid much of the unevenness. They then gathered all the black walnut shells and boiled them in water on the stove. After the water had cooled, Jess hunkered over the pot and dunked her cropped hair into it repeatedly, holding her hair in the water as long as possible.

The result, after her hair dried, was a mass of muddy brown curls, a marked difference from the long-haired blond she had been that morning. They both had stained fingers from the walnut shells. It turned their hands an odd shade of brown that did not go away for several weeks, no matter how many times they washed them.

They didn't discuss leaving, other than to begin making a pile on one side of the cave of things they wanted to take with them. The pile grew and shrank, then grew again as Jess and David tried to decide what was worth taking and what would be too much. They also experimented with expansions on their original backpacks, adding loops that could hold tools and Jess sewed the buckskins into cot lengths that could be rolled up and tied, then hooked onto their knapsacks.

Tina went out daily with Quincy by her side and picked the fresh greens that were just emerging... she brought back oxalis, wild violet, fresh new plantain, and handfuls of fiddlehead ferns. The greens were a welcome break from their stores of preserved meat and the last few packages of ramen noodles. The little dog acted as a guide and a hunter. Three times they returned with fresh rabbit as well as plenty of greens.

David had improved even further with the bow and arrow, whooping in excitement the first time Quincy pointed at a bird and he successfully brought it down. It was a scrawny pheasant, but Jess and Tina had both been excited to eat something other than squirrel or dried venison and encouraged him to continue trying.

Food on the trail would be scarce since it was still early in the year. Each of the packs included as much dried meat and fish as it could comfortably hold. The dog would help them catch food too, but that would only help if it was safe enough to build a fire and cook whatever she killed and brought back to them.

Jess wedged the beautiful leather book into her pack. She had read through the entries over and over the past few days, seeking the comfort of Madge's scribbled words. What she had read had brought tears to her eyes. The old woman had loved them so much, felt so thankful for their arrival, and Jess felt her loss keenly. She had become a mother to them all in the short time they were together. The other journals, mostly specifics around the work she was doing, were sealed inside a metal box and placed in the off-limits section of the cave. Jess added a note to the top of the stack before sealing the box. In the note, she explained who she was, how they had wintered with Madge in the cave, and their eventual destination.

Jess figured that anyone who knew where the cave was would be able to find the box and make their way to Belton and find her. She hoped it would be one of Madge's children and that she could meet them and someday share with them her special memories of their mother.

She kept one other notebook out and stuffed it in her jacket pocket. Madge had sketched many plants, some here at the cave, many not, and listed by each sketch the name and uses for each plant, along with notes on what part of the plant should be used. Madge had filled Jess's ears with more information than she could easily remember, but the little notebook helped with the tiniest of details.

She also had the names and last known contact information for Madge's family within the journal in her pack, for whatever good that would do her. How in the world would she find them when there wasn't mail service?

On the fifth day after Madge's death, they looked around and realized there was nothing left to pack. There were plenty of things, but nothing more they could fit comfortably in their bags or via the travois they had rigged to pull behind them. It was time to go. They ate breakfast, washing their meal down with bitter hot boiled chicory, and doused the fire.

Before the trees closed behind them, the little band stopped and looked at the cave opening, almost fully hidden unless you knew what to look for, and it felt like they were leaving home. They trekked down the trail to the rock cairn and thong tree, stood for a few moments, and then silently turned north and began to follow the waterline of the lake.

What little discussion they did have had come last night. Until they were given a reason to avoid them, they would try to find the nearest highway and begin the journey back to Belton that way. It would cut time off of their journey and kept the travelers near any remnants of civilization and possible food sources. It meant returning to Clinton, following Highway 7 into Harrisonville and then up 71 to Belton.

The air was cool and the sky clear. According to the pocket calendar they had kept in the cave, it was March 5th. This time last year, Jess had been planning her and Erin's escape from the camp.

"God willing and the creek don't rise. We'll be in Belton within two weeks. We'll head north until we meet up with YY and take it to Highway 7 'till it turns into Highway 71," she pointed on the map to David each step along the way. "If the fighting has died down, we might even hitch a ride and make it in days or even hours."

She glanced at his worried face. "Don't worry, we've got ammo and you are a great shot. You're our backup. Things get bad. They aren't going to expect a teenager with a baby and two little kids to haul off and start shooting."

His worried look turned into a smirk. "Who 'ya calling little?" He waved in his sister's direction, "She's the short one... I've grown two inches over the winter!" That earned him a laugh from the teenager. From the way his pants were riding high, he'd put on more inches the past summer as well. The kid was growing up fast.

They took pains to hide their weapons. Jess was right. What they had on their side was their youth and the element of surprise. It might just come in handy along the way. Madge had shown them a trail when they had first arrived and told them if they followed it, it would put them on a relatively straight course to Clinton. They followed this, thereby avoiding backtracking their path to the cave and avoiding the bodies to the north as well as the old farmhouse where Erin had died.

The first two days, they made good progress, winding their way back up to Route YY and then heading west back into Clinton. The town was deserted, and it looked as though there had been more fighting, as well as an extensive fire. It took some doing to find their old house. It looked as if there had been a fire.

Nothing was left, just blackened ruins and a flooded basement. Tina made a beeline for their parent's grave, plucked an armful of tulips and jonquils that poked out of the patchy grass of their old yard and laid it on the mound. The cross that David had set there had disappeared.

Jess saw that the children needed a little time. "We can camp here tonight. That shed where Jacob was born is still relatively intact." No one argued. One edge of the shed had been blackened by fire and a large tree limb had fallen and gouged a divot in the roof, but it looked better than camping out in the cold. The days were cool and the nights often dipped below freezing.

The previous night, they had curled up together for warmth. Jess on one side and David on the other, with Tina and Jacob sandwiched in between. The two on the outside had spent far too much of the night awake and shivering. The walls of the small shed would provide a break from the wind and contact with the cold earth.

David found a piece of limestone rock and scraped a cross and his parent's initials into it. Jess helped him pull it into position and, as had become their custom, they spent a few moments the next morning remembering who they had lost. She had never met them, but Jess knew David and Tina well, so she talked about how proud their parents would have been to see them and know they were doing well and learning and growing. Before moving on, they tried sifting through the blackened ruin of the house, but there was nothing left to salvage.

By noon they were on Route 7. The road was clear, but bodies in advanced stages of decay appeared at intervals in the ditches that ran parallel on each side. It made them all nervous, but none of these bodies were recent. They were dressed in an unfamiliar uniform. None of the group was willing to get close enough to the corpses to find out which army they were from. Quincy was their barometer. The dog was smart, more attentive than ever since they had set out, and she stuck close by their side at all times.

"Still think we should be using main roads?" David asked, in mid-afternoon, when the dog began to first whine, then growl deep in her throat. The day had begun sunny, but near noon the clouds had rolled in and the sky was gloomy and overcast. The wind had picked up, and they were walking into it, which made it harder. It was possible they could get snow. It was only March and snow this late in the season wasn't unheard of.

Quincy had begun to whine after they crossed over the South Grand River. They looked around, but nothing appeared out of place. Still, the little dog knew her stuff. Something was up.

"Let's get off the road and into that stand of trees over there." Jess pointed to a small patch of forest on the other side of a marshy section of land. It wasn't the best cover. The trees were still bare of leaves, but it was better than walking down the middle of the highway. They kept a sharp lookout, headed for the trees, and soaked their shoes walking through the marshy area. This was a problem, especially for Tina and David, who had barely usable shoes, having grown over the winter.

Their toes rested firmly against the ends of their shoes, straining against the fabric. The water was icy cold, and they were relieved to get out of the open as the wind continued to increase. Jess quickly began to realize the depth of the danger they were in. They did not have good shoes, there was still a strong possibility of snow and freezing weather, and they had no idea where to find shelter for the night. "What in the hell was I thinking, wanting to leave the cave so early?"

The small group plunged into the tree line, pushing on until the road was difficult to see. Quincy had stopped growling and was now only whining, as if she was picking up the scent of something familiar, but something that bothered her, nonetheless. The escape to the trees had only taken a couple of minutes and none of them were surprised to see several camouflage Army trucks motor down the now deserted road, full of soldiers and weapons. They were heading into Clinton, not out of it, so for now, the band was safe. If Quincy hadn't warned them, they would have never made it off the road and into hiding in time. Jess reached down and scratched behind the pup's ears with stiff, half-frozen fingers. "Good work, Quince. Now if you only knew how to find us some shelter for the night, we'd be set." The dog gave a little whine and licked Jess's fingers. Then she sprang away, nose to the ground, leading them west.

"It will take longer if we stick to the trees," David said as they followed the little dog, "But if we keep the road in sight, we'll have cover and some safety and still be following the main roads." Jess just nodded. It sounded like a good plan to her. An hour, perhaps far later, her stomach rumbled painfully. It had to be mid-afternoon by now and they hadn't stopped to eat any lunch. Tina was stumbling along listlessly to the rear. Even David looked worn out. Trekking through woods was far more difficult than the road.

Jacob sealed the deal by waking and crying fitfully. At nearly six months of age, he wasn't as impatient as he had been a few months ago. Then it had been a cycle of wake, scream for food, eliminate, scream to be changed, rinse and repeat. Now at least he gave her time to get settled, and would reach his arm up out of the sling to touch her face. He loved the necklace David had made for her and played with it for hours on end. She reached in, caressed his head, and put the disk of the pendant in his tiny hand. That would distract him for a while, but he would need to eat soon.

The sky was gray and ominous through the trees. It held an almost certain promise of freezing rain or even snow within the dark clouds. And although it was only mid-afternoon, the light was fading. David looked up at the sky as well, "We need to find shelter, Jess, shelter and food, and soon." As if to emphasize the point, Jacob whined again, kicking his legs against Jess's stomach in displeasure.

At that moment, Quincy, who had been heading west with her little nose to the ground, gave a short bark and dashed south, disappearing within the trees. "Squirrel? Rabbit?" Jess asked, looking in the direction that the little dog had gone. David shook his head and turned to follow. They could hear the dog give two sharp barks a few hundred feet away. Five minutes later, deep in the woods now, they found Quincy in a small clearing. The smell of wood smoke had made them nervous, but as they approached, they saw a small family and relaxed a little. There were four of them, a man and a woman and two small children, a boy and a girl.

Raiding Party

"*Give sorrow words. The grief that does not speak whispers the o'er-fraught heart, and bids it break. - Shakespeare*

It was mid-March and Chris had been working hard, preparing the beds for planting. The last frost date was a month or so away, not much different than it was in Chris's hometown, but there was much to do beforehand. He had climbed onto the roof of the barn and fixed the areas torn loose in a winter storm. It had, for a period, rendered one of the stalls unusable and they had moved Ichabod to a smaller stall until the hole could be mended. Chris had thrown himself into his work, stopping only for a bite of bread and cheese at lunch. These days he barely ate at all, and usually fell asleep early, holding Carrie close in his arms through the night.

A fog of grief had descended upon the Perdue farm. They had buried the baby as soon as Carrie was well enough to be carried to the small cemetery on the farm's southeast corner. The Perdue farm had been in the family for five generations and consequently it had its own private plot 100 yards due south of the original homestead.

Mrs. Jennings attended, along with the Carter-Owens family, and John Carter gently took the small coffin from Fenton. The old man looked as if he hadn't slept a wink in three days and his eyes were rimmed in red. Chris insisted on lifting Carrie, still weak and listless, and he refused all offers of help as he held his wife close and carried her to the family cemetery.

The plot was of decent size, perhaps twenty feet by thirty. Along the south fence were the Fenton's grandparents and parents. In the middle of the plot were the graves of his great-grandparents. There were also three small headstones next to his great-grandmother's headstone that were obviously those babies who had not survived to adulthood. Chris remembered Fenton mentioning that his grandfather had been the only child to survive, just as Fenton had been an only child, and Isaac after him.

On the north fence was Molly, with an open spot in the northwest corner for Fenton. Beside Molly's grave rested Isaac's. Isaac's wife Amy was the most recent addition. John had come early that morning to help dig the hole for the baby while Abigail made breakfast. She had given her son Carl a light push in Liza's direction and motioned for him to take her for a walk. In the small cemetery, Chris had pointed to where the other children's markers were and asked Fenton if it would be all right to bury her there. It seemed right somehow, that she should be close to other children, even if their little girl hadn't gotten a chance to be a child. The old man had just nodded and walked away, moving slow and looking as if every step, every breath was an agony.

The past few days had aged him.

Reverend Thomas, along with a small group of Tiptonville residents that Chris knew only in passing showed up by mid-morning and the funeral was subdued. Carrie made no sound, didn't cry at all, until the coffin was placed in the ground and the dirt began to be shoveled over it. She had insisted on standing as Reverend Thomas read the benediction and the Lord's Prayer and when they had begun to cover the tiny coffin she had collapsed on the ground, sobbing. Those who hadn't had tears in their eyes did at the sight of her sobbing, heartbroken, in Chris's arms.

In the weeks since, the cohesiveness of the family had been tested. Fenton had always insisted that the family gather for every meal. But Carrie stayed in bed and often refused to eat. She had grown gaunt and hollow-eyed. Liza was subdued, a stark contrast from her ebullient, energetic self, and she would disappear into the forest alone and walk to the old homestead or to the cemetery. Sometimes she would be gone for most of the day, slipping in only when the sun had set and the night shadows had stolen across the farm. Lunch as a family was nearly non-existent and breakfast and dinner were dismal, silent affairs.

The breaking point came at breakfast on a cool, crisp Sunday morning. Liza had slipped out before dawn and had not returned to make breakfast, a responsibility that she and Carrie shared, but one which she had shouldered entirely in recent weeks. Without his coffee, which was really a mix of chicory and coffee (heavy on the chicory), Fenton was not one to be trifled with. In fact, he was looking rather ticked off. Chris had been making the morning rounds of the livestock and had seen Liza slipping around the pond, heading towards the old homestead.

She'd taken the loss of the baby as hard as he and Carrie had. He suspected she felt responsible somehow, although he couldn't imagine how. Sometimes babies came early. If it was anyone's fault, it was his.

He shouldn't have gotten Carrie pregnant. She was too young to be having a baby. He remembered the 'family planning' classes in high school that had preached abstinence as their main theme. His teacher had explained that a woman's body wasn't fully developed until she is around twenty, and that carrying a child puts a lot of strain on any woman's body. She had even explained that teens had an increased chance of a premature birth and a host of other problems.

Dad had sat him down long before that class and explained to him in detail what sex meant. He had squirmed and wished he could shut off his ears. It is one thing to look at a pretty girl and let your imagination run wild. It is another to hear your parent remind you that sex is how you came into existence. The thought of his parents doing that still made him a bit nauseous, and that was an image he didn't need.

Michael Aaronson had laughed at the expression on his son's face and said, "Just think of it like this, son—every time you think of actually having sex, imagine that you will be making a baby with that girl. If you just 'sort of' like her, what's having a baby and having to raise a child for the next twenty years with her going to be like?"

Michael Aaronson had been pretty laid back. The only son of two hippies who had met and fell in love while attending college at UC Berkeley, he had spent the early years of his life in EastWind, an intentional community located in a remote area of Missouri.

He and his parents had left there and moved to Kansas City after an upheaval within the membership when he was twelve. His memories of the place had been rich, and he had shared many stories of growing up on the property—canoeing, exploring caves, and running through the fields and extensive gardens.

Fenton's bellow shook Chris from his reverie, "Where the Sam Hill is that girl?" He had been so lost in his thoughts that Fenton had called out twice before bellowing in frustration.

Chris snapped to attention, "Sir?"

Fenton frowned at him, looking irritated, "Stop callin' me that, boy."

"Yes, sir," Chris winced, "I mean... Gramps."

Fenton just rolled his eyes in exasperation and asked again, "Where's Liza?"

"I saw her heading around the pond a few minutes ago," Chris answered.

At that moment a scream came echoing from the trees. Both men reacted instantly, Chris dropped the bucket of water and began running through the open barn door. Fenton was right on his heels as he hung a sharp right and began to run along the path at the pond's edge. Some geese had nested for the evening by the pond edge and began to scatter as the men ran through them, honking loudly as they took to the air or waddled out of range flapping their wings in distress.

There was one more scream, which added wings to Chris's feet. Already Fenton was dropping behind, struggling to move his old bones faster.

Ahead of him a shot cracked off and Fenton bellowed and fell to the ground. Chris twisted in the air and threw himself to the ground as another shot came whistling by. It had been so close he had felt it zip by him in the air.

Here by the pond was a cover of sorts, the dead grass and weeds were still tall, undisturbed. He turned and crawled on his belly back to Fenton, trying to move the old man off of the clear path and into the weeds. He quickly examined Fenton's left shoulder, which now had a hole punched in it. He'd been lucky, a few more inches down and it would have hit his left lung, but it looked as if the projectile had passed straight through. He was bleeding and wheezing in pain. Holding on to Chris with his right hand he crawled into the brush as another bullet whizzed by overhead.

"You armed, son?" Fenton whispered behind clenched teeth; his shoulder was on fire.

"Yes sir, always." Chris had not forgotten the chaos of Belton. It had haunted him how easily the town had been taken; how easy it had been for the soldiers to round so many up. "I've got the .45, but just one clip. You?"

Fenton winced as Chris bumped his shoulder and pulled the gun out and into ready position, "I forgot mine. We're in a bad spot here and we got Carrie and Joseph in the house." His mind was spinning, working strategy.

Chris took the safety off and handed the .45 to Fenton. "I can crawl back, go 'round the barn and use the yard for cover and get back to the house and get more firepower. I'm just scared one of us will hit Liza if we shoot blind."

Fenton shook his head, "You need to get us some help. Get back to the barn, saddle the horse and ride to town."

"Sir, you're hurt. You go into shock and they've got Liza and an open shot at the house and our livestock with nothing to stop them." Chris knew Carrie and Joseph had heard the screams and shots. It was quiet out here, sound carried well. Right now, Carrie was probably arming herself to the teeth and keeping a close eye on Joseph. Another shot whizzed by and they could hear muted sounds of a struggle. Liza was fighting them tooth and nail, from the sound of it. But she was a slip of a thing compared to a full-grown man. There was no way she would be able to win a fight like that. He thought about Jess and burned inside.

What had it been like for her in that awful place? How long had she fought before being kicked and punched into submission? They had to get her back and defend the farm. If those raiders moved in, they would strip their stores bare, kill Chris, Fenton and Joseph, and then kill Carrie and Liza after violating them in terrible ways.

There had been months of silence since the raids in late fall. Were these men new to the area? Or were they the same ones, returned for more looting and murder?

"Send Joseph," The old man's voice was unsteady, probably shock.

"Send Joseph on Ichabod and get us some help. The Austins must be dead, 'cause that stand of trees backs up to their property, and we hadn't heard a peep all winter. Town is our only hope of getting extra firepower."

Time was of the essence. Chris knew Fenton would hold on as long as he could, but the man was no spring chicken and he was going into shock. Chris turned and began to crawl through the grass, moving as quickly as he could and ignoring the mass of goose crap that decorated the ground and oozed between his fingers. Several large ganders were still in the vicinity and they honked menacingly as he moved through.

He froze as one approached, its head low and wings spread, ready to attack. The shot that hit the gander was undoubtedly meant for him. With that shot, and the strangled squawk the goose gave out as it died, the rest of the flock rose into the air, honking and cartwheeling through the sky. Chris used the distraction to jump to his feet and race the final few yards to the shelter of the barn.

He could hear Fenton fire off one shot and a second as he raced to saddle Ichabod, the horse snorting and pawing the ground nervously. Chris figured it would be easier to ride out himself, and get help and get back here as quick as he could. He was so involved in getting Ichabod ready to go that he nearly jumped out of his shoes when a tiny hand tugged on his pant legs. "Jesus Christ on a stick!" Joseph jumped and cowered and Chris grabbed him and pulled him close, "Joseph, what are you doing out here?"

"I followed Gramps, and I was standin' there when Liza screamed," the boy looked scared and Chris realized Joseph thought he was in trouble. He hugged the boy.

"Joseph, you are going to get help for us. Can you do that for me, Joseph?" The boy nodded eagerly and Chris lifted him up to Ichabod as a third shot rang out from the pond and two shots sounded back.

"I'm going to send you out the back way. You stay down, keep close to the horse and go to the sentry towers. Tell them we need help right away. Can you do that, Joseph?"

The boy nodded again, looking scared and determined and Chris led the horse to the back end of the barn. The raiders would be watching the entrance and not expecting the barn had a back exit. He slapped Ichabod hard on the rump and the horse whinnied and bolted forward down the drive, Joseph flattened against the horse, past the house and into the distance. Chris dashed to the house.

It was a straight shot for him, just fifty feet and much of that obscured by the barn, and a line of fruit trees that lined the west edge of the garden. He flew up the steps, safe now from view and crashed into the front door. Seconds later, Carrie undid the bolt and pulled him inside, her delicate fingers running over him, checking him for bullet holes.

"Fenton's still out there. He's been hit and we need to get back to him." Chris's words tumbled out as he reached for the rifle Carrie had in her hand. He had to try to come up with a plan to get back to Fenton, rescue Liza, and stop the raiders in their tracks.

Carrie had already pulled every weapon she could find from the gun safe and other locations. She was half-dressed, just jeans pulled on under her pajama top and a windbreaker over that. Her hair was tangled, and she was barefoot. There hadn't been any more gunshots since he had run for the barn. Silence had fallen, except for the occasional outraged honk of the geese. Chris ran and peered out of one of the windows. He could just barely make out Fenton's boot sticking out of the tall weeds. "I've got to get out there. I sent Joseph for help and they should be here soon. You stay in the house."

"The hell I will! That's my Gramps and sister out there!" Carrie snarled as she loaded Fenton's prize shotgun, grabbed some extra shells and shoved them in her pockets. Her face was gaunt and there were circles under her eyes. But to Chris she looked more alive than she had in weeks. She headed for the door, turned and looked at him, "Well?"

"Shoes," he said pointing to her feet, "And we need Liza's med kit." Carrie glared at him, and ran down the hall to get the kit and shoes.

Chris listened carefully, peering out of the windows towards the stand of trees and trying desperately to see something, anything of the men who had been firing on the farm. Seconds later, Carrie re-appeared, shoes on her feet and the medical kit in one hand.

"I can't carry the kit and still shoot," she said, tossing it towards him. "And I'm the better shot, so, here you go."

It was true; she was dead accurate in her aim. It was a fact he had been made painfully aware of a few months back when the raids had been making everyone twitchy and Fenton had insisted that everyone except for Joseph improve their aim with a little target practice. Carrie had been a crack shot, and he'd been horribly jealous of the ease in which she handled everything from a revolver to shotgun.

His parents hadn't owned guns, and he was never trusted with one as a conscript. Carrie had better aim than him with her eyes blindfolded.

"Back of the garden, around the barn."

"Yeah, that's the way you need to go." She buckled a revolver on her holster. "I'm heading around to the north. I'll use the cornfield as cover and come in from that direction."

"Shit. At least wait for the militia to arrive!" Why oh why had they not had a plan in place for this?

"Get Gramps fixed up. Stop the bleeding and make sure he's okay." Chris started to object but the look on Carrie's face stopped him,

"Please Chris, help Gramps. I've got to get to Liza before they hurt her." She pulled him close and kissed him. "Please, Chris?" All objections melted in the face of her pained face.

As they exited the front door, each diving in opposite directions and running as fast as their legs could carry, there was silence except for their own feet running. Chris ran full out, behind the raised beds and cover of trees and to the edge of the barn. He peered around it, saw nothing and dropped to a crouch and ran the rest of the way, sliding to a stop on his belly next to Fenton who was still watching the tree line, his face chalk white and sweating. "I think they've taken off. I heard a truck start up, some ways off. That there engine don't sound too good, sounded rough." Fenton winced as Chris pushed a fold of thick gauze against the bleeding wound. "Damn that hurts!" He pushed at Chris, "Why the dickens you're worryin' over an old codger like me, I'll never know. Y'all need to be taking off after Liza and those men. I'll be fine."

Chris put his hand back against the wound earning a bark of pain from the old man. "Carrie's heading their way, armed to the teeth."

"What?! Why in the Sam Hill would you let her do that?"

Chris eyed him, his mouth tipping into a lopsided grin. "She's a Perdue, there wasn't any letting on my part. Besides, she's a better shot and even more stubborn than you. There wasn't any asking, there was only telling. She told me and that was that." He grabbed at the wound and the old man let out a sharp bark of pain. “Now if you would stop fighting me, I might be able to stop this bleeding!”

Behind them came the sound of horses. Behind the horses came the welcome sound of a truck. The truck screeched to a halt on the far side of the truck and Chris heard the door slam. Men on horseback were out of sight, but definitely there, he could hear the chuffing of the horses who'd just been ridden a half mile in a hot hurry.

“Fenton!” A voice called out, Chris waved his hand up out of the grass and sat up. He felt a flash of anger. Well, didn't it just figure it would be Wes Perkins come to the rescue? The man barely spared him a glance as he ran up at a crouch, keeping his eyes fixed in the direction of the old homestead.

“They've got Liza. I heard ‘em take off maybe three minutes ago.” The old man swayed dizzily as they pulled him to his feet. “Chris says Carrie's headin' round the other side so's don't you shoot her when she pops out of the cornfield. They ain't gotten much of a head start, so if you's think you can catch them in that rickety old truck,”

Wes cocked an eyebrow at the old man, unsure how to respond to his F150 Dodge Ram with reinforced steel and cattle bar on its front being referred to as rickety.

“You'd best take this young man here.” He waved a bloody finger at Chris, “He sure ain't any good at doctorin.'”

“On it.” Wes replied. He nodded brusquely at Chris, “Let's go, soldier.”

Two other men had arrived by now. One man covered the trees while the other put an arm around Fenton, turned him and slowly headed back towards the house. Wes spun on his heel, Chris close behind him and they sprinted towards the truck.

“We'll head south on Mooring Road and try to catch up to them.”

Wes started up the engine with a roar, put in gear and spun out of the gravel road.

“And then what?” Chris asked.

“What do you mean, and then what?” Wes sneered at him, “We shoot the bastards.”

"Yeah? Hey, I'm all for that except for one small detail. They've got Liza and how do we keep her out of the crossfire?"

"Anything's better than what those assholes will do to her."

"Damn it, Wes! We want her back alive! Why do you have to be such a..." Chris was cut short as Wes slammed on the brakes and Chris hit the dash hard enough to make his vision fill with stars.

"What do you care, soldier? Aren't them raiders your people?" Wes fingered the Bowie strapped to his leg, "Why do you give a shit about some little girl who you ain't even fucking? Or are you tapping that too?"

His lip curled and Chris could see he was begging for a chance to fight, it didn't really matter who he fought with.

"I'm not a soldier."

"Really?"

"They killed my family, raped and murdered my little sister, and when I wouldn't join them, I got to dig latrines and graves." Chris yelled at the man, "Now do we really need to have this discussion now? Or can we figure out a way to save Liza so I don't have to tell my wife and Fenton that I failed them too?"

Wes's lip curled up and his face held a strange mixture of smugness and approval. He unbuckled the leg holster, handed the Bowie and the strap to Chris and resumed driving. "You'll need that."

As he drove, he explained that when Joseph had ridden up to the sentry towers, Wes had been running down all the check-ins. "We've been having all the outliers check in monthly. Most, like you and the Perdues, show up in town at the Trade Mart and I tick you off our list. The Austins, over to the south of you, haven't been into town in over five weeks. I was just about to send Jeremy Black over thataways when little Joseph came riding in like the devil himself were after him. So that's where we're headin.'" He shook his head in grim satisfaction, "I knew you were caught up in that shit from the west, I just knew it."

"You don't know shit, Wes." Chris was still pissed. He strapped the Bowie on his leg.

"Yeah? Well, I know this. We'd be better waiting until after dark. They'll think they've made a clean break. It'll be an element of surprise on our side. That and the dark."

"No way. We got at most an hour before they..." Chris closed his eyes, Liza looked so much like Jess, there was no way he'd let that happen to her. "We have to get her away from those animals and do it now."

Wes sighed and shook his head, and turned onto Upper Wynnburg Road and then made another quick left, pulling off of pavement and heading up a bare rut of a road. It was nothing more than packed earth with grass and weeds sprouting up.

"I can take you in a ways, but, you'll have to go on foot for about a half mile. They'll hear the truck if I get any closer." He stared out at the road and saw faint tracks. "Shit. This is how they got in and got the slip on the Austin's, guaranteed." He stopped the truck.

"What are you thinking we should do?" Chris asked, his beef with Wes fading fast in the face of this shared enemy.

"I'm thinking we're screwed to be walking into this in daylight is what I'm thinking." Wes shrugged, "They didn't get what they wanted, which was your farm and all its food and livestock. They're probably already taking it out on her." He shook his head again. "Shit. Okay, let's think here. Jeremy will have secured the Perdue house and then followed through the woods behind Carrie. They definitely had to have taken the old access road. It runs up past the back of Perdue land and then heads northeast. I know the Wilkes family is fine, 'cause I saw Tommy two days ago, so they probably backtracked to the Austin's. The question is, are they in the new place or the old one?"

Chris was itching to get moving, but most of what Wes had just said was a mystery. "Map?"

Wes opened his door, grabbed a rifle from the rack and quietly closed the door. He looked around for a moment and grabbed a stick and began to trace in a patch of muddy soil. "Their old house is here, the new one is here, and then there's outbuilding, garage, outbuilding."

He drew and pointed. "Here's us and Carrie should come this way and be in position behind the new house. Now if Jeremy's caught up with her than we've got radio and can coordinate."

He checked his radio and there were a series of responses back and forth. In all, they had Carrie and Jeremy to the east, Chris and Wes coming in from the southwest, and two more men were on their way from town on horseback. Wes directed the men on horseback to head up the main drive to the house, which was further east on Upper Wynnburg.

"Now here is the north field, smack dab in between the old house and barn and the new one." He pointed with the stick at a stand of trees, "We stick to the trees and we'll have cover up until the last ten yards. I'm betting they are in the old place. Not everyone knows about it. It's been years since it was occupied."

After a bit of planning and an update from Jeremy when he caught up to Carrie they slowly closed in on the property. Chris and Wes approached the old Austin homestead from the south and Carrie and Jeremy approached the new farmhouse from the east. It was silent and there was no truck or men in sight. By the time they reached the old farmhouse, the smell hit them. There was definitely no one left alive in there. Wes double checked, pulled his shirt up over his nose, and went inside. A moment later he emerged, hard lines forming on his forehead, his brown eyes almost black with rage and pain.

Wes stopped outside of the old farmhouse and tried to calm his breathing. He spoke then, quietly, and Chris strained to hear his words, "They're all dead. It looks like they killed Lyle and the boys right away. They've been dead a while, maybe more than two weeks. But Katherine and Maddie, those bastards kept them alive for a long time." His voice caught, "It looks like a couple of days ago for Katherine and Maddie... well, maybe last night at most."

Chris's heart hurt in his chest. The raiders had been close, too close, and he and the Perdue's had never suspected, never thought to check, while an innocent family was slaughtered.

Wes pulled a rough hand over his eyes and Chris was sure he had seen moisture, even a tear run down the man's cheek. His view of Wes changed, altered, as he came to realize how deeply the older man cared for the residents of his tiny town. No wonder he had been such a dick, Wes had known how dangerous the Western Front was, and the thought of having even a deserter come moving in must have been disconcerting.

Wes looked up, focused on the new house in the distance, "Come on, we gotta meet up with the others." Ten tense minutes later, all parties converged in front of the Austin house.

Carrie looked pale, "The main house is empty. They must have killed everyone in the house, dragged them to the old place and been living in the main house for the past two weeks. There's blood everywhere in there." Indeed, Chris could see a long wide brown track leading from the front door onto the porch and down the steps.

Even Jeremy, a tough, greasy-haired man in his mid-30s looked sick, "Must have been at least five or six of them. The Austin's had two grown sons along with a teenage daughter. And I know Lyle Austin didn't go anywhere without at least a gun and a knife on him. It'd be hard for just one or two of them to get the jump on the rest."

Chris gripped Wes's arm, "You said something about the Wilkes being up that outer access road? Well, if the truck didn't head this way, then it could have headed back in that direction instead."

Wes turned without a word and ran for his truck. If the Wilkes family was still alive, they were fighting for their lives right now. A few minutes later, the entire group was careening along the rough access road, headed for the Wilkes farm.

A Tent for the Night

"I tried to talk Serena and Brad out of heading for Clinton. There was nothing left of the town, no supplies, no people. I had hoped they would come with us, more safety in numbers, but Brad seemed determined to return to his hometown. I warned him that we had seen troops moving that way and Serena got pale and worried, but she must have felt she owed him somehow for saving her from the camp. We parted ways the next day. She was pretty, a completely different person that the broken woman that came to town less than one year later."—Jess's Journal

"Hello!" Jess called out and the man tensed, then relaxed when he saw Jess with Jacob's tiny head peeking out from the wraps. They had a large tent, a fire, and several small pieces of meat roasting on sticks over the campfire. Probably rabbit, from the shape of them. Quincy energetically licked the youngest child's face, a boy who looked to be the same age as Tina and who was giggling in glee at the pup's attack. The girl beside him looked somber. She did not smile at the puppy. Jess figured she was about ten, maybe eleven years old.

"Hello to you!" the woman called. She looked young, a few years older than Jess perhaps, but certainly not old enough to be the mother of the two children. She stood up then, slowly, and Jess saw she was heavily pregnant. Then the young man stood and Jess stepped back quickly in alarm. He was wearing a Western Front uniform. David looked back behind him in terror, seeking an exit or quick escape in the woods behind them.

"Wait!" the young man spoke urgently. "It isn't what you think. I was forced to join them, and Serena here, well, we got out together, about four months ago." His arms were out at his sides. He stared apprehensively at the revolver that had appeared in Jess's hand without her even thinking about it. David and Tina were still as statues, ready to run.

"I'm Brad, Brad Osterman, I'm from Clinton." He put an arm around the woman. "This here is Serena, and she hails from Springfield. We found the boy, Max, about twenty miles south of here, just wandering in the road. The girl was in the camp, she don't talk, so we just made up a name. We call her Annie."

Annie stood there frozen, staring at Jess's gun. Her hair was a golden blond and her eyes were cornflower blue. She was a pretty girl, but Jess could see the look of deep, dark trauma in her eyes. Her breath caught in her throat as she replayed Brad's words. The girl was in the camp. It couldn't be. Surely, they wouldn't have had her in Tent 5, and she was so terribly young.

Silence followed. Quincy had stopped playing with the boy and moved closer to the young man, sniffing his outstretched hand and then licking it. Jess slowly lowered her gun. The dog trusted him, and Quincy was a good judge of character. If the pup thought they were okay, well then, they probably were. She hadn't been wrong yet. After all, she and Erin had been clothed in Western Front uniforms when they escaped and that didn't make them the enemy either.

Serena spoke then, "It looks like the weather is turning bad. We have some food we could share, and there's room in our tent if you need shelter." She was pretty, with blond hair and blue eyes. She smiled at Tina and David and gave Max a little push towards them. "Max, say hello to the little girl. What is your name, sweetie?"

The question jogged them out of their silence and the band began to talk at once, sharing names, setting down packs and pulling out dried meat and greens to share for dinner. Jacob once again made a loud, uncompromising demand for food and Jess adjusted layers and put him to her breast to nurse while Serena kept stealing glances. "How old is your baby, Jess?"

"Nearly six months now. He was born last August. His name is Jacob." She rubbed her son's head, petted his tiny button nose, avoiding Serena's steady gaze and the question that remained unspoken.

Serena rubbed her belly. "I think it's been about seven months now, maybe eight. I'm not totally sure." She leaned close so that no one else could hear, "Brad's not the daddy. Leastwise, I don't think he is. I sure wish he was. But he got me out of there. That's better than most. The bastard in charge, he has the women killed when they start to show."

Annie had moved away from them, and Serena pointed to her and leaned close to Jess. "She's twelve. What kind of monster would rape a twelve-year-old?"

Jess felt a cold chill. "Where was the camp when you escaped?"

Serena shivered. "Arkansas, near the Mississippi border. They were heading southeast, so we went northwest. We stole a truck, drove it as far as we could before the transmission gave out. Brad's mechanically inclined, but we just didn't have the parts to fix it. Highway 13 was taken out just north of Collins, so we took Route 54 west to Nevada. We holed up there for most of the bad part of the winter after the truck crapped out on us just outside of town. After that we followed the railroad 'til we hit Montrose. When we got there everything opened up onto fields then and, well, it seemed like a better idea to stick to some kind of cover." She shrugged, "Harder going in the woods, but we feel safer."

Jess switched Jacob to the other breast; he patted her free breast and gently tugged on her necklace. "My friend and I escaped right outside of Springfield a year ago," she winced as Jacob sucked harder, almost gnawing her boob; she wondered if he was teething. "She died a few months later. It happened last fall, just two day's walk east of here."

Serena's expression tensed. "Was she pregnant? Did she," she gulped and looked pale; "Did she die in childbirth?"

"No! Oh, no," Jess felt bad, obviously the woman was scared about giving birth without a doctor and a hospital, "Soldiers found us and I didn't get to her in time. They shot her." She realized it was the first time she had talked about Erin since a few days after the farmhouse, when she had told Madge their story. It was less painful this time, still a wound, but not as painful as those first few days.

"But you... I mean..." Serena looked uncomfortable, and looked down at her belly, "At least, well, you know what happened to me." She stole a glance at Brad, who was admiring David's compound bow and arrow a short distance away. "They weren't all bad. Brad came to see me often, and he got us both out of there when I told him I was pregnant." She shuddered, "That bastard Cooper, he..."

Jess interrupted. It felt like all of her blood had turned to ice, and "Did you say Cooper?"

"Yeah, Scott Cooper, I'll remember that sonofabitch's name till the day I die," Serena practically spat. "He raped me over and over the first night after I was taken. I could barely walk for most of a week. And little Lucy Abernathy, oh God, poor Lucy." Her body tensed. "Lucy was up on his roster the next night. He hurt her so bad she killed herself two days later." Tears welled up, "She was only fourteen, I mean shit, and I used to babysit her on Tuesday nights when her mom bowled in the league." Serena's hands were shaking. "I pray every day that this baby is Brad's. But I know it isn't. It's that bastard's, I'm sure of it." She looked up, gazed hard into Jess's eyes, "Y'think I'll be able to love it? Even if it is from him?"

A thousand memories flitted through her mind, but through the fog of pain and fear, Jess remembered the moment she had first held her son. The love she had felt, the strange and deep sense of healing. She stole a glance at Jacob, quietly nursing at her breast, his eyes locked on her necklace. His hair was jet black, but he had her eyes.

Jess's reply was simple and direct, "Yes."

Quincy's muffled bark disturbed their intense exchange. In her mouth she held a jackrabbit, the animal's long legs kicking futilely. "Damn! I like this dog!" was the only comment Brad made.

As the first flakes of snow began to fall, they had it skinned, gutted and roasting over the fire. A can of green beans was opened and passed around, along with a small bag of smoked venison and berries. Tina sat next to the boy, chattering away, the older girl Annie watching silently.

At their feet, Quincy gnawed contentedly on a handful of bones and the remains of a half-rotten squirrel she had dug up from somewhere. There wasn't much, but the meal took the edge off of everyone's hunger. The flakes began to swirl with intensity as dinner ended, and the light faded. They doused the fire to avoid any unwelcome notice and everyone piled into the tent. It was a tight fit, but the combined body heat soon made the tent toasty warm. When in doubt, sleep, and that is just what the group did, except for Jess.

The sounds of the others stilled and were replaced by relaxed, slow breathing, and the occasional soft snore from Tina, who had what sounded like the beginnings of a head cold. Jess lay awake on the hard ground, eyes wide open and staring into the dark.

Scott Cooper. Old Coop had said his son's name was Scott. But lots of people had that name, right? Cooper was a common name. It didn't mean that Old Coop's son was the same sonofabitch that had raped Serena, Erin, Jess and countless others. It could be anyone, right?

Jess's dad had once said that life was like a giant jigsaw and there were moments when, after trying to fit piece after piece together, two pieces slide together like butter and you know, for sure, that they are a perfect fit. "The pieces meld together, they become one, and you know that this is the way it was meant to be. This is it." He had said to her, "You'll know it, beyond a shadow of a doubt what the truth is, just by the way it feels."

Scott Cooper was Arno Cooper's son. He was also Jacob's father, and most likely, the father of Serena's unborn baby. She cupped her son's sleeping head in her hand. His hair was silky-smooth, and he smelled so damned good. She loved him so much. All that he was, all that he would grow up to be... would be of her and by her. His dark hair was the only suggestion of his father so far. Jess suspected Jacob would also be handsome, maybe have the same high cheekbones and dashing good looks. The devil himself couldn't be better looking than Scott Cooper. But she knew, deep in her heart, that was where the resemblance would end. Jacob would be good and kind, she would make sure of that. She would raise her son to be the antithesis of his father.

And what of Scott Cooper? The father of her son? The father of Serena's baby? She didn't love her son any less, but she swore to herself, on that night, that she would find him someday. She would find Scott Cooper. Maybe she'd even have to stand in line for the chance, but she would do her best to kill him. The thought made her smile. It was a good thing she was the only one awake, and that it was dark. The smile would have scared the shit out of the rest of the tent's inhabitants. And with that vow firmly in place, she allowed sleep to steal her away.

Hello and Goodbye

"We said our goodbyes, though I pleaded with them to change their minds. I thought of how they had sent soldiers in search of Erin and me. We hadn't even stolen a truck, and they had hunted us. We warned them, but they didn't listen, I really wish they had."—Jess's Journal

"Don't go to Clinton. There's nothing left there but bones and ash." Her voice faltered. She liked Serena a lot. The kids got along great, and even Brad was an okay guy. "Come with us to Belton. I know if my home is there, we could make a go of it. We have a little land; we're even set up for raising crops and small feed animals."

Serena looked interested, really interested, but Brad shook his head. "My family is here. They weren't in the camp, so I figure they kept their heads low. They'll be there. We'll be fine and my Ma will be awful excited about a grandbaby." He looked over at Serena and ran his hand down her back. "I hoping we have a boy. I want t'name him after my Gramps."

Jess sighed. She'd done her best; they weren't going to budge in their plans. She closed her eyes, willing away the certainty that these two would die. She wanted so much for things to go well for them. The cup of dandelion and chicory tea had gone cold. She emptied it onto the ground.

The snowstorm had been intense. During the night, it had dumped six inches onto the ground and then continued to snow heavily through the morning. David gathered wood, and they restarted the campfire so they could cook the two squirrels Quincy had managed to flush from their lairs. Because snow meant tracks, and tracks could mean problems for either party, they agreed to stay until it melted, which would probably be the next day considering how warm it had become after the snow stopped.

When Brad busied himself with gathering wood for the fire and enlisted the help of the kids, Jess took the opportunity to talk more with Serena. She shared more of her own experiences and begged Serena to change her mind and head towards Belton. "It's the opposite direction of those soldiers and any fighting."

Serena just shook her head. "You don't know that it's any better off than Clinton. You said yourself you haven't been there in over a year and a half. For all you know, the entire town could be occupied by the Western Front or in ruins." She grabbed Jess's hand. "Stay with us, we're stronger if we stay together, and I'm scared of being alone when the time comes to have my baby. You've been through it, and now you know all that herb stuff that you learned from the old Indian lady. Stay with us." She looked so desperate that Jess nearly said yes, but stopped short.

"I can't. I have to go home. I have to know if my parents are alive or dead." Jess hugged the woman to her. "You will be okay, you know. No matter what..." She took a deep breath, steeling herself for the words she had to say, "I think Jacob and your baby have the same father." She stared at the ground rather than meet Serena's shocked gaze. "I look at Jacob and I'm sure of it. From what you've said about the timing of yours, I think maybe it's the same way for you." Serena wrenched her hand from Jess's and started to turn away.

"Serena, wait, listen to me. I know this isn't something you want to hear right now, but... an old man told me something I didn't want to hear either, just a few weeks before Jacob was born. He said that Jacob was innocent, a child of God, and that he deserved my love. And he did, Serena, he did. I love him so much. I wanted him dead, I wanted to be dead rather than have him growing inside of me, but it all changed when he was born. I love him, completely, irrevocably, and I will until I die. It will be the same for you, Serena. No matter what, this baby is a part of you. Never forget that."

Tears were welling in Serena's eyes, "Oh Jess... I..." She searched for the words, as the tears slipped down her cheeks, took a deep breath and said bravely, "I'll remember what you said. And if things don't work out in Clinton, I'll tell Brad I want to head for Belton. I don't want our first hello to be a forever goodbye."

The next morning, bright and early, the two groups parted ways. Both Serena and Jess waved goodbye with tears in their eyes. Then one group turned and headed east towards an empty, burnt town while the other headed west and then north towards thc unknown.

Saving Grace

"*We achieve inner health only through forgiveness - the forgiveness not only of others but also of ourselves"—Joshua Liebman*

Grace Wilkes was looking forward to turning thirteen. Just three weeks more to the day. She secretly hoped for a surprise party, but she knew how unlikely that was. Just Mom and Dad and Tommy and Vic. Mom had promised she could have a sweet sixteen party in a few years and it seemed that was the best she could hope for.

She slipped outside the house with Danny, a still feisty twelve-year-old border collie and headed for the creek. Tommy was on her these days to stay close to the house and always within sight. Mom and Dad too, after hearing some whispered accounts of goings on recently. Tommy had come home several times sick and scared, and would say nothing to her, just go straight to Dad and tell him quietly about what he'd seen when out with the militia.

Two weeks ago, Mom had taken Grace aside and explained that sometimes bad men did things to girls, things she would understand when she was older. Grace knew what she was talking about immediately—on trips into town to the Trade Mart she had heard it from the other girls—rape, murder. She had walked carefully for days, spooking at the slightest sound, panicking if Danny ran too far from her. But everything was quiet. No one lurked in the woods, and her fears faded quickly.

She was just about to cross the outer road and see if the beavers were up and out of their den. She loved watching them and had even gotten Danny to stay silently by her side instead of barking and chasing after them. As she stepped out onto the road, she could hear a truck gunning its way through. It was running loud and rough.

As it came into view from around the bend, Danny began to bark. It was not his "who goes there" bark, but instead was loud and defensive. A ridge had formed along his back and his teeth were bared as he growled and barked furiously. Grace was surprised by his ferocity. The only one who came this way was Maddie Austin, or sometimes Thomas or James, come to visit her brothers. Maddie was two years older than Grace, but she was crazy for Tommy, even though he had nearly eight years on her. There had been a time when Maddie and Grace had been closer, but lately, with no one going to school in town any longer and things still being in such upheaval, it had been weeks since Maddie had visited or Grace had been allowed to visit the Austins.

The truck was slowing, and she tried to see inside the mud-streaked windows, wondering if James or Thomas had bought a fixer-upper. The truck stopped, its engine running loud and rough. Danny was in a complete frenzy by now, and Grace saw that there were two men inside the cab and two more in the back with a blond-haired girl. She was struggling when one of them, a dark-haired gorgeous looking one, backhanded her, sending her head thumping solidly against the truck bed. He looked up, took in Grace and Danny, the latter was still barking frantically, and smiled. It was a terrifying smile. She stood rooted in place as Danny's bark was cut short by the dark-haired man's knife.

He threw it almost casually, and it arced through the air, burying itself deep into Danny's chest. One of the men from the cab grabbed her, throwing her in the cab, sliding in after her and closing the door before she could even think of fighting. A knife at her throat and she shrank against the man holding her. He smelled bad. Danny was on the ground yelping and thrashing, a knife buried deep in his chest. Blood pooled from his fur.

"How many?" The man holding her asked.

"How many what?" she whispered, shaking so hard her teeth chattered. Danny had stopped making any noise. He jerked once more, then lay still.

"How many people at your house?" Riley gave her a shake to help her along.

"Just... just... my parents and my... my brothers." Grace faltered, too terrified to lie. The man squeezed one of her small breasts painfully tight. "My two brothers, but... but... Vic is just ten."

"Good girl." He nodded to the man in the back, "We can take them." At this, Eckhardt gunned the motor, and the truck started back down the Outer Access road, heading straight for the Wilkes farm.

It wasn't far to go. When they stopped a few yards from the house, all four men jumped out, pulling the half-conscious girl from the back, and Riley kept a tight and painful grip on Grace. There was no point in struggling. He was far too strong. Grace got a good look at the girl and realized it was Liza Perdue. She was the same age as Maddie Austin, but the two had never been close. Maddie was very much a girly girl and Liza was a tomboy, who hung out with the boys and read science fiction.

Liza's mouth was swollen and her nose was bleeding. On cue, she began to resist the good-lucking, dark-haired man holding her. He cuffed her again, pulled her close and whispered in her ear something that made her glance over at Grace and turn white as a ghost. Her resistance faded.

The group was mere feet away from the front door when it opened to the sight of Anthony Wilkes and a large shotgun in his hands. "You are going to put that down right now," the dark-haired man holding Liza said. He nodded to Riley, who put the knife back at Grace's throat. "He won't hesitate and you'll lose your little girl."

Anthony Wilkes didn't move, and Cooper barked, "Riley, slit that girl's throat if this stupid sonofabitch doesn't put down his shotgun in five seconds." He paused for one heartbeat. "One... Two... Three."

"Okay, okay, just don't hurt her." Anthony lowered his shotgun and placed it on the ground. At that very moment, a shot rang out from the south. None of them had noticed Tommy Wilkes peering around the barn. He had been milking the cows when he heard the truck approach. The gunshot entered Oliver Riley's right ear and blasted a chunk of bone and scalp into Scott Cooper's face, cutting him deep, and disrupting his hold on Liza. That first shot was followed quickly by a second that caught Derek Kimmel, standing directly behind Riley, square in his body mass, and dropped him to the hard-packed earth instantly.

Liza twisted away from Cooper and grabbed Grace's hand, pulling her away, towards the left. There was nowhere to take cover, no shelter of any kind. Eckhardt took aim and shot Anthony center mass, dropping him in the doorway. Inside the house, Grace could hear her mother scream.

Eckhardt turned towards the barn, firing off a shot randomly, and grabbing Cooper, who was bleeding profusely from a deep cut in the side of his face. Cooper also shot blindly in the direction of the barn.

Tommy ducked back into the barn. Liza and Grace ran then, full out back towards the woods that Grace had been walking in only moments ago. Behind them, Cooper and Eckhardt stumbled back to the truck, intent on retreating.

It was Karen Wilkes who fired the fatal shot into Eckhardt's back as he ran toward the truck. As Eckhardt slumped to the ground, a second shot grazed Cooper's side and neatly severed his right pinkie, effectively disarming him. He ran, started up the truck and whipped it around back the way they had come. A third shot shattered the back windshield, sending glass spraying in all directions. He gunned it and disappeared around the bend in the road.

Wes's F150 screamed with power down the rough and bumpy road. To the right, Chris could see flashing glimpses of Reelfoot Lake through the trees. Carrie was tucked in tight in the middle seat and Jeremy held on white-knuckled in the open back as they flew down the dirt and gravel road. They could hear gunfire ahead and to the right.

Sometimes, time can move so slowly. The next few minutes, time went from flashes of light and gunshots ringing in ears to a slow protracted growl. Chris would remember that moment for a long time afterwards.

He remembered seeing the battered old truck come around the corner, racing away from the Wilkes farm. He remembered turning and seeing the look on Wes's face as he struggled to turn the wheel in time. What stood out most for Chris, the thing that haunted him for nights afterward, was the sight of the face of the man driving toward them.

Despite the injuries and the blood, he knew him. He knew just who he was. In the half-second before impact, Chris Aaronson locked eyes with the man who had raped and killed his sister and brutalized countless other women. And then there was nothing but glass and noise and pain.

It would be days before he woke up. And it would be months before he could walk without excruciating pain. His left ankle, which had healed relatively well since last spring, broke again, along with his lower left leg. Several ribs had cracked, and he'd suffered a significant concussion. Wes and Carrie had sustained relatively small injuries as well, and poor Jeremy had broken both legs in the resulting crash. It had taken all the medical know-how that Liza could sum up to ensure that the man ever walked again.

It had taken nearly half an hour for Liza, aided by Tommy Wilkes and his grieving stepmother, Karen Wilkes, to reach the crash site on foot. By the time they had arrived, Scott Cooper had disappeared.

March had come and gone and the land was beginning to warm again. Already Carrie and Liza had been out preparing the raised garden beds for planting. Chris sat on the porch in a comfortable rocking chair, his leg wrapped in a splint, one of Fenton's walking sticks propped against the rocker. He jumped when Liza's voice sounded next to his ear.

"Wow, you were really lost in thought. I said your name twice!" She smiled at him. Her face had healed quickly, the bruises from the beating she had taken faded from purple to green to yellow, and then they were gone. She was still twitchy though and jumped at any sudden noise. She hadn't gone for any walks alone, either.

But Liza was tough, despite her youth, and she had only been punched and slapped. They hadn't had time for anything else. Chris had worried about that and finally asked Carrie to make sure. Somehow, the reassurance that there had not been any sexual violation of Liza or Grace made him feel a tiny bit better.

"You doing okay, Chris?" Liza's smile faltered a bit. She put on a brave front, but it was just that, a brave front. It had been a close call, and she had survived, but Cooper was still out there. That stuck in the Perdue's thoughts day after day.

Chris smiled back at his sister-in-law, "Yeah, I'm okay." He reached out and squeezed her hand. "When do I get to take this damn splint off?"

"Give it another week."

She turned to go and Chris held onto her hand. "Are you okay, Liza?" He'd heard her cry out in the night several times in the past few weeks.

Liza stopped, looked at him, and smiled. "Yeah. I'm going to go see Grace Wilkes on Friday. Carl's gonna come pick me up and drive me over there. Her mom's had a bad time of it, losing Mr. Wilkes like she did. I told her we'd help her and Tommy and Vic get the ground ready for planting. If we all stick together..."

Chris smiled, "We'll all be better off."

The sun was setting. Carrie and Joseph made their way from the barn, both armed. Carrie and Liza had spent several weeks with Joseph, making sure he understood gun safety and proper stance as well as accuracy. As for Cooper, if he was smart, he had gone far, far from here. The militia was still keeping a sharp eye out and had recruited double the members it had had prior to the raiding party. But in case Cooper decided to come back for a visit or to get revenge, the Perdues and the Aaronson's were ready for him.

Miles to the east, Scott Cooper walked. He was no longer handsome. The bone shards from Riley's skull had torn through his right cheek, shredding the skin. Then the impact from the collision had broken his nose and his jaw in two places. The fact that Cooper had survived the crash, ran away, and managed to get by with such injuries testified to his own dark will to live.

For now, Chris and Carrie, the Perdues and all of Tiptonville were safe.

Home

"My dad used to say, 'Jess, never underestimate the power of the mind to delude itself.' I never thought it could happen to me. I was tough and I was a survivor and all that. But really, that chick Pollyanna? She has nothing on me. I managed to delude myself for over a year. Maybe it kept me alive, maybe it gave me a purpose, but still, the truth, when I was finally faced with it, was devastating."—Jess's Journal

Thurman Banks watched the ragged group approach town. They came up Y, which was littered with burned out shells of homes. When the Western Front had torn through, the homes to the south had been obliterated. There were still one or two farms on the outskirts of town that were holdouts, but they were on their own, far too spread out for the Belton Militia to protect. Until Y intersected with Main Street, there was practically nothing and no one to sound the alarm. Thurman dialed in the zoom on the high-powered binoculars, Farley had insisted that all the police surveillance binoculars be assigned to militia members. They were mighty powerful. He'd been able to see the group clear as day for well over a mile and count their fingernails from a good half mile.

The tallest, a teenage girl with what looked to be a baby wrapped in a sling across her chest, looked somewhat familiar, but the two younger kids weren't ones he recognized. Damned if they didn't have some floppy-eared mutt leading the way. The dog trotted a yard ahead of the teenager, nose to the ground, ears cocked forward.

Belton wasn't a large town, but it wasn't that small either, and he couldn't see them well enough from the sights of the gun. They looked relatively harmless; certainly not any of those damned Western Front soldiers come to prey on the remains of his beloved town and home. He lowered the rifle, slowly slung it over his shoulders and stood up, stiff from sitting so long in one position. At least the weather was warm. Today was only the first day of April, but already the days were in the mid-70s. It was about time to start planting.

Since the invasion, those who were spared had formed an informal militia. They did what they could to watch the entry points to the small town and report on if they saw anything of interest coming their way. He pulled out a sheet of paper, scribbled on it a short message, and reached his hand out to the German Shepherd lying quietly at his feet.

Isa was at his side instantly, perfectly quiet, but her fur raised and stiff. These were strangers, but they were small, similar to the little ones who used to play in the nearby houses each day. Those children were all gone. Isa had smelled some of them, their fear scent, sometimes even the painful death scent, in the days back in the cold time, when they had been taken by the bad men. She missed the little ones. She sniffed the air, smelled the woman-girl and the tiny one cuddled against her, the sharp fun smell of a boy (they were the best for playing with), and a small girl-child beside him. The pup galloped in front of them and the sight of it drew a small territorial growl from the older dog's throat. Despite the distraction, her attention was still closely focused on her master. Isa knew her place, knew her part in the pack, and waited for orders from the old man she loved so much.

He spoke softly to her as he tucked the note into a small film canister that dangled from her collar. "Isa, go to Farley. Go!" The dog sprang forward, ran down the steep stairs along the side of the building and disappeared around the corner, heading west towards the old courthouse.

Thurman followed the dog to the stairs, moving far slower, joints creaking. The nights were still cold and his knees ached fiercely until midafternoon. He slowly moved down the stairs and off of the roof of the old grocery store. On street level, you could still see most of the sign, B—ks Grocers. Thurman had inherited the store from his father, bequeathed it to his son Mark and he guessed he owned it still, though it was bare to the bones now. The shelves were empty, had been half empty that fateful day when the Western Front had blown through. Now both windows were broken and nothing remained within to sell or steal—not even the shelves or cash register. He had washed the blood of his son from the walls and floor and buried him in the cemetery, next to his mother and Mark's wife Annette. Thurman thanked God and fate and all the rest each day since that his Mary had been gone and buried before that terrible day. It would have killed her to know her only son- and daughter-in-law were dead and her precious grandson missing and most likely lost to them as well.

He headed south towards the small group coming in. Farley would be along soon with backup if it was needed. Thurman doubted they were a threat, but Farley was mayor now, and he could make up his mind on that.

Jess was nervous, scared to death, actually. The endless miles they had walked, the dangers, the hunger, just so she could 'come home' suddenly seemed so ridiculous and foolhardy. How could she possibly know if Belton had been spared? What if her home was gone and enemy soldiers occupied the town? Serena's words echoed in her head and David and Tina both looked at her expectantly, even a little frightened. They too wondered quietly, what if this town was no better than the others they had traveled through?

She saw the old man approaching them and recognized him. Thurman Banks lived two blocks to the north of her parent's home. Old Thurman was Allen's grandfather, and he used to mow the lawn for granddad in the summer, then head down to Jess's house to see his buddy, Chris. That old Thurman was alive and here in Belton brought a whoosh of air back into her lungs. She smiled in relief. "Mr. Banks! Oh, Mr. Banks! Do you remember me? I'm Jess Aaronson, Michael and Julie's daughter."

"Jessie? My God, Jessica Aaronson," Thurman was amazed, none of those taken in the first wave had returned. He had written off the children and their parents as dead long ago.

"Where is Chris? Your parents?" He took hold of her and hugged her to him, and then pulled back, "Have you word of my grandson, Allen?"

All of Jess's hopes crashed and died in that moment. The past seventeen months had been filled with horror, struggle, and even success. My God, she was alive. So were David and Tina and little Jacob. The miracle of that had not escaped her notice. But all along, in the back of Jess's mind, she had clung to the belief that her mom and dad had made it through. They hadn't been in the camp, but then again, she had never seen Chris, although Allen told her he was there.

She didn't know when she had decided it, with such Pollyanna certainty, that Mom and Dad were still home in Belton. But she had.

And now it felt as if she had been shot in the chest.

"My parents aren't here? And Chris and Allen, they didn't make it back?" Her mind began to spin. She had been so sure, so absolutely sure, that Mom and Dad would be here, waiting for her. She had imagined their reunion over and over. Their joy at seeing her, the love they would show Jacob, and the surety that she would be safe again, for good, in their arms.

She had imagined, too, that Allen and Chris had made it out that night like Allen said they would. Surely, they had made it out. Guilt at not helping them, at not having a plan that included them and her and Erin together, it all exploded like fireworks in her head. Her legs felt like rubber and she slowly knelt down on the ground, her brain and heart spinning faster and faster. No Mom. No Dad. No Chris. Erin gone; her blood spilled in an abandoned farmhouse so far from here.

She remembered vomiting what little food she had in her stomach before the world turned to black, first at the edges and then all over. From far away, she could hear Tina scream her name and David yell for help as she slumped to the ground.

She was finally home, but those who had made it a home to return to were no longer here. Farley and several others arrived in time to see her pass out on the hard ground.

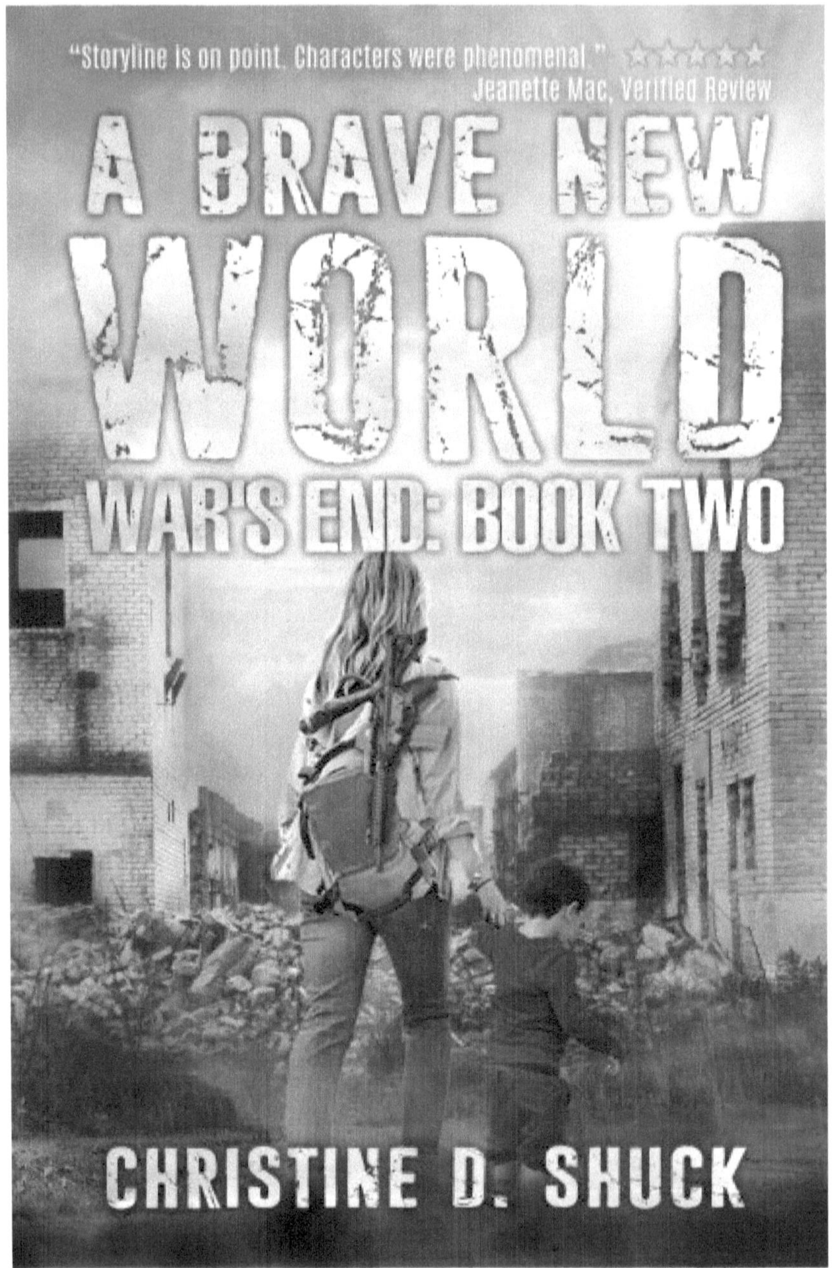
"Storyline is on point. Characters were phenomenal."
Jeanette Mac, Verified Review
A BRAVE NEW
WORLD
WAR'S END: BOOK TWO
CHRISTINE D. SHUCK

A Café on Main Street

"*We overstayed our welcome. We bullied, we pushed, we invaded... and when we were done, when the world had felt our presence in every corner of it, felt our hand on their backs, shoving our way into every aspect of their lives, faiths, even their very existence... we were hated. God, were we hated. In retrospect, I can feel no real surprise for what happened next. Our time had come. For our hypocrisy, for our crimes, we each paid such a terribly high price. The world we had known, the nation that our parents had been told to be proud of, a place of fast food and 'freedom fries', home of the consumer, center of capitalism, world leader, it all ceased to exist. It was a slow, painful end, an extended death rattle, as we slowly tore ourselves apart, and then allowed others to finish off what remained. What was left in the wreckage of the world that was? We were. And this is our story, my story, and the story of us all. We have survived. We have found a way to live on... in a world where ghosts haunt us and memories whisper in our ears. Life goes on, one day at a time, and by the skin of our teeth and the force of our will, we will continue. What else can we do?"—Jess's Journal*

"Drink it slow," an unfamiliar face in the crowd swam into focus.

The woman's face was prematurely aged, her brown hair streaked liberally with gray. Her brown eyes crinkled at the edges as she smiled at Jess. Jess blinked and accepted the steaming mug offered. She was sitting in a café, at a battered little table right across the street from Banks Grocers. It had been the last place she had stood before being ripped from Belton some seventeen months earlier. She couldn't see it right now; too many people were blocking the way, staring in through the window, staring at her. Some looked vaguely familiar, but most were strangers. The café, dimly lit and packed full of the mayor, Mr. Banks, and far too many others, was charged with excitement. Jess's fingers nervously traced the cracked Formica top of the table and tried to will away the rising anxiety. She hadn't seen this many people in a long time. God, they were close, so close; she could barely breathe.

Tina had scrambled under a table and buried her face in David's leg as he stood awkwardly. The little girl was shaking like a leaf. It had been a very long time since Tina had seen this many people in one place. David, his dark hair disheveled, a smudge of dirt on his cheek, wasn't doing much better. He kept attempting to move closer to Jess, seeking some amount of space between this overwhelming mass of strangers and him. Quincy stood at attention, glued to Jess's side, eyeing the crowd warily.

Another mug appeared before David, who sat down awkwardly, his sister wrapped around his leg, clinging to him with a tenacity that would rival that of a lamprey eel.

The same woman who had spoken to Jess lightly touched his shoulder. "Would the little girl like anything? I might have a packet of hot chocolate here somewhere."

David shook his head. "No thank you, ma'am. I'll just try to get her to drink out of my cup in a minute or two."

The woman nodded and smiled again before slipping back behind the counter, giving up the space to Todd Stevens, the militia leader, Mayor Farley, and old Mr. Banks, who had, after all, been the one to discover them in the first place.

Jacob mouthed a hard, dense biscuit.

Madge had shown Jess how to make them, pointing out their uses, saying, "They are good for traveling, since they never go bad, and when Mi'-da-in-ga begins teething, they will give him something to chew on." She had winked at Jess. "Believe me, Mi'-na, they are worth the trouble to make."

As with everything else she had taught them along the way, she had been right about this. The biscuits had provided countless boosts of energy, propelling Jess, David, and Tina down miles of road and kept Jacob from fussing. One tooth nub was finally poking through his little gums, with a second not far behind, and the edge of the sling was now dingy and encrusted with biscuit slime.

Mayor Farley and Mr. Banks had sat down in chairs around the small table. Jess thought that Mr. Banks looked much older than she remembered him. His hair was a shock of white and hadn't been cut in a while. The mayor, who had once been obese and shaped like a big round ball with skinny legs and possessing an overly large red nose, was now rather lanky, the extra skin hung in folds, but his nose was as red and large as ever. As she looked around the room, Jess couldn't see anyone who was overly large. The mayor spoke first.

"Now, you are, hmm, Angelica?"

Jess shook her head and Thurman Banks spoke up, "This here is Jessie, Michael and Julie's daughter." He said, correcting Mayor Farley's mistake, "You remember Julie baked bread, taught classes, and helped organize the farmer's market. Before the..." He looked distinctly uncomfortable, "Well... you know."

Jess could see by the slightly blank look on the mayor's face, who she still thought of as the president of Commerce Bank, where Mom and Dad had had all of their accounts, that he didn't remember her mother at all.

"Of course, Ang... err... Jessie," he smiled at her broadly, before turning his attention to David and Tina, "But who are these children? And this baby there?"

"This is my son, Jacob," Jess answered without any further explanation on that topic. "This is David and Tina Farnsworth. They are from Clinton."

"Your son?" The mayor blinked, looking scandalized. "And the father of the child?"

Jess felt a quiver of anger run through her. "He has none."

"I see." The mayor's voice definitely held a tone of disapproval now.

Mr. Banks, who understood far better than Mayor Farley, put a hand on Jess's thin shoulder. He could feel her bones sticking sharply through the fabric, and he suppressed a surge of fury at the mayor's lack of tact. Here was one of their lost children, who had gone through God knows what, returning to find only disappointment and misunderstanding.

"One of our own, everyone, Jessica and her family have traveled a long way to return home again." He said it loudly, so it would carry to the crowd outside, and he emphasized the words "family" and "home." He had long suspected the mayor was an officious, small-minded fool, and Farley was proving him right by leaps and bounds.

"What Jess and the kids need right now is food, a safe place to rest, and some time to settle in."

He ignored the mayor, who was trying to hush him and muttering something about the two younger kids not belonging.

He looked around at the crowd expectantly, "I think we can give them a good home-cooked meal while Todd goes and scouts out the Aaronson house to see what shape it's in."

Todd Stevens, who had been watching this whole exchange, nodded and stood up. "I'll go and do that right now. What's the address?"

Jess found herself stumped at such a simple request. Her address? When was the last time someone had asked for that? She closed her eyes at the memory of those tents, the group of men sorting the prisoners.

Name? Family?

But even they hadn't asked for an address. It seemed so immensely mundane, so normal, that her mind just went blank for several long seconds before memory kicked in. She rattled it off to him and he nodded, gave her a small encouraging smile, and slipped away through the crowd.

They could hear Sarah, the woman who had given Jess and David the steaming mugs of tea, talking in the kitchen of the small café, issuing directions to a young woman a year or two younger than Jess. Wonderful, mouth-watering smells began to waft their way and the kids' stomachs began to rumble painfully. Jess was so grateful for old Mr. Banks's intercession that she could barely speak. And then, of course, she remembered Allen and his visit to Tent Five, the first and last time she had ever seen him since she had left Belton.

She turned to the old man, leaning close so that the others could not hear, and said, "About Allen, Mr. Banks."

He set a large, callused hand over hers and shook his grizzled head, "Not now, Jessie. Later. You tell me later, all right?"

He could see from the look on her face that it was unlikely his grandson would ever return home. Despite wanting to know, even if the details hurt, he couldn't bear it in front of such a large crowd. Better to keep his grief close and to care for the living. The girl had obviously been through terrible trauma. And from the wary look on the boy's face, he and his sister had as well.

"Right now, we need to get you all fed, and a place set up to sleep for the night. I'm assuming you all want to stay together?" Jess and David nodded.

"Okay, I'll see what I can do."

Farley, who had been quiet far too long, felt the need to intercede.

"Now Ang... I mean Jessica, where exactly have you been all this time? In Clinton?"

"No sir, Clinton is in ruins, although there continues to be a lot of fighting and different troops moving through there," Jess answered. "I was held by the Western Front until a year ago. I escaped with Erin McGowen, discovered David and Tina in Clinton, where Jacob was born, and we over-wintered in a cave near Truman Lake before heading back through Clinton and up Highway 71."

"A cave? You lived in a cave?" The mayor looked incredulous.

He would have said more, but at that moment, the food arrived. Two large plates were set in front of Jess and David. There were eggs, thick slices of homemade bread with butter and a dollop of homemade jam, and slices of bacon still sizzling.

Jess winced as her empty stomach rolled ominously, reminding her of how she had just been sick not an hour before, and also that she hadn't had such rich food in a long while. Sarah Turner stood near her, her brown eyes soft and kind.

"Is the food too much for you, dear? Do you need something simpler?" David had already inhaled nearly half of the plate before remembering to offer a slice of bacon to his sister, who had folded herself neatly under his chair.

"I, um," Jess didn't want to be rude, but she felt exhausted. From hunger, from stress, and from the fear that her stomach would not be able to hold down anything she put into it right now.

Sarah patted Jess on the shoulder. "Don't you worry, honey. I'll scrounge up some oatmeal for you that should settle your stomach."

She bustled off and Jess slid her plate toward David and Tina. The offer of a slice of bacon had been enough to lure the little girl from under her brother's chair and a grubby set of fingers snatched at a piece of the toast while David eagerly cut into the eggs. Quincy whined once, licking Jess's fingers, and she offered the dog a piece of her bacon.

Quincy pulled it gently from her fingers and gratefully swallowed the delectable meat, staring at her mistress with a hopeful look, hoping for more. She wasn't disappointed. David slipped a triangle of toast under the table to the hungry hound.

Farley looked even more disapproving. Jess was surprised this was even possible.

"Dogs use up limited resources."

Her spine straightened and Jess stared the mayor square in the eye and said, "Quincy hunts for her own meals. Squirrels, rodents, sometimes a bird." She broke a piece of bacon in half and handed it to her dog, "She's helped feed us and she's protected us too."

Mr. Banks interceded again; he was sitting nearest to the dog, "Sounds like a fine hound, well worth keeping."

The corners of Mayor Farley's mouth turned down, but he said nothing. After all, he thought, if the girl was fool enough to get herself knocked up, and take on more mouths to feed along her journey home, there really wasn't much point in talking sense to her. Was there?

A bowl of oatmeal was set down in front of Jess and Mr. Banks introduced Sarah to Jess.

"Jessie, this here is Sarah Turner, one of our newest residents. She hails from back east, here with her two young 'uns for goin' on a year now. They were caught in a tussle between the Western Front and the Washington Guard; barely made it out of St. Louis. And Sarah makes the best lemon meringue pie I've had since my wife passed on. God rest her soul."

Sarah beamed with pride. "Not that we see many lemons these days, but I do manage to make a few each time we see a trader come from the Southern routes." She turned her warm brown eyes on Jess, who had managed a bite of the oatmeal. "Is that better, dear?"

Jess swallowed, her stomach settling some and said, "Yes ma'am, thank you."

"Call me Sarah." She reached out and petted the top of Jacob's head and then turned to look at David and Tina, both of whom had finished the food before them and were now running fingers along the plate to catch the last of the egg. Not a crumb had gone to waste.

"I would give you more, but that's a lot of food to eat after not eating much for so long. You take it easy, now." David nodded and thanked her.

Between bites of oatmeal, several in the crowd asked Jess questions about missing friends and loved ones. She shook her head no too many times to count. No, there was no one else she remembered seeing. Only Allen and Erin, but Erin and her family were dead, and she wasn't going to speak of Allen publicly. That would wait for a private moment with Mr. Banks. He deserved to know what little she knew—but in private, away from all of these eyes and questions. Jess found herself wondering if coming here was a good idea. No Mom, no Dad, no Chris. And the way that stuffed shirt, that bank president turned mayor, Jonathan Farley, kept eyeing Jacob—it made her angry. As if she had asked to have a baby. As if she could have stopped it.

Jacob began to fuss then, turning and nuzzling her shirt, picking up on her emotions and wanting reassurance, wanting food. He was just a baby, innocent and sweet. As her body responded to his need, the milk rushing into her breasts, she was filled with love for him. Never mind how he had been conceived, or the dark thoughts she had had about him while pregnant, walking those long miles with Erin. He was hers, and she loved him deeply. And wasn't that as it should be?

Jacob pulled at her shirt, more insistent now, and Jess looked for an exit. She wasn't going to breastfeed here, near this officious stuffed shirt and dozens of prying eyes. Her eyes met those of Sarah, who had seen the baby nuzzle at Jess's shirt. Sarah slipped out from behind the counter and made a beeline for her.

"I think that Jess needs to rest a little, away from everyone," she said diplomatically, "after such a difficult morning. There is a couch in the back, dear. Why don't you and the baby go in there and relax for a few minutes?"

Jess nodded gratefully, stood up, and let Sarah lead the way, the crowd opening for them.

Mayor Farley looked decidedly out of sorts. He had been in the middle of pressing for details on Erin and wasn't satisfied with Jess's short answer that she had died outside of Clinton. Jess suppressed a wave of anger; he hadn't even remembered Erin either, only Erin's brother Toby, who had been an Eagle Scout and the valedictorian of his graduating class. The mayor looked as if he wanted to follow Jess out of the room. He was the type who wasn't used to being told "no"—and his recent elevation to mayor had made him even more pigheaded than normal. Sarah Turner had quelled him with a stern look as he began to stand up and follow, and Farley suppressed a desire to push her out of the way. She wasn't even from Belton. But at that moment, one of the townspeople had tugged on his sleeve and suggested he update the crowd outside. The mayor's attention was successfully diverted to one of his favorite tasks: speaking authoritatively to crowds.

The back room was obviously where Sarah and her family lived. There was a large living and sleeping area and a candle gave them a dim light. Jacob was fussing, pulling at Jess's shirt, insisting on being fed. Jess sat down on the couch, eased her shirt up, and allowed the hungry infant to latch on. He made satisfied little grunts as he greedily sucked.

"Thank you, Sarah," Jess said. "How did you know?"

Sarah just smiled, moving a small box with the letters SAP carved into it, and put it out of view.

"How did I know the crowd was too much, or that you needed to nurse? Women's intuition, I guess." She busied herself clearing a chair free of books before adding, "That Mayor Farley is a real butthead. Don't you worry one second about what he thinks. He treated me the same when I showed up with two kids and 'no man to care for me,' is how he put it." She rolled her eyes. "As I hear it, they let him be mayor just to shut him up. He was carrying on so about how we needed 'structure and organization in this time of chaos.'" She grimaced. "I think it was because he just wanted to be able to tell others what to do." She winked at Jess. "And get out of serving on regular patrol in the town militia, like the rest of us have to do. They even look to me to participate in the patrols, now that I've been here long enough to be trusted."

Jess smiled in return and relaxed for the first time since returning to her hometown. Belton was the same cozy little town she remembered, yet different. But then again, wasn't everything? Everything had changed. Jess wondered if her home still stood, and whether they could go there, right away, because she wasn't used to this, the people, the questions, the judgment. Not from everyone, obviously. Sarah was nice, and so was Mr. Banks. The militia leader, Todd Stevens, was young, maybe in his mid-20s, and he had seemed okay. Belton was organized, well-defended now, which was more than she could say for any of the other towns she had traveled near since this whole conflict began. Jess sighed. Perhaps, just perhaps, they were truly home and safe.

She closed her eyes and melted back into the couch, switched Jacob to the other breast, and barely cracked an eyelid open when Sarah led David and Tina in. They had been walking since daybreak, in the cold, with nothing but the hard biscuits to eat. But that wasn't what pushed Jess into an exhausted sleep. It was all the people, the questions, and the prying looks. There was that and the black disappointment—after all this, all the running, all the struggles—her dream of returning to her family, to her mom, Dad, and Chris; to learn they had never returned was overwhelming. If they weren't here, if they hadn't made it back by now, then they really were all gone. That was the last thought she had as she succumbed to sleep, and it would be the first thought she had when she woke up two hours later.

What Happens Now?

"Sitting there, with so many people surrounding me. Knowing Mom, Dad, and Chris weren't there. That after all this time, they must be dead and that I was alone now—just Jacob, David, and Tina. I wanted to stand up and walk away from it all. Start down another road, to search for a place that the war hadn't touched and where no one would look at me with suspicious eyes, or pity, or disgust. But I sat there, I ignored their stares, and I kept telling myself, 'Here is where I belong. Here is where I need to be.' It didn't get any easier, not for a long while, but, eventually, I think I accepted it, and was accepted, by those who counted most."—Jess's Journal

"Hey Jess," a hand shook her shoulder lightly, rousing her. Sarah's warm brown eyes were smiling down at hers. "Todd is back from checking out your house. He says it needs work, but you can stay in it tonight if you would like. Or we can find you lodgings at some of the nearby houses if you would prefer."

A soft dog tongue licked her fingers, and she could feel Quincy's soft, warm weight against one leg. Jess shook off the fog of sleep. "How long was I asleep?"

"A couple of hours," the reply came from David. He was standing nearby, his arms full of a large box filled with cans of food and a large bag of oatmeal. "It's mid-afternoon, and they rounded up a cart and horse to take us over there. How far is it, anyway?"

Jess sat up, Jacob squirming in his wrap against her, also waking up. "Oh, about a 25-minute walk. By horse? Something less; I'm not totally sure." She changed Jacob's diaper, which was a cloth diaper lined with moss and sweet grass. She gingerly pulled a sodden wad out of the diaper, then added more of the dry mix before pinning it on the wiggling, and now fully awake, baby.

Sarah watched her, one eyebrow raised. Jess smiled at Sarah's dubious expression. "It helps absorb, and means I need to wash the diaper itself less often." Sarah just shrugged and looked thoughtful. She knew of several families who might try this out; one of the women had been complaining non-stop that there were no disposables left in the town stores. Of course, she also deemed cloth diapers disgusting so Sarah wondered how badly she would react to the moss and sweet grass. Not well at all, to be sure. Others might be amenable, though. She made a mental note to ask Jess more about it later.

They headed out of the tiny little apartment behind the café and into the crowd. The faces were different, but it was just as packed and just as curious. Jess saw several familiar faces and nodded to them. One of them had been her teacher at Kentucky Trails Elementary when she was a kid. Jess could see how much was changed in Belton. Many of the buildings were gone, especially those that bordered along Highway 71, which ran through the middle of the town, the old side to the west and the new side of town on the east of the highway. The town had never been large by city standards. There were three sets of exit ramps and overpasses, another to the south, halfway to Peculiar, and all of them were now blown up and gone.

Todd explained this to them as they followed Y under one of the ruined overpasses and the horses plodded on through a maze of concrete rubble and twisted rebar. "What the troops didn't destroy, we did. And then we put up rows of concrete barriers at the borders—on 155th and Highway 58 exits. Any single vehicles can usually make it at a crawl, but a big unit would be stopped in their tracks. Well, at least, that's what we hope will happen." He changed the subject quickly, not wanting to get into the long and steady arguments in the militia headquarters of why that was such a bad idea, considering they didn't have the sheer numbers of militia fighters they would need to defend against another major incursion. "Looks like the herd's been moved over toward your neck of the woods."

A large herd of cattle, some 100 strong by the looks of it, were lounging on each side of 163rd Street. Two of the town militia members were standing near a tall fence that stretched in each direction, north and south, until the ends disappeared into the trees. The militia wasn't just in charge of town security, but also the cow herd, Todd said with a grin, "Which means we handle the distribution rights when it's butchering time." He went on to explain that the herd had ambled in from Raymore one day, walking just as nice as you please down Highway 58. They had investigated the tags, driven through Raymore and south to just outside Peculiar, and found devastation wherever they looked. "If anyone had survived the massacre, they were long gone," Todd explained.

The cattle herd, along with about two hundred goats and literally thousands of chickens, had been the only things untouched by the rampage. "They killed the farmer and took what they could scavenge," Todd told them, "But the fools missed the huge corral and chicken house behind a stand of trees. We had gotten hit hard here in Belton. Raymore had pretty much been wiped off the map. We would have starved that winter if it hadn't been for all of those animals."

They approached the fence and one of the militia men approached, nodding at Todd, and casting a long, curious glance at Jess and the kids, before noticing Sarah and her kids and nodding again. He undid the chain and opened a section of the fence for them to pass through. The horse and cart proceeded through, and Jess heard the gate close behind her. It made her a bit nervous. They were being locked in?

Todd noticed her discomfort. "It's only for the cattle, you understand. We have several sets of gates and fencing systems in the area. And you and the others can come and go as you wish with no restrictions." Jess just nodded, feeling the fears rise up. This wasn't Tent Five, she reminded herself. I have nothing to worry about here. This is my home.

The surrounding landscape was both recognizable and not. She saw ruin where houses used to be. Some were still standing and showed signs of fire, along with broken windows. Others were water-filled pits, the houses gone and only the rain-filled basements remained. The devastation was widespread.

"It wasn't just the troops," Todd said quietly. "There was also a bad storm last year. Straight-line winds; some even reported seeing a small funnel cloud. But the lightning was what did several of these houses in. And it was summer, as well, and it had been dry for weeks. The lightning started fires, which spread to several of the houses and, before we knew it, a good part of the neighborhood was on fire. Your street had some damage, but your house is fine."

And with that pronouncement, they turned the corner, and she was on her street. Most of the houses were gutted and empty. After a year on the road, she could usually tell in a glance which was occupied and which wasn't. It was as if they had a certain presence, one that declared that they existed for a purpose, that of sheltering a family within. Seeing the surrounding devastation left her full of dread, and Jess stared in dismay at the state of her family's home.

Todd had been kind enough to do a quick fix on the front door.

"It had been hanging by a thread, mostly off its hinges," he told her. "The fix won't last forever, but it means you can at least open and shut the door for now. Maybe we can find a new one for you; there's plenty of abandoned houses on the west side of town to choose from."

She thanked him and walked into the house. It felt like a familiar stranger—someone she had known well and then lost touch with. Most of the nice touches, her mother's touches, the things that had made the house feel like a home, were gone. What wasn't gone was covered in thick dust and cobwebs. No wonder Sarah had insisted on bringing a broom.

Jess and the kids began by knocking down all the spider webs and sweeping what they could of the floor into the living room, kitchen, and front entry. Several of the townsfolk, including Todd Stevens, Mr. Banks, and Sarah, helped clear the house enough for Jess and the kids to sleep in the living room and had promised more help in the morning. Jess and the kids had met Sarah's two children, Cody and Laura. Cody was two years younger than Jess and Laura was four years younger, just one year older than David. She was delighted with the baby and insisted on holding Jacob while Jess helped clear out trash and broken glass from the kitchen. The clearing of the living room and kitchen was a good start, and the rest would wait until morning.

Night had fallen, and the house was chilly. Unbelievably, the pot-bellied stove in the living room was still in place, although it looked as though scavengers had tried their best to move it. Deep grooves were cut into the wood floor where the stove had been dragged. One leg had actually broken through the floor and the scavengers and simply given up at this point. It took all of Mr. Banks's, Todd's, Sarah's, and Jess's strength combined to return it to its original position and then re-attach the vent. David and Jess had then built a fire in it and lit two candles.

The back sliding glass door in the kitchen was boarded up and, along with the newly fixed front door, provided safety from any larger marauding vermin. The windows of the house were intact for the most part, with only one window in the master bedroom shattered.

The others had left and Jess and her little family were now huddled together on the floor of the living room, which had been swept clear of broken glass, dirt, and blown-in leaves. Outside, the moon had risen in the sky. Just a crescent sliver, with a vast array of stars surrounding it—identical to the moon she remembered, and the home she had grown up in. They had eaten a small dinner—two cans of green beans and one of Vienna sausage—straight out of the cans, too tired to bother trying to heat them up.

Sarah had instructed them to just come and eat at her café in the morning, and Mayor Farley had grudgingly offered some of the community food stores to get them started. Other families had offered them a rotation of daily meals. No one had much, but many were willing to share what they could.

The house had been ransacked, and not just by the invading Western Front troops. Every canned good was gone, and so was most of the furniture, clothing, and what little jewelry Jess's mother Julie had owned. Jess didn't blame the townsfolk; after all, she had done the same while on the road. For that matter, so had David and Tina—you did what you had to do to survive.

Surprisingly, nearly all the books were still there. Jess's mom had collected books the way some women collect shoes. The classics, science fiction and fantasy, some biographies, and stacks of antique books she had scouted from antique stores or inherited from her grandparents. Considering that most people had used books as kindling in the hard times, Jess was amazed to see most of the books right where they had been left, undamaged and untouched.

Mice had definitely moved in, along with spiders, and what appeared to be a nest of birds. The floors and walls were filthy and Jess suspected that, if she had been able to better see the extent of the damage and filth her family's home had suffered in the gloom, she would have been unwilling to stay the night inside. Only Jacob was able to sleep. The rest were huddled close together, jumping at every creak and groan, straining to listen for the telltale scurry of vermin, and uneasy at the thought of one of the large spiders invading their bedding.

"What happens now?" David's voice asked, just as Jess had begun to slip into an uneasy sleep. She jumped, and Jacob whined quietly and sucked on his fist.

Jess didn't answer at first, and they both could hear the subtle scratching and scuttle of a mouse nearby. No doubt, it was distressed to find so many large predators within its comfortable and quiet home.

"We get some furniture, plant the garden, and..." Jess paused, stunned by the realization that her parents' home and extensive gardens were now hers and, more importantly, her responsibility to care for. "We... survive, I guess. And... make this place our home—a place for all of us."

A few moments passed, and Jess listened to Jacob's and Tina's steady, rhythmic breathing. David spoke again, his voice thick with exhaustion, "It's... nice, Jess. I'm glad me and Tina came with you. It feels... safe." And with that, his breathing deepened and Jess lay there for a few minutes before also succumbing to the oblivion of sleep. It had been a very long day.

I Can't Forget

"*Two persons love in one another the future good which they aid one another to unfold."—Margaret Fuller*

Jeremy Deeds levered his body to a standing position, biting down on a scream. The bones in both legs had been put back together as best as possible, with their limited resources and the knowledge of a sixteen-year-old girl. And the left one was almost as good as new, some three months after the crash. The right leg, however, had been in worse shape, broken in three different places. Liza Perdue had done what she could, but it seemed that the leg was never going to be what it was. He would never run again, never serve on the town militia, and probably never marry. What good was he? He could barely get around.

He wasn't sorry he had done it. Liza Perdue was alive and unharmed, and they had stopped the murdering bastards and saved another little girl from an unspeakable fate. But there were moments when he wondered how in the world, he could ever be any good for anyone anymore.

When he had been able to get up and move around, albeit painfully, he hadn't left the parsonage. The Methodist church was now home to a long-term care facility of sorts. Two elderly citizens of Tiptonville were there, along with Jeremy, mainly because none of them had a family to care for them. There were also the orphans, just a handful of them, but the kids sought him out regularly. And of course, there was Reverend Thomas, who was growing more forgetful by the day.

Jeremy had never been much of a religious man, although his parents had been regular attendees of the Church of Christ nearby at 515 Church Street. That tiny church's ruined, fire-blackened bricks still stood, but not much else. Something appealed to him about the Methodist church, however, especially after something that Reverend Thomas had said to him early on in Jeremy's recovery.

The ward Jeremy was in currently held eight hospital beds, but only three of them were filled. Mr. Keenan silently rocked back and forth. The most recent stroke had robbed him of his speech. His wife, their only child, and all three grandchildren had died in the invasion by the Western Front nearly eighteen months before.

Mr. Asner, lost to dementia, was convinced that Jeremy was his old college buddy Jake, who had apparently died during Operation Speedy Express in Vietnam. At times, Mr. Asner seemed to think it was the end of their training at boot camp, other times it was after Jake's funeral, and most of the time, he seemed stuck right in the middle of a firefight. It was a rare night when he didn't scream at least once, "Get down in the foxhole, Jake! Them goddamn dinks have got us surrounded!"

Reverend Thomas had come into the main sleeping area the third week after Jeremy arrived. By then, the pain was bearable, at least when he lay still in the bed and didn't shift the wrong way. He had asked the small group whether they had a preference for what part of the Bible he read from. Jeremy, in a fit of pique and self-pity, had said, "None, there isn't any point to religion anymore."

Reverend Thomas had just eyed Jeremy for a moment, then smiled. "Let me share something about religion, as you call it. You might appreciate this." He winked and then said, "The Catholics say, 'The Virgin Mary says...', and the Baptists say, 'The Bible says...', and the Methodists say, 'Well, it seems to me...'"

He paused for a moment, and said, "It seems to me that we should believe in others because God is within all of us. There are plenty of people left in this town that are worth believing in. So, perhaps, Mr. Deeds, that in and of itself may be the point of it all."

Jeremy had been surprised by the reverend's calm answer. No threats of hellfire and damnation or of "cavorting with the devil"—and later that week they had engaged in a long discussion on the merits of Elvis Presley and other late rock legends.

They saw each other daily, and soon Jeremy was seeking out the Reverend, or vice versa, for an animated discussion on history, religion, or philosophy. He was surprised to learn that Reverend Thomas had served in the Korean War, not as a man of the cloth, but as a soldier. Looking at the white-haired man in front of him, Jeremy had difficulty imagining Reverend Thomas at war, with a gun in his hand. That is until the old man's face lit up with grim excitement as he described the fierce fighting during Operation Killer in late February 1951. It gave Jeremy a new respect for this man, who had seen war and yet turned to far more peaceful pursuits in the years since.

When he looked back on those days of painful recuperation in the church's infirmary, Jeremy was unable to explain how or why he decided to become a minister. Perhaps it was his way of paying back the reverend's kindness and patience with him, or perhaps he just didn't like to leave stories unfinished. A month into Jeremy's convalescence, he had been listening to a familiar story, one of his mother's favorites, the Book of Esther. Reverend Thomas had just gotten to the part where Mordecai learns of the impending slaughter of all Jews in the land when the reverend's face went slack. Not wanting the reverend to feel embarrassed or to lose the thread of the story, he quickly spoke up, recounting how Mordecai gave a copy to Esther of the king's decree, dooming the Jews. A few minutes later, the reverend snapped out of it and picked up the tale when Haman was being warned by his wife and friends to stop pursuing the death of Mordecai. Later, Reverend Thomas thanked Jeremy for his timeliness.

"I was diagnosed back in 2014 with it, and it has slowly been getting worse. Especially since there's been no medication to be had these last few years," the old man explained. They struck an unspoken deal of sorts: the reverend would share his sermons with Jeremy and, if he faltered, Jeremy would intercede, first with the kids' Bible lessons and the stories the reverend shared with the men, and eventually with the weekly sermons. He learned to recognize other signs of the disease, which included confusion and mood swings, as the Alzheimer's began to increasingly affect the reverend's daily life.

Before the year was out, Jeremy was helping Reverend Thomas with all other factions of his work—coordinating weekly church meals, writing sermons, caring for the orphans and new patients in the infirmary, and visiting parishioners. It was this last duty that brought him back in contact with Grace Wilkes, who had withdrawn after her father's death and the attack on the Wilkes farm. A visit to her mother from Jeremy and Reverend Thomas had revealed her mother's concern.

"She won't go much farther than the back porch there," Karen Wilkes said, gesturing to the back of the house. Jeremy and the reverend could see Grace huddled on the bottom step, close to where they had buried her dog, Danny. The devoted old Border collie had died defending her against the raiders. "And she won't say nuthin' but maybe a whisper in response to a direct question if she can't find a way out of saying nothing at all." Karen's face twisted in pain, "I don't know if she thinks Danny and her Daddy dying was her fault or what, but she just won't talk at all nowadays. Barely eats; I just don't know what to do, Reverend."

Jeremy stared at the girl. She was small for her age, just thirteen, and small for her age. She looked eleven at the most. What she had escaped. He shook his head, remembering what Chris had told him about the man who had tried to take her and Liza. She was just a kid. He turned back to the reverend and Karen Wilkes, "Ma'am, we could use some help with the orphans, if you could spare Grace. We could come and get her a few days a week, get her out of the house and around others. The kids are all small, she'd be of use, and," he paused, staring back at her silent unmoving form on the steps, "maybe it would help her snap out of it."

Karen Wilkes had been leery at first, but as the weeks wore on and Grace continued with her silence and sadness, she had quietly arranged for her stepson Tommy to bring Grace with him on his way to serve militia duty. Tommy had come by the church, Grace following a distance behind, and handed a note to Jeremy. "Mom said to bring Grace here and give you this." Tommy had been eight when his mother died and barely nine when Anthony had remarried and Karen moved in, giving birth a year later to Grace and then Victor just three years after that. Tommy was quiet, but his face bore the strain of filling his father's shoes as he struggled to keep the Wilkes farm going with a grieving stepmother and two young half-siblings to care for.

The note was difficult to read, and Jeremy had been surprised it was given to him, although this would become a growing trend in the months to come as the residents of Tiptonville increasingly turned to Jeremy for the things they would normally have gone to Reverend Thomas for. The note from Karen, full of misspelling and obviously written with difficulty, asked Jeremy to please help Grace "wit her leters" and noted that Grace was very kind and "thoughtful" and would be good with the children. Essentially, it appeared that Karen wanted to send Grace into town every Monday, have her stay at the church with the orphans and then have Tommy pick her back up on Friday to spend the weekend at home.

Jeremy smiled at the girl and handed the note to Reverend Thomas. The reverend read it with difficulty, squinting at the scribbled words, then nodded and said, "Grace, there is a cot in the girls' dorm where you can stay during the week. Why don't you have the girls show you where it is at?" Once she had gone, the old man turned back to Jeremy, "They don't have much in the way of food right now, and Mrs. Wilkes is terrified that Cooper will come back while Tommy is out in the fields or off on militia duty. She would feel safer if we could watch over the girl during the week while Tommy is away."

"How did you get all that from that note?" Jeremy asked.

The old man smiled. "I didn't. I just took a good look around when we were there visiting last month. They don't have much in the way of livestock, and Anthony never was particularly successful at farming. Figure in the bad soil, and not enough crop rotation..."

The old man's eyes had a faraway look and his mouth turned down as he added, "And from the amount of locks on the inside of their front door—I'd say Karen Wilkes is terrified, morning and night. She's doing the right thing, sending the girl away during the week. Fear like that is a poison."

Tommy would prove to be a far better farmer than his father, and eventually the Wilkes farm would help subsidize the church's infirmary and orphanage through bushels of produce. Grace's schedule never changed though, and as the months passed, she would stay with Jeremy, Reverend Thomas, and whoever was gracing the infirmary or occupying the orphanage. She slowly began to speak again, shot up three inches during the space of a few months, filled out, and Jeremy thought she looked quite pretty.

One day, shortly after Reverend Thomas's Alzheimer's had taken a turn for the worse, she and Jeremy were working in the kitchen. He sat on a chair at a low table, chopping vegetables. His legs ached constantly, and sitting was somehow easier. Grace was stirring a huge stock pot of vegetable soup which would serve for two of the three meals they would be eating the next day.

They worked so often in silence that Jeremy was startled by Grace's voice in the gloom of the large commercial kitchen, "I can't forget."

"Forget what?"

"What happened that day—the day Daddy and my dog Danny died." She continued to stir the soup, took the remaining vegetables he had finished chopping, dumped them into the soup, and then turned the heat down to the lowest setting. The blue flames sputtered for a moment and then settled, lightly flickering. Grace peered at him through a mass of brown curls. "You saved me. I heard what that man would have done to me if you and Mr. Perkins and Chris hadn't come and stopped him."

"We did what was right, Grace. No one deserves that. I wish we had known sooner. I wish we could have saved the Austin's, saved your daddy, and your dog." Jeremy closed his eyes, wincing at the memory of Karen Wilkes cradling her husband, soaked in his blood and screaming.

Grace stared at his legs; the right one was still twisted and Liza had tried to convince him to let her re-break it and set it straighter. But Jeremy had had quite enough of being bed-bound and in pain and told her no. "You can't walk right anymore 'cause of me."

Jeremy shrugged, "It wasn't you that caused the accident."

Grace nodded, "Well, I'm gonna do what's right too. When I'm old enough, I'll marry you and take care of you. Mr. Perkins is way too old and Chris is already married. And besides," she said, as Jeremy gaped at her, "I think you are plenty good-looking." And, having spoken more than she normally would in an entire week, she pulled her apron off, walked over to where Jeremy was sitting, and gave him a chaste goodnight kiss on the cheek. Then she left the room.

Jeremy sat there in the room for long minutes, in shock, turning over in his head what she had said. She's fourteen, he reasoned, just a kid. She'll grow out of this. And with that thought a reassurance to him, a man of thirty years, nearly old enough to be her father and terrified of being labeled some pedophile child rapist, he felt better. After all, he was way too old for her. Jeremy hobbled off to bed.

There's No Place Like Home

I took the news hard. David said I didn't talk much for days and that when I did, a huge piece of me was simply 'not there.' But in the weeks that followed, well, I didn't have time for self-pity. There were repairs to be made, seeds to be planted, and skills to be bartered. I guess the sorrow played itself out and was drowned in the sheer amount of work to be done. I survived. Somehow, I even survived understanding that there would be no answers, no bodies to lie to rest. But it hurt so badly. It still does; their loss haunts me to this day. I guess it will forever."—Jess's Journal

It was a beautiful, warm spring day. It had rained last night, a big booming thunderstorm with wild winds and strong rain. By the time the sun rose in the morning, the clouds reduced to wisps, drifting high in the clear blue sky. There was no wind now, not even a real breeze, and the earth was already warming. Spring had come early again this year and summer was close on its heels. Already finished with their blooming, the jonquils and tulips were now making way for the iris. The grass was green and lush where it had been left to grow wild, and already rows of lettuce and other greens were ready for harvest. A few feet away, Tina was quietly picking strawberries. From the looks of it, more of them were ending up in her belly than in the basket.

Jess pushed into the rich, loamy soil with her bare hands, setting in the last of the bush beans she had been given and pulling at the opportunistic weeds. Beneath all the neglect, there was richness waiting. This soil was dark and loose in her hands and the weeds came out easily when pulled. So many years of love and attention would trump the year and a half of abandonment.

She thought of her mother, Julie, hair piled up on top of her head, streaks of gray flying in wisps, and a halo of stray hairs around her head. Her hands had dug deep in the dirt, just as Jess's hands did now. Those memories of her mother struck so often. Julie Aaronson lived on in this garden and it gave her daughter bittersweet memories of her each day. Here in the yard, shaping, digging, planting, and weeding—Julie had poured her heart and soul into the rich loam. She had done her best to make this tiny patch of suburbia into a green paradise, despite her lawn-loving neighbors.

Jess remembered as a child that their neighbors would look at the family's trellises, fruit and nut trees, and raised beds and shake their heads. They would mow their perfectly green, dandelion-free lawns, and talk among themselves, convinced that the Aaronson's were just a little on the odd side.

That had all changed after Black Monday. When times had gotten tough, they had changed their tune and the rest of the neighborhood had transformed. "Victory gardens" had once again become vogue and sprung up in every yard, even the unoccupied ones. Julie Aaronson had taught class after class to their neighbors, and to scores of city-dwellers from the surrounding metro, who were all eager to learn how to raise their own fruits and vegetables. She had readily passed on her knowledge of composting, companion planting, cooking with fresh herbs and more. Jess's dad, Michael, had even caught the teaching bug and enthusiastically educated scores on how to construct and install rain barrels, build raised beds, and even—Jess grinned at the memory of the students' faces—how to compost human feces in buckets of sawdust. That last one had been a real winner.

Jess's mom had even begun writing a book on gardening in Missouri. This had become difficult when the power started going out regularly. She had begun writing notes longhand, muttering over the order of the pages and asked Jess for help with sketching the different plants. That had all changed when the Western Front troops had marched through, cutting through the streets, ransacking, burning, and taking whatever and whoever, they wanted.

It seemed that most of their neighbors had not made it. The yards and the pitiful remnants of their victory gardens were now full of weeds and lay untended. Half of the houses on their block had burned to the ground and most of the others were badly damaged. Jess's home was one of only two still standing. It was eerily quiet. Jess kept listening for the sound of a mower, but there was not a sound to be heard but the birds and a distant hammering, probably old Mr. Banks. He had said his shed needed a new roof.

She reviewed the list of projects in her head. Fix the northeast corner of the roof, install more raised beds, repair chicken coop, till the south side of the house, and plant a crop of corn. Each morning, she and David sat at the table in the kitchen and discussed the priorities for the day. Tina was good at fetching and carrying small items. And she could watch Jacob in a pinch, but it was Jess and David who shouldered the burden of getting the mountain of tasks done.

The townspeople had helped them enormously. They had dipped into the community stores and brought them jars of food, most of it grown fresh and canned the year before. The town was in better shape than any others they had encountered along the way, as well as well-armed and organized. Jess and David were required to put in time with the local militia each week, patrolling the outskirts of the town for intruders, much as Thurman Banks had been doing the day they arrived. There was a schedule posted on Main Street, and everyone adhered to it faithfully. Their survival, individually and as a community, depended on it.

Visitors to Belton were rare, but a returning native of the town was rarer still. The ones taken by the troops that bleak day now eighteen months past had not come back. If they had, it had been soon after. Wounded, they had trickled in half-dead, starving. Most had died within days of their return. The town's inhabitants had kept themselves alive by retreating from the rest of the world. They let in the odd trader, watched them at all times, and sent them on their way quickly. Any strange soldier was drawn down on and shot if he did not leave immediately.

It also helped that Belton had nothing that anyone else might want... at least not visibly. Well hidden from sight, they had a plethora of cropland and seed, and several large herds of cattle. In this new world, they were well placed. This area of Missouri had a decent growing season and an excellent water supply, with fertile land and livestock. There was plenty to trade.

Part of the roof, damaged in a recent storm, was actively leaking. Farley, who had been a banker and was now mayor, told her that it would have to wait until the crops were in the ground before fixing it, "You can't depend on handouts," he admonished her, as if he were speaking to a child, "You will have to make sure and produce enough food for you and yours to eat."

Jess refrained from pointing out that they had been surviving on their own for well over a year, and rather well at that, without his patronizing advice. Still, she had to admit that he was right; the repairs to the house would have to wait until the means for survival were well in hand. Meanwhile, to minimize the damage any rainfall might do, they draped a tarp over the affected area and held it in place with landscaping stones.

Jess's dad, an avid homebrewer, had planted hop plants along the entire length of the south side of the house. Already they were beginning to emerge from the ground. By summer, they would wind their way up the trellis mounted to the walls of the house. The vines would reach all the way to the roof of the house and then, a few weeks later, the first of the hop flowers would emerge. Jess figured they would be a good item for trade to those interested in brewing beer. She would keep some, as according to Madge's notes, the flowers could be used for stimulating appetite and also as a sedative.

The rest of the south side of the property they tilled and planted with corn. When the corn emerged and grew to half a foot, Jess would plant beans and squash at the base of each stalk—an ancient method of companion planting known as the 'three sisters.' Madge had spoken of this planting method and Jess wanted to try it and see how successful it was. By fall, they should have a lot of canning to do.

The back yard of the house was fenced and Jess and the kids' planted peas and beans along the entire perimeter, stapling chicken wire to the base of the fence for the plants to climb on. She realized, as she walked through the front yard, that many of the plants her mother had grown in it were actually herbs or beneficial wild edibles. Here was wild carrot, yarrow, and lemon balm. Madge had filled a handwritten journal and Jess's head with all kinds of details about how these plants could be used. Some were good for eating, others eased nausea, relieved menstrual cramps, and still others had antibiotic or healing properties.

Jess knelt on the ground, loosening the dirt around an emerging plant. This one was foxglove, also known as digitalis, a powerful heart stimulant. It was dangerous in just about any quantity. Madge had said that even nibbling the leaves could kill you. Jess debated on whether to keep it. Everything in the gardens and yard had to have a purpose. Mainly, that purpose was to ensure the survival of her little family. She worried that Jacob would get into it. He would be walking in a few more months and she had to think of what would be safe or not. As she debated, Tina walked over, hands caked with mud.

"Whatcha doin'?"

"Trying to decide what to do with this plant."

The little girl knelt beside her. "Grandmother showed me this one. It's called 'digee'...uhm, digee-tall-us..."

"Digitalis?" Jess asked.

"Yeah, digitalis." The girl didn't miss a beat, "For the heart, don't eat it." She recited, proud that she was able to remember. At four, the little girl's memory was unbelievable; she could remember hundreds of plants, their names, and their uses.

Jess smiled, "That's right, Tina, very good!" She gave the little girl a hug. "But we don't need something like that; maybe I should just dig it up and get rid of it. I wouldn't want Jacob getting his hands on it and eating it."

Tina shook her head. Her mouth was streaked with red juice and tiny black dots of the strawberries she had eaten. Despite this, the basket was heaping with strawberries. "We should keep it, Jess, so's we can be doctors and takes care of people when they're sick. Put a fence 'round it, a metal one likes you got on the big fence."

Jess looked at the girl with confusion for a moment, until she realized Tina was referring to the chicken wire. Putting chicken wire around it made sense. She grabbed the rest of the roll and cut a piece that was big enough to prevent a short little baby hand from reaching the plant and placed it around the emerging plant.

"Good idea, sweetie." She looked over at the girl again and asked, "So, you want to be a doctor?"

Tina nodded solemnly. "I am gonna be a doctor. Then I can go and fix Mama and Daddy and Erin and Grandmother an they can live with us again." Jess winced in pain. She thought of her own parents. Then she hugged Tina close to her again. If the kid wanted to be a doctor, so be it; it sounded good to her.

Jacob gave a small squawk beneath his blanket. She had laid him between two layers of blanket next to her on the ground while he slept, but now he was awake and kicking. Tina gave a small crow of happiness; she loved holding Jacob, which made Jess a little nervous since she was so small and he was a hefty fifteen pounds or so now. "Can I hold him? Can I hold him?" she danced up and down with excitement.

She deflated like a popped balloon when Jess shook her head. "You're all muddy, kiddo." The girl's sad expression was hard to take, so Jess continued, "Later, sweetie, after you have washed up." She dusted off her hands, picked up her son, and cooed at him. He grinned back at her, his wide smile showing the one lone tooth in his mouth, and then he shoved his entire fist in to his mouth. "Come on Jacob, you and me and Tina need to fix some lunch and figure out what to plant next." The baby gurgled happily in response.

The rest of the front yard was slated to become an orchard. Already they had three trees, two peach, one apple, and Mr. Banks had come by a week earlier to tell her he had several three-foot apricot and apple saplings ready to transplant. "They'll take a while, Jess," the old man warned her, "A few years at least before you have any to harvest." He came by regularly, bringing them extra items that would help make their lives easier, even volunteering to help with the roof later when it was time for repairs.

"Yes, I remember my dad planting the peach trees." She looked up at them, noted the blooms, and hoped they would get a lot of peaches. "I'll look forward to getting those and planting them, Mr. Banks. What can I give you in trade?" This was a phrase she had learned quickly. The jars of food, supplies of any kind. She had learned that these things came with a price. It was normal practice to ask what another would want in trade for such things. She had come to understand that even the food they had been given when they first arrived must be paid back. It made sense—for the community to survive, they were given a helping hand—but they were expected to return the favor as soon as they were able.

Mr. Banks had looked uncomfortable when she asked the question. He'd looked at the ground with his big hands stuck in his overalls and shuffled his feet. After much hemming and hawing, he had managed to explain that he was lonely. His wife Mary had died right before the invasion, his son Mark had died on the day of the invasion, his daughter-in-law, Allen's mother Annette, was gone in the fire that had leveled his son's home, and his only grandchild, Allen, was long missing and his whereabouts were unknown.

He had everything he needed to survive, extra even, and knew that Jess and her little family had a struggle ahead of them. They struck up an arrangement of sorts where he would bring by what he could spare, and she would fix him dinner and let him spend time with her and the kids. "Someday I'll be gone, Jess, and if Allen never returns, well..." He left the rest of it unfinished, but she understood him. All that was his would be hers if his grandson didn't come home. And as much as she appreciated his offer, Jess fervently prayed for the umpteenth time that Chris and Allen had made it out and were holed up somewhere or heading home, even now.

As she walked to the north gate, she glanced at the saplings, six in all, and smiled. In a few years, they would help shade the east side of the house from the hot morning sun and begin to produce fruit. She was looking forward to making peach preserves and pie.

Through the north gate, she ran into David. He had turned twelve three weeks ago and announced he was a man now. His reasoning was simple. Jess was "mom" and matriarch, so he had to step up to the plate and be the patriarch. He had actually used those very words. Jess maintained a straight face, restraining from laughing with some effort.

Later, it hit her that the kid was right in some crazy sense of things. When other townspeople came by, they spoke to either Jess or David with a level of equality they were unused to from adults. Mayor Farley was the only one who treated them like children or felt free to lecture them.

The brutal fact of the matter was that everyone was too damned busy struggling to survive. It didn't matter how young or old you were, merely that you were competent. It was what you did, how you carried yourself, and what responsibilities you took on that dictated how others perceived you. In the years that would follow, through acne and hormonal surges, David would earn that level of respect of his neighbors and the townsfolk through his hard work and courage.

He had his arms full of old tools and was struggling with the side door to the garage. "Whatcha doin'?" Tina asked her big brother as she opened the door for him.

"Organizing the tools and getting them oiled. Mr. Banks said they'd last longer that way."

"We have oil?" Jess asked.

"Yeah, the stuff that turned rancid from the heat, that big tub of peanut oil." He dumped the tools onto the open floor of the garage and said, "Might as well use it for something."

"It's gonna stink."

"I can handle it."

Jess grinned. She had watched him throw himself at projects around the house since they had arrived, always with that dogged determination to show no weakness. She wondered where it was coming from. Why did he feel the need to prove himself? Was it because he was worried that some part of her still thought of him as a kid? It wasn't particularly fair of her; four and a half years' difference wasn't a very long time. They were both still children when measured to the standards of 'before.' She reminded herself again to not slip up and call him 'kid' again, like she had two days ago. He deserved better from her.

"I'm gonna fix some sandwiches, you want one?" she asked.

"Sure."

"Wash the oil off before you come in."

"Okay."

There was no electricity in the house. Come winter, they would be dependent on the old wood stove in the living room for heat. The rapidly approaching summer was of far more concern to Jess. No air conditioning during the hottest days meant stewing in muggy, 90 plus-degree heat. If the mild winter was any indication, the summer promised to be a scorcher.

Jess had mastered the art of nursing while in motion. Jacob nursed contentedly against her in a wrap while she cut slices of cheese off of a block Tina had fetched from the cool basement, laid them on thick slices of homemade bread and added a dollop of pickled vegetables that they had received from the community stores. David walked in, wiping his wet hands on his pants. He ladled a cup of lukewarm chicory from the pan on the stove into a cup. He sipped and screwed up his face, "Eh, wish we had some sugar."

"You'll have to suffer until this fall. Mr. Banks gave me some heirloom albino beet seed last week, and it's good for making sugar. So, you planted all the seeds?"

"Almost. Got the okra, squash, cucumbers, and more lettuce in. Oh, the collards, carrots, and bush beans too. I didn't figure you wanted me messing with the herbs or the pumpkin or pole beans, but everything else is done. We'll want to keep at least 2-3 plants from each crop to use for seeds next year. Maybe more, 'cause Mayor Farley says they're gonna start asking for contributions to the community seed bank in late summer." Jess handed him a sandwich, and he took a huge bite, then his next words were impossible to understand as he tried to talk around the food in his mouth.

Jess snapped, "Don't talk with your mouth full. Now... what did you just say?"

David rolled his eyes, chewed, and swallowed. "Geez, who died and appointed you Mom? I said that I want to go hunting. I'm hoping to get us a good-sized deer."

"Well, if you want good-sized, you're going to have to wait. They're all still skinny runts after winter. Besides, after planting, we need to get started on some of these repairs. Aaannd," she said loudly as David began to object, "I need you to figure out how to fix the chicken coop and build a chicken tractor. Mr. Banks said he's going to bring us by some pullets so we can restart our own flock."

"Baby chickens?" Tina's interested was piqued. She set her sandwich down and Jess noticed her hands were still crusted with dried mud. "Can I take care of them?"

"Not if you can't even remember to wash your hands before you eat," was Jess's brisk reply, "Go wash those hands right now!" She finished the last word with a howl, as Jacob bit into her breast with his new tooth. The baby was so startled by her shriek that he let go and began to wail. As Jess swore and yelled, Tina and David exchanged looks and quickly disappeared outside, sandwiches in hand. Quincy trotted past them, heading for a shady spot in the yard. Even the dog knew when to make herself scarce.

They sat outside, near the small pond, and finished their lunch. Little of the sizable yard had grass in it. Instead, there were planters rising from the ground, filled with small sprouts and dark, rich earth. All the beds had been weeded now, and the weeds piled in the far corner of the yard near the damaged chicken coop. This place felt good, well-defended, thanks to the town militia. For the first time since leaving the cave, David felt safe. It wasn't home yet, but it would be in time. The four of them would make this a home and defend it if necessary. As they sat, ate, rested, and daydreamed, the clouds began to gather in the west. Later that afternoon, a heavy, life-giving rain began to fall, wetting the newly turned soil and waking the seeds from their slumber.

That evening, miles to the south, the storm was fully engaged over the pitiful remains of a ghost town once known as Clinton. A mile outside of the ruined town, a woman screamed. Lightning flashed and rain dripped through the roof of a dilapidated house.

Serena screamed at the top of her lungs for anything that could stop the pain. As Brad held her hand, he could see the baby's head crown then disappear back up. Another push and scream and the head and shoulders appeared. He let go of Serena's hand and reached down to cradle the tiny head, holding the baby as it slid out and coughed. A sharp, thin wail issued from its mouth.

He looked past the umbilical cord. "It's a girl. Baby, we got ourselves a little girl!" He smiled through his disappointment. He'd wanted a boy, but a girl was fine. What bothered him most was the baby's jet-black hair and ice-blue eyes.

He wiped her down, cut the cord, wrapped the tiny baby in a clean blanket, and handed her to Serena, who looked both excited and exhausted. The lightning lit up the room, and the baby squawked in fear at the loud thunderclap. Serena took in the baby's features and met Brad's steady gaze. He smiled again, reached out, and stroked Serena's cheek. "She's beautiful. What should we name our baby?

Relief washed over her. "My mother's name was Rebecca. We'll call her Becka for short."

"Becka it is."

Brad held Serena close and kissed her hair. Serena Kearney was a beautiful woman. Her blond hair was a mess and he could see she'd closed her beautiful blue eyes in exhaustion. It had been a long labor, and she'd been so frightened. Brad eased away from her, stood up, and lit a lantern. They were safe here; he was sure of it. Max and Annie were asleep in one of the upstairs rooms. He headed for the dark hallway and pitch-black bathroom, lighting the way with the lantern. His reflection gave him a start. They'd been on the road and away from mirrors so much that he'd grown used to not having one. He ran his hand through his light brown hair, peered in the mirror at his eyes, which burned and felt bloodshot. Damn, it had been a long birthing. He'd read up on it, so he wouldn't be a complete fool, but it had been hard for both of them.

He stretched, relieved himself in the dry, filthy toilet, and thought about the baby. Becka... huh. He'd figured it wasn't his, but it hurt in some strange way seeing the truth. He'd paid at least some attention in science class back in high school. Serena was blond, his hair was light brown. His eyes were brown; Serena's was this gorgeous deep blue. You didn't make a black-haired, ice-blue-eyed baby with that combination. For just those few moments, he allowed his thoughts to turn dark.

That bastard. Raping women, always blond, always blue-eyed. Raping them over and over until he filled them full of his seed and then, when they showed, he killed them. What kind of monster does that? His hands curled into fists at the thought. He picked up the lantern and headed back to the living room where Serena and the baby lay sleeping.

For just a moment, he thought of killing the child. Cooper was far away, too far away, and too damned powerful to kill. But he could... Brad felt his fingers clenching into fists... a moment passed... then the thought of wrapping his hands around her and choking her to death made him shiver. What was he thinking? The tiny creature whined slightly in her sleep. Black hair and blue eyes. The child was beautiful, even freshly born and red and a little squashed-looking. Brad shook his head, cleared it of the dark thoughts and smiled. He imagined her smile, thought of how it would sound to hear her say Daddy and reached down and stroked her cheek. Her tiny head turned and rooted for his finger. He smiled.

"Hi Becka, I'm your Daddy." He could have sworn she smiled.

The Face of Evil

"There is no good and evil, there is only power ... and those too weak to seek it."—J.K. Rowling

Cooper's skin felt hot and stretched tight. He hadn't eaten in two days, and, as he stumbled and fell over the tripwire, his last conscious thought was that he really hated the thought of dying like this, in some goddamn trap he should have had the sense to avoid.

The tripwire malfunctioned, however, and instead of filling him full of agonizing holes and more shredded flesh from the homemade bomb the tripwire was supposed to detonate, he simply ripped open his festering wounds on the gravel path. His head bobbed back, covered in blood, mixed with greenish-yellow pus, the infection from Riley's bone shards and the crash trailing down his cheek to mix with the blood. His vision faded to black, and he passed out cold. Not even the sharp kick of a booted foot in his ribs a few moments later revived him.

A slightly built, pale-faced teenager kicked again, harder this time, and earned a small groan in response. "Well, you ain't dead. Not yet, at least." She raised a hand to her mouth and trilled a bird call. There was a distant shout in response. She shifted her rifle from her shoulder, sat down on a rock nearby, and watched the man on the ground.

A few minutes went by. "Whatcha whistle for Delwen?" A young man in his late teens, followed by two younger boys, came to an abrupt stop at the sight of an unconscious man within the AR's borders. "Oh shit, ya bagged one."

Delwen eyed him and pointed to the tripwire. "You rigged it wrong. It shoulda gone off, but it didn't."

The young man glared at her for a moment before turning back to Cooper, still lying on the ground, unmoving. "He stinks," he grinned at Delwen, "what, ya want him for your boyfriend or something? Setting your sights awful low, aren't ya?"

Delwen returned his needling with a withering look, "Oh, shut it, Heim, he's as good as dead. I got a look at his face 'fore he face-planted. That blood isn't just from the gravel; he got messed up a while back, and it looks to have caught up with him." She stared at Cooper and thought for a minute, "Sul will want to talk to him, though. Look at his clothes... those are Western Front colors."

Heim chewed on this for a moment. "Think he's alone?"

"You see anyone else 'round here?" One of the younger boys sniggered at the sarcasm in her voice. Heim reached out and smacked him on the side of the head, and the boy yelped and slunk out of range.

"Right. Let's bag him and tag him, then." Delwen and the other younger boy fastened Cooper's hands behind his back with zip tie and then bound his ankles as well. After they were sure he wasn't going to jump up and make a grab for their weapons or their throats, Delwen patted him down, removing a large knife, along with a Hi-Point nine-millimeter. Heim barked in derision at the sight of the handgun. "What a piece of shit. Hell, he'd be better off shooting himself in the head with that damn thing."

"I afur nives," Cooper's voice was muffled and indistinct. His eyes had opened and the young boy jumped back, while Delwen jerked in surprise. The instant she did, she felt a sting of embarrassment. This bloody mess at her feet couldn't hurt her. If Sulwyn had seen, well, he was harder on her than the rest; it wasn't as easy as the other girls thought having the commander of Amerika Reborn for a father.

"Christ, Kerwin, stop being such a pansy. He's tied up like some damn Christmas goose; he can't hurt you." She rolled Cooper over on his back. "Now, say that again?"

"I said I 'afur nives," Cooper's mouth wouldn't stretch the right way. He could feel the crusted goo, and the grinding of the bones that obviously had not set right. Eating had been agony, and he hadn't had the need to talk to anyone in weeks... obviously, he needed practice.

"What the hell's he sayin?" Heim asked.

"He's saying he prefers knives," Delwen half-smiled at Scott, a bit of a thrill twisted through her. "My kind of guy, 'ceptin he's uglier than Camelia."

Camelia was their resident slave, as many of the Amerika Reborn members thought of her. She was Hispanic, one of the 'coloreds' they had picked out of a small group holed up miles from here. The rest they had shot or let burn to death in the fire the AR had set to the buildings during the fighting. Camelia had a jagged scar that cut across her face and down one arm. She couldn't walk right either. She had survived the Amtrak Train Bombings, but not without losing her looks in the process. Before the Collapse, she had been a nurse. Medical knowledge, even packaged in the wrong-colored skin, was a benefit the AR couldn't afford to discard. They had tied her up and dragged her out of that house of death well over a year ago now, and kept her busy cleaning wounds and patching everyone up ever since.

"Let's get him out of here and on back to Sulwyn," Delwen said, "he's definitely gonna be interested in this guy."

Half an hour later, with Cooper fevered and close to collapse, the group of child-soldiers had dragged him into the main AR camp. As soon as they had come into the clearing, within sight of a small assembly of cottages and low, dark buildings, a crowd of at least twenty adults had gathered immediately, all of them armed. Many sported tattoos that curled from under their heavy shirtsleeves and collars to wrap around necks and hands. Swastikas, skulls, and SS bolts adorned several of the men's shirts and coats as well.

The colors of the Western Front started a flurry of angry muttering among the adults, and two burly men stepped forward to help drag Cooper to a building near the center of the clearing. It was much larger than the rest, and the area had obviously been a popular campground pre-Collapse. The buildings were arranged in straight lines with neatly laid gravel paths winding between them, expanding as they approached what had most likely been a communal kitchen and social area. There were other buildings of newer construction, scattered about—as well as several yurts and large tents. Through another stand of trees, there were several fenced areas, one filled with horses, another held sheep, and Cooper could make out a cultivated field beyond that.

This camp was obviously organized and well-established. A wonderful aroma of cooking food wafted out of the building and into the clearing. If Cooper had felt even half-human, and not consumed with fever and exhaustion, his stomach would have rumbled in response. As it was, he was having difficulty maintaining consciousness.

A few moments later, Cooper's eyes focused blearily on a tall, bearded man. Sulwyn Kingmaker had gray hair and piercing blue eyes. He looked to be in his late 50s and had the appearance of a kind father. At one time, Sulwyn had had a different name, a rather mundane one at that. But that was before the Collapse, before Amerika Reborn had risen like a phoenix from the ashes of the broken fragments of the American Nazi Party.

"A soldier? And from the Western Front, I see." Sulwyn's eyes narrowed as he took in Cooper's appearance, and turned to Delwen, "Any sign of others?"

"No, Pops... I mean... no sir. No one," Delwen stumbled over her words.

"Hm. Well, take him to Camelia and have her patch him up." He started to turn away, and then turned back and added, "And tell that colored woman I don't want her wasting any of the remaining antibiotics on him. I've yet to see if he is of any use to us. Might be some cowardly deserter. Enemy or not, we don't need deserters."

Cooper soon found himself in a dim room, hoisted onto a hard metal table, with a scarred Hispanic woman bending over him, examining his face wounds in great detail.

"He's running a fever," she said out loud, mostly to herself.

"I can tell that, Spic," Delwen sneered, "anything else?"

Camelia didn't react to Delwen's insult; she was focused on her patient. "Yes. His jaw is badly infected, and he needs it reset and wired shut so it can heal right. He will need a good dose of antibiotics."

There was a pause as Delwen turned and met Heim's eyes. She stared at him, never breaking the gaze as she said, "Sul said to get him patched up and give him whatever he needs." As Camelia opened a large metal cabinet and began selecting instruments and some of the last of the antibiotic packs, Delwen closed the distance between her and Heim, "I know what Sul said, but I got a feeling about this guy." She said it in a whisper, brushing her lips against the older boy's ear. "You... won't tell... will you?"

She felt Heim shudder a bit in response, and he shook his head silently. Heim had been following her around like a puppy dog ever since she had started to fill out, and she used this obsession with her to full advantage whenever possible, teasing him, and then pushing him away. Little Eric Brown, now known as Heimdall Stonekiller, was nothing better than a tool. But he was her tool, and she liked it that way.

The chain around Camelia's ankle clanked as she moved back to Cooper, who had passed out by this point, and Delwen couldn't help but snicker. If the stupid Spic hadn't kept trying to escape, they would have left her unchained.

Sulwyn, Delwen's father and leader of Amerika Reborn, had explained to Delwen that some coloreds were worth keeping alive, although it was never acceptable to breed with them. "Their blood is full of disease, the muddy bastards. Never, ever allow a colored to touch you, Del," he had grasped her shoulder, bruising flesh and continued, "the only reason we keep that colored Spic around is for her stolen medical knowledge. We must keep looking for a better replacement so that we aren't exposed to her filthy diseases any longer than necessary."

Sulwyn had led the fight on the Spic compound over a year ago now. The Spics had been overwhelmed by the AR's superior firepower and guerrilla fighting tactics. Sul had ordered everyone killed. No point in keeping around some screaming brown babies, or helpless women. The Spic women weren't anything like the Amerika Reborn women—they were soft, helpless, and useless for anything except spreading their legs and giving the white man diseases, Sulwyn had explained to his group.

But when they had set it all on fire, they found Camelia in one of the back rooms, performing surgery on a mortally wounded boy. Sulwyn had recognized her abilities immediately and stopped one of the men from blowing her head off. They had dragged her away, fighting and kicking, screaming, until one of the men had cuffed her hard, sending her head flying back, cracking the glass of the side window in the lead truck and knocking her unconscious.

When she had woken up, she had caught on pretty quick to keep her fool mouth shut, Delwen mused. She had focused her efforts on trying to get away until Sul had her chained and told her if she tried again, he'd cut through the tendons in her ankles, laming her permanently. Delwen wasn't sure if it was the threat of never walking again, or the strength of the chain that had kept Camelia from trying again. But sure enough, she stayed put from then on.

It would take nearly a week before Cooper was able to stand unassisted. Camelia had managed to repair the half-healed wreck that was his jaw, but there was no hope he would ever be good-looking again. A large dimpled scar ran along his right jawline, jagged thick white scar tissue buckling and twisting the skin. It would be another month before he could eat any solid food.

As soon as he was fit to stand, however, Delwen dragged him back into the headquarters. Her father was sitting at a large, ornate desk, reviewing an almost illegible report from the man in charge of the barnyard animals. It looked as though they would need to raid if they wanted enough sheep and goats for breeding stock and plenty of meat. He paused, frustrated by the man's illiterate scrawl, and removed his reading glasses. Scott stood before him in the same stinking clothes he had been in when they found him, but he stood straight and waited for Sulwyn to address him.

"Name?" he asked Scott.

"Cooper. Scott Cooper."

"So... deserter or spy?" he asked Cooper.

"Independent agent... sir." Cooper managed to delay on the 'sir' just a fraction longer than was respectful.

"I see, and how does one become an independent agent?"

"One does the best with what he's got, sir. The Western Front collapsed, due to an improper mixing of color, sir." Cooper wasn't stupid; he had listened carefully and seen the tattoos. He figured it was the most expedient way to save his life, and possibly, just possibly, regain some of what he had lost in that raid.

"And I'm to believe that you share our values?" Sulwyn asked, raising an eyebrow in mock disbelief.

"Believe what you like, sir. I'm in need of a bath," Cooper said calmly, "That Spic medic you have, I wouldn't doubt that she has lice; more than likely scabies as well." Delwen sniggered quietly behind him.

Sulwyn Kingmaker, formerly John Stump, a former television repairman from Southie, smiled, "A bath then." He turned to Delwen,

"Have Kerwin take care of it and keep watch over him." He turned back to the reports and slid on his reading glasses, quite obviously dismissing him.

"My knives, sir."

Sulwyn glanced at Cooper. "You have not proven yourself to me, Cooper. When you do, we will discuss it further." He turned away, again dismissing the young man in front of him.

Cooper turned, as if he were capitulating, and then moved stunningly fast, his arms and legs a blur as he ruthlessly attacked the large guard standing at attention behind him. Within seconds, the burly man was dead on the floor and Scott Cooper stood there, the guard's knife in his right hand, covered in gore. Cooper slowly set the weapon on the floor next to his victim.

Delwen had an AK-47 aimed at his belly and the two other guards from outside the office were pointing their weapons at Cooper as well. He stood there, smiling. "Is that the proof you were looking for, sir?" He didn't move any closer to the leader, didn't move at all, which was for the best—he had three people within a hair trigger of killing him. Despite this, he was as calm and cool as ice.

Sulwyn spared a glance at the piece of dead meat currently covering his office floor with a spreading pool of blood and turned to Delwen, "Make sure he gets his knives back." Then he turned back to Cooper, "Stay within the boundaries of the clearing, and out of the armory, or I'll have my men shoot you on sight."

By the time he could eat solid food a few weeks later, Cooper had quietly carved out a comfortable niche for himself within the Amerika Reborn group. He refused to change his name, however, which had been a tradition among the AR since the Collapse. He quickly rose within the ranks, leading devastatingly brutal raids and bringing vast stores of food, ammunition, and other supplies, along with able-bodied men and women to swell the numbers of the neo-Nazi group.

Scott Cooper had found a new home.

First Summer

"I figured I would eventually get used to it. And we make do, because really, what other choice do we have? But I miss air conditioning. I mean I really, really miss it. It's been, what, over ten years now? And when that crazy hot, muggy summer heat hits, I just sit around like a limp noodle. Ugh. It's hard to believe that my grandparents grew up without it and all the generations before that. Of all the things I miss... having that ice-cold air conditioner is near the top of my list."—Jess's Journal

Sweat trickled down Jess's face. The sun beat mercilessly down on her as she moved through the backyard. On the back porch, the solar oven had two loaves of bread inside, and they had been baking for over two hours. The heavenly smell she kept getting whiffs of indicated it would soon be time to take them out. For now, she ignored the smell of the bread, and the heat of the sun, and continued tying the tomato plants up. The heat had spiked a few weeks ago and invaded every corner of the house and the yard. The tomatoes seemed to be the only living thing that thrived.

Jess and the others had all moved down to the basement; the slightly cooler temperatures were a relief from the unending heat and they slept, windows open at night, desperate for a breeze.

Thankfully, the screens on the two tiny windows were intact. This prevented a majority of the voracious swarms of mosquitoes from feasting on them. Some still made it through, as the itchy red lumps on Jess's arms and legs could attest to.

The unrelenting heat was hardest on Jacob, since he was only a baby and unable to regulate his internal temperature as easily as Jess and David. Even Tina struggled with the heat, turning red quickly and losing her appetite. She got her wish to hold Jacob more. The two of them relegated to the basement while Jess and David handled what they could of the gardening and chores.

Jess was worn out from struggling to pull a cart loaded with water from the creek. The only nice part about this duty was the messiness of it. They would pull a handcart loaded with one or two large rain barrels to the creek, then use buckets to fill them, which meant she was soaked down the front of her shirt and pants within minutes. When the barrels were full, they would turn the cart around and slowly pull it the three blocks back home, taking care to navigate the chewed-up blacktop and various obstacles—mainly bricks and wood from the collapsed and burnt houses—strewn about. It was hard work pulling the cart back. The slightest incline involved muscles she hadn't known she had.

Once back, they would hook up a short hose to the spigot near the bottom of the barrel, letting a barrel drain slowly into one or two of the raised beds. When the barrel was empty, they would switch to the other one and drain it as well. One trip in the early morning to water selected beds in the backyard and one trip in the evening, to water the backyard—thus avoiding direct sunlight. Until they could dig a well, it was their only option for keeping the plants alive. They had also decided to allow their new flock of chickens to run free of the confines of their protected chicken coop and yard during the day, after two of the younger hens, who had just begun laying, died from overheating.

The odd little flock of nine laying hens and one rooster had been cobbled together from donations by townspeople. For a few weeks, after they had help from Thurman Banks repairing the chicken house and coop, which was intact except for one smashed window, Jess and David received a bird here and a bird there. A neighbor would show up at their door, squawking chicken in one hand, a packet of seeds or some bread in another. One or two of the hens looked a lot like the Ameraucana birds that Jess's mom, Julie, had owned. Jess later concluded that they must be Ameraucanas when they found a stash of medium-sized pale green eggs. Others were larger breeds that lay large brown eggs. With a rooster to fertilize the eggs, it was possible that they could enlarge their flock quickly if they continued to have broody hens.

"If we just lock them up at night, so the 'possums and 'coons don't get 'em, then let them out in the morning. They can be free to find the coolest part of the yard," David had suggested. It had proven to be the perfect solution and the chickens could often be found resting under the shade of tomato plants in the cool dirt, or in a dark corner of the fence under the grapevines. It had its drawbacks, though; they tended to nibble on the tomatoes and had completely demolished the grapes before Jess and David devised a barrier with chicken wire.

A tiny warble at her elbow startled Jess. One of the hens was eyeing her curiously. She was one of the Ameraucana, one that looked distinctive enough from the rest to be named. Tina had decided to call her Little Miss Crankyfoot, or Cranky for short, but the young hen was anything but cranky. The rest would run from Jess and the others, but not Cranky. Jess figured Cranky's brain had to be just a tad bigger than the rest—she stayed close to Jess and David, watching as they dug into the earth, and was rewarded with tasty grubs, fat green tomato hornworms, and now, as the summer progressed, juicy grasshoppers. Jess spied one now and tossed it to Cranky, who devoured it quickly.

Work on the house was moving slowly now. Everything moved slowly in this oppressive heat. The rooms had slowly been cleaned out. Furniture, dishes, books, and more, some of it quite familiar, often appeared overnight on the front stoop. Old Mr. Banks had explained it kindly one evening when he showed up with a butchered goat for the family and then stayed for supper.

"Folks did what they had to survive, Jessie. Along the way, they maybe saw stuff that was nice, or made 'em smile, and they picked that up too. After all, someone who is gone, they don't need that stuff anymore, right? It wasn't stealing, per se, just filling a tiny desire. You understand, right, Jessie?" His eyes had pleaded with her to accept that what was taken would find its way back in due time. And Jess shrugged and nodded. Hadn't she done much of the same thing in countless other places along the way? The day her mother's cameo, handed down through three generations of women before her, returned, still nestled in its worn, velvet-lined box, she sat down on the front stoop and cried. It made her miss her mom even more.

The remnants of the once-thriving town of over 20,000 souls were tattered and threadbare. A mere one in thirty had survived. Despite this, or perhaps because of the loss of so many, those left pulled together wherever and whenever possible. Jess could count on one hand the number of meals she and her family had missed since their arrival in March. It was hard for her, though, to ask for help.

Sarah Turner had given Jess a stern talking to a few weeks before when she learned that there was a gaping hole in the roof, which poured rain straight into the master bedroom. "Don't be a fool, Jessie," she had said to her as she surveyed the damage. The floor had buckled and part of the drywall had collapsed. Soon it would affect their nest down in the basement. "This isn't safe for the baby, or any of you; the rain will lead to mold, and then you will have some real problems on your hands. If we can't find someone to help you fix it, you'll have to move into the dorms they've set up at Research. But that's been a hotbed for some bad strains of flu through the winter—I'd hate to see you or the kids get that."

Research had been the local medical center and part of it had been turned into a form of housing for orphans and the elderly after so many of the children lost their parents in a series of raids—first from the Western Front and later from bands of starving families holed up in the city. The old folks' home had been set on fire with most of the occupants inside, but the elderly who had lived on their own were now forced through need to live in the old hospital. In some ways, being around so many of the kids had saved many of the senior citizens from fading away to nothing. The kids needed them, after all.

The last two winters had been hard ones—food shortages in the first winter immediately following the first invasion had taken their toll. With lack of food had come higher susceptibility to illness. The last onslaught of flu had killed all but a handful of the senior citizens and put a serious dent in the younger population as well. Jess had heard the stories, and Sarah's admonition to get the house in order was taken seriously.

A week later, the ripped tarp was pulled away and a handful of the younger men from the militia were hard at work, with a former owner of a local construction company supervising their progress. Two days after that, the hole had been completely repaired, including the rotting drywall, patched from intact drywall salvaged from a home a few blocks away that had partially burned in the invasion. Jess had cleaned the room and, after a full-size mattress and box springs mysteriously appeared on their doorstep the next day, she had moved the bed and her meager belongings into the master bedroom. The heat had kept her downstairs, but she knew it wouldn't always be this hot. Eventually, the nights would cool and she would actually have a room to herself, mostly, considering that Jacob would be sharing it with her. It felt strange to take this room that had been her parents'. Looking around it, she could see the ghostly shapes of where each piece of furniture had stood, and the shadows of their presence still lingered in outlines on the floor.

One of the bedroom windows was broken. The former construction company owner, Mr. Kinsey, had offered to find a replacement window, but Jess had shaken her head and just asked that it be boarded over. She was relieved Sarah wasn't there to lecture her, or to go above her head and insist that Mr. Kinsey find a window for her. Having the roof intact was good enough, and she knew that she was already owed enough for all the help others had extended to her.

Jess had been lost in her thoughts for a while. Her back and knees were sore from crouching at the tomato vines and her fingers were rough and chapped from the twine she was using to tie the vines with. As she looked around, Jess found herself feeling almost... safe. Twice in the last month, the militia had repelled invaders, killing the ones who were armed, and no one from Belton had been hurt in the process. A small knot of cattle lowed peaceably nearby. The strong smell of them had become something of a comfort. All of her little family were filling out, the bones jutted less, and she had noticed her hair felt thicker and less brittle. Jess could also see the difference in Jacob's activity level, as well as his size. He had begun crawling and gurgled happily, keeping all three of them busy taking turns watching him.

She had even heard Tina, so serious and quiet for her four years, laugh freely the other day. For that matter, David, too, seemed happier. They were adjusting. It had been nearly a year now, Jess realized suddenly, since she had first met David and Tina. Nearly a year since Jacob had been born in the middle of that storm.

What had happened to that soldier who had found them that night? She remembered him standing there, ready to fire, the rain soaking him, the wind lashing the trees in the background. He had looked so tired, so sad, when he saw Jacob, naked, covered in afterbirth, his umbilical cord still attached. His young face had been lined with grief at the memory of his own son. "I had a son once. His name was Jacob."

She hadn't thought of the soldier for a long time. Not much at all since that first night, the memory of him lost in the simple and basic struggle for survival in the days, weeks, and months that followed. For the first time she found herself pierced by a sharp curiosity—all the stories, all the lives cut short or forever altered by the events of the past two years. What was Sarah's story? Where did she and her kids come from? And Grandmother Madge... where were her children now? How could she tell them the story of their mother?

Jess looked down to find her left hand clenched around a thin long shred of mulch, clutching it as she would a pen. Before it had all come to such a terrible end, her life here in Belton before the invasion had been filled with "scribbles," as her brother Chris had called them. "When you aren't reading, you're scribbling," he had teased her good-naturedly, "and sometimes it's both!" For nearly two years, she hadn't written a thing. The journals were gone and hadn't mysteriously returned on the stoop like so many other things.

Suddenly she felt that familiar longing, deep within her, an urge to write that was akin to a thirsty man begging for water. And not just write, but chronicle the stories of others, so that their words and thoughts and experiences would not be lost. A record, Jess decided, of all of those who will speak, for themselves and for others who are gone. So that we will not forget.

Jess stood up, brushed herself off, and went to look for a pen and paper.

A Hunting Expedition

"If we deny love that is given to us, if we refuse to give love because we fear pain or loss, then our lives will be empty, our loss greater."—Author Unknown

Wes twisted his wedding ring on his finger. It was a simple band, yellow gold, almost a woman's ring. It was so thin. There hadn't been much in the way of money, and with Cody on the way, there had been no time to save up for more. The mate to it, Sarah's, hung from his neck, next to Angie's ring, along with his dog tags. He toyed with taking all of them off, sticking them in a drawer and trying to forget.

He had done that once, when he started seeing Angie. She hadn't said anything, not a word of complaint, but one day he had realized he couldn't hang on to them and be with her, so he had slipped off his ring, and took Sarah's ring as well, and placed them in the back of his sock drawer in the box with the note from Sarah saying she was leaving him. They were memories of what could have been... if he had been the man he was supposed to be, a better husband, a better dad.

Cody would be, what, sixteen next week and Laura fourteen next spring. If they were still alive, that is. And in this crazy world he wondered... he wondered about that every day. Wes pushed his wedding ring back up his finger, until it nestled against his knuckle, a little loose; he had lost a bit of weight over the years, but the ring hung on, a part of his past that he couldn't let go, no matter that there would most likely never be answers, never be closure. He heard it clink against the metal of the rifle in front of him, currently in pieces, waiting to be cleaned.

It was nearly Thanksgiving, a time for hunting, and for Tiptonville, a time of terrible memories. Wes forced his mind away from it, focused on the rifle before him, cleaned and oiled it, then re-assembled it. As he did, Wes felt his thoughts turn to the outsider in their midst. Chris Aaronson was the one man in town that no one really knew. They certainly didn't know what Wes knew—that Chris had been a conscript with the Western Front. They had swallowed Fenton Perdue's story of Chris being a friend of the family. They had swallowed it hook, line, and sinker, especially after that raid and slaughter of the Austins and Anthony Wilkes.

And honestly, if Wes were to think on it long enough, he knew Chris had been telling the truth. He had been a conscript, and he had escaped. But the young man was the only one, the only witness to escape the Western Front. It was time they talked, time he learned more about the world outside of Tiptonville, Tennessee.

Wes slung the rifle over his shoulder, over his flak vest. Strapped to his left thigh was his Bowie. The flak vest held an arsenal of shells, blades, and a Magnum .44 was in a right hip holster. He had decided to bring the compound bow as well. As usual, Wes was a walking arsenal. There had been a time when he had not been, but he had paid for that mistake with tears and blood a hundred times over. He headed out of town, his F150 a dull roar as he passed the patrols and headed toward the Perdue farm.

The guarded look on Carrie's face when she greeted him at the door had secretly amused Wes. She ushered him into the house, looking pale and wan, more than a trifle suspicious, and sent little Joseph off for Chris. Fenton had been friendlier, but then again, Fenton seemed to have a knack for knowing your intent long before you did yourself.

"Wes," Fenton clapped him on the shoulder, "you look ready for war, young man."

"Just going hunting for deer, sir; thought I'd ask Chris if he'd like to join me, bring back some venison for Thanksgiving and all."

Fenton nodded, "The boy needs a bit of fresh air, been inside too much recently, what with Carrie... er... feelin' poorly. I prefer y'all bring back a nice tender doe, if you don't mind." He winked at Wes, and Wes found his mouth curving in response. He didn't get the chance to smile much these days, and it felt strange and somewhat uncomfortable.

Wes was spared any further small talk as the front door opened and some of the chilly air blew in with Joseph and Chris. Joseph was bouncing about, begging to go hunting. After the raid, early in the year, the entire family had made a practice of going out monthly and doing some limited target practice. Mainly, it revolved around making sure Joseph knew proper gun safety. The boy was now almost six years old, and had become a crack shot with a .22 caliber Beretta Bobcat. It was an elegant little piece, perfect for the boy's small hand. He had been attracted at once to the shine of the steel and the black grip. It had taken half of a hog in trade at the Trade Mart, but Chris had watched Carrie and Liza haggle over the deal for nearly an hour before the merchant, sick and tired of arguing, had thrown in two full boxes of ammo to go with it—a heck of a deal pre-war and a testament to the girls' bargaining skills.

Joseph had managed to net several squirrels and one skunk. Fenton had drawn the line at eating the skunk, but the rest had ended up in the stewpot with Fenton reminding everyone, "Y'all don't shoot what you ain't gonna eat."

Liza had rolled her eyes at that. "Sure Gramps, next time a raider comes by and we blow his brains out, I'll bring him to you to dress and prepare for supper." Fenton had eyed her sternly and grumbled under his breath about little girls getting too big for their britches.

Joseph was bound and determined to go hunting with Wes and Chris, but Carrie deflated Joseph's excitement in one fell swoop when she shook her head and said, "You have lessons, Joseph; it's time we practiced reading."

"Aw! Carrie, but I wanna..."

Carrie eyed him sternly. "You get what you get..."

The boy pouted. "And you don't throw a fit. 'Sides I never throw a fit. I'm not a girl!"

Fenton suppressed a snort of laughter and received an irritable glare from Carrie, all too reminiscent of her mother, as she pointed silently at the den. Now that Chris and Carrie were married, they had moved into her room. The den had been left empty and Liza had pushed to have it turned into a classroom of sorts. Joseph slumped, contemplated rebellion for two short seconds, and then slunk into the classroom muttering under his breath.

Fenton turned to Chris, "Now son, I want a nice, pretty doe brought back. She will make a fine addition to our Thanksgiving feast. Think you can manage that?"

Chris looked at Wes, then back at Fenton. He felt out of his depth. Was this some sort of twisted male bonding experience? Was he supposed to spit and then shake hands? "Uh... sure, Gramps... one doe... I'll do my best."

That earned him a gruff, aborted bark of a laugh from Wes. The jerk actually looked amused. Chris wasn't sure what was happening here, but he wasn't sure he liked it. Half an hour later, as the truck bounced along the ruts of something that might have been considered a road one hundred years ago, Chris was more than sure he was out of his element. What did Wes want with him? They had gone through town and taken Highway 78, nodding to the sentries outside of town as they headed toward Wright, now abandoned, hit by raiders long before Chris found his way to Tiptonville. They angled around Reelfoot Lake. Chris wondered how long the dead trees would stand upright, submerged in water, their leaves and beauty gone. It had been over two hundred years and it appeared that all or most of the trees still stood. It was as if they were waiting for something.

Wes followed Chris's gaze. "We cut 'em down every once in a while; more often these days since the Collapse. They make good firewood."

Chris looked at the trees, then back at Wes. "What are we doing out here, Wes?"

"We're going deer hunting, Aaronson." The older man spared a glance at Chris and smiled slightly, which caused a large knot to form in Chris's stomach. "You know, men go huntin', provide for the family."

"I provide for my family," Chris said evenly. "I help run a farm, if you'll remember." He briefly considered opening the door and jumping from the fast-moving truck. An image of him running for his life with Wes armed to the teeth in hot pursuit flashed before his eyes. Wes had pretty much left him alone since the events of last March. Could he have changed his mind?

Chris turned back to see Wes eyeing him again. Wes barked out a laugh, "Damn, Aaronson, if I didn't know better, I'd think you were lookin' to jump out of this here truck. What... d'ya think I'm plannin' on huntin' you?"

Chris glared at him. "Yeah, the thought crossed my mind."

Wes did laugh then, long and hard, and the truck swerved and heaved over the rough road. "Relax, if I wanted to kill you, I would've done it a long time ago." He raised an eyebrow thoughtfully, "and I would've done it from the woods. Fenton ain't the only one 'round here with experience in war, you know."

Chris relaxed a bit. Not a lot; that was hard to do when you were being tossed about a truck cab like a rag doll, bouncing along what was now a tree-lined hill in the middle of nowhere. Wes seemed to be the old-fashioned type, so Chris figured if Wes did intend to kill him, he'd get some measure of warning. "I heard you were in the second Gulf War."

"Yeah, now that was a screwed-up war, no winner, and it just dragged on and on. And it would've kept dragging on if the bottom hadn't fallen out of the war machine and every other damned thing here in the good ole United States." Wes's mood turned somber again, "It was just another messed up war, another excuse to kill good, honest folks who actually believed they were fighting for something more than sand and oil. What a crap-pie that turned out to be."

Chris felt a little more at ease; this guy wasn't the gung-ho, proud to be an American, gun-toting lunatic he had seemed to be at first, although Chris wasn't ready to rule out the gun-toting fanatic part of it. "Why are we out here, Wes?"

Wes eyed him. "You just get right to the point, dontcha, Aaronson?" When Chris didn't answer, he said, "Maybe I've got questions about the Western Front."

"After eight months you've got questions?"

Wes switched direction on the road with a spin of his steering wheel, and changed topics just as quickly. "Carrie looked peaked. She have another miscarriage?"

Chris's anger surged, "You leave Carrie out of this."

"Easy soldier, easy." Wes's eyes were glued to the road. That was good, because Chris sure as hell could not see any road at all. They hit a particularly large rut and Chris swore as his head hit the roof of the cab. "I ain't trying to rile you up, Aaronson."

"So you say, Wes. Then you go and call me a soldier again." Chris ground his teeth, "I'm not, and I never was."

"I believe you, Aaronson. Now relax; I've got no interest in fighting with you. I wanted someone to go hunting with, and I knew you weren't on watch. Most everyone else is, you know, 'cause of the anniversary."

And, of course, Chris knew exactly what he was talking about. They called it the Thanksgiving massacre. Just a couple of weeks after his hometown in Belton, Missouri had been invaded, Tiptonville had seen action. A different faction of the Western Front had smashed through town, toppling the water tower, setting fire to several buildings, including a bank, and killing nearly half of the population, including both of the town doctors. This was the two-year anniversary of the event. The entire town came together and held a communal Thanksgiving dinner; at least, those who weren't on watch. Then they brought food out to the militia, posted on all the roads that led into town, and took over the watch for them, standing in the night, armed, until the sun rose and the militia took back over the regular watch rounds again.

Chris had participated last year, on the first anniversary. The thought had occurred to him at the time that this was what true community and being an American were about. The United States was dead, but its citizens were not. He had been proud to be a part of the groups of townspeople watching out for the town. As an outsider, he hadn't been considered part of the militia and, until spring, had not been required to stand watch. After the raid by Cooper and his men, that had changed dramatically. It was a few days until Thanksgiving, however. Was there some kind of ritual hunting to be done before the anniversary? Knowing little about Wes, he could only imagine what was going on in the older man's head.

"Where were you on that day?" Chris thought to ask. It was like asking his folks where they were on the day the Twin Towers fell or Ronald Reagan was shot. And his mind flashed on the memory of the Amtrak Train Bombings, when nearly sixteen hundred commuters and train personnel perished when terrorists detonated multiple bombs placed around New York's Penn Station. That one had become even more relevant when Carrie had told him that it was how their father Isaac had died, just a few months before Joseph was born. They had never found Isaac Perdue's body.

The truck shuddered to a stop, and Wes's face looked grim. "We're here, gotta walk the rest of the way to get to the high hide," he said, not answering Chris's question.

Wes slid out of the cab and grabbed a backpack from the truck bed. He didn't look back at Chris; he just set off in a southwestern direction, along a barely visible path. Chris stared for a moment at the man's retreating back and realized if he didn't follow quickly, he would lose him entirely in the dense trees. Within minutes, Chris was well and truly lost. He could wander in these woods for hours, hell, maybe days, and never find his way back home. His ankle, now twice-broken and still healing slowly, ached as he picked up the pace. The last thing he wanted to do was lose sight of Wes. He had no doubt the man knew exactly where he was in the dense forest, but Chris himself was disoriented. After walking through thick forest and undergrowth, they were faced with a meadow and high hide. In the middle of the meadow was a salt lick. Silently, the two men climbed into the high hide.

Three hours later, as Chris shifted in the high hide, his left side numb from sitting still far too long, Wes finally answered his question.

"I was here," he said.

For a moment, Chris didn't have a clue what Wes was talking about. But his silence, once broken, opened the floodgates.

"I was sitting here, in this high hide, waiting for a deer when it all went down in town." Wes pulled his knife out of its sheath and dug at the wood plank at his feet. "I heard it, of course. We're what, eight miles from town? Thought it was thunder at first. Wised up pretty quick, but I was too far out. By the time I got to town, the water tower was down and the fighting was mostly over."

Two hundred yards away, Chris could see a deer step out of the woods into a clearing. He didn't know if he should let Wes finish his story, shoot the deer himself, or what.

He kept an eye on the beast and listened as Wes went on. "I guess you know a little about me. Liza and Carl always hanging together, and Abby and John comin' down for your weddin' and all."

Chris nodded, "I heard your wife took off with your two kids a few years back."

He hoped this was the politic thing to say, and he didn't elaborate on the details Abby Carter had given him. Chris didn't figure it was his place to mention the black eyes, the PTSD and abuse and alcohol. Wes knew the truth, and Chris didn't think it would be particularly conducive to his continued health to rub it in.

"That was over ten years ago now." Wes stabbed again at the wood, and still the deer stood in the clearing, calmly munching on the grass, occasionally raising his antlered head and looking around. Wes didn't seem to notice.

"I don't blame her."

Chris made some kind of strangled noise in his throat and Wes scowled at him.

"I know what Abby and half the town say. I was an asshole. I came back from that crazy, hotter 'n hell, sand nigger-infested place and I was well and truly messed up. Too many missions gone bad, IEDs, blood in the desert. We didn't belong there, none of us did. The government sending us to hell. And for what? So they could jack up the price of oil and talk about democracy while good men died for absolutely nothing."

The deer had four, no, six points, and looked well fed. There was a movement in the trees behind him, and a gorgeous doe stepped out next, head up, watchful.

"I was messed up, and by the time I figured out how bad off I was, Sarah had taken off with Cody and little Laura. I looked for them. God knows I did. I stopped drinking, cleaned up, and kept looking." Wes stared at Chris and continued, "When it all came apart, when war broke out and they nuked Austin, I knew I'd never find them. It was my fault, and the government, for making me into that messed up piece of crap I had become."

Chris watched the doe step out further, ears flicking, then nose-down to the grass, tearing off a chunk, slowly chewing it. "Why are you telling me this, Wes?"

The fury that still lurked within Wes surged to the surface and he pulled the action back on his rifle, aimed, and took two shots in quick succession. The two deer that Chris had been eying for the past five minutes fell dead in the clearing, side by side. Chris gaped as Wes slid the rifle back over his shoulder and began to climb down from the high hide, "C'mon, we need to field dress them before nightfall."

Chris's work with Fenton on the farm had given him ample preparation for field-dressing the deer, but Wes was able to give him some pointers, "Don't push the knife in too far, or you'll rupture the stomach and intestines." The two deer were strung up by their necks, hanging side by side from a sturdy tree branch. The men stood shoulder-to-shoulder and Chris watched and then mimicked each move Wes made. "Take care with the bladder here," he said, pointing with his knife towards the spine, "pinch the urethra closed and carefully remove it."

They worked for a few minutes more in silence, blood and gore covering their hands as they carefully detached the hearts from the lungs and plunged them into a bucket of water Wes had brought with them. The kidneys and livers also followed.

"I know what it's like to lose someone," Wes said, unexpectedly after nearly half an hour of terse commands as they finished gutting and prepping the beasts to transport back to the truck. "I had found someone, someone who didn't give a damn about my wife leaving me. She didn't judge me for the person I had been, just the person I was when I was with her."

Chris waited for the older man to continue. Wes strode to a nearby stream, knelt down, and washed his hands and blades in the clear water. Chris did the same, whistling sharply at the chill of the water. It wasn't long before Wes continued.

"Her name was Angie. She had been staying with friends just outside of town when all The Collapse went down. No family. No roots. We met at a 4th of July picnic and things just..."

Wes settled back on his haunches next to the stream. He set the knives down to dry, picked up a rock, and threw it hard into the trees on the opposite side. It hit the trunk high up and caused two birds to explode into flight from the remnants of greenery, chirping in alarm.

"She moved in a few weeks later and just two days before the Western Front blew through, she told me she was pregnant. I was off huntin' and she was left to die alone. She didn't make it out of the house more than a dozen steps before she was gunned down."

Although the circumstances were completely different, Chris couldn't help thinking of Carrie, her face pinched and sad, full of pain, crying softly where Chris found her hunched over in agony in the bathroom two weeks ago. This second pregnancy and miscarriage had taken Chris by surprise; he hadn't even known Carrie was pregnant when the miscarriage hit. The loss was still painful though, especially when he remembered how it felt to hold their first baby Amy Lynn, her tiny body so light, so impossibly feeble, for those few short moments she had lived.

Chris felt his throat catch on the words, "Carrie did have another miscarriage."

Wes nodded, "I figured as much."

They didn't say another word as both men rose and headed back to the two waiting carcasses. The sun was setting by the time they managed to haul the deer back to the waiting truck and load them up. As the truck bumped and jolted down the rough path, Chris said, "I'm sorry about Angie, Wes."

In the darkness, his face barely lit by the dashboard lights, Wes grimaced, "Yeah, me too."

Although Carrie asked, and Liza tried repeatedly to quiz him about that day in the woods, Chris never repeated what Wes had told him. Somehow, the relationship between the two men, despite the gap in years and the acrimonious way it had begun, changed that day. Slowly, over the years that would follow, Wes and Chris became regular hunting companions and Wes began showing up at both seeding and harvest time to provide much-needed assistance on the farm. Eventually, he would become a fixture at the family Sunday dinner.

On this particular evening, though, Wes delivered Chris and a large doe to a very pleased Fenton, remarking as he left, "Maybe next time that fool grandson-in-law of yours will actually shoot one himself. I waited for him to take the shot for five minutes before I gave up and took matters into my own hands."

And with that parting shot, he strode back to his truck and drove away into the crisp fall night.

Wounded Bird

"When my heart can beat no more, I hope I die for a principle, or a belief that I had lived for. I will die before my time, because I feel the shadows' depth, so much I wanted to accomplish before I've reached my death."—Author Unknown

Quincy barked once in warning before they heard the stamp of boots and a knock on the door. It was mid-January, late afternoon, the sky was overcast, and the house was gloomy and dim. Jess peeked out the peephole and saw it was one of the men who headed up the town militia. Her brain stumbled over his name, Ted... no, Todd Stevens.

Good God, we went out on two dates. Why can't I remember his name?

He looked worried. Behind him, Jess could see his horse tied to the listing mailbox across the street.

"Who is it?" David's voice sounded at her ear and she flinched slightly.

Even after all this time, she wasn't used to someone in her space, close to her, except maybe Jacob, who was walking now and clinging to her legs wherever she went.

"Todd Stevens here. I need to speak with Jess," Todd spoke through the door, his voice muffled by a scarf. He shivered slightly and bowed slightly at Jess as she opened the door, nodding gratefully when she invited him in.

He stomped the snow from his boots, unwrapped the scarf from his mouth and neck, and settled into an open seat at the kitchen table. Both Tina and Jacob were sleeping, curled together in a lump on the couch. They didn't wake.

"Something to warm you?" Jess asked, and Todd nodded gratefully, peeling his gloves off. His face was red where it had been exposed to the frigid air.

The cold snap had stopped everyone in their tracks, driving all occupants of Belton inside. Even the plants in the greenhouse Jess and

David had built died when the outside temperatures plummeted to the negative digits. It was one of the coldest winters in two decades.

Todd blew on his fingers and rubbed them vigorously, wincing as the blood flow increased to the cold-stiffened digits. "We have a woman down at headquarters."

Headquarters was a small building off of Main Street that had housed a tiny museum and once been City Hall some eighty years ago.

"She's asking for you, Jess."

Jess stared at Todd blankly. "She's asking for me?"

"Yep." Todd accepted a steaming cup of chicory from David gratefully and rolled his eyes to the sky after the first sip. "Good sweet lord, that's good. Where in the world did you manage to find sugar, anyway?"

"Sugar beets. They make a fine substitute for sugar." Jess smiled with pride; she had raised enough sugar beets to chop up and fill two gargantuan pots. She had then boiled them until they were soft. After removing the beets, she continued to boil the water, stirring it constantly, until it reached the consistency of honey. She had then set it aside to cool. Once cooled, the beet sugar had crystallized.

When they needed sugar, they simply chiseled off a small hunk and drop it into a pot of chicory that they kept on the back burner. It was an especially nice treat now that the days were so frigidly cold.

Todd closed his eyes and smiled, "It sure hits the spot." His thoughts returned to business as he slurped down the last of the chicory.

"The woman's got a baby with her and she's been hurt. She's got a badly infected gunshot wound to one arm and she looks half-starved. Says she came here from Clinton?"

Jess gasped and she and David cried out at the same time, "Serena!"

Jess began pulling on her coat and gloves and a pair of solid work boots. "There weren't any others with her? A man? A boy and a girl?"

Todd shook his head. "Nope, just her and the baby. She looks pretty bad off with that hurt wing of hers. The mayor told me to haul ass and come fetch you."

"I'll come too." David started to reach for his coat.

"We can't both go, David. Stay here, watch Jacob for me. I'll try not to be long."

Jess yanked on her two pairs of worn gloves. Each sported holes, but with two layers, she ensured that most of her wouldn't end up being too exposed. David looked rebellious for a moment, but then nodded. He was feeling a bit stir-crazy these days. It was so cold and inhospitable outside that it was difficult to stay out for long. But inside the house, only the main living room and kitchen could be heated. There were days when it felt like all they did was trip and stumble over each other. But as much as he would like an escape, he couldn't leave Tina and Jacob alone in the house and it was bitterly cold out, too cold to expose either of them needlessly. His shoulders slumped in resignation.

Jess smiled at him; she knew how he felt. "I'll make it up to you," she winked, "You can take my next watch shift."

With the movements of troops and scores of desperate, hungry people still out on the roads looking for something, anything, that could be better than where they had come from, the militia had upped the watches. Jess and David were tapped regularly, along with the rest of the able-bodied population, and every few days, one of them was sent to the town perimeter. There were miles of perimeter to watch, but in the two years since the invasion, the town had a rather effective system in place. Jess had seen towns that hadn't figured that out, and there wasn't much left of them.

"Gee, thanks." David replied sarcastically, while managing a half-hearted smile in return.

Jess finished pulling on her coat, three pairs of thick socks, and some overly large rubber boots that had belonged to her dad. They weren't great at protecting from the cold but, for now, they were the best footwear available to her.

"Okay, I'm ready," she told Todd, who quickly downed the last of the chicory and smacked his lips in satisfaction.

He pulled on his gloves, wrapped his scarf back around his head, and they left the house as quietly as possible.

"We can ride together," Todd suggested, and then a slightly worried look crossed his face, "If you don't mind."

Jess steeled herself for the close contact. They hadn't spoken since the disastrous second date. It hadn't been his fault; Todd was a decent guy in his early 20s. He had been "nothing but a gentleman" as Jess's mother would have said, but she just wasn't ready for any kind of close contact with anyone of the opposite sex. The wounds were still there, the memories too fresh.

"It's fine," Jess said, forcing a smile. "Besides, we'll make better time."

He smiled down at her and held the horse still to make it easier for her to climb up. Then he swung into the saddle behind her. It was a close fit, but at least some parts of her would stay warm. Less than fifteen minutes later, she struggled to slide off of the horse. Todd apologized even as he helped her safely down to the ground.

He's a good guy, she thought. Why can't I like him like that?

The old post office on Main Street was now the town militia headquarters. Here is where they coordinated the watch duties of all the town's able-bodied citizens. If you were old enough to hunt or work the land, then you were old enough to defend your hometown. Some of the townsfolk had objected to the term 'able-bodied' and the ages, which were ten for firearms training and twelve for serving in the militia. But the concept of 'childhood' lasting until the artificial age of eighteen was as dead as the concept of an intact United States of America was.

Jess followed Todd into the building. It was warm at least, toasty warm. Every citizen of Belton was required to serve the militia in some way, and not just on the active fighting side. There was wood to chop, bodies to feed, clothing to mend, and horses to care for. The low-slung building also contained several holding rooms for non-citizens and visitors, as well as a large barracks. Most of those who served with the militia did it in the same fashion as firefighters would have, on 24-hour shifts. Jess was exempted from this until Jacob was weaned, but she still had to serve lookout duty once per week.

They went directly to the front desk, where postal clerks had once stood, and a man that Jess couldn't remember the name of nodded at Todd.

"She's in the first room on the left. Doc's with her; she ain't doing well."

Jess could hear a baby wailing, and the wail seemed to be coming closer. As Todd led the way through the access door to the main warehouse room, the wailing grew louder and closer. The massive room had once been used to sort incoming and outgoing mail, but now the racks were replaced with several large gun safes, barracks, and an industrial kitchen. The scents of breakfast still lingered in the air. Pancakes, judging by the sweet, rich smell of maple syrup.

Sarah walked toward them, a dark-haired baby wailing in her arms. Sarah's face was drawn with worry. "Hi Jess, how are you?" She jiggled the baby, made shushing noises at it. Jess just stared at the baby's face, horror mixing with recognition. The baby looked just like Jacob. "I have Laura fetching a cup of milk to feed this little one. She is absolutely starving, and it looks like her mama might have dried up."

"Serena."

Sarah nodded, "You do know her, then. She says this little one's name is Rebecca, Becka for short."

Jess couldn't take her eyes off of the infant. "And the others?"

"There were no others, just Serena and the baby."

Jess's mind flashed to the two days spent outside of Clinton after they had left the cave. The man Brad, a very pregnant Serena, and the two kids, Max and... Annie? Yes, they had called the girl Annie. The baby continued to wail and Jess's breasts swelled in response, filling with milk, threatening to leak through her shirt.

"I'll take her," she said, and held her hands out to the baby. She was tiny, smaller than Jacob had been at that age, and she loosened her jacket and looked for a quiet corner. "I... uh..."

Sarah's eyes widened. "Oh, of course! Perhaps you should come into the other holding room. It's vacant, and there is a chair and a bed inside."

Jess nodded. "It won't take long. She's just hungry, that's all."

Sarah ushered her into the holding room while Todd stood back, looking uncomfortable. The door closed and Jess lay the baby down on the bed, slipped out of her coat and loosened her shirt. Little Becka did not hesitate and eagerly began to suck on a breast, drawing in the milk with a desperate hunger. How long had it been since this child had been fed? Jess could feel the baby's body relax; here was comfort, warmth, and food. It wasn't until that moment that it felt strange at all—nursing another woman's child—and Jess thought of how it must have been in ages past, before there was formula. Would a woman do this for another? They must have, and it seemed like the right thing to do. Moments passed and Jess could hear the baby's rhythmic gulps as she took in the nourishment. Sarah had said that she thought Serena had lost her milk; how long had she been without it? How long had this baby been hungry?

It would be a solid thirty minutes before the baby stopped nursing and fell deeply asleep in Jess's arms.

Young Love

"*Love possesses not nor will it be possessed, for love is sufficient unto love."—Kahlil Gibran*

The knock on the door came early; the sun was just beginning to peek over the horizon. Fenton, an early riser out of decades of habit, muttered with no small level of concern as he limped over to the front door. He peered out of the window first; the kidnapping of Liza and murder of the Austin family the year before had left an indelible mark on everyone. Even young Joseph was armed with a small pistol when he ventured outside the house.

In the gloom, Fenton recognized Carl Owens. His black hair was tousled, and he looked worried. He had just brought his hand up to knock again when Fenton opened the door.

He nodded at Fenton, "Morning, sir. I'm sorry to bother you so early, but I need to speak to Liza, if you please."

Fenton was perplexed. Carl was a nice young man, and certainly had his manners, except for the showing up at the crack of dawn part of things.

"Son, don't you think it's a tad early to come a'visitin'?"

Carl had become a regular visitor on the farm during the past summer. At first, he had come with the excuse of helping out on the farm, something he had done in the past, but when he and Liza would scoot off together to go "work in the field" or "check for blueberries," Fenton had been sure it was more than helping out.

He hadn't been so keen on Carrie and Chris, and Liza was a full three years younger than her sister. The world might be different from when he was growing up, but some things didn't change that quickly, so he had decided to keep a close eye on the two.

Carl blushed red, right to the tips of his ears, "No sir... I mean, yes sir, it's too early... I mean..." The boy took a deep breath and started again, "My mom's asked for her to come and see to Dad. He's not been feeling well. She said it's urgent, sir. She asked me to fetch Liza right away."

John Carter had been in Carl's life since he was a young boy. Fenton had always wondered why the man hadn't gone ahead and adopted Carl, especially since it was obvious how devoted he was to the boy and his mother. But for whatever reason, Carl's last name was different, and even after they had married and Tabitha had come along, that had not changed.

Chris had appeared at Fenton's elbow and Liza called from down the hall, "I'm coming! I'm coming! Just let me get my bag." Her voice still sounded heavy with sleep. There was still a congested wheeze to it. They were all recovering from the inevitable winter cold, with Joseph still in bed with a fever, coughing, and whiny.

Chris nodded to Carl, "It'll take her a minute, Carl. Why don't you come on in?"

Fenton looked embarrassed that he hadn't thought to ask the boy in out of the cold before Chris did. He shooed the boy inside, closing the door, and wished his knee didn't ache so during the winter. It made him more irritable than usual and he still felt bad for snapping at Joseph the night before after the little boy had whined about his congested nose.

If his wife Molly were still alive, she would have gently reminded him that children were only small for a painfully short time, and to be patient, and not to snap. He sighed; how he wished Molly had lived to see their son Isaac's children... she would have loved being a grandmother.

But Molly had died when their son was still in high school. Isaac had grown up, gone off to college, and found the girl of his dreams in that bustling metropolis of New York. Fenton had looked forward to each summer and winter visit when the kids were small. First, it was just the three of them visiting, Isaac, Amy, and little baby Carrie. Before long they had added Liza, and then long after Liza, when Carrie was a teenager and Liza not far behind, Fenton had gotten the news.

"We're having one more, Dad." Fenton had heard Isaac's voice, excited and tinny over his cell phone, "Amy and I decided we would try just one more time. She's just entering her second trimester, so it's safe to tell everyone. The baby's due in mid-March and we just had the ultrasound done. She's having a boy! Amy and the girls are so excited!

But hey, I gotta go. My train is here. I love you, Dad and we'll be heading down for Turkey Day. We'll see you then. Love you, Dad."

The phone had cut out before Fenton had a chance to tell his son he loved him, too. It was the last conversation they would ever have. Hours later, in the deep of the night, the phone rang again. He had answered it and heard the awful news. Isaac would never get the chance to meet his son. A series of terrorist bombings had taken the lives of over 1,600 innocent victims. Isaac's body, along with 83 others, was never found.

By Christmas, Fenton's home was full; Amy and the girls had packed up their tiny New York apartment and moved to Tennessee. Amy's parents had both died years before and she had been an only child like Isaac. With a baby on the way, and Amy a stay-at-home mom since Liza was born, it made the most sense. They settled into the farm and the girls adjusted to small-town life and living on a farm.

After little Joseph was born two weeks early, Amy's will to live just seemed to vanish. Amy had slowly faded away, consumed by grief at the loss of Isaac in the Amtrak Train Bombings, and the undiagnosed cancer that the doctors found far too late. They had buried her in the family cemetery, with Joseph barely six months old.

"He's been vomiting for a while now, but there's nothing left, and he's complaining of pretty severe cramping. Mom's worried it might be his appendix."

Fenton's knee ached, creaking painfully as he shifted his stance, bringing him out of the past and firmly back to the present. Liza was questioning Carl about John as she pulled on her boots. There had been a recent snow, and now the roads and paths around the farm were nothing but mud. Chris made a mental note to start collecting and hauling the smooth river rock near the cabin to pave the most heavily used paths. It would cut down on the mess, complaining, and cleaning that everyone seemed to be obsessed with by mid-winter.

"How long ago did he start vomiting?" Liza asked Carl. She was in her element, not fluttery or lovesick or making moon-eyes at her boyfriend. Instead, she was focused, intense, and professional.

"I think it's been since last night. He did some fishin' down at Reelfoot, spent the day," Carl answered, running fingers through his tangled hair, suddenly fully aware of his appearance, even if Liza wasn't.

Liza nodded and pulled on her coat, reaching down for the medical bag. "Right, well, let's get going."

Carrie appeared at that moment, yawning. "What's going on?" Chris explained and Carrie just smothered another yawn and offered to make coffee. Liza shook her head and headed for the door, Carl trailing uncertainly behind.

Liza kissed Fenton on the cheek as she left, "Love you, Gramps." She turned and waved to the rest of them. "See you all later, please make sure and cover for me on chores, I'm not sure when I'll be back."

And with that, she was out the door, Carl close on her heels.

Fenton stared at the closed door, unsure of what to do. Liza was barely fifteen years old, and people were sending for her as if she were a full-fledged doctor. It boggled his mind. This was the first pre-dawn trip anyone had ever made to the Perdue farm asking for the girl, but from the looks of it, it wouldn't be the last. For a moment, the old man was disconcerted and uneasy. What was this world coming to, that others would look to a teenage girl for their doctoring?

Chris put a hand on his shoulder. "We should all be proud of Liza, Gramps. She's taking on a lot, learning medicine like she is. She's taken care of you when you were hurt and I wouldn't be walking as well as I am if it hadn't been for her."

Chris was referring to the two separate ankle injuries that Liza had helped splint and heal for him. Fenton had managed to split his scalp open enough to need stitches more than a year ago. Recently the old man had figured out that Liza was adding some stuff to his coffee that thickened it up. He couldn't even pronounce the first word.

"Dia... diatom..."

"Diatomaceous earth, Gramps," Liza had told him patiently. "It helps with your blood pressure and cholesterol levels, and it helps a little with your knee pain and flexibility."

"There's nothin' wrong with my knee, young lady," he had told her, feeling old and weak and not liking the feeling of his own mortality at all that morning.

"Oh Gramps, just drink your coffee." She had watched him stand there, digging his heels into the rug at the base of his easy chair, the cup of untouched coffee in his hand. "Please, Gramps? It's good for you, I promise."

"Gramps?" Chris was still there, his hand on the old man's shoulder. Fenton came back to the present with a soft sigh and shook his head.

"That doggone girl left without givin' me that diatom, that diatom..."

"Diatomaceous earth, Gramps?" Chris asked, a small smile on his face. He turned toward the kitchen. "She's told me how much to add; come on, I'll make you some." And Fenton followed, lost again in thoughts of how proud Molly would have been of her grandchildren.

Carl had not driven the Carter's van, which had been converted to biodiesel. They still had to go to a great deal of trouble to make the biodiesel, so a horse worked best for trips that didn't require hauling the entire family. One of the other families in town had started a small horse-breeding business. It was just enough to ensure that there were horses available for riding at any time of day or night. They were housed in a communal stable near the Trade Mart and were guarded by the town watch at night.

A placid dappled mare was standing in the front of the Perdue house, reins lashed to the railing of the wrap-around porch. Carl held Liza's bag while she slid onto the horse and then climbed up behind her.

They hadn't been this close since the fall, when he had come out to help with picking the bushels of apples in the orchard. They had escaped to the woods, to the old cabin there, and made out for a few minutes, the most they could manage without Fenton's intervention. He had almost caught them kissing once, and Liza had told Carl to stay away for a full month afterward. Liza's grandfather had not taken well to how Chris and Carrie had started their relationship, and he was even more watchful now as a result.

The mare started out at a good trot. It wasn't far from town. Carl was distracted by Liza's warmth and proximity. He nuzzled her ear.

"He's been vomiting for most of a day. Did he bring back any catch?" Liza said all business and not the least bit distracted or interested in his romantic advances.

Carl sat back, embarrassed; after all, his dad was sick, and he should be focusing on that, not trying to make moves on his girl. What was he thinking?

"Yeah, about six bass, maybe seven."

"Did he eat any out at the lake?"

"I dunno... maybe. Why?"

"Well, it could be that he undercooked the fish and had gotten some parasite, but that would be awful fast. Or possibly if he drank the water that could be a contributing factor."

She stared off in the distance and the horse trotted along, working at the problem, occasionally asking questions that Carl struggled to answer. It was a different side of her, one he had barely seen. He stared at her, thinking she sounded so, so, clinical. Part of him, the young hormonal side, stung from the utter lack of response his advances had garnered. The other side of him was experiencing a dawning level of deep respect for Liza. She was focused and intense and dedicated. How often could you say that of a fifteen-year-old girl?

Carl thought about the hybrid bicycle he had been working on with Wes Perkins and Jim Dorian, who owned and ran the town's junkyard. Wes was his mom's cousin, and he had explained that Jim Dorian was autistic, but smart, "kind of like the guy in Rain Man," and then had to fill in the story since Carl had never seen the movie. Carl hung out with Wes far more than his mom knew or would approve of. Carl's mother, Abby, a kind and down-to-earth woman, was uncharacteristically disapproving of her first cousin and sternly ordered Carl to stay away.

Carl had heard the talk and he could barely remember his cousins, a boy and a girl, he had played with when they were all very young. Their mother had disappeared with them years and years ago, taking them away from the angry, hard-drinking, abusive man that had returned from the Gulf War.

Mom didn't see it, but Carl did. Wes had changed. Slowly, but he had changed. Although, the man had practically become a walking arsenal after the attack a few years back by the Western Front. Wes's girlfriend, Angie, had died in the attack while Wes had been off hunting.

That had really shaken Carl up; he had liked Angie. More than that, he had liked how Angie had settled with Wes and made him not so hard around the edges. For a while after she had died, Wes had taken to spending long days on watch and riding the others to establish the town watch in a more formal manner than they had before. It had saved lives, and there wasn't much anyone could argue with his methodology after that.

After the raid and murder of the Austin family and kidnapping of Liza, Wes had changed again, in a good way, at least in Carl's estimation. Even Mom had noticed.

Abby had said drily, "I didn't think it was possible, but Wes isn't quite the bastard I'd thought him to be."

Carl had overheard her say it, with her not realizing he was close by. When Carl had the idea of creating a hybrid bicycle and cart, one that would work on human pedal power but also carry a light electric charge and make pulling heavy loads easy for one person to do, he had stopped by Wes's and then they had headed for Dorian's Junkyard.

Pretty soon they had found an ancient moped, one that actually included pedals along with its tiny motor. At present, they were weighing the need for a bigger engine with the priority of keeping it as lightweight as possible, two conflicting goals. Every time he managed to escape from chores, or when he wasn't trying to see Liza, Carl had been at the junkyard, up to his elbows in grease and dirt as they worked to rebuild the ugly creation into a hybrid of lightweight efficiency and power. Like Liza, Carl was just as focused and intense. The realization struck him that it wasn't a bad thing, how clinical she was. Just as it wasn't a bad thing how involved he had become in the hybrid bike. It was the new normal.

They had passed the sentries, waved at the men in the towers and tried to ignore the ruined vehicles with the grisly blackened skeletons inside. Wes had explained what a deterrent the sight was to those infrequent visitors who came to town. They were usually traders, as Tiptonville didn't get many passersby since the town had never been on what would be described as a major thoroughfare, but Wes had told Carl and countless others that one never knew a man's intentions.

"They could be scouts, remnants of a renegade army, like those four men were. You never know. Those corpses on the side of the road will remind outsiders that we fight back and win. It's a better show of force than the men in the towers will ever be."

Still, the sight of the grinning, blackened skeletons turned many people's stomachs. They understood the necessity, but in a way it seemed inhuman. Those men had been people, and many of the residents murmured that they deserved a decent Christian burial. Carl wasn't so sure about the Christian part, but he agreed it was hard to go through here without feeling a crawling sense of disquiet. If Wes could hear Carl's thoughts, he would have pointed out that was exactly the point in having them there.

"I'm sorry," Liza's said abruptly.

"Huh? What for?" Carl asked, wondering if he had missed something she said.

She turned back and kissed him. "I didn't mean to ignore you earlier. I was concentrating on the symptoms and all that."

Carl grinned and kissed her back. "Never feel sorry for being who you are, Liza." He pulled her close, "I think it's pretty cool that you are the town doc."

As the buildings on the outskirts of Tiptonville appeared, they pulled apart and Carl quickened the pace of the mare with a click and sharp rap of his heels on the horse's side. Within moments, they had arrived at the small, nondescript house that John Carter had bought for his wife and stepson. Along with Tabitha, Carl's younger half-sister, they had lived there comfortably before The Collapse. Now the tiny yard sported a chicken coop, cold frames, and several projects at various stages of completion.

One of them was a windmill, inspired by the two that Chris had made at the Perdue farm. The first windmill that Chris had created powered the pump that brought water directly into the house from the well, just as was done in the days before city water. The water tower had been felled by the invasion of Western Front troops over two years ago and the citizens lacked the tools and materials to replace it. This meant that many wells had needed to be dug. Water became a precious commodity, hard to obtain and nearly impossible to store.

The second had provided some electricity—not enough to power the hot water heater that Chris had originally envisioned, but enough to allow them to extend the day somewhat with lights at night. It had helped immeasurably during the long winter months when the days were short on daylight but still long on tasks. When Carl had returned home from a visit to the Perdue farm, he had told John about it, which had prompted a visit to the Perdue's and then a trip to Dorian's Junkyard for parts.

Carl slipped off the horse and tethered it to the picket fence surrounding the small house. Then he reached up and helped Liza down. Not that she needed the help, but Carl had been taught well by his stepfather.

Normally, John would be out by now, rummaging about in his project piles. The man rose with the sun, which was now lighting up the sky, a fiery ball in the east, and would putter about for hours outside. Today, though, he was in the house, vomiting and shivering violently. For a man so seldom sick, it was concerning for all of them to see him in such a state. It was a small wonder that Abby had sent her son to fetch Liza.

As they entered the house, the smell of sickness hit them like a cloud. Liza winced; this was definitely one of the areas of her new role that she wished she didn't have to endure. She had always had a sensitive nose and today was no exception. After leaving the cool, clean wood smoke-tinged air of the outside, the smell was an affront to her nasal passages.

Carl's mother, Abby, leaned out of the hall bathroom, peering through the gloom of the hallway, and called out, "Thank goodness you're here, Liza. He just keeps throwing up... and other things... I hope you can help."

Carl watched as Liza bustled down the hallway, doctor bag in hand, and on into the bathroom with Abby. Tabitha had woken to the sound of Carl and Liza arriving and stood in her bedroom doorway, rubbing sleepily at her eyes.

Carl smiled at his little sister. "Hey Tabby, mornin' kitty-cat."

Tabitha smiled at her brother, "Morning Carl." She looked confused then, "What's Liza doing here?"

"Just checking up on Dad, he's feeling kind of sick." He reached down and scooped her up. "Want some breakfast?"

He turned and headed toward the kitchen. He could hear Liza asking questions about John's fishing trip and whether he had eaten any fish there.

"Daddy's sick?" Tabitha asked, "Oh, poor Daddy!" She paused for a moment. "Carl?"

"Yeah, kiddo?"

"Is Liza your girlfriend? Joseph says you and Liza kiss each other when Grampa Fenton isn't looking."

Carl grinned, "Yeah, she's my girlfriend. But don't tell Grampa Fenton, okay?"

Tabitha grinned back, "It's a secret?" She was very into secrets recently and had finally figured out that secrets were something you didn't blab to everyone, otherwise they wouldn't be secrets.

"Yeah, sort of. So, let's cook up some eggs for everyone, okay kitty-cat?"

Tabitha giggled, "For Liza too, okay?" Carl nodded, and then the little girl asked, "Is Liza the town doctor now?"

"Yup, she sure is." Carl felt a curious thrill of pride. In the world that was, one that Carl barely remembered, he and Liza were merely children. But in the world of now, the one they all seemed rather stuck in, Liza was a doctor, and he was, well, what was he? Carl had yet to figure that out.

As Carl and Tabitha prepared breakfast, and Liza diagnosed John's illness as probably due to some undercooked fish, Carl thought about the future and what his place was in it. In the world that was, his thoughts would have been surprising and unusual for his age. But in the world of now, it seemed he was right on target. He had an attractive, brilliant girlfriend, two loving parents, and a sweet little sister.

But for the first time, it struck Carl that he should be thinking about what he wanted to do. Did he want to putter with the bicycle hybrid that he and Wes and Jim Dorian had been working on? Did he want to become a farmer like Fenton Perdue and Chris? Was his future in hunting and fighting like Cousin Wes?

Later, as most of the family settled in for a hearty breakfast of eggs and greens from the cold frames, Carl looked over at Liza, her blond hair a rumpled mess from her hurried departure this morning, and saw his future. He might be just a few months shy of sixteen, but he knew what he wanted.

He wanted her.

Another Orphan

"Seeing Serena, and holding Becka for the first time, it brought back all of those memories. I looked at Becka, took in that straight, dark hair and those pale-as-ice-blue eyes, and it just shook me. Here was Jacob's half-sister, both of them, fathered by that monster. Life had emerged from such evil and pain and death. Others would have taken her, wanted to take her, but I told them 'no'. I told them Serena wanted me to take Becka, had begged me to, and that I could handle it. It was the least I could do for her. If only I had tried harder. If only I could have convinced her and Brad to come with us. In the end? Becka was family, she... fit. And I can't imagine life without her. —Jess's Journal

Anthony Ridley, the town doctor, was waiting by the closed door. He shook his head slightly at Jess as she approached the room where they were holding Serena.

"She's in and out of consciousness," he told her, "If I had been able to treat her sooner... but she's got blood poisoning, a high fever, and we don't have any antibiotics. I take it you know her?"

Jess nodded. "I met her on the way back here. We were on the outskirts of Clinton. Her group was moving toward Clinton and we were leaving. From what I could see, there wasn't anything left for them to go back to. A lot of troop movements back and forth—different factions, and Clinton had practically been burned to the ground." Todd had rejoined her and was listening intently. "I asked her to come with us, but she had a man with her, a boy and a girl..." Her voice trailed off and both men looked grim.

"She was definitely on her own," Todd said. "One of the militia patrols found her on the edge of town, unconscious, in the trees. If it hadn't been for the baby crying, we would have never known she was there. But I know this; there wasn't anyone else with her."

"Can I see her now?"

The doctor nodded. Sarah offered to take the baby, who was sleeping peacefully in Jess's arms, and Jess shook her head. If Serena was awake, she would want to see Becka. The room was dark, except for a small light in the corner, and it held a certain unexplainable smell. Serena was a tiny mound in the bed, barely breathing, her arm bandaged and hair matted with filth. Her skin was covered with a sheen of sweat and it looked mottled, red and white blotched, except for one eye which was swollen, and the eye socket looked fractured. She was painfully thin, and Jess was sure this had affected her ability to produce any milk.

The baby, Becka, was deeply asleep in Jess's arms, her tiny belly swollen and full of milk. Serena's eyes fluttered when Jess said her name, but she didn't stir. Not once.

Hours passed, people came and went, and Jess sat in a small chair by Serena's cot. Waiting for Serena to wake up, worrying about the others and wondering if she should send for David and the kids. In the end, a diaper change with Becka awake and fretful decided the matter. The baby kicked at Jess irritably, reaching for her mother, over and over. Serena finally roused, her eyes dull and confused. She turned her head and saw Jess.

"Jess?" she whispered, "They found you."

Jess smiled at the woman and took her cold hand in her warm ones. How could Serena be sweating and cold at the same time? Anthony Ridley had been in twice since Jess sat down to check on Serena. He had explained again, quietly, that there was nothing more that he could do for her. His knowledge was limited, after all. He was actually just a medical student and had been away in medical school before the Collapse. He had explained that the mottled skin, the difficulty breathing, all of these things pointed toward a steady decline and eventual death. The end was coming soon.

In some ways, it was harder to deal with. Here was a living, breathing human being. There would be no sudden death, only a slow journey into oblivion. Jess had seen plenty of violent, sudden death. This was new and uncharted territory.

She waited for Serena to say more, but she had slipped away into unconsciousness. Jess sat there, watching Serena and Becka. Becka had cuddled against her mother and fallen asleep again, her tiny body curled against her mother, reassured by her presence. Jess wondered for the hundredth time what had happened to Serena, Brad, and the two children. Her eyes became heavy and, just as she was about to slip into a doze, Serena spoke. Jess's eyes flew open. Serena was awake and looked... lucid.

"You were right, Jess, we never should have gone to Clinton." She whispered it, her voice weak and cracked. Jess leaned in close so that she wouldn't miss any words—words were precious now, numbered and limited. Serena continued, "They're all gone. Brad, Annie, and Max. All of them. I just... ran. I didn't know what else to do. I... took Becka... and I... ran." Her words came in short spurts; she sounded winded and exhausted.

Jess tried to shush her, to tell her they had time to talk later, but somehow Serena sensed how little time they had left.

She touched her sleeping baby's face gently. "Dark hair, and those ice-blue eyes, Jess. She's Jacob's sister." Serena turned and smiled at Jess.

"You were right about everything. It was okay at first, a struggle, and Brad loved her even though she wasn't his." She stopped, and Jess thought she had fallen back asleep.

"Please love her, Jess. Be her mother."

The last thing Jess needed was another baby to care for. They were struggling to survive as it was, and she closed her eyes so she couldn't see Serena's face begging her. She didn't want this baby. Jacob, with his dark hair, sometimes brought back nightmarish flashes of those dark months inside of Tent Five. But he was hers and had her deep blue eyes.

Becka was what Cooper surely looked like as a baby. She was beautiful, no question, but it would be like having a reminder of that monster day in and day out in her own home. How could Serena ask this of her? She opened her eyes and saw Serena's gaze had not wavered.

"You'll be better soon."

"Don't lie to me, Jess. I'm dying and I know it. Please take Becka. Take her now and do this for me, please. I know I've no right to ask this, but I need your promise. I need to know that," again Serena paused and gathered the strength to continue to speak, "she will be with family who loves her."

Jess felt a huge surge of panic. "Serena, I don't know if I can love her like that. She looks so much like him. I..." She felt such a horrible dread at denying this dying woman her request, but the fear it evoked was overwhelming.

Serena smiled weakly. "Do you remember what you said to me when we met, Jess? You said that Becka was a part of me and that I would find the love inside me when she was born. You were right; she's my child. She's all things good, despite her beginnings." She took a deep breath. "Jess, I'm asking you to love my child as your own. Please. You... no one else. Let me die knowing she is loved, because you have that in you, like no one else I know."

And after a long, painful moment, Jess had said yes, the tears welling in her eyes. There had been no more words between them. Serena's plea had taken every last bit of life and strength that she had in her. Moments later, the woman fell into a restless sleep, her breathing hitching and rattling in her throat. Dr. Ridley assured her there was nothing more to be done, and Jess asked Todd for a ride back home.

They bundled the baby up in a swath of blankets. The night was full of stars and frigid. Jess covered Becka's face lightly, trying to keep the baby as warm as possible. The horse's hooves rang out on the cement, echoing off of deserted buildings and past the lowing cattle. They rode back to Jess's little house in silence.

As they turned off of 163rd Street, Todd spoke, "She asked you to take the baby, didn't she?"

"Yeah."

"Are you going to be okay?" he asked kindly.

"Sometimes I wonder if any of us will ever be okay again," Jess said softly.

"Jess, if anyone can make it, you will. You are stronger than you realize. That woman made the right choice." Todd's kind words warmed her in the bitter cold of the night.

Jess didn't trust herself to answer. The day had been overwhelming; the near future seemed just as daunting. She hugged the squirming baby close and then handed Becka to Todd to hold while she slid off of the horse.

"I'll make sure someone lets you know when she wakes up again," Todd said. But Jess knew that Serena probably wouldn't last the night. All of her dwindling energy had been put into making sure Becka was here with Jess and Jacob.

"Come in for a cup of coffee?" she found herself asking, her voice cracking with the effort.

"No, I'm headed home." Todd reached down and touched her cold cheek with his gloved hand, "Get some food and rest, Jess."

In the months that followed, he visited often, bringing extra meat and provisions for Jess and her little family. So did others. The baby thrived and Jess's small family did as well. Before long, they couldn't imagine their world without Becka in it.

What Are They Good For?

T*he soul is healed by being with children."—Fyodor Dostoevsky*

Camelia tried to ignore the growing agony; this was not the time. The lights flickered for the third time since she had begun surgery on a badly wounded Amerika Reborn soldier. He was young, maybe nineteen at most, and had tried to make a name for himself by rushing a small settlement a few miles to the east. Like the Amerika Reborn group, their target had chosen an old campground and was just a little more successful at farming than the AR. Small surprise there.

The only thing these idiots know how to do is shoot guns and run their mouths about "coloreds," Camelia thought to herself.

The raid had been a failure. Two men dead, this one on her table badly hurt, and no food to show for it. As much as she hated him, Camelia knew that if Sulwyn hadn't held Cooper back from the raid, it would have probably been successful. Alenoush had heard that the other settlement, in addition to the crime of sheltering a black "colored" family, had also had a small herd of goats. Meat was in short supply these days, and Camelia's mouth watered at the thought of it.

"I need those lights to stay on," she snapped. If she could just get the artery sutured closed, he would have a chance. If he hadn't lost too much blood, that is. The lights flickered a fourth time and her belly rippled, agonizing pain shooting into her buttocks, up her back and down her legs. She didn't have much more time before... she bent over in agony, her sight temporarily blurring.

"What's wrong with you?" Alenoush hissed in panic. Blood still terrified her and despite a year of training, she couldn't even handle a simple surgery without turning green at the gills.

Camelia would have laughed if it weren't for the agony she felt. Sulwyn sure knew how to pick them. Her belly twisted again and her sight blurred. It had been a hard pregnancy. She'd been sick for more than five months, barely able to keep food down, and then when it had finally subsided, she had dealt with more difficulties.

She glared at the fool girl who had been sent to her to learn doctoring. Sulwyn had turned her over to Camelia only because Alenoush was completely hopeless at warfare, guns, or much of anything else. Months before, while handling a gun in weapons training, she had accidentally shot and killed her training partner. Sulwyn had been disgusted with her, but stuck her with Camelia as a last resort. Like the rest, she had taken on a white name. At eighteen, Alenoush Swiftblade wasn't very swift with any kind of blade and looked as if she were close to vomiting.

Camelia snapped at the girl, "I'm in labor, you fool. Now hold this clamp and don't move."

When her condition had become apparent, Sulwyn had summoned her, questioned her at length. And although she was tempted to tell him who the father was, she was far more frightened of what would happen to her if she did. Cooper had already firmly entrenched himself into the Amerika Reborn's leadership. He would find a way to hurt her, or the baby, who hadn't had a choice in any of this. Add to that severe leg swelling, back pain, and spiking blood pressure, Camelia would count herself lucky if she managed to keep this baby.

Sulwyn had not been pleased, and he had looked positively enraged when she blithely replied, "Immaculate conception." If the Amerika Reborn group hadn't needed her doctoring skills so badly, he probably would have had her shot where she stood. As it was, he had knocked her to the ground with a sharp crack of his open palm on the side of her head.

She gathered her strength as another massive contraction hit, breathed through it, and then focused on the man lying on the table. The lights flickered on and off twice more before she was finished. It looked as if the generator was going out, or that the AR had managed to steal a batch of bad gas on their last raid. Either was possible, and by the time she finished with the AR soldier on the table, she was in too much pain to care.

Hours later, Alenoush washed and swaddled the tiny red-faced baby while Camelia cleaned herself up. The child was quiet; he had barely cried when he was born and was staring about in wide-eyed wonder at the new world he found himself in. This quiet demeanor would serve him well and allow him to survive the years to come.

Alenoush, known once upon a time as Trudy Denkins, smiled at the baby and cooed at him. She wasn't a complicated girl, rather simple-minded really, which made Sulwyn's choice to establish her as the next doctor so laughable in Camelia's eyes. She wasn't even as rabidly racist as most of them, and was delighted with the baby.

"He's beautiful, Camelia. And he's not so brown-skinned like you," the girl said, smiling, truly unaware of unbelievably stupid she sounded, "He could pass for white."

"Could he now?" Camelia's response was dry.

"Oh yes!" the girl replied, then cooed again at the baby. Her admiration of the infant was interrupted by a voice in the doorway.

"So, this is what has everyone in a dither," Scott Cooper said, leaning against the frame.

Camelia felt a line of fear run through her. "Is there something you need, Cooper?" she asked as evenly as possible.

She reached out and took the baby from Alenoush. He was so impossibly tiny in her arms, so perfect.

His eyes flickered over the child for a brief moment, taking in the dark hair and eyes, the pale skin. The boy was several shades paler than Camelia's bronze skin. "What are they good for, anyway?"

Camelia wouldn't respond; she couldn't. This man had given her a baby, but it certainly wasn't out of love, or even kindness. He obviously cared nothing for children. He had told her as much, told her that there had been other women who showed, and that he had ended their lives.

The fact that she was the only doctor, and therefore under Sulwyn's protection, however limited that might be, meant that he hadn't killed her. But he had warned her that if she told, thereby endangering him and his progress inching up the racist neo-Nazi group ladder, that he would end her life and the baby's.

Sulwyn had suspected that Cooper was the father of the baby. It wouldn't do for Sulwyn's new right-hand man to be coupling with a disease-infested colored Spic—especially since his precious daughter Delwen had professed an interest in pairing with him. It was why he had held Cooper back from the last two raids, which had had devastating results. Three men dead, one badly injured, and two horses lost to the group. The men had grown to depend on Cooper's tactical knowledge and fought well under him. Without him, they fell into a state of disorganization, worse than they were before his arrival.

Cooper strode into the room and with one quick move pulled the baby from Camelia's arms. She screamed, "Wait!" she thought a moment and then blurted out, "I'm not telling you who the father is, but if you kill my baby, you can just forget about me doctoring another person, because I won't do it. That's my price. Let him live, let me care for him, and I'll keep doctoring." She felt a presence in the doorway, but ignored it. "I swear to you, I'll help no one if you hurt my baby. He's mine."

Sulwyn spoke from the doorway, "Give her back the little brat." He glared at her, "Threaten me again and I'll kill you and your half-breed runt. Caring for it had better not affect your doctoring or any other duties."

And he walked away, satisfied that Cooper couldn't be the father—otherwise why would she have said to Cooper she wasn't going to tell him who the baby daddy was? For all he knew, it could have been one of those idiots who had died on recent raids. Cooper was clean. It looked as if Delwen would get what she wanted after all.

Inside the room, Cooper handed the tiny bundle back to Camelia, gave her a cold smile, and left the room. She released a breath she hadn't realized she had been holding until that moment. He was hers; she could keep him. She looked down into his warm brown eyes, his perfect face, and soft downy black hair. Hers.

Alenoush moved closer and touched the tiny patch of soft, downy hair on his tiny head. "What are you going to name him?"

Camelia's thoughts turned to a memory of a smiling Hispanic man, standing outside her car window, with soft black hair and warm, brown eyes. The rifle strapped to his back was unusual, but then again, the whole trip from New York had been surreal. Military everywhere, helicopters and unusual military aircraft filling the skies, checkpoints and questions about where she was heading, and long stares at her scars.

She had answered them all calmly, "I'm heading to Texas, and I've been offered a nursing position there."

The nursing home was filled with a mixture of elderly residents and a special wing for burn victims. The perfect place for her, she had thought, a place she could fit in and not be stared at every day.

"Run out of gas?" he had asked her.

"Yes, it looks like it. I hoped I could make it to the next gas station. The ATMs were all down, and none of the bigger gas stations were willing to take my credit card," she had said to him. "I turned off the main roads, hoping to find a smaller place, but..." She tried not to feel nervous; after all, he didn't have the rifle in his hands.

"I'm Armando," he had said, reaching out a hand, "Armando Velasquez." She had taken his hand, shook it, and then he had said, "I'm really sorry I can't help with gas. There's been nothing but shortages in the area, but my house is just up the hill there."

He pointed and continued, "If you like, you could try calling someone to come pick you up."

"There's really no one to call." She realized as the words were coming out how bad that sounded. What if he were some crazy serial killer?

"I mean, I was headed to Texas, and..." She stopped when she saw the man shake his head and look sick. "What?"

"It's just that I heard over the emergency radio. Well, there's been a nuke in Austin," Armando told her.

"What?! That's, that's... I mean, it's impossible. You can't be serious. What, who..." She stopped and took a breath, struggling to conceptualize of a nuke inside U.S. borders, "Why would someone do that?"

Armando shrugged, "I don't know. Things have been getting rather scary in the last few days. The military is putting up barricades, shutting down borders to the southern states. It looks as if... well, as if the United States is at war."

"With who?"

"With itself."

Camelia stood by the side of her car in shock. A thousand questions raced through her head.

Eventually, she let him help her move the car off of the road and bring her bags, and eventually her boxes of books and other necessities she couldn't live without, up to his large, sturdy home. There, they would listen to the increasingly bizarre news reports on the emergency radio. Armando lived there alone. He was a widower; his wife having died in a car crash several years before. Slowly she told him the story of her scars, the remains of what extensive plastic surgery could not fix. She had survived the Amtrak Train Bombings, when so many others had perished. The scars, she said, were a testament to her will to survive.

He had touched them, ran long gentle fingers over the ridge of scars on her face, and told her she was beautiful, inside and out. She had stayed in his house, and they had fallen in love, quietly survived the chaos in the secluded mountain retreat. They had soon welcomed two more Hispanic families when the sentiments of the area had turned ugly and desperate.

A racist group, a leftover of the American Nazi Party, had been blaming the war and the nuke in Austin on Mexico. Between shortages of food, no power, and an intermittent water supply, the few Hispanic families in the area stuck out like sore thumbs. They had banded together, worked the land, traded with those who weren't spouting racist rhetoric, and kept to themselves. Camelia hated the memories of those last few moments, when the Amerika Reborn group had attacked them without provocation, seeking to rob them of what little food and supplies they had.

Armando had fought. All of them had. When Maria, the smiling, round-cheeked mother of two teenaged boys had fallen, though, Camelia had laid down her gun and got to doctoring. She had tried in vain to save the woman who had come to be her closest friend and confidante next to Armando. After that, the boys, Maria's husband, even Armando, had fallen while she was busy trying to save Carlos, a young newlywed. As she worked, the southern wall of the house caught on fire, set by the attackers.

The Amerika Reborn soldiers had grabbed supplies, ripped the medical supplies from the table next to her and even the needle and thread from her hand after Sulwyn stopping them from shooting her, seeing her medical expertise in action. She had been a fine ER nurse prior to the bombings, but scars like hers scared the patients too much. She had screamed and fought them, even as they pulled her from the burning building and past Armando's lifeless body. She had kicked them, bit at them, and tried to get away, until a hard punch had knocked her out and carried her away into the darkness, away from everyone she had come to love. And here she had been ever since, nothing better than a slave, nothing more than a tool to be used at the whim of Amerika Reborn.

Until now.

Tears came then, as she held the infant in her arms. How she and Armando had tried to have a baby, despite the troubles surrounding them. Armando had called it an act of faith, that the world would get better, that life would return to normal. But each month, there was such disappointment, no matter how often she prayed for just one chance.

She stared at the baby's beautiful brown eyes and saw instead the eyes of the kindest man she had ever known. He reached out from her memories to brush her hair from her face and tell her she was beautiful, telling her that the scars didn't matter to him. *You should have been his.*

She turned to Alenoush. "His name is Armando," she said.

No Shotgun Required

"T*he first symptom of love in a young man is shyness; the first symptom in a woman, it is boldness."—Victor Hugo*

Chris stopped in at the house for lunch, rinsing the dirt off his hands. It was April, and planting season was in full swing. He felt an almost electrical current of stress in the air from the moment he walked in. Carrie and Liza were both in the kitchen and Liza looked tense. He gave his wife a quick kiss and tilted his head at Liza. "What's up, Liza?"

His sister-in-law was chewing nervously on a slender fingernail. She glanced toward the den. "Gramps is in the den with Carl."

"What for?" Chris began to ask and then thought of Carl and Liza's more outward signs of affection recently and groaned. "Oh, boy." He had caught the two kissing and holding hands several times. It was just a matter of time before Fenton caught on, if he hadn't already. Carl had been a regular visitor on the farm for over two years now, and it wasn't as if the writing wasn't on the wall. The two had been an item for quite a while.

Liza was quick to defend herself. "I'm not pregnant!" Her face flushed at the thought. "We just...Carl and I...it's just time, that's all. He asked me and I said yes."

"Yes, to sex? Or yes to getting married?" Chris asked, a playful smile on his lips. Carrie slapped his arm. Her mouth turned down disapprovingly, but her eyes crinkled at the corners, a sure sign of amusement.

Liza glared at him. "Oh yeah, Chris Aaronson, you're one to talk!"

She had a point. He and Carrie had mixed up the natural order of things, as her grandfather had put it. That had been nearly three and a half years ago, and their marriage was a good one, despite the losses they had endured. Carrie's first pregnancy had ended in a premature birth, and there had been several heartbreaking miscarriages since. Fenton had come around, eventually, although the sight of the shotgun still gave Chris pause.

"If you must know, Mr. Smarty Pants, Carl asked me to marry him. They've been in there for a few minutes." She bit off another fingernail and said, "I think it's going well. He hasn't started yelling yet."

That hopeful moment was shattered. "Where's my shotgun?" Fenton bellowed from the den.

Chris winced, "Oh yeah, Liza, that went really well." He then grinned at Carrie, remembering several moments of shotgun-induced terror that the old man had brought on for him. His wife rolled her eyes at him and walked toward the den to head the old man off.

Carl came out of the den first and made a beeline for Liza, who grabbed his arm and pulled him close. She wrapped a determined arm around his waist and whispered something in his ear, then kissed him. This earned another bellow from Fenton, who was limping down the hallway, Carrie slowing him down only the slightest bit.

"Are you pregnant, young lady?" Fenton was unusually brusque with his youngest granddaughter.

Liza stood her ground, holding Carl in his place and shushing him with a determined look. "Nope, Gramps, not yet." Her hazel eyes snapped with mischief. "But if you give us a half hour, I'll see what I can do."

Fenton gaped at her. For that matter, they all did. Carl looked terrified, "Uh, sir, I don't think she meant that."

"Oh yes, I did!" Liza said, her jaw firmly set. Chris looked bemused, Carrie stood wide-eyed, and Carl's face had broken into a sheen of sweat.

"Gramps, I'm not a kid anymore."

"You are sixteen years old!" Fenton bellowed.

"I'm seventeen years old, Gramps, almost eighteen. And I know what I want," Liza countered.

Chris watched with admiration. The Perdue women were strong-willed, and Liza was probably the most strong-willed one of them all. Carrie held some of her mother's quiet calm, but Liza was fire and ice, especially when she felt strongly about something. She stood there, back straight, immovable, in the face of her grandfather's wrath.

Fenton faltered ever so slightly, his wrath fading as he grasped at straws.

"What would your parents say to you getting married this young?"

His eyes began to redden and the old man looked exhausted. "You are barely more than children."

His gruff demeanor was nothing but a façade, and the vulnerability Fenton tried so hard to keep hidden came sliding into view. Above all things, he loved his three grandchildren and his grandson-in-law. He loved them fiercely, deeply.

Liza's tone changed in response. "The world is different, Gramps. Carl and I," she pulled Carl closer and stepped forward toward her grandfather, "we've talked about this for a long time. And we love each other."

She stared into the old man's eyes, eyes that reminded her so much of her father, gone for nearly eight years now. Isaac would have liked Carl, just as Fenton did.

"We're getting married, Gramps." Her words were a statement, not a question. A moment passed and no one spoke. Then Liza continued, "So, will you give us your blessing?"

Fenton closed his eyes in exhaustion. He did not understand these young people, so eager to hunt for blueberries and get married. But he knew resolution when he saw it—and his granddaughter was full of it. Heck, the girl was overflowing with resolution. He thought about all the smiles, the surreptitious hand-holding he had tried his best to ignore, and the way Carl fit into the farm, just as Chris had. A good fit.

Fenton opened his eyes and looked at Liza, standing there, Carl at her side. She looked so beautiful and so resolute. She had always known her own mind, and fearlessly faced her future. Just last fall, she had successfully operated on one of the town boys who had come down with acute appendicitis. She had saved that nine-year-old's life and firmly established herself as the town's doctor.

Since then, there had been a stream of steady visitors who would knock on the farmhouse door, day or night, with varying degrees of injuries and illness. At seventeen, Liza was accepted by Tiptonville residents as "the best at doctorin' in the area," as old Otis Liles had said to him at Christmas while Liza looked after a nasty cut the frail centenarian had received after he fell in his cluttered parts shop.

It seemed that Fenton was the only one who still saw the wide-eyed child who had stood waiting with her mother and older sister at the airport. Her hair parted down the middle and fastened into two neat braids. All of them wearing black and still reeling from the loss of his son Isaac in the Amtrak Train Bombings. Amy, heavily pregnant, Carrie, her thin young face drawn with grief, and Liza, who had just looked up at him, opened her arms wide for him to pick her up, and said nothing. She had nestled her face in his neck and wrapped her small arms around him tightly. To him, she was still that little girl. But it was time he saw her for what she was: a young woman who knew her own mind.

Wearily he mustered a half-frown. Why oh why did they all have to grow up so quickly? "Fine," he said, "you have my blessing." Then he pointed a gnarled finger at Carl who looked very relieved. "And you just wait on any fun stuff until after the weddin', you understand me, young man?"

"Yes sir," Carl nodded. And despite Liza's efforts to the contrary, he kept that promise.

They had a June wedding.

Their first child, Molly Ann Owens, was born on Valentine's Day the following year.

A Gift on Our Front Stoop

"I saw her huddled there on our front stoop, red curls matted with dried blood and piercing green eyes. She looked up at me, as if she knew me. Like Erin had been reborn into her. She's not the Erin I knew, however. She's kinder, gentler, and almost magical. But at that first moment, when I saw her shivering there for the first time, it felt as if my friend had come home to me. How could I turn her away? In some way, it was as if I had a second chance. To make it right, to be there when she needed me. I know they are different, and that my friend is long gone, but still..."—Jess's Journal

Jess and Becka were digging out the last of the potatoes, and David and Jacob were hard at work on the carrots. David's sister Tina was sitting cross-legged on the ground some distance away, oblivious to the cold, studying a new plant that had sprouted that year and comparing it carefully to a sketch in an old worn leather book. The skies were overcast and gray; there was a sharp bite to the wind. Any time now they'd see rain, maybe even a freezing drizzle. Winter had come late this year. But now it was clearly on its way. Some distance to the north, there came rolling echoes of gunshots—one, two, and three—in quick succession. Quincy tensed, delicately sniffing the air, her hackles in the air.

Jess couldn't help wondering what the dog smelled. Quincy's reaction was far from comforting. A small whine sounded in her throat as she continued to stare in the direction of the gunshots, her ears pulled back against her head and her nose twitching.

"D'ya think Mr. Banks bagged himself a deer?" Jacob called out from the far side of the garden where he had been put in charge of digging up the garlic bulbs.

Jacob was lean, with tousled black hair, dark blue eyes, and a handsome face. He was seven now, and his last growth spurt had turned his pants into waders. His shirtsleeves ended well before his wrists. Jess made a note to ask at the community center for larger-sized clothes. Several of the kids over at Research were taller than Jacob; perhaps they would have some hand-me-downs to spare.

The boy looked hopeful, positively dreamy-eyed, at the thought of some fresh deer meat. They hadn't eaten venison in well over a month, and the old man would make them a fair trade in meat for some of the apples they had finished picking last month.

Jess had shown Becka and Jacob how to wrap the apples carefully in paper so they didn't touch skin to skin. There would be less rot that way. And there they would sit, deep in the crawlspace of the basement where it was dark. The apples would stay fresh for months. Whatever did rot would be made into applesauce or fed to the chickens or put in the compost, depending on how bad off it was.

Jacob's mind filled with images of a nice juicy roast, or ribs, and resolved to beg his mother again to let him learn how to hunt.

Jess just shook her head and frowned. "Thurman never shoots like that. He fires once and waits; I just heard three in a row. That's a stranger or one of the town militia."

The town militia had changed drastically since Mayor Farley's son, James, had taken over. For that matter, the town had changed as well. Farley's influence was a powerful one. He was still the mayor and there had been no open elections held in over five years. As soon as James Farley had turned the respectable age of twenty, Mayor Farley had pushed, pulled, and threatened a position for his son. Unbelievably to Jess and several others, he had finally dislodged Todd Stevens, who had been designated the head of the militia three years back, after saving the town from a devastating raid.

A group of well-armed men and women had tried to cut into the town from a little-used road on the northeast side, a weak area of defense, and steal the entire herd of cattle. The raiders had been occupying a series of caves to the north along the tattered remains of I-435, which had formerly been used for storage for years. The problem with cave dwelling was lack of sunlight and space, both needed for raising livestock and crops. Pale and malnourished, they had still been savage in their attack. Several members of one family living on the outskirts had been murdered, and three of the town militia had also lost their lives before the attack had been repelled.

That had been a harsh but necessary lesson. The Western Front may have disintegrated, but there were still plenty of people on the edge, desperate to survive, and few left worth trusting. The waves of disease and malnutrition that had turned Kansas City and the surrounding metropolitan area into a tsunami of death long before the Western Front ever arrived on its doorstep were still pulsing through. The townships and their local militias were the only thing keeping most of them alive. Todd Stevens had understood this all too well.

Todd had been interested in Jess and actively courted her that first year after her return to Belton. He was a good man, and she had thought highly of him, but having a man look at her with interest, any kind of interest, had been absolutely terrifying. She had quietly defined their relationship as being a friendship only. He had been disappointed, but accepted it. He had eventually turned his sights toward Laura, Sarah's daughter, courting her on a daily basis at the café on Main Street, where Jess and her family had stayed their first day back in Belton. They now had two small children.

After Mayor Farley had propelled his son into power, Todd and Laura had spent more time with Jess's small family. His parents were dead, and he had talked to her, revealing a snapshot of the struggle from the inside of the higher echelons of the town militia, for power, for control. "I don't want to deal with the politics," he had said to her the summer before. "I just want to keep us safe. Why does it have to be like this?" A week later, the announcement had come that James Farley was now in charge of the militia.

In a matter of a few months, the mayor's son had undone, if not destroyed, the seamless network of militia members. Those who had dedicated themselves to ensuring the town borders remained safe were pushed aside and the decisions and leadership positions farmed out to the untested and cronies of James Farley and his father.

Since he had assumed control, the borders had seen a dozen incursions. The last one had resulted in the death of an entire family. The raid before that had ended without any deaths of residents, but half of the old hospital—now an orphanage, old folks' home, and college rolled into one—had burned to the ground. No one would be attending classes in the near future. Several groups were struggling to find intact housing, and there was no lumber to fix what had been destroyed.

As a one, their heads turned toward the north, waiting for more noise, a shot, a yell, but there was only silence. After a moment of listening to the wind, and nothing else, Jess turned back to her chore.

The temperature was dropping, rain was coming, and they couldn't afford to lose these roots to an overnight frost. "Come on you, let's get these out of the ground and into the basement." She nudged Becka, and then tossed a tiny potato at David, hitting him in the butt and giggling at his startled look.

He put on his sternest face. "You just better watch it, lady! You'll start something you can't finish! I'm armed with pointy carrots... hiya!"

He flourished the carrot in his hand like a deranged fencer, which set the younger kids to laughing. The bit of humor made short work of an otherwise long and tedious job. When they were finally done, the sky had begun to spit fat drops at them, daring them to stay outside for any longer.

Tina had gathered up the old leather journal and her pencil, absently brushing at some plant matter that had attached itself to her patched and worn pants. Recently, she had been adding to the book that Jess had inherited from Grandmother Madge, the old woman who had sheltered them over the winter in a cave east of Clinton. Tina was nearly eleven now, and she was a quiet girl who already showed an incredible knowledge of healing herbs. Her hair, once a muddy blond, had darkened to a golden brown. She kept the unruly curls cropped short, and they seemed to be the most lighthearted part of her otherwise solemn demeanor. Her smiles, which were rare, were usually used exclusively for smaller children, like Jacob and Becka. Although she could not remember her parents, their abrupt loss, and the loss of Grandmother Madge less than a year later, these events had marked the child in a way that Jess or David seemed unable to change.

Despite this solemn demeanor, Tina was gentle and loving and cared deeply for her brother and the rest of their adopted family. It just seemed that she existed in a world of her own so much of the time. Few understood her. The town doctor, Anthony Ridley, was the exception to the rule. He had spent time with her one day while checking on Becka, still a baby at the time, and making sure everyone was surviving the winter without trouble. Todd Stevens, the militia leader, had urged him to drop in on them, worried that Jess was exhausting herself with so many children to look after. While looking over the entire little family, a strange mix of related and unrelated teenagers and children, Dr. Ridley had been surprised by an offering of some strange dried flowers and stems.

Tina had looked up solemnly at him, barely five years old, had handed the bundle to him, explaining that it was echinacea, "Missouri coneflower, it's good for keeping away colds."

He had looked intrigued and asked her to tell him more. "You can put the flower petals in a tea. Dry it first." He had asked her more questions, and he had returned the next day to talk with her more and ask her for two other herbs she had pointed out, sitting next to her and gently holding the herbs she handed to him.

Over the years, through illnesses and injuries, he would always take an extra few minutes to discuss with Tina her latest miracle plants. After that first encounter, he had made an effort to learn more about herbs and, after a while, he began requesting that Jess and her family grow certain herbs or that Tina make certain poultices. He continued to encourage her to learn more and broaden her knowledge with the books that Jess and David collected for her. As time went by, more and more of Tina's infusions and decoctions helped heal the residents of Belton.

Despite this, most of the residents remained blissfully ignorant that their medicines were supplied by a girl who wasn't even in her teens.

Inside the house, Becka staggered under the weight of the potatoes she was carrying. Jess lifted the basket from her hands before the six-year-old could drop any of the precious cargo. Becka had jet-black hair that held long curls. Her eyes were still a hauntingly familiar ice-blue, but that was where the resemblance to Scott Cooper ended.

Becka was soft-spoken and thoughtful. Jess was struck by the memory of Becka's biological mother, Serena, and the way she had spoken on the two times that she and Jess had met. Serena had been right; Becka was good and kind, just as Serena had been. The only reminder of her paternal heritage was in her features. Jess had spent hours studying the girl's face, seeing Scott Cooper in a completely different way. Had he ever been good and innocent? He must have been.

Jess wanted to believe that all children were, and she wondered what had changed. She had learned to love Becka, just as Serena had said she would. It wasn't hard; the child was sweet and loving, and it was obvious how well she fit in their family unit. Jess leaned down and kissed the little girl, who was protesting that she could carry the heavy load. Becka was also fiercely independent—a trait she shared with the rest of them.

For the first winter in years, she could count on keeping most of this harvest and not losing it to marauding rodents—now that they had Lord Flea. Lord Flea, short for Lord of the Flea-Bitten, Bent-Eared, and Generally Ragged Felines, was a tattered-looking cat of indeterminate age. He was not friendly, and Jacob and Becka had learned to leave him alone after the first round of scratches and bites, but he did a bang-up job on the rodents. Nothing to complain about there!

And with the biggest harvest in three years, thanks to David's research into composting methods, they would have enough root vegetables to last them all winter with extra for trade, as well as seed for next year's crop. Thurman Banks, their nearest neighbor, would be happy to trade his meat for vegetables and for some of the herbs that Jess had painstakingly tied and dried in the heat of the summer.

Icy, stinging drops of rain on the edge of becoming sleet were falling by the time they finished with the last of the vegetables. Everyone was worn out and ready for a bath by the time they finished. "Rinse off as much of the dirt from your hands as you can in the pond and then help with carrying the buckets of water," Jess directed the younger children.

There were already four large pots of water on the stove, water boiling merrily away. If they conserved, the icy cold water from the well mixed with the boiling hot water wouldn't cool things down too badly and they could all get through their baths.

Bodies washed, stomachs full of fresh vegetable soup, the small family gathered in the living room around a few beeswax candles. Night had fallen soon after the rain began. Jacob snuggled up to Jess, his body transmitting warmth and comfort to her.

"Mom, will you read from the story tonight? The Harry story?" he asked her, sleepily.

He was very tired from the hard work of the day. David had found a set of books on a recent trip into the southern part of Belton and brought them back for Jess to look over. She had smiled when she read the titles in his hands, and remembered reading the series when she was a child... Harry Potter... now there was a fine set of adventures! She had not noticed his flushed face when she had hugged him in thanks and excitement, and he had scuttled away before she could see how her affection had affected him.

"Yes, sweetie, but just a few pages tonight," Jess stifled a yawn, "I'm all worn out."

She carefully opened the book to the marked page and began to read aloud. Barely a few paragraphs later, she set the book down with a soft laugh and looked around. David, Becka, and Jacob were all fast asleep on the floor—softly snoring lumps buried under blankets and cradling pillows. She slowly stood and lifted Jacob up into her arms. He was lanky yet light, thin arms and legs, tall for his age, but she could still lift him easily in her arms. She carefully stepped over and around the others and quietly carried him to bed. The others would be fine sleeping the night out on the floor, but she was happy to burrow under the covers of her bed and listen to the tiny taps of ice-laden particles hitting the glass windows before she drifted off to sleep. For the moment, life was bearable and the winter could come—they were ready for it.

The light from the candle on her bedside table guttered and spit as she struggled to keep her eyes open and read over the latest narrative she had collected. For the past five years, she had been slowly chronicling the histories of the local residents. It had started out with the question, "Where were you on November 4th? The day the Western Front invaded Belton?"

Slowly, the stories had changed, taken on different shapes and focus, and she was now chronicling Sarah Turner's life. Sarah Turner, who was actually Sarah Perkins, a woman who had run away from an abusive husband, changed her name and created a new life for herself, as well as for her children, Cody and Laura.

She reviewed her notes, which she had taken two days ago while sitting in the café Sarah ran. She had asked Sarah what she wanted to contribute to the town's oral history and had been stunned by the life story that Sarah had shared.

The older woman's face looked haunted. "I did what I thought was best. To protect myself, to protect Cody and Laura. But I always wondered. If I had stayed... if I had managed to get him help for his PTSD..., could we have made it?" She had smiled wanly. "In so many ways, I still love him, Jess. I never saw another man I wanted as much as I wanted him. I guess that either makes me a fool or..."

She had left the sentence unfinished. Jess's eyes fluttered closed, slipping into sleep as she thought about all the unknowns, all the lost loves in the world—her folks, Chris, Allen, and so many more. The papers slipped from her fingers. The candle guttered next to her in the growing pool of wax and then quietly extinguished.

To escape the nightmare, Jess woke up abruptly, surprised to see that it was already light out. The details of the dream were already fading quickly, but gunfire and the memory of a sobbing child were all that remained. She shook her head, as if to rid herself of the last vestiges of the nightmare. The nightmares came every night, but in different forms, and it was a relief to wake up and spend her days too busy to remember the night's horrors. Jess pulled her clothes on quickly and tried to peer out of an open crack in the wood planks covering one of the windows.

There wasn't much to see; the icy rain must have tapered off early in the night. Winter, it seemed, was delayed for just one more day. She pulled on tattered wool socks and her boots followed. A sweater completed her, and she headed out the bedroom door and into the living room where the others were stirring. Jacob was already awake, sitting at the table and eating an apple.

"Hi there Sweetheart, you're up early." She smoothed his unruly hair with her fingers. The boy looked wide awake. He mumbled incoherently from his apple; eyes fixed on a picture book in front of him.

"Say that again?"

"I've been up 'cause of the cryin,'" the boy repeated. "She just won't stop cryin' no matter how nice I am to her. She don't talk, and she won't look at me or nuthin.'" The little boy looked disgruntled.

"Who won't talk, sweetie?"

"The girl on the front porch."

Jess considered this statement for a moment. "There's a girl on the front porch?"

Jacob rolled his eyes at his mother. "Uh, yeah, I told you she woke me up. But she don't talk or nuthin'; maybe she's 'tarded or somethin.'"

Jess automatically corrected him, "Anything, retarded, something, and that isn't nice, Jacob, calling someone retarded."

She headed for the front door as David struggled to a sitting position, still in the same place on the living room floor where he had fallen asleep, "Wha,' who, what's goin' on?" she heard him mutter sleepily as she unbolted the heavy front door.

David received no answer as Jess simply stared at the small child huddled against her storm door, blocking it from opening.

Jacob walked up behind her, "You'll have to go around; she won't move 'tall," he commented calmly and walked away down the hall.

The small, huddled child did not react, simply rocked back and forth, shaking in the cold. She was tiny, smaller by far than Jacob or Becka, maybe two or three years old. One thumb was firmly stuck in her mouth and her hair was a bright red, tangled, and full of burrs and leaves. Her face, what Jess could see of it, was filthy and tear-streaked. She was dressed in jeans or overalls, and a thick pink coat that had seen cleaner days. Her tiny sneakers were covered in mud.

"Oh my God," Jess jumped at David's voice in her ear, "What the hell?" He was rubbing the sleep from his eyes and looking as confused as she.

Jess said nothing, just turned and ran out of the living room and through the kitchen, the pantry, out through the garage, which was now used as a small barn, and around the house to the front door. She skidded to a stop in front of the stoop, half expecting the tiny child to have vanished before she arrived. But the little girl hadn't moved, not an inch. She didn't even flinch when Jess reached down and gently picked her up in her arms. David held open the door for her then, now that the girl wasn't blocking it from opening.

By now, Becka and Jacob were both at the door behind David, Becka still bleary-eyed from sleep and Jacob curious enough not to be as annoyed with the girl now for not talking to him. Tina had not yet made an appearance.

The group of them moved like a school of fish toward the center of the kitchen, where the light was brightest. Jess set the tiny girl on the floor and sat down cross-legged in front of her. Now she could see blood caked on her face, hands, and the front of her overalls. It was mixed in with dark black river mud and dissolved in tracks from the child's tears. She was shivering from fear and cold, and now she looked up at Jess with the most startling, piercing green eyes. "Erin," Jess whispered to herself, reminded painfully of the childhood friend she had lost. The child did not react, merely stared at her with tears welling up in her eyes, spilling down cheeks, and shivering.

The sight of tears was like an electric charge that sent Jess into action. Without taking her eyes from the child, she began snapping orders.

"Becka, round up some towels and a washcloth. David, please draw some water and set it to boil; get more from the well in the other buckets. Jake, honey, see if you have some old clothes that are too small for you in your closet or help Becka find some of hers. Someone get me a lamp lit and put it in the bathroom. Get the first aid kit from my bathroom!"

As the others rushed in various directions, she gently removed the dirty pink coat, pulled the child into her arms, and gently stood up. Above all, whatever had happened to the little girl in the past day or more, Jess was intent on helping her feel safe. She had to make sure that she wasn't hurt, get her clean and warm, and get some food in her.

David briefly laid a hand on her shoulder and said, "I'll take care of breakfast and the kids will help with chores; you take care of her." At seventeen, he was every inch of a man in height and Jess was reminded suddenly of how mature and thoughtful he had always been. She could rely on him to take care of the details while she sorted out what injuries were under all the blood and dirt on the little girl.

The next hour was a flurry of activity. Jess closed herself and the small girl inside of the hall bathroom and talked to her softly, speaking of the small family mostly, as she gently removed the girl's clothes and worked to remove some of the larger twigs and burrs from her fine hair.

"Jacob is my son, and he's seven years old now. He really likes to have stories read to him. Right now, we are reading a neat book called Harry Potter and the Sorcerer's Stone. Have you ever heard of it?" There was no response, but the tears and the rocking had stopped.

Jess just kept talking until there was a soft knock on the door, "Mom," came Jacob's low voice, "the bathwater is ready." In the background, she could hear Tina's sleepy voice asking the others what was going on.

"Just leave it there Jacob, I'll get it in a minute," Jess replied encouragingly. She smiled at the little girl, who had jumped at the knock, and began rocking again. "I'm going to open the door and get the buckets for the bath, so you just sit right there."

She kept her movements slow and deliberate as she pulled the buckets of water in, alternately steaming or cold, and poured them one by one into the tub. No one appeared near the open door, and she silently thanked David for his help. Becka and Jacob were as curious as cats and would have been right there in the bathroom with her if he hadn't had warned them off or kept them busy with other tasks.

With the buckets left empty outside the door, and the bathroom once again closed with just the two of them inside, she gently held out her hands to help the little girl into the bathtub. "And then there is Becka, who was Serena's daughter, but she died, so now Becka calls me Mom. She's a few years older than you; she's almost six years old now. She has five dolls, and maybe later on, after we get you cleaned up, she will show them to you. We've made very pretty dresses for them to wear."

She dipped the washcloth into the water and gently washed the little girl's face. Most of the caked-on blood did not appear to be hers, but there were a few scratches on her pale skin. She was a beautiful little child underneath the grime, and she stared at Jess with an intensity that Jess found both compelling and heart wrenching. Again, she was reminded of Erin, her best friend, and her heart contracted in pain. Whatever had happened, this child had seen something awful and, considering the amount of blood, whoever had been with her was either gravely wounded or irrevocably dead.

She put on her most encouraging smile. "I need to talk to David for a moment, sweetie; will you be all right for a minute or two?" She was surprised to get a small nod. "Okay, I'll be right back. Oh, wait," she turned around and began to rummage under the sink, pulling out two toy boats and a handful of battered plastic figurines. "Here, you could play with these if you liked." She plunked the toys into the water and slipped out of the door.

She was not surprised to see David standing outside, a plate of warm eggs and browned potatoes with the steam still rising from them. His face was knotted with concern as he asked, "How is she; is she hurt bad?"

She smiled a brief reassurance at him, "No, let's talk out in the kitchen." He followed her, still carrying the plate. "The blood on her face and clothes definitely is not hers. But there's so much of it, David... whoever she was with, whatever happened to them." Jess closed her eyes and shook her head. "It doesn't look good. She's in shock and she hasn't said word one. I know she can hear and understand me, so I think she's just been horribly traumatized. Take the shotgun and head north, scout around and see if you can find anything... tracks, blood, anything. But be careful, for God's sake, and don't be out long or Jacob will want to follow along."

He nodded and looked over at the kids standing quietly in the pantry, trying not to be noticed.

Jacob looked sheepish for a moment, then rebellious, "But Mom, I..."

Jess quieted him with a glance, "Don't you 'But Mom' me. You stay here and help with the chores, Jacob; I need you here with Becka." She flashed a look at Tina, who was looking quite awake and alert now and said, "Tina is in charge and you had better listen to her or answer to me later for it. Now you and Becka go find me some clean clothes for the little girl."

And with that, she took the plate of food from David, turned away, and headed back for the bathroom, ignoring the small mutter of complaint she heard issuing from her son.

When she slipped back into the bathroom, the toys had floated to the far end of the bathtub, untouched. And the tiny girl just sat there looking at her with those big green eyes.

Jess smiled brightly at her. "Hi, sweetie, I'm back to clean the rest of you. But would you like some food first?" She wrestled the fork around until she had a small bite of egg on it and held it out to the little girl.

The child opened her mouth like a hungry baby bird and ate the bite Jess deposited inside silently. The plate of food was nearly gone before she heard quiet scuffling outside of the door and Becka's quiet voice, "Mom, we brought some old clothes of mine."

"Just leave them there, hon, I'll get them." She heard the floorboards creak as the children departed. She had kept up a line of chatter all the time she was feeding little 'Erin.' But there had been no word from the child, just quiet chewing and that intense green-eyed stare. When Jess had asked her what her name was, the child had simply stared at her and said nothing.

"Well, we have to call you something. Otherwise, it will be 'Hey, you over there' or 'What do you know, little miss, so and so!'" Jess looked the tiny child over, now out of the tub and a towel wrapped around her small body. "I had a friend once, and she was my best friend. We grew up together, played together, right here in this very house."

Her eyes blurred for a moment; her voice caught. "She saved my life, and no matter how bad things got, we always had each other. Her name was Erin. Perhaps, until you are ready to tell us your name, we can call you Erin. Would that be okay?" Little Erin stared up at her, eyes unblinking, and gave a small, almost imperceptible nod. Jess smiled in relief. "Well then, Erin, it is. Now let me see what the kids found to dress you in."

The small pile of clothing outside was an insane mix of tiny clothing, worn-out boots, and only one thing that looked like it might fit... pajamas. Well, that would work for now.

She grabbed the pajamas and pulled them inside, closing the door behind her. When Erin was dressed in the pajamas, and Jess had made another trip out to find a pair of oversized socks to cover her feet, she was ready to meet the rest of the family.

Jess held Erin's tiny hand and led her out of the bathroom and into the kitchen and pulled up a chair for her to sit on at the table. She was so small her head barely peeked over the top of the table. There was a small pitcher of milk on the counter and Jacob had just finished rinsing the blood from his finger and wrapping it in a small rag. Tears of pain coursed down his cheeks.

Jess gave him a hug. "Oh Jake, I'm so sorry, sweetie."

The boy pulled himself up taller. "It's okay, Mom, Satan didn't hurt me too bad," his brave expression belied by the drying tears.

That damn goat was always trying to nip Jess or David, but today little Jacob had been the one to milk her and, of course, gotten bit for his trouble.

She turned to Becka, who was eyeing little Erin with barely contained curiosity, "Becka dear, get those old phone books out for her to sit on."

The door from the garage opened, and David walked in, shedding his coat and wiping his boots. He shook his head. "I didn't find any tracks, Jess, nothing at all. And there's a big one blowing in from the West; looks like we'll get snow before nightfall." His eyes took in the small girl seated at the table and he smiled at her. "She looks better, clean at least."

Becka bustled up with the phone books and Jess lifted Erin up for the books to be slid underneath her, elevating her to a normal level, straightened up, and placed a hand on the child's shoulder. "Everyone, this pretty little gift that Jacob found on our front stoop is a bit shy and doesn't feel like talking right now. And since we don't know her name quite yet, I've told her we will call her Erin until she tells us different."

She smoothed Erin's damp hair with her fingers. "Now, she's heard everything about you, and I know everyone here is very eager to make friends with you, Erin." She looked down into the girl's eyes and spoke softly to her, "Here you are safe, and you can stay with us and be part of our family until we find out where yours is." She felt the girl give a small shudder under her hand. "And no matter what, if we find your family or not, you can always stay here with us; we've plenty of room, food, and love to go around."

The rest of the group murmured affirmatives and Becka edged closer. She smiled at Erin excitedly, obviously overjoyed at the idea of having a playmate. "I have five dolls, Erin, but I'll let you have one of them for your very own. Her name is Stacey, but you could give her a different name if you liked. I'll go get her." And off she ran to retrieve the doll.

Jacob carefully picked up the pitcher of the goat milk and poured a glass full to the brim. "Here, drink this; it's really good when it's warm."

He set the glass down in front of her, then ran to fetch a rag to mop up the slopped mess. David sat down at the table and watched her, taken aback by how pretty the tiny child was now that the grime and muck had been washed away. Erin reached forward and pulled the glass toward her slowly, taking sips, while never taking her eyes off of the other occupants.

Jess considered it all great progress when little Erin didn't pull away from Becka's reappearance next to her or the ragged doll that was suddenly thrust into her face. She just eyed Becka solemnly, and slowly took the doll from her. Jess sat down near her and ate the remaining eggs and potatoes that had cooled on the stove.

And the rest of the family slowly settled around the table in the kitchen, recognizing a need for calm and normalcy around the traumatized little girl.

It wasn't long before Erin's eyes began to glaze over and her head began to droop. She didn't pull away when David stood, walked around to her side of the table, leaned over, and carefully picked her up in his arms, cradling her like a baby. He said nothing, simply walked to the bedroom that Becka and Tina shared and placed her gently on Becka's bed, covered her with blankets, quietly tiptoed out of the room, and shut the door silently behind him.

"Who knows how much sleep she might have gotten, or how long she was out in the cold," he said, shaking his head and sliding into a chair at the table. He scratched through his long hair, looking frustrated. "I couldn't find any kind of tracks... maybe I should go out further."

Jess took his hand in hers. "There's no need. If she had family, which she must have had, all that blood belonged to someone else and there was plenty of it. Her clothes were absolutely soaked in blood. If she showed up on our front stoop, it was because there wasn't anyone left to take care of her. Those shots we heard yesterday, it's all connected, David. You and I both know she's probably here for good." She missed the flush in his cheeks as he stared down at their entwined fingers and turned away seconds later as she disengaged her grip and busied herself with clearing the dishes from the table. "Kids... water from the well and dishes now, please."

The children obeyed without complaint, quiet, putting together for themselves what had probably happened to little Erin's family. No strangers to loss or death. It was sobering nonetheless, and all members of the little family were once again reminded of how easily ended life could be.

It seemed that the gift on their front stoop was here to stay.

Wedding Bells

"L*et me not to the marriage of true minds admit impediments. Love is not love which alters when it alteration finds, or bends with the remover to remove."—William Shakespeare*

"Reverend?" The woman's voice came from the doorway to the church office. Even now, after taking over all of Reverend Thomas's duties completely for the past two years, Jeremy still didn't associate the title of Reverend with himself. He looked around for Reverend Thomas out of habit, but the old man had passed away in March, a withered, gibbering shadow of his former self. It was a hot day, the hottest yet this year, and Jeremy had just been wishing he was out under a tree, hanging out with the kids, watching them run and play. His head jerked back to the door and a large drop of sweat that had been collecting along his forehead dripped into his left eye, momentarily blinding him in one eye as he peered through his open right eye at Grace Wilkes's mother.

Crap.

Karen smiled tentatively at him as he wiped the sweat from his brow and cleared his left eye and motioned for her to come in. "Good morn... afternoon, Mrs. Wilkes," he stumbled a bit; the sermon he had been working on had been a difficult one and it had apparently taken him through the morning and into the early afternoon according to the antique clock in the corner of Jeremy's small office. The room was filled with Reverend Thomas's books and belongings. Jeremy kept looking at them and wondering if he should keep them or give them away. Reverend Thomas had never been married, never had children, and Jeremy was at a loss to find any known relatives.

"May I speak with you, Reverend?"

Jeremy winced at the title. He had never attended seminary and was unsure what the Methodist church would have thought about him, a conflicted half-agnostic and lapsed member of the Church of Christ.

Half the time he wasn't sure he believed in God, but it sure seemed to reassure some of the older crowd. "Please, call me Jeremy."

Karen smiled, "Well, I guess, considering you and Grace and everything." Jeremy winced; he knew what was coming next. "Grace turned nineteen last month, you know."

"Yes, ma'am, I know."

"Don't you dare, ma'am me, Jeremy Deeds. I'm barely two years older than you and you know it." Jeremy's discomfort grew. Karen smiled again, perhaps to show him her words were just that, words, and that she wasn't offended. "It feels strange coming here, though, because it should be Anthony here, the right of the father to speak about his daughter, and all that." She looked around the tiny room and tugged at her clothes, which were clinging from the miserably humid heat. "Shall we go outside?"

"Sure." Jeremy stood up. The heat actually felt good on his legs; it was the winters that were the worst for him. He could predict bad weather better than the old-timers from the strong aches he felt in his damaged legs, but in the summer there was some relief, as if the sun could reach through skin and muscle and warm the irrevocably damaged bones beneath. Still, it wasn't easy to walk far, no matter what.

They walked slowly out the door; the sun was bright overhead and the waves of heat rippled across the empty parking lot. Grace and the orphans were nowhere to be found; perhaps they had gone to the creek to swim. It certainly was a good day for it. Karen pointed to a tree a hundred feet away, and they walked over to it and sat down. Before Karen could say anything, Jeremy said, "Mrs. Wilkes..."

"Call me Karen."

"Um fine, Karen, I... I just wanted you to know... that I... I've never done anything inappropriate with Grace," he said, fumbling over the right words to say.

Her loud peal of laughter surprised him. "And well I know that!" She smiled and looked concerned. "Is that what you thought I was doing here? Warning you away from her?"

Jeremy had a hard time meeting her eyes. "I just..."

"Do you like Grace, Jeremy?" Her question was soft.

"Of course, I do. I mean, she is a great help around here. The kids love her, and... she was a great comfort and help with Reverend Thomas, especially in those last days."

"But do you like her?"

"Mrs. Wilkes," he couldn't manage the informality of her first name to such a serious question. This was Grace's mother he was talking to. "I'm thirty-nine years old and Grace is..."

"And Grace is an adult, capable of love," Karen interrupted. At his shocked expression, she smirked a bit, "I didn't choose you; she did. And twenty years between you is a sight better than the 23 years that separated me from my Anthony. That marriage worked just fine," her eyes filled, "right up to the end of our time together." She shook her head, choking back the memory of her husband lying dead on the ground.

It had been six years, and yet it had been the blink of an eye. The loss of him had not abated; she still expected to see him walk through the door, or be there in bed with her when she woke up at night. "I'm not in judgment of you and I'm less worried about the age difference than you apparently are." She stared into his eyes. "What I want to know is this: is the love that Grace feels for you returned? Do you feel for her as she feels for you?"

He started to stammer out a response, and she stopped him. "I've put you on the spot, and that isn't fair. Listen to me and think about it. Grace is in love with you. She has been for years."

He started to disagree, and she stopped him with a wave of his finger. "You think she is too young to know what she wants, but she isn't. She was practically a mute when I sent her to you. The only time I heard anything from her was at night, when she would scream from the nightmares of remembering that awful day. I didn't know what to do, but I knew she was lost and I hurt so much from losing Anthony that I could barely help myself, much less her."

Karen stopped for a moment, collected the emotions threatening to burst out now. Even after all this time, the wounds were fresh. She gazed at the horizon, and in the distance, they could see the children returning, tumbling through the grass. In a few moments, they would be back in the church parking lot.

"I sent her to you, Jeremy, because I remember your face when you saw her that day, sitting out on the back porch. And you helped her; both you and the Reverend did, but mostly you. She focused in on you like you were her own private lifeboat. At first, yes, when she first talked about marrying you, I dismissed it too. She was a child, with simple beliefs and a good heart. But as these years have passed, she's grown up and never deviated from it. She's waiting for you to reciprocate. You think about that, Reverend Deeds, and let me know if my daughter's feelings for you are something you can return."

Jeremy squirmed again at the title of Reverend. "Please, I really wish everyone would stop calling me that."

Karen shook her head, "You are the Reverend here now, you know. Long before Reverend Thomas passed, you were doing his job and we all know that. Let your parishioners call you Reverend Deeds; it's for them, not for you." And with that piece of advice, she hugged him, then got up and walked off, leaving him to sit under the large oak tree with a completely new point of view.

She was gone before Grace and the kids returned and he couldn't help but smile when one of them flung herself into his arms, half-damp and covered in grass. Collette, the youngest, just an infant when her father and mother died during the assault by a faction of the Western Front on the tiny town of Tiptonville, giggled as she squirmed in his lap. She was an adorable child, with curly red hair and lively brown eyes.

"Mister Jeremy, we went swimming in the creek and I catched a crawdad but Miss Grace said I hadda put it back." She pouted slightly, her eyes dancing with mischief.

"Quite right," Jeremy smiled down at the child, and then flashed a smile up at Grace, "Leave that crawdad in his home. Besides, you are lucky he didn't pinch you," he said, eliciting a scream as he tickled her side. And with that, the rest of the kids dove in and began wiggling, tickling, and shrieking in Jeremy's lap while Grace looked on and shook her head in mock disapproval.

Jeremy looked up during the ruckus and caught Grace staring at him with a look he hadn't seen before. Or perhaps it was better to say he hadn't bothered to notice. It seemed that, when Grace came around, he spent a great deal of time looking at everyone else but her. And why was that? Why was he so worried about what others thought of him? Or of her?

This thought continued to plague him, through an early dinner, through the evening games and storytelling, through the baths and bedtime rituals, and he found himself sneaking glances at her throughout the evening. Grace was petite, like her mother, with curly brown hair and big blue eyes. She still slept in the girls' dorm every Monday through Thursday night, and went back to the family farm Friday evenings after supper, returning early Monday in time to help him fix breakfast for the kids. Today she was wearing a pair of patched and tattered jean shorts and a short-sleeved top. She was slim, and seeing her in a new light after Karen's visit still had him feeling like he was some kind of pervert. There were twenty years between them, for crying out loud, and he felt wrong just looking at her that way.

Just then, as the last of the kids were put to bed and they were alone, tidying up the communal living spaces, Grace turned to ask him a question and caught him staring at her. Jeremy's face flamed red, and he quickly turned away. For crying out loud, he was thirty-nine years old, and here he was, blushing like a pimply faced teenager trying to get to first base. He was so busy trying to hide the flush on face that he missed the big grin that lit her face at his sudden interest.

It would be two weeks before he mustered the courage to visit Karen Wilkes and answer her question about how he felt about her daughter and another five more before the church was able to play the wedding march for the couple. Despite Jeremy's fears, none of the townsfolk or members of the church had concerns about the age difference. Too many things had changed in the world, and if the Reverend was happy, and Grace was happy, then they were too.

In the years to come, the disparate age gap would matter little, and the couple, their adopted children, all orphans, and their two biological children would be instrumental in bringing healing to the community.

To Each a Trade

"The idea of apprenticeship was a term that seemed to hark from the Middle Ages. But here was this opportunity for Tina, for us, and we accepted it. I think it was one of the best decisions we made as a family, but it was hard, real hard. Watching her leave was hard for me and hardest by far for David. But we were facing a bleak, cold winter. A late start to the spring planting, along with a freak frost in mid-May, had wiped out all the fruit tree harvest and a freak cold snap in late August had wiped out most of our remaining crops. We were in bad shape and we knew it. We said our goodbyes, watched her walk away with her hand firmly in Penelope's, and hoped we would all survive our first winter apart."—Jess's Journal

Jess didn't like the smell of the lamb's ear. She had cut the dried, dead flower spikes off of the plants and began trying to extract the seeds. Jess had done this with all the plants currently in the garden. So far, she had managed to harvest hundreds of sage seeds. The sage hadn't bothered Jess a bit, but David had run out of the house protesting the strong scent and howling that his eyes were burning.

It was early September, yet the days were still quite warm. The sun beat down and there was a light breeze, keeping it from being unbearably hot. Everyone was busy with something, making use of the slightly cooler weather to get a long list of needed tasks done. At the moment, it was almost impossible to imagine the impending winter. The tomatoes were still producing and the apples that had escaped the late frost were just about ready to harvest. David had announced he would be clearing an area on the other side of the block where they hoped to start a new orchard and plant the ten small apple trees, he had helped Mr. Banks graft last year. There were also numerous peach and cherry trees that Jacob and Tina had planted as seeds which were now in their second year of growth and ready to be transplanted as well. They had all headed over to the area that morning and were clearing areas of weed cover and prepping the soil. That left Erin and Jess and Quincy behind.

Erin sat quietly next to Jess, her red hair shining in the sun. It was curly, just as Erin's had been. Sometimes Jess found herself wanting to believe that she was Erin, or even Erin's daughter, a piece of her best friend come back to her, a piece she could keep close.

She had seen her friend die. But it didn't matter; she still caught herself hoping for a different reality. The little girl was so quiet, still mute, unlike her namesake in so many ways, yet Jess loved having her nearby. The child had a gentle, kind spirit, which spoke louder than words ever could.

Jess had also harvested the dried pods from the kale plants that had flowered. She had uncovered a garden three houses down beneath a dense carpet of weeds and discovered a persistent kale plant in the mix.

That little gem had yielded hundreds of seeds. She had planted handfuls of kale seeds in areas close to the chicken coop where the chickens could feast on them. Then she had planted long rows of kale two houses down, which still had a privacy fence mostly in place. The flock never strayed too far from their coop and, hidden behind the tall fence, the rows of kale grew thick and lush. The plants would be perfect for adding to salads and soups, and for trade as well, since most of the townspeople still seemed to be in a rut of growing the tried-and-true vegetables, without thought to nutritional powerhouses like kale.

She didn't know what to do with all of these lamb's ear seeds, didn't even know if it was worth her time to do this, but she persevered. Jess gathered every seed she saw come available; basil looked to be next, and some lettuce that had bolted in the rows next to the kale. She wrote on scraps of paper and shoved the drying plants into bowls, boxes, anything that would hold them. She sat on the front stoop, slowly picking at the stalks of lamb's ear, trying not to breathe through her nose. The flower stalks of the plant had an odd smell that made her almost nauseous.

The smell seemed to bother Erin equally. She wrinkled up her nose and made a face at Jess, which made her laugh out loud.

Quincy let out a small whine and one short bark. This usually meant that someone familiar was approaching the house. Jess looked up, surprised to see a stranger approaching. The woman looked to be in her late 40s with slim, long legs, and she was tall. Her hair was long, straight, and dark and she had it braided in one thick rope down the middle of her back. Her temples showed gray, as did one long streak that ran the length of her long hair. Despite the cool fall day, she was wearing shorts and a sleeveless tank top with a durable rucksack resting on her shoulders.

She met Jess's gaze and smiled, raised her hand in greeting. "Hello there! You must be Jessica Aaronson." She reached down and scratched the dog's ears, "And this must be Quincy."

Quincy licked the woman's hand, then settled down at Jess's feet again, her tail a steady thump against the ground. Her latest litter of puppies squirmed on a blanket nearby, mainly sleeping, and Quincy didn't seem alarmed at all by the stranger. Jess had long since come to rely on her dog's instincts—she had found them to be quite accurate.

Still, Jess knew nothing about this strange woman, but she already seemed to know a great deal about Jess and her little family. "Uh, hello." It sounded lame as it came out. Who was this woman?

"I'm Penelope," the woman said, sticking her hand out to shake Jess's. Jess fumbled with the lamb's ear and quickly stood up to shake Penelope's hand. "I see you are collecting lamb's ear seeds." Her eyes were a dark brown color, full of warmth as she asked, "Do you work with other herbs?"

Jess nodded, and did not elaborate. The truth of the matter was that the lamb's ear, along with the basil and some other herb seeds she could barely identify, would probably be handed over to Tina. Despite being just ten years old, the girl had become a fount of knowledge.

Penelope smiled. "Do you know anything about the properties of lamb's ear, Jess?"

"Only that it's making me feel sick to my stomach. I don't like the weird smell."

The woman laughed then, and it was soft and free. "Stop for a while and I'll take over. I've gotten used to it." She sat down on the stoop, took the bucket from Jess, and began plucking at the dry flower heads. Jess could hear the intermittent scatter of seeds as they fell and hit the bottom of the bucket. "The leaves can be picked early, before it flowers and can be dried and used in tea. You could also eat it in salads, or steamed, but most people object to the furry aspect of it. The best use of lamb's ear is for small wound care—it is absorbent and soft, and plentiful.

But that isn't why I came here." She finished with one stalk and started on another.

"I've come to speak with you and David about Tina and a possible apprenticeship."

Jess looked at her, trying to gauge whether the woman was joking, "Tina's only ten years old."

Penelope's hands didn't stop moving as she turned toward Jess and gave her a long, appraising look. She had spent time in the heart of the town, talking to Sarah Turner. She had described Jess as the go-to person for information on the town and its residents. After a few days of trade and work, Penelope knew enough of the girl's history to know that she and her house full of kids had struggled through some pretty tough times in the past six years. Sarah Ann had been forthcoming with details about Jess, informing her that Jess was busy writing down the lives and accounts of most of the residents of Belton and compiling a history of the area.

"She goes from house to house, usually during the winter when there's not so much to do," Sarah Ann had said, "She writes down whatever memories they have—of this war, of their families, of the time before—whatever someone wants to talk about, really." The woman had shrugged. "I wasn't born here, but she even wanted my story."

Penelope had been as circumspect as possible. She had been searching a long time for the author of the letter she had found in the cave. She was sure, however, that this Jess Aaronson was the one that had seen Mom through her final days, and buried her in the cairn outside her beloved cave.

If you are reading this, then you undoubtedly know Madge. My name is Jess Aaronson. I'm sixteen years old.

The letter was crumpled and tattered now, worn from reading and re-reading it over and over.

"Well, I've heard from Dr. Ridley that she knows a lot about herbs and healing." She smiled and turned back to the lamb's ear. "I've also come for a different reason. I've been looking for you for a long time now, nearly five years. You see, you knew someone very important to me."

She let Jess digest this in a long moment of silence. Jess's fear was rising slowly. This woman wasn't a soldier; she had no weapons... could she have come from the camp? Her memories of Tent Five and the camp haunted her dreams each night, but her days had been bright and full of love for long enough that she had learned to cope with the nightly terrors.

Penelope must have sensed her fear, as she stopped and said, "I'm sorry; I didn't tell you my full name. It's Penelope Falling Water Aster... Dr. Madeleine Falling Water—you may have known her as Madge—she was my mother."

"I, she, oh my God. Grandmother Madge. She..." Jess couldn't put the words together. And the tears came then.

Penelope watched her for a moment. She had read the letter so many times, but she had still had her doubts. Had this girl and the other children truly loved her mother? Had Madge been at peace, surrounded by someone, anyone, who may have cared for her? Had they said the prayers the old woman's spirit required in order to find peace in the hereafter? Watching Jess now, it seemed that the letter had spoken true.

Before I tell you how your friend or mother died, I want to tell you how she lived. How she gave us sanctuary and saved our lives, by leading us here, to this cave...

The four of us, my newborn son Jacob, David, and Tina, both orphans from Clinton, and I have been here since September.

Penelope reached out and hugged Jess to her as tears began to slide down her nose. David found them that way a few minutes later and just stood and stared at the two sobbing women. A moment later, Tina also wandered up and took in the scene.

I am sure I do not need to tell you how special Madge was—or how much she came to mean to us. I lost my best friend in the world just days before she found us. I couldn't think; I was scared and lost.

"What's going on? Who is she?" Tina asked her brother. He just shrugged and kept staring at Jess and Penelope. Tina's voice, however, was enough to reduce the crying and elicit some basic explanation of who Penelope was. This was followed immediately by an invitation to dinner.

Two hours later, the sun had slipped low on the horizon and dusk was gathering. Penelope's husband Kip had joined them and they had just finished nibbling the last kernels of corn off of the cob.

Penelope had been fascinated by little Erin, who at nearly four years of age was in a growth spurt and had lost most of her babyish looks. The young girl was slender and pixie-like, her freckled skin slightly sunburnt, and her hair a mass of bright red curls. She still did not speak, and Jess wondered about it from time to time. Would she ever? She had been with the family for just over six months and was obviously happy with everyone. She understood what was asked of her, nodded, smiled, and shook her head when she disagreed, but never spoke a single word, except for the occasional giggle when David tickled her.

As dinner wrapped up, there was a quiet silence that descended upon the group. Penelope looked at the bunch of them and marveled at their resilience. Jess was tall and graceful. Her skin was tanned a golden brown from working in the sun, and her hair fell in long curls down the middle of her back. David was in his mid-to-late teens, and his arms and chest were muscled and lean. They had served some stew with turkey and wild greens in it and Jess had pointed to David, noting that he was the one who had landed them the turkey using his bow. It was the same bow that Grandmother Madge had taught him to use.

The end was peaceful. We were with her, holding her hands, and my baby Jacob nestled beside her. She loved to hold him, and he adored her. We all did.

The sun had slipped down beyond the horizon, pink and red streaks colored the clouds, the crickets had begun to sing, and the evening had a chill. They had spent hours describing their time with Grandmother Madge in the cave. Penelope and Kip had asked many questions, Kip was amazed that they had all spent a winter there. As dinner had wound down, they had put a pot of chicory coffee on to boil, sweetened with the sugar beets Jess had cultivated in the yard two houses down.

They had expanded their gardens to several yards, those they identified as having good soil, and others that simply had intact tall fences. Especially when it came to foods that deer liked, the high fences had been effective in keeping out the local deer population that was exploding in spite of regular hunting.

"Grandmother Madge said you were in Europe, or was it Africa?" Jess asked, dying to hear about the outside world. "How did you get here?"

Penelope's and Kip's faces grew grim. They glanced at each other for a moment and Penelope held out her mug to Kip for a refill. He was nearest the coffeepot. "That has been an adventure, let me tell you. Have any of you heard much of what is going on in the outside world, outside of the former United States?" she asked Jess and David. The word former raised David's hackles a little. What did she mean by former? They were still in the United States... weren't they?

Jess answered, "We heard that The Collapse spread past our borders. That it was kind of like a domino effect. First the economic collapse and then multiple civil wars and uprisings in places like Greece, the Middle East, even China after the U.S. dollar collapsed."

She dug into old memories from before the invasion by the Western Front, "There were a lot of problems with the Euro before the Collapse. But afterwards," she shrugged, "we lost power and internet and my parents stopped talking about what was happening out there."

She stared into the gathering darkness. "Maybe it was too big, too frightening even for them. And then afterwards, after I returned with David and Tina and Jacob, well, we haven't exactly welcomed outsiders in Belton until more recently. The world has changed, I'm sure, but we only know what is nearby. There have been plenty of false starts into reasserting government on a broader level, but nothing that's stuck." She gestured toward the town center, "We have a militia, a mayor..."

"For whatever they are worth," murmured David in disgust.

Jess shot him a glance, "... and a basic town government in place. Every so often someone gets their britches in a knot and wants something more, and starts talking about money and taxes and the federal government. That doesn't last long."

Penelope nodded. "When the United States collapsed, much of the world was already on the brink of complete chaos. The riots in Greece were just the beginning of what became an uprising, civil war, and eventually a full war through Europe."

She gave a dark laugh. "Even Switzerland couldn't sit this one out. And Africa had already been a hotbed, right along with the Middle East; so much infighting, along with the scourge of HIV and so many young people growing up without any parents, without any direction in their lives."

She took a sip of the dark, heavily sweetened chicory and continued, "We were traveling with an independently funded humanitarian aid mission in Uganda. The Lord's Resistance Army controlled much of the north at the time. The word got out that every American had better get out now, or else." Her face had a wry look, "As if it were that easy."

Her husband Kip, who had said little until this point, took up the story. "It took us nearly two years just to get out of Africa. Everything that could break down did—communications, monetary systems, and the American embassies, or any embassies friendly to United States interests were either closed, burned to the ground, or abandoned. The fact that we were Americans was suddenly a very bad thing. Luckily, we had friends, those who had been helped by our organization, by us. We stayed with a string of them until it became dangerous for them to keep us there. We eventually found our way to the Mediterranean and tried to enter Europe via Italy, and later Spain." He shook his head.

Penelope continued, "It seemed that all of Europe was either involved in uprisings, civil war, or fighting each other. More than anything, though, we, well, any Americans were turned away. We ended up with several others from our aid group on a freighter, bound for Port-au-Prince. It was the closest thing we had to the U.S., although anyone we spoke to told us there had been nukes set off in the south and there were plenty of pointed fingers."

She took another sip of the chicory, now cooled in the mug, and continued, "In the end, we don't know how it started, or who pushed what buttons, but there were nuclear detonations recorded in Austin, D.C., and Los Angeles. It looks as if the Star Wars defense program took out most of the satellites in space at right around the same time—effectively ending world-wide communications."

David remembered some of the talk, overheard through closed doors and muffled conversations between his parents. Hearing it so clear, so real from two people who had experienced it, it was surreal.

Jess remembered more, and hearing Kip and Penelope describe it brought back the memories of the internet, intermittent, and her father shouting about the nuke in Austin before everything went down for good.

Penelope stared at the bottom of her cup; her vision clouded by the events that came next.

Kip waited for her to speak and then he continued the story. "We knew the chances of finding Madge were unlikely. There had been such chaos in the cities. We wondered if she ever even made it out. Not to mention that she had told Penelope and her other children of her illness and that she didn't have long. Penelope had been scheduling a trip back to the States when everything went to hell. We just didn't hold out much hope. We stayed in Haiti for nearly eighteen months trying to stay alive and figure out where to go next."

Penelope sat there for a moment, her eyes and mind miles away, lost in memories of Haiti. She didn't want to tell them of the disease, the murders, or how many times they had fought for just enough food to survive. She didn't want to talk about the children she saw lying dead in the streets.

Penelope roused herself. "Florida was impossible—there were nearly a dozen naval bases there that banded together once communications with D.C. ceased. They patrol the waters and allow no one in. It's a fire first, ask questions later situation. We couldn't get close enough to tell them we were American, not that it would have mattered. They had locked it down to Florida residents, anyway. Texas was a fallout zone, as was much of the Caribbean and the southern states." she pursed her lips. "Not that they told Florida citizens that. They actively denied it even after the first reports of radiation sickness. Once the Western Front started moving east into the Plains states, other factions of former military, along with extremists, rose up to define their own areas of control."

Kip chimed in, "The Allied South struggled to consolidate Louisiana, Arkansas, Mississippi, Alabama, Georgia, and South Carolina. Mexico had surged into Arizona, New Mexico, and the most southern section of California and there was chaos there—lines drawn between the white, Hispanic, and Native American populations. The drug cartels made a move for power. The east coast had three different contingents—the Northern Allies who were struggling to define the borders of half a dozen small states, the Unionists that controlled some parts of the southeast, and the Patriots who were hopelessly divided through infighting in Kentucky, Ohio, and Indiana."

Even Jacob and Becka, who understood little of the states being discussed, having been born after the Collapse, were silent. Erin, just four years old, had curled up in David's arms, and was sucking her thumb, listening intently to Kip and Penelope's account.

Penelope continued, "We finally found entry just west of Biloxi, Mississippi. There had been a radiation fallout scare, and much of the area was deserted. We headed up Highway 49. After that it was a zigzag route. We entered Tennessee, tried to go through the northwest section, but there was a chain of small towns, all with militias, and we were turned back at Tiptonville." She took another sip. "The Western Front had torn through that region and everyone was on edge. If you weren't a resident, they turned you away, no questions, no argument." She smiled wryly. "After all, they were the ones with the guns. You can't argue much with the business end of a gun."

Kip spoke, "We spent a winter in Arkansas. There were migrant groups moving through the areas, many of them working crops, building or reinforcing town borders, living like gypsies as they searched for a place to stay. We moved in and out of these groups—diseases we hadn't seen in decades in the Western world ran rampant. Cholera, bouts of dysentery, and a host of other illnesses could be found in any group we joined. But the alternative was to go it alone, without some of the protection a group could provide. Sometimes it was worth it, other times it wasn't."

Penelope spoke, "And eventually we moved through parts of Oklahoma, Kansas, and then finally Missouri. Once we hit Missouri,

I was determined to find my mother. I had thought about it a lot, wondering what she would do, where she would go if she knew she only had a short time to live. I doubted that she would have stayed in her home there in Kansas City, and we were close to the archaeology site she had been working on for the last few years. I had been given the opportunity to visit the site the first year they had begun work, so I was familiar with where to find it. I figured if she wasn't there, I would try finding her in KC. I wasn't holding out much hope either way."

She paused, drained the last of the chicory from her cup, and said, "I noticed the cairn immediately. When we arrived at the cave, I was convinced that the full team had to have been there, since there was evidence of more than just Mom. It took me a while to go deeper into the cave. I was wondering where everyone went, even though it was obvious it had been a while. I had completely forgotten about the long passage. Finding your letter, even as it raised more questions, gave me some measure of peace."

Her eyes brimmed with tears. "She wasn't alone when she passed. That means so much to me to know that she had someone with her as she passed into the world of spirits." She wiped at a tear that had escaped and began trickling down her cheek. "And eventually we came here, looking for you, Jess."

Jess realized then that her own cheeks were wet with tears. The few months they had spent with Madge had been beautiful ones. The old woman had given her so much—love, acceptance, and peace—even now, six years later, she remembered it like it was yesterday. Just when her faith in humans and life in general had been so sorely tested, Madge had reminded her of all she had to live for, all that she could be for Jacob, the others, and for herself. Healing during those months in the cave had allowed her to have some trust in others again. She had emerged from the cave as more than just a ghost filled with grief over the loss of her friend Erin.

Grandmother, that is what she asked us to call her, took us in, and taught us how to survive here, in this cave through the winter. It is now March, late March, and no snow has fallen in several weeks. The temperatures are rising and it is time for me to try to finish my journey home.

"I have her journal. The personal one that she kept," Jess remembered suddenly. "I can get it for you."

Penelope held up a hand. "Tomorrow. Can I come again tomorrow?" The sun had set, and the darkness had closed in. "We are staying in town. That they let us in at all was a surprise, but apparently the militia is allowing traders and migrant workers in these days, so we will be here for another day or perhaps two."

Jess nodded, "Yes, yes, of course. Come by tomorrow." They said their goodbyes, and she watched Penelope and Kip walk away into the darkness. It was a new moon in the sky, and the darkness seemed overwhelming as they disappeared into the night. She gave a small start when David put his hand on her shoulder.

"She wants something, doesn't she?" he asked, his voice quiet in the gloom.

"Yeah..." Jess didn't know how to say it better, "She wants Tina."

"What?!" David sounded outraged, and he looked as though he was ready to run after the couple and confront them.

Jess hastily explained, "There's a group of doctors, healers, working together in the city, or what's left of Kansas City, to create a new learning center for the healing arts. Sarah Turner told her about us, about Tina, and Penelope says it would be an apprenticeship." She grabbed his sleeve. "They are coming back tomorrow. We will learn more about them then. Okay? Let's not jump to any decision right now. They seem alright, and you can say no, but at least let's hear them out. It might actually be a chance for Tina to become a doctor... someone necessary... a future she might want."

David pulled away. "She isn't your sister, Jess. You can't just make this decision for her, or for me." His tone was defensive, even bitter.

Jess felt a surge of pain. They had spent years together, and she loved Tina just as much as she loved David or Jacob. "Of course not... I'm not trying to make a decision for her. I'm just... I'm just saying we should listen to what they say."

David walked in the opposite direction, away from where Penelope and Kip had headed into town, away from the house and Jess. She watched him go, feeling hurt and defensive. She knew he had a right to his feelings, but his abrupt departure wounded her. The last thing in the world she wanted to do was suggest that she wanted Tina should go away.

I don't know you, and you don't know me. But I'm writing this letter and then hiding the box where only someone who knows Madge and inner twists and turns of this cave will be able to find it. I have to be sure; you see. It still isn't safe. They have sent out soldiers hunting for us and I don't know that they aren't still out there looking.

The next day, David seemed better. They had worked on the house, repairing a section of the roof, and then weeding several of the beds of potatoes and lettuce. Jess had made up her mind to tell Penelope they weren't interested, that Tina was far too young. What possible apprenticeship could apply to a young child? As she watched Penelope approach, her long-legged stride fluid on the broken pavement of the street, Jess could see that Sarah Turner had joined her and that Penelope's husband, Kip, was not with them.

Sarah was a kind woman. She had always treated Jess as an equal—and during those first months and years, she had championed the younger woman's cause, and that of their motley group of children more than once. Sarah was quite protective, in fact, which made Jess wonder about the older woman's past, and that of her children, who were nearly the same age as Jess. Sarah had always been rather close-mouthed about where she had come from, or where Cody and Laura's father were.

What would Sarah have to contribute to all of this? Jess wasn't sure what to think. A quick glance at David's face signaled trouble. Tina was his sister, and he had a right to his opinion, but for the first time, Jess wondered what Tina wanted. Stay or go, wasn't it up to her? After all, Tina was nearly the age that David had been when they all first met in Clinton. He had been old enough to make a decision then, a decision that taken him away from everything familiar, everything that reminded him of home. Shouldn't Tina have the right to make that same decision? Even at the age of ten years?

Jess was conflicted, and she knew it showed in her face. Sarah took it in, smiled at her, and gave her a warm hug. "Good morning, Jess!" Since her daughter Laura had married Todd Stevens, the laugh lines on her face had deepened. The births of Laura and Todd's two boys had brought happiness, along with something Jess could only describe as longing to Sarah's face. Jess wondered if Sarah was thinking of the husband she had left behind. Jess had listened to so many stories, so many unfinished, unknown fates of loved ones. It was perhaps the most haunting part of her job as historian — the unknown fates of so many. Sarah's story was one of dozens.

It was hours before dinner and they had had lunch just two hours earlier, but Sarah produced a loaf of her sourdough bread, a favorite of David's. That was combined with a bag of fruits that Kip had sent along, payment for some picking work they had both done earlier in the day. Jess and David, along with Tina, Sarah, and Penelope, sat down for a bite to eat and some conversation. It was stilted at first, mainly due to David, who felt cornered and resentful. Jess laid her hand on his knee, reminding him silently that she was his ally. He stared at her hand as she made small talk with Penelope and Sarah, concentrated on the long, tapered fingers. They were rough with callouses, but still delicate. He looked at them and tried to calm his fears—of losing his sister, knowing how much she wanted to go.

Tina had come to him that morning, the sun barely peeking over the horizon, and quietly folded herself on the floor of his room, quietly so she didn't wake Jacob. Her room was right next door, shared with Becka and Erin, when one or the other wasn't curled in bed next to Jess. "I want to go with her," was all that she had said when he opened one bleary eye and focused on her. They had engaged in a silent contest of wills, him glaring, her just staring back, until he had finally turned away and pulled the covers over his head and tried to ignore her. When he had turned back over a few moments later, she was gone.

The small talk had progressed while he was woolgathering. Penelope was describing her mother's house in Kansas City. "It's over 130 years old and solid brick. Surprisingly, it's rather intact considering the dire situation that most residents were in before and during the collapse.

Most of her books are still there," Penelope smiled at Jess. "She wrote about all kinds of recent history, as well as anthropology. She had quite an obsession with Jesse James and also had notes on Pendergast, a corrupt political boss in the early 20th century." She turned toward David, who just shrugged and shook his head. He had never heard of Jesse James or Pendergast.

"In any case, the house was gone through, but not much was taken and it was empty when we visited it last week. We are planning to stay there and work with a medical group that is forming." She looked at Tina and smiled at her, then back to David where her smile faltered a brief second. "If it would be all right, Tina could come with us to Kansas City, and stay in the house. There is plenty of room and there are other students who she would be learning side-by-side with. You could come too, David, to see for yourself, if you liked."

A long silence ensued. All eyes were on David, until Tina spoke up. "I want to go to Kansas City with you, Penelope. I want to learn how to be a doctor. It's all I've ever wanted to do."

David closed his eyes for a moment, remembering her tiny hand in his, her matted hair in those weeks and months that had followed the deaths of their parents. The feel of her tiny body nestled against his. He remembered farther back, the first time he had seen her in the hospital, a tiny red face, impossibly small, mewling cries that sounded like a tiny, sad kitten. They had never fought; with nearly eight years between them, he had always been the oldest, the one she looked up to. And when they had been alone, lost in the rubble of a dead and broken town, she had depended on him for everything.

It was only here, in Belton, that she had come into her own, as young as she was, defining her future, writing it on the wall with nothing short of an indelible marker. Her abilities, her intuitive understanding and curiosity about the healing arts had given her this opportunity. And who was he to say no? How could he? David thought of her being absent, not someone he saw every day, not in the garden or walking into town with freshly picked herbs for Dr. Ridley, and something deep in his chest twisted and pulled. She was all that he had of their former life. The only evidence he could show of the parents that he had lost. The words to say all that seemed to elude him.

In the end, he simply stared at Jess's hand, still on his knee, and said, "If Tina wants to go, then, I guess that's what she should do."

But if you find this, know that she died surrounded by people who loved her. She was at peace, and I miss her dreadfully.

Yours, Jess

Jess, David, and the kids stood there for a long time the next morning and watched Tina walk away, her tiny hand in Penelope's, Kip alongside her. They watched until all three became dark specks that simply disappeared over the horizon.

Ascension

"*Good can imagine Evil; but Evil cannot imagine Good*"*—W.H. Auden*

Sulwyn leaned back in his chair, his arms crossed in front of him, and shook his head. His gray hair had been cropped close—there was an outbreak of lice going around the camp—and even some of the women had chosen to cut most of their hair off rather than scratch all day. "Slaves? I just don't see how it's gonna work. Slaves have to eat."

Cooper had surprised everyone by returning with three black women from the last raid. He had insisted on putting them in a half-burned cabin where they huddled, tight-lipped and bloody, under armed guard. The raid had been quick, brutal in its efficiency.

The cabin had belonged to one of Sulwyn's chief lieutenants. Two weeks before, deep in the night, a fire had sparked, and others woke to the cabin fully engulfed in flames. The man had burned to death while the rest of the camp had concentrated on making sure the fire didn't spread to the rest of the nearby cabins and tents.

Despite part of the roof missing and some gaps in the charred timbers, the body of the cabin was intact. They threw a tarp over it, chained the captives, and attached a lock that opened only from the outside. Situated in the middle of the clearing, the captives would have to run by scores of armed Amerika Reborn soldiers in order to escape.

Cooper shrugged in response to Sulwyn's question. "Who says we need to feed them well? Slaves are for working, and if one or two dies," he shrugged again, "oh well, there's more out there." Sulwyn thought about this for a few moments and while he did, Delwen came to the door of the cabin.

In her arms, she held a small baby. Cooper felt a wave of disgust wash over him. He didn't know who he despised more, the mewling brat that was his daughter or the unattractive woman who held her. He found himself wondering how his life had gone so wrong. In the Western Front, he could have had any woman he wanted, he could have ordered any man's death, or done it himself with impunity. And here, he closed his eyes; here he was, bound by Sulwyn's rules.

It had been hard to break into the upper echelon of leadership—there was Sulwyn, his wretched daughter Delwen, and several others that had been with Sulwyn from the beginning. Albus had been as close to Sulwyn's right-hand man as you could get, and Cooper had made sure to get rid of him when the short-sighted man had refused to align with him.

Albus had been the one Sulwyn listened to the most and Cooper had gone to him with the idea of capturing slaves and eventually using them for drug production. Plenty of people wanted an escape from what they saw as a dark new world. Cooper would never understand that way of thinking, but he was certain he could benefit from it. Manufacturing the drugs that gave them those ways to escape could be very profitable.

Albus had been fine with the slavery part, but the drugs? "No way," he had said, "what kind of idiot are you, Cooper?" Drugs had killed his wife and young daughter over a decade before, something he said little about, but the images of the crumpled car and blood haunted him even now. He warned Cooper that if he persisted in his plan, that he would push Sulwyn to throw him out, whether he was married to Delwen or not. Cooper held himself back from doing violence to the man. A week later, he made sure that Albus would never bend Sulwyn's ear again. The flames had destroyed all evidence of the crime.

Delwen's hard-edged voice broke through his reverie. "I ain't seen you around much these days." Her tone leaked resentment in every syllable. Her face and body were heavier now; she had put on a few pounds with the brat that hadn't come off. Perhaps if she actually did something besides sit around and feed her fat face, she'd get back her body, which would be some improvement, but not much, to her looks.

He stared at her, wondering if there was any way he could get away with killing her in some handy accident. "I've been sleeping in the hammock outside. I thought that would be better than disturbing you when I got back late." The raiders, led by Cooper, had returned late the night before. It was September, and the nights were still quite warm. Sleeping outside in the hammock had meant he didn't have to listen to the squalling baby, or to his wife's snores, both of which disturbed his sleep and peace of mind.

They reminded him all too often of his new, disturbingly domestic life, which he didn't want and certainly hadn't asked for. A few wordless meetings in the dark, the only ever instigated by a woman instead of him, and he had ended up facing Sulwyn, and a quietly smug Delwen, one cold March morning. "My daughter tells me she's pregnant, and you are the father."

Cooper hadn't known what to say. Scuttling through his brain had been the question he'd wanted to ask but didn't. How do I know she's just slept with me? But he knew Sulwyn well enough by now not to ask a question like that. In another time and place, this man would have been a baron. He was a good leader, yet he was definitely removed from the others. And after four years with the Amerika Reborn, dealing with Sulwyn nearly every day, Cooper knew that questioning whether the man's only child was sleeping with multiple men would have been a mortal mistake.

Sulwyn had given Cooper a minute or two to realize how badly he was hosed before saying, "We don't have a preacher, so I guess I'll have to do. We'll have some kind of ceremony tomorrow." And with that, Cooper's fate was sealed. Once the leader of a hundred plus faction of the Western Front, and now a lackey of Sulwyn's. With every caterwaul that came from the brat he had sired, he thought of where he had been, and where he was now, and regretted it. Somehow, he needed to take back his life—and that meant that Sulwyn had to die. But before he could just kill the man, without question or retribution, he had to make this group into a fighting power that the region had not seen before. They had to see him as a leader in his own right—then, and only then, would the men follow him. When that day came, he could and would kill Sulwyn with impunity.

Delwen just glared at him and jiggled the infant. From the sour, scrunched-up look on the baby's face, it appeared as if she was getting ready to begin howling any moment. Cooper hadn't had any say in what the child was named, not that he particularly cared anyway, and Delwen had announced that the baby's name was Sulwen, the feminine version of Sulwyn, which meant white sun in Welsh.

Once she had come out, Cooper had been convinced she was his kid, but it hadn't changed his mind about children in general. He despised the mewling brat. At least Armando had been quiet, but this creature screamed all day and all night, given the opportunity. Sulwen's name was quickly shortened to Sully, in order to differentiate her from her grandfather more easily.

"Well, I want one of those women you rounded up to help with Sully," Delwen said, "I can't get any sleep and you sure aren't any help." And with that input, it was decided. The slaves would be put to use, and the first part of Cooper's plan fell into place. First slaves, then drug production and sale, and then he would find a way to get rid of Sulwyn, along with Sulwyn's daughter and grandchild. It all felt perfect.

Camelia didn't just handle the doctoring; she had also been put in charge of bodies and burials. Two weeks before, Armando had watched with grim fascination as his mother gave the grisly burned remains a cursory examination, her focus honing in on the skull for just a second longer than normal, and then turned back to the business of digging the hole. Later that night, when the others were gone and Armando was alone to snuggle next to his mother, he asked her in a tiny whisper, "Why did you look at his head, Mamá?"

Camelia pulled him close. "Promise you won't ask again? I'll answer, but you must promise not to speak of it to anyone."

Armando wondered who she thought he might talk to, since he had been ostracized from anyone his age due to his 'color' and nodded, "I promise, Mamá."

"Someone killed him," she said flatly.

"Why?"

"Because he was in the other man's way—then he burned the cabin to hide what he had done."

"It was Cooper, wasn't it, Mamá?"

The conversation had been conducted in whispers, and all of it in Spanish, but Camelia had flinched at the name and pulled her son even closer. "Sh, do not say his name."

"Well, was it?"

"Yes, I think so. Now go to sleep."

Morning

"*Like a morning dream, life becomes more and more bright the longer we live, and the reason for everything appears more clear. What has puzzled us before seems less mysterious, and the crooked paths look straighter."—John Paul Richter*

Light peeked in through the boarded-up window in Jess's bedroom and she opened her eyes instinctively, knowing that the daylight was wasting and there was much to be done today. Becka lay curled up next to her, hair sticky and moist with sweat from the fever she had been fighting for days. A small hand fisted the covers, and one leg lay over Jess.

She slowly slid from the bed, quietly cursing the bitter cold that cut into her as soon as she left the warm layers of bedcovers. Becka murmured and shifted, curling into a small ball. Jess pulled on a thick sweater and slid her socked feet into tattered and taped-over work boots.

Her feet guided the way to the hall where the light did not, for the years spent in this house were many and she knew each squeaky floorboard, each corner of furniture, and doorway within it. Her hand was reaching for the doorknob of the door of the bedroom at the end of the hall when it opened and nine-year-old Jacob spoke quietly in the darkness, "Mornin', Mom. How's Becka?"

Jess sighed, "No change. I left her sleeping. Breakfast or barn?"

"Breakfast... are eggs okay?" he replied.

"Sounds fine," Jess reached out through the gloom and smoothed his hair with her hand. "Wake up the others, but tell them to be quiet and let Becka sleep."

She walked through the living room and on through the kitchen and small pantry next to it. Next was the door leading to the barn. In a former life it had been an attached two-car garage, but now it was a shelter for the family's two goats, a large rabbit hutch, and feed supplies.

Sounds of the others moving about in the house could be heard dimly through the walls as Jess set about feeding each of the animals. Later, she would let the goats out into a corral to stretch their legs. After feeding came cleaning, and after that came her daily war with Satan, their female goat, for her meager pitcher of milk. Satan, as her name implied, came straight from hell and was meaner than any goat had any business being. Jess once again resolved to finish off the wretched creature as soon as she produced female offspring. Satan was also resolved to produce only females. Consequently, her life and future seemed safely assured. Apple, the male goat, kept out of Satan's way and always seemed to have a henpecked, desperate look about his whiskered face.

"Damn it, Satan," Jess exclaimed as she wrestled the goat into place, only to be sprayed by the first drops of milk she squeezed out. The goat had moved suddenly. As she wiped her boot off, the goat took the opportunity to nip the unprotected finger.

"Sonuva...aw jeezsus!" Jess held her bleeding digit to her lips. "Goat curry! That's what I'm gonna make you!" She waved her fist at the goat half-heartedly, knowing the threat was empty.

The door to the garage swung open and Erin stepped through, shutting it quickly so as not to let out what small amount of heat was emanating from the kitchen. Erin was now six years old. There was a quiet maturity about the child that belied her tender age. Without a word, she took hold of Satan's head and offered the beast a withered crabapple. She was the only one in the family who could coax the blasted goat to stay still, and she also was the only one of them to never have been nipped, stepped on, or even so much as butted by Satan.

Jess smiled and quickly began milking the goat, stopping only after the last drops of milk were squeezed out. Satan had long since finished the apple and was standing still patiently as Erin stroked the recalcitrant beast's head and whiskered chin. The girl's eyes held the goat's gaze steadily. It was as if they were speaking a silent language, telling secrets and exchanging memories with each other.

"All done." Jess broke the silence, Erin let go of Satan, and the goat instantly left to graze on the fresh feed set out for her. Jess reached over and smoothed the child's tangled hair with her hand and smiled down at Erin. "Any words for me today, sweet Erin?" she asked the girl, cupping her chin in her hand.

The fey child only smiled and shook her head, saying nothing at all, and instead she held out her arms to be picked up and hugged. As always,

Jess took Erin in her arms and hugged her gently against her, marveling at how such a small creature could so silently charm all those around her—man and beast alike.

Erin had appeared on the doorstep over two years ago. Jess had rounded the front of the house, saw her crouched there and instantly drew near, crouched down, and gathered her in her arms. The trembling creature had wrapped her arms and legs around Jess and buried her face in Jess's neck. She had not uttered a word then, or in the two long years since. But where her voice failed, her eyes and hands spoke volumes, and she had instantly become a part of their family, without question or reservation.

The spring following Erin's arrival, a body was discovered a mile to the east, along the creek bank. It was the remains of a man with red hair, much like Erin's. He had been shot. There had been a well-loved teddy bear tucked inside a child-size knapsack lying nearby.

Thurman Banks had found the body and told Jess about it the following day as he brought by some potatoes in exchange for fresh eggs from the chicken coop Jess and the kids kept in back of the house.

He had buried the body where it lay, he said, and put up a rough cross for the unknown man. He looked over at the small, silent child sitting in the garden patch, placed the bear in her lap, and went away quietly with his eggs. He visited often, and never failed to bring by something special for Erin when he did, for the child had enchanted him.

Jess gave Erin another quick hug before setting her back on the ground. "Go help Jacob, sweetheart. He's in the chicken coop and surely having trouble with Maude and Beulah by now," she directed the child, envisioning her son struggling to get the eggs from two of the older, more aggressive hens.

Maude and Beulah, like Satan, were destined for the stockpot one of these days. But they were still quite reliable layers, so Jess held off from ending them, despite the inevitable pecks and scratches they handed out so liberally. Erin slipped away silently and headed out the side door toward the back of the house.

Jess headed back inside the house and promptly ran into David, who was still rubbing his eyes, trying desperately to wake up. "Mornin' Jess," he said yawning, wincing as he saw her bloody finger. "Satan git you again?"

Jess nodded and headed for the medicine cabinet to dose her injured finger with iodine, leaning in first for a peck on the cheek from the young man as she passed by. David was now twenty years old, and his hair was nearly shoulder-length, dark brown, and tousled, his eyes a soft, friendly brown. Like the rest of their hodgepodge family, he was of slender build—obesity had all but disappeared in the past decade when food was scarce and most lived at bare subsistence level. Though harvests were better now, they were still far from being safe from starvation if a winter came early enough or lasted too long.

"So, what's on tap for today? Lessons, hunting, or washing?" David asked as Jess busied herself with lighting a small fire under one burner.

"Well, we could use some meat, or even fish, if you could get them to bite. Take Jake; he's itching to get out there and do 'manly' things." Jess winked at him, and David snorted and nodded. "I'll see how far Erin and I can get with the wash, but make sure and gather it up for me, okay? Then maybe some lessons for Jake tonight if you two don't get back too late."

Jacob slipped in as she was talking. "Hunting? Really? Right on!" Then his face managed to twitch into a somewhat serious expression, "But Mom, you know how far we have to go out to get anything; it might be really late when we get back. We might not have time for lessons tonight." He tried unsuccessfully to look disappointed.

Jess turned and gave him a look. "Well then, perhaps, young Jacob, you should stay here with me and help with laundry and still have plenty of time for your lessons afterwards. It seems to me that you should be farther along in that book by now, and your math needs work too."

Jacob practically stumbled over himself getting his objections out. In the end it was a wail, "But Mom!"

She raised an eyebrow. "I can depend on you being back by sundown?" He nodded excitedly. "Glad to hear it. Now be sure to pack a lunch for the two of you while breakfast gets cooked and wear your warm wool socks that I made you." As he prepared to launch himself like a rocket into the living room and on through into his bedroom, she called out in a loud whisper, “And quietly! Becka’s still sleeping!”

Saying Goodbye

"I *can't stay here. It isn't home without him. Chris will say, 'What about our babies?' And what about our babies? Our babies are gone, gone before they drew their first breaths. If I stay here where I have lost so much, I will taste the ashes of regret in my mouth forever."—Carrie's Journal*

The little graveyard didn't have much room left. Not with its newest addition. And unlike the four previous, mostly private, ceremonies, this one was well attended. Practically everyone in Tiptonville was here. Carl had whispered to Chris that they had even shut down the Trade Mart for the day.

To the right stood Joseph, looking quite tall and somber for his fourteen years. Beside him, seated in a well-padded chair with a blanket, was Mr. Liles. The man was 116 years old and looked so frail and thin that Chris feared a stiff breeze would blow him away. His rheumy eyes watered and he clutched a much-abused handkerchief in one hand while the other plucked randomly at the blanket that swaddled him. Joseph said that Mr. Liles slept a lot these days and ate little.

The teen had volunteered to stay with the old man after a recent fall had left him weak and fragile. Joseph had developed a knack for working with motors and he had begun helping out Mr. Liles a few years earlier in the shop. Now he stayed and cared for the old man, fixed meals, and made sure the stove stayed lit. He also manned the store and helped the infrequent customer.

Despite the attention, Mr. Liles had declined steadily during Fenton's illness. Chris wondered what it must be like to outlive your children, your grandchildren, and to see your friends pass before you. How many funerals had Mr. Liles attended? How many goodbyes?

Liza and Carl, along with their three children, Molly, John and little Abby, stood on the left. Liza's face was a mask of grief, her eyes red-rimmed, and her nose blotchy. She would not cry, however, in front of the children. Abby, not quite two years old, wriggled in her arms, itching to be set down so she could run through the tall grass. Little John, just three and a half years old, stood holding his dad's hand and looked puzzled by all the people and the mournful tone in the air. Molly Ann, who would be six in less than two weeks, clutched Carl's other side, her tiny face sad. She had been Fenton's favorite, the first of his great-grandchildren, and he had doted on her.

Outside of immediate family and Mr. Liles, it appeared that the rest of Tiptonville stood outside of the waist-high metal gates. Everyone wore black armbands. Mrs. Jennings, the town librarian, stood close to the fence, grasped it with one frail hand, and wept softly into her handkerchief.

Reverend Deeds stepped forward, leaning heavily on his cane with one hand, the other arm around his young wife, Grace. He opened a well-worn Bible riddled with tabs and papers marking different passages.

Carrie leaned against Chris. She had miscarried just a week before, and was still weak and tired. She closed her eyes, trying to stop the tears from sliding down her face.

Gramps had suffered for so long, and Liza had done everything she could. In another time, when the world had been whole, Gramps could have had bypass surgery. The doctors would have been able to open him up, clean out the clogged chambers, and give him a decade more.

But that time, like the country they had long identified with, was gone. The recovery and founding of the new nation was taking its time. This had all taken too long for Fenton. This life they led was harder, with no time for the weak or the sick to heal. Not when there were fields to be plowed or the bare necessities to be met. Slowly, his heart had reduced his ability to walk very far or exert himself in much of any way.

There were rumblings of a Reformation, now that the Second American Civil War was officially over. Life was slowly going back to normal. However, that seemed to be happening with more speed on the east and west coasts, not here, not in Tennessee, or even the larger southern cities. The citizens of Tiptonville, along with so many other small towns, were still on their own.

It had been a difficult thing to see, watching Fenton slowly succumb to heart disease. It had been especially hard for Liza, there in the house, pulled in so many directions. She had three small children, the duties of the farm and the townspeople, who now regularly visited for their doctoring needs.

Jeremy—Carrie still had a hard time thinking of him as Reverend Deeds—stepped forward and began to speak.

"We are gathered here today in memory of our friend, a beloved grandfather and member of this community, Fenton Perdue." He opened it to a marked page and began the sermon. "Jesus tells us that we will know not the hour of our death..."

Carrie's attention wandered from Jeremy to the markers in the small family cemetery. Her gaze came to rest on her father's and mother's graves. Her heart ached at the memory of them, especially her mother, Amy.

That last time she had seen her, she had been in the hospital bed looking so thin, so insubstantial. Carrie had been afraid to hug her, afraid that Joseph, who had just begun crawling, would hurt his frail mother as he wiggled in her arms. It had been three days before Thanksgiving and the hospital reeked of turkey and disinfectant, an unpleasant and disconcerting combination.

Fenton had stepped out of the room with Liza and baby Joseph to get a bite to eat at the cafeteria, and Amy had beckoned her daughter closer. "Carrie, sweetheart, come here." Her bony fingers were cold in Carrie's hand. A tear trickled down her mother's pale cheek. "You are so beautiful, and I love you so much. You know that, don't you?"

Carrie had nodded, unable to say anything. There are moments when you know it, whether the words have been said or not, that things are not going to get better, that life will never be the same again. Dad was gone and now Mom was dying, as well. Carrie could see there was little time left, but her voice seemed to have deserted her. She wanted to tell Mom everything and beg her not to leave, to just fight harder.

"Carrie, sweetie, your sister and little brother need you right now. Even Gramps needs you. And these next few weeks and months will be hard. I know they have already been hard and that you feel lost and scared right now." Her mother stopped, struggled to breathe, and then continued, "Someday, though, someday you will find love. You will make a family of your own and you will have babies and you will laugh and love. Promise me that you will do these things—that you won't wait for the perfect moment—but jump into life and live it and love every moment of it. Promise me that you will find happiness and that when the time comes to leave, you will do it, and you will go where you need to go and be who you need to be."

Carrie nodded, her eyes full of tears, "I promise, Mom." A moment passed before Carrie mustered the courage to admit, "I stole five dollars from Dad's wallet the day before... the day..." her voice faltered.

Her mother managed a small chuckle. "I know you did. Your dad told me." She squeezed Carrie's hand with remarkable strength. "Anything else you want to confess?" she asked, her voice cracking with the effort.

Carrie struggled for a moment to form the words. "I blamed Joseph at first. For making you weak, for making you get sick. But... I know it isn't his fault and I promise I will be a good sister and not fight with him or Liza." She could see her mom slipping into sleep, exhausted from their brief discussion. "I love you, Mom."

Jeremy's words interrupted Carrie's reverie, "Even though I walk through the shadow of the valley of death, I will fear no evil, for thou art with me." He continued the Lord's prayer, and she could hear the others murmuring it softly all around her.

Gramps had loved them, grouched at them, guided them... and now he was gone. The memory of her mother's words fell like arrows on her heart. Jump into life and live it and love every moment of it. What had she been doing?

Carrie couldn't help but feel she had ignored her mother's advice, at least some of it. She had found love and embraced that, but she had somehow lost her way on the rest. As the coffin was slowly lowered into the ground, and her tears, along with many others', flowed freely, Carrie could not shake the feeling.

Somehow, I need to change. Somehow, I need to be more than I am right now.

Love Finds Us

They say, those soft-spoken romantics, that love finds you when you least expect it. Somehow sneaking up behind you after all of that loneliness and searching. It hits you dead on in your brain-pan and touches your very soul. It sucks you in and steals your heart. It is a moment when you are looking down at the ground, trudging forward, innocently aware that fate is coming down the highway, barreling along, making time, a load of bricks on its back. This deep and great love that takes you and sweeps you away with no regrets or time for compromise. —Christine Shuck

In the end, it was really Satan's fault. If it hadn't been for that awful creature, and a very bloody finger, who knows how long it might have been before Jess realized that she was in love with David and he with her? In the end, that damned goat got to live, despite her violent tendencies.

Satan grunted and her bloated stomach convulsed and twisted. David stared at the rear of the animal. "I think I see the head!"

Jacob sidled up next to him and stared as well, "Oh gross! That is so cool!"

Jess had had enough of everyone. "Out! Out!" she ordered Erin and Jacob. Satan had been laboring for well over four hours now and Jess had missed breakfast and lunch and was hungry and cross and done with the circus act the pregnant goat seemed to be putting on.

David eyed her warily. "You all right?"

She just glared in return and eyed the retreating kids. Jacob foolishly spoke, half inside the sanctuary of the house, half of him still in reach, "But Mom, I..."

"I said OUT!" The door slammed shut, and she relaxed somewhat and turned back to Satan. "This effing goat had better have a girl this time."

"Still going to turn her into stew?"

"You're damned straight I am!" Despite her tough words, she stroked the pregnant goat as the kid's head slowly began to emerge. "Come on Satan, you can do it!"

Out slithered a kid, covered with blood and definitely, oh quite definitely, another damn male. Jess cussed low and furious. "Damn you, Satan, another boy?"

The goat's stomach convulsed and writhed again. David stopped staring at Jess's tousled blond hair and turned back to the goat. A few seconds later, he was holding a tiny, damp newborn kid and grinning.

"Looks like a girl to me!" Satan made a strange sound, and David's grin slipped as he stared at Satan's rear in puzzlement.

"What is it?" Jess asked, sounding concerned.

"I... uh... think she's having triplets!"

"You are shitting me." David arched an eyebrow in mock shock. It was a rare thing to hear Jess curse, and she was always after him to watch what he said in front of the kids.

"No... I'm uh... ah crap, here it comes!" David shoved the slimy, damp newborn kid into Jess's arms and reached up in time to catch the third one before it slid out onto the hard concrete. He examined it quickly and looked up with a grin. "Would you believe it's another girl?"

As if sensing her days were numbered, Satan reached back and bit down hard on the hand resting near her flank. Jess dropped the floundering newborn kid and recoiled away from the vicious animal. Blood flowed freely and brought tears of pain into Jess's eyes. "Oh, damn it all to hell, that really hurts!"

David was at her side in an instant, applying pressure and wrapping the finger in a clean cloth. They had a pile of them there on the floor for toweling off the newborn kids.

The minute he touched her, smelled her hair near his face, it made him crazy. And today was no different. He'd been avoiding being alone with her for weeks now. It was just too much, these feelings he had when she was nearby. The slightest touch, the smell of her, even her smile—and his body would vibrate from deep inside.

And all the while, he wondered if she even knew how much he wanted her. At first, he had told himself he was just horny. It was natural, normal, and they weren't related after all. But it seemed as if they had known each other forever. He told himself that she couldn't see him that way, because he was younger and she'd taken care of him when they first met.

He'd only been eleven and her fifteen and pregnant and both of them as lonely and scared as could be. For years he'd thought of her just like that, just like the moment they had met. A big sister figure, alone, just like him and Tina.

But something had changed. First the dreams had come, bringing visions of soft lips, deep blue eyes, fantasies of her lying naked in his arms. After a few of those dreams and blushing furiously when he looked at her across from him at the breakfast table, he'd headed east on a week-long hunting trip, hoping to get his head (both of them) screwed on straight. Along the way, he had found Elle Beringer alone picking mushrooms in the woods and she'd showed him what he'd only dreamed and fantasized about. It had taken the edge off for a while.

Whenever it got bad, he went on another hunting trip and looked up Elle at her cabin where she lived alone and traded mushrooms and wild carrots for some fresh goat's milk or eggs. She'd asked him to stay once, and he was tempted—the sex was phenomenal—but something kept pulling him back to the little house in Belton.

One day, after nearly a year away, he'd stopped by Elle's. He found her with a swelled pregnant belly and a man by her side. The tiny cabin had doubled in size, new wood gleaming in the sun. Elle was a good woman; he was glad to see her settled and happy. She introduced her man, Mike, and they sat and ate supper together before parting ways.

"You're a million miles away," Jess's voice brought him back to reality, his face inches from hers, "you okay?"

He looked into her eyes, they were a deep crayon blue, and before his brain could come up with a million reasons not to, he leaned in, reached one hand up into her soft blond hair and pulled her close and kissed her. The kiss lasted several seconds. Her lips were soft, and she made a quiet almost purring sound in the back of her throat. He found it to be incredibly sexy.

When they broke apart, he was terrified to even look her in the eye. What if he looked up and saw pity? What if he saw a look that said 'sister' or 'friend' and not lover? He had wanted to kiss her, to know the feel of her skin and lips against his own for so long. He could not bear the thought of her not wanting him back.

Jess was stunned by the kiss. More than anything, she was shocked by her response to it. Her whole body thrummed! She had avoided men for so long, kept herself safe by sticking to the family, hiding behind the children and their needs in order to never have to be attractive or attracted to another man for the rest of her life. So why did she want to grab him by the shirt, pull him back up against her, and have him kiss her again like that?

At that moment, the door to the garage opened and saved them both from whatever foolish words they might have uttered next.

Jacob flew into the room, "Oh wow! THREE baby goats. Satan had triplets!!!!"

Becka was at his heels, bouncing up and down, and Erin followed silently. Although she could speak, she still chose silence more often than not. Old habits die hard. Jess and David had practically jumped apart when the door opened and while Jacob had eyes only for the newborn kids, little Erin gave them a once over and smiled secretively at them before turning her attention to the newborns. She was a perceptive little girl.

The rest of the day was consumed with cleaning up the afterbirth and making sure all three newborns were nursing well. Satan was looking fine, despite the strain of multiple offspring, and Apple kept his distance from the tiny family unit after Satan bit his neck when he sniffed the newborns.

Jacob was singing some impromptu song about goat curry, stopping only to ask what exactly curry was and Becka had asked to name the newborns Damien, Lucifer, and Beelzebub. When reminded that Lucifer and Beelzebub were both male names, she was quick to note that angels were androgynous and after all, and that Satan wasn't particularly a girl's name either. The names stuck.

In later years, their names would prove to be frighteningly accurate. Both girls took after their mother and exceeded her in viciousness. Damien ended up being the gentle one. Lucifer and Beelzebub ended up in the stewpot long before their mother did.

Jess and David avoided each other's eyes and busied themselves with chores and dinner, and cleaning. Jacob and Erin ran and played for most of the day outside and fell asleep, dead asleep, in the middle of the living room floor by the fourth page in the book Jess had begun reading to them, Harry Potter and the Half-Blood Prince. Jess's voice faded to a whisper as she surveyed the limp bodies at her feet. They were wrapped in blankets and breathing even and deep.

She raised her gaze to meet David's. He had been staring at her steadily for the past ten minutes, slowly convincing himself that she hadn't said "no" to that kiss. She had even touched his hand lightly, caressingly, earlier when asking him to pass the salt. She smiled at him nervously, broke eye contact, and stood up. Negotiating around the limp sleeping bodies was difficult; the floorboards creaked noisily and caused Jacob to shift and mutter in his sleep. Jess negotiated her way to the dark hallway and the open door to her bedroom. Her heart gave a thump of surprise as she realized that David was inches from her.

He had been silent in his approach. Standing this close, she realized he was nearly half a foot taller. "When did that happen?" she asked herself. Damn it, he was close; mere inches separated them.

"Maybe we should talk about this..." she began to say to him, her body beginning to thrum.

"Mm hm," was his only reply. He pulled her against him gently, sought out her soft lips in the darkness, and kissed her. Unlike their first kiss, there was no question in this one. Their tongues met, entwined, teased, and intensified.

She made one more attempt, "The kids, they might wake up." She felt annoyance, not at David, but at herself for even mentioning the kids. It wasn't what she was worried about, not really. By this time, they had somehow made their way inside of the bedroom. He closed the door firmly and quietly behind them and pulled Jess close to his body.

He threaded his fingers through her soft blond curls. She had cut it short just the one time before their journey back to Belton. Ever since she had let it grow long, only trimming the rough split ends away, and it was now past her back, a riot of curls and waves.

He leaned into the curve of her neck, whispering against her skin, “This has nothing to do with the kids. This is between you and me. The kids will be fine out there.”

Before she could protest any further, he pulled her down onto the bed and covered her mouth with his. She found her hands moving along his body, pulling at his shirt, sliding her hands along his ribs. Clothing melted away, her shirt tossed over there, a shoe clattered to the floor. His tongue and mouth moving along her neck, down to her breasts, sliding a hand into the hem of her pants. She stiffened, almost imperceptibly, but he felt it.

He stopped, his voice was soft in her ear, “I love you, Jessie, and I would never hurt you. You know that, right?”

She nodded, unable to trust her voice; the fear and memories had just hit her and then, just as quickly, passed through her. And a few moments later, the unexpected pleasure of lovemaking, not just sex, was mind-blowing. For years she had avoided men, avoided the thought of ever being close to another. But this, this was physical love, with someone she had spent the last ten years living and working next to. It was familiar, yet completely new, and she hadn't felt anything like it before.

Tears followed. There were so many tears that he became confused and worried he had frightened or hurt her. At least until she told him that she loved him, too. He held her then, covered her with a quilt, and pulled her close to his body until she stopped crying and fell asleep in his arms. It was now that he could see so clearly the horror that she had experienced in the enemy camp those ten years past. Nothing could erase those memories, and he knew there had been no one since, no man to show her any different. He fell asleep that way, holding her close, listening to her soft breathing.

David was having an amazing dream; more of a fantasy, really. In it, Jess was running her mouth and tongue along his neck, stroking his chest.

“Wake up.” He opened his eyes and saw her above him in the gloom, her hands on his chest. She nibbled his fingers and smiled at him in the dim moonlight, “I promise I won't cry this time.”

They made love again, her body writhing in pleasure beneath his. His heart was racing and her body, dear lord, it felt so good to be inside her. He held her close afterwards, their bodies wrapped around each other, legs and arms entangled.

"David?"

"Mm?" he had been slipping back into sleep again.

"Is this..." Jess's voice faltered, "Is this for real?"

"God, I hope so," David laughed, nuzzling her neck, kissing her shoulder lightly.

Jess squirmed a little; his face was scratchy, and it tickled a little.

"How long have you, I mean, have you felt this way for me for a while?"

"The last year, give or take a few months," he said, kissing her again.

"How did I not notice?" her tone was tinged with wonder and exasperation.

He shrugged. "I did my best to hide it. I figured you wouldn't take me seriously."

Jess laughed, "Wow. If that's what I've been missing out on for the past year, I... I don't know what to say."

"You don't need to say anything." And he leaned over and kissed her again, his hands caressing her body. "Not a single thing." Their lips met in the dark and after that there were no more words until morning.

Dark Horse Riding

"B*etrayal is the only truth that sticks."—Arthur Miller*

Delwen rolled over, leaning away from Heimdall, and reached for the half-smoked joint. She struck a match and lit it. She had to pull hard on it; the weed was still a bit wet, the taste harsh. They had started growing the plants a few years ago. They had the slaves tend it, along with working the meth lab, and Amerika Reborn had a decent "honest" income going now that the Reformation was spreading.

The Reformation, however, was a double-edged sword. With a return to normal life, or some semblance of normalcy, the demand for drugs that Amerika Reborn had become so good at supplying had begun to climb. However, the ways in which they produced the products, namely using the slaves, was beginning to garner the wrong sort of attention. The raids, something that had diminished significantly in the last year as more and more of the localities began to solidify their loyalties with the Allied South, were also attracting the wrong sort of attention from militias and local governments re-forming to the east. The group had begun as a few remnants of military units in the region and slowly evolved into a large governmental unit with tentacles in nearly all the larger towns and cities that stretched through Louisiana, Arkansas, Mississippi, Alabama, Georgia, South Carolina, and the eastern edge of Texas.

Soon Amerika Reborn would have to give up the slaves and possibly move to a different part of the country if things continued in their current trend. It wasn't time to close up shop though; the demand for drugs was higher than it had ever been before. It seemed like everyone needed an escape from reality at some time or another.

Heimdall's acne had faded over the past ten years, but the scars remained. So, it seemed, had his lovesick obsession for her. He'd had it bad since they were kids, always following after her, with his greasy, lank blond hair, the occasional whopper of a bruise from his volatile alcoholic mother, always volunteering to go on guard duty with her.

When she had first pulled him aside in the woods after a mission a few months ago, he had been surprised, but responsive. He wasn't a bad lay, she mused; he had been attentive to her needs, something that Cooper never was, and had kept his mouth shut about it, something she needed him to do until the time was right. When the first encounter hadn't produced the desired outcome, she had pulled him aside again.

Later, she had done it for fun, even after she was sure. Getting pregnant was her insurance policy—and finding a guy like Heimdall, all muscle, not much brains, was essential.

Delwen's father, Sulwyn, had made a big mistake. Despite all of her hard work, her dedication to proving to her father that she could lead, he had given the reins of power to Cooper. But that was about to change for Sulwyn and Cooper both.

While Scott Cooper had never truly liked her, or even trusted her, over the years she had learned to read him better than anyone. Delwen knew he was planning something, and it probably had to do with taking Sulwyn out of power... permanently. Cooper wasn't the type to take orders. From what he said of his time with the Western Front, he had made a determined and calculated effort to kill his way to the top, and she knew it was just a matter of time before he took her old man out, and probably her as well.

Delwen had her own ideas about who should be in charge—and after years of being ignored or marginalized by her father, just because she had breasts and baby-making equipment instead a dick and balls—well; it was time for a change. She smiled to herself, her homely face curving. Sulwyn had made a big mistake in underestimating her. So had Cooper, for that matter. And she was nearly ready to give them both what they so richly deserved. Just a month more and she would enter into her second trimester. Her father would be dead. Cooper would either be dead or on the run, and she would hold the scepter of power in her hands.

Heimdall reached his hand out and caressed her hip. His hand was rough with callouses, but he had a gentle touch. Delwen handed him the joint and was about to reciprocate when there was a scratch at the door.

"Shit!" she whispered, grabbing for her clothes. They had used Heimdall's cabin for their tryst, and she felt stupid for allowing herself to relax. Who could have followed them? Was it Cooper? Or one of Sulwyn's cronies?

Behind her, Heimdall stubbed out the joint and was hurriedly pulling on a pair of pants. He went to the door first, easing it open, and then opened it all the way to the person standing on the other side. It turned out to be Sully, Delwen's six-year-old daughter, looking every inch of her father. She was a pretty girl, with ice-blue eyes and black hair, just like Cooper.

The girl was quiet, reserved, her intelligence kept hidden from most. With neither of her parents particularly interested in her, she had naturally gravitated toward her grandfather, Sulwyn, after Camelia had died in the outbreak of dysentery that had halved the ranks of Amerika Reborn four months ago. Camelia had become nursemaid to Sully a few months after her birth, just as Camelia was weaning Armando. Delwen hadn't had enough patience to nurse for long, and with no formula, there hadn't been any other real option. Long after the child was weaned, Sully had stuck close, as if sensing that Camelia cared more for her than her own parents did.

Camelia had found it ironic, the similarities between the two children, who were, after all, half-siblings. They were the only children in the camp and Armando and Sully did everything together, something that was often frowned upon by the Amerika Reborn leaders. Yet no one challenged it, no one wanted to take care of a small child. But it had all changed when Camelia died.

Delwen and others blamed the Hispanic woman for the disease, despite the fact that several members of the AR had sickened first, and inevitably transmitted the dysentery to their one and only doctor. Alenoush, who had studied for several years under Camelia, had gotten sick as well and died just two days after the Hispanic woman, leaving no one with any medical knowledge. The Reformation's tentacles were spreading, though, and the group hadn't had any major illnesses since the dysentery's spread had been halted. There was a town a few miles away that still turned a blind eye to the group's unsavory aspects—in no small part thanks to the mayor and his town council, who were happy to indulge in the AR's samples of meth and weed. They had a doctor available if the AR suffered another medical emergency.

Sully had missed Camelia deeply, but she said nothing; even at the age of six, she could see the way of things. She feared her father, avoided her mother whenever possible, but had found a small measure of kindness from her grandfather Sulwyn. She stood at the doorway, understanding on a level that belied her years that her mother was engaged in something she wished hidden.

"Grandpa is looking for you," she told her mother, staring at the dirty wood floor of the cabin.

Delwen nodded to her daughter, "Go to the woods out back, stay there, and pick some of them greens. Don't come back until you have a good armful. If anyone asks, I was there picking and gave 'em to you to take over." She said it tersely and stared at the girl until she nodded and ran toward the woods.

After the girl disappeared, Delwen shut the door, finished dressing and grabbed a handful of mint from a patch growing near the cabin to chew on and stuff in her pockets. It wouldn't do for Sulwyn to smell either of her two sins on her.

He knew what a bastard Cooper was, but had told her many times over the years, "You made your bed girl, now you are going to damn well lie in it."

Having an affair with Heimdall, no matter how careful they were or how uninterested Cooper was in her (he hadn't slept with her in well over two years), was simply unacceptable in her father's eyes. And as for the weed, her old man thought it was all well and fine for others, for the "weak" ones to do that. But heaven help her if he caught her at it. Her mother had been a crack whore on the avenues. Sulwyn reminded her of it time and again.

"She was weak and stupid and wanton, and I did what I could to save her from herself."

Her mother had died when Delwen was a baby, long before she had held the name Delwen Kingmaker.

When she arrived at the central cabin, a large meeting room that doubled as their communal dining area, she watched the old man carefully. He had sent the one lone guard away, and he was looking bad, sipping at the tea she had begun lacing with belladonna months ago, his skin pale and sweaty, his pupils large. He blinked when the door opened, letting in a surge of light, and turned away. The light hurt his eyes and Delwen couldn't help but smile; he was steadily worsening.

Sulwyn was alone in the dark room. He barely glanced her way when she shut the door behind her and advanced toward her father. The older man's hand shook as he waved her closer.

"You kept me waiting a bit, girl; where were you anyway?" His speech was slurred, and he compulsively licked his lips.

"Pickin' greens, sir," she answered him promptly, in the way he expected her to. He lifted the cup of tea. It settled his nerves, at least for a while, which seemed shot these days. He hated watching his fingers shake, the cup slopping liquid out as he brought it unsteadily to his lips. It seemed to him as if he was always thirsty these days, and tired, so tired. The dreams were the worst, waking nightmares of the Collapse, but different. Instead of human beings, the military were actually monsters, hiding in their uniforms, pretending to be saviors and instead eating their victims alive.

"I need that damned slave woman to come attend me," he said, slurping at the tea and trying to ignore the stabbing pain in his head.

Delwen wondered if she had made the last batch too strong—Sulwyn was degrading fast.

"Camelia?" she said and tried to think fast. "She's off with Cooper on a raid, don't you remember?" Now was not the time to remind him that the Spic had been dead for months.

Her old man blinked, confusion filling his haggard face. "A raid?"

"Yes sir, you said Cooper couldn't be trusted and neither could that colored woman, so you sent them both off on a raid. You said Cooper wanted to kill you, remember?"

His jaw was slack, his eyes confused, and he reached up with one hand to his head. Everything was so confusing these days, like some kind of waking nightmare. Delwen looked at her father and realized it was now or never; he was suffering deeply from the effects of the drug, and he was now susceptible to her influence, as he never would have been otherwise. She knelt down beside him and began to whisper quietly in her father's ear.

Painting Disappointment

"*I know he loves me, but this pain is mine. It's mine to keep, mine to bear. If I cannot bear his children, at least I can bear the brief memories of their existence, their time inside of me. They are the faces I see on the canvas. Chris doesn't understand why I paint. It's remembering them. How they would have been, how they come to me in dreams. I will never get to hold them, never hear them say they love me or watch them grow up. The paintings are all I have of them."—Carrie's Journal*

It was her weeping that woke him. Muffled sobs in the dark. Chris fumbled for a candle and matches. Back at the main house, there were solar panels and a Bloom box, signs that the Reformation was slowly trickling into the backwater towns. As the town doctor, Liza had qualified for the latest in gadgets that were making their way from the East Coast, but here in the old homestead they were roughing it. The simple four-room stone structure had been steadily rebuilt over the past five years. After Liza and Carl had married and began having babies, it was easier on all involved for Carrie and Chris to make the old homestead their home.

After all, they didn't need as much room. In all, they had suffered four late-term miscarriages and countless others earlier on. It had left Carrie devastated, and she grew thinner and frailer with each failed pregnancy. Liza and Carl's two oldest children, Molly Ann and John Fenton, absolutely adored their Auntie Carrie, which made seeing them even harder on her. Chris could see it in the tight line of a smile and stiffness in her shoulders; even as she opened her arms and let them barrel into her. How she wanted just one to call her own.

She hadn't argued at all when Chris first suggested rebuilding the old homestead in the woods. It had been Fenton's childhood home. The old man had looked positively touched when Chris first asked him for permission to rebuild, and eventually add on, to the crumbling ruin. The plan had been simple—just one bedroom, a kitchen, bathroom, and living/dining area. It followed the original plan of the building and included a loft, which had been semi-private, open to the living room below. The loft area had been Fenton's, but now it was a place for Carrie to write and paint in. A large bank of windows, different from the original design of the house, allowed plenty of natural light in. She had taken up the writing and painting after her second miscarriage nine years ago. It seemed to help distract her and ease the pain and loss.

Chris fumbled over the matches and struck one, lighting the lantern by the bed. "Baby? You okay?" His voice cracked and his eyes were still encrusted with sleep. Outside, the darkness was absolute. He picked up the lantern and headed for the tiny bathroom. Inside it, Carrie had pulled off her nightgown, and a large blotch of red stained it. "Oh, Carrie, I..."

Carrie's voice was strained. "Please don't say it, Chris. Don't say anything. Okay?"

Chris reached out a hand to her. "Carrie... I..."

She pulled away. "I have to clean up. Just, just, please go back to bed. I'll be fine. I, I just need to be alone, okay?"

With each loss, the gulf between them seemed to widen. She kept the pain close to her, embraced it like a friend, and pushed away Chris, Liza, and anyone else who cared. Chris didn't know if she was trying to spare them from it, or if retreat was just a coping mechanism, but each time, his own misery grew. How much more of this could their relationship take? This terrible feeling that they were growing apart, isolated from each other, lost in their own private pain?

Chris retreated back to bed. She hadn't even told him this time. And how long had she been pregnant this time? A few weeks? A month? With Fenton's passing and Liza's new baby on the way, work on the farm was busier than ever. Usually he tried to pay attention, to know, so that he could be some kind of support for her. But he had been so busy.

The lantern light was blown out, and he heard Carrie navigate her way back to the bedroom. She moved silently across the floor—only one or two creaks gave her position away—and then she was sliding into bed beside him.

"How long?" he asked her.

"Two months, six days," she replied, and her voice sounded hollow. "I didn't want to get your hopes up."

Chris closed his eyes in pain and guilt. He hadn't noticed at all. Two months, and I didn't even notice.

"Sweetheart, I..." he began.

"Please Chris," she cut him off, "I'm just really tired right now."

He pulled her close to him. She stiffened at first, sighed, and let him pull her against him. They lay there, unmoving, for a long time before either could sleep again.

The next day dawned, sun bright over the tips of the trees and the warmth of the early summer sun already warming the tiny homestead. Chris awoke with a start, realizing he had slept late, later than he had in a long time. He could smell hot chicory percolating on the stove and quickly dressed. Usually, he was the one who rose first.

After splashing some cold water on his face, he walked into the kitchen, poured himself a large mug of the brew, walked into the living room, and looked up. Sure enough, there she was, sketching away. She usually threw herself into a new project or series right after a miscarriage. He could see her now, intent on sketching out the details on the canvas, which she would then fill in with the paints she made from plant extracts. I'll have to let Liza know, he thought, have her check in and see if Carrie needs any extra iron supplements and also to keep the kids away for a week or so.

He knew he would also have to push Carrie to stop working, to eat something, and even to come to bed. The painting would consume her. It was her escape, but it came at a price. She had broken her ankle shortly after her fourth late-term miscarriage. She had gone into labor at just 22 weeks and given birth to a stillborn baby boy. That had been almost three years ago. By that time, Chris had finished the loft and moved Carrie's painting supplies in there. She had gotten out of bed way too soon, insisting she was fine, climbed up into the loft and began painting with single-minded intensity. The third day of painting, with little food and even less sleep, she had tried to climb down the ladder, slipped and fallen, breaking her left ankle. Since then, Chris kept a sharp eye on her, which caused friction between them, and insisted she regularly stop for meals and rest.

"Morning sweetheart," Chris called, "ready for some breakfast?"

"I'm not hungry." Carrie didn't look up from her sketch. Her eyes were red-rimmed and drawn tight with exhaustion. He wondered how long she had waited before slipping back out of bed and climbing up the ladder to the loft. Probably not long.

Chris tried again. "I could make you something simple. An egg or..."

Carrie flushed with anger; she was right on the edge. "Chris, leave it be."

He took a deep breath and fought the desire to argue with her. He had half a mind to go up and drag her down from the loft by force, but he couldn't bear an argument right now. Better to go talk to Liza and see what she had to say. He knew his sister-in-law would shake her head and beg Chris to try to convince Carrie to stop trying. The last miscarriage, just seven months ago, had shaken them all. She had lost a great deal of blood, collapsed, and Liza had feared for her sister like never before. Between that and Fenton's slowly succumbing to heart disease, it had been an incredibly difficult year for everyone. And Liza didn't need any stress either. Carl had quietly pointed that out to Chris the other day. After all, she was in her final trimester and they were expecting the baby to come any day.

With one last look at Carrie, who sat less than ten feet from him sketching with an intensity he admired and hated at the same time, Chris left the tiny homestead and headed for the main house.

A Time for Writing

"*The role of a writer is not to say what we all can say, but what we are unable to say."—Anais Nin*

It had already been an excellent day for trading. David felt on top of the world. He and Jess had made it official with the kids, and even shared the news of their new relationship with a trusted few: Thurman Banks, who had dropped by unexpectedly and caught them holding hands, and Sarah Turner, who had smiled and nodded her approval.

It was a moment in time when everything seemed bright, anything was possible, and there were no clouds or harsh words that could mar their happiness. Jess had reminded him that there was a trader leaving town soon and asked if David could find her some paper. "I'm running low. I'm finishing up with Sarah Turner, and then I'm hoping to speak to Mr. Stevens and write down his story." Jess had been writing down the various townspeople's stories for a while now and filled several notebooks. There was a large stack of them in one corner of her room, filled with personal stories, accounts of the invasion of Belton, descriptions of lives before and after the war, and so much more.

Jess had earned quite a reputation around town, and residents now sought her out and volunteered their stories. She had heard heartbreak and tragedy, but also, she had listened to the young and the old alike as they smiled and relayed tales of falling in love, of babies born and accounts of a world now that was harsh, simple, and, in some ways, more real than the old one. Through the people and their stories twined hope and love like threads of shining gold. She had filled countless notebooks with delicate script and was close to running out of the last battered one in the stack.

"Whatever you can find would be wonderful."

David caught the trader just in time. He had been packing up, having stayed in a small room in a decrepit building across from Sarah Turner's café for two full days. When David had asked for paper, he had rustled around in the back of a still overly full van filled with boxes overflowing with a wild medley of tools, fabric, shoes, and more. A moment later, he had handed over two simple student notebooks with lined paper.

"I think I have something more here," he had said, and began digging further into the stacks of items. David marveled at the man's ability to find anything; it looked for all accounts like a hodgepodge with no rhyme or reason, but the trader always seemed to know exactly where to look. He pulled out a large tote, shifted another to the left and began pawing through a third one. "Ah yes, here it is." The trader handed David a journal encased in a soft leather case. It had obviously been handmade, was soft and supple, the pages within were thick and sturdy. It was thick as well, the paper roughly cut and of different shades of cream and pale yellow. The thick leather smelled vaguely of lemon.

"I got a whole crate full back in Tennessee a few months ago. This kid, Joseph Perdue, lives in this hole-in-a-wall town, makes Belton look positively metropolitan, and he makes them all by hand. Traded 'em for auto parts." David felt the well-cured leather and noticed a small raised area on the back—the initials JP were embossed on the back. "He does quality work," the trader added, anxious for a sale.

Neither of them had noticed Sarah Turner's face when the name Perdue and Tiptonville had been mentioned. She had turned pale and excused herself without a word. As she slipped away, Sarah couldn't help but wonder who Joseph was. Possibly a grandchild of old Fenton Perdue? She recalled that he had a son who had moved away to New York. In a small town like Tiptonville, everyone knew everyone else. It had been years since she had been there. More than half a lifetime since she had run away in the night with her two small children and left Wes Perkins behind. For the first time in twenty years, Tiptonville suddenly felt close enough to touch. She wasn't that frightened young woman any longer. She disappeared into the café and lost herself in making preparations for the lunch crowd.

Neither the trader nor David had noticed her departure. David looked at the well-made hand-crafted journal in his hand and nodded. They began hashing out a trade. The trader was itching to return home after a month on the road. He had accepted five dozen eggs and three jars of preserves, along with a bag of deer jerky in trade for the journal and the two notebooks. It was a good trade, and they had plenty of extra eggs these days with the expanded chicken house and yard and an overabundance of fruit to can into preserves. The trader had also given him three clean and empty jars in return.

David brought it back to Jess that night after visiting with Sarah Turner, who seemed quite distracted and quiet; not her usual ebullient self. He had also run a handful of errands for old Mr. Banks, who had been having trouble getting around lately due to swelling in his knees. The old man was having more and more difficulty getting around, and Jess, David, and Jacob visited him often to help in whatever way they could.

As he handed over first the notebooks and then the journal, David hadn't thought much of it. Jess had asked for something to write in, and he had dutifully found it. It was paper and leather, nothing special in David's eyes, but the reaction Jess had to it made his heart stutter. Even now, three months into their new relationship, a simple touch or look in her eyes brought on such overwhelming feelings of wonder and desire. Knowing that she returned his feelings was staggering, new, and each day he wondered when he would wake up from this beautiful dream he was having.

Her fingers stroked the leather cover and then opened the book to fan the pages within. She smiled, unconsciously, her eyes soaking up the thick, rich paper, and like David, her fingers found the embossed initials. "JP?" she asked, her eyes flashing up to him.

"Trader said it was some kid in Tennessee who made them all by hand. A Joseph Perdue, I think."

"David, it's... it's beautiful." Her crayon-blue eyes smiled up at him. "Thank you." She couldn't imagine what she would write in this thing of beauty, but she knew it would have to be something special, something different.

David had been surprised at the force with which she hugged him. Later that night, after they had made love, she had slipped out of bed. "I'm going to stay up a while," she had said, kissing him.

She had selected the leather journal, slipped quietly down the hall, and sat down at the kitchen table. The night was quite warm, now that it was early June, and the cicadas were thrumming noisily outside. In the far distance, you could occasionally hear the low of a cow. The horse and goats inside the garage-turned-barn were silent, and the stars glinted in the clear night sky.

Jess sat at the kitchen table, a small candle glimmering and expanding on the moonlight that spilled in through the window. She stared at the journal, touched the soft leather with her fingers, and wondered what to do with it. Several minutes went by before she slowly opened the journal and began to write...

"There are moments when all of it is too much, too painful to remember. Yet then I look around at those I love and realize I would not be here, with these people who I love and who love me, if those awful things had not happened to me. How do you reconcile that?"

I Can't Stay Here Anymore

"W*here we love is home, home that our feet may leave, but not our hearts."—Oliver Wendell Holmes*

The soft creak of the box springs woke Chris. Carrie had slipped into the bed quietly and, once she heard his breathing change, she slid close to him and kissed his ear softly. He shifted, turned toward his wife, and pulled her close.

"Is the painting done?" he asked.

"Yes."

"I've missed you." She had slept each night for the past two weeks in the painting loft on a small couch. It had been a compromise early on to the all-nighters she pulled when lost in a new painting.

"I know. I missed you too." The past two weeks had been hard. There had been words exchanged, harsh ones, mainly from her. He didn't understand this need that she had to finish a painting before returning to him, to her life and family.

Carrie sat up, her hair reflected in the moonlight, cascading down and brushing Chris's chest as she straddled him. He started to speak, started to object that it was too soon, but she shushed him and put a slender finger on his lips. It smelled vaguely of turpentine.

"No more arguing," she said, "Not tonight."

Her hands moved and Chris felt his body respond, just as it always did, to her touch. They made love, slowly coming to a climax together. Afterward, they spooned, wrapping their bodies around each other, their bodies replete. They may not have children, but they had love, so much of it that it sometimes hurt. He wasn't always sure where he ended and she began. They lay there and said nothing for a long while.

"Chris?" he jerked awake at Carrie's voice, having just dozed off.

"Yeah, babe?"

"I can't stay here anymore."

"Here in this house?" he asked, confused.

"No... here on this farm... in Tiptonville."

"Wait, what are you saying, Carrie?" He feared hearing the words. Had he just gotten some crazy, twisted goodbye screw? Was she leaving him?

"I'm saying I can't stay here anymore, Chris. Not on this farm, not in this town; hell, maybe not in this state. I've got to get away from all the memories—my mom, the babies, even Gramps. I see him everywhere, you know, and I miss him so." Her body shook with emotion and he could feel her tears drip onto his arm.

"And what about me, Carrie?" he asked, terrified of her answer.

"I don't want to leave you," she said, sounding affronted. "I love you, Chris. And through all of this, you have loved me and stayed by my side. I don't want to lose that. You aren't tied here, you know. Come with me, we can travel the roads again and be safe. The Reformation has taken care of that."

Relief flooded through Chris. After everything they had been through, she still loved him and wanted him by her side.

Carrie continued, "Remember the trader who bought that box full of journals from Joseph and several of my paintings from the Trade Mart? The one who insisted on meeting me? He talked about the new government, about the new Capitol in Denver. He told me I could get good money for the paintings, that there has been a resurgence in American art in the past three years now that The Collapse is over."

Over was a bit of an overstatement. Wes had said that there were two stories circulating. One proclaimed that The Collapse was over, that life was back to normal. As if by simply saying it enough, the bigwigs in D.C. could make it so. The truth was, much of the country, especially a wide swath of the central states, was not back to normal. The coasts had their electricity, more cell phone towers than ever before, and in no small part due to the European contingent in the East and the Chinese contingent in the West, back to normal was a relative term.

"Sure, we're back to normal," Wes had growled, "as long as you ignore the fact that the Chinese occupy California and a huge swath of the West Coast. Christ, they own us, and they're gonna make sure they get their money's worth. And don't even get me started on the fucking East Coast. Goddamn sellouts."

Chris thought about all of this, about the quiet life that he and all the Purdue family led here in Tiptonville. He rested his nose against Carrie's head, breathed in her unique scent of sage and wood smoke. He thought about Missouri and home. It did, after all, hold a huge part of his heart. Mom, Dad, Jess, his friends. His thoughts drifted west to Colorado, and his grip tightened around Carrie.

"Yeah, baby. Let's go. We can do this; we can head west, to Colorado, or wherever you want to go."

Only The Hunted

"B*etrayal is the only truth that sticks."—Arthur Miller*

"That... whore," Cooper fumed, as he stabbed into the hunk of meat he had taken off of a deer. It had been a perfect opportunity; the fool thing had just stood there in the clearing long enough for him to get a shot off. And it was a good shot at that; it had killed the creature instantly. "I'm going to kill her. Stick a knife right into that pregnant belly and..."

Armando sat a few feet away from Cooper, saying nothing, his eyes on the small amount of food on his plate. There was plenty to be had, although it was a little stringy and not evenly cooked, but Cooper had only given him a small amount, commenting that the boy was useless and lucky he got anything at all. At the moment he was back on the same old subject—his cuckolding—Mama had always made sure Armando had learned plenty, despite the lack of books. And Cooper had definitely been cuckolded by his wife and her new lover.

Cooper still wasn't sure how she had done it, but whatever Delwen had done, it was enough to get her appointed as leader in Cooper's place when her father suffered a series of convulsions two weeks prior. And right after that, she had announced she was pregnant... with that idiot Heimdall's child.

"I'll cut that little bastard out of her and shove it down her throat..."

Armando let Cooper's curses wash over him. He chewed on a hunk of venison. It was dry, tasteless, and Armando remembered with longing his mother's cooking. They were never given much, despite her being the camp doctor, but what she made with those scraps of food and the wild edibles she taught him to collect for her was a feast compared to this.

He took another bite, forced it down, and thought of her face and her words, "Eat, Armando, eat and be strong. It is fuel, and you cannot stay strong without it." How many times had she said that to him? How many times had he nodded obediently and eaten whatever was on his plate? He knew too that Cooper would just as soon not feed him. The older man only kept him around because he was small and could fit into tight spaces. A couple of days ago, that had come in handy. Cooper had ordered him to find out what lay within a small shed on the outskirts of a farm. It had been difficult, but he had managed to squeeze through between the bottom of the shed wall and the dirt floor beneath. There had been grain, some farming equipment, and several knives, including one tiny and one half buried in the dirt.

Without really thinking about it, Armando had slipped one of them into his pocket. It was a small Swiss army type, just one blade, a space for a toothpick—although the toothpick was no longer there—and a small screwdriver as well. He wondered how he could get away from Cooper. Armando was nearly nine, and he had had to be rather self-sufficient, but making ends meet in the middle of Tennessee was frightening, especially since anyone he encountered was either shooting at them or dead or dying from Cooper shooting them first. Cooper didn't seem to have any other setting—killing seemed to be his primary way of dealing with people.

"Choke on the blood... you damned whore!" Cooper was still ranting. Armando's thoughts turned to the knife in his pocket. How he wished he had the strength to end this terrible man's life. The tiny, dull knife certainly wouldn't do it—and he was no killer, despite his genetic inheritance. The fact that he was here, in the middle of nowhere, hungry and cold, was Cooper's doing. The boy hadn't exactly been welcomed there in the neo-Nazi camp, but when Delwen turned her sights on him, declaring Armando to be Cooper's illegitimate son, the rest of the camp had been happy to see the back end of him along with this monster.

Armando missed Sully, his only real friend; she had stood silent, tears streaming down her face as he and Cooper had been thrown out of the AR camp. Cooper had been so angry, so furious at everyone, that Armando had wondered just how long it would take before Cooper turned on him. How long before he too was dead by Cooper's hand? The man might be his father, but he didn't give a damn about him insofar as he could use him to serve his own needs.

The last of the light disappeared from the horizon. The nights were dark, even more so than the Amerika Reborn camp had been. In the last two years the camp had cobbled together a small system of electric lights that ran off of a series of solar panels they had acquired during a trade or raid, Armando wasn't sure which. The light from the campfire gave off a dark red glow, and Armando knew better than to add any fuel to the fire. They hid in the shadows, traveling mainly at dusk and dawn, and slept during the day.

Cooper was still ranting, although it had grown quieter, and Armando pulled his knees up, lowering his head and hoping the man didn't turn his rage onto him. The swelling from Cooper's last fit of rage was finally going down, although his cheek remained mottled in yellow and red bruises. All that Armando could think of as he slipped into a doze was that he wished his mom was still alive. Even if it meant being back at the AR camp... anything but this.

The next morning found them on the outskirts of a small town. It was early still, barely light out, and there were no signs of activity; everyone in town was still sleeping. They edged around the town, Cooper muttering quietly to himself as he scoped out the town's defenses.

"Sentries, at least one there at the end of the street. Another up in that high hide in the south. Burned vehicles with skeletons... nice touch." He rambled mainly to himself, noting the defenses, before turning his attention on Armando. "You'll go in there. Tell 'em you're an orphan, ask 'em for food. I'll watch from here and come tonight; you'll let me in so I get what I need."

He nodded, narrowed his eyes. "I've been to this shithole before. They grow some nice tail 'round here." He stared at Armando, "You do what I say, or I promise you, you'll be sorry you were ever born. I'll come at midnight." He gave the boy a rough shove toward the small town.

As Armando walked toward the town, the boy thought about the past few weeks. Three times now, Cooper had sent him in to farmhouses, isolated, alone. Three times, the boy had done what Cooper demanded. He'd convinced an old farmer he was all alone, then two men, a father and his grown son, and finally a young couple who had just lost a child to a fever. The last one had been the worst. He didn't want to think about what Cooper had done to the woman.

He had hidden in an outbuilding after being tasked to remove the husband's body and the bloodstains from the front porch, just in case someone came by. Afterwards he had hid in the shed several hundred feet away and tried desperately to not hear the woman's screams. When they had gotten back on the road several days later, well outfitted now with a rifle and plenty of ammo, Armando had thought about what Mama would have said to him.

At the camp, she had always kept him out of sight of most of the more militant ones. His skin was dark; not as dark as hers, but still darker than acceptable when surrounded by racist white men. The neo-Nazis hadn't been eager to include him in their fighting lessons, other than to use him as a punching bag. One or two of those sessions had taught him to lie low, but here, with Cooper, there was no lying low. Mama would have stopped them, threatened them by saying she wouldn't patch them up if they kept going, but Mama was dead, and he was all alone.

As he put distance between him and where Cooper was hiding, a set of high-powered binoculars in his hands watching his every move, Armando realized he had to make a decision. He thought of what his mother would have said, would have thought, if she had known that he had had a part in the deaths of five innocent people. She would have been horrified and she would have reminded him that God would judge him, most severely, for what he had done. Part of him wanted to wail and cry, to hide his head in her lap and beg her to help him. He was so very lost without her.

As the town drew near, he heard a sentry ring a bell. They had seen him. Soon he would have to tell the lie, how he had been orphaned, that he was all alone. The shame he felt at his part in the old farmer, the two men, or the young couple—it felt like a lead weight in his heart and his steps slowed.

"Reverend." Jeremy Deeds looked up from the sermon he was preparing to honor Mr. Liles and saw Joseph Perdue standing in his office. According to the town records, the ancient man had died just three days short of his 116th birthday. He had been so involved in writing down notes for the sermon he hadn't even heard the teenager come in.

"Reverend, I'm sorry to bother you, but we have a situation down near the Trade Mart. Some kid just walked in on the main road."

Jeremy gave Joseph a befuddled look. Kids, and plenty of other people, had been making their way into town for years now, and for the most part, things went peacefully. Either way, they had never needed him involved. "The kid is asking for a priest, so Wes sent me to get you."

"Is the boy ill?" Jeremy asked.

"Not that I can see, sir. Although he's got plenty of bruises on his face and arms. He just won't say anything past that he needs to speak with a priest and confess his sins." Joseph shrugged, "And he looks scared."

Jeremy stood up painfully. His badly damaged leg, nearly pulverized in a car crash over nine years ago, would always give him terrible pain. During the winters, when he felt every step even more keenly, the congregation had grown used to seeing him give sermons from a tall chair. It was hell getting into it, but once he did, he was good for the entire service. Joseph stepped forward to offer his assistance. Jeremy had learned to accept others' help, and he leaned on the young man and slowly walked to the door of the church where a small crowd was gathering, the boy at their center.

The boy was thin, painfully so, with large brown eyes and jet-black hair. His skin was tanned, and Jeremy could see the remains of several bruises on his face and arms. He was dressed in a ragged T-shirt and worn blue jeans that had patches; his feet were bare. The boy stared back at Jeremy, "You don't look like a priest."

"And what do priests look like?" Jeremy asked in return.

The boy shrugged his thin shoulders, "I don't know; I never saw one. Mama said they had funny little collars, and they lived in the church."

Jeremy nodded thoughtfully, "I see... well, I do have a funny little collar I wear on Sundays and I do live here in the church. My faith may be different from your Mama's, but in the end, we believe in the same thing. Will that do?"

The boy nodded solemnly, "I must confess my sins."

Jeremy nodded as if it were the most normal thing in the world.

"Come up to my office with me and tell me what you need to say." He shooed Joseph and the others who offered to help, and slowly made his way back to the office with the boy, closing the door firmly behind him.

A few minutes later, Jeremy stuck his head out and asked for a large lunch for two to be sent up. It was nearly half an hour after that before Jeremy asked for Wes to join them in the office. An hour later, and Cooper watched through binoculars as the church bell rang and people began to gather outside.

He cursed as he packed up his binoculars and began to run north, putting as many miles between him and the small town as he could. He ran for the backwoods, where cars and horses alike would have difficulty following. He was gone long before Armando, surrounded by well-armed militia, led the townspeople to the camp he and Armando had made the evening before.

Armando stared into the distance. The stark dead trees that populated Reelfoot Lake stood in the far distance. He knew Cooper wouldn't be back, no matter what he had threatened. The priest, no, not a priest. They called him Reverend here, had told him he would be safe and that, no matter what he had done, God would forgive him if he only asked. Armando wasn't so sure about that last part, but he made a silent promise to his mother that he would do his best to earn that forgiveness.

The Reverend's wife had been kind as well. Heavily pregnant, and awkward with her big belly, she had still found a place for him to sleep for the night there in the sanctuary. Most of the children the makeshift orphanage had housed were now living with foster or adoptive parents. The large room was still filled with beds, but it was mostly empty. Miss Grace had explained that she knew someone very special who was looking for a child to take in.

She patted his shoulder, "You'll like Abby; she's raised two kids of her own and just has Tabitha still at home now. She's got room and I've told her all about you."

Within a few weeks, Armando had shortened his name to Andy and fit in seamlessly with the Carters. He missed his mother, more than he could even say, but for the first time in his life, he finally felt safe.

Miles to the west, Scott Cooper walked on.

Count Me In

"The best day of your life is the one on which you decide your life is your own. No apologies or excuses. No one to lean on, rely on, or blame. The gift is yours - it is an amazing journey - and you alone are responsible for the quality of it. This is the day your life really begins."—Bob Moawad

"Are you insane?" Wes barked at Chris. "Completely certifiable?"

Chris was packing a large backpack at the moment, trying to puzzle out how to fit the clips of ammo and the rest of the loose shells into one of the smaller sections.

Wes stared at the mounds of packs as well as boxes of paints and supplies.

"You can't just waltz out of here with a bunch of..." He waved his hand at the far corner that was occupied with a maze of paintings, "A bunch of... art. The roads are still dangerous, the Reformation is a frigging joke, and you are both going to end up dead."

Chris ignored him. Wes was plain-spoken, and Chris had grown used to that over the years. The older man glared at him for several long moments before stalking out of the tiny house. Chris suppressed a twinge of regret. Despite their difference in age, or a host of differences, Chris had found a solid friendship with Wes. Despite his angry façade and harsh words, the man cared for others far more than he could admit, even to himself. Since the raid that had killed his fiancé and the mother of his unborn child, and even before that, years before, when his wife Sarah had left him, disappearing into the night with their young son and daughter, Wes had been unable to give voice to the part of him that was good and kind. He rarely smiled, other than a sarcastic sideway smirk, and still called Chris "soldier" far too often.

The older man hid behind his gruff exterior so that others wouldn't get close, so that he wouldn't ever be given love or acceptance, only to risk losing it again. That was what Carrie had once said, and Chris knew she was right. Wes worked hard, spent long hours toiling on the Perdue farm and then heading up to see Jim Dorian, who had recently had a stroke and shortly after that fallen down his rickety old stairs, breaking his leg in the process. The simpleminded man was now in his mid-50s and had trouble understanding why his body was betraying him in such a strange manner.

Outside of the stone house, he could hear Wes start his truck up and gun the engine, driving down the rough dirt road and back toward town. They were leaving tomorrow, first thing in the morning. He had hoped Wes would stay for dinner at the Perdue farm, where Carrie already was now, saying her goodbyes. She had put on weight the past few weeks, inching away from the skeletal frame and looking younger and less haunted. It was as if the decision to leave had taken a weight off of her she hadn't realized existed. She had sent letters ahead to the art gallery in Denver, but there had been no response. This wasn't surprising; mail was still rather spotty and there were still some routes that took longer than others—the highly efficient system of mail delivery had been lost with the collapse of the country and they were still struggling to put it back to rights, along with a host of other creature comforts that most people took for granted decades before.

That evening at the Perdue's was not easy. Liza, expecting her fourth child, was exhausted and beside herself at the thought of her older sister moving away. The children, even little Abby, were voicing their own distress. Abby climbed onto Carrie's lap at one point, and said in her tiny baby voice, "Au Cree, no go!" Which caused tears to spring in both Liza and Carrie's eyes.

Liza's husband Carl said little. He wasn't a talkative man, but obviously he, too, disapproved of Chris and Carrie leaving. Chris turned to him at one point in the evening and asked, "Did Wes say if he would be by for dinner?" Carl just shook his head.

Chris thought briefly of running into town and seeing if Wes was holed up in his house or at Dorian's ramshackle trailer, and decided against it. Perhaps this was for the best. He couldn't explain it to anyone. Not Carl or Liza; not even to himself. What mattered was Carrie. If she thought leaving would make it better, then leaving is what they would do. As it was, he found himself thinking more and more of Belton.

Mom, Dad, Jess, and Allen—they were all dead. But the town was probably still there. He found himself wondering about it; how much had it changed? Was there anyone left that he knew? He had resolved to make sure they stopped there, at least for a day, before moving on to Colorado. Just to see the old house, just to say goodbye properly this time, and take a moment to remember the happier times. He knew that Carrie wouldn't begrudge him that, even if the detour was slightly out of their way.

"Chris?" Joseph was standing there in front of him.

Chris hadn't even noticed his arrival from town because he was so lost in his plans for visiting Belton. The little kid was now grown into a rather self-assured, yet quiet, teenager. He was fourteen now and had taken over Mr. Liles' automotive store more than a year ago, caring for the aged old man, crafting leather-bound books out of deer hide Wes shot and then taught him how to cure. The books were then lined with paper from a printing supply company that had sat abandoned for more than a decade. The kid had weathered Fenton's death, then Mr. Liles's less than two months later, with a quiet reserve that belied his years. His blond hair was spiky and short, his haircut a parting gift from Carrie, who wielded more than just a paintbrush with quiet accuracy.

The boy had a box perched near the front door. "I brought you more of the journals. Thought you might use 'em for trade."

The journals were made from rich cream vellum he had found beneath boxes of envelopes and cheap stationery. The butter-soft deer hide was embossed with his initials. Chris picked one up and ran his hands over it.

"These are great Joe; you really have been improving, and the hide seems quite supple. No more shrinkage?"

The teen winced a bit at the memory of his first attempts at curing the hides Wes had brought him. There had been a trial-and-error phase, but he had quickly learned how to mend his mistakes and create quality hides. Books were his first project. Now he was starting on working leather belts.

"Yeah, I've got the hang of it now." Joseph paused, looked down at the ground, "I wish I could go with you Chris."

Chris laid a hand over the boy's shoulders, but said nothing; he knew Liza would lose it completely if both of her siblings answered the siren call of the West. He felt a sharp pain in his chest, and he couldn't help wondering how long it would be before he saw the boy again. Tiptonville had been his home for over ten years, and Joseph was the little brother he never had.

That evening, they spent a restless night in the small stone house. One last night of banking the fire, checking to see if there was anything they had missed, anything that just had to be included. The van they were using had been the Carter's—Carl's mom and stepdad—but they had given it to Chris and Carrie when they first heard the news that they were leaving.

"We barely use it, and it's in good shape and you can carry the gas cans on top. It should be enough to get you all the way to Colorado," John Carter had told Chris.

They had accepted the gift gratefully, then packed the van full of paintings, items to trade, foodstuffs, and a handful of belongings. There was barely any room left for them in the front, and even the open space between the two front seats was piled high, every inch of space spoken for.

As the pale rays of the sun lightened the treetops, Chris scrambled some eggs and wrapped up a fair-sized bag of sandwiches for them to eat on the road. He walked outside just as Wes's truck came rumbling around the bend. The truck had a camper shell on the back, something Wes usually only put on when he was going hunting. It wasn't really hunting season, but perhaps the older man felt the need to kill something soft and furry in response to Chris and Carrie's departure.

Chris grinned at the sight of his friend. He had been sick at the thought of not saying goodbye. After all, they had no idea when they would return, if ever. "Hey there, Wes, come to see us off before you go off on a hunt?"

Wes shook his head. "I'm coming with you, you damned idiot." Typical Wes; kind and heartfelt words were not his strongest suit.

"You're what?" Carrie asked, having just emerged from the house with the last of their belongings in her arms.

"I'm comin' with you. The two of you'd end up dead 'fore you got halfway there and then damned if Fenton would raise outta the grave and give me what for," Wes said, taking the bundle of food from Chris, who stood there in shock. "Besides," he said, "it's high time I saw more of the world 'sides sand and them damn sand-nigg..." he glanced at Carrie's stern look, "Yeah... lotsa sand. Figured I'd get out and see the world."

Carrie burst out, "What about Jim Dorian? He's still hobbled up with that broken leg."

Wes nodded, "Yup. Dropped him off with Reverend Deeds last night. Jim'll be right as rain in a few more weeks and then he can help out 'round the parish. 'Sides, they need some help now that little KG is in the world."

Jeremy Deeds and his wife Grace had just welcomed their second child, a little girl named Karen Grace, or KG for short, after her mama and grandma just two months ago. They already had a very boisterous little boy, Anthony, who adored Jim Dorian. "Dorian needs to be with others; ain't good for him to be livin' alone in that leaky old trailer."

The older man lifted up the back of his truck and displayed a host of items to trade or sell. "Hell, I gotta get rid of this crap, and you ain't got any more room in that van. The way I see it, you two could use the company." Wes had his trademark smirk plastered on his face. He had thought of everything, it seemed.

Chris felt Carrie's eyes on him. This was far from what she might want, but the more Chris thought about it, the more he couldn't help but like it. An extra eye, an extra gun, and, despite his gruff and taciturn ways, Wes was a good friend.

"Well, all right then. Let's get moving."

A few minutes later, they drove away from the tiny stone house—the van in the lead and Wes in his truck behind. Within an hour, they were making time down the cracked highway heading west.

Reunion

"*The most important thing in life is to learn how to give out love, and to let it come in."—Morrie Schwartz*

"Morning, Mom. Thanks so much for taking Hunter; I totally forgot about working at the food bank," Sarah's daughter Laura said as she gave her mother a quick kiss and hug, awkwardly balancing the sleepy toddler on one hip. "Are you sure he won't be a problem?"

Sarah smiled at her daughter. Hunter was a little hellion, and that was for sure. But he certainly came in handy at times. The last time she had babysat her grandson, he had broken two plates, burned his fingers on the stove, and then finished off the day by biting Mayor Farley on the arm after the overstuffed shirt had complained about the serving size on his plate. Considering his shirt was straining its buttons, and that Sarah had already served him a helping nearly twice that of the other diners, she hadn't concerned herself much with his opinions. The plates were a bit of a problem—she was getting low on the larger dinner plates—and the little boy had cried so when his fingers were burned, but the mayor's effeminate scream that followed the toddler's bite was well worth the trouble. She would have paid good money to see the mayor leave and never darken the door of her establishment again.

"Oh, don't you worry a bit. Hunter is a sweetheart, and I just love having him here," Sarah said, her smile full of mischief. It was a Tuesday, after all, and the mayor often came by for an early lunch. She wouldn't mind a little more biting on Hunter's part; perhaps the mayor would catch the hint.

"We will have a great time, won't we, Hunter?" She adored both of her grandchildren. They were the spitting image of their mother, except for the red hair, which was all her son-in-law Todd's contribution.

She reached out and took Hunter from her daughter, and hugged him close; he nuzzled her shoulder and sighed sleepily. "Bah, Mama. 'Unter tay wit Gamma."

Laura laughed and gave him a kiss on the cheek, "Be good for Grandma, sweetie, and don't touch that stove!" She headed for the front door of the café, turned and called, "I'll be back by sundown, Mom; just let me know if you need me to come sooner!" Laura had already dropped Melody, her three-year-old, off with Allen and Gina Stevens, Todd's father and stepmother.

Sarah hugged her grandson close and said, "We have a busy day in front of us, don't we, sweetheart? Well, I guess we best get started."

She fed him some pancakes, his favorite, and watched him as he ate with single-minded intensity. He looked so much like his grandfather. It startled her to see him in her grandchildren's faces, especially Hunter's.

Despite the long years apart, she still thought about him from time to time—more now that the grandkids had come. The what ifs came frequently to mind. If she had stayed, if he had changed back to the man she had married, what would their life have been like?

Sarah wondered about Tiptonville often. No traveler would even really remember if they had stopped in a tiny town in the middle of nowhere—but she asked, anyway. It was always the same answer, a shrug, a shake of the head, or, from those who had been out on the road way too long, "Those little towns just kind of blur together after a while." She had long given up asking. It had been a shock when the trader had mentioned it last month. Ever since she hadn't been able to stop thinking about it, or kicking herself for not having stopped the trader to ask a hundred questions about that "little Podunk town" he had visited.

There were customers to wait on, and Hunter had shaken off the last vestiges of sleepiness and begun running up and down the length of counter, without a care for who he might run headlong into. Sarah distracted the boy by setting him up with some dough and a cookie cutter. "Will you make me some cookies, Hunter?"

"I make cooees!" the boy crowed and got to work, cutting the dough into ragged shapes with one hand, while stuffing handfuls of dough into his mouth.

The front door bell clattered as a small group of strangers walked in. The café had been busy all morning, but now, at just after ten a.m., it had fallen quiet. The noon rush would start up in an hour, and with it would come the mayor. Sarah suppressed a sigh; she had hoped for a moment's peace before having to prep for lunch. The first two to walk through the door were young and in their mid-20s.

The woman was blond, with striking green eyes. She carried herself with a quiet dignity that also conveyed a sadness beyond her years. Sarah wondered what had made the girl sad, for the young man beside her was quite obviously her husband. He was tall, also blond, and had beautiful crayon-blue eyes. He looked familiar somehow, but Sarah was equally certain that she had never seen him before.

Then the third person came into view and Sarah's heart stopped. Standing before her was an impossibility, and she felt terror and wonder and hope all at the same time. The man stared at her for a moment, blinked, and said wonderingly, "Sarah?"

Carrie searched her memories for the details of a woman she had not even known, one who had disappeared years ago, fleeing from her husband and taking their two young children with her. No one had ever known where she had gone, but it had been the talk of the town for years. And here she was, apparently, in Belton of all places, where Chris had insisted they stop and visit, if only to see his childhood home.

Chris had talked with Wes once about his family. Well, better to say Wes had talked to him, and Chris had simply listened. The older man had admitted he had returned from the Second Gulf War messed up, suffering from PTSD and mad at the world. He had taken it out on Sarah one too many times, and the last time had culminated in her disappearing with the kids. Never to be seen or heard from again. And here, apparently, is where she had ended up.

Sarah stood there in shock, "Wes?" She didn't say anything, none of them did, until Hunter, tiring of the dough, covered in the remains of it, tugged on her hand, trying with his chubby little toddler hands to open her fingers and place a lump of dough inside.

"Gamma... eat!"

Wes stared at the little boy, then back at Sarah, and then back down at the boy again. He took in the boy's features, which reminded him of Cody at that age. "Is he...?" Wes stopped and sat down heavily in the nearest chair, staring at the little boy, a look of wonder settling over his face. He had a grandson. A grandson.

There they all stood, wordless. Chris and Carrie didn't know what to say, and quite obviously, neither did Sarah nor Wes. They might have stood there until sundown if Mayor Farley hadn't chosen that time to walk in the door. He had been craving a plate of Sarah's famous biscuits and gravy all morning. It was distracting him from his duties, these visions of the creamy gravy and fluffy biscuits, and he had headed over to the café early to avoid the rush.

He preferred to be given more preferential and individual service, which seemed impossible when other diners hogged Sarah's attention. And although biscuits and gravy were a breakfast item, and he was a stickler for eating the proper three meals of the day, he would make an exception in this case. After all, he reasoned, it was technically still morning and certainly too early for lunch. That made it perfectly reasonable to order his second breakfast that day. The mayor was surprised to see people in the café at this late point in the morning, and even more surprised to see three strangers. Well, that was all right; it was a fine time to establish himself as the authority in town. He straightened himself, sucked in his gut as best as he could, and boomed out a greeting.

"Good morning, Sarah! I've come for a plate of your biscuits and gravy. Make it a double and add extra gravy to that, would you?" His voice broke through their immobility, and Chris and Carrie stared at the rotund man for a moment before slipping to a back corner and sitting down. The mayor sat in his customary seat in the center of the café.

Wes, however, didn't move. He continued to stare at Sarah, and Sarah could not take her eyes off of him. She ignored the mayor.

Wes found his voice first, "Sarah, I'm, it's good to see you. I've wondered, I mean, I've wondered if you were all okay. Are the kids... are Cody and Laura, are they here too?"

Sarah relaxed, just a bit. She allowed a small smile and nod to appear. He had a right to know his children were alive, healthy, and happy.

Wes was older, visibly so. He had white sprinkled liberally through his brown hair and his face had lines where there had not been when she had last seen him. He seemed steady, not drunk, not angry, and she felt a small ray of hope. Would he forgive her for running? For taking his children?

Wes stared at his estranged wife. Wife... it felt so odd to think of her as that. But there had been no divorce, no day in court, just an empty house. She was older, the laugh lines had deepened, and her hair was streaked with wiry gray hairs that she had plucked out ruthlessly when they first arrived in Belton years back, and eventually given up and allowed to grow.

Her shape was thinner than he remembered, but then she had been a bit heavy after Laura was born. His cheeks burned at the memory of himself, drunk and angry at the world, pointing out her defects—her weight being one of the many ways he berated her. He looked into her eyes, warm and brown, but a little scared. Scared of him, he realized, scared of what he might do.

Wes tried to imagine what she must be feeling. Was she scared that he was still that man? That he still carried that war inside of him? He stared at her, wondering how he could explain, wishing he knew the right words to tell her how different he was. That time had healed him.

He wanted to tell her how sorry he was, how much he had missed her and the kids, that he hadn't deserved to have them, that he had nearly died when they left. He stared into those brown eyes and everything else melted away. It didn't matter how long it had been or the changes they had come through alone; he was hit by the memories of her, younger, full of laughter, heavy with child, his child, and the frenzied, tearful reunions when he would come home on leave from boot camp.

The mayor, who had at first been interested in this odd scene only because it was the chance to impress new and different people, was quickly becoming incensed at being ignored. Who was this upstart, anyway? And the two young ones, who were they? He grumbled at the thought of the militia just letting them sashay on in this way, armed to the teeth from the look of the older one, and no one to watch them.

Oh sure, sure the war was over and there was talk of a new centralized government. But that wasn't much more than a promise of taxes and some damn bureaucrat trying to wrest control away from him.

He had built himself a nice little empire here, one that he would pass on down to his son one day if that boy didn't stop screwing up everything he touched. James had been a disappointment in many ways, the most recent being his loss of control of the town militia and some damned girl he had managed to knock up. The boy spent more time carousing about in one of the few working trucks and drinking moonshine than he did keeping the town safe.

And that damned Todd Stevens, who had re-assumed control of the militia, had the audacity to lock him up for two days after he accidentally sideswiped one of the town's cattle, breaking its leg.

Mayor Farley felt his pulse increase, beating an angry rhythm in his neck. His face flushed hot. Why, damned if they weren't all ignoring him! He was sitting in his regular seat waiting for Sarah to snap to and fix him up her delectable biscuits and gravy, and she was just staring at this man like he was a ghost. Couldn't she see he was waiting? It was bad enough she had that damned grandson again today. The little beast had bitten him, bit him, and she had simply apologized and let the boy go without tanning his behind. His eyes traveled to where the little beast had been sitting, covered in flour and dough, but he had disappeared.

Wonderful, Mayor Farley thought, she can't be bothered to do her job and now she's let the little crapper wander off. What was the world coming to?

"Sarah Turner, have you gone deaf?" Farley said loudly, startling Chris and Carrie and earning a sharp look of displeasure from Wes. "I'm waiting for my biscuits and gravy here. And pour me a mug of that hot chicory as well; I'll take it black as usual. And make sure you add some bacon and..." the rest of what he was going to say was lost in a howl of anger and pain.

Hunter had crawled under the tables, wound his way around to the table that housed the mayor's large bulk, and bit down firmly on a fat ring-encrusted finger.

It was Wes who was able to scoop the wayward child out from under the table before the mayor got some bright idea to kick out at the child. As it was, the rotund man roared from his seat, maddened that the little beast had bitten him not once, but twice, and without any kind of consequences.

"You hand over that little brat, right now, I'm of a mind to show him the back side of my hand," the mayor panted with fury, "but I'll settle for one good crack of my belt," and his hand went to loosen his belt. "Teach him once and for all not to bite honest, hard-working men, by God."

Sarah bristled. Honest and hard-working most definitely did not describe the mayor, and she would be damned if he was going to show her grandson any kind of violence. Instead, it was Wes who quelled the red-faced mayor with a look, the little boy struggling in his arms to get another chance at biting the offensive man. Wes didn't say a thing, just stared at Mayor Farley in a manner that made it clear he would tolerate no violence toward the child.

Jonathan Farley had never been a particularly bright man. His father had quietly maneuvered him into positions of power, taught him a few tricks on how to make others look dirty while he appeared clean, and generally railroaded him into the bank president position he held for nearly two decades, until the world had been set on its ear. Through a little luck and happenstance, perhaps his daddy's spirit guiding his steps, he had managed to convince the shell-shocked remains of the town populace that he should be mayor, and he had quickly taken control of the reins of power and held on tight.

To say that Mayor Farley was used to getting his way was an understatement. But standing there facing this grim-faced stranger—who held the toddler with such ease and showed such certainty in his ways—Farley realized for the first time the adversary before him. He had no idea what the man was capable of, but he doubted it would be anything short of violence.

Suddenly, biscuits and gravy didn't sound appetizing at all. In fact, his appetite had plumb vanished. Mayor Farley turned silently on his heel and slipped out the door, intimidated enough to say nothing, and leaving Sarah gaping in silence at the effect her estranged husband had on the pompous, rotund old man.

Wes didn't bother looking at the mayor's departure. He was examining his grandson closely, damned if the kid didn't look dead-on like Cody when he was two. The only difference was the shockingly red hair the boy had—which was a mess of sharp angles and coated on the sides in flour.

The little boy stared back, his eyes warm brown pools, just like his grandmother's... grandmother, my God, that makes me... a grandfather, Wes turned that realization over in his head, as the boy grinned and giggled, then wiggled impatiently to be let down. He hadn't been the least afraid of this tall, strange man. Wes set him gently on the ground and the boy ran on his short little chubby legs toward the back door where he knew there were toys to play with.

Chris looked a bit disconcerted; the fat man had looked familiar somehow, but he couldn't put a name on the face. This woman, Sarah, didn't look at all familiar, yet Wes had called her Sarah.

The Sarah? Wes's long-disappeared wife, Sarah? This was getting crazier by the moment.

Wes watched the boy disappear and then focused again on Sarah. He managed a small smile. "Turner? So, you've remarried, Sarah?" Why did his chest squeeze tight at the thought of her married to another? No ring on her finger, but not everyone wore one. Their wedding rings, along with Angie's, were still there, solid, warm and heavy on the chain against his chest. He had worn his wedding band for years before finally slipping it off again and adding it to the chain.

He had thought briefly of leaving all of them there in the drawer in the house in Tiptonville. Those days were so long past, his children a snapshot of a memory. Grown or dead, they were gone forever. And Angie, along with their unborn baby, gone before they had any chance at a good life together. He had pulled the chain off of his neck, stared at it for several long minutes, and then quietly put it back on. They were a part of him, his memories of a life he hadn't deserved but wished he could make right.

Sarah shook her head, "I took my name from a highway sign, changed the kids to that too; I figured you wouldn't let us go without a fight." She was right.

He had done plenty of searching for her himself, hired a private investigator for a short time, before the world had gone to hell in a hand basket. The trail had gone cold in Texas and when word of the nuke had come, he had feared the worst. Now, thinking back on it all, he simply nodded; of course, she would have done just that. He had looked under her maiden name, tracked down every boy in middle school or high school that had looked twice at her, dated her, tried to date her, and got nowhere. She had disappeared, slid into a world full of people, full of opportunities to remain anonymous, to remain hidden. He tried to summon anger or resentment, but it was impossible. He had hurt her, emotionally, verbally, and, finally, physically. He'd deserved nothing less.

Chris leaned close to Carrie. "Perhaps we should leave them to talk. We could walk over to the house; see if it is still there. It isn't more than twenty minutes or so from here." Carrie nodded, and they slipped out. Wes and Sarah didn't even seem to notice. They were too busy staring at each other in a way that seemed peaceable enough. A few years ago, Chris wouldn't have thought it possible that Wes would be able to hold it together like that. Now? Chances were pretty good that he would be reconnecting with his long-lost family. His mind reeled at the thought. He missed Mom and Dad. He missed Jess. Damned if it isn't a small world. How he wished the impossible could happen for him, too.

The bell on the door quietly chimed as the young couple made their exit. Sarah and Wes stood frozen, their memories, their ghosts between them, plenty of questions in their eyes. Sarah broke the silence first, "Let me get you some coffee."

She slid behind the counter, her mind awhirl with the shock of seeing a man she had loved once upon a time. She poured the coffee with both hands to stop the shaking that had suddenly started up. He had always taken it the same way, black, with one spoon of sugar. But this was chicory, not the real stuff, and she suddenly panicked; what if he didn't like it? She looked up, startled, as he closed a hand over hers. He'd moved with cat-like stealth, silently slipping behind the bar. She looked up, her heart thumping hard, wordless.

"I take two spoons now; the chicory is so doggoned bitter." He smiled. "Sometimes I even add a splash of milk as well." He paused; his expression turned sober. "I'm glad you are alive, Sarah. You and the kids. The world seemed a darker place without you in it." His hand still covered hers; it felt calloused, strong. "Can we sit a bit? And talk? I'd like to hear about Cody and Laura... and you."

Sarah nodded, her eyes filling. The man she had married, full of hope and youth and love, was standing before her. He was different, but so was she—older, wiser, perhaps. She didn't see the Wes she had run from. Instead, Sarah saw the Wes who had loved her.

She squeezed his hand, walked to the front of the café. She closed the curtains, turned the "Open" sign over to "Closed" and locked the door. The townspeople could go elsewhere for their lunch today; it was time she and Wes had a talk.

"Come on," she said, "let me introduce you to your grandson."

A Ghost Returns

"H*ow do I even describe today? There was so much joy, such indescribable joy. Shock too, for both of us. I had given up hope and so had he. Standing there, face to face, was like a page out of one of my dreams. How often had those dreams haunted my nights? I hated waking up and realizing I had only dreamed of it. I think tomorrow I will pinch myself, and check here in this journal, before I believe that it is really real."—Jess's Journal*

Chris and Carrie walked down to the end of Main Street and turned right, heading first north and crossing over Highway 58. It wasn't much of a highway, just a two-lane road running from east to west.

"Do you think Wes and... what was her name... Sarah?... will be all right?" Carrie asked.

The look on the older man's face was one that neither of them had ever seen. It might have been twenty years or more, but the woman had run off with his kids, and no matter what had prompted her to do it, would Wes be able to forgive her for it?

"Yeah," Chris said, and he squinted in the bright sunlight; it was a hot day, "I think they'll be okay."

He stared at the remains of what had been the new Price Chopper, which had opened just a handful of years before the Collapse. The walls had collapsed in, the insides blackened with fire. He wondered when it happened. It had been cleaned out early on, after the trucks stopped showing up with food and goods. One of the first signs of the Collapse had been the breakdown in the chain of deliveries. Slowly, stores found themselves out of one item, then another, until finally a cascade of outages, combined with ever-increasing blackouts and a panicked rush on the foodstuffs that remained, had caused the store to close. Chris could still see a portion of one of the handwritten signs that had been placed in the glass windows. It should have read, "store closed until further notice," but all that remained was "store clo" and the rest of the sign was long gone, as was the glass window it had hung on inside.

Now they were passing the road to nowhere—an access road that had been planned, along with several miles of walking trails, and never finished, yet another victim of the financial troubles years before the actual collapse. The pavement was now cracked and warped. Several trees had pushed through the tarmac and were flourishing, undeterred by their asphalt surroundings. The road was clear, and there was little traffic, either on foot or by auto. It was obvious that the town's population had been severely decimated. Prior to the collapse, there had been more than 20,000 residents in Belton. From the looks of it, there was perhaps ten percent of that number now.

The day before, they had made their way slowly through parts of Kansas City. The highways were in tatters, all overpasses had long been destroyed, and huge swaths of the city appeared to be nothing but blackened ruins. Wes had spoken with a few others shortly outside of St. Louis and learned that Kansas City had endured several large fires over the course of a decade of hot and dry summers.

It had destroyed most of the inner city, sparing only a few homes in the historic Northeast district, and leaving the West Bottoms full of blackened and crumbling brick buildings. Most of downtown had been lost, as well as nearly all the poorer neighborhoods where the old houses were filled with dry, brittle wood just waiting for an excuse to go up in flames.

The city had suffered greatly in the aftermath of the Collapse. The loss of many of its inhabitants from the inner core had occurred years before the Collapse, but it was hit hard when the country descended into anarchy and war. In wide swaths throughout the state, homes were left abandoned, crime rose, and those who could fled to the suburbs and surrounding countryside. This had all occurred years before the Collapse, but it had set the tone for what came next.

Despite the efforts of many to re-populate the city at the turn of the century and try to save some of the historic, yet crumbling, buildings, when the Collapse finally came, it hit hard and fast. The loss of utilities—clean water, dependable electricity, and finally gas main breaks—was only the beginning of Kansas City's woes. Quickly, food shortages and water-borne illnesses due to the lack of utilities began to take a horrific toll on the inhabitants who were left. The hospitals collapsed next, due to the shortage in supplies and loss of infrastructure—it was a scene that played out in city after city; one that resulted in mayhem, death, and the panicked flight of the remaining population.

Kansas City had become a ghost town filled with collapsed buildings and a general sense of empty decay. There were a few pockets of civilization—certain areas that had held out and refused to fall into ruin. Here and there, scattered through the city, people bustled about, tending large gardens in empty lots, repairing what they could of the damaged buildings closest to them, and working toward opening trade routes.

Belton was a world of difference from the chaos and destruction they had seen when passing through the city. Chris had winced as he pointed out much of the cultural center of Kansas City, which was now abandoned, looted and destroyed; even the grand stone edifice of the Nelson-Atkins Art Museum had reflected the devastation of the Collapse and the warring troops that had fought for control of the ruins of the former United States. It had been heavily damaged during mortar fire, and most of the roof in the older section had collapsed.

The highway overpass that bisected the town of Belton into its east and west sides had been obliterated. The ramps still remained, but they were closed into narrow sections, of which a normal car barely fit through. This had been done intentionally. Military vehicles, large trucks, especially a tank or Humvee, would not be able to pass through the choked-off passage ten feet high on each side of twisted rock and metal rebar. The van and truck waited for them near Main Street, but it felt good to stretch their legs, and gas was too difficult to find to waste on a little side trip.

As they walked, slowly approaching a large network of fences and walls with the obvious smell of cattle emanating from them, Chris was experiencing what could only be described as double vision. The memory of what had been a United Rentals and Casey's gas station next to it was clear in his memory. How often had he taken a run with his dad to rent an auger or chipper? How often had he and Jess begged for a treat when stopping at the Casey's for gas? It was, however, overlaid by what now existed—blackened ruins with amorphous lumps within. His memories of his hometown were sharp; it felt as if the past twelve years had passed in a quick snap of the fingers, and Chris felt as if he was waking from a dream. He wondered why he had never come back, never tried, not once, to find out what had become of the home and the family he had lost.

In the distance, coming toward them, was a man on a horse. He wore a bandana, most likely to soak up the sweat from the heat of the sun pounding down on him. Chris stared at him, thinking he looked vaguely familiar and the man stared back, a look of shock on his face.

"Chris Aaronson?" the man asked, a tone of wonder in his voice. His hair was red, and Chris couldn't place him, but he appeared close to the same age, late 20s, early 30s at the most. He certainly knew Chris, which made Chris uneasy and embarrassed he couldn't place him.

"Yeah, I'm Chris, and I'm sorry, it's been a long journey... you are...?" he stared at the man as he dismounted.

"Todd Stevens. I was a couple of years ahead of you in school and at Scouts." The man grinned, and shook his head, "I just can't believe it's you! Where in the hell have you been, Aaronson?"

Chris's memories of a red-headed lanky teen a couple of years older than him came flooding back. They had bunked in the same tent one year when the Scouts went on their annual camp-out. Todd had been a cool guy, and he hadn't been a jerk to Chris and Allen; he'd shared his homemade beef jerky and shown them some tips during archery lessons.

"Man, Todd, I remember you now." He reached out and shook Todd's hand and turned to Carrie, who had been quietly watching the exchange, "This is my wife, Carrie. I've been in Tennessee for nearly twelve years now, in a small town by the name of Tiptonville. We're moving on, going on to Denver, but I had to stop and see the town before I went. See if the house is still standing." He shrugged. "Pay my respects to anyone from before... you know."

Todd had a strange look on his face. "Well, your house is still there, Chris. Still there." He looked as if he wanted to say more, but thought better of it. "Let me walk you over there." He waved at one of the other sentries, which Chris had noticed were posted every few hundred yards, watchful, with horses saddled and ready to go nearby. "Most won't remember you, and we don't allow visitors through the gate without an escort." He shrugged, "The Reformation may be in full swing on the coasts, but I guess we have got a way to go before it stops being the Wild West 'round here." He nodded to Carrie, "Nice to meet you, Carrie."

They walked for another block, passing a sentry along the way. It appeared that everyone was heavily armed and quite watchful. "Have trouble with raiders?" Chris asked.

"Yeah, now and then. It just makes sense to be more watchful. Word gets back to 'em, and they stop trying. Leastways, the attacks have petered off to nothing, down from a swarm of them last year. We lost two men and 20 head of cattle, including two beautiful heifers we were hoping to breed."

They passed through a set of heavy metal cattle doors. Half of the block had burned, but the houses here had been torn down, hauled away, and the empty lots filled with gardens. Every possible space was being utilized. They were quickly approaching Chris's old street.

As the small group turned onto the street, Chris's pulse quickened. He could see his childhood home, just barely; it was hiding now behind tall trees and massive blackberry bushes. Most of the houses were gone on this street, but there were fruiting bushes, fruit trees, and rows of in-ground plants in various stages of growth. From the looks of it, the land was intensively planted, every bit of it utilized to grow something. It was a riot of green growth.

Chris stopped in the middle of the road as a boy, aged eleven or twelve, popped out of a long line of corn, chasing a dark-haired girl, pelting her with what looked like overripe grape-sized tomatoes as she screamed and laughed. One hit her square in the back as she skidded to a stop in front of the group. The boy, also dark-haired, was so intent on chasing her that he nearly ran into the back of her, crashing to the ground to avoid knocking her over. Both kids stared at Chris and Carrie curiously.

Todd Stevens laughed, "You kids are sure working hard, I see." He reached a hand down, helping the boy up. Chris thought the boy looked eerily familiar. But he couldn't possibly know this boy; he would have been an infant at most on the day Belton was invaded. Todd asked, "Where's your mom? Tell her I've got someone she would like to meet."

Chris stared as the boy, who looked so strangely familiar, as did the girl, they were obviously siblings, gave Chris a short, appraising stare with his crayon-blue eyes and ran off calling to his mother.

"Mom! Hey Mom! We got visitors." He disappeared around a row of trees, and several hens squawked in alarm at his passing.

"Someone's living here, then," he said, a statement, and a question rolled into one.

Todd nodded, a peculiar smile forming on his face—as if there was a joke that Chris should be clued in on. Chris's heart twinged a little at the thought. The memories, some of the best memories of his life, were of that house. It felt both good and painful to think that someone was living here. The house looked relatively well cared for, and the garden would have made his mother proud. How she had loved her garden and teaching her neighbors how to grow luscious fruits and vegetables out of soil once reserved for immaculate lawns and ornamental flowers.

A young man with unruly dark brown hair and patched jeans came around the corner with a wheelbarrow. He was in his early 20s, and his arms and chest were tanned dark from the sun.

"Hey, Todd, what do you know?" He asked with a friendly smile on his face, a look of curiosity at the strange man and woman in front of him.

"Hey, David, I have some folks here you'll want to meet," Todd said, nodding to Chris and Carrie. "This here is Carrie, and this is Chris... Aaronson."

David's face changed from a look of welcome to one of shock. He had been in the act of shaking hands with Carrie and he froze at the mention of Chris's last name. "Aaronson?" He glanced at Todd. "Does she know?"

Chris wondered who she was. He began to page through his memories. Had there been a girl or woman here who knew him? For a brief moment, his hope surged at the thought that possibly his mother was still alive. As quickly as the hope came, it died. Allen had been sure. Chris had wrested the memories from his friend, insisting he know in every detail. They had both died, his mom and his dad, and the children who had fallen behind and slowed them down had died with them. Allen had been certain and God knows Chris had tried to convince himself that it wasn't true, but reality was harshly indifferent to hope.

And Jess; those scumbags had told them all about how she had died, her and Erin. The dull ache of her memory thumped in his chest. Losing Jess, knowing she was gone, and he had failed to protect her, that was the worst part of it. And it is what had set his feet walking far, far away from the only home he had ever known.

There was a woman approaching now. Lean, slender build, golden hair tumbling in curls over her shoulders and down her back. She was preceded by the dark-haired boy, and followed by a girl with red hair who was perhaps six, maybe older. The young woman drew near and Chris's heart stuttered to a stop. She was equally shocked, stopping in mid-stride with a gasp, her mouth a perfectly round 'o' of disbelief.

"Oh my God... Chris?"

Chris blinked in shock and finally found his voice. "Jess?"

I'm What?!

"What you need to know about the past is that no matter what has happened, it has all worked together to bring you to this very moment. And this is the moment you can choose to make everything new. Right now."—Author Unknown

There would be little sleep in the long evening that followed the reunion. There was far too much to catch up on. Far too much to share and learn about each other.

Tears, anger, sadness—and the stories. They tripped over each other's words, eager to describe the lives they had lived since that fateful stormy night so long ago. Jess mourned once again her friend Erin as she recounted the few months of freedom they both had before losing her so tragically in that abandoned farmhouse outside of Clinton.

The others, Becka, Erin, and David, along with Carrie and Todd, circled about in the background as Jess and Chris laughed, cried, and hugged and described the past dozen years. It would be hours later that a meal was set before them, eaten and barely tasted, as Chris described old Fenton and his cleaning the shotgun, or Jess spoke of Serena and adopting Becka as her own.

She did not elaborate more on Jacob's beginnings, other than to describe his birth in the ruins of Clinton, tousling his hair, and pleading silently with her eyes for Chris to not ask for more details. The boy stared at Chris silently, his face and hair so reminiscent of the nightmare they both had endured. It wasn't anything the boy said or did; just the way that he looked so exactly, exactly like that monster... except for Jess's crayon-blue eyes.

Chris swallowed the revulsion he felt with difficulty, tried to remind himself that where the boy had come from was not who the boy was.

We are defined by the responses we make to the circumstances that surround us, not the circumstances themselves.

Although his mind reasoned this, his stomach churned at the thought of what his sister had gone through, all alone.

In the days that followed, the plan to move on to Denver was delayed indefinitely. It was high summer and there was plenty of farm work to be done. Chris stepped up when Jess came down with a strange, intermittent flu. It would hit her especially hard in the morning, so Chris took over milking the goats, two of which were vicious beasts well known to bite when one least expected it. Carrie found herself painting murals in the old downtown where they now had a small school set up, and lunching with Sarah regularly at the café.

Chris had made a special visit on his own to visit with old Mr. Banks. He had explained what he knew of Allen's death, filling in the details that no one else had known. The old man's grandson had died a hero, protecting the information of which direction the girls had fled that stormy night a dozen years past. His silence had cost him his life and given Jess and her friend Erin the small window of time they desperately needed to escape.

The old man had listened, nodding as Chris told him what he knew, a small tear trickling down his weathered cheek. A week later, he had turned over the farm to David and Jess and headed into town to register as a challenger to Mayor Farley in the upcoming election. It was an odd move for the old man, who had been happy to keep to his homestead on the outskirts of the town for years.

It was several weeks after arriving in Belton that Carrie suddenly found herself between painting jobs. She walked over to the house, looking for Chris, and found Jess instead, looking miserable and ill. "I just don't understand it, this horrible flu," Jess said, her face pale with dark circles under her eyes. "Just when I think I'm over it, it comes back."

The two women were less than a year apart in age and Jess had been disappointed when she came down with the flu and wasn't able to spend more time with her new sister-in-law. She wanted to ask Carrie so many things, personal things. She suspected that her brother's wife couldn't have children. At first, she had just assumed it was by choice. Then she had seen Carrie interact with little Erin, joke and laugh with Becka and Jacob, and kindly volunteer to paint a mural for the new school, which had been re-established just two years ago in the remains of an old hardware store on Main Street.

The school was only open in late fall through early spring half days, allowing for children who lived in the surrounding countryside to attend around their family's farming schedules. The school had dismissed for the summer before Chris and Carrie had arrived, but the building was now being retrofitted with a small kitchen and other improvements. The mural that Carrie had painted was the crowning jewel to that.

Carrie leaned close to Jess and gave her a hug. She missed Liza and Carl and the kids. She hadn't realized how badly she missed them until she stopped long enough from painting to interact with her sister-in-law. What a miracle it was for Chris to find Jess alive here. And after so many years! She smiled at Jess, who looked beautiful even when she was sick. And then, as a click of recognition slammed into her brain, she gasped and covered her mouth.

"What is it?" Jess looked confused.

"How long have you been sick with the flu, Jess?"

"I don't know." Jess shrugged. "Maybe a week or two?" As she said it out loud, a conversation from the past exploded into memory...

"How long have you been sick, Jess?" Erin's voice was clear of any sleepiness now, and she sounded frightened.

"About... ohhh!" Jess listed back toward the stream and heaved again, "Oh man, this sucks! Um... going on," she bent and retched, "about three weeks now. Oh!!! Why?"

"When was your last period?" Erin persisted.

Jess looked at her oddly. "I dunno, a month, maybe two."

"When exactly?"

"How the hell should I know?"

"Well, do you think it's possible that..."

Jess stared at Carrie with wide eyes. "Oh my God. Oh, oh, oh my God, I," And without saying another word she turned and retched into a nearby trash can.

Carrie had smiled and brewed some raspberry tea for Jess, searched out some dry, stale biscuits from a couple of days ago, and hugged her sister-in-law and congratulated her. Then she had locked her own pain down and given Jess some space to herself to think about the life growing inside her and form the words that she would say to David and the rest of the family. It was mid-afternoon by the time she made her escape, and Carrie aimlessly walked back into town and into Sarah's café.

Sarah had been well occupied with Wes and her children and grandchildren during the past few weeks. Carrie had sensed a very kind soul in her, but had not had a chance to speak with her much. The lunch rush was long gone, and the café didn't serve dinner. Sarah had almost finished cleaning up, and Wes had gone with Chris and David on a trip into the city to trade for supplies. When Carrie appeared at the door, Sarah opened it and insisted she come in.

A few pleasantries aside, Sarah stared at Carrie sharply and said, "You have something weighing on you terribly, girl. What is it?"

That simple question had broken the dam. Carrie burst into tears. It took several long minutes before she was able to explain. She spilled about Jess being pregnant and sobbed again as she described the miscarriages and stillbirths. "We have lost so many babies, Sarah. It has been so hard, so painful. I guess..." She stopped and brushed her tears away, "I just... so many times over the years I have wondered why Chris even stuck with me."

The older woman nodded, placing a warm hand on Carrie's. "I see how much he loves you."

"He'd have to... every time, every time... I get so sad, so angry..." she shook her head, "I push him away."

Sarah laughed softly, "Oh Carrie, that man loves you far too much to be deterred by a little push away now and then. I'd imagine that it might actually prove an irresistible challenge." She squeezed the younger woman's hand. She stroked Carrie's hair. "It's okay to cry, to be sad, and to want what you want."

The older woman was so kind, and for the first time in what seemed like forever, Carrie simply gave in to the years of disappointment and loss and sobbed in Sarah's arms. She cried until she couldn't cry anymore. Sarah just held her, stroked her hair, and rocked her.

Carrie couldn't help thinking of her mother, and the hole her absence had created in their lives, even more so than their father's. She had been the eldest, and she had had to be strong for Liza and for their baby brother for all of those years. Learning to hide her pain from her parents' loss had provided an easy segue into hiding her pain during the stillbirths and miscarriages. After Carrie had cried herself out, Sarah had given her a cup of tea and led her to the back rooms to a comfortable couch to lie down on.

Sarah hugged her again. "There now, you are safe here. Get some rest, my dear; you have just let out a flood of sadness. And there's nothing like a little nap to set you right after that."

She closed the door quietly, leaving the younger woman in the room alone. Carrie had tried to fight it at first, telling herself she should return to the house and help get dinner started, or work out in the yard. But every part of her felt hulled out by the storm of emotions. Her eyelids slowly became heavier. She closed them, thought of the look of terror and joy on Jess's face, and smiled sadly at the thought of her husband's sister in love and expecting a child. The world spun around these children, born into a different time than she or her parents had been born. It spun around and around. Babies were born, people died, and still the world kept spinning. She slipped into a deep sleep on the soft couch, barely aware of the bustle in the kitchen and restaurant outside of the door.

Traders and Raiders

"*The first evil choice or act is linked to the second; and each one to the one that follows, both by the tendency of our evil nature and by the power of habit, which holds us as by a destiny.*"*—Tryon Edwards*

In the end, the old man hadn't gone peacefully. Cooper found himself fascinated by how some people fought so hard against the inevitable, while others simply faded away. Sulwyn had once talked about some Eastern religion, where there was an endless cycle of birth, death, and rebirth. The object of the game, from how Sulwyn explained it, was to get off that cycle of rebirth, somehow ascend to a higher plane of existence. He had said, "Some people are closer to that higher plane than others, so they don't fear death; they welcome it as the next step."

At the last house, the bright yellow farmhouse that sat outside of the tall fence surrounding the town's cattle herd, the mother had gone quickly. In truth, after he had killed the woman's husband, she had frozen, unable to cope. The girl had struggled. But she was young, sixteen or seventeen at the most. No matter what horrors life had dealt, she desperately wanted to live. At the end of three days there at the house, the most he dared to stay, he had moved on to the old man's house, leaving the flies and blood behind for others to find.

Cooper hadn't known any of the people he had killed to welcome their imminent death, but there were some who seemed to go with only a small show of resistance, while others fought tooth and nail to the bitter end. The old man had been one of the latter. Every breath he had taken was impossible, a fight against all odds, as the blood pooled around him and his breaths became shallow and far apart, ending in hitched gasps. He had stared at Cooper as if he knew him, but said little. "You... it's you." Cooper was pretty sure he had never met the old man before, but who knew? Maybe he had.

Thurman Banks had taken a long time to die. Cooper had watched it with the clinical detachment that comes from not just seeing death, but dealing it out with regularity and precision.

He had waited until the last rattling breath had come and the light had died from the old man's eyes before exiting the bedroom and shutting the door behind him. He figured that he had a day, maybe two, before the summer heat would betray what had happened here. Meanwhile, he would have a nice nap on the living room sofa and see what there was to eat.

He had tricked his way into the farmhouse, and now this old man's house, by pretending to be a trader. In reality, the items he had for sale were nothing more than the loot gathered from his previous stopovers—a trail of bodies and trauma that extended through three states now.

A few blocks away, Jess had gone to the west garden to pull weeds and collect some tomatoes that were heavy and ready for picking. She had asked Carrie not to say anything about the pregnancy. She was still struggling with the reality of it and the complicated memories her condition brought up.

There was a tiny pooch to her otherwise flat stomach, and she felt exhausted by midday. But other than that, there was nothing to indicate a child growing inside of her. Despite this, Jess knew it had to be real.

Once her shock had receded, she had found herself excited at the prospect. But there was a deep sadness, as well as guilt, as she recalled her first pregnancy. Although she reminded herself time and again that the circumstances had been drastically different, a part of her felt great guilt at not having wanted Jacob from the beginning. Those months, filled with fear and running and escape with her friend Erin, had left a mark deep within her. She had hated the child growing inside her, actively hoped it would die, and been horrified as it had grown and thrived, taking over her body, before finally finding herself in the throes of labor and delivery.

If that soldier had not thrown open the door right then, his presence reminding all of them of how close death was and how important being alive could be, would she have ever loved him? She loved Jacob now—deeply, irredeemably—even as she watched her brother's face as he struggled with the reality of his nephew's grim origins.

So, in addition to feeling happiness and excitement over this new life growing inside her, Jess also felt guilt and shame at not feeling this way about Jacob, so she said nothing, hoping she could reconcile these different feelings, and also wait until she was a little further along and sure before sharing it with everyone else.

A car horn sounded from the street outside the front of the house. The Jeep was obscured behind the rows of corn, now over five feet tall, and the fruit trees. The family emptied out of the house and grounds, converging on the front road. It was Todd Stevens and his face was pinched with exhaustion, his mouth set.

"Hey there, Jess." He nodded to Chris and David and the rest who had come from their work in the garden and inside of the house. "We have a problem."

Todd's presence at the house, along with a serious look and the word "problem" raised all the adults' hackles. Todd had been re-established as the head of the town militia after the mayor's son had made a royal mess of it, too busy riding on his wave of new power to follow the tried-and-true strategies of protecting the town from raids.

Entire families had died, but the raiders had been run off over the past year, thanks to Todd's leadership. Once again, all able-bodied adults in town were required to do their part and serve on a rotating schedule for the militia. The raids had fallen off dramatically, and there hadn't been a problem in months. That, however, appeared to have changed.

"It looks like the Franklin place was raided a week ago," Todd said, looking grim. The Franklin home was north off of Kentucky, outside of the outer fence. They kept pigs and chickens on their ten-acre plot and came into town every couple of weeks to trade. "They were due in last week. When they didn't show, Sarah let us know they were overdue for a delivery of chickens she had ordered, I figured we needed to drop by there."

Jess felt her heart thump in her chest. "Raiders?"

Todd looked over at the kids clustered around. "Yeah. Looks like they stayed a day or two." The Franklins had two kids, both in their late teens. The daughter Mary had helped out a handful of times caring for

Jacob and Becka when they were smaller. A sick dread spread through Jess's stomach.

Todd met her eyes, "They're all gone." He said it with finality. His even tone did not betray the turmoil he had felt when faced with the reality of what he had seen. He beckoned to Chris and David. "I'll need you two to help me search. We think they are still out there."

Both men were already carrying a small sidearm at their waists. Chris nodded and opened the back door, but David hesitated, staring at Jess. He didn't want to leave her, not if there was danger in the area. She caught the look and gave him one of her own that clearly said she could take care of herself. Her hand strayed to Lady, a tiny revolver that hadn't left her side in years, not since Old Coop had given it to her as a gift all those years ago.

Thinking about him now, she wondered if the old man was still there, raising his hunting dogs and setting traps. He had been a good man, and she could still remember the last thing he had said to her, his hand on her rounded belly.

"I can't blame you girl if y'think you hate this creature inside you, but it's a blessin' and someday you'll see it that way."

Old Coop had been right; Jacob was one of the best parts of her life, and she wished she could tell the old man that.

"Go," she said to David, "I'll be fine and we have Jacob here as well."

David had spent the past few summers teaching Jacob archery, how to handle a small or large firearm, and tracking techniques. Todd Stevens had taught Jacob and others hand-to-hand combat as well once he resumed control of the militia.

David smiled at her, kissed her, and then he jumped into the Jeep as well. "See you soon."

It was nearly dark when they returned, both men grim-faced. Jess had extended the offer of dinner to Todd, but he had politely refused, his eyes haunted, saying only that his wife and kids were waiting.

"Anything?" Jess asked.

"No tracks past the creek." David said, his lips set, "It looks like only one guy, but we aren't 100% sure. Todd thinks he might have headed north, but I'm not convinced. I think we need to keep a sharp eye out, keep everyone close."

Chris nodded, "Me, too."

Dinner was a muted affair, and Chris looked tense and on edge. Danger was lurking far too close to home for anyone's comfort.

The Truth of the Matter

"Are you willing to believe that love is the strongest thing in the world - stronger than hate, stronger than evil, stronger than death?"—Henry Van Dyke

Chris was angry, uncharacteristically so. Perhaps it was the fear of raiders in the area. The Franklin family, not more than a mile away, all dead—it brought back all too familiar memories. Dead, staring eyes, the violation of the women, and the stench of death. Would he ever escape this endless cycle of death? Would he ever be able to unsee the terrible sights he had been witness to?

The boy hadn't said or done much of anything, just made a joke, and Chris had stridden off into the house, unable to think, to speak, past the blinding hatred he felt rising up inside of him. What had Jess been thinking? Keeping a reminder like that near her all of these years. Jacob was a carbon copy of the man, except for his crayon-blue eyes of what had come to be the main character in his worst nightmares. He fought for control. Carrie didn't understand, Jess didn't, none of them did.

God, how many times had he dreamed of Jess, dead by that monster's hand? Finding her alive, realizing that he had his sister back, that she had been here for years, rebuilding her life even as the ghosts from their previous life haunted her. How could she stand to look at that boy? How could she force those words, "I love you," out of her mouth?

He heard a soft tread behind him, and Jess's hand reached out and squeezed his shoulder. "He didn't mean to make you angry, Chris. He's just a boy."

"He's rude," Chris ground the words out, "A real smartass."

Even saying the words, he knew they weren't true. He knew his emotions were colored by the past, by what was long gone. He had tried so hard to close off this anger, to recognize that the boy wasn't to blame, but it was all too much. The way the kid's lips had twisted, almost in a snarl, reminded him of blood and death and darkness, months of it, and the years of grief that had followed. How could he look at that boy and see anything else but that?

Jess couldn't understand where all of this anger was coming from. Chris had never been like this; he'd been kind and patient. Why did her brother hold such animosity towards Jacob? Above all, she wanted peace. They were all family, all together now, for the first time in years. Underneath one roof, an impossible and beautiful thing. Why was he being this way?

"Chris," Jess fought to keep her tone even, "please understand."

"Understand what, sis? That Cooper, that raping bastard, is his father? That he destroyed your life? That Jacob was born because an evil man, who raped and murdered countless women, put his seed into you?"

Jess stood in shock. "You... know?"

Chris practically snarled, "How could I not know? Looking at him is like seeing that bastard's face over and over and over again. It makes me sick, seeing what he did to you, knowing what you went through."

Her tongue felt heavy, unwieldy, and she couldn't form the words to explain that Jacob was nothing like Scott Cooper, that he was good, that she loved him more than she had ever loved anything else, more than life itself.

"Chris, you don't know what it's like. Jacob is my son. I love him. He's not like that... that monster. He isn't."

Her brother stared at her, his mouth turned down at the edges, "For Christ's sake, Jess, how could you stand to keep him? After what happened to you? Knowing who his father was... hell, still is, for all we know. We never caught him. How can you stand to look at him knowing what Jacob is?"

There was a small sound behind them, a soft scuff of shoes on the worn floorboards, and Chris and Jess turned to see Jacob, his eyes round, full of anguish and betrayal.

Jess gasped in horror; the very thing she had dreaded happening had occurred. She had told no one, not even Sarah Turner. David hadn't even known who it was, although he had sussed out the overall idea of it all long ago.

"Jacob! Oh baby, no, no, no! Listen to me, I..."

The boy was already backpedaling out the door. "You told me my dad had died. You said he..." overwhelmed by the sheer horror of his origins, he turned and fled, quickly disappearing into the dark night.

Jess screamed after him, "Please, Jacob, please wait! I can explain!" She turned back to Chris, her face chalk-white. "How could you, Chris? How could you? He's my son. It doesn't matter who his father is. It doesn't matter, because he's my son and I love him. That's all we have ever needed... love... oh, how could you possibly understand?"

And she ran then, shoving past him, running blindly into the night.

Chris took a step to the doorway to follow her, to try to help, as Carrie arrived. She had heard everything. She reached out a hand, firmly grasping his arm. Her face was hard, tight with anger.

"Let them go, Chris. You've done enough, don't you think?"

"Carrie, I... I didn't mean for him to hear," he said, taken aback by her fury.

Seeing her face made him realize how his dislike of the boy must look to the others. They couldn't understand, they didn't see him like that, they didn't see Scott Cooper sneering out at him through that face. What Carrie and the others saw was his unreasonable disgust and contempt for his sister's only biological child, a boy who had done nothing to him. Jacob didn't deserve this.

Chris watched her go, a sickness rising up inside him. What had he done?

Collision

"L*ife is a series of collisions with the future; it is not the sum of what we have been, but what we yearn to be."—Jose Ortega y Gasset*

Jacob suddenly remembered being five and hiding from his mom.

"Come and find me!" he had called while huddled under the blankets.

He had heard his mother's steps on the floor. She stood for a moment by the bed and then reached out and patted him. Her voice had a playful lilt as she said, "Ah, there you are, kiddo!"

"How do you always know where to find me?" Jacob had demanded.

Jess had smiled and had hugged him and said, "I just do." Her smile faltered for a moment, her eyes far away, caught in a dark memory. "I'll always find you. I'll always come to you. You can depend on that."

How many times through the years had she told him that? Not just when he was playing hide and seek, but when he had gotten separated from her at the town picnic a year later, or when he had wandered off in the woods when they had been hunting for morels? She had always found him. And when she did, she would wrap her arms around him, kiss the top of his head, and say the same thing, "I'll always find you, Jacob. How could I not?"

His head was aching painfully. The man had hit him hard on the head, stunning him, and then dragged him inside of the dark house. Jacob felt tears coursing down his cheeks.

He closed his eyes, repeating silently, over and over, "Please come find me, Mom. Please."

His father was a rapist. A murderer. Someone his Uncle Chris obviously hated and probably his mom too. He had run away into the night, his eyes burning and his stomach heaving. He had run, without direction, without purpose. Everything he had understood about his life turned upside down, even as he heard his mom's voice in the distance calling his name. He ran fast, and before too long her calls faded into the distance. How could she have lied to him like that?

Jacob felt as if something dark and unclean had occupied his body. He had asked a handful of times about his dad. Mom had always looked so sad, so haunted, that he had backed off and accepted the short, unsatisfactory answers she had given.

"Your father, he, lots of people, died, Jacob. Lots of people died."

He had figured that she must have loved his father a lot, and that it hurt to talk about him, so he had stopped. But now, to realize that his father probably hadn't died, wasn't someone his mom had loved, and worse, was a rapist, seemed overwhelming. His footsteps slowed, his heart pounding in his chest, and he looked around for the first time.

The moon was out, and its bright sliver of light added enough illumination for him to see where he was. Over the rise, the herd of cattle gave off little noise, their nightly routine barely affected by the boy so nearby. To his right, Jacob saw Mr. Banks's house. A dim light glowed from one window. And Jacob, not knowing who to turn to, approached the house to see if old Mr. Banks was still awake. The old man was like a grandfather to him. Since Chris and Carrie had come, the normal routine of having him for dinner each Sunday had fallen by the wayside.

And if there was anything that could be done about the strange and disturbing situation at hand, Mr. Banks would be the person to know what to do. Jacob crossed the yard, realizing for the first time that he had run off without shoes as his feet encountered a mostly dry cow pie.

When he knocked on the front door, there was no response. It wasn't that late, but Jacob wondered if the old man was all right. He hadn't been feeling well last month... and Mr. Banks was getting up there in years; what if he had slipped and fallen and was lying on the floor of his bathroom? What if he had suffered a heart attack?

These questions and concerns emboldened Jacob to try the front door. It was locked.

He knocked, called out to the old man, "Mr. Banks? It's Jacob... I... uh... Mr. Banks, are you all right? Can I come in?"

Jacob missed Mr. Banks. He wasn't much of a talker, and he would retreat into silence when there were more than a handful of people in the room. Like most of the residents of Belton, he had seen great loss.

In the outbreak of war, he had lost his wife, along with his only son and grandson. His grandson Allen had died before Jacob was born, but since Chris had returned, he had heard more details about him, and his death.

Jacob stopped in his tracks. Chris had said that Lieutenant Cooper had killed Allen. And just a few minutes ago, he had said his name again.

"That damned Lieutenant Scott Cooper destroyed your life! Jacob was born because an evil man, who raped and murdered countless women, put his seed into you... looking at him is like seeing that bastard's face over and over again."

He could hear those words repeating in his head.

Cooper was his father. And he had murdered Mr. Banks's grandson Allen. Perhaps, upon hearing the news, Mr. Banks wouldn't want anything to do with him. Jacob faltered, uncertain, fearful. He was about to turn away when he heard a creak on the floorboards inside. Jacob turned back toward the door in time to see it quickly open and a man who was definitely not Mr. Banks step into the doorway. Everything moved too suddenly. Jacob was still trying to puzzle out who this man was when the man's right hand lashed out and clocked him hard on the side of the head. Jacob slumped to the ground.

Scott Cooper stared at the unconscious boy at his feet and contemplated whether he should kill him now. The boy was dark-haired, thin but wiry, and looked to be around twelve or thirteen. He wouldn't pose a problem to Cooper, and he might actually come in handy.

He looked out into the night filled with dim moonlight. No one else in sight. The kid might have some information. He might know if that family out on Kentucky Road had been found yet. He probably also knew about militia watch schedules. He was old enough to participate, by the looks of him. And it was time that Cooper was moving on.

Cooper reached down and grabbed the boy's arms and dragged him inside.

The Reckoning

"Life moves on, whether we act as cowards or heroes. Life has no other discipline to impose, if we would but realize it, then to accept life unquestioningly. Everything we shut our eyes to, everything we run away from, everything we deny, denigrate or despise, serves to defeat us in the end. What seems nasty, painful, evil can become a source of beauty, joy, and strength if faced with an open mind. Every moment is a golden one for him who has the vision to recognize it as such."—Henry Miller

The roads were empty and Jess couldn't hear anything but the distant lowing of the town's cattle. They had been moved to one of the eastern paddocks the day before. Jacob could be anywhere. The night sky was free of clouds, allowing the sliver of moon to light it well. Well enough that Jess didn't need a lantern to see, although she occasionally stumbled on debris.

Her heart ached in her chest at the memory of her son's face. He had looked so bereft, so betrayed and horrified. She had never wanted that for him, never wanted him to know the darkness that had helped make him. She had tried so hard to forget.

Jess's hand strayed to her stomach, to the small bump of the unborn child was already pushing its way out, making itself known. She hadn't told David yet. In fact, no one knew except for her and Carrie, and she knew her sister-in-law was waiting for her to say something, for her and David to announce the news.

Jess couldn't help but make comparisons. Her first pregnancy had been filled with such horror, such disgust; she winced at the memory of wanting her unborn child dead. The condition had been forced on her, and she had hated every moment of it, as her body was taken over by another's, distended, changed, slowed down, and exhausted. She had been frightened, terrified the soldiers would find her again and kill her or, worse, take her back there.

This pregnancy was different, and how often had she reminded herself of that? And yet, the memories she had of being pregnant with Jacob gnawed at her—filling her with guilt and sadness. She felt she was somehow betraying him if she allowed herself to be happy with this child, one created in love and passion instead of fear and pain.

She was startled out of her thoughts by the sound of footsteps behind her. She whirled around. "Jacob?"

The gloom resolved into a taller shape, "No, it's me." It was David. He reached out and hugged her to him. "I'm so sorry he had to find out like this." Jess let him hold her for a moment, took a small measure of comfort from his embrace.

"You knew?"

"I didn't know his name. But I knew something terrible had happened to you. That was obvious." He kissed the top of her head. "You are one of the bravest people I know. Jacob is lucky to have you and he is a great kid. Chris just needs time to see that."

"I don't really want to talk about Chris right now." She could feel the anger building inside her. How could he judge her? How could he judge Jacob? He hadn't been there when Jacob was born, when her friend Erin had died, or Madge, or... she knew that David was right, that Chris needed time, but her son had deserved better than to find out like this.

"I know you don't. Carrie made sure he stayed there at the house and didn't come after you." He hugged her, "Come on, let's find our son."

"Our son?"

David put his face close to hers, "Yeah... our son."

David could just barely make out her smile in the dim light of the moon.

"Okay. Jacob first and then, then I need to tell you something." She looked around at the empty street. To the east were a couple of homes and families. To the west was Mr. Banks' property—Jacob could be at either, and she wasn't sure who to target first.

"What do you want to tell me?" His arms were still around her and he leaned in to kiss her neck.

"After," Jess insisted, wiggling away, "you take the Stevens's and Devonly's houses to the east. I'll check in on Mr. Banks."

"Okay," Dave said, and released her, his hand lingering on her arm. "I'll meet you back at the house in half an hour. Just in case he heads back in that direction."

He turned away and walked toward the two nearest occupied homes. Jess watched him go for a moment before turning and heading toward Mr. Banks's small home two streets over. She nearly fell twice, thanks to the cracked concrete and various sticks and rubbish strewn over the roadway after the creek flooded last month during a heavy rain.

It wasn't long before she was knocking on the door of the darkened house. It was probably past ten at night by now. And Jess felt rude for knocking on the door and possibly waking the old man. Mr. Banks had been feeling under the weather, a late summer cold, and she had been so busy with having Chris back in her life that his inclusion in their day-to-day lives had fallen off dramatically in the past few weeks.

There was a muted sound coming from inside. Jess stopped knocking and leaned close to the door, trying to tell if the old man was coming toward the door.

"Mr. Banks?" she called softly. "It's Jess. I'm sorry to bother you, but has Jacob come by here tonight?"

There was no answer, but there was another sound coming from within the house, a thumping of some kind, a muffled yell.

Jess felt a small panic. Had the old man fallen? Was he hurt and unable to come to the door on his own? She tried the doorknob and knocked louder, calling to him, "Mr. Banks? Are you okay?"

More thumps came from inside, and she turned the doorknob in her hand. It was unlocked. She gave the door a shove, and half fell through it when it opened suddenly. The living room was dark. Mr. Banks had to be in his bedroom or the bathroom, and probably hurt if he wasn't answering. She stepped inside the house, her eyes struggling to adjust to the gloom. She never noticed the tall man step out from behind the open door and reach out for her until it was too late.

The blow he delivered stunned her. She had had a nanosecond to react. A soft creak of the floorboard and a rush of air as he closed the distance between them had been her only warning. She spun through the air, fell to the floor, the air whooshing from her lungs with the abrupt contact with the floor and Cooper on top of her in a tangle of limbs.

His breath was rank and she couldn't see much detail. This was not Mr. Banks, or Jacob, or any other of the town's residents. Her jaw ached and she could taste coppery blood where her teeth and tongue had connected in his initial blow. And now, as they wrestled on the floor, the memories of those first few days in Tent Five came flooding back. Jess felt her breath coming in hitched gasps, terror over just who this man was and what may have happened to Mr. Banks flooding through her, adding to her panicked punches. In the other room, she could hear the thumps clearly now, the sounds of someone trying to break free of his bonds. Her attacker's hands closed on her throat, narrowing her world, edging it in blackness. She tried to reach his eyes, to tear them from their sockets. She kicked with her legs, hoping desperately to connect with some part of her attacker that would be made of soft, vulnerable flesh. He blocked every move, pinning her beneath him. The blackness closed in and Jess's arms and legs felt heavy, impossible to move. She tugged at his hands weakly, scraping him with her fingernails before succumbing to the all-encompassing dark.

Consciousness returned slowly. Air moved over her. Jess struggled to remember where she was. A small lantern now lit the room, and she pulled at the bindings around her wrists. Some cord tied them tightly together above her head. It was immovable, and it cut painfully into the flesh of her wrists.

"I know you." Her attacker's voice sounded mildly amused. She felt his hand on her leg, felt his knife cut through her pants, slicing the fabric from her body. "You are the whore who got away."

Jess felt a scream bubble up in her throat. He had gagged her though, and all that could be heard was a guttural whine as she struggled to free herself.

"I was on top of the world before that," he continued, now running his knife up her other pant leg. Her shirt was already gone, and she shivered in fear. "Right after you and those others took off, things really went to shit." He reached out and grabbed her right breast, squeezing it painfully in his hand, "But I'm thinking that you and I are going to have some fun now. I'd take the gag off, but I really can't risk it this close to others. That family over on Kentucky sure was a lot of fun. And I must say I even enjoyed slicing on the old man."

He cut the last of her clothing off and settled himself on top of her; Jess felt the tears slide down her face. His voice was soft, almost conversational, and she wanted to scream, to buck him off, to stop him, but all the horror, the memories of those months of hell, they had made her limbs rigid and unresponsive. In her mind, she was screaming.

He sighed in her ear, "I really, really wish I could hear you scream. I think it would make me feel better." His mouth was at her ear and she shuddered in fear, "And the time I would spend with you, let it last for a few days, maybe even a week; it is a shame that I can't. In fact, I'm pretty sure I'm out of time already. But life isn't any fun if you don't take a few risks. Don't you agree?"

The cold blade of his knife slid along her side, before viciously slicing into the muscle of her upper arm, her right arm. Hot agony flooded her, and she did scream then, although the gag blocked most of it. She felt him reach down, fumble with the waist of his jeans and her limbs were energized with a new panic. Her mind screamed in terror, the thought of him raping her now, all of these years later, violating her body after she had spent so many years trying to forget, terrified of ever having any man come near her. She thought of the baby inside her. He would kill her and her child. David's child.

The fear lent her body more energy than she thought possible. She bucked against him, kicking, pulling at the bindings at her wrists with such violence that her skin was torn and began to bleed.

He laughed with delight. "Now that's the whore I remember!" She could feel him becoming even more excited, struggling to push her legs apart, eager to take her violently. His hands once more closed on her throat. She wondered, as her vision began to narrow, if he even particularly cared if she was alive or dead when he got around to raping her.

The thumps from the other room had stopped, and as she struggled against Cooper, as the will to fight slowly left her body, she looked up and saw why. Jacob had managed to break loose. He stood above them both with a baseball bat in hand. She blacked out again as she watched the bat come crashing down on Cooper's head.

"Mom? Mom? Mom!" Jacob's voice sounded very far away. Jess coughed and tried to roll to her side. Her bones felt like mush. Jacob's hands were on her, helping her to turn on her side. She felt his absence keenly for the few seconds it took for him to run to the other room and find a blanket to cover her.

"Jacob?" her voice sounded as if it were full of gravel. Her throat ached. She coughed again.

"I'm here, Mom. I'm here." His hand draped the blanket over her, covering her exposed skin, his work-chapped hands busy trying to loosen the bindings on her wrists.

"Where is he?" she managed to croak. She struggled to sit up.

"He's here. I think I killed him." Jacob looked over at Cooper's limp figure. "He isn't moving."

"Good." With her son's help, she sat up. The boy nestled his head against her and she crumbled, dissolving into tears. "I love you, Jacob. I've always loved you. I'm so sorry I didn't tell you about him sooner. I just didn't know how to. I never wanted you to think less of yourself, to think you were anything like him. Because you aren't. You are good, you are kind, you are my son. You are nothing like him."

Jacob clutched at her, staring at the prone form of the man on the floor. Jess winced as his hand tightened on the stab wound on her arm.

"Is it him, Mom? Is he the one?"

It was hard to force the word out, "Yes."

"He killed Mr. Banks."

Jess felt a stab of deep pain. The old man had been so kind to them. He hadn't deserved that kind of end. How many times had they sat together? Eaten meals side by side, planted trees, harvested crops, and more. He had been like a grandfather to them. He had held baby Jacob in his arms. After all of these years, he had been family. She had imagined him passing someday, but in a non-specific sentimental sort of way, surrounded by those who cared for him as much as if they shared blood with him. The thought of him dead at the hands of that monster on the floor was too terrible to comprehend.

She looked around the dimly lit room. How long had he been here? How long had Mr. Banks been dead or dying in this house and they hadn't even known? She clutched her son to her and felt a deep cold inside and out, despite the lingering summer heat. She reached out with her left hand and took hold of the knife lying on the ground near Cooper's body. Her right arm was bleeding freely, but she barely noticed.

"We need to get out of here, Jacob."

She levered herself up painfully. Her head was pounding, and the side of her face that Cooper had struck felt like raw meat. One of her teeth felt loose and the coppery taste of blood was still on her tongue.

"We need to make sure he's de..."

Her words fell away as she turned and saw Cooper rise up, blood running in a thick rivulet of gore down the side of his scarred face, and absolute murder in his eyes. He reached for her throat.

Hope and Loss

"*Life is not measured by the number of breaths we take, but by the moments that take our breath away."—Hilary Cooper*

David stood at the graveside, clutching Tina's hand. She had returned from Kansas City with Penelope and Kip when she had heard the news. She was fourteen now, and she had grown nearly as tall as her brother. She stood quietly by his side, her long fingers clutching a bouquet.

The masses of people gathered around the graveside were a testament to the mark left on so many. In their loss, and everyone had lost so many in the past ten years, the grief had not lessened at the passing of someone so intrinsically a part of the community.

Nearby, another grave had been dug, but no one paid any attention to it or cared. It had already had a body lowered into it, been filled, but there was no marker. It wouldn't take long, perhaps a few years at most, for the wound in the soil to become grass. And then no one, not a single person, would remember that he was buried there. And that was for the best.

On David's left side stood Tina, and on his right was Jess. Her arm was heavily bandaged, and her neck bore livid bruises, the sharp outlines of fingers now smudged in red and purple. Her left eye was black and her cheek still swollen. Despite her appearance, Jess felt stronger than she had ever thought possible.

That night, as Scott Cooper's hands had closed around her throat, she had held his knife tightly in her hands. The nightmares, filled with darkness and fear and hands groping her, touching her body, using her—those nightmares had resolved into one clear and focused thought.

This man before her had to die. Despite his strong grip on her already bruised throat, despite the screams of her son as he struggled to stop the man he shared a genetic heritage with, she had kept that one thought firmly in mind. She hadn't panicked.

The knife had slid in... softer, easier than she had expected. Scott Cooper had looked... surprised... and rather shocked. She remembered to use a sideways motion, a quick slice to the left, and to the right, severing arteries, intestines, spilling waste inside the abdomen, ensuring a horrible, elongated, and certain death.

As if in slow motion, his hands had fallen away. His body angled backwards... slowly... as if time had reduced itself to a crawl, especially for them, in this moment. She fell with him.

Together, Jess and Cooper connected with the floor, Cooper's knife between them, slamming into the carpet, the knife finding his spine beneath. This close to him, she could feel his heartbeat, strong at first, but slowing as his life drained away. Cooper's face wore surprise, a look of mild alarm, and he stared as Jess slowly pulled away, Jacob frantically searching her for wounds, asking if she was hurt. His voice was muted compared to the dull roaring in her ears.

All she could do was stare into Cooper's eyes—locked in that moment. She would not look away until it was over. There was so much blood. It was black in the weak moonlight, warm and wet, bathing them both in a pool of it.

It wasn't her blood though; at least, not the majority of it. She let Jacob wrap the blanket around her once again, never breaking eye contact with the man on the floor. Jess stared at the monster from her dreams... bleeding out... his body disjointed and slack, a puzzled look on his face. There was a pounding at the door and Jess could hear David, her brother, and others. The door crashed open and people poured inside—militia members, her brother and David, everyone heavily armed.

The moment, though, stood suspended. Like a mosquito in amber, a fish frozen in ice. She stared into Cooper's eyes, ignoring the surrounding sounds, the shouts of the others as they moved into the house and found the old man's body. She ignored David, asking her if she was all right.

Nothing else mattered at that moment. Cooper stared back at her, his eyes slowly glazing over. She stood there, unmoving, unresponsive, until she saw the life leave him. The eyes are the windows to the soul. She had heard that once. She waited until the lights turned off for the very last time.

Only then had she allowed David and the others to lead her away.

Now, standing at Thurman Banks's graveside, she felt a strange sort of bittersweet peace. The old man had been Cooper's last victim. And he was mourned. Not just by her little family, but by most of the town. There were people all around her, and their low murmurs saturated the air, reminding Jess that even in death, life goes on. The pastor had given a short speech and now it was her turn as the town historian. She stepped forward, out of David's protective embrace, unfolded a piece of paper and began to speak.

"I shared many moments with Mr. Banks over the years. The first two years after we returned, he made sure we stayed fed. He shared his harvests with us, the meat and eggs from his chickens, and his knowledge. He was the grandfather I never had." She paused, and felt the emotion swell up inside her. "Last year, he asked me if I could write down his story, and I of course told him that I would. And here it is..."

"Thurman Banks was born on a hot September day in 1946..."

Hours later, after the grave had been filled, and the tears had been dried, the dark beauty of the late summer night stole over them. The cicadas hummed noisily, their rhythm rising and falling in a cadence known only to them. The house was full, but everyone inside was preternaturally quiet. Jess felt as if everyone was hovering around her, nervous and watchful. Jacob and David had maintained a regular, almost obsessive presence around her, barely leaving her side at all in the past two days. She could feel them watching her now as she pecked at her food, not really seeing it, the vision of Cooper's death replaying in her mind.

David's hand on hers, "Jess? Are you okay?"

She returned to the kitchen, looked around and saw all those who she loved. David, Jacob, Becka, and Erin, along with Tina, Penelope and her husband Kip, Chris and Carrie. There was concern written on many of their faces, held quietly in their eyes as they stared back at her.

Jess felt her mouth tug and re-shape, lips curving into a huge grin. "Yeah," she said simply, "I'm okay. I really am." She took David's hand in hers. "We are going to have a baby."

The room erupted with surprise and excitement.

Outside, the cicadas sang.

Life is Precious

"I *finally understand it. The meaning of life. Life is love and hate, pain and bliss, gain and loss, life and death. And in between, among the cracks of all that we have endured, life is precious."—Jess's Journal*

The room was full. David was on one side of Jess, Carrie and Erin on the other. Tina stood at the foot of the bed with Dr. Farley and was speaking in low tones to the doctor about the healing properties of a certain native plant as they finished putting the room in order.

The baby lay nestled in David's arms, her blue eyes wide open and staring at the world, a look of bewildered amazement on her tiny face. David stared at her intently, surprised when he had discovered his cheeks were wet with tears. He gazed at his newborn daughter, shocked at how tiny she was, and how perfect.

Twin wails began piercing the room as Chris bustled in, a tiny bundle in each arm. As usual, they were wailing in symphony, one after the other. "I held them as long as I could," he said to his wife, "but they definitely want their mama." Carrie's thin face lit up, and the circles beneath her eyes were testament to the lack of sleep she had been receiving as of late.

"I think they just wanted to meet their new baby cousin," Carrie said, as Michael and Julie instantly quieted in her arms.

Her heart surged with happiness. Her pregnancy had coincided with Jess's, but Carrie had been terrified to hope, even once her belly had pushed out to an enormous size and Dr. Farley had told her he thought she might be pregnant with twins. Her labor had been quick, and the babies had been tiny, not quite five pounds each, but perfect. There hadn't been a whisper of complications and both were thriving, despite being born nearly a month early. That had been nearly two weeks ago.

How many times had she despaired of ever having a child? Of being able to hold her own flesh and blood in her arms? And yet, after all the years of pain and misery, of miscarriage and stillbirth, she held two perfect and beautiful babies in her arms. How she wished Gramps could have seen them.

Joseph, newly arrived from Tennessee, stood uncertainly in the doorway. He had come out with traders and a stack of hand-bound journals to sell, somewhat rudderless, since Mr. Liles had passed away last summer. Tall and handsome, he had locked eyes with Tina and suddenly a short visit had turned into a semi-permanent stay. He had stayed in the city, welcomed instantly into the large, brick Victorian that housed Penelope and her husband Kip, along with a small health clinic and dorms for the interns. There they had stayed until two months ago, when Chris had asked for Joseph's help to clean up Mr. Banks's home.

There were new families moving into the area, but Mr. Banks had willed it to Jess and David, and they had in turn given it to Carrie and Chris. It didn't feel right letting it sit vacant, despite what had happened there, and the homes were close to each other, allowing the siblings, along with their families, to be within walking distance of each other.

Chris and Jacob's relationship had smoothed out in the months following the deaths of Cooper and old Mr. Banks. Seeing how much the boy had tried to protect his mother from the psychopath's attack had brought home to him how different Jacob was from his father, and how much of Jess's goodness he held within him.

Jess smiled at Chris's brother-in-law. "Would you like to hold her?" she asked.

Joseph nodded, and David handed the newborn gently to the teenager. Joseph was well familiar with babies, from Liza's to the recent birth of Carrie's twins, and now this one.

Her tiny eyes opened briefly, and he smiled at the flash of blue. "What is her name?" he asked, staring transfixed at the newest member of his extended family.

"Hope." Jess was surprised as she uttered the name aloud.

She and David had stayed up late so many nights, working through names, trying different combinations. Nothing had seemed to stick and eventually they had agreed that they would just have to wait and see who their baby was—boy or girl.

"We will know when we see the baby," she had told David. "We will just know, I will know, in that moment."

And that moment had arrived.

For all that they had been through. For all that they had endured and lost and for the friends and family gained along the way.

For the nation they had seen crumble and the new world that they had built with their hands, sweat, blood, and tears.

Hope.

The rays of the sun peeked through the window. The warmth crawled along the floor and lit up a newborn baby and the family she belonged with.

It was a brave new world, and a beautiful life had just begun.

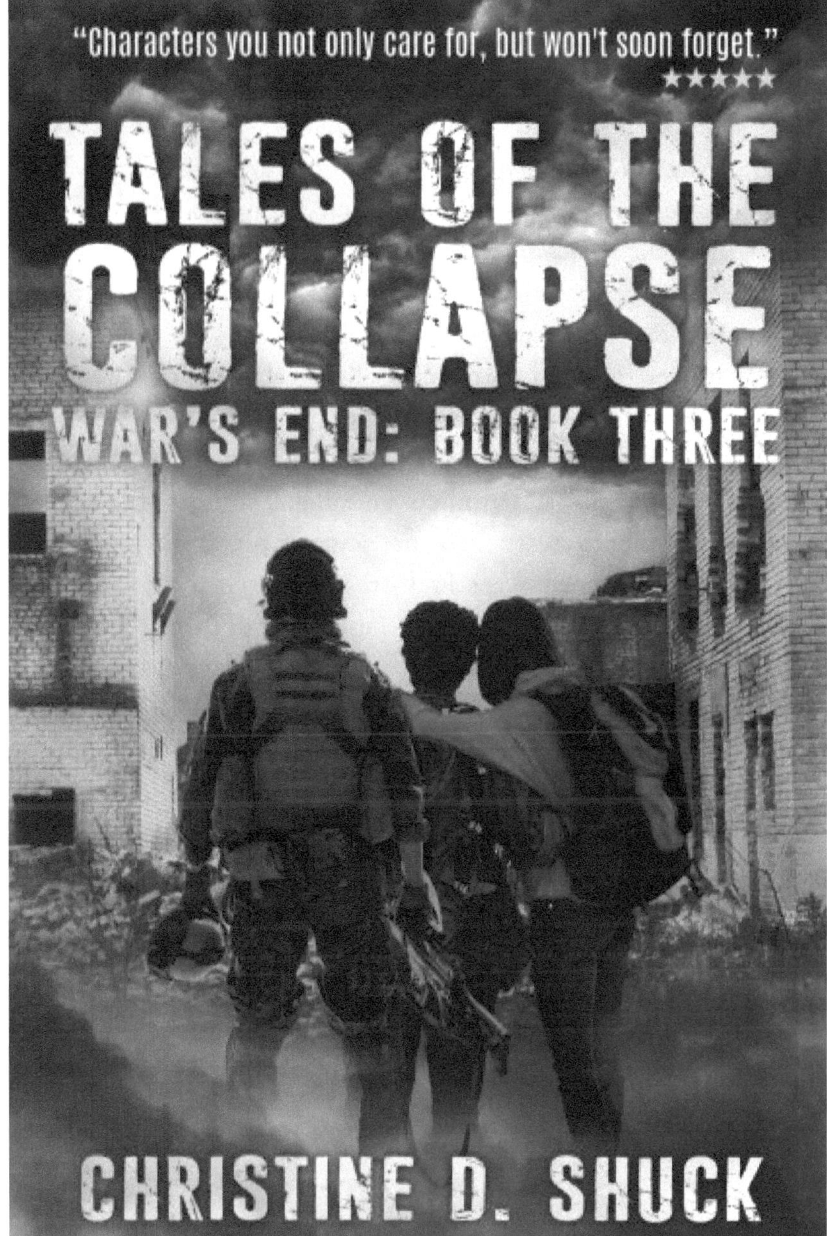
"Characters you not only care for, but won't soon forget."
★★★★★
TALES OF THE COLLAPSE
WAR'S END: BOOK THREE
CHRISTINE D. SHUCK

Introduction

Stories swirl around each of my characters begging to be told. Sometimes a song lyric will get me started, as it did in 99 Problems. Or I imagine where this character came from and what happened to them after their lives intersected, even for the briefest moment with another. Jacob's story, for instance, in All Roads Lead to Austin was an example of that momentary exchange that meant so much.

In others, I wanted to tell more of the backstory of how a character came to be where they were, or why they were who they were.

A societal collapse, even a civil war, does not happen overnight. Instead, it is the slow and insidious undoing. It consists of multiple facets coming together to create chaos, fire, and destruction.

When I imagined War's End - that is what I thought of. Not one single problem, but a slow, yet growing cascade of them.

Viruses growing out of control and wreaking havoc, killing hundreds and even thousands.

Social unrest that leads to a rise in factions, including white supremacists.

Terrorist acts on American soil.

An economy in ruins.

If this is sounding eerily familiar, well, call me Cassandra. But by all means, read on. The Collapse is coming. In fact, it might be just around the corner.

Leave Now

"It's coming. You have been warned."

Sarah could hear the news reporter on the television in the living room talking about the Hong Kong H1N5 virus. Deaths from the particularly virulent strain of flu had grown to over several hundred now and the news anchor was advising people to wear masks and stay home if they showed signs of the illness. Sarah sighed; the television was something she tried not to be bothered by. Gina kept it on all day, even when she was gone from the bungalow. Sarah, on the other hand, had grown up with a television relegated to just a few hours of use a day. The idea of keeping it on constantly had been irritating at first, but now it usually served as background noise. It wasn't much different from the hum of cars from the freeway now.

She stared at the ocean and sipped from the tall, slender coffee cup in her hands, wincing as the liquid scalded her tongue. The Santa Ana winds were warm, and she could smell the brine of the ocean, hear the gulls scream as they dove into the surf. Hunting, she supposed, for their next meal.

Gina Abernathy stretched out with a sigh on the chaise lounge to Sarah's left, "My God, Sarah, you are up at the crack of dawn. Just like your Pops, God rest his soul." Her hair was already styled, stiff with what had to be a half of a can of Aqua Net holding it in place, and her fingers encrusted with several large, gaudy rings. Sarah smiled at her friend. Gina had been a longtime live-in girlfriend of Scotty Abernathy, Daddy's literary agent, and now was his widow for the past five years. A month after Sarah's husband Theo had passed of pancreatic cancer, Gina had rousted Sarah out of her gray haze of grief, shoved her on a plane and taken her to Fiji. That had been two years ago, and Gina had been a constant companion ever since.

"I have to be at Cedars-Sinai by ten to meet with Dr. Carlson, and you know traffic is far more difficult here than in Kansas City."

"Oh Honey, you don't know the half of it. It takes an hour to go twenty miles! It's worse than New York, and that's saying a lot." Gina flapped her hands as she spoke, her East coast accent creeping through. "I just don't know what you hope to do there, girl. You do know they're all crazy, right?" She turned and stared at Sarah as if the thought had just occurred to her. Despite the early hour, Gina was made up, thick foundation caked on her face, blush, eyeliner, and mascara - the works. Gina Abernathy contributed to the livelihood of the cosmetics industry and single-handedly propped up several, by Sarah's estimation, something that was both awe-inspiring and slightly terrifying.

Sarah's mother, June, had tolerated the younger woman's presence with patience, graciously including her whenever she invited Scotty to visit her and Dad while they had both been alive. She had known and been close friends with Lucinda, Scotty's first wife. Gina had been such a sharp departure from the mousy woman that Mom had once confided to Sarah that she couldn't imagine what Scotty had seen in Gina, "Unless it is simply that he knew Lucinda could not and should not be replaced, so he found her exact opposite."

Gina would have been a pain in the ass, what with her clownish makeup, gaudy decor and garish clothing - except that she was also one of the warmest, kindest human beings Sarah had ever met. She was the type who would do anything for a friend, especially in the aftermath of the worst possible loss. Theo's illness had not only taken them by surprise, but it had robbed them of any time to enjoy a retirement or indulge in the bucket list of dreams they had slowly accumulated over the decades.

They had fallen in love in college, and for Sarah, there had never been any other man she could imagine sharing her life with. Theo had matched her - intellectually, emotionally. Being with him, spending more than thirty years together, it had been a comfort. While many of her girlfriends from high school had gotten married at the same time as her, most had divorced, at least once, and Sarah knew they had envied the close, steady relationship that she and Theo had shared.

His abdominal pain, weight loss, and repeated bouts of nausea had all tied in so neatly to a particularly nasty round of flu that had been going around. Sarah's heart panged at the thought of the six long weeks in which he had gotten progressively worse until she had insisted on getting him in to a doctor for tests. Two weeks after that, they had learned the truth, and just six weeks later, Theo was gone. There had been no time to mount a defense, no time to try any alternative treatments or aggressive chemo. The man she had thought she would spend her golden years with was gone, and Sarah had descended into a miasma of grief and loneliness that no number of visits from friends and family could shake. That is until Gina had come around and forced her back into the world again.

She was lucky she had Gina. Very lucky.

Gina waved her jewel-bedecked fingers in Sarah's face. "Earth to Sarah. You still there, Honey?"

Sarah shook herself, tried to shake off the memories, to turn her focus to the present. "Sorry, Gina, I was miles away."

"I'm just saying, girl, some of those people they have in there are crazy and violent."

"Not the one I'm seeing today. She wouldn't harm a fly."

Gina snorted. "That's what they say right before the patient tries to claw your eyes out. I just don't know why this was your choice of writing career. Honey, you could be a travel writer. My friend Blanche, she traveled to China, stayed in the finest hotels, saw the Great Wall, all on Conde Nast's dime. And her writing is shit compared to yours. With the genetics you got from your Pops, you might as well have been born with a pen in your hand." Gina whistled, "But you decide to write an expose on mental health care in America. Who the hell is gonna read that, Sarah? Especially when it is gonna be thicker than a textbook by the time you are done?"

She took a slurp of her coffee and shook her head, the scent of Aqua Net pouring off of her in a cloud.

Sarah's nose twitched, and she fought off a sneeze. The older woman made her smile, something that seemed a rare thing now that Theo was gone. The only other things that made her happy were her rather grim writing subject, and her two grandchildren, Chris and Jess. Sarah had spent two weeks visiting them during the summer, staying at their house in Belton, Missouri. They were teenagers now, which seemed impossible, because she distinctly remembered holding each of them in the hospital, exclaiming over their tiny little hands and wrinkled, red faces. Michael and his wife, Julie, had raised them right, however, and despite being teenagers, they were as kind as ever. Every morning, Jess had brought two large mugs of tea, Earl Grey with milk and sugar just the way Sarah liked it, down to the basement guest bedroom and sat with her grandmother planning what they could go and do that day. Chris had made it a point to introduce her to his friends, a unique combination of jocks and gangly nerds who were polite and said "yes ma'am" with regularity. One of them, Allen, who was slightly thicker around the middle, loved reading. He had spent hours talking with Sarah about their shared love of books. Good kids, all of them.

Sarah sighed. Michael kept asking her if she would consider moving in. "We could even build a mother-in-law cottage in the back if you would prefer your privacy, Mom. I just wish you were closer. You would get to see the kids more often."

She hadn't been able to stay in the house she and Theo had shared for more than 35 years. It had felt so empty. Instead, she had rented it out and, after Gina had shoved her on a plane, ended up traveling for more than a year before settling down in the spare bedroom at Gina's -first in New York and later at her beach house in Southern California. A week's stay had turned into a month, and except for visiting Michael's family, she had found a sense of peace here in this small bungalow with a view of the Pacific Ocean. It was a sharp departure from the low, rolling hills of flyover country. Even the clouds in the sky were different. They were long and thin and wispy, compared to the fat cumulonimbus in Missouri. Everything moved faster here, people, automobiles, the public transit - all frantic to get from one point to another. And it was here that she had gone back and re-examined the paperwork from her parents' files, the order to commit her father in 1954 that had been begun but never finalized, and the remaining mystery surrounding his death decades later. Fifteen years had passed since then, but the answers had never come.

She thought about it now as she took another sip of coffee. The question of what had happened to Dad, what had really happened to him, remained a mystery. What do near-death experiences and psychotic breaks do to people? Dad had always seemed fine, he'd just been Dad to her, but her sister Betty had often described Dad as being very different when she was young - angry, indifferent, and resentful.

"That all changed after the accident, though." She had mused when Sarah pressed her. "He took an interest in us, and that's also when he started writing, sold the company, and soon after that, you were born." She had shrugged, "You know, they say that head injuries change people. Maybe it changed Dad for the better."

Those words had haunted her. Had the accident truly affected Dad for the better? If so, he was one of few. Head injuries like his, and she had examined the x-rays and spoken with numerous doctors on the subject, tended to change a person, but not for the better. And then there was his letter, one that spoke with certainty of this other life he was sure he had experienced with Mom, Betty and Danny dead, and he remarried to a nurse, Theo's mom no less! And a child born after, with her own name, Sarah Magdalene. That had been the other woman's name, Magdalene or Maggie. And it wasn't as if she could ask Maggie, for Maggie had died, just nine years after Mom and Dad's accident, in 1962. Theo had been orphaned by it. His father had never been in the picture and he had ended up being raised by relatives in a large rambling brick farmhouse in Raymore, Missouri, just a few miles south of Kansas City, where she had grown up. Their shared geography had been the first connection when they met in college - something that brought them closer and given them something to talk about.

It was mysterious to say the least, but even now she struggled to find a realistic explanation. One that was grounded in facts, not fantasy. It was this quest that had led Sarah down a somewhat winding path to where it was now. A focus on mental health in America and with it, the unique and odd interpretations of reality from the mentally ill's perspective.

She had spoken to individuals who were involved in intense psychotherapy, under the care of psychiatrists and therapists. She had spoken to several who were incarcerated in the penal system because the mental hospitals were now the last bastion for only the luckiest of the mentally ill.

Today, she was meeting with Dr. Carlson, who was treating a young woman who claimed to know the future. Dr. Carlson had reached out to Sarah after reading one of her articles, noted that she was writing a book, and asked if she was looking for more patients to interview. Their schedules had been full of conflicts for nearly two months, but now, today, she would finally get a chance to meet him, and his patient, for the first time.

Gina's voice interrupted her thoughts, "Sure you don't want to go shopping with me? I've just got to stop by Prada and see their new handbag line. And besides, right around the corner is Jimmy Choo, and there is a young man there that is a ridiculous flirt." Gina laughed, "The things he promises an old lady like me are, well, who knows, he might just jump start this dead as a doornail libido of mine, you never know."

Sarah suppressed a smile. Gina was loud, over the top, and full of chutzpah. She gave off an air of rich widow and that had plenty of strapping, young, pretty-faced boys drooling after her wherever she went. Whether it was over her money or her still-voluptuous body, Sarah couldn't say for sure, but Gina strung them along like puppets, never indulging, just teasing them and flirting outrageously. She had done it when Scotty was still alive, and he had pretended to be out of sorts over it, but really wasn't. Gina, despite appearances, hadn't wanted anyone but Scotty. Even after Scotty, for that matter. It was obvious to Sarah that the older woman had loved her husband, body and soul. There was no one who could replace him.

"Maybe next week, Gina. But I've been trying for over two months to get this appointment and as a bonus, I'll get a read on the future. Who knows, maybe she'll have some good stock tips or tell me who is slated to win at the races." Gina was an avid horse racing fan and hadn't missed a race at the Kentucky Derby in over ten years.

Gina snorted, shook her head, and drained the last of her coffee. "Sarah, honey, you are missing out. That fine, strapping lad is just the jolt to a woman's ego that every one of us fifty-something's need." Gina was in her mid-sixties, but far be it from Sarah to correct her.

"But make sure and ask her if Black Shadow has a chance of winning. Best to hedge our bets, after all." Gina had been hitting the horse races more often since one of her major investments had tanked. She still had enough money, and she was actually fairly good at judging winners, so recently her betting had been a boon instead of a bust.

There were whispers in the wind that the American economy was not what it had been. Sarah had moved most of her portfolio into steady, low-interest-bearing bonds as the Dow alternately tanked and then exploded. The rapid seesawing made her nervous, and Michael had recently sent her a text again asking for her to come home to Missouri and stay with his family. "It's not looking good, Mom, I've been reading that we are heading for the mother of all depressions," he had written, "the likes of which will make the Great Depression look like a walk in the park in comparison."

His concern was sweet, and she knew that his wife, Julie, was very involved in producing their own food and believed in self-sufficient living. She had turned their suburban yard outside of Kansas City into a food-producing paradise filled with fruit and nut trees and bushes, as well as raised beds that grew everything from asparagus to zucchini. Sarah loved walking through the raised beds and gathering herbs and fresh vegetables when she visited. It felt like a miniature garden of Eden.

Gina interrupted Sarah's thoughts again, "There's also Shenanigans, check on that one as well. I've got a good feeling about that horse."

Sarah laughed, finished her coffee, and stood up. She leaned over and hugged her friend, holding her breath so she didn't pass out from the hairspray fumes still off-gassing and polluting the air. It was enough to give Sarah a thumping headache if she took a big enough whiff. She couldn't understand how Gina managed to stop herself from passing out.

"I'll catch lunch out, but let's make plans for dinner, okay?"

Gina gave her a fierce squeeze back, "I'll make some cannoli."

"Sounds wonderful!" Sarah had put on five pounds since she had quasi-moved in to Gina's guest room. Her friend's cooking remained out of this world and she specialized in delectable, albeit fattening, Italian cuisine.

The drive into the city was hair-raising and frantic for the first twenty minutes and then slowed to a maddening stop and go as Sarah encountered two different fender benders. She was relieved she had left a half hour earlier than planned because she had a long hike to the entrance of the hospital. All the nearby parking lots were full, and she had to park several hundred yards away. The last fifteen minutes before her appointment with Dr. Carlson were eaten up going through security, a necessary precaution for the locked psychiatric unit she would be walking through.

At just two minutes to ten, she sat down in a hard, plastic chair to wait for Dr. Carlson to respond to the page announcing she was here. She didn't have long to wait. He strode over to her and shook her hand. "Mrs. Aaronson, it's a pleasure. Please, let's meet in my office."

His office was small and held a desk, filing cabinet, and two chairs. She looked around it and realized that he must see patients elsewhere. Papers were in haphazard heaps here, there, and everywhere. Pictures of his family were half-buried by them, showing only tantalizing glimpses of a trio of tow-headed children laughing in a park.

"Thank you for taking the time to see me, Dr. Carlson."

He nodded. "I found your article on the high percentage of incarcerated mentally ill to be rather fascinating, Mrs. Aaronson. Truly, the pleasure is all mine." The psychiatrist was slim, with a receding hairline and thick coke-bottle spectacles. He wore a rather plain plaid shirt and khaki-colored pants. She had caught him sucking in his gut and smothered a smile. Even after all these years, her own frame was slim, her hair only now beginning to show white and gray hairs intermingled with blond. She still found men turning their heads when she passed. It was a lovely feeling, one that she appreciated but felt no desire to act upon. Theo had been the love of her life, but that part of her life, the one that hoped for a partner to walk through the world with, that was gone, buried with Theo.

"Can I get you anything? Coffee? Tea? Water?" he asked.

"No, thank you, I'm fine." Now that she was here, Sarah was eager to meet the patient Dr. Carlson had spoken about in his email.

"Well then," he settled into his seat and reached for a rather thin folder, "I don't have as much detail as we normally would have at this stage. Usually, by the time someone is committed, the medical history is quite complicated, and there are multiple incidents. In Cibil's case, however..."

Sarah blinked. "Her name is Sybil? As in Sybil Dorsett?" Sybil Dorsett had been the pseudonym for a woman plagued with multiple personality disorder. At the time the book had come out in the early 1970s, it had led to a movie starring Sally Field as Sybil.

"No, no, her name has a different spelling. Cibil Zradce is her full name," he pronounced it "zuh-rad-chee" as he pushed the thin file folder towards Sarah. "She was found on Rodeo Drive, screaming at the top of her lungs that her child was missing and that there was no time, that everyone needed to leave now." He shook his head, "She alternated between telling anyone who would listen that the collapse was coming, whatever that is, and that her baby is gone, that she had been taken by someone."

"So, she hadn't done anything illegal, and she wasn't placed in custody?" Sarah asked, her eyes focused on the photograph of a disheveled, raven-haired woman with piercing green eyes staring up at her.

"Initially, yes, because she ran out into traffic, screaming that her child was in the road, in a car seat, no less. Swore up and down she could see her there in the road."

"But there was no child?"

"No." He tapped the report attached to the other side, "No drugs in her system, and an examination here at Sinai determined she had given birth recently, but we have no records of a child's birth, no records of a Cibil Zradce for that matter, and no fingerprints in the system. Cibil Zradce had no identification, could tell us nothing about where she had grown up, where she had lived. Hell, it was as if she had appeared, freshly made, with no history, family, or records."

Sarah stared at the file and then back at Dr. Carlson, "That's..."

"Impossible?" He smiled then, and she was struck by a sense of longing. It reminded her of Theo's smile in some strange way. "Tell me about it." His smile disappeared, replaced by a more hopeful look. "That's why I contacted you. I was hoping that perhaps you could write about her, and that we could find her family, perhaps this child is in danger, we could find them and see if they could help provide the background that we need to shake her out of this muddled state. She's calmed down, somewhat, but I think that if we could just find out more about her, I could create a more effective treatment plan."

Sarah nodded, finally understanding why he had contacted her. His voice said it all. He gave a damn, and that was rare. She looked again at the photos on his desk and he followed her glance, reaching out with his left hand to fish the photo out of the tall stack of papers and handed it to her. It showed him surrounded by two boys and a girl, all tow-headed to his dark-brown hair. The children were obviously related to each other, but they looked nothing like him.

"Roger, Amelia, and Landon," he said, "I guess you could say I inherited them. My stepsister and her husband died four years ago, auto accident, and our parents were too old to take on three kids." He smiled wryly, "In a way, the kids are the best thing that ever happened to me." His grin faded. "Cibil has had a child within the last few months. The doctor who examined her was sure of it. And maybe that baby is in danger, somewhere out there." He looked back at the photograph. "There are all kinds of hair-raising stories I hear in this line of work. Abuse, neglect, drugs, even human trafficking. The situations some of my patients have endured, the worst possible of childhood and even adult trauma." He stared at the photo, his eyes betraying his devotion to the children. "I just want to make sure Cibil's baby is safe. I spoke with one of the psychologists on staff at New Jersey State Prison and he told me that you got more information out of Charles Cullen than he had in five years of therapy."

Sarah smiled and shook her head, "I got lucky."

Dr. Carlson leaned back in his chair. "No, I think it's your demeanor, the way you carry yourself, the sound of your voice - everything. Heck, I never talk about my kids. If I do, I just say they're my sister's kids and leave it at that. You've got something, Mrs. Aaronson, a gift if you will. And that's why I contacted you. I could see it in your articles, the way you have managed to interact with the people you write about. They trust you. I wanted to see if you would be able to get some details out of Cibil. Something, anything, that would help us track down that baby."

He set the picture down on his desk, gently moving the stacks of papers away from the frame, giving it a few inches of space in each direction, and stared at the photo again before turning his attention to Sarah. "The police terrify her; she clams up and won't say a word. And with me? She cries. When she isn't crying, she's telling me stories of another world, one filled with magic that hovers in another dimension in the same space as Earth. She says it fits over Earth 'Like the skin of an onion' and she insists she needs to return to that world soon, before the coming collapse. Perhaps she will talk to you, give you some details you can share with us. If not," he glanced back at the photo of his children, "then I fear for that baby."

Half an hour later, Sarah found herself face-to-face with a frail version of the disheveled woman in the photograph. According to Dr. Carlson, Cibil had been in their locked ward for nearly ten weeks. From the look of it, she had lost weight, a lot of it, in a rather short amount of time. Her raven hair was limp and stringy. Her green eyes were lackluster and half-closed. She didn't acknowledge Sarah as they sat her down in the chair on the opposite side of the table.

The door shut quietly behind the two orderlies who had escorted Cibil Zradce into the room, but Sarah knew they were right outside in the hall, in case anything went wrong during the interview.

"Good morning, Cibil, my name is Sarah."

Cibil blinked slowly, and then raised her head and stared at Sarah without speaking.

Sarah began her standard introduction, "I'm not with the police, I'm not a psychologist, I'm a journalist and, if you would like to share it, I would very much like to hear your story."

"My story?" The woman stared at her, her eyes held dark shadows under them and her skin sallow, tinged with a hint of gray. She looked haunted, and Sarah couldn't help wondering if perhaps this woman had killed her baby. It wouldn't be the first time she had spoken with a woman who had.

"Yes, your story, or whatever you want to share with me. I'm a journalist," Sarah repeated, "My job is to listen to people."

Cibil gave a strange sound, dry, like the leaves in winter, and Sarah realized the woman was laughing. "No one listens. I tell them what I see and they never listen."

"I will."

Sarah watched as Cibil looked at her then, the disheveled woman's strong psyche pushing through the haze of sedatives and anti-psychotics the staff had been feeding her and sneered, "You might listen, but you can't understand, you can never understand, and I see your death, along with others, so many others. You will be the first of many, so many."

Sarah felt a small chill crawl down her neck at Cibil's words. It lasted but a moment. She was far less afraid of death with Theo gone. It wasn't that she wanted to die, quite the opposite, but seeing it happen had changed the way she thought of life. She persisted, "Tell it to me, anyway."

Cibil's lips trembled, and Sarah could see her wrestling with a decision, "You're a journalist? Yes?"

"Yes."

"You will write down what I say?"

"Yes." Sarah fumbled to open the recording function on her cell phone. "I record the conversations. That way I don't misremember any details. Would that be okay?"

Cibil twitched, then twitched again, more obvious this time, and Sarah realized the woman was nodding. She pressed the button, "It's recording now."

Cibil sat for a moment, unmoving and silent, before she said softly, "They say I'm confused, that I'm showing signs of postpartum psychosis. They think I killed my child."

Sarah pushed the phone closer towards Cibil, hoping that it was able to pick up her words. Cibil, in turn, leaned towards it. "I didn't kill her. Natalia is alive and well. I've seen it. I know she is safe, but she doesn't belong there, and neither do I."

"Here at the hospital?" Sarah asked.

"No, here in this world." Cibil replied, an edge creeping into her voice.

Sarah nodded. The key to dealing with the mentally ill was to affirm what they said and to provide a listening ear. "Where would you go with Natalia if not here in this world?"

"To Fyrsta Heim." Cibil replied, a dreamy look on her face, "Where my people come from."

"Tell me more about your people, and Fear... Fear..."

"Fyrsta Heim," Cibil said, her eyes sharp on Sarah's. "It means First World. It is where I and the rest of my people come from."

Sarah kept her face serene. "Another world? Is it in a different solar system?"

Cibil glared, "You mock me." She pulled back and let her dark, stringy hair fall across her face. Sarah's heart skipped a beat as she was reminded of that awful horror movie, The Ring. She had happened across it when she had been laid up with a broken ankle several years ago, long before Theo had died. She had watched the entire movie, pillows clutched in her lap. It had given her nightmares.

"I'm sorry, Cibil. I did not intend for you to feel disbelieved or mocked." Sarah kept her voice steady and calm, but Cibil turned away from her, averting her gaze. "Cibil? I am very sorry. Please, will you tell me if Natalia is on Fear... Fyrsta Heim?" The memory of Dr. Carlson's face, his earnest concern for this missing baby, it filled Sarah's heart with fear as well. The baby was innocent, and if she could just get Cibil to speak, they had a chance of finding it, no, her, alive.

A tear slid down Cibil's nose. "You don't believe me. No one does." Her voice was even quieter now, a cracked whisper as she fought emotion, struggled to stop the tears that had followed the first. They dripped off of her chin, a splat of liquid on the battered Formica table. "I wish I knew where Natalia was," she said, her voice rising ever so slightly. "I know she isn't in Fyrsta Heim. None of the Njerez know of her. I didn't tell them. The Arbre Genealogic controls who breeds and when, and Natalia, she wasn't planned by them. It was a chance encounter." She turned, her eyes agonized, desperate, "If he hadn't died, I would have told them. Perhaps it would have been excused. But most have moved beyond the World Walls. I was..." she hiccupped, the tears falling faster, "I was supposed to go through them too. I was told to travel to the East Coast, to board a private plane had been chartered, to join the others heading for a thin spot in Germany. But on the way to meet the others I had a vision."

Cibil wiped her tears away, a trail of tears and snot combining together into a stringy mess. She wiped again, smearing her hospital-issued sweatshirt with a glob of sticky goo. Sarah swallowed hard, doing her best to ignore her queasy stomach and not react. The woman was talking, and that was a big step.

"Tell me what happens when you have a vision, Cibil."

The younger woman shook her head. "It hurts, a lot. I black out. When I came to, I was in a hospital. They thought I had been mugged." She stopped, stared off into space, staring with a confused look at the opposite wall.

Sarah sighed to herself. Inside of locked wards like this one, the use of sedatives and anti-psychotics was liberal and often heavy-handed. Communicating with Cibil was going to be difficult if they kept her dosage at this high level.

"But instead, you had a vision? Is that right?"

"Yes." Cibil answered but did not elaborate, once again her concentration slipping away.

"What was in your vision, Cibil?"

Cibil's eyes blinked and re-focused on Sarah. "Hm?"

"You said you had a vision on your way to meet the others. What was your vision about?"

"A train bombing. In New York."

"A train bombing? Not the Twin Towers?"

"No. It was underground, fire, explosion, and the blood." Cibil stared past Sarah's shoulder, a thousand-yard stare that did not see what was in this room, but somewhere far away instead.

"What happened then, Cibil?"

At the sound of her name, her head swiveled back towards Sarah and Cibil stared at her as if seeing her for the first time. "Hm?"

"When you woke up in the hospital and they thought you had been mugged. What happened then?" Sarah prodded gently.

Cibil smiled. "I knew better than to say anything. Humans never listen. They can't imagine a world where there is no science, only magic. If you say that you can see the future, then obviously you are mad. I said nothing, only that I couldn't remember what happened, and they let me go."

"Were you pregnant then?" Sarah asked, hoping to establish a timeline and possibly pinpoint Cibil's hospital stay for Dr. Carlson to follow up.

"No, no," Cibil said, shaking her head.

"Okay. Would you like to tell me what happened next?"

"He found me."

"Who found you, Cibil?"

"Why, Conor, of course." Cibil gave her a sideways look, as if Sarah should have known the answer.

"Does Conor have a last name? Is he Natalia's father?"

The tears welled up in Cibil's eyes. "Yes. But when she quickened in me, he told me I wasn't her. I wasn't Maggie. He said that I meant nothing to him. That no one existed but Maggie and his son, Theo."

The small chill Sarah had felt at the beginning of the conversation returned when Cibil spoke Theo's name out loud. And at that moment, Cibil nodded, her green eyes intense. She held up a thin, bony finger. The fingernail had been chewed to the quick.

"You know now. Brother in one timeline, husband in the other, as if fate couldn't keep you apart. Fate's highway, it has many twists and turns." She smiled then, her teeth yellowed and stained, madness rising in her eyes. "Your father knew it, the moment you took Theo home to meet your family, to tell them of your future child." She leaned forward, her eyes sparking with interest. "Your father told you about it, didn't he? He did, I just know it. I can see it in your eyes."

Sarah stood, her chair knocking back and falling to the floor. She pressed the stop button on her recording app. "Cibil, I..." The chill hadn't left her. If anything, it had grown. Who was this woman? Who was she really? "I need to take a bathroom break, if you don't mind," she said. The words came fast, spitting out as she backpedaled, phone in hand toward the door, knocking on it briskly.

An orderly opened it and she slid through, suddenly out of breath, as her heart raced and stuttered. The burly man, dressed in the standard blue scrubs that all the workers there wore, coughed wetly, and she could feel and see the fever racing through him. He asked, "Are you done speaking to the patient, ma'am?"

Before she could answer, Dr. Carlson entered the hallway, walking briskly out of the observation room. "Mrs. Aaronson? Are you feeling alright? You looked as if you had seen a ghost."

Sarah plastered a smile on her face. "I'm fine, Dr. Carlson. Just surprised. If I may ask, what did you share with Cibil about me prior to my meeting her?"

His concerned expression faded slightly, replaced by a confused frown, "Nothing really, just that a female journalist wanted to speak with her. I didn't follow that last bit, something about brother and husband, and..." His voice petered out as Sarah backed away.

"I'm sorry, I," she looked around, "I need to visit the Ladies Room, if you don't mind."

"Oh certainly, it's just down the hall. Through the security doors. I'll have them buzz you through."

She nodded her thanks and walked briskly towards the doors, hearing the tinny buzz as she strode over to them and pushed her way through. She found the restrooms on the left and slipped inside, her heart hammering. How had Cibil known? About Theo? About Theo's mother, Maggie?

Maggie had died in a car accident when Theo was barely twelve years old. Her loss had left him orphaned, his father... My God, she just told me that her child and my Theo have the same father. But it was impossible. It had to be impossible. A gap of, what, sixty years between the two siblings? Sarah felt lightheaded, as if she had entered this alien world Cibil had spoken of, this Fyrsta Heim. She called it First World. But referring to the letter, something only she and Theo had read, no one else, not even Betty, God rest her soul, her older sister had gone to her grave never having read the letter that Dad had left Sarah. In the end, after reading it, and re-reading it, Sarah couldn't make sense of it. It had frightened her in many ways, as if this other world had reached out and taken some of her family with it.

She stared at her reflection in the mirror, clutching the sink, her knuckles white, her reflection pale in the cheap fluorescent light that flickered from the ceiling above.

Of all the parts of the letter from her father that she had read and re-read until the words were memorized, Cibil's comments brought one back with full force.

Of all the emotions or fears this letter might stir in you, reading that Theo is, in my memories, both your brother and your husband might be disturbing to you. Believe me, it took me by surprise, and yet it also made absolute sense. It felt as if the world was put right again in some way by Theo's return to our lives. Perhaps your souls sought each other out, reuniting that which had been lost.

"Occam's Razor. The simplest explanation is usually the correct one." Sarah whispered as she stared into the mirror. "So, what, magic and time travel and other worlds really do exist? Sarah Magdalene Edmonds Aaronson, do you realize how insane that sounds?"

A knock sounded at the door. "Mrs. Aaronson? Is everything all right in there?" Dr. Carlson's voice was muffled, yet his concern carried through the thick metal door.

She looked down at her hands. Her wedding band was set firmly on the right hand, a clear sign of widowhood. Her hands showed her age more than her face, which had only a handful of wrinkles to betray the fact that she was edging out of her fifties and would soon celebrate six decades on Earth. Or would she? Cibil had said, "I see your death, along with others, so many others."

"Mrs. Aaronson?" The muffled murmur of a second voice. A woman, possibly one of the unit nurses, joined Dr. Carlson's. It was followed by a brisk knock at the door.

Sarah stared at her hands for a second longer, reached into the stall to flush the toilet, and called out loudly, "Just a minute." She ran the water, splashed it on her hands and dried them, her ring catching and tearing the paper towel.

She marched out the door, a professional smile on her face, "My apologies, Dr. Carlson, my friend took me out to a new Thai restaurant last night and I think it must have upset my stomach. Let's get back to it, shall we?" She ignored the curious stare of the young unit nurse standing beside the doctor.

His face was full of concern, and a flash of confusion. "Oh, I thought perhaps Cibil had said something that bothered you. Are you sure you are feeling well enough to continue?"

"I'm fine, really, just a bit of stomach upset at the worst possible time." She smiled wider, perhaps too brightly, because Dr. Carlson cocked his head and looked as if he were about to object.

A commotion from beyond the locked doors distracted him, however. One orderly shouted for help, another ran from the nearby nurse's station towards the room where Sarah had spoken with Cibil. Dr. Carlson turned and hustled down the corridor, Sarah on his heels as he used his key card to buzz through the doors, his legs moving in a fast trot that Sarah was challenged to keep up with.

At the doorway, her way was blocked by Dr. Carlson and another duty nurse, but she could see inside it quite clearly. Cibil had fallen from her chair, her body locked in what appeared to be a grand mal seizure. Her back arched, impossibly far, and her hands and legs contorted into impossible angles. The carotid artery bulged out of her neck and she seemed to be drooling and choking at the same time. It was her eyes that Sarah couldn't stop staring at. The vivid green eyes that had locked onto hers just moments before were black. And not just the iris, but the entire sclera, which was normally white with the odd blood vessel twisting through - all the eye, was black. Sarah wasn't the only one who noticed. The duty nurse on the floor stood next to her. She gave a small gasp and muttered, "Her eyes, my God, what in the world?"

Cibil's slight body shook violently and Sarah winced at the sharp crack of the woman's head on the floor. Dr. Carlson pulled his white lab coat off and handed it to the orderly who shoved it under Cibil's head as her spine arched again, impossibly high, rigid, and her head lifted off the ground, only to slam back down again. Dr. Carlson shoved the table and chairs out of the way and knelt beside his patient, his hand light on her wrist. He spared a cursory glance in Sarah's direction and spoke softly to the orderly holding Cibil's head, cushioning her skull with his hand and lab coat as he looked up at Sarah.

"Mrs. Aaronson, my apologies, but it looks as if we are done for the day. It will take a few hours for Cibil to recover from her seizure. If you could return tomorrow at the same time, I would be happy to arrange access to her again at that time."

"Yes, of course," Sarah responded, backing away from the doorway. In truth, she was taken aback by the ferocity of the woman's seizure. In high school, she had once witnessed a friend of hers have an epileptic seizure. It had been terrifying for her. This one, however, had been far more violent. And it was still happening. Her spine arched repeatedly, her limbs shook, and her head slammed up and down against the orderly's hand and Dr. Carlson's folded up lab coat.

Sarah turned, the duty nurse still by her side, and walked down the hall, her mind spinning.

"Those eyes," the duty nurse murmured, "I've never seen anything like it before."

Sarah said nothing until they arrived at the locked doors. The other woman produced a key card and, seconds later, escorted Sarah through them, down the hall to the elevators. They slowed to a stop, and the woman sneezed violently twice. "Ugh, sorry. I've been fighting the flu bug all week!"

"I hope you feel better soon. And that it isn't that Hong Kong variant that is going around." Sarah said.

"Me too. My nephew's family were felled with it last week. It was touch and go with their two-year-old for a few days there." The woman produced a worn Kleenex from her pocket and blew her nose into it.

"Oh goodness, I hope everything has turned out for the best."

"It did, Tommy is back to running his parents ragged. Damned if they don't recover fast!"

"Well, thank you, Ellen," Sarah said, noting the name tag on the woman's uniform, "I know the way from here."

The woman nodded, flapped her hand at Sarah before she turned and began walking back the way she came.

Sarah pushed the down button at the elevator, her mind occupied with Cibil. She kept replaying the words over and over, returning to the woman's claims, the people she shouldn't even know about, even the train bombing, the one in New York she mentioned. Try as she might, Sarah couldn't remember hearing of any train bombing. She clung to this fact, desperate to cast any kind of doubt on the woman's words, because if she didn't, well...

The long drive home flew by as Sarah reviewed, and reviewed again, Cibil's words, her mannerisms and reactions. She drove in the slow lane, knowing it was the safest option for her since she was used to the less frenetic Midwestern drivers. Despite maintaining the speed limit, other cars passed her on the left, honking in frustration. She ignored them as she listened to the conversation play from the voice recorder.

Sarah had listened to the recording with Cibil so many times she had lost count. Finally, she had just sat there in the stark white living room, Gina's latest minimalist obsession had been a sharp departure from her Liberace days. She stared out at the sky, filled with orange and red hues from the setting sun. Gina bustled in, shopping bags in one hand, and what smelled like Thai takeout in the other.

"Girl, you would not believe what I found! The most delicious flats you have ever seen in a cherry red!" Gina crowed, "They have them in your size, honey, and I insist we go back there tomorrow. They..." Gina took in Sarah sitting in the dark and stopped and set the bags down on the counter. "Sarah, honey? What's wrong?"

Sarah managed a smile. "It's nothing, Gina, really."

Gina, far more empathic than anyone past Sarah or the long-departed Scotty knew, shook her head. "Right, and I'm Genghis Khan." She dumped her bags in the corner of the living room and set the Thai takeout on the counter. "I'll fix you cannoli tomorrow night."

She pulled two plates out of the cabinet, opened the myriad of boxes and beckoned Sarah over. "Food, even takeout, makes everything better."

The edges of Sarah's mouth twitched. There was no such thing as secrets when it came to Gina. And despite the older woman's flamboyant ways and addiction to shopping, Sarah had found her friend to be intensely loyal and rather grounded. She reached for the plate and began poking through the boxes.

"Try the pad krapow moo, it's delish." Gina flapped a hand at another box, "And you haven't lived until you've tried the yum nua. It'll light you up, but it's worth it." She leaned over her plate and sucked in a large mouthful of noodles, her eyes closing in pleasure as she chewed.

Sarah dug into the food heaped on the plate. She hadn't eaten breakfast or lunch. After leaving the hospital and seeing Cibil's body contorting, her eyes as black as coal, any appetite Sarah might have had for lunch had deserted her. She had driven back to Gina's beach house on auto-pilot, her mind turning and turning again on the interview with Cibil Zradce.

There was silence for a few minutes as both of them attacked the takeout with zeal. Sarah sighed as she ate a mouthful of the yum nua. Gina was right, it was better than any Thai food she had ever tasted before.

As soon as the last bite of food had disappeared from her plate, Gina stood up, "I'm making us decaf, and then you are going to tell me what happened today." There was no question in her words, more a statement of fact. Gina was used to getting her way after all, and after she set the steaming cup of decaf down in front of Sarah, she plopped down in the chair opposite and barked, "Spill it, sister."

Sarah pressed play on her cell phone and Gina listened in silence until it was done. "Where's the rest of it?"

"When I returned from the bathroom, she was in a grand mal seizure the likes of which I had never seen before." Sarah answered quietly, "Her doctor said I could return tomorrow."

Gina stared at the phone and then back up to Sarah, "Honey, she's crazy. All that talk of another world and some guy and a train bombing. You realize she's completely off her rocker, right?"

"There was just something about her, Gina. I can't explain it. The way she looked at me, the things she said, and she knew things. Things she couldn't have known."

"Sarah honey, a broken clock is right twice a day. I figure it can't be far off from that." She took Sarah's hand, "Listen, you need to relax, and stop thinking about this for tonight. Go back tomorrow if you must, but meanwhile, sit down and watch Dancing with the Stars with me, will ya? What's his name is so hot! I hear their ratings have skyrocketed since Mr. Hot Pants has been shaking his patoot off for all to see. Sit down for a few minutes, take your mind off the crazy people for a while, and I guarantee you will fall in lust with him right along with me."

Sarah giggled. Gina was an unstoppable force and she let the older woman pull her over to the plush white sofa and click on the large flatscreen television on the far wall.

"We missed the first few minutes, but that's okay, Mr. Hot Pants isn't on until later. He and his partner are performing nearly halfway through the hour."

As the screen jumped to life, Gina frowned and stared at the display, "What is this?"

Sarah stared, too horrified to answer as the television showed blood and gurneys and fire trucks instead of scantily clad women and their dance partners. The headline across the bottom of the screen said it all - Terrorists Strike at the Heart of the Atlantic Railway During Morning Commute.

"Oh my God," Gina whispered, "I've traveled through that station more times than I can count." Her normally ebullient self was muted in shock as she read the words trailing across the screen. "Multiple incendiary devices, fire, and..." her voice petered out.

"Over 5,000 people reported dead or missing." Sarah breathed beside her. "Cibil saw this in a vision."

The two women stared in shocked silence, occasional gasps from each of them as they watched the images rolling across the screen. The commentators themselves looked haggard and raw.

"How did we miss this?" Sarah asked.

"I had Sirius on all day," Gina replied, her perfectly applied makeup streaked with tears, "Oh God, Sarah, all of those people!"

It brought back the memories of 9/11 hard and fast, and both continued to watch the screen, Gina's hand creeping over to hold on to Sarah's, seeking the reassurance of another. Gina reached her for her phone a dozen times, only to set it down again.

"I don't think I'm ready to know," she said quietly when Sarah asked. "I just, I just can't, you know?"

Most of Gina's life had been spent on the East coast, around the very area affected. The dark closed in outside and the two women watched the television without speaking until nearly midnight. Sarah stood up finally and pressed the Off button and turned to Gina.

"Enough, we can't do anything tonight, but if you need to go home tomorrow, I can help you find a flight."

"No." Gina's reply was quiet, almost inaudible. "I'd only be a burden. Look at me, I'm good for shopping and makeup tips, Sarah." She flapped her fingers, the rings flashing in the dim light of the room, mascara streaking her cheeks. "I have no place there."

Sarah had never heard her friend sound so alone, so bereft. She sat back down on the couch and took Gina's hands.

"That's not true, Gina. You make the best damn cannoli I've ever tasted. Go home, volunteer to help with meals for the rescue crews, but wear flats, for crying out loud. Those Jimmy Choo's will kill your arches."

Gina snorted, stifling laughter, and then met Sarah's gaze, "Do you really think I could make a difference?"

"Gina, love, go home. Go cook up a storm. I know it will help."

"Did you get a lick of sleep?" Sarah asked blearily a handful of hours later as Gina bustled about the small house, packing, it appeared, for a small army to descend on New York. There were three large suitcases in addition to her carry-on and voluminous purse. Sarah sat on the edge of the sofa and tried to order her thoughts, but the lack of sleep, combined with the horror of the previous evening's news, had left her foggy-brained and slow.

"I'll sleep on the plane. Believe it or not, I get the best sleep on planes." Gina's face was excited as well as determined. It had taken a little more convincing last night from Sarah, but by the time Sarah headed for bed, Gina had been on line searching for flights. Her steps were fast, purposeful, as she strode from one end of the house to the next. "The cab should be here in five minutes and my flight isn't for three hours. That's more than enough time to get to LAX, go through security and have a coffee before takeoff."

Sarah nodded, and the motion made her head and stomach spin. Perhaps it was more than just lack of sleep. Was she coming down with something? She swallowed, noting a painful patch in her throat. Now is not the time to be sick!

Gina's voice intruded, "Sarah, honey, are you okay? You don't look as perky as you normally do."

Sarah glanced up at her friend, whose expression had turned from barely contained excitement and nervousness, to concern.

"I'm fine, Gina, probably just the beginnings of some stupid head cold. Absolutely nothing to worry about."

Gina walked over and held one cool hand up to Sarah's forehead, "You're a little warm. Perhaps some Tylenol would help." She bustled away to the bathroom and returned, pills in hand, frowning slightly. "Perhaps I should stay here."

Sarah laughed, ignoring her symptoms, pushing past the haziness she felt, "Don't be silly, Gina. I'm a grown woman and can take care of myself. I'll be fine, don't you worry about a thing."

The doorbell buzzed at that moment, which was perfect timing to keep Gina on track. Sarah bent down and lifted one of the smaller suitcases, her muscles aching as she did, and walked to the door to meet the cabbie. As he loaded the suitcases in the trunk, Sarah hugged Gina, "Go see your family, Gina. Cook for them, hug them close. Call me when you land."

"You'll be okay? Call me if you need me to come back and I'll make it happen," the older woman snapped her fingers, "lickety-split."

Sarah nodded and hugged her friend again. The last thing she would do would be to ask Gina to come back. Sometimes her friend could lose herself helping others. Most of Gina's family was the same way. They were brassy, affectionate, and loud. Sarah had met Gina's sisters and brothers, of which there were six in total, on several occasions and knew that Gina's presence in their midst would help.

By the time Sarah had woken up in the morning, Gina had received a text telling her that two of her nephews were among the missing. According to Gina's brother-in-law, Gina's sister, just two years younger than Gina, was in hysterics not knowing where her two sons were.

Sarah couldn't help but smile as she saw her friend out the door. Gina was a true friend, but Sarah was relieved to see her off. Her friend needed her family just as much as they needed her, especially in this time of crisis.

She waved goodbye until the taxi rounded the bend before shutting the door on the pre-dawn darkness. She hadn't slept well, not at all, and her throat was sore, her eyes ached, and Sarah wondered again if she might be coming down with something.

A little more rest, and I'm sure I'll be fine.

The large, comfortable bed swallowed her up, and she pulled the covers over her, slipping into a deep sleep within seconds, despite her mind's best efforts to dwell on yesterday's interview with Cibil, and the massive seizure that followed, or the terrible scenes from the train bombing. When her eyes slowly opened hours later, it felt as if she hadn't rested at all. The sun shone bright, and she struggled to focus on the clock on the bedside table. She groaned when the numbers slowly resolved to a more readable blur. It was after ten in the morning. And she felt worse than when she had first laid down.

Her phone blinked with messages.

How did I miss it ringing? It had been less than two feet away from my head on the nightstand!

Blearily she placed her glasses on her nose and peered at the screen. Two missed calls from Dr. Carlson and two texts from Gina. She read the texts first, one from her friend saying she was at the airport and the plane was late, another as the plane taxied down the runway ready for takeoff. Her head thumped in pain as Sarah tried to estimate how long the flight would take her. "Still in the air, I imagine." Her voice sounded rough, congested.

She closed her messages app and stared at the phone. There was a voicemail. She pressed the speaker button and played the message.

"Sarah, er, Mrs. Aaronson," she smiled, hearing Dr. Carlson's voice as he stumbled over her name, "John Carlson here. I wanted to let you know that Cibil has, erm, gone missing overnight. We are making all efforts to locate her, but we are unsure of her location at this time. Please feel free to call me if you have questions. I wanted to pass along to you some other information as well. Perhaps you could join me for lunch?" His voice wavered again, "I mean, if you wanted to, that is. Uh, well, anyway, call me back when you get this."

Gone missing? From a locked unit? How was that even possible?

She pressed the button and listened to the phone ring once, twice, before John Carlson's voice answered. "Dr. Carlson speaking."

"Dr. Carlson, it's Sarah Aaronson."

"Sarah, er, Mrs. Aaronson, so good to hear from you. I trust you received my voicemail."

"I did, and I am free for lunch if the offer is still open." She pushed past the exhaustion and body aches, curious to learn what other information he had. It was worth pushing her body a little, just to learn how a woman as frail as Cibil had managed to escape a locked psychiatric unit. Flu be damned, she wanted to know more!

Dr. Carlson's voice had an ebullient tone to it as he gave her directions on how to avoid a majority of the traffic and meet him at a local taqueria that he promised had the best burritos in all of L.A.

"Great, I'll see you in two hours," she said, doing her best to sound spunky. As soon as the call disconnected, Sarah's hand fell to her side, heavy, aching. Her entire body felt as if she had just run a marathon, instead of sleeping past ten in the morning. She couldn't remember the last time that had happened.

Two cups of the strongest coffee she could manage, along with a hot shower, relieved some of her malaise, enough for her to convince herself she was fine. Following the doctor's directions, she made decent time, and it was half past the hour when she arrived. The small, nondescript restaurant was packed. Dr. Carlson had waited outside for her, his face lighting up when he saw her. He waved and as she approached, the tense lines in his face smoothed, and he reached for the door. "Believe it or not, we have a table waiting."

Sarah raised her eyebrows, the restaurant didn't seem the type to have reservations, and it was standing room only when they entered. He waved at the hostess and walked to a small table in one corner. He pulled out a chair for her, waited until she was seated and then sat down.

"Okay, I really need to know the story behind this," she said, laughing after the hostess brought her a menu and gave Dr. Carlson a kiss on the cheek.

He looked embarrassed. "I wish they wouldn't do it, but I know better than to argue. Once, I came in and didn't say anything and

Ramon, he's in the kitchen, chewed out their new hostess for not seating me immediately ahead of the others."

"Go on."

"I was in the emergency room with Landon. He had twisted his ankle falling out of a tree and it wasn't supporting his weight, so he was having it x-rayed and I saw the signs of a myocardial infarction in Ramon's grandmother who was also there in the waiting room. He's a widower, with five young children, and Abuela Vasquez," he stopped and looked sheepish, "yes, that's what I call her. Anyway, she was there with Jacinta who had a high fever." He shrugged, "She was so concerned with little Jacinta, that she was ignoring her own health. I called a nurse over. I mean, Abuela was obviously in distress, and they admitted her immediately. She underwent a quadruple bypass the next day."

"Oh, my goodness!" Sarah gasped; her hand was over her mouth.

"In any case, the family was very grateful. I was visiting her a couple of days later and Ramon came up to me and introduced himself and told me to come to the restaurant. I didn't, not for months, but finally I went by and the second he saw me, he ran out of the kitchen and gave me a huge hug." He smiled, "I was invited to Lola's quinceanara last month. She's the oldest, and my kids get along with the others so well, it just feels like family."

"That's beautiful, Dr. Carlson."

"Please, call me John."

Sarah nodded, "Only if you call me Sarah."

"Fair enough."

He looked as if he wanted to say more, but a pretty young girl arrived at that moment, "Tito John! You brought a friend!" She was small and looked far too young to be working in a restaurant during what had to be a school day.

Ben's eyes lit up, "Teresa! It must be spring break for me to see you here. How are you?" He gave her a gentle hug.

She grinned, "I'm good. Papa says he will come by later, it's very busy right now, but could Amelia come to my birthday party?"

"Of course. This weekend?"

"Yes."

Sarah felt a surge of heat, not unlike a hot flash, and then a wave of exhaustion crashed over her. She was definitely ill.

Why in the world did I think going out for lunch was a good idea?

She stared at the menu while they chatted and when there was a pause, she glanced up and found them staring at her expectantly.

"Oh dear, what did I miss?" she asked, slightly flustered.

John frowned, a look of concern on his face, "Are you feeling okay? You look exhausted."

"I'm just tired." She forced a bright smile on her face and turned to Teresa, "I understand that your father makes the best burritos around. What do you suggest I try?"

The girl smiled, her brown eyes lighting up with pride and she said, "My favorite is the chorizo, but it has a bit of heat."

"That sounds fabulous," Sarah smiled, "I don't mind a bit of heat." She handed the menu back to Teresa.

"And I'll have the usual," John said, smiling at the girl. She nodded and slipped away to the kitchen.

"What is the usual?" Sarah asked, her interest piqued.

"It changes," John answered, shrugging, "The first time I came here I said, 'Surprise me,' and they do, every time. Everything is amazing, by the way. Truly the best in the valley." He cocked his head and stared at her, "Are you sure you're okay?"

Sarah waved her hand distracted, "I'm mostly just tired. My friend Gina, her two nephews are missing in the train bombing, and she flew out on a red-eye this morning. Between watching the news late and Gina leaving early, it's been hard. And I might be coming down with something, I'm not sure. God, I hope not, I don't want to get you ill."

"Don't worry about me, I've got the constitution of a goat. I'm never ill," John assured her.

Sarah sipped her water and nibbled at the chips and salsa, "Enough about me, though. I'm dying to hear how Cibil has gone missing. When did it happen? Was there anything on the security video?" She had noticed the cameras throughout the hospital, their dark, round black eyes in most of the hallways as well as the room she had interviewed Cibil in.

John sighed, setting his water down and fiddling with his napkin, "Let me start with what happened after the seizure."

Sarah settled back, "Yes, please do. I had never seen a grand mal seizure that was as violent as that."

Carlson shook his head, "Nor have I. To tell you the truth, I was shocked at the severity of it. And typically, the stronger the seizure the longer it takes to recover from, but less than an hour later, she was screaming - I could hear her down the hall." He rubbed his forehead, his hair thin. Sarah could see where his hairline had originally begun.

"In any case, she was lucid enough to tell me about a highway, a Highway 49 and a sign for a town, one called Beldon or possibly Belton? I have my secretary looking into it. She believes that is where her baby is at."

Sarah's mouth flew open in surprise, "I know exactly where that is!"

John cocked his head, "What?"

"Highway 49 runs through Belton, Missouri, just south of my hometown of Kansas City."

"Seriously?"

"Yes! My son and his family live in Belton. I'm quite familiar with the area." She pulled out her phone and typed a quick message to Michael, groaning with frustration as it refused to send. "Another service failure, these are getting more and more frequent, and not just with Connect Now."

John had his phone out, shaking his head over the connection icon. "Same here. Between the outages and the rolling blackouts, it sometimes feels like we heading back to the dark ages."

"Hey now," Sarah managed to smile at him, "I grew up in the Dark Ages!"

He had the good grace to blush, and began to stutter an apology when Teresa returned, balancing two plates, each loaded with a burrito, Pico sauce and more. They smelled amazing. Despite feeling an ever-increasing sensation of weariness, Sarah's stomach growled in anticipation. She was thankful for the full restaurant and its ambient noise.

"Papa said you will like this one, Tito, it is a mix of barbacoa and carnitas with extra hot sauce."

John grinned at the girl, "Thank you, Teresa. And thanks to your papa, I've been looking forward to this all week!"

Sarah's burrito was deliciously spicy, but she could only manage a few bites before her body, now thoroughly convinced it needed to be in bed, rebelled. She set it down and drank some water instead, "It would truly be amazing if Cibil's baby is found in Missouri. I must admit, the thought of a baby out there, somewhere, missing and perhaps injured or worse, it keeps cycling around in my head. I can only hope we manage to get a happy ending to this."

"Indeed." Carlson said, wiping a bit of sauce from his mouth.

Sarah leaned forward, in part so she could rest her body on her two elbows and hopefully hide her malaise a little longer. "I'm dying to know how Cibil escaped from a locked ward, however."

John shook his head, "We are still trying to figure that out. Truly, I'm stumped. I'll tell you what I know, but this is off the record. Insurance and public relations are both an issue, you understand."

"Of course. I completely understand."

He took another large bite of the burrito, finished chewing and swallowing and sighed in contentment. "I wasn't kidding, I look forward to my lunch here every week. If I ate here every day, I'd end up too wide to fit in the door!" He frowned slightly at Sarah's burrito, "Was yours too spicy?"

"What? Oh God no, I just can't manage to stuff myself with any more of it right now." She waved her hand, "Too much coffee, perhaps."

"You might be catching that virus that is going around. We're operating on a skeleton crew today, two more of my staff called in sick."

"I really hope I'm not, but I'll be honest, I feel worse than I did before I left. I'm so sorry, the last thing you need is to get some nasty virus." She leaned back in her chair, hyper-aware now, feeling warmer than she had earlier.

"Like I said, I am rarely ill, no worries, seriously." He wiped his fingers, "Back to Cibil, however."

"Yes, please."

"All we know at this point is that she was in her locked room last evening, that the orderlies logged her as present up until five a.m. when there was a shift change. The incoming staff performed a routine check of the corridor and found Cibil's door unlocked and open and her bed empty."

"Well, surely the security cameras show something. Perhaps the orderlies skipped a walk-through or two, it's been known to happen." Sarah asked, frowning as Dr. Carlson shook his head.

"That's the weird part. The cameras show nothing. Not only that, but there is no lapse or lost time. I went through them myself. No one can explain it. It's as if she vanished from her room."

"Through a window?"

He laughed, "Through the bars? Six stories off of the ground?"

Sarah flushed in embarrassment, "Oh." She looked up at the doctor, met his eyes, "Then how?"

"Believe me, I'm flummoxed. I've got nothing."

"What about external cameras?"

He frowned, "I haven't checked them."

"Well, perhaps you should." Sarah shrugged, "I am as befuddled as you, but I'd double-check the exterior cameras just to be sure."

"That's not a bad idea. I'll do that when I return to work." He caught the eye of the waitress and asked for two takeout boxes and dug into his wallet. "Now is when I get to be sneaky. You ready for it?" He pulled two twenty-dollar bills out.

Sarah looked around "Sneaky? Um, why?"

"They won't accept payment. No matter how often I return, so I have to get inventive. Help me out?"

"What do you need me to do?"

"I'll distract her, you slip the money into her apron pocket." He grinned at her and Sarah was struck by his open, kind smile. It reminded her of Theo, despite Dr. Carlson being at least twenty years younger. Theo had brought out the best in her and everyone around him. She missed having that in her day-to-day life.

Sarah found herself smiling back and taking the money from his hand. When Teresa returned with the takeout boxes, John distracted her by asking for her help and winked at Sarah as she managed to slip the bills into the girl's pocket.

"You make a fine co-conspirator, Sarah, thank you for that." John took her arm gently and guided her out of the restaurant after Teresa moved on to the next table.

"That was the highlight of my day. Intrigue, conspiracy, and..." Sarah's body finally rebelled, and she stopped abruptly, dizziness and fatigue now fighting with nausea. She swayed and John's grip on her tightened.

"You aren't well at all!" John exclaimed, there was concern in his voice.

"I really thought I would be fine, but," she swayed again and she could feel sweat beading on her forehead, her cheeks flushing. "I am so sorry, John, I..."

"Here, my car is right here, let's sit you down until you can get your bearings." He guided her to the passenger side and helped her slide into the seat. The car was warm from the sun and Sarah was hit with a wave of dizziness. At that moment, all she wanted to do was curl up and sleep. She put her right hand on the dashboard and leaned forward, waited for the world to stop spinning all around her.

John's voice held concern, "I really think I should take you to the Emergency Room, or would you rather see your primary doctor?"

"I don't, oh," another wave of dizziness, "would you believe I don't have a doctor here in L.A.? It sounds so stupid now, but honestly, I've been so healthy that I haven't bothered finding one. I do my annual when I go to visit my son and his family in Missouri each summer. And, oh, I don't want to be sick in your car." She tried to stand up, but Carlson wasn't having it.

"Sarah, I'm happy to take you to the ER. I'll get a bag in case you feel nauseous, but you have no business driving right now. Especially not with some of the drivers I see loose on the road!"

She knew he was right. "Okay, but honestly, I just need to go home and rest."

"Are you sure?" He handed her a thick, insulated bag. "I'm worried about you."

"Really, I'll be fine. I'm sure it's just a nasty virus. A couple of days and I'll be right as rain."

The ride back to Gina's beach house was subdued. John had assured her that her car would be safe there in the parking lot and had double-checked that it was locked. Sarah concentrated on not throwing up, her stomach was spinning and she felt sweaty and feverish. When they arrived, John parked the car in the drive, got out, and opened Sarah's door. Everything was moving faster around her, while she sloshed through a thick mire, her brain fogged and her body miserable.

Why did I ever think I was okay to leave the house this morning?

She was dimly aware of the doctor's hands steadying her as they walked together to the front door. All she wanted was to be in bed. If she could just lay still, surely the nausea would pass.

"I am so sorry," she mumbled, "I had no idea I would feel this ill." She kicked off her shoes and tried to smile up at John. Two or three copies of his face swam in front of her.

"Please let me take you to the ER, Sarah." There was such deep concern in his face, and despite him being at least ten years younger than her, she was reminded again of Theo.

She reached up, her hand hot against his cheek, "Really. I'll be fine. I just need to lie down and rest. You'll keep me updated if you hear anything? If they find the baby? Or if they locate Cibil?"

"Of course. May I check in on you later today and see how you are doing?"

She nodded, and he backed down the hall towards the door, "And if you need anything, anything at all, you will call me?"

"Yes, of course." She managed to smile. He was a kind man and for the first time in years, she felt a spark of desire. More for the companionship than anything else. The steadfast presence of another person in your life. She felt Gina's absence, and Theo's, keenly at that moment. "Once I have a rest, I'll feel much better. I'm sure of it."

She fought to stand steady on her feet until he left, the door closed and locked behind him, before she tottered to her bed, and collapsed.

Nightmares, and bouts of semi-conscious wakefulness stole any real rest from her sleep for the next several hours. At some point of it, the nausea finally gave way to a panicked run to the toilet where she managed to get most of the contents of her stomach into the bowl. Unlike most bouts of nausea, she felt worse after, not better. The room spun as she levered her way into a standing position and rinsed her face, hair and shirt. She felt ridiculously guilty for not keeping the tasty burrito down, even though she knew it wasn't her fault. Also, it had burned worse coming up.

As the afternoon sun sent the rays of light sliding around to the west, her room cooled. A relief from her fever at first, but she was soon shivering uncontrollably. Her phone buzzed intermittently. Gina would have landed by now and Sarah's thoughts landed in a murky gray half consciousness that kept needling her to answer the phone. She couldn't though. Her body was stripped of energy for any other activity than running to the bathroom and laying on her rumpled bed. She closed her eyes, ignoring the phone, the cold descending over her limbs, and lost herself to the darkness.

"Sarah? Sarah!" A voice intruded on the dark oblivion. Theo's voice was calling to her. What was he doing here, anyway? She tried to open her eyes, but it seemed like too much effort.

Maybe in a little while, once I've had more sleep.

She sank back into the darkness, a part of her noting that the voice couldn't be Theo's, but sounded familiar. He was talking to someone else now too.

"Right this way, she's in here."

"Sir? If you could please give us some room." An unfamiliar voice. A cool hand on her wrist, hands gently rolling her onto her back. She was too tired to respond. As she cracked an eye open, a blinding light caused her to flinch. "Are you her husband, sir?"

"No, no, I'm a friend." He sounded distraught, "I should have taken her to the emergency room earlier, but she said she just wanted to go home."

"Don't beat yourself up, we've been seeing this a lot in the past week. The virus hits fast and hard, especially in the very young and the elderly."

Gentle hands, a gloved finger opening one eye. She flinched again and then, without her normal ten second warning, found herself retching up a dark green bile. It dribbled down the side of the bed and onto the white carpet.

"Okay, Mrs. Aaronson, okay. I think it's time for a quick ride to the hospital." The man turned away, speaking to his partner, "Let's get an IV hooked up with a saline drip. She's dehydrated and her temp is at 104.2. Also, call ahead and let them know we have one for potential admit to the ICU."

Sarah heard Theo, no, not Theo, it was John, John Carlson pacing at the far end of the room. "I should have taken her straight to the ER," he muttered. A young woman's voice then, "You couldn't have known, Uncle John. And besides, you got help for her. Come on, we can drive ahead to the hospital."

She felt hands lift her, then she was settled onto a hard surface before Sarah slipped back into the abyss.

Hours later, as the sun's rays turned the skyline from a midnight blue to a rosy pink, John pulled out his phone and dialed home. It rang twice before Amelia answered, her voice husky with sleep, "Still at the hospital, Uncle J?"

He looked out of the window. To the east he could see the sky lighting up with salmon, pink, contrasting sharply against the low foothills in the distance. His chest felt heavy, constricted. "I am. I just wanted to check in and see if Mrs. Almeida could take you to practice. I'll be home by noon, and I don't want you to be late with the championship coming up."

"Okay, I'll ask her in a bit, after I take a shower."

"Are the boys okay?"

"They're still sound asleep. They watched some horror flick and Landon curled up in my bed." She sounded annoyed. John smiled briefly, Amelia was the oldest, and at fourteen, was full of the typical teenage angst.

"Is your friend any better?"

John's smile dropped away. "No."

Amelia's tone changed, "Oh. I'm sorry, Uncle J."

"Yeah, I have to finish making calls now."

"Okay. I'll make sure and make breakfast for everyone." She paused, "And Uncle J?"

"Yes?"

"It was really good of you to stay with her, you know? She wasn't alone."

John nodded, even though his niece couldn't see it, "I'll see you after practice, Am."

The bed they had placed her in was empty, Sarah's body had already been transported down to the morgue. The sheets had been stripped, and the room cleaned with speed. There were more ill patients being brought in. He had been downstairs, the ER and the halls near the admissions desk were clogged with scores more who had arrived sick with the flu.

He had sat there, next to her bed, against the rules and held her hand and talked to her. He told her that the baby had been found. The story seemed impossible, the infant had been strapped into a baby seat, still spinning in the middle of the road when a couple had very nearly hit her. She was in care now, with the very people who had discovered her.

"The craziest part of it, Sarah?" he had said, her hand limp in his, "The baby was found on the same day as Cibil was taken into custody."

There had been no response. She hadn't stirred, not once, never gaining consciousness, never learning the news that had compelled him to first call and then come to her door the night before.

He had been too late to save her, and he felt wretched at the thought of her passing from the world without anyone but him by her side. They had been practically strangers. Despite this, he had felt a connection with her, one that ached with loss, grief, as he imagined what could have been if they had just had more time.

He glanced down at his watch, noted the time and headed for the door. Her son's plane would be touching down soon. He had found Michael's name in the contact info on Sarah's phone and called him near midnight as her breathing became uneven and the doctor had shaken his head, the look on his face betraying the truth. Michael had been first suspicious, who wouldn't with a call from a stranger in the middle of the night? But once John had explained the connection, and the dire situation, Sarah's son had made reservations on a red-eye and headed for the airport, calling John from the runway before departure to give him the flight information.

It would be close to two hours before he landed, just enough time in rush hour to make it to the airport.

John parked his car and as he oriented himself to the correct terminal, Sarah's phone buzzed in his pocket. He thought of letting it ring. Who was he to answer a dead woman's phone? He saw the number was local, however, and pressed the green button.

The woman on the other end was already talking, "Sarah honey, I've been trying to reach you since I landed yesterday. Where have you been? Oh girl, you were so right, aren't you always?" This had to be Gina, Sarah's roommate. Sarah had described Gina as someone who could talk a mile a minute without taking a breath. "Coming here was the best thing I could have done. My sister was losing her ever-loving mind and everyone was coming over and just standing around. I mean, really, just working themselves up something fierce while we waited for word and so I fixed that cannoli like you suggested and Carmelina and Lucina went from crying and screaming to calm in nothing flat. And the best news, Sarah, honey! They found both the boys. I mean, they're not boys any longer, Mario's pushing forty, and Silvio's not far behind, but they are both okay. Beat to hell, Mario's got a broken leg, ribs, and missing a pinky for the love of God, but Silvio walked out with scratches. He was helping get others out and both of them lost their phones in the confusion.

By the time the cannoli were out of the oven, we got word he was alive and fine. Though I'm pretty sure Carmelina is gonna kill him for not calling home. And I'm running on fumes, the pull-out in the front room is lumpier than my auntie's mashed potatoes..."

"I'm so sorry, but..." John interjected.

Gina gasped, "Who is this? What have you done with Sarah?"

"My name is John Carlson, I'm the department psychiatrist at Cedar-Sinai. Sarah fell ill with a bad strain of flu, Gina."

There was silence from Gina's end, just a whoosh of air, then a door closed, and Gina didn't say anything for a long moment. When she did, her ebullient tone gone. "Is Sarah all right?"

"I'm sorry... she's... not. We met for lunch yesterday. She was obviously ill, but insisted she would be fine. Later in the evening she wasn't answering her phone. I came by and found her very ill. I called for an ambulance. They admitted her to the hospital, but unfortunately, she worsened. I am so sorry to tell you this, but she passed away early this morning."

"Oh God." Gina began to sob, "Oh, I should have been there for her. That woman, that patient of yours, she told Sarah she would die. I never should have left. Never. She was right. About the bombing, about Sarah dying, everything."

As he stood there, he could see the plane taxi up, nestling against the gate. He watched as the first passengers appeared from the long hallway. John's fingers felt numb. He hadn't thought of it until now, what Cibil had said in the observation room. How could he have forgotten it? He'd written it off, certain of her mental instability, that he'd barely given the words credence save for any mentions of her child. How had she known?

Gina was still talking, "Cibil was right. She was right about the bombing; she was right about the flu. What else is she right about?"

A group of three women appeared first, behind them a short, older man, a sour expression on his face.

"I'm so sorry, Gina. I wish I knew what to say." John told her. "I, I have to go, her son flew in and his plane just landed." Whatever she said next, he missed it, his eyes fixed on a taller man who had appeared, a backpack in one hand. He looked anxious as his eyes searching the crowd waiting for the passengers to disembark. John could see a strong resemblance to Sarah in him.

"Michael?" He stepped forward and the younger man zeroed his attention on John.

"Dr. Carlson?" He asked, his brilliant blue eyes laser-focused, "How is my mother?"

John shook his head. "I cannot tell you how sorry I am, Michael. Sarah passed away two hours ago."

The younger man, shook his head, his mouth opened and closed in shock and grief.

Hours later, John returned to his house. It was empty, Amelia was at practice and the boys had left a note that they were at a friend's house and would be back after they ate dinner.

John peeled off the clothes he had worn for more than 24 hours and stepped into the shower.

The baby had been found, even if her mother was now missing. And the world had lost a talented, kind woman. John Carlson closed his eyes as the water ran in rivulets, washing his body clean, the steam billowing over the top of the shower doors.

A storm was coming. He could feel it building.

Reek of Bone

"Not with a bang, but a whimper."

"Hi Dad, it's me, Isaac. Did I wake you up?"

The man's voice pulled Camelia from the depths of the paperback she had been reading. *A Life Relived* was a sharp digression from Dean Edmonds other books, which she had enjoyed immensely. This one, however different, was enthralling. She was nearly done, just a handful of pages left, and she found herself re-reading the pages, unwilling for it to end.

She peeked up and took in his blond hair and dark brown eyes. Their eyes met momentarily. He gave her a small smile and nod, and kept talking, eyes flitting elsewhere.

His accent was definitely not East coast. Hm, possibly a Southerner, maybe from Georgia? He had smiled as well, something that New Yorkers rarely did when making eye contact with a stranger. Camelia had dated a guy from Georgia right before her mom was diagnosed. He had been obsessed with her skin.

I've never felt anything so silky smooth.

He would touch her endlessly, his hands almost obsessive in their need to connect with her. Whether it was to slip his arm around her waist, even touch her hand or press his lips against her hair, he had been attentive and kind. Too bad his family had been such racist pricks. They had threatened to cut off his funding and him with no job and a full-time student.

She had been the one to break it off.

Her eyes traveled up to his face, admiring the fine stubble, the few stray white hairs interspersed in the blond. She had always had an attraction to older guys.

Hm, handsome.

"No? Oh good. I... no, no, nothing's wrong. Everyone is great, actually. I have some exciting news and I wanted you to be the first to hear."

Her gaze traveled to his left hand, which was clutching the seat in front of her.

Married. Damn.

"We will be adding a new Perdue to the family! Yes, you heard me right. And Dad, we just learned it is a boy."

The tall blond man laughed, his warm brown eyes sparkling with excitement. "I knew you would be happy to hear that. Who knows, he might just take over for you there on the farm!"

He laughed again, "Well, you will just have to hang in there another twenty years. That shouldn't be a problem, right?"

He glanced out of the window.

"Hey Dad, look sorry, but I have to go. We are almost at the tunnel and the connection will cut off in a few more seconds. I just wanted to tell you the good news and I promise we will head down there soon. Next month, for sure, during Thanksgiving break. Yeah, I promise. Yeah, I love you too."

Fumbling with his cell phone, the man accidentally stepped on Camelia's toes, "Oh, I'm so sorry, ma'am, my apologies!" His smile was replaced with an embarrassed look of apology as he reached out and grabbed the back of a seat to steady himself again. The train swayed and continued to rumble down the track. Outside, the concrete walls were rising as the tracks angled down towards the tunnel.

"No worries." Camelia said, smiling up at him. "Congratulations, by the way." she added. "I couldn't help overhearing. How many children do you have?"

He grinned happily, "Baby boy will make three. I have two girls, ages ten and thirteen."

He was dressed in a suit, an expensive leather briefcase wedged between his feet. His right hand tucked the cell phone into his pocket while he steadied himself with the left. The train was crowded, unusually so. A bridge shutdown, along with several road repair projects, had impacted the entire area, and the passenger trains, normally with seats still available, were now full to capacity, with standing room only.

"How wonderful for you."

The train slipped into the East River tunnel and darkness enfolded them. The interior lights blinked twice and brightened.

His smile stretched wider. "Thank you! It's been a long time coming, I'll tell you! We have been trying for just one more for over three years. My wife, she's forty-one, and, well, it isn't as easy now as it was with the girls. We didn't want to say anything, at least not until we were in the second trimester and the baby was doing well."

"I did a rotation in Obstetrics. I miss it. There's nothing that beats catching babies. But Sinai had an opening in Oncology and it meant better hours, so I had to say yes. Having a regular schedule, well, for the most part, is rare in the medical field."

"Are you a doctor?" He asked, his gaze slipping to her scrubs.

"No, I'm an RN, but I hope to begin studying for my MSN next semester, after I've got a good feel for the department."

"Well, you are definitely in a growing field. Especially with all of these aging baby boomers."

"When is your wife due?"

"The last week of February. The first two went over, so it might end up being the first week of March."

Camelia laughed. "Babies seem to have a mind of their own. You never know, this one might surprise you."

"Indeed, he might." He grimaced then. "It means moving, though. We have a two bedroom in Auburndale, and my wife is campaigning for a brownstone in Brooklyn. She wants the girls to go to Berkeley Carroll."

"I've heard of it. It's K through twelve, if I remember right. Very expensive, but worth it."

"Tell me about it, I might have to take on a second job just to pay for tuition!"

"There's nothing better than a good start, though. Berkeley Carroll is a great choice. A girlfriend of mine has her daughter enrolled there. The scholastics are far and above other schools in the area." Camelia smiled. "Someday I'll find Mr. Right and make a family of my own. Kids are our piece of immortality, after all."

"Indeed." He nodded at her book. "Dean Edmonds, eh? My favorite book of his is *Fate's Highway*. What about you?"

"I'm really enjoying this one. It's completely different from anything he ever wrote before and it almost feels like memoir instead of his tried-and-true speculative fiction, but my hands-down favorite is *Touched by Light.*"

"Oh wow, I remember that one! It was good. I saw an interview with his daughter back in 2002, at the release of the 20-year anniversary edition. She said it was her favorite book."

Camelia opened her mouth, but before either of them could say anything more, a tremendous roar and concussive blast hit the train. On its heels came darkness, pain, and screams. A blackness descended, but there was no silence. Instead, the screams of passengers blending with the high screech of twisting metal, the floor of the car bending and gravity shifting around them.

The blast knocked the breath out of Camelia's lungs, and she felt as if her entire body was being thrown—legs and arms pinwheeling, before she crashed back into place. The train car itself twisted, screaming in metallic agony as the skin of it tore and the train, what was left of it, ground to an agonized stop.

There was a strong crack as something hard connected with the side of her face.

And then blackness descended.

How long it lasted—whether it was seconds, minutes or even hours—waking to darkness was unnerving.

What happened? How long was I out? Where am I?

Camelia took a breath, and instantly her throat closed, choking on the grit, dust, hair, and more. She coughed, spit it out, and tried to remember where she was.

Above all, rational thought was a grinding, overwhelming pain. It felt as if it were consuming her whole body in electric jolts of agony.

In the distance, a shower of sparks elicited weak screams and moans. She could hear coughing, the sound of a woman, or possibly a man, wailing, their words rapid fire and foreign. New York was a melting pot, in this train alone they could have a hundred nationalities. Nearby, at her elbow, she could hear choking and coughing, labored breathing.

The world felt off center, unsteady. In the nearly consuming black, there was no reference to up, down, forward or back.

I was on the train. Going to work. Going to Sinai.

Camelia felt around her. The padded seat she had been sitting in was tilted, crumpled from the feel of it. Sharp metal stuck through the padding and there was a wet stickiness everywhere. She could smell smoke. It had a greasy, oily taste to it.

The darkness was not as absolute as she had first perceived. There was a light, in the distance, in the direction of the front of the train. At least, she thought it was the front of the train.

If her skin and bones could speak, they would have been screaming curses, not unlike the others in the distance. Her training kicked in.

Assess the situation. Possibly cracked, even broken ribs?

Her right arm wasn't moving, and the right shoulder hurt like hell. She dragged her left one out from under her and flexed it experimentally. She bent the elbow, and although all the arm felt bruised, she could move it. The fingers of her left hand gently explored her chest and ribs. The pressure of her fingers generated new agony.

Cracked, probably not broken.

What the hell had happened? The train must have jumped the tracks.

She had been talking to the man about his kids.

Where was he? What was his name?

The massive sound, an explosion perhaps? It had obliterated his words, turned the lights into showers of sharp, shards of glass, and lifted the train from its tracks.

The dampness was spreading. She could feel it everywhere now. The fingers of her left hand traveled, probing her right arm and stopping at a response of white-hot agony. She was curled on her side, in a half ball, as if her body had known what to do even if her mind had not. It had sought to protect itself, to gather in, but was prevented by something. Her traveling fingers found a head of hair. It had to be him under her fingers. He was warm, still breathing, but with a choked liquidity to it.

Not good.

"Hey,"

Damn it, what was his name? Wait. He had called himself Isaac on the phone.

"Isaac?"

God, it hurts to talk. My face feels wrong, somehow.

He moaned, moved slightly, and gasped. His head was near her stomach and her hands explored his blood-soaked hair and face, tapping him lightly with her fingers. "Hey Isaac, can you hear me?"

Her words sounded garbled, just like they had after a visit to the dentist and several fillings, her cheeks numb and tongue heavy.

"Christ, what happened?" he mumbled, rising slightly only to collapse again with a pained groan. "I can't move."

"Don't try to get up."

The smoke was increasing and now she was sure there was a fire.

Was it the train engine? Is that what had caused whatever this was?

Isaac coughed, and Camelia felt a spray of wetness on her arm. "I couldn't move if I tried. My legs, they're pinned."

"I'm sure there will be someone here soon. Just try to stay still."

"We are about midway through the tunnel; it's going to take them a while." He coughed again and Camelia felt another shower of droplets.

She reached for her purse, fingers reaching in the darkness until she found it. In the destruction it had upended and she ran her fingers over surfaces, sharp edges, and under a limp, obviously dead hand before she found her keys. A flashlight was attached to the chain. She pressed the small button on the side and the light revealed a scene out of hell.

Blood and bodies, parts of bodies, interspersed with twisted metal, the remains of seats, and wreckage surrounded them. A shoe without a foot in it, another with just a foot inside, grisly bone and meat, shocked her into letting go of the tiny button. Darkness descended, and Isaac coughed again. It sounded wet, and his breathing bubbled in and out, his head cradled against her stomach.

She pushed the button again, and he winced as the light filled his eyes. He was twisted, his body bent. He shouldn't look like that. A human body doesn't turn that way.

His head was against her, his body caught in an impossible grip of metal and the remains of chairs. Near where his feet should be was a twisted conglomeration of body parts, blood, and metal. Blood covered his face. She winced and wondered what she should do. More likely, what could she do? He had internal bleeding. He needed to be in the ER.

The train no longer resembled the sleek, gleaming machine she had boarded in Long Island. Instead, it was sharp, bloodied, and broken, just like the bodies it held within its bowels.

In the distance, she could see that the fire was growing, expanding, and beginning to move slowly towards them. It was yards away, but still, they couldn't stay here.

"I smell smoke." Isaac wheezed.

Forget the fire. The smoke will kill us first.

"Yeah, something up at the front is burning. Maybe that's what caused this."

He shook his head slightly, which was enough to induce yet another coughing fit. "No, that was no accident. That was a bomb." He said it with certainty. "We have to get out of here. Now."

Camelia nodded, "Yeah. I know." She took a breath, which felt like she was breathing in broken glass and motor oil, and shifted. Isaac's head rolled to the right, and he hissed in pain and began coughing again. It burbled out of him, wet and thick.

Camelia wiggled while her ribs and right shoulder screamed objections, and slowly pushed herself to a seated position. The fire was gathering strength, and the flames lit up patches of the twisted train car, illuminating gore and death in every corner. No one else in the car was moving except for her and Isaac, but she needed to check on them, try to provide assistance if she could. She coughed and tried to breathe shallow. It hurt less when she did.

"Your arm doesn't look so good." Isaac noted, staring at her right arm hanging limp.

"I'm pretty sure it's dislocated. I can't move it." She stared at him, "Don't worry about me, I'll be fine."

They were both silent for a moment, and Camelia used her flashlight to assess the situation. The train car had been full, with some of the passengers, like Isaac, standing.

"I need to check on the others." Her legs were shaking, and she was dizzy.

He nodded and coughed again.

The car was crushed beyond recognition. She tried to get her bearings. They had been in the front of the last set of three cars, hadn't they? There were two more cars behind them, with the rest of the train on the other side of the fire, deep within the tunnel.

As she looked around, it was obvious that, at least in this car, they were the only two who had survived.

Was it really a bomb?

Her face pulsed in pain, especially on the right side. She set the flashlight down and touched her face. She quickly pulled her hand away when her fingers touched teeth and bone where her cheek was supposed to have been.

She made her way back to Isaac.

"You need to get out of here." He said, his voice already sounded tired, defeated.

"Don't you mean *we* need to get out of here?" she fired back. As if she would leave a patient who needed her.

"What's your name?" He asked, then coughed again, another gout of blood escaping and dribbling down his cheek. "You know mine, but I don't know yours."

"It's Camelia. Camelia Garcia. I work at Mount Sinai Beth Israel."

He smiled and then winced as he tried to shift his hand. She realized he was trying to reach out and shake her hand. His right arm was badly broken from the looks of it.

"I'd say that it was a pleasure to meet you, Ms. Garcia, but circumstances being what they are." He coughed again. He managed to pull his head back enough to see the blood. "This isn't looking good."

Camelia's ears strained to hear sounds of any kind of rescue effort, but she couldn't hear anyone other than the handful of survivors screaming, crying, and the sound of the fire crackling and spitting.

She could smell it then. There was nothing quite like the smell of burning flesh. She had learned that after a stint in the ER and a bus crash. Most of the passengers had been trapped as the fuel line had ignited and began to burn them alive. The horror of that experience had stayed with her for weeks and Camelia had sworn there and then to find a field that would take her far from burn units or ER work. It was the smell that was the worst. The distinctive greasy reek of flesh and bone that stayed in her nose long after she had finished her shift, stripped off her scrubs, and showered.

Her fingers rested on his wrist and took his pulse. It was thready and irregular. Combine that with internal bleeding and the lower half of him trapped, if not crushed, in the twisted remains of the train car, and Isaac was right, it didn't look good at all.

She tried to reassure him again. "We just need to wait for the rescue team. Hang in there."

"Tell me what you see, Camelia," Isaac gasped, coughing again.

"About as much as you see. Darkness, twisted metal, and a fire that is spreading."

"Any others alive? There had been a woman and her child who boarded after me. I let them have my seat."

She could see a tiny limp and bloody hand beneath a section of collapsed concrete. "There's no one else alive in this car."

"What about me?"

"What about you, Isaac?"

"Why can't I move?"

"You're pinned. The rescuers, they'll be here soon." She took a breath and cued the professional voice, the one that had calmed scores of stressed patients. "They will have tools and equipment. They'll be able to get you out."

"My body, it doesn't feel right. Like it is turned wrong. What do you see?" He asked again, stopping every third word to cough and choke. More blood seeped out of his mouth, dark red, mottled with black clots.

Camelia stared into the darkness. The opening to the tunnel was far behind them, around several bends. There wasn't even a spot of light to betray its presence. Her ears strained for any sound of voices or movement from that direction. But there was nothing.

"Camelia?"

She settled back next to him. "I wish I knew what to say, Isaac."

"Tell me the truth."

Had she ever been this honest with a patient? "You are seriously injured. Spinal injuries, internal bleeding. The rescuers must be on their way, but they aren't here yet. Just hang in there, okay?"

"Listen, I need you to do something for me." His skin held a sheen of sweat. "I need you to find my wife. Her name is Amy Perdue. I need you to tell her how much I love her. How much I love our life and tell my girls..." He coughed again, the thick blood choking him, his words mixed with bubbles of red escaping from his lips, "Tell them that," the rest of his sentence was obliterated by a fresh gout of blood.

Camelia shined her light on the man's legs and where they disappeared into the twisted metal. It would take hours to get him out, and Isaac didn't have hours. He had minutes.

"Shh, Isaac, you can tell them all of this, just..."

"Please, don't. Let us have truth between us. I'm dying, I can feel it." His fingers closed on hers. The act of moving the badly damaged arm had to be excruciating. She could feel his eyes on hers, the flickering of the flames growing closer. "Tell my girls to be strong and love their brother and their mother. Tell them to leave New York and get out of this death trap."

He gasped and choked on more blood. It was bright red. "You need to go, Camelia. There are others who need your help."

She knew he was right. Camelia could see the man's death approaching. It couldn't have been clearer if the angel of death had appeared before them.

The flames were beginning to crackle, and the heat was building as it inched closer. More screams and moans now from other cars. In their own ruined train car, there were only the two of them and this moment.

Her chest hurt. Not from the cracked ribs, but from the thought of the handsome man lying half in and half out of her lap. She imagined the family he was leaving behind. His wife, her belly swelling with a boy who would grow up knowing his father only through pictures and stories. His daughters. Girls needed strong, kind fathers like this one.

Camelia reached for the cross around her neck, praying silently for the dying man.

"You'll find them?" he asked, choking out the words.

"Yes. I promise I will."

"Go now." The fire edged closer. "You must go. So that my children and wife know. I don't want them left without answers."

She couldn't just leave him. Not like this. "May I pray with you, Isaac?"

"I'm not, I mean, I haven't," he faltered and coughed again, choking on the blood, "I haven't prayed in a long time."

She took his hand in hers. She wondered if it was for her more than it was for him that she was praying. Did it matter?

"Hail Mary, full of grace. The Lord is with thee. Blessed art thou amongst women, and blessed is the fruit of thy womb, Jesus. Holy Mary, Mother of God, pray for us sinners, now and at the hour of our death. Amen."

"Amen," he choked in response, blood bubbling past his lips. He squeezed her hand.

The fire was inching closer, the reek of burning flesh and bone a now omnipresent smell, the sulfurous odor of burning hair mixed with the coppery metallic smell that was both nauseating and sweet.

Camelia pulled her way upright, her eyes never leaving Isaac's. As she stood, shaking from the effort, he managed to smile at her, and then he sighed. One last bubble of red, and his eyes fixed and staring. He was gone.

She sucked in an agonized breath, her body reminding her in a thousand ways that she was alive but in desperate need of medical treatment if she wanted to stay that way.

She reached down, closed his eyes, crossed herself and whispered, "Vaya con Dios," before crawling away. She had to get out. The fire was growing, and the air was now thick with the choking smoke.

The train was shredded. Strips of metal littered the concrete and track and there was a steady wind coming from behind, feeding the ever-expanding fire. Crawling out of the wreckage, Camelia had glanced back to see only a handful of others heading her way. The train cars behind were just as damaged as hers had been and she wondered how it was possible she had survived the initial explosion, if that was what it really was.

Her face, ribs, and right arm were all agonized points of heat and pain. She could hear a steady hissing, the fire flaring and burning hotter with every passing moment.

"There's no one back there alive." An older man said, reaching for her right arm. She bit back a scream of agony.

"Your arm," he winced, his hand falling away, "I'm sorry, I was trying to help."

She clenched her teeth, focusing her energy on staying upright. "It's dislocated. Are you sure there is no one else back there?"

He shook his head in the orange-hued gloom, coughing as some of the oily black smoke rolled past them.

"Only the dead."

One of the others, a guy with a buzz cut and Carhart pants and coat, flapped a hand at her. "Come on lady, we gotta go."

"I'm a nurse, I should check."

Buzz Cut shook his head, "Look lady, unless you are Jesus Christ himself, come to raise Lazarus, you ain't gonna be able to help them. Everyone is fucking dead. Whatever that was, it cut the train in half and capsized parts of the tunnel. We gotta head back to Astoria before this fire catches up to us."

Camelia knew he was right. And as hurt as she was, there was little that she could do for the other victims. As they trudged through the dark, she tried to calculate how many passengers had been on the train.

Each car could hold, what, fifty seated, plus those standing, so maybe sixty-five, seventy tops? And there were, what, fifteen passenger cars?

Her brain struggled to complete the math.

Somewhere around nine hundred, maybe more, maybe less.

She shook her head and lurched dizzily to the side, leaning against the concrete wall as she struggled to comprehend it. She had been in the last set of cars. Perhaps the front of the train, on the other side, hadn't been as devastated.

Camelia stumbled and fell against the older man, her feet refusing to cooperate.

Shock is setting in.

Blood caked her neck on the right side of her face. She must look bad. Both the old man and the younger one had avoided looking at her. Their gazes sliding away from her face, concentrating on anywhere but there.

Buzz Cut pulled her up, and they kept going. Behind them, the fire was turning the tunnel, and the ruined train into a hellscape of death and destruction. No one was screaming, not anymore.

Each step seemed harder than the last. No matter how hard she concentrated, her knees kept buckling. As they made their way slowly, painfully, down the tunnel, they were joined by two more. An older woman and a young girl, both had been sitting on the tracks, staring in blank-eyed shock as the others approached.

The tunnel was narrow, barely three feet wider than the train that was now fully engulfed in flames, the hissing growing louder and louder. Chest high on each side, the walls were lined with a concrete ledge. Camelia stared at them, wondering if she and the others were supposed to be walking on them instead of down below on the track.

The older woman, her scalp torn and bloody, her business suit in ruins, put Camelia's fears to words, "What if another train comes?" Camelia noticed the woman was missing one of her shoes and limping badly on the other.

"Just keep moving, we should see the end soon," came the clipped response from Buzz Cut. He stopped occasionally; his face contorted with pain. The piece of jagged metal protruding from his left elbow had rendered the limb useless. They shambled, all of them, lurching through the tunnel, guided only by the dim, intermittent lights of cell phones and Camelia's keychain flashlight.

Far ahead in the distance, a dim sliver of daylight could be seen. The lights that normally lit this length of tunnel were dark, and glass from the broken bulbs crunched under their feet. The woman without a shoe said nothing more, only occasionally hitching her bare foot reflexively as she encountered more broken glass or rocks.

"Walk in the middle, as far from the glass as you can," Camelia mumbled, her cheek now swollen, her teeth aching. Her injuries were affecting her speech.

In the far distance, Camelia could see the dim light momentarily blocked and the sound of voices.

"Oh, thank you, Jesus," the older man said, "We're here!" His voice ricocheted against the tunnel walls, and Camelia heard one of them shout back. Lights and movement were headed towards them. The hissing behind them had turned into a low roar that was growing. The fire was now something else entirely, a white-hot light behind them that lit up the track, the tunnel, and even the rescuers, still hundreds of feet away.

"We gotta go, the train's gonna blow up." Buzz Cut grabbed her arm and Camelia bit back a shriek of pain.

"The train already blew up!"

"Nah, that was a bomb, this is something else. Come on, we gotta move!"

The rescuers were running faster, and within moments, they reached the small group of survivors. By this time the whine, turned roar, turned white hot light, had completely engulfed the tunnel behind them. Camelia's legs collapsed under her just as two sets of hands lifted her and everyone ran from the inferno. If she had looked back at that moment, she would have been temporarily blinded by it.

But by then, Camelia had already passed out.

Two days later...

"The terrible events of the past forty-eight hours have shaken New York and the East coast to its core. Once again, our nation has found itself attacked by the lowest of the low. These cowardly, vicious individuals have sought to strike at the core of our hard-working community."

Camelia heard the newscaster first, recognizing her without needing to see her. She was a stunning blond with a perfect body. She had stridden into the ER a few years back on the heels of a hot story. Her stiletto heels had clicked on the hospital floor tiles like gunshots. Camelia had found her revolting.

She opened her eyes and stared at the television. The thick white bandages on the right side of her face obscured her vision.

"Due to the nature of the blasts, all apparently timed to go off at the peak rush hour when the LIRR and Amtrak trains were deep within tunnels, and..." the reporter paused, intently listening to her discreet Bluetooth headset.

A brief flash of giddiness crossed her face before it morphed into a mask of fake concern. "Oh my, it seems that we are now receiving confirmation of a series of bombings on the BART train systems in the San Francisco Bay Area. One of which may have damaged the tunnels that run under the San Francisco Bay. There are reports of capsized tunnels and flooding."

Camelia could hear a hum of voices rise outside of her room and someone say, "And thousands already dead in the New York train bombings, by God, somebody's gonna pay."

"Why look who is awake!" Camelia turned to see a portly, red-haired nurse beaming at her. "You are in Sinai—Queens, and I'm Jackie." Her hands were warm. "We have been waiting for you to wake up and tell us your name, Miss..."

"Camelia Garcia." Her mouth felt full of cotton, her words still garbled. "I'm a nurse, at Sinai Beth Israel."

"Well, Camelia, you are lucky to be alive. Not many made it out of those tunnels after the bombs went off. The fire afterward, well, I'm sure you remember that."

Camelia nodded. "I do."

"You have been through so much Camelia; I can't even imagine how you must be feeling. I'll let the doctor know you have woken up, and there's a team of trauma counselors who will be adding you to their rotation, but who else can I call for you? A friend? A family member?"

Camelia thought about it. Work would need to be notified, but more importantly, "I need to find Amy Perdue. Can you help me with that?"

"Sure, what's her phone number?"

"I'm sorry, I don't know her number."

The nurse nodded and picked up Camelia's chart. "You were brought in along with four others. They are all still here and I can check and see if there is an Amy listed."

"No, she wasn't on the train. Her husband was, and, well..." She could picture those last moments, the life fading from his eyes, "He didn't make it."

"Ah, I see." The woman set down the chart. "I can ask around. Is there anyone else I can contact for you? Family? Friends?"

Camelia thought of her mother, Esperanza, in a nursing home upstate. She had begun to show signs of Alzheimer's when Camelia was in middle school. And there had just been the two of them since Dad had died in a highway crash shortly after Camelia's fourth birthday. She barely remembered him.

The Alzheimer's had intensified by the end of high school and if it hadn't been for Camelia's excellent grades and the chance at a scholarship, she would have had no way to go to college. Mom no longer recognized her and the decision to place her in a home had been a hard, but necessary one.

The tenuous friendships made in high school washed away in the bustle of everyday life. The city had swallowed her up, and she fell into a routine of school, work, and then back home to the tiny efficiency apartment. One day didn't much differ from the next.

"No, there's no one."

Jackie clucked her tongue sympathetically, "Well then, let me see if I can find this Amy Perdue and we will go from there. Now you rest, Camelia, and I'll let Sinai know you are here."

Camelia thanked her, and the woman bustled away, moving quickly.

Hours later, after meeting with the doctor who informed her, she would need several surgeries to repair the injuries to her face, and being told how lucky she was to have survived when over 800 passengers had not, Camelia closed her eyes in exhaustion.

There had been a total of fifteen survivors—ten emerged on the Manhattan side, and the five in her group in Astoria. The train had not only been blown to hell and back by the bomb, which had capsized several sections of the tunnel, but it had also contained thermite, which burned so hot, that it had immolated the passengers trapped inside. The fire had turned the twisted remains of the train car into slag and made identifying the bodies impossible.

And it hadn't been the only one. Three other trains and two subway lines had been targeted and the simultaneous attacks had been carried out with precision. The news reports were still trying to put a total on the number of dead, but it was threatening to exceed the World Trade Center bombings, possibly even double that grim number.

"Excuse me, Miz Garcia?" A soft voice at the foot of her bed woke her from her half-doze. She opened her eyes to see a pretty blond woman clutching her purse. Behind the purse, Camelia could see the woman's rounded, protruding belly. Her eyes were red and swollen, and they had dark circles under them. This had to be Isaac's wife.

"Are you Amy?" Camelia asked in return, "Isaac's wife?"

The woman's chin trembled, "Yes, I am. I understand you were on the train that was in the East River tunnel. Is that right?"

"Yes. I was sitting near your husband at the time of the explosion."

Tears filled the woman's eyes then, and Amy's shoulders began to shake. "He's gone, isn't he?"

"I'm so sorry. Yes, I was there with him when he died. He asked me to find you."

The woman began to sob uncontrollably. Camelia reached out her hand, and Amy took it, squeezing hard.

"Please, tell me everything."

And Camelia did. The two women shared stories and tears and Amy hugged her and cried again.

Hours later, after the sun had slid behind the buildings, its orange glow lighting up a sky still tainted with the black smoke of death and loss, Camelia thought about Isaac's words.

"Tell them to leave New York and get out of this death trap."

Camelia had lived in New York her entire life. But there had been something in his words, in the fear in his voice. Camelia wondered if, standing there on the edge of this world, looking into the next, he had seen something she couldn't. And ever since the train tunnel, no matter how many times she scrubbed at her skin with her favorite lavender vanilla soap, her nose remained filled with the reek of burning bone.

Perhaps it is time to leave New York.

And the following week, after visiting one last time with her mother, that is just what Camelia did.

Other Mother

"Sometimes, you can't hide, no matter how hard you try."

Enid hid in the tall grass at the edge of the field and watched a column of ants move past her outstretched bare toes. It was late summer and everything was dry and crackling. Most of the insects, so numerous in the wet spring and early summer, were now hidden from view. Except for the solitary line of ants. Where were they going? Perhaps to the shade of the forest? She watched them pick their way around a large clod of earth, all marching in the same direction. Heading, it seemed, towards the trees.

She was far away from the farmhouse, too far to hear Other Mother, and that was as it should be. Mom was gone, replaced by Other Mother and Enid didn't know how long it would be until she returned. She had watched the change happen this time. Mom had stiffened when Enid handed her the scissors. A coldness had replaced the warmth and love that her mother opened each day with.

Mom would fling open the curtains, "Wake up, sleepyhead! It is a new day and full of possibilities!" And Enid would stretch and smile and be caught up in a warm hug.

When Other Mother made an appearance, the best possible option was to leave, to hide. It was safer that way. She sat at the edge of the cornfield in the tall, dry grass and watched the ants march and tried to ignore the heat of the sun beating down on her neck and arms. She would have a sunburn for sure.

Enid tried to imagine what it would be like to be Dorothy from The Wizard of Oz. Mom had read the book to her a few months ago, during a calm spell. As she read it, she had run her hand down Enid's long, dark hair, stroking it, her fingers occasionally catching on the smallest of tangles, working the hair with her fingers until the knot disappeared. Enid marveled at how Mom could read for so long without stopping, her fingers working at Enid's hair, her voice almost hypnotic in its ability to act out the various characters' voices. Enid would find herself lost in the story.

What would it be like to be picked up, sucked into a maelstrom of wind and rain and noise before finding yourself in a magical, far away land? Enid had her very own ruby slippers. Well, they were a pair of house slippers decorated with sparkling red sequins. They had been purchased on a road trip to Kansas City when they stopped off in Wamego and visited the Oz Museum. She would slip them on at night and pretend she was walking down the Yellow Brick Road. She wished she could be Dorothy. Instead, she was simply Enid Walters, aged seven years, on a farm near Atchison, Kansas.

A rustling caught her attention. Someone was moving through the cornstalks corn. Someone tall. The stalks had grown high, far above her head. The deeply tanned neck and face of her dad appeared. His face held concern. "I came looking for you, Half Pint. You weren't at supper."

Daddy had taken to calling Enid Half Pint, just like Laura Ingalls. Pa had called her Half-Pint in the Little House on the Prairie books that Mom had read her last year. He had listened to the stories right along with Enid, although sometimes he had dozed off. Enid couldn't help but giggle when he began to snore softly.

He handed her a sandwich, and she took it.

"You all right?"

Enid shook her head and looked away from him, trying not to cry.

"I didn't mean to make her mad, Daddy."

"Sure, and I know that, Half Pint. You haven't got a bad bone in your body. So, what did you say this time?" He asked, slowly easing his body down next to hers. His boot crossed the line of ants, disrupting the dirt, and with it the chemical trail they had laid. The back of the line scattered, and the ants began milling about in panic.

"I just handed her the scissors. That's all."

"Had she asked you for them?"

"No."

"Then why..."

Enid's eyes filled with tears. She had known Mom needed the scissors. She knew that she was going to reach for them in her sewing bag and that they wouldn't be in the right place. She knew, just as sure as if it had already happened, that Mom would reach too deep and find a stray pin instead. It would have stuck in her finger; it would have bled. She had seen it. But she had done it too soon. When the vision had hit her, she'd just got up and went to the sewing box and pulled out the scissors. She had placed them in Mom's hand, and returned to playing, like she normally would. But Mom wasn't sewing. Not then, at least. If Enid had been paying attention, she would have remembered that in the vision the short clock hand had pointed to the one and the long one to the twelve. If she hadn't been busy thinking of a story she had read in school on Friday, she would have avoided giving Mom the scissors until after supper, not at the moment she was layering the sandwich meat onto the homemade bread.

She told her dad the whole long explanation, just as she had Mom when Mom asked why she handed her the scissors.

"I think that I scared Mom and so she went away and Other Mother came out."

"Other Mother." He said it slowly, letting it roll off his tongue. "That's what you call it when Mom gets a little off?"

Daddy didn't understand. He didn't see what it was like when Mom went away and Other Mother came out. She hid it well. Mom did. She waited until he left a room, was out of the house, and then Other Mother came out and those same arms that could hug Enid could also grab, twist, slap, and more. It was a physical transformation. She walked harder; her step heavy on the floor. Her touch was iron-hard, and no emotion showed on her face. Enid knew to be scared when Other Mother came. She knew to run away if possible or to crouch down and let the blows come and just keep saying "sorry" until Other Mother stopped.

Enid nodded. A tear slid down her cheek. "I just wanted to be helpful. But I made her mad instead."

Her dad sighed. "I know, Half Pint. I know you didn't mean anything but good by it. She's just a little off today. I guess you had best avoid her for a while. She'll be better by dinnertime. These spells, they pass. Like yours did, a couple years back, we just need to be patient with her."

"Okay, Daddy." Enid gave her dad a brave smile, and he slipped a candy from his pocket, kissed her head and headed back to the house feeling more troubled than ever.

Enid's unexplained collapse into tears and sobbing two years back had lasted for days. Until then, everything with the little family had been perfect. The tiny infant they had found had grown into a vivacious, adorable preschooler. The walls were lined with photos of those happier moments.

Leo closed his eyes, envisioning the long hallway covered with pictures of them both holding her, their faces betraying their adoration.

The joy they had both felt after all attempts to find the girl's biological parents had failed and Enid was theirs to keep. She had been everything they ever dreamed of and more. But when that long week had hit, when the girl stopped laughing and began to cry, it was as if a switch had been flipped. She was old enough to speak by then, but she only shook her head and wailed, tears flooding down her cheeks. It had been terrifying at first, and then, at least for Deena, it had become something different, something far worse.

"I don't know how to explain it, Leo, but just seeing her like that, this feeling came over me, and all I could think was, not mine, not mine, NOT MINE." His wife's lips had twisted, her eyes haunted. "I didn't care about why she was crying, only that she suddenly didn't belong. She isn't ours, really. And maybe she doesn't belong here."

"Deena, listen to yourself. What do you mean she doesn't belong? She's ours, in the eyes of the law and in our hearts. We have loved her and hugged her and cared for her for over four years now! More than half of her life! If she doesn't belong here, where would she belong?"

Deena had said nothing, simply muttered, "Exodus 22:18."

How many times had he reached out and pulled Enid into his arms, only to say, "Your mom, she had a rough childhood?" An understatement, to be sure. Deena's childhood was one of the reasons why they had chosen to foster and adopt. Raised by her mother, a heroin addict and prostitute in Kansas City, Deena had spent the first ten years of her life saving her mother from choking on her own vomit while fending off the advances of her mother's customers. She had been at a summer camp, sponsored by one of her teachers, when a social worker arrived with the news her mother had died of an overdose. And after two years of bouncing between foster homes, Deena had eventually gone to her maternal grandparents' home and learned firsthand why her mother had ended up an addict.

Leo rubbed his chin as he walked. He'd picked up Deena hitchhiking, helped her find a job at the diner in town, and one thing had led to another. Five years of marriage, with not so much as a missed period, and Deena had been the one to suggest it. She'd been so excited, and so good with Enid, until the girl had her episode. After that, well, things had been different.

And it wasn't just Deena, Leo reasoned, Enid was different.

Even he had to admit that. After a week of crying, refusing food, and just rocking back and forth, she had suddenly stopped one day. Not just that, but she'd brought him a bolt.

"What's this for?" he had asked her.

The little girl had shrugged. "You're gonna need it. Just keep it in your pocket."

Later that day, the combine had started to shimmy from side to side while he was in the north field. When Leo stopped to take a look at it, he could see the hitch was missing a bolt. He reached into his pocket and pulled out the bolt Enid had given to him. It was a perfect match.

Sure, it had been unsettling. But it hadn't stopped there. Enid had woken a few weeks later, crying and sobbing again. Not so different from the first time except she kept asking for Leo's dad, her Gramps. The crying jag didn't last long. It stopped abruptly when the phone rang.

His brother James on the other end, "Dad died this morning, Leo, I just got word from the hospital that he had passed."

That was the first time that Deena had invoked the bible, and especially Exodus 22:18 and the quote about not suffering a witch to live, but it wouldn't be the last. The last two years had not shown a relief, but instead an acceleration in conflict. Enid continued to evidence premonitions that were often dark and foreboding.

Her best friend, True, watched her brother die in a freak accident days after Enid woke screaming from a nightmare. The neighbor's dog, a purebred Golden Retriever, contracted rabies shortly after Enid warned its owner not to touch it. And the decline of the country, the rumors of financial collapse and the increasing utility outages and food shortages, all of them appearing just as Enid described, her childish print filling a Hello Kitty journal with dire glimpses of the future. Each time she let one slip, Deena grew more fearful, and Leo was at a loss for what to do.

That night, after Deena had performed her perfunctory duties, and it was Leo's turn to read to Enid, she had sat there in bed, sober, her piercing green eyes tormented.

"Daddy, I'm afraid." She had rested her head against his chest, errant black curls tickled his nose. Her words chilled him. What had she seen now? And what would Deena say? He'd actually seen her raise a hand to the girl last week, descending sharp and fast in an open-handed slap that sent the girl sprawling. He'd intervened, but honestly, how could he keep her safe? He was in the fields most days.

"What did you see, Half Pint?" At least she had learned to keep her mouth shut around her mother. With him it still flowed out, although he'd pay a ransom to wish it away.

She was silent and that in itself was telling. Enid told him everything, all the bumps and warts. Her mother's anger and fear had caused her to retreat in confusion and hurt, but she needed him. He could see that. He didn't shy away. It was as if the child was holding down the brake on a revving engine. She couldn't unsee these things, and with it being summer, hell, with everyone so damned spooked by her visions, she was all alone. He was the only one she had to talk to.

"I saw men," she said finally, "Soldiers, but not the good kind. They're coming, Daddy. And you..." Her voice faltered, wobbled with unshed tears, "Daddy, I can't make the things I see change. No matter what I do, they still happen."

"I know, Sweetheart." He had to wonder if such things ran in families. With her raven-black hair, pale as milk skin, and piercing green eyes, she was out of place in this sunbaked land. Who were her people? Where had she come from, anyway? And who would have been willing to abandon a child such as this? She was beautiful, sweet, and Leo's love for her grew with each day.

Sure, he reasoned, *the visions scare the hell out of me, but it isn't her fault. It can't be.*

In this, Leo and Deena took opposing positions, which was no surprise when his wife's childhood was examined. Shuttled from one foster home to another before her maternal grandparents were found and she was handed over without so much as a by your leave. Their spare the rod and spoil the child philosophy hadn't worked so well with her mother, so they doubled down on it with Deena, all while hauling her to a church that felt more like a cult the scant handful of Sundays that he had stepped inside it. Speaking in tongues, flailing about in the aisles, and handling snakes had all been part of the weekly repertoire. It had been doses of fear and hatred and then more fear and hatred on its heels - twisting teachings of the bible into warped judgments on anyone who was different in any way. Leo shook his head. How could Deena embrace that twisted world? He couldn't understand it. Although he could imagine what his dad would say.

"We all got our ways of returning to our roots, son. Good or bad, we fall back on what we know." Leo missed his dad in ways that no words could properly describe.

"Daddy, I'll try to change it this time. Okay?" And her words suddenly sunk in.

"Enid, honey, did you see something happening to me?"

The child nodded, her fist clenching his shirt. "I keep seeing it, Daddy. But it happens when it's cold out, not hot like it is today. I keep praying for it to stay summer."

"I see." A black hole opened in his stomach, and he could feel it spiraling through his body. It wasn't fear for himself, not really. Leo had always been a pragmatist. He figured when God called, you went, and that was that. Instead, the blackness was fear of what might become of Deena and Enid. Most especially Enid, without him to soothe Deena's dark moods. And then it occurred to him. What if it was more than just him? What if Deena and Enid were on borrowed time as well? Somehow, the thought of anything happening to either of them was more than he could bear.

"What about you, Enid? What about you and Mom?" Heart in throat, he dreaded hearing more, but couldn't help but want to know.

"Me and Mom will be fine, but she's going to be Other Mother. It'll get worse, lots worse, way worse, Daddy." Her face was solemn, pinched with fear as she stared into the distance, her eyes not on the pretty pink dresser in the corner, but far in the future. "Mom will be Other Mother until she dies."

"Can you see what happens to you, Enid? Can you see your future?" Leo couldn't help asking, his heart breaking for the child. It was a curse, of that he was certain, but not in the way that Deena saw it.

Enid nodded, her face damp with sweat, a sour smell of fear rising from her damp hair.

"I see me all growed up, Daddy. But sad too, and," she shuddered, "like Other Mother 'cause seeing all of it and not being able to change it, it makes a person bad in the head." Her tiny fingers dug into his. "Maybe I can change it, Daddy." She choked back a sob. "I don't want you to die. I need you."

He hugged her tight. "I love you, Half Pint. And no matter what happens, no matter where you go or how long you live, I want you to remember that. Promise me that you will."

"I promise, Daddy."

She had tucked herself against him and said nothing more while he read to her from Harry Potter and the Chamber of Secrets. Deena had objected to the books, but Leo had overridden her.

"They teach powerful lessons of friendship and good, Deena. It isn't the worship of the dark arts and witchcraft like some churches are preaching."

Many days, after he had done the bare minimum needed to keep the farm running, they sat in the field together until the sun began to creep low in the sky. The smell of frying chicken would lure them back to the cool farmhouse and out of the summer heat. Deena would make a pie or even ice cream. His wife was calm, placid even, and Leo couldn't help but hope that whatever was coming, whatever dark horse was headed their way, Enid might be wrong for once. Who knew? Perhaps she could manage to change the doom that approached.

That evening, the power failed again, the condenser slowly spinning down, the cool air all too quickly replaced by the hot, humid Midwestern air. The next day it wasn't on, nor the next, nor the day after that. When the natural gas piped in from town stopped working two months later, they switched back to the propane tank, a relic from before Leo had modernized and had the farm added to the gas line when the small town expanded and suburbs were laid in not too far away. The pipes had been laid on the way to a large, sprawling suburb that had been half-built before the 2008 housing collapse and never finished. It had cost a small fortune to connect, and now it appeared that they were better off with the propane for as long as it might last.

"We got at least three months longer if we use it judiciously," Leo told his wife. "I'll go into town and see what the word is."

Enid had bitten her nails down to the quick in his absence. The days had grown cool, but not cold.

Please come back, Daddy, please come back.

And when he had appeared at the tree line, she had run through the stubbled field and thrown herself into his arms. She could feel the dark horror of what was coming, slowly, inexorably marching toward them.

As the days grew colder, Deena's mood turned dark as she watched Enid cling desperately to Leo. "That creature won't give you a minute's peace," she said one evening, hours after Enid had been sent to bed. Her tone was sharp. "She follows you closer than a lovesick cow."

"She's scared is all," he answered in the darkness, "She isn't bothering me."

"Well, it bothers me!" Deena snapped. "What's she seen? I know it's gotta be that, so what unholy vision did she have now?"

He hated talking to her when she was like this. All hard edges and sharp words, the fear of what she saw in the child, freezing the love in her heart. Leo wished he knew what to do to make it better, to change it in some way. He didn't have much time. From the way the child clung to him, her anxiety and desperation increasing, he knew his life could be measured in days.

"Deena, stop. Just..."

"I'm not the one who needs to stop, Leo Walters! What has she seen?"

"It's nothing, Deena, nothing at all. All of this will wash away and the world will right itself again." Even as he said the lie, he knew she saw through it.

Deena sucked in a breath. "Oh no. No, no, no, no, no. You can't leave me with her, Leo. She's got the Devil in her. It's an unholy thing to see what's coming. Unholy, against the will of God." She ran out of air, the last words spoken in a rasping whisper.

"Enid isn't unholy or evil, Deena. No matter what she sees." Leo's voice hardened. "And I'm begging you to see that. This little girl is the same little girl we found in that baby seat, spinning in the middle of that highway. The same one we nursed through the croup, through every nightmare, even the fractured tibia when she fell off the swing. Surely you can see that. She needs your love. You withhold it, and she will turn into the very thing you fear. Mark my words, she will."

Deena gasped, and he could feel her tremble in the bed next to him. "I'm scared, Leo."

He sighed and pulled his wife close. "You and me both. Promise me you will show her kindness, Deena, she's just a little girl."

And in the days that followed, Deena did her best. A week later, with Enid sick in bed with a cold, Leo headed out to town to see if he could barter for some cough syrup and aspirin to bring down the girl's fever. At a quarter past two that afternoon, Enid awoke with a banshee wail. In the distance, mother and child could hear gunfire. Tears rolled down Enid's cheeks. Deena, her hopes crumbling to dust, shushed Enid.

"You stop carrying on. There's no need for such a racket!"

The child continued to keen, her body folded up, her entire person a sculpture of grief. She hadn't been this bad off since the week all the visions had started, some two years past. And Deena knew then, her heart crumbling to dust in her chest, that Leo was gone. There was a snap, a bowstring break in her soul as she watched Enid sob uncontrollably in the bed. Deena could feel everything good and kind wither up and dissolve to dust along with her heart.

If Enid had been looking, she would have seen the transformation come over her mother. It was more than mental or emotional, it was a physical transformation. One moment, it was Mom, her mother, the woman who had a place in all but her earliest memories. The next, it was Other Mother. The warm brown eyes went dark with pain and rage. Her body stiffened, hardened, her skin no longer warm and soft, her hands now bony, painfully wrapped around Enid's wrist, ice cold.

"Stop that unholy noise, you and your visions, you have brought this to pass!" A hard slap knocked the girl off of her bed and onto the wood floor. It hadn't been the first time Other Mother had hit her. It was, however, the beginning of a descent into darkness that Deena never recovered from. Enid marked it as the moment when Mom went away, never to return, and Other Mother emerged. As if the good and light had not just been locked away, but purged from her mother's body, until only darkness remained.

The days were cold, Enid's world stuck in the cycle of the seasons, held in place by duty and dread. She had seen what would come next, and in a way, Other Mother had seen it too. Especially in the last year, confined to her bed, the curtains closed in a dark, oppressive room. She couldn't say much of anything, grunts and gestures with the one hand that hadn't frozen and curled up in the wake of the powerful stroke from the year before.

Enid wondered why she stayed. Every year, as the spring thaw came sliding through, warming the frozen wasteland that had once been a thriving farm, she asked herself why she stayed. For Daddy, mostly. The memory of his kindness, his love, still strong ten years later. And partly for the woman Other Mother had once been - a kind woman who had held her and rocked her at night. Enid thought of leaving, but despite no words of love, and certainly no kindness, her dreams still showed her that Mom was there, inside of Other Mother. And especially now, in this past year, Other Mother was really nothing but a shell of the monster her mother had become. Enid could see both of them trapped inside the body that could no longer speak, or move, or care for itself.

The weak light of an early spring dawn brought a groan from Other Mother's room and Enid turned from stoking the fire in the old stove.

She fixed a small smile on her face and marched into the room. "Morning Mom, how are you today?"

The contorted figure in the bed groaned, her mouth struggling to shape a sound. "Naa... nah.. nat..." She had been repeating this for days now.

"Nat?" Enid didn't know a Nat in town and certainly couldn't remember any family member or family friend by that name. She had woken this morning with a deep certainty. The woman who had dominated her life for as long as she could remember, first in the form of love and protection, then as a creature to fear, and finally as an object to care for - she was dying.

Enid could see the end coming. She had seen it a decade ago and now, finally, it was here. It was a dark cloud of certainty, approaching with deliberation and intent. Mom, or Other Mother, hell, Deena - her life was measured in moments, in hours. This Enid had seen for far longer than she cared to admit. It was what had kept her here on the farm, long after Daddy was taken from them. The dream of a life he had wanted for his small family long gone. Evaporated with invading troops, a bullet to the chest, and the fallow fields that followed. She had stayed, partly out of duty, but also because she had seen a clear, defined end to it all.

She perched herself on the edge of the bed and leaned in to wipe her mother's face with a clean cloth. Deena closed her eyes for a moment, seconds ticking by as she seemed to relax, even be soothed, by Enid's gentle touch. Despite everything, the blows, the curses, and now this complete helplessness - Enid had stayed. After all, her last fragile link to Daddy lay in the bed. Enid was no longer a child, yet some part of her needed to honor what Daddy had always seemed to stand for - peace, love, and commitment. She hadn't handled it with grace, not always, especially when Other Mother had raised her hand in anger or screamed excerpts from the bible at her, but she had done her best.

In some ways, it was more than that. It was destiny, just as her vision of the end of the world, the one filled first with plague and finally with a fireball that promised to scorch the earth like no other, was coming. She could see it so clearly.

"Nat... Natal... yuh..." The wretch in the bed groaned again and her left hand flopped and twisted on the bedsheet, a single bony finger raised shaking in the air. Enid watched her, following the finger as it rose in a spasm, shaking, pointing to the small chest in the corner of the bedroom.

"Do you need something from the chest, Mother?"

"Nat... Nat... all... yuh." The finger jabbed into the air for emphasis before collapsing back onto the bedsheet. A sheen of sweat had formed on Other Mother's face from the effort.

Enid found herself rising, moving with purpose to the chest. It was locked, the key missing, and the wood chest had strong hinges. "It's locked and I don't have the key, Mother."

Her mother said nothing, eyes closing from the effort she had expended, a tiny slick of drool sliding down her slack jaw.

And Enid suddenly felt energized. The key, it had to be in the room, it just had to be! She shoved open the curtains, dust motes dancing in the rays of the sun that shone through. Other Mother didn't flinch, her eyes were shut, her breathing shallow and erratic. Enid glanced at her and began to search the room methodically. It had to be here somewhere. And Mother had wanted her to open the chest, practically ordered her to do it. She opened drawers, rifled through Daddy's now moldering belongings, still in the drawers they had been in since the day he died. Enid pawed through underwear, then Mother's jewelry box, before finally finding the key tucked beneath a lock of hair. Hers, it seemed, a few jet-black wisps of curls with a pale pink ribbon tied around it.

The key fit into the hole with ease, and Enid turned it first to the right and then to the left, stopping when she heard the click of the lock releasing. A glance back at Mother, who lay there unmoving, barely breathing, her eyes shut. Enid opened the chest. A puff of dust and stale air, along with a faint odor of baby powder. Inside of the chest was another lock of hair tied with pink ribbon, along with a note in Deena's hand:

First haircut!

Below was her christening gown. Although they had rarely attended church, especially after her visions created a gulf between her parents and the other townsfolk, Enid knew she had been christened. Dad had mentioned it, partly in rebuttal to Mother's fears, that she was possessed by an evil spirit that sent her visions.

Something crackled then, deeper in the chest, and it took some digging to find the source. A yellowing newspaper clipping slipped into a clear plastic cover.

Mystery Baby in Car Seat Identified

The toddler was still fastened in her car seat in the middle of the Highway 49 just outside Topeka when it was discovered by a couple who hail from Atchison, Kansas last week. The couple called police after the discovery and the wife swore the car seat was still turning in a slow arc in the roadway when the couple's truck approached it.

"She was so tiny, and I thought it was a doll at first, she was still asleep!"

The couple, who had recently completed foster care training, were able to take the child home as an emergency placement until the biological parents are located. Yesterday, Cibil Zradce was identified as the child's mother. Cibil is currently in custody and awaiting a competency hearing pending her release from The Oaks Mental and Rehabilitative Facility outside of Topeka, Kansas. The child will remain in state custody until Ms. Zradce is fully evaluated.

Enid took in a deep breath. "This is me, isn't it?" She glanced back at Mother, who lay unmoving in the bed.

She dug further.

Two more articles appeared.

Patient Disappears from Mental Health Facility

Authorities report that a patient from a mental health facility in Los Angeles, California, with ties to the baby found on Highway 49, has somehow escaped custody.

Cibil Zradce is not considered to be dangerous, but anyone seeing her should call authorities immediately. She is described as medium height with a thin build. Black hair and green eyes.

Missouri authorities were advised that Cibil may try to return to her child, who is in state custody at this time. Her mental state is reported as unstable, confused, and manic.

And nearly a year later...

Child Found on Highway Adopted by Local Couple

The infant found in a car seat in the middle of a highway has been adopted by the couple who found her.

The local couple has requested privacy for their child...

She could barely breathe. The air in the room was stifling. The final document was a birth certificate, listing her name, Enid Walters, along with the original certificate. Enid scanned it. The mother's name, Cibil Zradce, was listed and the name of the father was blank. A baby girl, weighing six pounds two ounces, 18 inches in length, named Natalia Zradce.

"I'm Natalia, aren't I, Mother? The baby in the car seat?"

The only answer was a soft rattle, the last breath of a woman who had both comforted and terrorized her for most of her seventeen years. Deena lay unmoving on the bed and her eyes, once closed, had opened into a fixed stare. She was gone.

Enid couldn't breathe, couldn't think here. She gathered up the papers, slid them back into the chest, and lifted it all up. It was heavier than she expected. She staggered out of the thick, dead air of the bedroom, down the hall, through the living room and out into the gathering sunlight on the front porch. Bright beams of light lit up the documents in her hands, and she sucked in mouthfuls of the clean morning air.

Natalia, not Enid.

That was her name.

Her mother, lost.

Her adopted family all dead.

"I'm Natalia." She said, the word sounding odd, different on her tongue. Had her mother sung her to sleep? Had she whispered her name in the dark and held her close?

There was so much she didn't know.

Natalia looked towards the road. A few weeks ago, a town meeting had announced that the war was over and the Reformation had begun. Washington was gone, lost to a nuke, just like Austin, but now the provisional government of the Reformed United States of America had been formed in Chicago. Things were changing.

She turned her gaze to the barn, the fallow fields, and the farm that had been her world since she could remember. She didn't belong here. She wasn't Enid Walters. Instead, she was Natalia Zradce. It felt as if she had been reborn.

By the time the sun set in the sky, she was ready. A pack on her back carried everything she needed, and the fires had been set. By the time the townsfolk saw it, she would be long gone. The walls of the empty barn and the house blazed up in the gathering darkness, the fire gaining speed, fast, hot. Natalia Zradce walked away. Away from the farm, away from the small town of Atchison, and onto the smooth highway leading east. She walked away from the life that Enid Walters had, that Deena and Leo had, and into her own. As she did, she hummed softly, a lullaby, one filled with nonsensical words she could barely remember on her lips. Perhaps Cibil was still alive. Perhaps she wasn't. But Natalia knew one thing for sure. She knew who she was for the first time in her life. And that was enough.

There was darkness coming. Darkness and then fire. "Darkness and death, cleansed by fire," she whispered as she walked. "It's coming."

99 Problems

"This is the way the world ends."

"I dunno, Cal. What do we need with them, anyway?" Donnie slid lower in the bucket seat and stared at the house. "And what's for sure the old man has even got 'em?"

The plan was simple. Most of them were. Cal wasn't particularly bright, but he was sneaky and good at working out solutions to pesky problems. He excelled at finding weed when they were running low. And he could slip a six-pack out of the store right under the clerk's hawk-eyed stare when what was left over from their meager paychecks wouldn't cover it. Hell, given a chance, he could get them a hooker to share and pay her off in meth he'd made in the basement a few months back.

This, however, this was bigger than rolling some dude fresh off the farm with more homegrown than sense or stealing beer from a guy who didn't own the place. This was stepping over the precipice into dark territory.

"Shit, Donnie, don't wuss out on me now." Cal fiddled with the settings on the radio. No one was talking. The music was on an endless loop, ever since the news out of Austin. As the power outages continued, the stations were dropping off one by one, vanishing from the atmosphere as if they had never truly existed.

If you're having girl problems, I feel bad for you, son
I got 99 problems and a bitch ain't one.

"Damn, this a fucking great song." Cal turned up the volume, and the speakers gave short static bursts. Cal ignored this, slapping his hand on the steering wheel in time.

"Cal, c'mon man, let's just go back home. I don't got a good feeling about this."

Tip my hat to the sun in the west,
Feel the beat right in my chest.

Cal turned and stared at him, his eyes turning mean like they did when he didn't get his way. And everyone paid the price when Cal didn't get his way. Donnie looked at the floor, but he could feel Cal's eyes on him.

"Wake the fuck up, Donnie, the world has changed, and we gotta change with it. We need those guns and pretty soon we're gonna need food and a hell of a lot more."

At the crossroads a second time,
Make the devil change his mind.

"It's just a power outage, Cal, they'll fix it soon." Donnie protested, knowing even as he said it that it wasn't that simple. The power had been out for two days now, and there had been no crews on the ground, no one fixing whatever was broken.

And more than that, there were no cops, no government vehicles. Hell, not even the 24 Independence bus was running. And while some of the more tight-knit communities through the metro had come together and tried to fill the hole left after the desertion of the police, forming citizen watch groups, the rundown street that Cal and Donnie lived on was certainly not one of them.

It's a pound of flesh, but it's really a ton
99 problems and a bitch ain't one.

"Look, if you're gonna be a pussy about it, Donnie, you can just stay here. I mean, shit, I wouldn't want you to have to break a nail or pee your little panties." Cal sneered.

Donnie flushed. "I'm just saying maybe this isn't the best place to do it." He looked out of the windows. There wasn't any trash, not like on their block, and the houses were quiet and dark.

"We go up north of Independence and we'll get our asses handed to us," Cal snapped. "They got something to protect."

"What and this guy doesn't? Look at his house!" The house, its outline dim in the gloom, was large and well-built. Cal hadn't been inside it, though, only Donnie, when he was contracted to do some work there installing a tile floor in the spacious kitchen. Which was, of course, how this had all started. The man's sign, in the window of his side door no less, had been the giveaway.

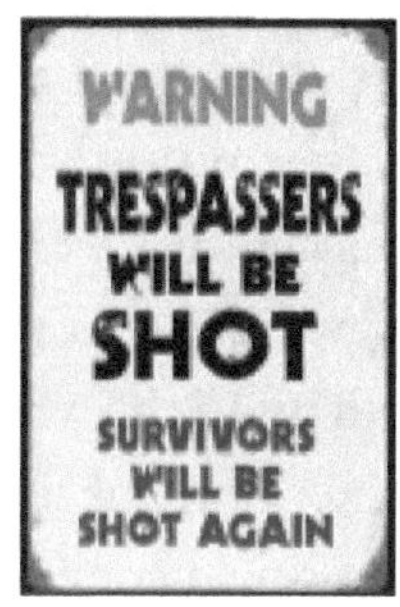

IF YOU'RE HAVING GIRL problems, I feel bad for you son,

I got 99 problems and a bitch ain't one

"I'll bet he's got plenty of booze and cash besides the guns." Cal replied, ignoring Donnie's last comment. "Look, we need those guns. Look around you Donnie, this shit isn't getting better, and it's gonna get a lot worse. The water and gas still work, but for how long? Hell, Price Chopper was cleaned out of everything except the goddamn produce section and half the workers there were running scared. We need to defend ourselves."

"You got a gun already," Donnie pointed to the revolver sitting between them.

"Yeah, and it's got four bullets in it and the gun shops were cleaned out afore the grocery store was!" Cal barked back at him, "We need this, Donnie, or we're gonna be deader than doornails in a few weeks' time without those guns."

99 problems,

But a bitch ain't one.

Donnie sucked in a deep breath and blew it out, "Fine. I'll do it."

"Yeah?" Cal grinned at him.

"Yeah."

Cal reached over and punched his arm. "Cool, let's do it. Just like we talked about, right?"

"Right."

Cal had come up with the plan after he had driven by the area, nice and slow, during the day. No one had been out even then. Folks were staying inside now. Not like they had been in the first few days, when the garbage trucks were still picking up the trash each week and the bus was still running. Now, with the lights off and fall quickly approaching, there were plenty of rumors, but no real, hard facts. Still, folks stayed inside, checking their smartphones that were slowly running out of juice and debating whether to run a generator which would give them a connection to the world but draw all the wrong attention in the process.

Yesterday had brought news of a nuke in Austin. Shortly after that, all but a handful of radio stations had gone silent. The tv stations were all off the air and there wasn't just a general sense of unease anymore, now it was more one of terror.

They were on their own.

Like broken glass under my feet

I could lose my mind in this heat

The sound of their footsteps crunching over gravel was far too loud. Cal hissed at Donnie, "Remember to stick to the plan." Then he disappeared into the shadows.

They had gone over it back at their cheap rental house off of St. John. Cal had said, "I'll take the way around back and set myself up around the corner of that back door. You go on up to Old Man Nichol's door and get him to come out."

That had been Cal's plan, and Donnie had gone along with it. As he approached the door, he couldn't help wondering exactly how he was going to get the guy to come outside where Cal could get the drop on him.

He knocked on the door.

Looking for the prize, but I don't want blood

I order one drink, then I drink the flood

One minute stretched into another and he knocked again. "Hey, Mr. Nichols, you there?"

"Who's there?" Donnie heard Nichols' voice on the other side of the door.

"Uh, it's uh me, Donnie. I worked on your kitchen floor this past spring and you said to come by if I, uh, if I ever needed more work." As the words left his mouth, he realized how stupid it all was. This guy wasn't going to let him in. Why would he?

Rather improbably, he began to hear the locks turning, chains rattling seconds before the door opened. The older man stared at him. “Donnie? You do realize it's almost midnight, right? You okay?”

And now, staring at Nichols again, Donnie understood why Cal had been so hot to take this guy down. Especially after Nichols had given Donnie a ride home all those months ago. He hadn't really thought about it at the time, but now, staring at the man again, he could see what Cal had been hinting at.

The smile on Nichols' face was more than friendly, a lot more. So was the hand he had placed on Donnie's arm, the sensual slide down it, like a woman would do if she was looking to get some.

Donnie suddenly remembered Cal questioning him about Nichols.

“Any signs of a woman ‘round there?” He had asked. And there hadn't been. Donnie had just figured that Cal wanted to make sure there were no woman or kids to get hurt.

“He's all artsy fartsy and shit,” Donnie had told Cal, “Like the carved Roman statues and naked guys and all that.” And Cal had rolled his eyes, shook his head and laughed.

Well, you can come inside, but your friends can't come

99 problems and a bitch ain't one

Before Donnie could say anything to Mr. Nichols, Cal stepped forward, the weapon in motion, hammer back, the pistol pressed against Nichols' forehead.

“What the hell!” Nichols squawked in surprise as Cal shouldered past Donnie, backing the man up until he slammed against a cabinet on the opposite end of the small enclosed porch.

“Shut your mouth,” Cal said, pressing the gun hard against Nichols' forehead. He tipped his head at Donnie, “Donnie, get your ass inside and shut the door.”

Donnie did as Cal instructed, hands shaking as he twisted one of the deadbolts into place. Rolling some kid for weed and a handful of cash was one thing, but this was far different. They were in this man's house. A house is a man's castle.

“Where are the guns, old man?”

“What guns?” Nichols gasped as Cal jabbed harder with the revolver.

"Cal, wait, just let me talk to him."

"Nah, Donnie, I got this." He sneered at the older man, "Fuckin' freak. You hot for Donnie here? Stop looking at him, you look at me. I'm the one with the gun to your head. Now you tell me, where are the guns?"

"I don't know what you..." His words were interrupted by Cal punching him hard in the gut, knocking the air out of him.

"Fine, we'll play it your way, old man. I bet that shit is upstairs, right?"

And then Cal made a mistake. He looked away. It was just a second, and that was all it took for the man to shove him hard, and then run from the room.

"Shit, he's getting away!" Cal shouted, no longer worried about making too much noise as he stumbled, struggled to regain his balance, and then pivoted and ran after Nichols.

Donnie stood there, unsure of what to do, the light from the oil lamp that Nichols had set by the door flickering. Cal turned, slowing for a short second before he disappeared from sight, "Come on Donnie, move your ass, we got to catch up to him!"

Rooms, doorways, curtains, and old furniture—it all passed with a blur—the darkness of the house far more intense than the dark of the night outside. Here there were no stars, no moon, only Donnie, Cal and Nichols, playing a nasty game of keep away. And they were running out of rooms.

It was Cal who found it first. The door ajar betrayed the light flickering within. "Holy shit, Donnie, he's got a goddamn arsenal in this room."

It was the last thing he said, past gurgling. The bullet caught him in the throat and he collapsed like a sack of potatoes on the immaculate wood floor.

Nichols stepped out of the shadows and pointed his gun at Donnie, "I liked you, kid. And I never would have hurt you. But this, you have brought this to my door. And what am I to do?"

Donnie put his hands up. "Mr. Nichols, I'm sorry. I should have never told Cal about you. It was wrong and I..."

"It's best you don't talk right now, Donnie, I'm liable to shoot where you stand and I already have this friend of yours blood fixing to stain my wood floors."

Cal gurgled and bubbled, the blood flowing freely from his throat. His gun had fallen from his grasp when he was shot, and Nichols had his foot firmly over it, ignoring Cal's efforts to claw his way toward it.

Nichols shook his head and clucked, "What to do, what to do?"

Cal had almost reached the gun and Donnie watched him with horrified fascination as Cal reached not with his right hand to grab the gun, but with his left, which held his Muela. He raked it down the back of Nichols' leg and the older man screamed, and Nichols' leg buckled, blood spraying. He fell to the floor, the gun booming in his hand as he collapsed.

If you're having girl problems, I feel bad for you, son

I got 99 problems and a bitch ain't one

Donnie felt a searing pain in his chest and struggled to understand why. Nichols was on the ground, Cal's knife cleaving gouges in his flesh, gurgling sounds from both of them as Cal put the last of his energy into murdering the man whose house they had invaded.

Donnie looked down, confused, at the bloom of red, that spread slowly from a hole in his chest. His eyes glazed, his vision blurred, and he felt cold.

So cold.

Falling to the ground felt as if it were happening to someone else. More that gravity changed, morphed, and broke the laws of physics. The floor came up and greeted him in a rush. He could hear the tchotchkes clattering and breaking as they tumbled off of the side table, victims of his bulk collapsing onto the fancy spinets and arches of a Victorian era.

The floor was cold, hard, unyielding.

I got 99.

The blood pooling on his chest was filling his lungs, and he gasped, trying desperately to suck in air and finding only blood. There wasn't pain so much as what felt like a heavy rock pressing on his chest. No matter how much he tried to suck a breath in, there was simply not enough air.

99.

The darkness, which had been nibbling at the edges of his vision, now was rushing in. From far away he could the pounding and yelling. A splintering of wood from the door being broken down. Voices. The floor shook imperceptibly as others entered the large, rambling house.

99.

"What the hell happened here?"

99.

"Oh man, they got Nichols! Shit!"

99 problems.

Another voice, "Are they all dead?"

A foot nudged Donnie, and he tried to speak. He wanted to tell them he hadn't wanted to do it, that it hadn't been his idea, but the words were just bubbles drowned in blood.

But a bitch ain't one.

"This one's still kicking, but not for long."

99.

Donnie couldn't see anything now. Instead, he felt lighter than his body, his soul slipping from the flesh and bone that lay dying on the floor.

"A hidden door? Holy shit, Nichols was hiding the mother lode in guns! I can't believe it. He kept telling us that sign was just bullshit. We could have handed it to those fuckers who came barreling through last week with the AKs. Could've handed them their asses. That stingy old piece of shit!"

99 problems and a bitch ain't one.

And then Donnie was gone.

All Roads Leading to Austin

"Hope is a dance with the impossible."

Jacob

The heat of the late summer was far worse here in the Midwest. He was used to a drier heat, and the humidity in the air here just sucked the energy out of a man. His men were lagging behind, their steps slowed by exhaustion. Jacob wiped away the sweat beading on his forehead and eyed the approaching storm. It was humid, and the clouds were gray and ominous. Thunder rumbled in the distance and occasionally he could see the twist of light strobe through the thick, roiling layers. It was a bitch of a storm headed their way. It would cool them off. It already was now that the wind had picked up, pushing his damp hair away from his forehead. He needed a haircut. Hell, he needed to stop walking and fighting and watching what was left of his unit die for no damn good reason.

This town, Clinton, was a destroyed shell. Most of the buildings were either partially collapsed, burned, or mere skeletons, reaching fire-blackened brick chimneys to the sky. After weeks of fighting in June between the Western Front and the Allied South, most of the inhabitants were either dead or had fled. His orders were to clear the east side of town, confirm that the Western Front had moved on out of the area, and reconnoiter with Bravo unit before nightfall. Jacob just wanted to sit down and sleep. But sleep brought nightmares, dreams of a blond-haired boy, mushroom clouds, and radiation warnings.

His men were spread out, dog tired and stretched to their limits, thanks to the endless muggy heat and meager rations. Scouts hadn't found any food locally either. The shelves of stores had been stripped bare for nearly a year now, and it was every man, or soldier, for himself.

He had heard talk that most of the men in Tango unit had melted away in the night, disappearing like cockroaches under cover of darkness, likely heading for home or whatever was left of it. He wondered if it was time to do the same. Could JJ and Nancy still be alive? He knew how unlikely it was. But still, his heart wanted to hope against hope that they were both still out there. Divorced or not, he loved her still. No one else had come close to giving him the feeling he had when he was with her.

Nancy hadn't wanted to be a military wife. She'd wanted more. She'd wanted to finish her Master's in Art History, and who was he to hold her back? When the end had come, she had already moved to Austin and served him papers. He'd managed to come and visit and see them as often as he could on leave. But it wasn't enough for little JJ. He would cry and beg him not to leave at the end of the visit.

They had been too close to ground zero. Likely still asleep on that sunny Saturday morning, when the nuke blew a crater into the northeast section of the city and annihilated anything within a twelve-block radius of the Arts District and the University of Texas. That's where Nancy was a student, just a year left until her degree that she had fought so hard for. He wanted to believe it had been quick, that his boy hadn't suffered, and that he hadn't died screaming like the scores of others who were farther away from the detonation site. It still gave him nightmares. The carnage that they had showed on the enormous viewscreens in the Fort Hood Commons before the blackouts took out the internet had haunted him ever since.

His scheduled leave had been that morning. He had stood there, bag in hand, planning on hitching a ride with friends after missing the train out the night before when the news hit.

"All roads leading to Austin have been closed until further notice. Authorized medical and emergency response personnel only are allowed in."

The bag had dropped from his numb hands, the ground rushing up to meet his knees, the air leaving his lungs. Hollowed out, empty. His family was gone.

Leave had been canceled; all troops recalled. Not all the men had returned. He knew of plenty who had family in Austin, and had likely been there at the wrong time, good men that he would never see again.

What am I doing here, anyway? How does this solve anything? We fight each other, and for what?

He knew the company line, had parroted it back to the senior officers, shouted "Yes, sir!" and told his men to keep going. But as the days had turned into weeks, and weeks into months, it had all seemed so pointless. Communications were down, and their orders, when they received orders at all, were often conflicting. The reality was, they weren't fighting an outside enemy, they were fighting themselves. And those were battles that no one could win.

Nancy

Nancy woke from the dream, a scream dying on her lips as she sat up in the pre-dawn darkness. Uncle Ray stared at her from his well-worn seat in the kitchen.

"Y'alright?"

"Bad dream." Jacob, alone in a wash of radioactive hell, bleeding, burned. The vision of it hung there, painted in her mind, the taste of ash in her mouth. She should have called him. But she hadn't, and now he was gone, lost in the blast or the radiation that followed. All it would have taken was a phone call. The father of her child, one of the best men she had ever known, gone.

Uncle Ray coughed. It sounded wet, thick. He always sounded worse in the morning. Eventually, given a shot of strong black coffee to loosen it up and he'd cough up a mass or two, thick yellow globs shot through with blood. On a bad day, it would be mostly blood. He should be in a hospital, but since the blackouts, and the shortages, and then the Very Bad Day, the hospital was no longer a place you went to get better.

The Very Bad Day had struck more than two months ago. And Nancy had given thanks to God every day after, for where they had been, and where they had not been, when the nuke struck Austin.

Over a million dead, probably twice that.

The fate they would have suffered, at least for her and JJ, that close to Ground Zero. It would have been quick, but still. She had seen what it had been like for those who weren't as close. Burns that wouldn't heal, hair that slipped from scabbed heads in clumps, blowing on the floors of Davis Medical Center like listless furballs, impossible to keep up with.

She did her best, though. When not changing bedpans or scrubbing the sheets clean by hand now that the power was out, she pushed a broom and tried to round up the errant hairs. It seemed to her that those strands of hairs had deserted their posts, leaving behind hollow-eyed, bald skeletons that did not seem to notice their absence. For that matter, they appeared to see nothing, eyes staring and lost, their radiation-sick bodies wasting away before Nancy's eyes.

There were dozens of them. Specters that had driven, walked, even been carried from the highways and byways leading from Austin. They had spread out, like a sickness, meandering through the country like broken homing pigeons. One foot in front of the other.

JJ mumbled in his sleep and turned over, curling up against the table leg. His hair was slick with sweat, his cheeks red from the heat. Nancy could see it was early still, the sun a weak specter sliding up into the sky, barely pushing its way through the thick cloud cover. It was hot, stifling in the small single-wide mobile home, and she sat up slowly, her back aching from the rough bed on the floor.

"I made coffee." Uncle Ray coughed again, turning away, grabbing for the handkerchief he kept in his shirt pocket. His bony frame shook, convulsed, and Nancy winced at the rattling sound that accompanied each of his breaths, in and out, in and out. He bent over, let the cough take him and gave himself to it, almost retching. He spit into the handkerchief.

"Christ."

"You watch your tongue, Raymond Withers," Aunt June said, tottering out of the bedroom at the far end of the narrow trailer. Her face was a pasty shade of gray and she said it halfheartedly, as if it took too much out of her to say more. "We give thanks to God, not use His name for curses." She looked for a moment as if she would fall, gently swayed back and forth, then slowly regained her equilibrium, and shuffled to the easy chair. It occupied the corner opposite of the table that JJ still slept restlessly underneath.

"Where's your oxygen, Auntie?"

"Out."

"What? But we got that last Tuesday! It was supposed to be full!"

"Well, it wasn't. I knew it felt light when you brought it in. I took it easy on it, just like you said," she paused, caught her breath and continued, "Ain't nothin' to be done 'bout it. I'll manage."

Nancy shook her head. "I'll see if I can't get another. Maybe if they pay me less in potatoes for my work, I can ask for an extra can. You need it, Auntie."

June reached out her hand and touched her niece's arm. "Don't you... dare... that child needs food more than I need that... silly oxy... gen. You hear me?"

Hard, hot tears pricked at Nancy's eyes, "Yes, ma'am, I hear you."

June and Ray had raised her, without complaint, after the mother she barely remembered had died of leukemia. She had been four years old when the social worker had brought her to the small one-bedroom trailer, looked it over with a jaded eye and said, "Kids are made of rubber, just let her sleep on the floor under the table. She doesn't need a room of her own." She had leaned close, speaking low, but Nancy had heard her all the same. "Better with you than with strangers and a ward of the state. You got no idea how bad it can be." And they had just nodded and taken her in.

It felt as if Uncle Ray and Aunt June had been sickly in one form or another all of her life, but not this bad, never this bad. They had moved slowly, were in their 60s by the time Nancy entered their lives. That first fall, when it was time for kindergarten, Nancy had held June's hand and walked with her into Midlands Elementary on the southern edge of Elkins. Everyone else had young moms and dads, but Nancy's had white hair and wrinkles. It was a different way of life. Simpler, with no frills, but they had loved her and made sure she grew up healthy, with decent clothes on her back and food in her belly. Sleeping under the table hadn't been that bad, wasn't bad now, and JJ loved it. He had drawn stars on the underside of the battered Formica table and called it camping.

They had taken her in and never once complained. When Uncle Ray had called three months ago and said Auntie was in the hospital, Nancy had dropped everything, picked up JJ from his daycare and drove straight on through to Elkins, West Virginia. They had only stopped for gas, fast food meals, and what had felt like every damned rest stop along the way because JJ still couldn't hold it for long. She hadn't even thought to call Jacob until it was far too late.

They had just checked Auntie out, driven her home and settled her in her easy chair when the reports had started coming in. Chaos, screaming and crying from the folks in the park as they watched the mushroom cloud over and over and over again on the television. JJ had snuggled close, despite the muggy heat, and whispered, "It's a very bad day, Mom. It's a Very Bad Day."

The entire cell phone array was down within minutes and it wasn't long after that the rolling blackouts started. Each one longer than the one before, until finally the power shut off completely. How many times had she tried to call Jacob over the next few weeks? Hundreds? The calls wouldn't go through, and one of the power surges that had accompanied one of the last blackouts had taken out the phone and Uncle Ray's computer, the A/C unit, and the television in one go. They were down to a radio that produced nothing but static. And no word from Jacob, none.

Nancy sighed, staring at her son on the floor. JJ asked every day, as hopeful as the day before. She hadn't told him that his dad had told her he would be visiting them in Austin, that he had bought the train tickets a month before the nuke and swore he'd be there. She had forgotten all of it in the panic of getting to Auntie's side in the hospital, scared she would lose her. And then, staring in horror at the images on the screen she had been afraid to tell JJ his father was dead, hoping beyond hope that he would magically appear, walking down the cracked macadam with his duffel bag in one hand, clothed in the familiar fatigues.

The Very Bad Day, Nancy sniffed, JJ's name for it had stuck. And not just with Uncle Ray and Aunt June, but the rest of the scattershot inhabitants of Happy Hollow Trailer Park, which was neither happy nor in a hollow. With the loss of power over a month ago, many of the park's residents had packed up their station wagons or trucks and headed away.

"I got family out West."

"I'm a fixin' to see how Canada is right 'bout now."

"I hear the power is on in New York."

And slowly they scattered, sometimes in the morning, others in the dark of night, but most when the sun was high in the sky. JJ, who was as outgoing and gregarious a child as Nancy had ever seen, saw most of them off, waving goodbye to the frail and weak Longbottoms and their disabled daughter. Hollering "Safe travels!" to Jolene Nichols, who made the best angel food cake in the world, and the Larabies who were determined to find their youngest son.

"Not all the roads leading to Austin can be closed. He's at the University there, studying architecture, and we'll be back once we fetch him." Amber Larabie had said, her face determined, a small brave smile on her lips even as her eyes betrayed the truth of it. Their son had been in campus housing, so close to the epicenter that even his bones weren't dust. A brief millisecond and hundreds of thousands of sleeping, innocent people had vaporized.

They would never find him. And chances being what they were, they would never come back, either.

Nancy looked down at Aunt June's gray face, which held so many familiar lines and wrinkles. June smiled up at her grandniece, "Be a dear and fetch me a cup of that black tar Raymond's brewed up. That will put some power in me."

Nancy fetched her the cup, added two sugars, and noted how low the packets were in the bowl. A few more days left if she went without any, but they would run out of coffee before that. Hell, they would run out of everything by tomorrow night. She closed her eyes, her heart stranded in the dream of her ex-husband, terrified she would have to choose between eating and buying more oxygen for June, and wondering if she would be digging two graves in the next few months.

Jacob

The storm hit, fast and strong. It had been threatening it for an hour, perhaps longer, the dark clouds massing, rotating in the brisk breeze, the branches on the trees swaying. There had been a battle here, not long ago, and most of the houses were in ruins - burned and broken. The rain was falling, thick drops, and there was little or no cover. If Jacob and his men could make it just a half mile further to the north, there was a hill with a rocky outcropping they could camp underneath. Lightning flashed, and he heard something coming from a small shed up ahead. The fence that had surrounded it, along with the house that it undoubtedly belonged to, were both splintered wooden ruins. The house had gaping holes in the roof, one wall blown completely off, and there appeared to be crude graves, complete with tilting, rough crosses.

He could no longer see his men; they were spread out too far. The same noise attracted his attention again. It was definitely coming from the shed and almost lost in the crack of thunder and the rushing of rain. What had he heard? An animal? He walked toward the shed, his finger sliding into the trigger.

He carefully swung the door to the shed open, surprised to see four faces gaping up at him in fear and shock. He stood for a moment, taking in the scene before him.

There were two young children huddled in a corner and two teenage girls frozen in fear at his feet. In the red-haired girl's arms was a tiny, pasty, limp newborn. Another flash of lightning showed he was a boy.

The baby had obviously been born mere seconds ago; his umbilical cord was still attached. They all looked at him with undisguised terror.

Corporal Jacob Daniels Sr. turned his gun to each in turn. A rifle was propped in the far corner of the shed, but no one moved. He stared at the newborn and remembered the day his son had been born. The nurse had handed JJ to him, wiped clean and wrapped in a soft blanket, and he had stood there in the Army hospital in Fort Hood, stunned at how tiny and fragile the child was.

A thousand images of his little face flickered through the Corporal's memories like a home movie. He had grown so quickly from a tiny infant to smiling toddler and finally into that precocious four-year-old who slept with a battered G.I. Joe doll that had belonged to Jacob and insisted that he was going to grow up and be just like Daddy.

The children at his feet were holding their breaths, eyes wide, terrified.

They were all children, even the older two, who couldn't be out of their teens yet. What in the hell was he doing here? As if losing JJ wasn't enough. This war, it was killing them all, ripping apart families and destroying lives. He could hear his men moving closer, calling over the radio for his status. Soon, they would be close enough to see the shed and its occupants.

Inexplicably, almost unbelievably, he lowered his gun. His body sagged slightly. He was so tired of fighting, so tired of war. All he wanted was his family back.

In a voice that was surprisingly soft, barely audible above the thunder and wind, he said, "I had a son once. It seems... so... long ago. His name was Jacob." Then, without another word, he turned away, softly shutting the door behind him and disappeared into the raging storm.

Outside, the storm raged on as he called over his radio to his men, "Move north. There's nothing here but the dead."

And the troops marched on, with Corporal Jacob Daniels, Sr. leading them. He marched through the mud, past a row of bombed-out houses. He barely noticed the crude grave markers, or the bodies lying in ditches far north of the small town. Instead, his memories were consumed with the laughter of a blond-haired little boy who had died far too young.

Nancy

"We dig one bigger grave, put 'em both in it." Harvey said, nodding to a shaded spot, "That's good soft dirt there, easier to dig into."

Nancy nodded wearily. She had found them, hand in hand, side by side on the bed that morning. The way she figured it; Aunt June had likely gone first. She had been struggling since the last canister of oxygen had run out the week before. When Uncle Ray had realized she was gone, he had gathered her up in his arms, and just let go, too. Anyone who tells you that can't happen doesn't know a married couple who have spent more than sixty years day in, day out with each other. Uncle Ray had been devoted to Aunt June. There was no sense in his living if she was gone.

The coffee was long gone, had been for weeks, but Uncle Ray would still get up every morning, shuffle into the kitchen, open the cabinet door and stare at the spot the coffee was supposed to be, as if it would magically reappear. It was as predictable as an alarm clock and Nancy would wake to the sound of the bedroom door creaking open and usually be sitting up by the time the old man made it to the kitchen. When Uncle Ray didn't wake her up that morning with his usual routine, she knew something was wrong.

A quick glance in the bedroom had confirmed it and she had slipped out of the front door of the trailer quietly, thankful that JJ slept so soundly. She had walked down to Harvey's trailer at the end of Row 3 to ask for help. Now in his late 50s, Harvey wasn't any spring chicken, but there wasn't anyone else to ask and she wasn't sure she could manage it on her own without waking JJ. He didn't need to see that. Her son was a gentle soul, even if he did keep talking about becoming a soldier like his dad. He had cried inconsolably three nights straight when his hamster died, just two weeks before they left Austin.

The trailer park was empty now. The trailers that were capable of travel had moved on, leaving gaps that felt like missing, rotten teeth. The remaining trailers sat uneven and rusting in places.

Harvey had suggested they pull the bottom sheet, wrap it around the bodies of Uncle Ray and Aunt June, and slide them on out, down the hall. Nancy had covered the open edge of the dining table with a sheet and prayed JJ would continue to sleep soundly.

It hadn't been easy, but they had done it, easing the sheet-wrapped bodies down the narrow hall and out of the trailer, down the three short steps, and to the cover of the trees.

Harvey's breath rattled in his throat. He wheezed and coughed, hacking until he shook it loose from his lungs and spat into the dirt.

"Lemme catch my breath, then I'll help you. I got me another shovel in the shed out back of my trailer."

"I got it, Harv, you rest."

Harvey harrumphed, "You ain't got nuthin' girl, you's as skinny as a rail these days." He scratched at the tufts of white hair that still sprouted in odd patterns on his mostly bald pate, "You gotta eat more to keep that energy a'going. Hate to say it like this, but, hell, leastways there'll be more t'eat now you got two less mouths to worry about."

Nancy felt a surge of anger, followed by a wash of sorrow. Harvey was plain-spoken, and she knew he didn't mean anything by it, but damn it, she wished he'd shut his trap. As if she hadn't thought of it herself, and not just today. She dug the shovel into the ground and it yielded easily, just as Harv had said.

"The previous owners had a goddamn sandbox right around here. They figured they'd have it for kids to play with. Only thing that got in it were the damned cats. There was more shit in this sandbox than there was sand. But I figured that'd make it easier to dig in, huh?" He smiled at her; his teeth yellow. One of the front ones chipped away at a sharp angle.

"Sure does," she grunted as she dug deep. The sweat was already rolling down her back and onto her forehead, the flying dirt sticking to it. Hot work, dirty work. She hadn't remembered the sandbox until he mentioned it. She'd tried to play in it a couple of times as a kid and been turned off by a rather fresh cat turd. After that, she'd stuck to the tiny yard that went with the trailer.

"Mommy?" She could hear JJ calling in the distance.

"Shit."

"Here," his rough hand closed on hers, "you go take care of your boy, I'll keep at it." He flapped a hand at her as she cast a look at the bodies, the hole, and then back at the trailer in the distance. "Go on with you, I can handle this."

"I'll be back soon." She jogged away, trying to formulate the words to say to him.

Jacob

He woke up on the hard ground, the sounds of fish splashing in a nearby lake. It wasn't quite dawn, and by now they would have noticed he was missing. It was time to move, put some miles between him and his unit, and, more importantly, the superiors who would do their best to find him and make an example of him.

He wouldn't build a fire and heat up one of the MREs. He'd just down a protein bar, some water, and get going. Later he could chance a fire, but not yet, maybe not even tonight.

It'll have to depend on how far I get.

Jacob felt a cold knot of dread form in his stomach at the thought of them hunting him as a deserter. The Army was all he had known. They were more family to him than the laundry list of foster homes he had stayed in.

That's what drew Nancy and me together - a wish for family - both of us missing out growing up, even if she did have her aunt and uncle.

Jacob paused mid-swallow.

That's it. If she and JJ are alive, they'll be in West Virginia. I need to head there, not to Texas.

No one would think of looking for him in West Virginia, or on any roads heading north or east. They would expect him to go to Texas, which made sense. But Nancy's family was in West Virginia.

She loves Uncle Ray and Aunt June. If she made it out, that's exactly where she will be.

He dug out the protein bar, swallowed another gulp of water, and filled the canteen with lake water, using the carbon filter. The filter wouldn't really help make it taste good, but he'd avoid getting parasites and would stay hydrated. After all, he had a hell of hike in front of him.

Jacob hefted the pack onto his back. He had maybe twenty meals, twenty-five if he stretched it. That could get him pretty far along before he needed to look for more. And he had his gun, so he could hunt in a pinch. He pointed himself towards the east and began walking, slapping at the mosquitoes that were beginning to gather in the cool, shaded areas.

He tried to calculate it. West Virginia was over eight hundred miles away. If he maintained an average of 3.0 miles per hour, and walked at least six hours each day, it would take at least forty-five days to reach his destination.

I could have stolen a Hummer and been there in a couple of days of driving.

He shook his head and kept walking. Hell, if he'd stolen a vehicle, they would have tracked him down and locked his ass up in the brig. That is, if he was lucky and didn't get shot on sight for desertion. At least this way, he had a chance they'd just give up. He wasn't the first to desert, and he certainly wouldn't be the last.

Nancy

The trailer park was quiet. The fall morning air was crisp, just a hint of what was to come in another month, perhaps two. The garden was full of fall crops - kale and spinach, along with a bumper crop of carrots. Nancy had helped Harvey cannibalize several of the older trailers for their windows, and they had built several cold frames that would allow them to continue to produce through the winter. The park was far away from main roads, and she was thankful they were isolated.

Elkins had been hit hard. First by the Allied South duking it out with the Central Unionists, then some damned neo-Nazi group had come in a series of deadly raids, scooping up drugs from the pharmacy inside of Davis Medical Center and kidnapped a Somali widow and her two children. Anyone who stood in their way was shot with terrifying efficiency. Fearing another raid, Nancy and Harvey had downed a large tree across the cracked and winding mountain road that led to Happy Hollow Trailer Park and dug out the battered sign that advertised its presence.

Two families, both from Elkins, had picked their way down the road, over the fallen tree, and brought a large dog kennel full of chickens with them. Later, a pregnant goat, loose in the woods, had been rounded up and given birth to a kid. With luck, they would find another and have some breeding stock that could add meat to their diet. With extra hands on board, the garden had tripled in size, the earth surprisingly rich as it yielded forth bountiful harvests over the long summer. With hard work and no small amount of luck, Nancy was reasonably sure they would make it through the winter.

Nancy had climbed the radio tower twice before and she climbed it a third time, braving the winds that tore at her and stared out at the mountains, curving roads, and ruins of Elkins in the distance. Here and there, she could see campfires that rose up and blended with the fog that often crept over the mountains and married the treetops to the sky. Their corner of the world was quiet for now.

"Jacob, if you are out there, you need to come back to me." Her words were snatched away by the wind and her eyes hurt as much as her heart did. "I'm sorry I didn't try harder, but I know now how much I need you. Not just JJ, but me too. Come back to us."

She clung to the tower, half-sitting, half-standing, her legs and arms firmly wrapped around the rungs. The cold was creeping into her fingers through her gloves, though, and it was time to go back down. Nancy took one more look at the road that led to the trailer park, a speck of movement catching her eye. A deer, perhaps? They had bagged one over a month ago, and nothing since.

What I wouldn't do for some venison.

The tree cover was too dense. She thought she saw something, but what it was, she couldn't be sure.

Jacob

The thin mountain air held a chill. It had since he approached the edge of the Monongahela National Forest two days ago, skirting his way around a settled area, and heading towards Elkins.

Day 62 - Damn, but it's taken a lot to get here.

His boots, designed for war, for marching, along with his fatigues, were still in decent shape, although his clothes were stiff from dirt and he wondered if any amount of cleaning could be able to get the stench two months of living out of them. Everything hung loose on him. He had seen his reflection in a glass window, one of the few intact ones in the town of Elkins, and been shocked at how gaunt he was. He had walked through the town, unnerved by the silence. Several times, he was sure he had seen a curtain twitch as he moved past some of the more intact buildings, but no one had ventured forth. This had become routine as he walked the highways and streets. His uniform marked him as a soldier, but no telling which faction, and most of the countryside had seemed to have had their fill of soldiers. They didn't venture out, but he hedged his bets by not approaching, either. He had walked too damn far to get shot now.

The last week had been the hardest. The miles had been eaten up quickly the first two or three weeks of his journey, especially once he had made it to Interstate 70, which was, barring bridge collapses and warring factions, still a nearly straight shot to the beautiful mountains and the outer edges of the Monongahela National Forest.

He had been born there in Elkins, and lived the first eighteen years of his life in one shitty foster home after another. The only bright memory was of Nancy and a couple of other high school friends. Nate had made it out and had been in California last he heard. His foster brother Joe had ended up serving time for burglary in Tygart Valley Regional, and Perry had been studying to be a mortician like his dad. And, of course, Jacob had ended up marrying Nancy. It had been a no-brainer to get hitched when she realized she was pregnant. He had loved her, still did.

If I had been better at those little things, the little gestures, maybe we would still be together.

Instead, he'd focused on his role in the Army, moving them from town to town until she had had enough.

"I'm always having to leave my friends behind, Jacob. I can't go to college. JJ won't make friendships that will last more than a few months, and it's just too damn hard to live like this."

He had brushed her concerns off, ignored them, until the papers were served and she had taken JJ and moved to Austin. He didn't blame her, not one bit. He'd been the one to take her for granted, to not listen, and here they were.

He was getting close. If they were here, and he wanted to believe they were, how would she feel about him showing up. Would she welcome him back into her life again? Or would he just be an unwelcome reminder of the past?

He stumbled, tripped on an uneven portion of pavement, and nearly fell. He was tired, bone tired each and every day. Not enough food, lips dry and cracked, dehydrated since losing the water filter last week crossing a ravine to avoid troop movements.

His feet guided him to the lonely, tree-lined road that led to the trailer park. Just a few miles now. He looked up and saw a small flash of sunlight, some lookout up in a tower, and slipped to one side of the road where the trees covered him. What was he walking into? He had stopped at a farm a few days back, helped the old man with the harvest in exchange for food and gotten an earful about a group of extremists in the area, making trouble.

"You see anyone moving in a pack bigger than two and do what I do, hide," the old man had said, waggling a bony, spotted finger in his direction. "Those damn neo-Nazis been rounding up women and kidnapping any of them ethnics that they can find. I hear they use 'em as slaves. Goddamn slaves!" He had spat on the ground then, shook his head, "As if we didn't learn nuthin' the first time 'round."

He had offered Jacob a permanent place to stay, shaking his head when the younger man refused. "The offer stands. It's dangerous out there, son, so find what you gotta find, and come back if you can. You and yours would be welcome."

Jacob saw the tree straddling the road in the distance. The sign he had seen a thousand times, battered yet legible, was missing. He moved off of the road, stepping quietly now. The world, even one he knew like the back of his hand, had changed. Who knew what was waiting for him up ahead? He slid the rifle off of his back and double-checked it. There was a round in the chamber. The safety was off, and he crouched slightly, bending his knees and choosing his steps carefully, taking his time.

He swung around, moving higher up the north incline, moving carefully as he circled around to a side of the trailer park. They wouldn't be expecting him to come in on, on the opposite side from where the road led in. The sounds of children playing, laughing, were the first signs that someone still remained. As the trees thinned, he could see an extensive garden located in the sunny, central patch next to what had been the trailer park office. Many of the trailers were missing, but the ones that remained were a mix of obviously occupied as well as others with gaping holes where the windows had been. A hundred yards from the garden was a rough corral that held a handful of goats. Chickens strutted about, loose, pecking at the grass and winding their way through the cold frames on the ground.

A burst of laughter and several children came into view. Jacob blinked, barely able to believe his eyes. A tow-headed boy was being chased by two smaller children, a boy and a girl, all of them screaming and laughing as they tore around the garden, chickens scattering in their path. Jacob stepped out from the last cover of trees and the boy looked up, stopping in his tracks so suddenly that the other two slammed into him, collapsing on the ground in surprise.

The little boy looked up at him and grinned and hurled himself into Jacob's arms.

"Daddy!"

Jacob hugged his son to his chest and sucked in a breath, "Hey JJ."

After all these months of not knowing. Hoping against hope. He had found him. He opened his eyes and saw Nancy running towards them.

"Jacob? Oh my God, JACOB!" The strength of her embrace took his breath away and his fears dissolved as her lips found his.

His son was alive.

Nancy, his first kiss, his first and only love, was here, in his arms.

And after far too long away. After miles of endless road and plenty of hungry days, Jacob knew one thing.

He was finally, and incontrovertibly, home.

Run While You Can

"When you can't save others, at least try to save yourself."

Arriving at Clinton had been a letdown. Serena had seen it in Brad's face. When it came to the town, there wasn't much to be done. Brad had stopped dead at a burned hulk of timbers and said nothing. His face held a mixture of fury and anguish, his lips worked silently, and his fingers whitened as they gripped the pack on his back. After several moments of silence, he had turned away. Which really said everything. His family was gone. So was his home.

Max and Annie hadn't said a thing, not even a whine of complaint. They followed as he turned on his heel and marched them towards the east, to the outskirts of town. There they had found the same scene; the only difference was the wide space between the farmhouses. The corpses of horses, and of other animals of an uncertain breed lay rotting on the ground, spread out randomly across the wide drive. The farmhouse they stopped at was in ruins, nothing but the blackened bricks of a chimney stood among the collapsed, burned timbers. Nearby, a barn was in the same shape, but several smaller buildings appeared relatively intact and they ended up bedding down for the night.

It wasn't their final destination. A half-collapsed building in the forest marked the end of their journey the following day. A tree had fallen against the house years ago. Its branches poking through what were now open holes along the back edge. The house hadn't been occupied in years, and the remains of the front of the property were desecrated with graffiti and empty bottles of beer and whiskey. And it seemed that someone had collected the cigarette butts, arranging them in what were now moldering pyramids, black with mold.

"It's remote," Brad had said, "off the beaten path." He shrugged at Serena in what might have been an apologetic way, but he'd been so quiet since seeing the remains of his family's home that she wasn't sure he was even capable of that. His expression had settled into a blank darkness, and he pulled away from her that night, instead staying up to provide watch, despite the proclaimed safety of the location.

The first night, they slept in the filth and mess. By the next morning, however, Serena was determined to make a go of it. She didn't have long, after all. The baby would be here soon. Any day, by her estimate. So as the dull rays of the sun peeked intermittently through the low cloud cover and the chill of the morning hung around them, she roused Max and Annie and set them to work. Some of the bottles could be rinsed in the nearby creek and made use of. Others could serve as the base for an outdoor cooking pit once the clay soil warmed enough to be dug up and shaped into an oven. By the third day there, they had settled into a routine of sorts. There were plenty of destroyed buildings to pick through. There were only so many clothes or blankets people could take when running for their lives, and from the looks of it, the troops that had blown through the small town had killed anyone foolish enough to stay. Serena thought about what Jess had said as they parted ways. "Don't go to Clinton. There's nothing left there but bones and ash."

Jess had been right. There was no one left in Clinton. If there was, they hid themselves well. Most of the homes in their area hadn't even had a good pick-through. Serena had certainly seen her share of empty homes in the past few months as she and Brad had slowly made their way, mostly on foot, from the time they had escaped the Western Front in Mississippi. By now she could tell when one had been picked over versus one that had not. Most of the places they scavenged were untouched, and Serena couldn't help but feel afraid. Untouched did not mean safe, not at all, and she listened carefully for sounds of footsteps, anything really, that would betray the presence of others. No matter how quiet it was, she couldn't shake the feeling that they were being watched. The night that they had spent with Jess and the kids was the last snow of the season. It had melted away within days and the air had warmed quickly. The warmer temps and the discovery of a cache of seeds in a dented old box near the ruins of another farm had curtailed any additional scavenging and instead become a race to get the ground ready for the spinach, kale, and lettuce seeds. The storm clouds gathering in the west promised them a wet reward and Brad had pointed out that any seeds they could get in the ground now meant not starving in a few months when their supplies ran out.

It was there, in the middle of the fourth row, that Serena had stared down at her legs, confused at the sudden rush of warmth and wetness. She stared at her legs, rooted to the spot, and felt panic wash over her.

Why didn't I insist we go with Jess? There was a hospital there, Research Belton. I can't give birth here!

Brad, consumed with the work, had moved ahead of her down the row with his shovel, Annie followed behind with a hoe, breaking the dirt up further. Serena felt Max tug at her hand. "Sweena? I plant more?" His hands were covered in dirt. He had followed behind as she carefully dropped seeds at intervals and gently pushed the dirt over them. Brad turned back then, took in the wet pants and dropped his shovel, pushing past Annie to close the distance between them.

"Is it the baby? Is it time? It isn't those hick contractions again, is it?"

"Braxton Hicks, and no." The contractions were coming, fast, hard. She stood there, lip trembling, tears running down her face, "It's different this time, way different." Her stomach twisted, and she felt the baby slide down even further, pressing hard against her pelvic bone.

Brad was at her side then, holding her steady. "Okay, it's gonna be okay, babe. We planned for this, remember?"

In a moment of wild optimism three days ago, she had told him that women had been giving birth for thousands of years, and all they needed was some hot water, towels, and something to cut the umbilical cord.

Prepared? Oh God, I want a hospital. I want doctors. I want a fucking epidural! Why did I let him talk me into coming to Clinton?

Slowly, they moved back to the house, and she gritted her teeth as the next contraction knifed its way through her.

That evening, the storm was fully engaged over the pitiful remains of a ghost town once known as Clinton. Lightning flashed and rain dripped through the roof of a dilapidated house, forming a puddle.

Serena screamed at the top of her lungs for anything that could stop the pain. Another push and scream and the head and shoulders appeared. Brad let go of her hand and reached down to cradle the tiny head, holding the baby as it slid out and coughed. A sharp, thin wail issued from its mouth.

He looked past the umbilical cord. "It's a girl. Baby, we got ourselves a little girl!" He smiled, yet Serena could see he was disappointed. He'd talked endlessly about having a son and the evening before he had brought home a stack of baby clothes, all in blue. Serena fell back against the blankets, exhausted and exhilarated at the same time. She'd done it all without a hospital or doctors or even an epidural. She wished her mom was here. Mom hadn't thought much of her, always chiding her for being a delicate flower - she would have been in awe of her girl managing such a feat.

Brad gently wiped the baby down, cut the cord, and then wrapped the tiny infant in a clean blanket, and handed her to Serena, who looked both excited and exhausted. The lightning lit up the room, and the baby squawked in fear at the loud thunderclap. Serena took in the baby's features, her shock of jet-black hair, and met Brad's steady gaze. He knew the baby wasn't his, didn't he? For just a moment, the same look Brad had on his face when he saw the remains of his family home resurfaced as he stared at the tiny infant swaddled in a soft blanket. But he said nothing, shook his head quietly. Was it sadness? Anger? Hurt? She wasn't sure. She felt a lump of fear and guilt form in her throat. She hadn't ever come out and said the baby was his, but as the months had passed and they had become a family of sorts, he'd just sort of stepped up. He'd been excited, especially after they found Max huddled alone and starving as they made their way out of Mississippi.

"I always wanted kids," he had said, his gaze landing on Annie and Max as they walked down the road hand-in-hand behind them. "I guess I never imagined it quite like this, though."

She had relaxed a little, hoped for something good to come out of it, and started thinking of Brad as the baby's father. Now she had to wonder, had she been wrong? Would he reject the baby, hell, maybe reject her as well?

He smiled then, reached out, and stroked the baby's cheek. "She's beautiful. What should we name our baby?

Relief washed over her. "My mother's name was Rebecca. We'll call her Becka for short."

"Becka it is."

It stormed for two days and the wet and the cold returned. Not as bad as it had been in winter, but certainly far from comfortable. They huddled inside and Brad and Annie handled the meals while Serena breastfed Becka in a pile of bedding and pillows scavenged from the wreckage of a partially burned home nearby. The smell of smoke riddled most of bedding, sometimes overwhelmingly so, but Serena soon learned to ignore it.

When the storms passed, the warmth of spring returned in earnest. The seeds sprouted and were soon joined by new rows of carrots, parsnips and potatoes. Serena nursed Becka, and Brad took care to see that she ate plenty of food. Occasionally, when he didn't realize she was watching him, she could see his true feelings on the subject. Especially when the standard blue of her newborn eyes began to pale and become the all too familiar ice-blue. They were quick flashes of anger, possibly resentment, but Serena could see that he was trying hard to push the negative away and focus on the good.

"Which do you think trumps the other, nature or nurture?" He asked once, in an offhand way.

The kids were outside playing in the warm summer evening, the sun low in the sky. Annie still wasn't talking, but occasionally Max would do something exceptionally cute, in a way only a three-year-old can do, and Annie would giggle softly. At the moment, he was covered in dirt and so was she, as they dug into the soft earth underneath a nearby tree. It was the day that Becka's eyes had changed, lightened to the ice-blue she remembered so well.

She said nothing for a moment. Becka was already fast asleep. She was a good baby, and by the end of two months was sleeping well through the night. Serena thought of the monster who had raped her and wondered, just for a moment, if he was still alive. She hoped not. Men like that, rapists, murderers, they didn't deserve to live. But how Becka had been made, how Jess's son Jacob had been made, that was nature. What happened next was completely within their power.

"Nurture," she answered, looking up at him. "It's the one thing we can control."

In the gloom, Brad's face was difficult to read, but she saw him nod slowly. "Yeah, that's what I think too."

Serena saw an opportunity then and took it. "I knew this boy in middle school. He was quiet, shy even, but really sweet when you got to know him. We studied together after school. Totally platonic, just great friends. He had to move, though. Out of the area, East coast. His mom wanted to return to the family there. We kept in contact for years. He finally told me about his dad after the man died in our junior year. He had been a long-haul truck driver. That is until they sent him away for multiple rapes and murders when Joe was twelve. Joe was the gentlest person I ever knew. Once, we were walking home from school and we saw a little squirrel get hit by a car. Killed instantly. He insisted we bury it." She paused, "If a kid can have a dad like that and turn out okay, then I have to believe its nurture."

It was a small lie, the story. She hadn't known Joe, not personally. Sure, she'd waved hello to him in the hallways and shared several classes, but he was on the outer edge of her friend's circle. Instead, her best friend Shelly had known him, even kissed him once behind the bleachers on a dare. The rest of it had been true, so really was it a bad thing to lie about?

Nonetheless, it had the desired effect. After that quiet summer evening, she hadn't caught him looking at Becka with anger or resentment. Which was a relief, to be sure.

By the end of summer, they had managed to accrue six hens, three of whom managed to survive a rash of raccoon attacks that stopped abruptly when Brad brought back a large roll of chicken wire and reinforced the tiny doghouse turned chicken coop.

Brad spent most of the daylight hours ripping the damaged back wall off of the house, patching sections of the roof, and framing in a new section. It wasn't pretty. He wouldn't be winning any architectural awards, but it would keep out the elements. And that was important, come winter. They didn't have much in the way of meat, which was a problem. However, the garden had produced more vegetables than they had expected, thanks to the warm temps and regular rain showers. It was a delicate balance. Too much rain and plants suffered, not enough rain, and their growth was stunted, but the growing season had been kind. Even better, Brad and Annie had discovered hundreds of empty dust-covered canning jars in a church basement a mile to the west.

Whatever they could can, and probably even some of the things they shouldn't, had been quickly put up in the old jars with their zinc covers. Serena hoped desperately that they weren't setting themselves up for a nasty case of botulism, but Brad was insistent.

"Hell, my mom canned everything, even potatoes, chicken, you name it, if it could fit in a jar, she canned it and we ate it."

Serena had her doubts, but Brad was so self-assured, so certain, that eventually she just went with it.

They hit gold in early October after a particularly violent storm toppled a length of fencing. One adolescent bull wandered away from a small herd that had evaded all of Brad's efforts to catch them now that he was out of bullets. His mistake was fatal. He crossed a section of the downed fence and ended up tangled in the barbed wire. Wet, wounded, and wrapped up like a present, he roared his distress, which woke them in the pre-dawn hours.

Serena watched as Brad killed the young bull quickly and efficiently. He definitely knew what he was doing in this department, and he grinned like a schoolboy as he began the butchering process.

"Steaks for dinner, Babe!"

She was thankful for the abruptly cool temperatures. The flies were few and far between and the mosquitoes had already died off, were hibernating, or whatever mosquitoes do when the temps drop into the 30s and 40s. Serena didn't know or much care, as long as they weren't buzzing her ears at night and raising welts on the kids' arms.

Most of the meat had to be smoked in order to preserve it for more than a few days or weeks, and Brad set into doing that. There was already a smoking shed on the property, luckily. Brad had pointed it out when they first arrived. Meat had been in such short supply that he hadn't gotten a chance to smoke any of the fish he caught. There was no need to smoke what they desperately needed in their bellies at the moment. But the bull was a different matter. It wasn't possible to eat the meat before it went bad, even in the colder temps.

"I know where I can find some mesquite wood, up there at the Ace Hardware," he said as he hacked away at the meat, his knife cutting off strips of steak. They had been eating beef for the better part of a week and the newness had worn off, Serena was happy to add it to a soup filled with spinach and root vegetables, but she was well and over the thick steaks they had eaten day in and day out. "I saw it near them chimney things when I was over there scavenging."

"Chiminea," she corrected, laughing. Becka cooed from her spot on the blankets at the far end of the room and gummed at a piece of dried meat in her hand. She had cut two teeth in the past week and been an angry, fussy mess until Brad had handed her the meat. She had chewed on it constantly, the two lower incisors working their way through the gums, a mess of drool and meat juice on her chin.

"What?"

"It's not a chimney, it's a Chiminea."

"Whatever. Anyway, that's where I saw it." He flapped a hand at her, "I'm just wondering if going there is such a good idea."

"Why?" Serena asked, frowning.

"Well, I know there's got to be others around here. Seen evidence of 'em. Stuff moved. Just wish I had bullets for that rifle I brought home last week." He had found it lying underneath a body, not far from where it appeared, at least from the bodies and spent ammunition, as if the Western Front had engaged a different faction, likely the Allied South.

Serena's hands felt clammy and she could feel her heartbeat increase. "Others? As in... soldiers?"

Brad slid his hand around her and pulled her close. "It's just folks who live around here, Babe, nothing to worry about. I'm just being cautious is all."

Serena still had nightmares. At first, they were so bad that she had punched and kicked Brad a couple of times, her sleep-addled brain convinced she was back in the camp, back in Tent Five. After months on the road, and the birth of Becka, they had slowed down. Instead of having them nearly every night, it had dwindled down to once a week, then once a month, but it made no difference. Unless the others that

Brad had seen evidence of were a woman or a child, they weren't safe, she was sure of it.

When Brad announced he was heading out to scavenge later that day, after washing the blood and gore from his hands, she had asked if he was going by Ace. She hadn't even realized she was biting her lip until the taste of copper flooded her mouth.

"Don't worry, Babe, I'm not gonna go anywhere near there," he had told her, his eyes avoiding hers, "I'll be back in an hour, two at tops." He'd kissed her forehead, turned and walked away, heading into the forest to the northeast. He had devised several routes this way, varying his paths, in order to avoid creating a visible path back to their small family.

Serena watched him disappear into a thick copse of trees, his brown hair and camo jacket quickly disappearing into the last of the greenery. Soon, the leaves would be gone from the trees and they would have to face a cold winter.

Serena found herself wondering yet again if she had made the right choice. Jess had seemed so certain that her home, a large town of over 20,000 people, would still be there. Clinton hadn't even had half of that number, and from the looks of it, those who hadn't fled had died either in the fighting or when the Western Front had done its best to torch the town. Those that were left seemed to have no interest in showing their faces. Between being pregnant and then caring for a newborn, she didn't have an opportunity to get out, but Brad had. He provided her regular updates that were curated, no doubt, to avoid alarming her. Two months ago, he had come back scraped up, a black eye, and blood on his ripped shirt. She knew he had been lying when he said that he had fallen, but she hadn't said anything. He'd stayed close to home for weeks after that.

By the time the sun slipped behind the trees and darkness set in, Serena knew something terrible had happened. Either he had run into someone armed and dangerous, or he was afraid to return and bring whoever was around back to their small family. She stamped out the fire in the smoke shed and buried the haunches of meat after wrapping it in a sheet. She would have preferred to sink it in the creek, but that was too far of a hike to risk, even in the dark. Becka had already fallen asleep, as had Max, but Annie was wide awake and Serena could see the girl watching her every move, eyes wide, lip trembling. She still didn't speak, not a word, but Serena could tell the girl definitely had something to say.

That Brad hadn't returned was a bad sign. They were exposed, unsafe, here. Serena cast about in her mind for any potential solutions, her thoughts interrupted by terrifying questions.

Was he dead?

Did whoever had killed him know where she and the kids were?

Were they coming for them?

Sleep was elusive and fragmented that night. And the next. And the one after that.

"Where is Brad dad?" Max asked. The little boy was relentless, asking over and over until Annie would reach over and put a finger against his lips and shake her head in warning. He wouldn't listen. Becka, only six months old, had been fretful and fussy. It wasn't a new tooth, Serena had checked. No, it was Brad's absence, and the rising fear in all of them. Becka could sense it the same as the rest of them.

Brad would have returned if he could and by now Serena was sure he was dead. Nothing else explained it, nothing else made sense.

Despite the chill in the air, Serena's hands were clammy with sweat. As the sun set each night, she found herself shaking uncontrollably, her leg muscles tight, ready to run. Day in and day out, the fear did not abate, and she was a shaky, sleep-deprived mess by the time a week had slipped by.

Annie tugged at Serena's sleeve. Becka had been fussing and unwilling to take a nap, but the baby had finally collapsed in her mother's arms, drunk on milk and stripped of the energy that had caused her to fuss for nearly two hours straight. Serena glanced down at Annie and raised her eyebrows in the gloom.

"What?" she whispered, then winced as Becka moved restlessly against her chest.

Annie pointed towards the back of the house and tugged again, clearly indicating she wanted Serena to go with her. Serena nodded, turned back to the baby long enough to settle her gently in the bed and pull another blanket over her before she followed the girl into the gloomy interior.

Without any intact replacement glass available, Brad had simply boarded over the broken windows. This made the back half of the house dark and somewhat treacherous to walk through, thanks to some rotting flooring. The kids slept upstairs and seemed to manage just fine while Serena, Brad and the baby had occupied the front room near the front door. It meant less privacy, but it was warmer near the fireplace. Max had been complaining about the cold and Serena had known it was just a matter of time before they would all be crammed into the same room. Winter was here, and with it the bitter cold.

Along the back wall of the house next to the stairs going up, Brad had patched the wall where a large hole had been knocked out by the tree. His repair job hadn't been pretty, but it had done the trick. Water wasn't getting in, despite some strong storms during the spring and late summer. Annie walked over to one part of the back wall and knelt down, pulling and shoving at a small piece of wood that had been tacked in place. With some effort, she wrenched it up and to the left and then pointed out the newly made hole.

"A way out?" Serena asked, "In case people come for us?"

Annie nodded.

"That's good thinking, Annie. Thank you."

She fought to keep the tremor out of her voice as her stomach dipped, thinking again of Brad, wondering what had happened to him.

He's dead. And really, what else do you need to know other than that?

She winced at the thought of it, leaned over, and hugged the girl gently. "We'll be okay, Annie, don't you worry." She sat there for a moment, wishing she could do something to help the girl feel safe.

"I think maybe it's time we headed for Belton. Maybe we can find Jess and her family. What do you think?"

Annie's head nodded and the girl, normally so reticent, reached her hands around Serena and hugged her back with a strong grip. It took Serena by surprise.

"Okay. Make sure and get a bag together, keep it by this back wall and we will just see if we can't plot a course for Belton before it's too cold."

Hell, it's already too cold. But what else can I do? Chance staying here all winter without him?

Serena reviewed her options.

I can try staying here and likely starve halfway through the winter. I could try to find whoever is still out there and do whatever it takes to stay alive. Or I can take the kids and head for Belton, maybe even Kansas City.

She knew the chances of them all surviving the winter were slim to none, with the first two options. With a tiny baby and a preschooler, the entire burden of survival would rest on her and Annie's shoulders, and Annie was barely more than a child herself. The chances that whoever was out there would take her and the kids hit her anxiety triggers like nobody's business.

Whoever was out there likely killed Brad. The only way they would want to use me or Annie would be nothing better than a return to Tent Five. And Annie already tried to kill herself once before I got her out of there. As for Max and my baby, who knows what they would do? All I know is that I can't risk it.

Serena tried to remember how far away Belton was. Some fifty, no, close to sixty miles away. Her brain nearly stuttered to a stop as she tried to imagine how they would get there, the four of them, all alone, on foot. How fast could a child walk in a day, anyway?

A brisk walking pace is three miles an hour, so figure half of that through mud, off-road. And maybe six hours a day of walking per day, tops, between Becka and Max. That was, what, a week of walking every day? They would need to carry food too, and how will I take care of Becka's diapers?

Brad hadn't had any luck finding diapers, so they had made do with strips of cloth and safety pins. There were only so many cloths, though, she'd run out just a few days in and have no way to clean and dry more. The image of a baby crying loudly as they made their way through unknown territory was enough to send her shaking uncontrollably.

Shit, shit, shit. No matter what she did, no matter how she chose, she couldn't see this ending well. And as the night closed in around them, Becka hugged to her chest, with Max and Annie now spooned against each side of her. Serena was more afraid than she had been in a long time.

Serena silently cursed Brad for carving up the tent to use for several projects, including a cover for the front door, which had been hanging on by one hinge and hadn't even been good for anything more than kindling. Without the tent, they were going to be cold, damn cold, as well as exposed at night as they walked all that way. Not to mention the fact that she would have to be carrying Becka and likely Annie would have to help Max. In the end, just two days later, there ended up being no choice at all.

They came late in the day, the sun had long vanished behind thick, heavy gray clouds and the temperature had plummeted. They had just finished eating dinner, a large jar of green beans and onions, along with a side of the beef she had kept in the house. It had begun to turn, but not enough that she was willing to waste it. Becka had slipped off into dreamland and Max as well, curled around the baby, a thumb in his mouth. It was Annie who heard it first. An errant step onto the now frozen ground, and a branch snapped. Her eyes rounded, her head snapping to Annie, who had been carefully adding another blanket to the heap. She froze in the gloom, stiff, alert, and stared back at Serena.

Serena said nothing, just pointed to the back of the house and reached for Becka. There was no time to do anything more than slip her sleeping daughter into a backpack, zip it up as far as the surrounding blankets would allow, and try to move without sound to the back of the house where the escape hatch was. Annie passed her, a very sleepy Max in Annie's grasp. They could hear voices now, several, and despite the cold, Serena felt a rivulet of sweat trickle down her back as she waited for Annie and then Max to slip through the hole before handing out Becka in the backpack. The sounds they made were small, but in the night, they sounded so loud. Luckily, whoever was out there had been drawn to the remains of the bull, which they had slowly continued to strip off all meat over the past few days since Brad had disappeared.

"You were right, Buddy, damned if that young bull didn't end up getting snatched," an older voice commented. He sounded grizzled, old.

"I knew that guy wasn't alone, either." A younger voice said from inside of the house, "There are more. Got the remains of a vegetable garden over near the smoke shed. Blankets are still warm and I smell food."

Serena prayed to whatever gods were still there that Becka would stay asleep. She eased the straps over her shoulders, keeping the pack against her front, and tugged at Annie's arm, pointing in the direction of the trees. They needed cover, and to be out of sight, but there was at least one hundred yards to run across open field, something they needed to do as quietly and as quickly as possible, before the men thought to look behind the house. Max, despite his age, seemed to understand enough to keep quiet. He took Annie's hand, and they all began to run.

"We got movement!" The old man shouted, "Buddy, get over here! There's movement in the back field!"

Time didn't stop, so much as blur. Serena heard rifle shots and increased her speed, legs flying across the stubbled, uneven ground. Max and Annie fell slightly behind and Serena didn't falter, couldn't bring herself to slow down in the slightest. In truth, she felt nothing but horror and panic - the rest of the world washed away in white noise. Her only focus was the dark shelter of the trees. They were close, so close, and the fire in her lungs barely registered as she willed her feet to go faster. Becka was making small squawks of distress as the backpack strapped against Serena's chest heaved and thumped with every footfall.

She felt, rather than heard, the gunshots. One came close as she entered the woods, hitting the tree next to her head. The bark exploded into shrapnel and she dove to the right, into a thicker part of the woods, as an agonizing streak of what felt like an electric shock tore down her left shoulder and arm. Serena didn't allow herself to think of it, or to stop. She just kept running. The men back at the farmhouse continued to shoot. The bullets, such small and seemingly inconsequential things, parted the surrounding air.

Behind her, she heard the children doing their best, but losing ground, falling behind more with each moment that passed. Then there was a strangled scream, a thud of a body hitting the ground, and then nothing more but her own feet grinding through the forest, a stampede through the fallen leaves, rustling, sliding.

Her arm hurt. A deep ache that finally turned to a throbbing stab of agony. She slowed, the darkness fully encapsulating her now, her breaths hoarse, ragged. She couldn't continue like this.

Serena slammed into a tree with her right shoulder and wheeled about, unable to go on. She had run so far, and for so long, that she could no longer see Annie or Max or anything but the thickness of the trees all around her, even in their leafless state. The sky above was dark, as was the forest that surrounded her. She couldn't even hear the men now.

I didn't even try to save them. Oh God, I just let them fall behind and be shot!

Serena felt the guilt surge through her. As she regained her breath, Becka stirred, the sudden lack of movement waking her where the panicked run had not. She whimpered, twisting in the tightness of the backpack and blanket, her tiny feet kicking. Becka quieted quickly when Serena pushed up her shirt and pressed her breast into the baby's mouth.

"Shh," she whispered, and Becka's body relaxed against her, slowly nursing before falling back into a deep sleep. While she sat there, her body pressed against the hard, cold ground, Serena listened, trying to ignore the heartbeat that still roared in her ears. Had they stopped? Or were they still following her? It was dark now. So dark that Serena could barely see beyond the small clearing she was in. Worse, it was beginning to snow.

If I can get to the highway, walk it at night, I could make better time. And now that it is just me, I can walk faster, maybe twice as fast.

She felt another surge of guilt at that last thought.

As she slipped Becka off of her breast and struggled to place her back inside the backpack, her left arm burned in agony. She realized then that the wetness on the blankets was blood and her right hand crept up to feel the wound on her arm. It burned like fire when she touched it, and she hissed at the pain of it.

Is the bullet still there?

She couldn't tell, but the blood was still coming. She dug into the pack and found one of Becka's spare diaper strips and wrapped it around her arm. That would do until daylight, when she could see it better. Now she just had to figure out where the highway was and get moving. It wouldn't do to stay here; the blood trail would make it all too easy to find her come tomorrow morning. There was no point in going back. She knew she couldn't help the kids, even if they had survived. She suddenly remembered a story she had read in high school, from a former soldier in Vietnam who had been the lone survivor of his regiment.

"When you can't save others, at least try to save yourself." At the time, reading those words, she had been horrified. But now she understood it better. There was no way she could have saved them. Hell, she would be lucky if she could save Becka and herself. Still, the tears tracked down her cheeks, freezing in the cold of the night. She began to walk, her feet slipping on the leaf-covered forest floor, heading west toward the highway. Becka's warmth was heavy and still against her chest. She was thankful that the baby had not been woken, and that she would likely sleep most of the night through while Serena walked. And walk she would until she could move no further. Her life, and Becka's, depended on it.

Serena put one foot in front of the other. The mile markers would have told her how far she had come, and how close she was, but she was no longer in any shape to read them. She struggled to keep her focus on putting one foot in front of the other.

Her left arm was swollen, hot to the touch, and her feet felt like two lead weights soldered crudely on. She had walked and walked, stopping only to rest, if she could, for a few hours at a time. The snow had continued to fall. This was unusual for the area. Typically, the storms blew through, dumping a couple of inches before moving on, never lasting for more than a day. This snow, however, had turned to sleet and then back to a powdery fine snow that felt hard and painful. The infection in her arm had begun almost immediately, and it had turned Serena's thoughts to mush, especially once the dull headache had set in.

She walked, chewed on a piece of bark from a willow tree, remembering that it could help with pain, and winced at the terrible bitter taste before spitting it out. Pieces of the bark stuck to her tongue.

Her mouth was dry, her lips cracked, and after three days of walking, she had moved beyond hunger and into something else. Becka cried against her chest, but Serena couldn't help. It had started with a clogged milk duct on the left and then the fever and infection had set in and all Becka did was cry when she tried to nurse.

Serena ignored her child. It did no good to stop. Every time she did, it was the same. Her breasts were on fire as well now and there was no sustenance, no respite for the hunger her baby felt. Becka would suck at the breast, flail and beat at Serena's chest with her tiny fists, and then wail in frustration. She hadn't eaten in over a day. The only thing Serena could do was somehow make it to Belton, and hopefully find Jess or anyone who might help.

Jess will help, I know she will.

She remembered what Jess had said to her, in those quiet moments when the children were playing and Brad was off gathering wood for the fire. Serena had been overcome with fear, afraid of how she would feel about Becka when she was born. She had leaned close to Jess, so the others couldn't hear and whispered, "I pray every day that this baby is Brad's. But I know it isn't. It's that bastard's, I know it is." She had looked up, gazed hard into Jess's eyes, "Do you think I'll be able to love it? Even if it is from him?"

Jess's reply had been simple and direct, "Yes."

Serena had liked the girl. Why had she listened to Brad? If she had put her foot down, insisted on taking the kids and going with Jess, she wouldn't be here right now. Max and Annie would still be alive. Her mind occupied with these thoughts; Serena barely noticed the sign by the side of the road. It had been cut down and covered up, only the metal supports jutted out of the ground. As she concentrated on her putting one foot in front of the other, her eyes were caught by the sharp stubs barely peeking out of the snow. She stopped, tottering in place for a moment before she left the road and she pushed the branches away from it.

Five miles. Just five more miles to go.

Night was coming. And with it, darkness that was impossible to navigate through. Her foot slipped, then the other, and Serena fell. It wasn't the first time. Her knees ached from the impacts of multiple falls. She got up, slow, and continued to walk down the empty road.

One mile.

Another mile.

When Serena lost her way in the dark, she slipped hard on the slick macadam, tumbled down the small embankment, and landed, unconscious in the ditch. She heard nothing. Not the wails of her child, who had somehow been shielded from harm by Serena's body as she rolled down the hill, and certainly not by the two young men who realized with shock that she was still alive. It wasn't until they moved her, jolting her injured arm, that she woke with a scream of pain on her lips.

"It's all right, we got you. We're gonna get you to a doctor, ma'am, just hang in there." The one who said it was young, maybe late teens. He and the other man each had rifles slung over their shoulders. They exchanged glances, one crouching beside her, the other letting out a low whistle as they pried away the blood-encrusted bandage.

"She's in bad shape, Jake. We best get her back to town and have Ridley take a look at her."

Serena struggled to speak. It impossible. The world was bright and white, but she felt so heavy, so tired. "What... town?"

"Belton," was the younger one's quick response. "Where you from?"

"Clin... ton. Tell her."

"Tell who?"

"Jess Aaron..." her words slurred and Becka, all cried out, gave a pitiful whine in the backpack still strapped to her chest.

"Jess Aaronson?" The one standing above her asked. "You know Jess?"

Serena managed a small nod before her eyes slid closed. She had done it. She'd managed to get Becka to Belton and these men would help her find Jess. Becka would be safe. She smiled then, a thread of gratitude and relief intertwined. As she felt herself lifted, Serena relaxed for the first time in more than a week. She was safe now.

Loved and Lost

"In war, there are no winners."

Wes held the receiver so tight that the plastic creaked in his iron grip. "What do you mean, you've got nothing?"

"I'm sorry, Mr. Perkins, sometimes these things take time." The private eye's voice crackled and faded; his cell phone connection as poor as ever. "I tracked them to Memphis, but then the trail went cold. She might be here, working for cash, staying under the radar, or she might have headed for a big city, like New York."

Wes gritted his teeth, his jaw tight and aching as if he had chewed on an entire half pound bag of House of Jerky in one go. His free hand clenched as hard as the one holding the receiver and he could feel his short, stubby fingernails digging deep into the flesh of his palm.

"It's up to you," the private eye said as if he didn't have a care in the world, "but I'll need another two thousand if you want me to keep working the case."

How he wanted to reach through the phone line and rip the smug little bastard's throat out. He had damn near zeroed out his savings as it was. And now with his boss cutting his hours down to thirty hours a week "until the financial crisis blew over" he had even less coming in. Where the hell could he going to find another two thousand dollars?

"Keep looking," he ground it out, his knuckles showing white on his left hand. He opened his fist and counted the four crescent moon shapes his fingernails had left in his skin.

The line crackled and the private eye sighed. "Mr. Perkins, I'll need that deposit by tomorrow evening."

"Stay in Memphis. Find them. You'll get your goddamn money." He slammed the receiver down and punched the wall. The drywall, which was already sporting a sizable dent from the last time he had hit it, crumbled, leaving a gaping hole. A splinter of wood from the edge of the stud dug a gouge into his hand. "Fucking shit!"

He stumbled away from the phone, his mind spinning on how he was going to generate two thousand dollars by the end of the day tomorrow. He tripped over a Power Puff doll and slammed his hip into Laura's beloved rolltop desk. It rocked back and forth and a figurine of a dolphin that Cody had given her last year for Mother's Day fell and smashed on the floor, breaking into several pieces.

Wes limped into the small, dark hallway cursing, and fumbled for the light switch. Nothing happened when he flipped the switch on, which wasn't surprising. The rolling blackouts had become more frequent in recent weeks, and it seemed like the power was off more than it was on these days. The sharp edge of the medicine cabinet raked his hand, and he fumbled in the dark for a box of band-aids only to find the damned box was empty.

"Fucking kids," he muttered and tossed the box, now smeared with blood, toward one of the children's rooms. Sarah had probably used the last of them on her baby dolls or herself. The smallest of wounds, imaginary or real, were instantly solved by his daughter raiding the medicine cabinet for a band-aid.

He wiped his bloody hand on his pants and walked back into the living room, grabbed a bottle of whiskey from the corner table where he had put a serious dent in it the evening before, and settled into his easy chair to drink some more. The fridge was empty, and he had finished off the last of the canned soup and crackers on Sunday.

Fuck it, whiskey for dinner sounds just fine to me.

He didn't bother with a glass, just tossed the cap in the general direction of the overflowing trash can and tipped the bottle up to his lips, feeling the liquid burn as it slid down his throat.

In some ways, having Laura and the kids gone was pretty damn nice. No nervous looks from Laura or the kids, no scuttling about like they had something to hide or were somehow scared of him sitting there. No complaints about how there wasn't enough money to buy food because he'd gone and bought an economy size of the Jim Beam, or her pursing her lips in disapproval like his mom used to do to his dad.

It has to be a thing they all learn at their mother's knee, that tight-lipped look that gave the appearance of a stick being shoved firmly up their asses while simultaneously saying without words what a disappointment a man is to them. All the women I've ever known had that look mastered. Like it's a fucking art or something.

He took another hard swallow. The alcohol burned less this time and he could feel the slow heat spreading from his stomach to his limbs, loosening the angry set of his shoulders.

Four weeks now and not a goddamn word. No phone call, the bank account hadn't been touched, and that damned useless private eye had lost them in Memphis. They had stayed in a rundown roach motel for two days, cash only transaction. Wes knew that much. But the private eye had fucked it all up, spooked Laura before he could get off his shift at the plant and head for the address. He was left holding his balls, the television in the corner still warm and set to Channel 39, the Disney Channel.

He'd only hit Laura that one time. Hell, he'd apologized, brought her flowers, everything. But it hadn't mattered. He'd seen the wary look in her eyes and she'd tiptoed around for two days before taking the kids and disappearing, poof, with no one willing to look him in the eye up at the police station or help him fill out a missing person's report.

"Ain't a missing person if they leave of their own volition," the deputy had said. "Go home, Perkins, maybe she'll come round. Things are really tough right now. She'll have a hard time finding work. Hell, she'll be back with the kids before you know it."

But she hadn't been back. And the house wasn't the same without the kids squabbling over who got to watch what, or Laura in the kitchen whipping up something amazing.

Did I tell that private dick to check the diners and cafes? She could've gotten a job as a cook easy as pie. She was that good.

He frowned, downed another jolt of liquid medication, and jumped to his feet at the loud backfire that sounded outside on the street. Standing there, Wes swayed a little, unsure of why he was standing there or why his heart was pounding so damned hard, his pulse jumping in his neck, the hairs on his arm pricking up.

Just old Dowsey's car backfiring. Nothing to worry about.

He sat back down. It had been like that ever since he came home from Afghanistan. A loud noise, a car crash or siren. Hell, he was a fucking mess when the 4th of July came around.

His hand ached, and the blood was drying, except around the wound, which continued to leak. He looked down at his dingy white shirt. It was covered with red smudges of blood. That would have set Cody off big-time. Laura had been worried he had autism or Asperger's or some kind of fucked up syndrome of some kind. When the kid saw blood, he freaked the fuck out.

That's what comes of having a woman raise your son while you're off killing sand niggers and defending America.

His lip curled in disdain at the memory of Cody losing his shit in Wal-Mart when Sarah fell down and got a bloody nose. She was crying, but Cody, two years older and lacking the balls a boy his age should have, had started screaming bloody murder over the blood on his sister's dress. Wes had taken him into the men's bathroom and backhanded him, shocking the boy into silence.

And how Laura had given me The Look then. As if it was my fault the boy had no balls and screamed like a girl over blood.

Wes hit the bottle again, then again, until suddenly, the last drops were dribbling out on his tongue and everything felt warm and fuzzy. A nice big blur that intensified as he tried and failed, to stand up. He tried again, and the room tilted as he wobbled towards the dark hallway. The last light of the day was pouring in through the living room windows cloaking the room in red and he heard the hum of the electric start up, the fridge motor turning on, as if after hours of being off, and a checkered past two weeks of infrequent electrical spikes that there would be anything inside worth preserving any longer.

He wove his way into the bathroom, belching as he peed into the toilet. The light in the bathroom was dim, probably because all but one of the three lightbulbs had burned out. He turned and tried digging in the closet for a box of bulbs. He was sure it was in there somewhere. And just as quickly as the lights had come on, they flickered once, twice, and were down again.

Wes backed up, but not far enough. In the pitch black, and in his drunken state, he stood up too soon and cracked his head on the shelf above. He didn't see stars so much as streaks of hot white light burning across his retinas, his head exploding with pain.

"Fuck!" He fell back, the ground tilting and moving under him, and passed out on the floor of the bathroom, too drunk to try to find his way back to the living room or the empty bed.

Dawn came stealing in from the east, lighting up the hallway in a weak orange light. But the dawn wasn't what had woken him. The impatient honk of the truck outside had. Wes groaned and clutched his head as Maynard pounded on the front door and rang the doorbell.

"Perkins!" He could hear his friend's muffled yell, "We're gonna be late!"

Wes struggled to his feet, removing the Hot Wheels car that had slid up his pant leg and lodged painfully against his ankle. It clattered and slipped away, banging into the far wall. He winced. The back of his head had a lump where he had slammed it into the shelf, but that was the least of his ailments. His tongue felt thick and coated, swollen, yet also dry and parched, and his injured hand ached, the wound having finally stopped bleeding. The weak sunlight filtering in was enough for him to see his reflection and he instantly wished he hadn't. He looked like hell. He looked worse than that.

Eyes sunken, dark smudges under them like he'd been in a fight, and his lips cracked. He stood there, shaky, a sour taste in his mouth, and his teeth were coated with gunk.

How long's it been since I brushed my teeth? Or took a damn shower?

Maynard pounded again and then thought to try the door. It was unlocked, of course. In a town the size of Tiptonville, everyone knew everyone. You needn't bother locking your doors.

Maynard turned the handle and walked in, saw Wes shuffling out of the bathroom and shook his head in disgust. "Christ, Perkins, you ever give that whiskey bottle a break? We're gonna be late to work and you look like the walking dead. What the hell? Did you forget we got the early shift the rest of this week?"

Wes flapped his hand and shuffled to the bedroom. "Gimme five minutes, I gotta change my clothes."

It took seven minutes, and Maynard revved the engine of his truck as Wes slid into the passenger seat. "I can't afford to be late man, you're gonna have to find someone else to take you if you do this again to me."

Wes mumbled under his breath and his friend looked at him, his lips set in a thin line before he squealed the tires and pulled out of the gravel drive with an impatient jerk. The plant was just to the north of town, and there was no traffic to speak of. The men were silent. Maynard fiddling with the dial on the radio the entire way, flipping incessantly from channel to channel. They made it with one minute to spare, sliding into one of the last parking spaces left in the small lot.

"Best avoid Boss Man, you reek of whiskey," Maynard said in a low voice as they approached the building.

His warning, however, was in vain. Boss Man, also known as Ethan Hurlbut, the owner of Hurlbut Manufacturing, was waiting at the door. Maynard nodded at the man, "Mornin' Boss," and sidled past. Wes wasn't as lucky.

"Perkins, if I could have a word." The older man's face was grim, and Wes felt his guts twist.

Maynard threw him a sidelong glance that spoke of pity mixed with unease and scuttled out of sight around the corner. Wes could hear the punch of the clock seconds later and the far door open, releasing the loud hum of machinery, before clicking shut behind his friend. He knew he would not be walking onto the floor today, and possibly any other day.

He licked his lips, which felt dry, stretched, as if the whiskey had sucked every ounce of water out of him. Hell, his skin felt so dry that his eyeballs ached in their sockets. He hadn't felt this bad coming off a drunk since Afghanistan and the IED that had blown up his patrol vehicle, sending him to the hospital with a concussion, lacerations, and a week's stay in the infirmary. And he had been the lucky one.

"Don't bother, I got a feeling about where this is heading," he rasped, glaring at Ethan Hurlbut.

Boss Man had spent time in the Marines, been drafted into a stint in Vietnam, and then re-upped for one more tour. When he had come back, he had taken over Hurlbut Manufacturing from his dad after the old man suffered a massive heart attack and died in the dingy cafeteria directly under a hand painted sign that read, "Here at Hurlbut we don't haul ass, we hurl butt!"

And Ethan ran a tight ship. A lesser man, a man who hadn't served his country like Wes had, wouldn't have lasted a month coming to work hung over. But Boss Man had watched Wes, even given him an advance two weeks ago so he could hire the private dick, and even let him take off that one day to find Laura and the kids in Memphis.

"Wes, I've been where you're at," Hurlbut began.

"Save it for someone else, boss. I don't need an intervention."

"No, you need to stop killing yourself. Which is what you're doing. And I can't have you operating machinery when you're still sauced from the night before. No can do."

Wes waved a hand, weaving slightly as he walked away, heading for the road. "Right, got it." He didn't look back, but he could feel Boss Man's eyes on him.

The walk back to town took most of an hour. It gave him time to think about how fucked he was.

No wife or kids. No job. No fucking money.

He sobered up as he walked, the May sun warming his bones, the brightness of it painful at first. He stopped when he got to Main Street and instead of heading home, he walked into the Sinclair gas station and dug into his pockets for the wrinkled dollar bills he had dug out of Cody's piggy bank that morning before getting in the truck with Maynard.

Leslie Cobain and her husband Phil owned the gas station. They alternated shifts, and it was Leslie's turn to man the station. She looked up with a smile that faltered at the sight of Wes.

"Hey there, Wes, you look like you have been through the wringer." She clucked her tongue, "I heard about Laura and the kids. You had any luck on that yet?"

Wes knew it was all over town.

Hell, can't take a dump without the entire fucking town hearing about it.

He shook his head, his mouth dry as a bone.

"Well, grab a cup of Joe and sit for a bit."

He didn't want to head back home to an empty house. He had no job to go to, and Wes couldn't remember the last time he'd just sat and talked to anyone. He grabbed a cup of coffee, added a couple of pieces of ice to cool it off enough to drink, and pulled up a stool next to the counter. He had dated Leslie for a few months in high school. It hadn't been serious, a casual friendship that got a little hot and heavy and then, once the anticipation was done and over, had dwindled back to casual again.

Phil wasn't the jealous type. A year ahead of Wes and Leslie, he had been friendly, and Wes and Laura had been invited to several get-togethers over the years. Hell, Phil had drunk him under the table a few years back now.

"So how are you, Wes?"

"Shit, you got eyes. I feel like hot shit bagged in a layer of lava." Leslie wasn't blind, and he knew he looked like hell.

She laughed and stood up, walked to a cooler and grabbed three large Smart Water bottles and two orange Gatorade, then set them down on the counter in front of him. "On the house. You'll feel better if you can flush some of that whiskey out of your system."

"Hell, whiskey's a food group, Les, didn't you know?"

Her eyes were kind, full of empathy, "Drinking it like its water isn't going to bring Laura and the kids back."

He cracked open one of the Gatorade bottles and downed half of it in one go. He could feel his body sucking it in, felt the cells expand, and his skin felt a little less tight.

"Well, now that I'm fired, I got nothing to buy any more with anyhow." His headache, although still a whopper, began to ease off. His stomach growled, loud and long, and Leslie looked amused as she tossed him a bag of jerky.

"You'll be in good company soon enough. Ethan doesn't have the funds to keep anyone on after the 18th, anyway. All this financial mess, the power issues, and more..." she shook her head, "It's gonna get worse before it gets better."

Wes took a piece of jerky and began to gnaw on it. The taste of the teriyaki-flavored meat filled his mouth and soothed his angry stomach. "Whatcha heard?"

"Mostly it's been through Phil when he's up at the clinic getting his dialysis treatments. They are saying things are going to get a whole hell of a lot worse soon."

Wes shrugged, "Economy goes up, it comes down, it goes back up again. Big fucking cycle. What's to worry about?" Before Leslie could answer, the question struck him. "Hey wait, what's going on with Phil that he needs dialysis?"

Leslie's face twisted in pain, her lips quivered a little as she tried to smile, to put a brave face on her fears. "His kidneys are failing and his liver is starting to fail. What with all that's going on in the world, the list of donors has dropped off. Especially here in flyover country. The doc says it's likely they won't find a donor liver in time, so he's got maybe three, six months if we're lucky."

"Jesus, Les, I'm sorry." He reached out and took the woman's hand, his mind reeling at the thought of Phil, full of life, father of four, dying. Hell, they weren't even middle age. "This shit isn't supposed to happen in our 30s, damn it."

She shrugged helplessly, "It was the drinking. He drank like a fish for years. Nobody really saw it. He started in high school and just never really stopped. I don't know why I didn't say something, do something, especially after seeing my dad and mom kill themselves slowly. Instead, I was living with it, covering for him, enabling him instead of drawing a line in the sand. I covered for him here, at home, and it just got bad, really bad. And one day he went in for a checkup. He hadn't been feeling well, been vomiting blood, peeing blood, the works. And they told him he was going to die if he didn't change his ways."

"Overnight, he changed. He checked himself into English Mountain, that rehab center up in the Eastern hills, and he got himself clean and sober. It was amazing and wonderful. I got my husband back; the kids got their daddy back. And things were good, better than good, until late last year." There were tears in her eyes. "And now, well, now I get to watch him die, just when things were turning around."

Wes squeezed her hand, unsure what to say, when suddenly Leslie grabbed his hand and held onto it with a strength that took him by surprise. "You only get this one life, Wes. This one, here and now. You can waste it or you can make the best of it."

Before he could reply, there were voices, shouting, a flurry of activity from down the street near the Trade Mart.

"What the hell is happening now?" Leslie asked, her eyebrows furrowed as she stared out of the glass. A handful of men and women, more than the usual group that held court in front of the Trade Mart and smoked cigarettes and gossiped, were gathering.

One of the women shook her head and Wes and Leslie could both hear her shouting, "No, no, NO! The news reports are wrong. They have to be!"

Wes stared at Leslie, "We better go see what's going on."

Wes untied the body of the deer from the pole. He had gas in the truck, but instead of driving he had walked the ten miles, choosing to enjoy the stars and camp for a day or two before taking the buck, field dressing it, and returning to town.

He'd spent the past two months clean and sober, even though the DTs had hit him hard soon after the news of the limited nukes in Austin and D.C. had come out. That day, standing there in front of the Trade Mart, listening to the scant, and often contradictory, news coming over the radio, reality had struck him like a freight train.

Thanks to his PTSD and heavy drinking, he had lost Laura, Cody and Sarah. Most likely forever. There was no way of finding them, no clues as to their whereabouts. Thanks to The Collapse, the United States was in shambles, the government gone, and rumors of civil war were spreading. The country he had known, the one he had gone to a foreign land filled with sand and violence to defend, was no more.

There in the gravel driveway, he glanced up and saw Leslie sitting on his front stoop. She looked as if she had aged ten years in the last two months. But then again, losing your husband and your only way of making a living thanks to The Collapse will do that to you. No tankers to bring gas, as of a month ago, no gas to sell, and Leslie had finally just walked away from the gas station. The shelves were empty by then, nothing to sell, certainly nothing to steal, and she had sat by Phil's side until he drew his last breath.

Wes had been bringing her hunks of meat since May. He knew that others were helping in whatever way they could, as well.

"Hey there, Les. I got a nice-sized back haunch for you."

He eased the carcass down off of the sling. A combination of metal poles, wheels, and a heavy-duty tarp had made hauling the deer back to town relatively easy. As it was, he was feeling more fit than he had since his high school days. He spent most of his time hunting, alone in the woods outside of town, and the isolation had helped. Having meat helped. He traded it for other things, like produce from the Perdue's farm, or the heavy home-style bread that Sadie brought every Tuesday and Friday to the Trade Mart to barter for her family's other needs.

Leslie smiled, a small one that faded fast. She looked tired. No big surprise there. She had four little ones to look after and her husband hadn't been gone three weeks now.

"Hanging in there, Wes." She looked at the deer carcass. "No head?"

"Already dropped it off at the Perdue's on my way in. Old man says he's gonna make head cheese with it and the tongue."

Leslie nodded. "I wasn't coming by for meat, although it's kind of you to offer, but I wanted you to come to the Fourth of July picnic folks are planning for tomorrow."

Wes snorted, "Fourth of July? Hell, there ain't no Fourth of July anymore."

"Don't be silly, of course there is." She waved a hand in the direction of Main Street. "Hell, I know how you feel. I'm not really up to a picnic myself, but it will be good for the kids. They haven't been out much since the funeral."

"Yeah, well, I ain't going."

"Wes, stop it. You cleaned yourself up, everyone can see that, and some of the menfolk they've been asking about your military experience. We could use a militia in case those rumors turn into something more. You've got training, experience."

"Yeah," Wes snorted, "I got really good at getting shot at."

"Don't be a pain in the ass, Wes Perkins. Come to the picnic and bring some ribs. You need to be part of the community; this town could use your expertise." She stood then, and she moved slow, slower than she should at her age. "I'll expect to see you there."

The next day had dawned and with it, storm clouds on the horizon. Wes looked out the window and thought of what Leslie had said. She'd been right about his drinking, and she was probably right now. He hated the 4th of July. At least he had these past five years or so, back from Afghanistan where a damn car backfiring had him on his feet looking for an attack.

The rumors that were swirling of the supremacist militias and the remnants of soldiers left unpaid and leaderless in the economic collapse, all of it added up to bad news. Wes cinched his belt a notch tighter. He'd lost two waist sizes since Laura had left, taking her mad cooking skills with her. He ate meat, usually jerky, and wasn't drinking, so the extra pounds he had put on since he'd been overseas had melted off.

Hell, maybe I can fit into a size large shirt again.

He dug into the back of the closet and found a stack of old shirts Laura had put away when he'd drank enough to make them too tight. His mouth quirked up at the third one down from the top, an outrageous red and yellow Hawaiian shirt, garish in design. It had been a Father's Day present shortly after he'd returned from overseas. Back when things were still good, or relatively so, a time when Laura had still loved him. He slipped it on, buttoned it up and felt his mouth turning up in a happy grin. The first one in months.

It fit. It actually fit well.

Fuck it. I'll go. It'll shock the shit out of most of those gossipy old busybodies to see me show my face.

He stared at his reflection in the mirror and his smile slipped as he thought of Laura and the kids. Chances were, he might never see them again. He had hoped, when things got bad, that they would come back. He dreamed of it, waking up in the middle of the night sure he had heard Sarah's voice, or Cody's husky whisper, the one where they think they are being quiet but instead are shout-whispering. But there had been nothing. No sign of them, not even a postcard or letter before the mail service had shut down completely. They were gone, and he was here in this empty house, reminded of them at every turn. Reminded of how he had failed to be the husband and father they deserved.

Hours later, as he stood on the edges of the crowd, the rack of ribs he had brought slowly browning on the large grill that had been set up in the middle of the street; he found himself questioning why he had come. Most of the women wouldn't meet his glance, and the men were all gathered in a group, with Ethan Hurlbut at the center, talking about starting a town militia. Leslie had come over, smiled and squeezed his arm, gave him a small hug before having to run off and deal with her youngest, four-year-old Eva who had fallen down and had a nasty scrape. The girl was wailing, a mess of tears and snot over a tiny little patch of blood on her knee.

He stood there, alone. His shirt felt like a damned neon sign that proclaimed, "Look at me! My wife left me and took my kids thanks to me being a drunken asshole!"

Another hunt in the woods sounds really good right about now.

"Hi."

Wes blinked. The woman standing in front of him could not be talking to him. He looked around, first to the left and then the right, before he turned back to her. Her lips twitched in what could only be amusement.

"Me?"

She said nothing, but a smile grew on her face. She handed him a slice of cake tilting on a cheap paper plate. "Leslie said that lemon cake is your favorite. I'm Angie, by the way."

She tipped her head back towards the group of women where Leslie was holding her youngest. Leslie looked up, winked at him and smiled before returning to petting Eva's hair and wiping the last of the little girl's tears away.

Dessert before dinner. Why the hell not?

"Uh, thanks." Wes took the cake from her and managed a weak smile in return. "I'm Wes." He took a bite of the cake. It was delicious. How long had it been since he had eaten lemon cake? At least six months, probably longer. It wasn't as moist as Laura's, but still.

The light shifted, dimmed, the clouds that had been in the distance had finally moved in and the day took on an unprecedented coolness as the storm began to move in, thunder beginning to rumble.

"Uh oh," Angie looked up, grinning, "it looks like we are about to get some real weather."

The way she said it, her odd accent, and the fact that her face wasn't familiar, reeled Wes in. He stepped closer. "Where are you from? Not from around here, I'm guessing."

"No," she said, shaking her head. She cocked it sideways and grinned like a fool at the darkening sky. "California. I was visiting friends, and well, things went to hell and I figured why not stay here for a while."

She turned away and studied the clouds, her eyes examining them as they roiled and moved, the wind picking up her hair, blowing it. Behind them, folks were scrambling to pull the tables inside of the Trade Mart. Even the grill was being moved to under the overhang of the building as fat drops of rain began to fall.

"You act like you've never seen rain before." He shoveled half of the cake into his mouth, watching her with obvious delight.

She turned back. "There's plenty of rain, but without the thunder and lightning. Just a downpour, no light show." Her grin stretched impossibly wide, her teeth were uneven, but bright white. "Do you think we might get a tornado?" She said it with a hopeful look, eyes wide with excitement. She jumped as a streak of lightning lit up the horizon and thunder boomed.

"I think we are more likely to get hit by lightning if we stay here." He swallowed the last of the cake, licking his fingers. "C'mon, let's get under cover."

Without thinking, he took her hand and led her away. Not towards the Trade Mart, but towards home. It was instinctual. He had been ready to run when faced with the crowd already, and somehow, having just met her, he didn't want to say goodbye. She didn't question it, didn't look nervous, just laughed as the rain began to fall, heavy and their feet were soon splashing through puddles as they ran through the side streets.

The heavens let loose as they made it to his door. The rain hammering the roof, filling the gutters and gushing over in two places, the water overwhelming the gutters, and spilling down in a solid line where Cody had dented the spot of guttering over the eaves with a football the year before. The kid might be a pansy over the sight of blood, but he was strong.

"Wow, that changed from sunny to downpour in nothing flat!" Angie laughed, pulling at her soaked t-shirt and wiping at the drips that ran in rivulets from her hairline. She looked around the living room and Wes felt a wave of embarrassment crash through him.

What had he been thinking when he brought her here? The bottles of Jim Beam were all gone, but he hadn't cleaned, not once, since Laura and the kids left. Dirty laundry lay scattered on the floor, a pile of dirty dishes covered the coffee table, and he was suddenly acutely aware that he hadn't cracked a window to let fresh air in. It smelled almost feral, as if he had brought her to a wolf's den, not a home. He grabbed a tall candle, a floral scented one Laura had liked so much, and lit it with a match. He shook the box. He was down to the last handful of them. Hopefully he could pick up a box at the Trade Mart next time he had some meat and skins to trade.

"I, uh..." Wes was surprised to find he felt nervous, worried this stranger would want to leave as quickly as she had arrived. "I didn't really think about how messy it was in here. I, uh..."

"You weren't expecting a strange woman to come home with you?" Her face was guileless, and she cocked her head to one side, assessing him with her warm brown eyes.

"Yeah, I guess so. I mean," he paused, suddenly out of his depth, "I mean, is that what we are doing here?"

She threw her head back and laughed. It rang out, so bright and melodic, that he was shocked by it. "You tell me, Wes, you led the way. I just followed along!"

He felt attraction then, a strong pull of it. It wasn't just the fact that a real, live woman was standing in his living room. That she could have taken home top spot in a wet t-shirt contest or that he hadn't had any for longer than he could remember. There was something about her. She was confident, yet not brash. She smiled at him and he felt like he could lose himself in that smile. It reminded him of how Laura had looked in the early days - when the first blush of their love had been simple and overwhelming and pure. Before Afghanistan, before Cody, and responsibilities and bills had replaced those hedonistic moments of making love on his narrow futon in a sun-drenched apartment with neighbors bickering on the other side of the wall. Before the explosions and the whiskey, he drank to keep his nerves from feeling like white-hot pokers in his brain.

He smiled back at her, felt the unfamiliar stretch as the corners of his mouth lifted up. She nodded then, "That's better. You looked so solemn before. A smile looks good on you."

It slipped then, and he looked away. "I'm not so good with people these days."

She stepped closer, reached up, and touched his cheek. "Really? Maybe you just haven't been with the right people." She leaned in, her breath smelling of lemon cake, and kissed him lightly on the lips. He returned the favor by putting his arms around her, pulling her close, and losing himself in a deep, passionate kiss.

He slept late that next morning for the first time in forever, opening his eyes to hear Angie moving about in the living room, humming away. She had stayed the whole night, and the sun was pouring in the bedroom window, promising a hot, muggy morning after the odd weather of the day before.

He stretched, listening. What was she doing? He sat up, grabbed his jeans, and slipped them on. Her back was to him and she gave a small yip of surprise when he spoke, jumping as she turned, toys filling her hands. He looked around the living room, saw it neat and clean, the dishes washed, the tables cleared.

"You're awake." she looked down at the toys in her hands. "I'm an early riser and, well," she shrugged, "I like to clean. I hope you don't mind."

He didn't and realized his face probably told her something different. The scent of meat cooking got his stomach rumbling, though, and it let out a large, low growl.

Angie laughed, another one of her carefree, musical laughs that had him grinning in return. He scuffed his bare foot on the floor, "I guess I worked up an appetite last night."

Her eyes widened, eyebrows arching, her grin infectious, "Same here, I'm positively starving!"

It felt strange to see her in Laura's spot at the table. But as she talked about the life she had left in California, "It was so expensive to live there!" and her life here in Tennessee, "Did you know that cows actually do that?" he found that she fit in some odd, refreshing way.

After breakfast, they sat on the front porch and she waved at Dowsey as he walked past, his decrepit Buick neatly put away in the garage. The old man was pushing ninety. He had lived on his own since his wife of sixty-five years had passed the year before, and he still didn't even need glasses. He nodded at the two of them and kept on walking.

"Tell me about your family," Angie asked, matter of fact, right to the point.

Wes stared at her. "I imagine you've heard the stories."

She shrugged, "I'd rather hear it from you."

Yep, and this is when she's gonna high tail it out of here.

"Laura, my wife, she took Cody and Sarah and left about four months ago now. I hired a private eye to try to find them and he got close. By the time I got to the motel in Memphis, they were gone and there's been no word since." He paused. "Is that about what you heard?"

Angie nodded, then asked, "Would you consider yourself a good husband and father?"

She's direct. A woman after my own heart.

He drew in a breath and let it out, sighed, "No, I wouldn't. I tried to be. I really did. But I fucked up. I drank too much, yelled at the kids, and lost my temper with Laura. She didn't deserve it, not one bit of it." He looked away, down the road, wondered where they were, whether they were okay, if they were safe. He wondered if he would ever know the truth.

"She did what she had to - to be safe, to be a good parent to the kids. She did it because I wasn't changing, and the situation was getting worse, not better. I was mad as hell, ready to drag her back by her hair if I found her. I lost my job, lost most of my friends, and I've sat alone in this house and wished I had another chance to make it right."

He stared into the distance, afraid to look at the woman by his side. She sighed too and slipped her hand into his. It was small, delicate.

"Thank you, Wes. For your honesty."

He snorted and shook his head. "And now is when you're gonna run for the hills, right?"

She laughed and bumped her shoulder against his. "Nah, I think I'll stay awhile if you don't mind."

Relief flooded through him. He'd been lonely and there was something about Angie that captivated him. His voice was gruff, "I don't mind."

"Good."

Five Months Later

They sat there in silence and listened to the town wake up around them.

"I fixed you the last of the tea." Wes set the steaming mug down on the dining room table and turned back to his packs. The first cold snap and a hunting trip were long overdue. He added his fletching knife, which he had sharpened the evening before.

Angie's hair, normally neatly coiffed in a bun, was in disarray and she was still in a nightshirt, a thick woven blanket around her shoulders, her knees drawn up to her chest, heels balanced on the worn wood of the chair, a faraway look in her eyes.

Wes looked back at her. She hadn't touched the tea. "You okay?" He pulled up a chair, sat down next to her. Something was wrong.

She looked up, uncharacteristically somber. He attempted a smile. "I suppose you could keep your nightshirt on while hunting, and just flash the deer. The shock of it might keep them from bolting."

A corner of her mouth twitched, but it was fleeting, and he could see an anxious look in her eyes. "I think I had better stay here. I'm not feeling so well."

"It was that damned Anderson kid, wasn't it?" She had been helping out with running the small school in town, reading to the younger children while others taught the older students. Bella Anderson, a normally feisty four-year-old, had been rosy-cheeked with fever, glassy eyes and a runny nose when he stopped by with lunch for Angie the day before. "I swear they've got some cold or flu on a constant running basis. With seven kids in the house, it's practically a rotating array of disease."

"It's not little Bella," Angie picked up the tea, sniffed it, and then set it down again and pushed it towards him. "I can't enjoy it, my stomach's all crazy right now, you go ahead."

Their fingers connected and Wes felt a ball of wonder beginning to rotate in his stomach. Laura had been the same way with both Cody and Sarah.

"Oh shit." He breathed it out, shock mixing with anticipation, even joy. Her eyes met his, worry and even fear so clear in her soft brown eyes. "You're pregnant, aren't you?"

"Do you want me to go?" Her voice was childlike in that moment, and he could see she was waiting for him to give her a sign, anything that would indicate decisively how he was feeling.

"Do I want you to go?" Why would she think that? And then he thought of Laura and Cody and Sarah. They had spoken of them, many times, and in all of those times, she had never once asked what would happen if they did come back. For that matter, he hadn't wanted to think of it either. And now the question was there, in front of them. This existence, this thing that they had together. What was it?

His mouth opened. And then it closed. He couldn't explain it. He couldn't put it into words, the emotions he was feeling. That if he told her how he felt about her, it meant closing the door on the life he had with his wife and children. What if they came back? This child, this baby growing inside of her, it changed everything.

"I can't... I can't talk about this right now." The words sounded harsh, distant, and they fell out of his mouth before he could stop them, before he could explain how complicated this all was. The love he felt for her, so different from the love he had felt for Laura. Different, because they were different people. He pulled back, hating himself as he saw his retreat in her eyes.

He reached out then, took her hand, stared at how the fingers were bare of jewelry, no ring that said she was his, and his own still wearing his wedding ring. It was simply part of his hand, it had never occurred to him to take it off, not even after Angie had moved in four months ago.

Four months, they had done nearly everything together. She had hunted with him, sleeping on the hard ground, cussing out the mosquitoes that swarmed near Reelfoot Lake, and learned to trap right alongside him.

"Stay here. I need to think. I need to..." His brain was spinning, "I just need some time, okay?"

He could see the beginnings of tears in her eyes, "Okay." It hadn't been the response she had obviously been hoping for, more of one she had feared.

Her fears manifested. Will I ever stop hurting the people that I love?

He squeezed her hand. "I'll be back tomorrow, next day at the latest."

He grabbed his packs and left then, escaping to the woods where there were no people, no noise, nothing but the woods and him and the creatures he was hunting. All of his cares, all the things that pulled him back to civilization, they fell away and he could think.

Wes walked; each step chosen carefully. No high hide this time. A bullet in the chamber, locked and loaded, and he picked up fresh tracks near the stream's edge, heading away into a deeper brush.

A baby. He remembered Sarah's birth so clearly. Cody's, he had missed, thousands of miles away in the desert city of Kandahar when he got the news that his son had been born a month early, two weeks before his scheduled leave. Laura had been young, just seventeen, and he had gotten leave to come home and see his new wife and son. Red and small and squalling, that had been his impression of him.

And if he were honest, that was pretty much how he had always found Cody, at least the squalling part of it. Sarah, despite her love for baby dolls, was tougher. She had been a happy baby, seemed impervious to pain, and had climbed trees better than her brother. He hadn't been there for them. Neither of them.

And he would be there, every step of the way, every moment for this one. Not fucked up, or desperate for the alcohol to blunt the noise, the memories.

The tracks intersected with another creature's prints, and Wes could see he was on a main thoroughfare for the animal life here. A superhighway to the watering hole. Ahead he saw the path open up, and there at the edge of the lake, a doe and her two fawns had stopped to drink. He lowered his rifle. He wouldn't take a doe, not one that had babies to care for. Across the way, a hundred feet away where the land held on, fighting the lake for dominance, he saw a majestic stag. No doubt the sire of the two fawns that drank water silently, mere yards away from him.

He lifted his rifle once again. It was a long shot, but he could see just where to put the round. There was no wind, nothing to interfere with a quick death. It would take a good twenty minutes to walk through the brush and around the edge of the lake to retrieve the kill, but it was a good one and Wes smiled, eager to return to Angie, to say the words she needed to hear. The stag's ear twitched, but it didn't move.

He closed an eye, sighted down the barrel, and focused on the place where the round would hit. Center mass, slightly to the right of the breastbone, a tad elevated to account for distance. His finger tightened gently on the trigger. And in the split second before he fired, the sound of gunfire erupted from the distance. The stag wheeled around, sprinted away with a mighty crash and was out of sight in less than a second, random crashes in the brush betraying his existence as the creature fled for its life.

Wes stopped, looking in vain to see if he could see anything. It was a lot of gunfire, and it was coming from town. He dropped the two packs he had brought with him. They didn't have anything he couldn't retrieve later, and certainly nothing that he needed. What he did need to do was get home as quickly as possible.

He ran, settling into a steady lope. A ground-eating pace he had learned in the service, one made easier by not having the sixty-pound pack of camping supplies and tools on his back. The '65 Enfield was strapped to his back and at this rate he would be back in town in less than an hour.

Too long, gotta get there faster.

He lengthened his stride, felt his boots dig into the brush, crackling with frost, following a game trail rather than seeking the road.

There had been rumors of troop movements, in at least two directions, one from the west, and others to the north. Tiptonville was small, remote even. The initial tension and attentiveness to the world around them had faded as the months stretched on and the small town was forgotten by the world at large. An oasis of calm, it went unnoticed for so long that many had come to believe they would be able to ride out The Collapse with little more than inconvenience. They had taken their peace for granted, assuming it would continue. And now, from the sound of the gunfire, the town was paying for that mistake dearly.

He was winded, his heart pounding in his chest, but he continued to push his body forward, yards disappearing beneath his feet, his entire focus on returning to Angie. Would she stay inside? Or would she step out of the door, run towards danger?

In the past three months, Angie had proved herself to be strong, capable, tough. He had shown her how to fire a gun. She had lain on the hard ground beside him, handled gutting and cleaning the kills, and even taken a buck of her own over a month ago. A clean shot to the chest, with the creature dead before it hit the ground.

Stay inside. Hide. Stay inside. Hide.

The silent plea repeated itself over and over. If only his wishes were enough to keep her safe.

He faltered, his ankle a hot pulse of pain as it twisted on a rocky section of the trail. He ignored it, followed the tree line, and burst out between two backyards a block over from his house. The fence between the two yards had been on the decline for a decade, but it was helped along by a particularly strong spring storm. The neighbors, an older couple on one side, and the other house long empty, had not bothered to fix it. A quick road trip to Home Depot was no longer an option.

He slipped through the gaps, avoiding the fallen panels and crossed the road. The gunfire was concentrated in the north part of town, to his right.

Perhaps they hadn't even come through this area.

His hopes were dashed when he saw the first body. Dowsey lay crumpled on the ground on his stomach, one gnarled, aged hand lying limp at his side, the other tucked under him. He wasn't moving and there was a wide circle of red in the middle of his back. Wes didn't stop. He passed another and another.

His heart hammered in his chest as he turned the corner, and he saw her then, her dishwater blond hair splayed out, half on, half off the front stoop. His Ruger, the one he had given her to practice with, lay on the ground next to her limp right hand. And blood, so much blood.

If he had any breath to spare, he would have screamed then. But each molecule of oxygen served to move him forward to bring him to her side. He slid to a stop, his lungs desperate for more air than he could give, his heart shattering as he brought her up to him and held her against his chest.

Minutes passed. Time enough for his heart to slow, for his breathing to return to some semblance of normality. He sat there and held her. When he could speak again, he told her how much he loved her, that he was sorry he hadn't said it that morning, that he was a fool. He told her all the words he knew she had wanted to hear, all the words that had occurred to him on the long walk out. He spoke of his dreams, the dreams made real by the news that he had another chance, another moment, a life to spend with her and their child in this house. That he didn't want her to go anywhere but instead be here with him. He held her, rocked her, and described what it was like to see Sarah born. To know that a piece of himself had become a person, something whole and separate from him, and that, no matter what, they would make it work.

And when he was done. When there were no more words and her blood had drenched his shirt, his jeans, he laid her gently on the ground, carefully closed her eyes, and went to find the men responsible.

Hours later, in the darkness, in the burning flames of the buildings the invading troops had set on fire, Wes exacted his revenge on the last two soldiers left.

He had been far too late to catch the men responsible. Those who had commanded the troops were long gone, on to another town, and better conquests. The town militia was in tatters. Their head, his former boss and ex-Marine Ethan Hurlbut lay dead, partially crushed by the fallen water tower, his body riddled with bullets. Of all of them, Ethan's voice had been the loudest, warning of the possibility of this happening. He had been their leader, but most of the men in the militia had never seen combat. They were gun owners, hunters even, but not soldiers.

The two soldiers, wounded, left behind when their Jeep headed down the wrong side street, separated from the Western Front, if the violent, murderous remainder of the army could even be called that now - the two soldiers were taking a long time in dying. Both of them shot in the legs, they couldn't walk or run or even crawl. Hell, they couldn't escape from the Jeep which was now on the side of the road into town, pushed there after Wes had assumed leadership of what few remained of the militia.

It was Wes that called for the gasoline can. And as he set fire to the Jeep, he ignored the screams of the men inside as they begged for their lives. He had stood there, long after the crowd had dispersed, long after they had scuttled away, back to the ruins of their homes and their lives, and he had waited for the men inside to be burned clean of their sins. He had waited until only their skeletons remained.

He walked away, into the dark.

"Wes?" Leslie, her arm in a sling, put a hand on his arm.

A new day had dawned. He hadn't slept. He'd cleaned Angie up as best he could, but there was no water pressure left in the lines now that the water tower was down. He'd wrapped her body in a sheet, loaded her onto the tarp they had used to bring back the deer carcasses and begun the long walk out to Reelfoot Lake.

He hadn't noticed Leslie following behind.

He had dug the hole there in the first campsite he had taken her to. It was on a hill, surrounded by willow trees and carpeted in wildflowers. He had just been settling Angie's body into the grave when Leslie spoke.

"I'm so sorry." Her voice was flat, her eyes bloodshot.

"She loved this place. Said it was magical." His hands shook, and he stared at the shovel, realizing he hadn't washed the blood off of them yet. Her blood.

"It's beautiful." Leslie said, her voice choking. "She is, well, she was..."

"I know. She told me." He took the shovel and prepared to begin digging.

"Those soldiers," Leslie's voice was a whisper, "the ones in the Jeep."

"I thought it would make me feel better." He said, his eyes taking in her burns, the dried blood on Leslie's clothing, her hands. "Seeing them burn after what they did to Angie. What they did to this town."

"And did it?"

"No."

"In war," Leslie said slowly, "there are no winners."

"No, there aren't."

And with nothing left to say, Wes dug the shovel deep into the soft earth.

This Fractured Nation

"The world is not what it was. Our nation is in ruins."

I noticed the dog first. She watched me, at attention, her body close to a small girl with red hair who sat near a young woman with golden blond curls snaking down her back. A few feet away, a blanket was covered with a small mound of tiny pups, all of them sleeping deeply.

The dog gave a short bark, then wagged her tail at me. The young woman looked up, surprise on her face. I wondered if it was surprise at the dog's reaction, or was it that I was a stranger? Perhaps few people came this way, I wasn't sure.

This had to be her, though, the girl I had been looking for. She was younger than I expected. She looked to be in her late teens, perhaps early 20s.

I thought for a moment that, given the right set of circumstances, this girl could be my daughter's age, if Anna had lived. And for a moment, the pain slammed into me, barely dulled by twenty years, still as gut-wrenching as ever. When menopause had come on last year, early at the tender age of forty-six, it had been a relief. I didn't need the monthly reminders that my ovaries and uterus had conspired against me, that they were not capable of bringing viable life into the world. It was a relief, really.

I forced the memory away, met Jess's gaze, the corners of my mouth turning up in a friendly smile, and I raised my hand in greeting. "Hello there! You must be Jessica Aaronson." I reached down and scratched the dog's ears as she nosed my leg, "And this must be Quincy."

Quincy licked my hand, then settled down near Jess's feet again, her tail a steady thump against the ground. Her latest litter of puppies squirmed on a blanket nearby, beginning to wake up, their bodies of mass of tiny noses and twitching tails.

I wondered what Jess must think of me. Now in my late 40s, I had slim, long legs, and I was taller than most women, far taller than my mother had been. My hair was long, straight, and dark, and I kept it braided in one thick rope down the middle of my back. The hair at my temples had begun to show gray last year, as did one long streak that ran the length of my long hair. Despite the cool fall day, I was wearing shorts and a sleeveless tank top with a rucksack resting on my shoulders. When Mother was younger, they had often pointed to me and called me her mini-me. They said it even as I grew taller than Mother, eventually towering over her by nearly six inches. So much for a mini-anything. But that had been years ago.

Jess stared, "Uh, hello." She sounded hesitant, but polite. Not afraid, but not overly friendly.

"I'm Penelope," I said, sticking my hand out. The girl fumbled with the lamb's ear and then quickly stood up to shake my outstretched hand. "I see you are collecting lamb's ear seeds." I said, "Do you work with other herbs?"

Jess nodded, but did not elaborate.

I smiled, curious about the girl's knowledge. Perhaps she was the one I needed to ask after an apprenticeship, not the young girl that the town doc had mentioned. "Do you know anything about the properties of lamb's ear, Jess?"

"Only that it's making me feel nauseas. I don't like the weird smell." The young woman grinned ruefully back.

I laughed, "Stop for a while and I'll take over. I've gotten used to it." I sat down on the stoop, took the bucket from Jess, and began plucking at the dry flower heads. "The leaves can be picked early, before it flowers and can be dried and used in tea. You could also eat it in salads, or steamed, but most people object to the furry aspect of it. The best use of lamb's ear is for small wound care—it is absorbent and soft, and plentiful. But that isn't why I came here." I finished with one stalk and started on another. Suddenly I wasn't sure what to say, or how to say it. Here was the girl I had been looking for, for nearly five years, I was sure of it. But how do you jump into that? Instead, I found myself saying instead, "I've come to speak with you and David about Tina and a possible apprenticeship."

Jess looked at me, frowning slightly, "Tina's only ten years old."

My hands didn't stop moving as I turned toward Jess and gave her a long, appraising look. I had spent time in the heart of the town, talking to Sarah Turner. She had described Jess as the "go to" person for information on the town and its residents. After a few days of trade and work, I knew enough of the girl's history to know that she and her house full of kids had struggled through some pretty tough times in the past six or seven years. Sarah had been forthcoming with details about Jess, telling me that Jess was busy writing down the lives and accounts of most of the residents of Belton and compiling a history of the area.

"She goes from house to house, usually during the winter when there's not so much to do," Sarah had said, "She writes down whatever memories they have—of this war, of their families, of the time before—whatever someone wants to talk about, really." The woman had shrugged. "I wasn't born here, but she even wanted my story."

I had been as circumspect as possible. I had been searching a long time for the author of the letter I had found in the cave. I was sure that this Jess Aaronson was the one that had seen Mom through her final days, and buried her in the cairn outside her beloved cave.

If you are reading this, then you undoubtedly know Madge. My name is Jess Aaronson. I'm sixteen years old.

The letter was crumpled and tattered now, worn from reading and re-reading it over and over.

"Well, I've heard from Dr. Ridley that she knows a lot about herbs and healing." I smiled and turned back to the lamb's ear. "I've also come for a different reason. I've been looking for you for a long time now, nearly five years. You see, you knew someone very important to me."

I let Jess digest this in a long moment of silence. When I looked over at Jess, the expression on the girl's face had turned from one of curiosity to one of fear. Sarah had hinted that the girl had been through terrible experiences before she returned to Belton nearly seven years ago.

I stopped and said, "I'm sorry; I didn't tell you my full name. It's Penelope Falling Water Aster... Dr. Madeleine Falling Water—you may have known her as Madge—she was my mother."

The girl said nothing for a moment, her mouth falling open in shock.

"I, she, oh my God. Grandmother Madge. She..." the girl couldn't manage to put the words together. And I watched as the tears welled up in her eyes.

I watched her for a moment. I had read the letter so many times, but I had still had my doubts. Had this girl and the other children truly loved my mother? Had Mother been at peace, surrounded by someone, anyone, who may have cared for her? Had they said the prayers that my mother's spirit required in order to find peace in the hereafter? Watching the younger woman now, seeing her reaction, it seemed that the letter had spoken true.

Before I tell you how your friend or mother died, I want to tell you how she lived. How she gave us sanctuary and saved our lives, by leading us here, to this cave...

The four of us, my newborn son Jacob, David, and Tina, both orphans from Clinton, and I have been here since September.

I reached out and hugged Jess as my own tears began to slide down my nose. We were still hugging and crying when a young man in his late teens walked up a few minutes later, followed by a girl who looked very much like him. They both stood and stared at the two of us sobbing, frowning.

I am sure I do not need to tell you how special Madge was—or how much she came to mean to us. I lost my best friend in the world just days before she found us. I couldn't think; I was scared and lost.

"What's going on? Who is she?" The girl asked the young man. He just shrugged and kept staring at us. The young girl's question, however, was enough to reduce the crying and elicit some basic explanation of who I was.

Two hours later, the sun had slipped low on the horizon and dusk was gathering. My husband, Kip had joined them and they had just finished nibbling the last kernels of corn off of the cob.

I kept stealing glances at little Erin, the little girl with red curls. At nearly four years of age, she appeared to be in a growth spurt, her pants coming to rest high on her ankles, her top stretched tight, and her sleeves ended long before her wrists began. She was slender and pixie-like, her freckled skin slightly sunburnt, and her hair a mass of bright red curls. She maintained a steadfast silence, never speaking, except for the occasional giggle when David, the young man who had come upon them crying, tickled her.

As dinner wrapped up, there was a quiet silence that descended upon the group. I looked at the bunch of them and marveled at their resilience. Jess was tall and graceful. Her skin was tanned a golden brown from working in the sun, and her hair fell in long curls down the middle of her back. David was in his mid-to-late teens, and his arms and chest were muscled and lean. They had served some stew with turkey and wild greens in it and Jess had pointed to David, noting that he was the one who had landed them the turkey using his bow. It was the same bow that Grandmother Madge had taught him to use.

The end was peaceful. We were with her, holding her hands, and my baby Jacob nestled beside her. She loved to hold him, and he adored her. We all did.

The sun had slipped down beyond the horizon, pink and red streaks colored the clouds, the crickets had begun to sing, and the evening had a chill. They had spent hours describing their time with Grandmother Madge in the cave. Kip and I had pelted them with question after question, Kip especially seemed shocked that they had all spent a winter there. As dinner had wound down, Jess had put a pot of chicory coffee on to boil, and handed out mugs full of it. I tasted it and was pleasantly surprised at the sweet taste. I raised my eyebrows, and Jess grinned.

"I sweeten it with sugar beets. We grow them over there, two houses down." Jess said, pointing to the east.

They had expanded their gardens to several yards, those they identified as having good soil, and others that had intact, tall fences. Especially when it came to foods that deer liked, the high fences had been effective in keeping out the local deer population that was exploding in spite of regular hunting.

"Grandmother Madge said you were in Europe, or was it Africa?" Jess asked, dying to hear about the outside world. "How did you get here?"

My face grew grim, as did Kip's. We glanced at each other for a moment and I held out my mug to Kip for a refill. He was nearest the coffeepot.

"That has been an adventure, let me tell you. Have any of you heard much of what is going on in the outside world, outside of the former United States?" I asked Jess and David. David frowned and said nothing.

Jess answered, "We heard that The Collapse spread past our borders. That it was kind of like a domino effect. First the economic collapse and then multiple civil wars and uprisings in places like Greece, the Middle East, even China after the U.S. dollar collapsed. There were a lot of problems with the Euro before the Collapse. But afterwards," she shrugged, "we lost power and internet and my parents stopped talking about what was happening out there."

She stared into the gathering darkness. "Maybe it was too big, too frightening even for them. And then afterwards, after I returned with David and Tina and Jacob, well, we haven't exactly welcomed outsiders in Belton until more recently. The world has changed, I'm sure, but we only know what is nearby. There have been plenty of false starts into reasserting government on a broader level, but nothing that's stuck." She gestured toward the town center, "We have a militia, a mayor..."

"For whatever they are worth," murmured David in disgust.

Jess shot him a glance, "... and a basic town government in place. Every so often someone gets their britches in a knot and wants something more, and starts talking about money and taxes and the federal government. That doesn't last long."

I nodded. "When the United States collapsed, much of the world was already on the brink of complete chaos. The riots in Greece were just the beginning of what became an uprising, civil war, and eventually a full war through Europe."

"Even Switzerland couldn't sit this one out. And Africa had already been a hotbed, right along with the Middle East; so much infighting, along with the scourge of HIV and so many young people growing up without any parents, without any direction in their lives."

I took a sip of the dark, heavily sweetened chicory and continued, "We were traveling with an independently funded humanitarian aid mission in Uganda. The Lord's Resistance Army controlled much of the north at the time. The word got out that every American had better get out now, or else." I grimaced, "As if it were that easy."

Kip, who had said little until this point, took up the story. "It took us nearly two years just to get out of Africa. Everything that could break down did—communications, monetary systems, and the American embassies, or any embassies friendly to United States interests were either closed, burned to the ground, or abandoned. The fact that we were Americans was suddenly a very bad thing. Luckily, we had friends, those who had been helped by our organization, by us. We stayed with a string of them until it became dangerous for them to keep us there. We eventually found our way to the Mediterranean and tried to enter Europe via Italy, and later Spain." He shook his head.

I continued, "It seemed that all of Europe was either involved in uprisings, civil war, or fighting each other. More than anything, though, we, well, any Americans were turned away. We ended up with several others from our aid group on a freighter, bound for Port-au-Prince. It was the closest thing we had to the U.S., although anyone we spoke to told us there had been nukes set off in the south and there were plenty of pointed fingers."

I took another sip of the chicory, now cooled in the mug, and continued, "In the end, we don't know how it started, or who pushed what buttons, but there were nuclear detonations recorded in Austin, D.C., and Los Angeles. It looks as if the Star Wars defense program took out most of the satellites in space at right around the same time—effectively ending world-wide communications."

I stared at the bottom of my cup; my vision clouded by the events that came next.

Kip waited for me to speak and then he continued the story, "We knew the chances of finding Madge were unlikely. There had been such chaos in the cities. We wondered if she ever even made it out. Not to mention that she had told Penelope of her illness and that she didn't have long. Penelope had been scheduling a trip back to the States when everything went to hell. We just didn't hold out much hope. We stayed in Haiti for nearly eighteen months trying to stay alive and figure out where to go next."

I sat there for a moment, my eyes and mind miles away, lost in memories of Haiti. I didn't want to tell them of the disease, the murders, or how many times we had fought for just enough food to survive. I didn't want to talk about the children she saw lying dead in the streets.

I shook it off with some effort. "Florida was impossible—there were nearly a dozen naval bases there that banded together once communications with D.C. ceased. They patrol the waters and allow no one in. It's a fire first, ask questions later situation. We couldn't get close enough to tell them we were American, not that it would have mattered. They had locked it down to Florida residents, anyway. Texas was a fallout zone, as was much of the Caribbean and the southern states." I pursed her lips, "Not that they told Florida citizens that. They actively denied it even after the first reports of radiation sickness. Once the Western Front started moving east into the Plains states, other factions of former military, along with extremists, rose up to define their own areas of control."

Kip chimed in, "The Allied South struggled to consolidate Louisiana, Arkansas, Mississippi, Alabama, Georgia, and parts of South Carolina. Mexico had surged into Arizona, New Mexico, and the most southern section of California and there was chaos there—lines drawn between the white, Hispanic, and Native American populations. The drug cartels made a move for power. The east coast had three different contingents—the Northern Allies who were struggling to define the borders of half a dozen small states, the Unionists that controlled some parts of the southeast, and the Patriots who were hopelessly divided through infighting in Kentucky, Ohio, and Indiana."

Jacob and Becka, who likely understood little of the states being discussed, having been born after the Collapse, were silent. Erin had curled up in David's arms and was sucking her thumb, listening intently.

I continued, "We finally found entry just west of Biloxi, Mississippi. There had been a radiation fallout scare, and much of the area was deserted. We headed up Highway 49. After that it was a zigzag route. We entered Tennessee, tried to go through the northwest section, but there was a chain of small towns, all with militias, and we were turned back at Tiptonville." I took another sip. "The Western Front had torn through that region and everyone was on edge. If you weren't a resident, they turned you away, no questions, no argument." I smiled wryly. "After all, they were the ones with the guns. You can't argue much with the business end of a gun."

Kip spoke up, "We spent a winter in Arkansas. There were migrant groups moving through the areas, many of them working crops, building or reinforcing town borders, living like gypsies as they searched for a place to stay. We moved in and out of these groups—diseases we hadn't seen in decades in the Western world ran rampant. Cholera, bouts of dysentery, and a host of other illnesses could be found in any group we joined. But the alternative was to go it alone, without some of the protection a group could provide. Sometimes it was worth it, other times it wasn't."

I picked it up from there, "And eventually we moved through parts of Oklahoma, Kansas, and then finally Missouri. Once we hit Missouri, I was determined to find my mother. I had thought about it a lot, wondering what she would do, where she would go if she knew she only had a short time to live. I doubted that she would have stayed in her home there in Kansas City, and we were close to the archaeology site she had been working on for the last few years. I had been given the opportunity to visit the site the first year they had begun work, so I was familiar with where to find it. I figured if she wasn't there, I would try finding her in KC. I wasn't holding out much hope either way."

I paused, drained the last of the chicory from my cup, and said, "I noticed the cairn immediately. When we arrived at the cave, I was convinced that the full team had to have been there, since there was evidence of more than just Mom. It took me a while to go deeper into the cave. I was wondering where everyone went, even though it was obvious it had been a while. I had completely forgotten about the long passage. Finding your letter, even as it raised more questions, gave me some measure of peace."

My eyes brimmed with tears. "She wasn't alone when she passed. That means so much to me to know that she had someone with her as she passed into the world of spirits." I wiped at a tear that had escaped and began trickling down my cheek. "And eventually we came here, looking for you, Jess."

Jess's cheeks were also wet with tears. "Those months we spent with Madge were beautiful ones. She gave us so much—love, acceptance, and peace—even now, I remember it like it was yesterday. My faith in humans and life in general had been sorely tested and Madge reminded me of all I had left to live for, all that I could be for Jacob, for myself and my family."

Grandmother, that is what she asked us to call her, took us in, and taught us how to survive here, in this cave through the winter. It is now March, late March, and no snow has fallen in several weeks. The temperatures are rising and it is time for me to try to finish my journey home.

"I have her journal. The personal one that she kept," Jess said suddenly. "I can get it for you."

I held up a hand. "Tomorrow. Can I come again tomorrow?" The sun had set, and the darkness had closed in. "We are staying in town. That they let us in at all was a surprise. We tried months ago and were turned back. But apparently the militia is allowing traders and migrant workers in these days, and we had goods to trade, so we will be here for another day or perhaps two."

Jess nodded, "Yes, yes, of course. Come by tomorrow."

As we walked away from Jess and her family, I could feel their eyes on our backs, watching us. Kip slipped his fingers into mine. "Have you asked after Tina? She's pretty young, younger than I thought."

"The town doc vouched for her. Says she's smart as a whip. Young as she is, it's kids like her who will help us climb out of this hole we are in, and return to a better future."

I don't know you, and you don't know me. But I'm writing this letter and then hiding the box where only someone who knows Madge and inner twists and turns of this cave will be able to find it. I have to be sure; you see. It still isn't safe. They have sent out soldiers hunting for us and I don't know that they aren't still out there looking.

The next day, David seemed better. They had worked on the house, repairing a section of the roof, and then weeding several of the beds of potatoes and lettuce. Jess had made up her mind to tell Penelope they weren't interested, that Tina was far too young. What possible apprenticeship could apply to a young child? As she watched Penelope approach, her long-legged stride fluid on the broken pavement of the street, Jess could see that Sarah Turner had joined her and that Penelope's husband, Kip, was not with them.

Sarah was a kind woman. She had always treated Jess as an equal—and during those first months and years, she had championed the younger woman's cause, and that of their motley group of children more than once. Sarah was quite protective, in fact, which made Jess wonder about the older woman's past, and that of her children, who were nearly the same age as Jess. Sarah had always been rather close-mouthed about where she had come from, or where Cody and Laura's father were.

What would Sarah have to contribute to all of this? Jess wasn't sure what to think. A quick glance at David's face signaled trouble. Tina was his sister, and he had a right to his opinion, but for the first time, Jess wondered what Tina wanted. Stay or go, wasn't it up to her? After all, Tina was nearly the age that David had been when they all first met in Clinton. He had been old enough to make a decision then, a decision that taken him away from everything familiar, everything that reminded him of home. Shouldn't Tina have the right to make that same decision? Even at the age of ten years?

Jess was conflicted, and she knew it showed in her face. Sarah took it in, smiled at her, and gave her a warm hug. "Good morning Jess!" Since her daughter Laura had married Todd Stevens, the laugh lines on her face had deepened. The births of Laura and Todd's two boys had brought happiness, along with something Jess could only describe as longing to Sarah's face. Jess wondered if Sarah was thinking of the husband she had left behind. Jess had listened to so many stories, so many unfinished, unknown fates of loved ones. It was perhaps the most haunting part of her job as historian—the unknown fates of so many. Sarah's story was one of dozens.

It was hours before dinner and they had had lunch just two hours earlier, but Sarah produced a loaf of her sourdough bread, a favorite of David's. That was combined with a bag of fruits that Kip had sent along, payment for some picking work they had both done earlier in the day. Jess and David, along with Tina, Sarah, and Penelope, sat down for a bite to eat and some conversation. It was stilted at first, mainly due to

David, who felt cornered and resentful. Jess laid her hand on his knee, reminding him silently that she was his ally. He stared at her hand as she made small talk with Penelope and Sarah, concentrated on the long, tapered fingers. They were rough with callouses, but still delicate. He looked at them and tried to calm his fears—of losing his sister, knowing how much she wanted to go.

Tina had come to him that morning, the sun barely peeking over the horizon, and quietly folded herself on the floor of his room, quietly so she didn't wake Jacob. Her room was right next door, shared with Becka and Erin, when one or the other wasn't curled in bed next to Jess. "I want to go with her," was all that she had said when he opened one bleary eye and focused on her. They had engaged in a silent contest of wills, him glaring, her just staring back, until he had finally turned away and pulled the covers over his head and tried to ignore her. When he had turned back over a few moments later, she was gone.

The small talk had progressed while he was woolgathering. Penelope was describing her mother's house in Kansas City. "It's over 130 years old and solid brick. Surprisingly, it's rather intact considering the dire situation that most residents were in before and during the collapse. Most of her books are still there," Penelope smiled at Jess. "She wrote about all kinds of recent history, as well as anthropology. She had quite an obsession with Jesse James and also had notes on Pendergast, a corrupt political boss in the early 20th century." She turned toward David, who just shrugged and shook his head. He had never heard of Jesse James or Pendergast.

"In any case, the house was gone through, but not much was taken and it was empty when we visited it last week. We are planning to stay there and work with a medical group that is forming." She looked at Tina and smiled at her, then back to David where her smile faltered a brief second. "If it would be all right, Tina could come with us to Kansas City, and stay in the house. There is plenty of room and there are other students who she would be learning side-by-side with. You could come too, David, to see for yourself, if you liked."

A long silence ensued. All eyes were on David, until Tina spoke up. "I want to go to Kansas City with you, Penelope. I want to learn how to be a doctor. It's all I've ever wanted to do."

David closed his eyes for a moment, remembering her tiny hand in his, her matted hair in those weeks and months that had followed the deaths of their parents. The feel of her tiny body nestled against his. He remembered farther back, the first time he had seen her in the hospital, a tiny red face, impossibly small, mewling cries that sounded like a tiny, sad kitten. They had never fought; with nearly eight years between them, he had always been the oldest, the one she looked up to. And when they had been alone, lost in the rubble of a dead and broken town, she had depended on him for everything.

It was only here, in Belton, that she had come into her own, as young as she was, defining her future, writing it on the wall with nothing short of an indelible marker. Her abilities, her intuitive understanding and curiosity about the healing arts had given her this opportunity. And who was he to say no? How could he? David thought of her being absent, not someone he saw every day, not in the garden or walking into town with freshly picked herbs for Dr. Ridley, and something deep in his chest twisted and pulled. She was all that he had of their former life. The only evidence he could show of the parents that he had lost. The words to say all that seemed to elude him.

In the end, he simply stared at Jess's hand, still on his knee, and said, "If Tina wants to go, then, I guess that's what she should do."

But if you find this, know that she died surrounded by people who loved her. She was at peace, and I miss her dreadfully.

Yours, Jess

Take the Shot

"How far would you go?"

Jonathan

Farley's underground bunker was a well-kept secret, one that the mayor took pains to keep. No one needed to know the extent of his wealth or his resources. During the past two winters, especially. He had said nothing, not a word about it to anyone, since the Western Front had overrun the town, looting, snatching people up to join their ranks, and burning half of the damn town to the ground in the process. After that, food had been scarce, and he had even considered, if only in passing, limiting his intake of the food stores he had collected in order so as not to bring attention to his door.

He had thought of it, sure, but continued to avail himself of the fine foods, the rare liquor, while others in town starved. The fact was, he didn't give a damn what the other people in this town had to go through. It was their fault, for being the mindless sheep that they were, and this was the natural order of things.

The only exclusion to this was his son, and sometimes Jonathan Farley wondered if he had made a mistake allowing James to know as much as he did. The boy was hotheaded, impetuous, and worse, loose-lipped, with a few drinks in him.

Farley shook his head and swished the glass of port in his hand gently. It was chilled, thanks to the reusable ice cubes he had plucked from their bin in the freezer. Here in his hideout, his secret lair at the end of a fifty-foot-long tunnel dug fifteen feet deep in the earth, the only access to a rusty hatch hidden behind the hay bales in the barn, he could relax. Not even James bothered him here. Well, not usually. Really only at Farley's behest. Tonight, or in the morning, he would be coming by to report on how the transaction had gone.

James had never shown a preference for port, or any of the near priceless bottles of wine Farley had trucked in here, one case at a time. And he hadn't told his son about the rest of the liquor, the higher-end stuff that he didn't feel he needed to share. He had made sure to throw everyone off the scent by installing a significant number of items that he could use as a trade. The rest, everything stored here in his hidey-hole, well, that was for his personal use.

In the depths of the earth, it took some juice to keep the coolers full of meat, seafood, and more running. But not nearly as much as it would have on the surface, where it could exceed a hundred degrees in the summer. The humidity often brought it to a heat index of 103 degrees, and despite the chilly temperatures now in play, Farley could still remember how the sweat caused his clothing to cling to his body. He shivered at the thought in the cool of the wine room. It was late November, and the winter had long since descended, capturing the Midwestern states in its icy grip.

There was one oversized chair of tufted leather and a high back in the middle of a room surrounded by wine racks, the outer circle of which held the freezers full of foods against the outer stone walls. This deep underground, with nothing but stone surrounding him, and it was a constant fifty-five degrees. The only thing that varied was the humidity level.

The port was sweet and heavy on his tongue. Since the Collapse, Jonathan Farley had placed his fingers in even more pies than he had already had them in as the bank president and town alderman. The town was lucky to have him, though he was sure that the sheeple wouldn't see it that way. His wheeling and dealing had helped ensure that no one else invaded, and that was important, because the town of Belton, a mere 26,000 souls before the Collapse and invasion of Western Front troops, was now down to a fraction of its size. And it wasn't as if the land surrounding them was empty or devoid of life. Before the Collapse, there had been more than two million people in the Greater Kansas City area. Two million, and while many had fled, or died in the fighting or of starvation and disease, there were plenty left. It was enough to warrant more than just a town militia to defend their borders. It meant deals, brokered arrangements, and shady compromises.

Belton had always been a rather white town, but before the Collapse, you could still see diversity, however limited. It was that small amount of color difference that had been the first to fall. When the chief of police

James Wingo had sensed a change in the wind, one that would eventually carry the Western Front to their door, he had sat Farley down and had some strong suggestions for how the future of their vulnerable town could be secured with a few changes. Those few changes had included dozens of well-placed evictions. That several of the evicted had the temerity to suggest that Belton, Missouri, had become a sundown town was met with ridicule, even if it was accurate. Shutting down that talk had led to what seemed inevitable, a slippery slope into what some might even call human trafficking. He preferred to think of it as improving their community with a side benefit of getting some folks a future they were far better fitted for. Farley sniffed and took a large gulp of port, then nibbled on a rich brownie that Sarah Turner had baked with the last of the chocolate. At least, it was the last chocolate that she had. He had at least thirty pounds of it in a box down the hall. His thoughts briefly strayed to exactly how he was going to "find" some more chocolate, and better yet, not have it shared with the others in town. Sarah wasn't a native to Belton, but his control over her and what she was able to do at her small cafe on Main Street had slipped slightly as the years wore on. He grimaced and swallowed more port. She was rather popular now, no doubt thanks to her mad baking skills. Those who hadn't learned how to go back to basics and bake their own bread often brought their rations to her and she managed to make the magic happen. The fact that she didn't ask anything in payment for the work also worked in her favor. It was hard to argue with people's stomachs and it had led to her and her two children being welcomed into the fold by most.

The trade in people, more specifically those less fortunate or those who were not raised as well as they should have been, had been an unfortunate, yet necessary, course of action. His town, as Farley liked to consider it, needed the best. People who would work hard and follow his directives. Those who couldn't, or who asked too many annoying questions, well, they needed to move on, disappear even, so long as they stopped interfering with Farley running the town in the manner in which it needed to be run.

People disappeared all the time these days, after all. Wingo had already taken the lead on handling the drug production and trade in the area, something that kept those undesirables left who still had some use, quiet and compliant, but he had tasked Farley with making sure that a steady trickle of people - unwanted or non-compliant - were provided to the surrounding areas in exchange for protection from invasion. What they did with the unwanted. Well, that wasn't his business, was it? The Collapse had changed everything but human nature. There would always be the haves and the have nots, and Farley was determined to fall into the latter category.

As the bombs had fallen, and the world at large had descended into chaos, losing the electrical grid and communications array had sent their once-proud nation back to the Dark Ages. And here, in what Farley thought of as the unlikeliest of places, they had found some kind of balance in what could only be described as a form of city-state. The remnants of the political structure had shifted and morphed into a mix of "get whatever you can and hold on to it" and a territorial shifting of priorities, one that re-created the warring city-states of ancient times.

What most of the citizens of Belton didn't know or understand was that the currency had changed. They no longer operated in fiat currency, instead it was trade. And while food crops, even cattle, were highly prized, the trade he personally specialized in was not trade that most people accepted. In the new, post-Collapse world, food, drugs, and human beings were the new currency, and Farley and Wingo, working together, controlled them all.

James was heading up the collection of a woman who would provide a tidy solution to an imminent problem. An addict with loose lips, and one time worker for Wingo, she had become a problem that needed solving. He had told his son to check in with him once the deed was done.

Farley gathered the last rich crumbs of brownie goodness from his plate and drained the last drops of port from his glass. He didn't let morality interfere with his life. That was something Evelyn would have done. His late wife had been the religious one, the moral one. At least, she had been until the cancer began to eat away at her brain. It had turned her into a hate spewing, paranoid creature. Their son, James, had been in young, ten maybe, when the delusions had really set in. Farley had put her in an institution immediately. That kind of behavior, created by illness or not, simply had no place in his orderly existence. It had been a short stay. The cancer, while relentless, had been mercifully quick. Just six months from diagnosis to death, and Farley had found himself raising the boy all on his own. For a child he hadn't particularly wanted, it had been an onerous burden. Figure in the Collapse a handful of years later, and it was almost too much to bear.

He'd increased the enormous life insurance payout in a number of financial wheeling and dealing, which had quickly tripled the amount he had been paid. He had then engaged an out-of-state contractor to dig the tunnels and lay in the solar when the rumors of a financial collapse began to circulate. While most of the nation was focused on elections, or Black Lives Matter, the latest epidemic, or rising food costs - Jonathan Farley was stocking foods, supplies, weapons, and any other creature comforts he could think of. Let the world burn. He was ready for it.

The Western Front blowing through had both helped and hindered his position. He'd been lucky that he had the sniffles that day and not gone into work. He had been an alderman with dreams of more power, but with several seasoned candidates in his way. Almost to a man, they had died during the invasion. The one who had been left, the lone female alderman with plenty of clout and her fingers in every pie, had been spared, only to lose her husband and grown son in the attack. Marjorie Brown hadn't lasted long. The first round of a bad flu had taken her that first year and the path to the mayorship had been cleared for him. In that sense, he certainly had the Western Front to thank. But the damage they had done had been substantial. By the time the fires had been put out and the dead and missing accounted for, Belton had less than one-tenth of their population left.

From a town of more than twenty thousand people to one that hovered in the range of around eighteen hundred.

Farley shook his head at the thought. His father, had he still been alive, would likely have been sorely disappointed in him. The old man had aspired to far more, and he had dabbled in politics as well while making his fortune in several investment firms that were nothing better than Ponzi schemes. But power was power. If the town had still had its population intact, it would have been far more difficult to control. Farley knew this for a fact. He wasn't a pie in the sky dreamer, and he understood people rather well. He knew himself better than most, and he could see that others respected him only for the power he wielded, not for his sparkling personality. He was good at making money, better at keeping it, and he made sure to keep his supporters well-plied with the occasional rare gift.

Farley was as happy as could be expected in these trying times. And if he positioned himself right, he would continue to profit, and grow, come what may. That was the goal, at least. And the challenge of profit, through cold, hard cash or the wealth of choice when others had little of either - that was one he embraced.

He poured more of the port and picked up a remote, aiming it at the enormous speakers on one wall. A moment later, Vivaldi blossomed forth. Farley smiled and settled back to wait for his son.

A warm glow was beginning to spread through Farley's limbs when a chirp of alarm sounded. "Front hatch... open," chimed his security alarm. It was disabled. He'd been expecting his son, but not for a few more hours. He was handling a transfer tonight. The girl was a particularly troublesome one. And Farley had certainly been happy to assist Wingo when she didn't make good on payment for services rendered. The girl had made certain promises in return for a hefty amount of meth, and she hadn't kept up her end of the bargain.

As far as Farley was concerned, the ones who couldn't afford their addictions tended to be the worst of the riffraff, causing troubles in other areas - theft, disruptive behavior, and more. The fact that she had been one of the former alderman's kids made it all the sweeter. He would be all too happy to hand her over to the gentleman's club that had been restarted some forty miles outside of Kansas City on I70. His connection there had made sure to take care of his son James' needs as well, but Farley had little time or inclination for such cheap things. In truth, he had hoped for a little more with Sarah Turner, even though he could see she had no interest.

Better that I live a simple life, monastic in nature, he mused as he slipped the last crumbs into his mouth and followed it with the last mouthful of port. He stood up and turned to greet his son as he emerged from the long tunnel.

James looked worse for wear, and that was being kind. His nose, chin, and the front of his shirt were a bloody mess. His eyes were wild with panic. Jonathan felt a rush of fear flow through him.

"What happened?" he barked at James.

"We have a situation, sir." His boy looked afraid, but at least he kept up decorum. Long ago, likely long before the boy's mother's cancer had eaten her brain, Farley had insisted the boy call him sir, just as his own father had done. It was the small, yet meaningful traditions like that which kept them above the simpler folk.

Farley set his glass down and wiped his mouth with a cloth napkin. He kept his composure, but he hated the sight of blood, and James' face was covered in it.

"Go on."

"The crazy bitch got the drop on me. Damn near broke my nose and hit me on the head with something. By the time I came to, she was gone."

Farley stared at his son incredulously. "Why are you here? Get Wingo, and a couple of men you can trust and go after her!"

"I just thought..."

"No, no, you didn't think. If you had been thinking, we wouldn't be having this discussion, would we? Get Wingo, get Payton and Trey and get her back. Now! Before she flaps her mouth to anyone in town."

The chances that anyone would believe Cici Baker, daughter of drug addicts and an obvious addict herself, were small, but if they got wind that James Farley, the son of the mayor, was involved, then things could get sticky. Farley shook his head.

Stupid boy. Should have known better than to expect him to do this job right.

He dusted a few crumbs off of his shirt and barked at his son, "Go on! Round her up and I'll get Wingo to pitch in. She isn't going far. Stupid girl has alienated anyone willing to help her long time back."

And if she got out, if she talked to anyone, it could mean real trouble for all of them. Until the girl had shown what a real mess she was, they had used her for production and distribution. It had been a while, a year or more, since she had shown herself to be unreliable.

Why didn't I push for her to be removed back then? Hell, I could've had Wingo give her too big a dose and just had her OD. Too late for that now, though.

He felt anxiety ratchet up his pulse. Best they caught her quick. There was talk on the wind of a Reformation, and there hadn't been any fighting for quite a while. The time for these murky transactions was coming to a close and that little skank Cici had been involved in far too many of them. She wasn't particularly smart, but now that she knew James was involved, it didn't take much for anyone of any basic intelligence to look farther past the boy to the real source. And Farley couldn't have that. Uh, uh. In a few years, the world would reset itself, climb out of the darkness and society would go back to what it had been before the dollar had collapsed and the bombs had fallen. Life was cyclic like that. The bad times didn't last, but neither did the good. Existence between birth and death was far messier than most would care to recognize.

"Find her, and I'll meet you at the rendezvous north of town." Farley barked at his son.

James, who had been gingerly wiping at the caked blood from his face, nodded, his shoulders hunched, and disappeared down the tunnel without another word.

Jeremiah

Jeremiah Flanagan woke from a doze, the ground hard and cold beneath him. Dani, her tiny body spooned against the inside of his, slept hard, a bundle of warmth tucked in tight. He did his best not to wake her. She was exhausted, dark rings under her eyes from lack of food and the endless walking. She hadn't said much, not since they had left New Mexico behind some four weeks ago.

He slid one leg out of the thick extra-large sleeping bag and then the other. Easing out of it, wincing at the cold air which sucked his energy away. His stomach grumbled, and he knew they would need to find a town soon. One that might take them in, if only for a day or two. One that would have work for him to do, so they could re-stock on supplies before hitting the road again.

He'd been a fool to try to do this now, in winter, but really, what choice did they have?

Dani shifted as a gust of cold air invaded the sleeping bag in his absence. She didn't wake, however, and Jeremiah slipped on his gloves before he tried to stoke the campfire back to life. He winced at how stiff they felt, the cold affecting him in a way that he had never experienced until now. New Mexico got cold, sure, but this, this was bone-aching cold. It slipped in and surrounded you, enough to make you wonder if you could ever be warm again. And it would only get worse, especially when he thought of where they were heading. Canada in winter. He shook his head.

What kind of fool heads north, on foot, with a preschooler, in winter?

It hadn't been cold when he left, not at all. The weather had been warm, short sleeve weather, as Shannon had called it, and consumed with grief and loneliness in the wake of her passing, it had seemed like the right thing to do. His mother's older brother, his uncle Jaime, had settled outside of Winnipeg not long before the Collapse. His last emails, before the power had failed, and the nuke hit Austin causing a string of chaotic events, had been to invite Jeremiah and Shannon there to his farm, an extensive parcel that was self-sufficient and safe. But Shannon hadn't wanted to leave. New Mexico had been home to the de Silva clan for generations, and she had never so much as stepped foot outside of the state in her entire life.

Neither had Dani, for that matter. Shannon had given birth to their daughter nearly five years after the Collapse, surrounded by her mother and sister and a cousin who had been a doula since before Shannon was born.

Jeremiah poked at the fire, pushing aside the layer of white to reveal the glowing red embers beneath. He added a piece of old, weathered fencing, all that he was able to gather the evening before, and tossed a handful of dead grass on top. The glow intensified, smoke curling, a crackle and spit, before the flame jumped to life, heat emanating from it which felt good on his chilled face but also pulled the already dry skin tighter until it felt as if he were wearing a tight mask. He added another piece of fencing and watched the flames lick up the worm-riddled wood.

Dani stirred then, stretching at his feet, her eyes fluttered open for a moment before she burrowed deeper, out of sight, in the folds of the sleeping bag. Her red hair was a mass of tangles. He'd forgotten a brush, and it had descended in a matted mess of snarls and the occasional twig or mashed leaf.

I suck at this, Shannon. God knows I do.

He watched the flames grow, hypnotized and lost in thought. Those last moments with Shannon, watching the fever take her in its clutches and not let go.

"It's dysentery. I'm sure of it. The Lakewood's down the way had it and it presented just like this," Shannon's mom had said at the end of August, shutting the enormous tome she regularly consulted in times of illness. The Lakewood family had all died within days of each other as they ran high fevers and vomited and shit themselves. It had been sudden and fatal. But the antibiotics were gone, long gone, and although there had been rumors of the Reformation, it certainly hadn't made it to their little hamlet of Hatch, New Mexico.

Jeremiah closed his eyes, turned, and let the heat of the flames warm his back. Rosalia de Silva had survived the dysentery that gripped her and her daughters. It had left her a weakened wreck, however, especially after Shannon and Sonora had both died. He stared at Dani's small shape, now completely hidden within the sleeping bag. Her torso rose and fell rhythmically. Rosalia had been a formidable woman when Shannon had brought him home to meet her, and it was only her own bout with the disease, and the loss of her daughters, that had robbed her of the strength to fight his departure.

The heat pulsed into his back, the fire crackling merrily now, spitting sparks, the ancient wood engulfed in flames. His stomach grumbled, and he reluctantly left the warmth of the fire to dig through the backpack for the last cans of food they had.

Dani roused from the sleeping bag, her tiny fists rubbing at her eyes.

"Hey sugar plum."

She mumbled, "Hi Da," and pulled the sleeping bag close to her, a tiny shiver racking her body.

"We've got corned beef hash and peaches for breakfast."

Jeremiah watched as her lower lip began to tremble. She said nothing, but tears filled her green eyes.

"It's all we have, kiddo. At least until we get to the next town." He reached out and plucked a crumpled leaf out of her rat's nest of tangles, paused and remembered how his wife had been with her. He leaned down, cupped her tiny chin in his hand and kissed her forehead just as he had seen Shannon do a thousand times.

"Did you sleep okay?" He asked, reaching for the cans of food. Nights were the worst for her. There hadn't been one night without tears, not one.

Dani nodded, but said nothing more. He felt his chest tighten. His baby girl missed her mom. Hell, he missed Shannon so badly it felt as if his heart had shriveled up and died with her. But for Dani, who had been Shannon's shadow since the day she could walk, the loss of her mother had been the most traumatizing event of her life, seconded only by leaving the only home she had ever known.

You goddamn fool. You should have stayed in New Mexico.

Was it a fool's errand, this quest to find Uncle Jaime's farm?

Most likely you'll both die out here. At best, you don't, and you actually find this damn farm only to learn he's moved on or died or the place has burned to the ground.

At first, they had ridden a sweet 3-wheeled bicycle he had bought shortly before everything went to hell. But after a couple of close calls on I-35, the third time of which had seen them running for cover as troops moved through, Jeremiah had more than enough. Which faction of troops they were, he had no idea, and he wasn't willing to find out. He had ditched the bike, and they had hidden within the forest, moving deeper as he watched several of the soldiers stop at the bike and then look toward the line of forest. He hadn't wanted to know whether they would take what little the father daughter duo had, or simply shoot them. Later, as dusk stole over the land, he had snuck back close enough to see that the bike was gone, no doubt taken by the soldiers. That was okay. Two of the three tires had already begun to leak. And without a spare, he was on borrowed time with it, anyway.

They had stuck to smaller roads and occasionally cut through forests or wide grassland. It was better to avoid the towns when possible, and the terrain had been slow-going, but they hadn't managed to get as far on foot as he had hoped. His back, neck and arms ached from carrying her on his shoulders and Dani's shoes were sporting cracks in the soles, and the thin canvas wasn't enough to keep her feet warm as she stumbled along the ground beside him.

Something had to give. They still had at least 800 miles to go and winter was here. Jeremiah struggled to remember how in the hell he had thought it would take a month, maybe two at most, to travel over sixteen hundred miles with a three-year-old. The math had seemed simpler somehow when he was imagining them riding the bike, Dani perched on the custom seat he had built in the back, the wind blowing in her hair. On foot, however, reality had set in. Still, he could have turned back. He had been closer to Hatch, easier to return, admit defeat.

It was his Irish blood. That's what Shannon would have told him, laughing as she threaded her long delicate fingers through his red hair or spread aloe vera over his ever-present sunburn. Shannon, with her dark brown curls, olive skin and hazel eyes. God, he missed her. The dysentery had taken her so fast, faster than any of them could have been ready for. In his darkest moments, he had hated her for leaving him, for leaving Dani who hadn't smiled once, not once in the eight weeks and five days since they had lost her. Shannon had been the glue that kept them together. The one who had stood up to her mother and insisted that Jeremiah was her choice and her love, defiant in the face of maternal disapproval. Without Shannon, he had no chance of withstanding the hurricane that was Rosalia deSilva.

Jeremiah slipped off a glove and hooked the pull tabs on both cans of food with his fingers. Gently easing them back one at a time. He couldn't afford an injury or cut. Not now, not on the road. A week earlier, he had stepped wrong. One minute he had been fine, the next he had been on his knees. It had hurt for days and slowed them down. The ground was uneven here, whether it was forest or open prairie, and occasionally, after examining their surroundings well in both directions, he would slip onto a gravel road, grateful for a more even-footed stretch to walk on. Still, it wasn't a good idea. He'd seen what some of the troops that barreled through the main roads had done. Whatever side they were on, it wasn't that of anyone unfortunate enough to run into them. There had been one hair-raising encounter at least two weeks past, with three men dressed in fatigues, all armed. Jeremiah had been lost in thought, and Dani had been draped over his shoulders, a slick of drool escaping from her mouth, dozing as he walked. He'd been so busy picking his way through the forest he had walked into their encampment before he had even realized they were there. The dark muzzle of a shotgun in his face had nearly caused his bowels to loosen, but it had been the larger of the three men, sitting on a fallen tree next to their campfire, and the lascivious look that he had fixed on Dani that had turned Jeremiah's blood ice cold. It had all happened so quick. But the man holding the shotgun had waved Jeremiah away when he learned he wasn't a local.

As he had put tracks between them, picking up his pace to a jog shortly after their camp disappeared in the trees behind him, he had wondered if they really were soldiers.

There had been plenty of talk, rumor really, of what was happening in the country. After the reports of nukes, a wave of silence had hit. It had left them to wonder, fear, what was really happening. Rumors had flown thick, especially from anyone who dared to travel. Several factions of soldiers were fighting for control of what remained of the United States.

Although really, what is left, after all? Jeremiah had wondered more than once. D.C. is a nuclear wasteland, so is Austin.

Nevertheless, the various factions found something to fight about. Considering how dirty the three soldiers had been, Jeremiah couldn't help wondering two things - was there anything worth fighting over and were the men deserters of whatever faction they had originally sworn allegiance to?

Dani's small hand on his arm brought him back to present. She handed him the can of corned beef hash. There was more than half left.

"Sugar plum, you gotta eat your share. Here, take one more bite." His daughter made a face, but opened her mouth obediently to the spoon he held out to her. He looked at the can of peaches, untouched, in his hand, and speared several slices with his fork. "And I need to take my own advice, don't I now?" He shoved the sweet, dripping mess into his mouth, wiped the drop of juice that escaped down his chin, and handed the can to his daughter.

They would need to find food soon. Dani was looking peaked, tiring earlier and stumbling along the way as they walked, and he wasn't faring much better. Walking took a lot of calories out of them, more than they were taking in, and that was for sure. Especially now that the weather was colder. Perhaps he could find a way to pay their way to overwinter in the next town.

"Da? Carry me?" His heart wrenched at her request. He was tired, exhausted even after a night's sleep, and he forced a smile on his face.

"Sure Sweetheart, just for a little way, though, okay?" He could manage a short distance, maybe the first mile or two, even. She sat and watched him as he broke down their camp, rolling their sleeping bag up and zipping everything away neatly before he lifted her onto his shoulders. She felt lighter as he lifted her, but as soon as she was settled on his shoulders, he regretted having agreed to carry her. Her little butt was bony and dug into his shoulder blades. She had lost weight over the long journey, of that he was certain, but so had he, and it was hard enough carrying all of their equipment. He teetered off balance for a mere moment, and she clutched at his hair in fear.

"Easy there, Sugar Plum. I need that hair to keep my head warm," Jeremiah said, wincing as she clawed for safe purchase.

The sooner they got to the small town of Belton, the better. He grimaced, hoping that Dani's elfin face turned their hardened hearts into puddles of kindness. If it didn't, they had a day, maybe three at the outset, before either of them would simply stop being able to travel at all.

It was simply bad luck what happened next. If Jeremiah had known whose field he was stepping into, if the sign that read Keep Out hadn't been felled by a recent storm, and if a particular, highly private trade between two parties who prized their anonymity above all else had not been happening at that very moment - Jeremiah and Dani's lives would likely have been very different.

Dani had seen the sign. Her head, a good foot above Jeremiah's, had given her that extra range needed. It was on its side, wrenched from its hole and turned away by the tree that had felled the section of fencing they were now walking through. She recognized the letters, at least some of them. Her mother had been teaching her letters earlier in the spring, tracing the shape of them in the dirt outside of their house. Dani could see a K, which was a letter she loved.

"K is for Kitten," Dani could still hear her Mommy's voice in her head, see the stick in her mind as it scratched through the dust, making shapes.

Dani had been trying to find out where mama cat had hidden her new kittens for days and days. Likely under the front porch, which was off limits due to fears of snakes or scorpions. She had wanted a kitten more than anything. And the K, well, it looked perfect, a shape that promised happiness. Just a moment to glance at the sign, though, before Da moved on into the small clearing surrounded by trees. The K had been followed by two Es and a P.

"Da? What's K and E and E and P?" she asked.

Jeremiah lurched to one side beneath her as he stepped over the uneven terrain.

"K... E... E... P, Sugar Plum?" He lurched again, swearing under his breath, "That spells keep."

Dani nodded and said nothing more. She hadn't read the bottom half of the sign. There hadn't been time, after all. The small clearing was not empty. There was a series of low-slung buildings in various stages of disrepair. No wood smoke, though, so likely they were abandoned. It was too cold out for there to not be wood smoke and both of them started with surprise at the sound of voices coming from the boarded-up house to the left.

It was two men at least, and their voices sounded angry. A second later, and a woman's voice. The words were not clear, but the woman sounded scared.

Jeremiah stopped in his tracks and gently slid Dani off of his shoulders, bringing his face down close to hers, a finger to his lips.

Dani

"Da?" Dani began to speak, and Jeremiah shushed her. The look on his face was clear. He was afraid. Before Mama had died, he had only looked like that once, when Tuna, Grammy's doc, had gotten bit by a rattlesnake by the back shed where Dani liked to play. Tuna's leg had swollen up, impossibly big, and he had died. Da had grabbed her arm and told her not to go anywhere near the back shed. The next time he had looked like that, Mama had died. And the time after that, it had been when the soldiers took their bike.

Dad didn't get scared very often, but if he was afraid right now, so should she be. Dani clamped her mouth shut, eyes widening, and took his hand, sticking close to his left hip.

The voices were louder now, clear, despite there being boards over the windows and the others being inside while they crept by. There was a small creek in the distance, along with another thatch of trees. Da pointed to them, making sure she understood. That's where they needed to go. That's what would get them away from this place, and the angry voices.

"You can't treat me like this! I kept my mouth shut, never said nothing to no one!" That was a woman talking.

"She knows too much, Farley. We can't trade her to the whorehouse, she'll open her goddamn mouth and now, thanks to Jimmy screwing this up, she knows you are in it too." The voice was low, closer, and Dani realized with a start that the two men were standing outside of the ramshackle house, in clear view. They hadn't noticed Dani and Da, but they would at any moment. The taller one, the one who had been speaking, left the shorter, fat man standing there and walked inside.

"Oh, shit!" shouted another younger man's voice inside, and an aborted scream from the woman as a shot rang out. A loud thump followed.

Dani had tried to be silent. But even she knew something bad had happened. A sharp gasp from her, and the fat man's eyes shifted, suddenly seeing the father and daughter there, and he jumped a little in surprise.

Da said nothing. Nothing at all. As he grabbed Dani's hand in a brutal grip and began to run through the tall, dead prairie grass. Dani could feel her feet flying, the grass whipping against her, feet not even touching the hard, cold ground. If she could have looked behind her, she would have seen the fat man turn back to the house, wave at his partner to come back out, and the man give chase. Instead, she simply held onto Da's coat as they flew, everything a blur of browns and yellows and golds mixed with snow and eventually ice-cold water as they entered the stream and then the trees and did not stop. It felt like an eternity. Eventually, Dani could hear Da's breaths coming in rasps, huge heaving gasps of air as he continued to run. The trees that had closed around them had twisted and turned with the stream, lining it, providing cover, but also a challenge of twists and turns. They rose and lowered on each side of the stream, the terrain far from even. The man shouted at them to stop, but Da didn't listen. He kept running, and with him, Dani simply held on. She felt like she was flying. It might have even been enjoyable in any other circumstances, but this, this was all too fast and scary.

"Someday, Sugar Plum, I'm gonna take you on a roller coaster." Da had told her. "They're all closed right now, but soon, soon the world will turn right again and I'll take you on a roller coaster and you'll scream and be scared and love it all at the same time."

Da had traveled all over the world. He'd been born in a place really far away called Ireland. "Across the pond," he'd said, but a bigger one than they had near the farm. A super-big one that was deeper than anything she had ever seen. Da had told her about coming to the United States, traveling all over, and that his car had broken down in a tiny town in New Mexico and, "I fell in love with your Mama, Sugar Plum, and suddenly traveling the world didn't seem half as important as staying right here and being with her."

Da's red hair and bright green eyes were an oddity there in their small hometown. But his voice, it was his voice that always drew the stares. Dani loved it more than anything.

As he ran, slower now, his breaths coming ragged and harsh, the trees thinned out onto a large open patch. Nearby was the continuing line of forest and trees. It had diverged from the stream, charting its own path.

In the far distance, she could see the tops of what looked like houses. A town, possibly. It was then that the shot rang out and Da jerked and fell into the stream. They had come so far. Dani couldn't even see the ramshackle house or even the men that had been chasing her, but Da lay in the water and Dani, flung in a sprawling heap at the side of the stream, stared at Da, waiting for him to get up. Her backpack had ripped as they fell and it cushioned her fall, only a small tear in the knee of her jeans and a pinprick of pain to show for such a heavy, abrupt fall.

Looking at him, he didn't seem hurt. There was a tiny rip or hole in the back of his jacket, but nothing else. She pulled on his arm and he moaned. That was when she saw the water moving away, sluggishly, and colored a dark crimson red.

Dani couldn't make words come out of her mouth. A whine of fear escaped, similar to the one that had caught the fat man's attention back at the clearing, but nothing else.

Da shifted, groaned, and blinked. His mouth was bloody. Dani could see it now that he lifted his head, barely moving, just lying there in the icy water. His lips moved, and she knelt down in the stream, ignoring the ice-cold water, trying to hear what he was saying. It wasn't louder than a whisper.

Closer. Closer.

"Run, Dani. Run away." The words were Da's, but they were so quiet, so low, it felt like a nightmare where nothing sounds or works right. Dani shook with fear, her teeth chattering with her feet and knees soaked in the ice-cold shallow water. Da raised his head again and choked, blood speckling the smooth rock in the stream next to his head. "GO!"

And somehow, she had. She picked herself up, focused on the nearby forest, and ran. As she did, she could hear men's voices. Mainly they shouted at each other, but once or twice they shouted at her to stop. She didn't listen. Da had told her to run and run she would. As she entered the trees, a second shot rang out. Dani didn't stop, however, she just kept on running until she tripped, her small body catapulting over a half-buried tree branch and then sliding to a stop in a culvert filled with brush and leaves.

It hurt. Vegetation scraped her face and hands, and she winced as she tried to tuck the injured hands into her pockets. The culvert that she had landed in was rather deep on the side she had fallen in on. To one side was an enormous dead tree protruding on the edge of rocks and a dark crevice of dirt and leaves provided a nest of sorts. She crept into it, pulling the leaves up and around her like Da had taught her the other day.

"Sugar Plum, if you ever get too cold out here and for some reason you are all on your own, just make a little hole and pull the leaves and dry vegetation up all around you. It'll help warm you."

She could hear his voice in her head, warm and rich. A tear slipped down her cheek, then another, and another. It mingled with the dirt, fat drips falling muddy onto her hands. The men were coming. She could hear them now.

"A little kid, by the looks of it. She can't have gone far." The older man's voice rang out, dangerously close, and Dani tried to hold her breath. She flattened against the earth and rocks, her body disappearing from view, the leaves thick and comforting, a great thick blanket of them. She tried to hold still though, for fear that the very things keeping her safe and helping to warm her would be the same things that gave her away. She listened as the man's footsteps came closer.

A younger man's voice, his breathing labored, spoke up, "She's just a little kid. What's she gonna do, really, Chief?"

"She could point. Tell someone we shot her daddy." The older man, Chief, responded.

Another body came in, his breath rattling as he wheezed to a stop. "Christ, Wingo, why the hell did you do that? You shot that man. There's no covering that shit up. Cici, back at the farm, that was justified, but I could have talked to the guy, sent him and the kid on their way or something."

Dani couldn't be sure, but she thought it might be the fat man that had been back at the ramshackle house that was talking, well, wheezing. Three men. The older one that had been outside with the fat man and was called Chief or Wingo, and the young man, who had been inside the house.

She wanted to make herself smaller, but she was afraid the leaves would make noise and give her away. They were close, so close.

"Any sign of her?" Was all that the older man said in response, ignoring the other two.

"Not that I've seen."

"How old d'ya think she is?" Wingo asked.

"I couldn't tell you," The fat man responded, still wheezing, "Small, maybe two or three years old?"

"Old enough to talk then."

In the trees above, a soft pattering began and, as Dani watched, ice particles began to fall, landing with ever-increasing rapidity on the fallen leaves all around them.

"The storm's rolling in," Wingo said, his voice further away, back the way they all had come, "A kid that small will be dead by morning from exposure. End of problem." Dani could hear him walking away, twigs snapping and the leaves crunching as he left. "I'll take care of the mess back at the house."

"What about the guy in the creek?" the younger man called after him, still standing close to Dani's hiding spot.

"Fuck him. He's no local. Folks won't give a damn about someone who got shot after he was creeping around fixing to rob them." Wingo's words hung in the air, and then there was silence.

"Damn, but this all went to shit." The younger man whistled slowly.

"You think?" The fat man spoke, his breathing mostly back to normal now, and he sounded angry. "You made a mess out of it. I should have never agreed to this human trafficking bullshit, not with you making a hot mess of it from the get go. And shooting that man, hell, Wingo's damn near lost his mind."

A branch snapped above Dani's head. "He's right about the kid, though. She's likely to die of exposure out here, so I'm thinking we might as well be on our way. I've had enough nasty business in the past hour to last a lifetime."

Dani could hear him slowly walking away, his departure noisy, his feet heavy on the forest floor.

"You coming? We need to get that nose of yours looked at."

"Yes, sir." The crunch of leaves signaled his departure as well.

Dani listened as the men left. Part of her was sure that they would be waiting, like the bogeyman from a nightmare, just out of range of hearing, waiting to grab her and hurt her like the Chief Wingo man had wanted them to do. She took a chance, adjusted herself deeper into the drift of leaves, and closed her eyes. Just as quickly, she opened them, looking at the empty woods. Around her, the storm began to pelt the forest with sleet. She would have to leave soon, likely go back to the stream where Da was.

Da. I need Da.

The leaves were warm, however, warmer than she had felt in a long time. Dani's eyes slid shut, and she sunk into a fragmented, restless doze.

When Dani's eyes opened, the small amount of weak sunlight that had greeted her that morning on the road with Da was gone, replaced with gray. Sleet now fell solidly, a relatively loud, continuous sound. For a moment, Dani didn't remember where she was. The momentary confusion that had her back in New Mexico, staring at the alien forest around her. And then it all surfaced at once, the argument in the ramshackle house, the gunshot, their panicked run and Da falling in the streambed.

Her mouth formed his name, but her lips failed to speak it aloud. The leaves that covered her exploded out as she scrambled out of her hiding place, intent on getting back to the stream, back to Da. Her feet scrabbled up the embankment, up out of the culvert, slipping and sliding on the newly wet and slippery leaves.

It was cold, ice cold now, but she didn't notice. All of her focus was on returning to Da, to the streambed, to the only source of safety and comfort she had left since Mama had died and Auntie Tia too. She slipped and fell twice before emerging from the cover of the trees. As she ran out into the open, she could see his form, dark and alone, still sprawled in the streambed. Some part of her gabbled in fear at the thought of the men that had chased her and Da, could they still be here? But she kept focus on reaching Da. That was all that mattered.

Her chest was heaving, her breaths sharp and ragged in the bitter cold, as she slid to a stop next to him.

She had seen Mama, right after, before they had sealed her in the box and lowered her in the ground. Da, he looked like that, only covered in blood and his eyes open, not closed like Mama's had been. Still, she couldn't help but cling to him.

She thought of a rhyme Mama would say at night, while they sat on the porch and looked up at the dark, night sky and the panorama of stars.

Mama had smiled and whispered, "Star Light, Star Bright, first star I see tonight. I wish I may, I wish I might, have this wish I wish tonight."

But there were no stars out. It was still day, although it was dark and gray and the sleet kept falling, a steady patter as it covered the browns and golds of the dead vegetation. And there were no wishes that could bring back the dead.

How long she stayed there, Dani could not have known. Long enough that she felt cold all the way into her middle, and her fingers and toes were stiff, cold and aching. Tears she hadn't realized she had shed, coated her cheeks, mingling with the pellets of ice. Dani was alone. Worse, she had no one left to run to. Her stomach rumbled, but she had no way of accessing the last of their food, Da's backpack was wedged underneath his body and there was no moving it, nor accessing the zipper. And even as her stomach rumbled, Dani felt too scared to do much about it.

In the end, she had kissed Da on his cheek and stumbled away. Not back to the forest, but slowly, in the growing gloom, towards the buildings she saw in the far distance. Her feet and legs automatically moving, one step, then another. Away from Da, toward the unknown. By the time she reached the first of the homes, her coat was coated with ice. Her limbs felt stiff, unwieldy, and she kept falling.

The first house was a burned-out ruin. So was the second, and the third, and after the fourth one she lost count. It seemed that most were burned, but others were simply dark, empty things. Their doors gone, their contents removed, whoever had lived and loved and laughed inside of them long gone. She wandered up and down the streets, past burned hulks of cars, and skirted the edges of roads.

The house wasn't big, or even much different from the others she had seen walking in, but Dani was drawn to it. It had signs of occupancy. The large yard in front had been cultivated. Not now, of course, but Dani could see the remnants of orderly rows that had once held plants. The rest of the houses on the block were either in ruins or obviously empty, but this house, someone lived here. The smoke curled from the chimney and one of the windows allowed for a small glow from the fireplace within.

By now, the darkness of night was complete and Dani was afraid. What if the bad men were here? What if they wanted to hurt her? She was tired, though. So tired. And the front stoop she found herself standing in was well-protected from the wind. The snow, piled high just a few feet away, actually seemed to insulate the entryway and Dani slid down in place against the front door, seeking warmth, but also trying to marshal her reserves. Every part of her ached with exhaustion, grief, and her eyelids felt like heavy doors that would not stay open. Outside in the open, the wind howled its own grief, and she cried with it, the tears leaking down her cheeks in the darkness. Somehow, despite the cold and the hunger and her grief, Dani slid into a restless sleep.

The day dawned bright and light. The storm had moved on, the clouds pushed away in the wind the night before, and the sky was clear and blue.

A boy had appeared at the door. The inside door, that is, whereas Dani was against the outside door, huddled in tight. He had talked to her, but Dani had been so tired, so cold and scared by then, that she had no words for him. No words at all to encompass this yawning chasm of loss. It had hit her then, that Da was gone, and Mama was gone and everyone she knew and loved, who knew and loved her back, were gone. She had ignored the boy. Turned away and cried. Perhaps she should have stayed with Da, back at the stream. Just as she was considering going back there, if she could even find it, a woman appeared at the front of the house.

She was pretty. Her long blond hair hung out over her coat and she had the prettiest blue eyes that Dani had ever seen. She didn't say a word, just reached down and picked Dani up, her arms warm and strong. The outer door swung open then, the boy inside wasn't the only one there, and Dani ducked her head against the woman, tucking in close, suddenly terrified by all the strange faces.

There was a tall boy, almost a man, and the boy she had already seen, and even a girl not much older than Dani. They stared at her curiously and Dani, suddenly surrounded by warmth, began to shiver uncontrollably. The tears started up again as well.

The next few hours were a blur of being bathed, new clothes, and a hot meal. No matter where she went in the house, Dani saw no evidence of the bad men. The voices weren't the same, and these people were kind. Still, Dani could not seem to make her lips work. No words escaped. She didn't have anything to say, nothing that could compare to the howling loss she felt. The little girl pressed a doll into her arms and Dani thought of her bear, her lovey as Mama had called it, still stuffed in her backpack which lay abandoned by the stream. The food in her belly was more than she had eaten in a long time. She sat there, propped up in the chair, two books wedged under her to raise her to the height of the kitchen table and, despite the staring eyes, found her eyes slipping closed.

She barely noticed when warm, strong arms picked her up, carried her into a room, and tucked her in.

"It's okay, Sweetheart, you're safe now." The man's voice was kind, reassuring.

As she slid deeper into sleep, Dani let go of her fear. The bad men weren't here, and instead, this family was kind. She missed Da, just as much as she missed Mama and her aunties and Grandma. Here she was safe. And she liked her new name. The woman had called her Erin. Da had a sister named Erin, back in Ireland. Maybe someday she would tell her new family about Da and Mama, the aunties and Grandma. Perhaps she would tell them about the farm that her great-uncle Jaime had in Alaska, or what she and Da had seen and heard outside of town. But for now, she didn't need to talk, and she really didn't particularly want to. She just wanted to sleep in a warm place, eat good food, and not be afraid anymore.

And as the winter snows fell, melted, and gave way to the sunny days of spring, Dani became Erin, a quiet, peaceful child who said nothing aloud but made herself perfectly understood, nonetheless.

Johnathan

At a ramshackle house north of town, Farley met with Wingo. They hadn't had any contact in months, not after Farley had decided that the trade in flesh was simply too dangerous as the Reformation began to solidify. The world was going back to what it had been, or at the very least, it was returning to a shadow of its former self.

Alaska and Hawaii had declared their independence. So had Texas, California, Oregon and Washington. The states that remained, however, were quickly rebuilding and the new capital of the country would be located in North Carolina.

Wingo leaned back in his chair, poking at the charred remains of a fire in the fireplace. "I hear they found the body."

Farley nodded, "Yes, Thurman Banks found it last week."

Wingo said nothing for a moment, then turned to stare at Farley. His direct gaze, unblinking, made Jonathan Farley more nervous than he had been when word came through the town of the little girl's discovery a few days after the incident. He broke eye contact, stared out the grimy window with its broken panes. Somewhere out there Wingo had buried the body of Cici Baker. Why he hadn't felt it necessary to bury the traveler, Farley had not a whit of an idea, especially now that Wingo had called this meeting.

"And the child survived."

He forced himself to turn back to Wingo, "She's a mute. Hasn't said a word since she showed up on their front stoop right after that storm."

"Mute, huh?"

"I sent one of the men over to check it out after I heard she'd shown up."

"Not you?" Wingo's eyebrows raised, "Or young James?"

Farley felt a flash of discomfort. He had thought about it, sure. But she'd seen him. What if she remembered something, freaked out, or reacted in a way that caused questions?

Kid that young, she'll forget given enough time. She won't remember what it was like anywhere else in a year or two. And Jess and her family are rarely in town with all the kids.

He kept his face as serene as he could manage, "Didn't have time to. There were other things to attend to at the time. Didn't see a reason to follow up once I heard she was mute."

Wingo stared at him silently.

"Look, the kid is no danger to us. Jess Aaronson says she's young, barely three years old. Kids don't remember stuff that happens when they are that young. If you had kids, you'd know that."

"I have kids. Grown now, but I'm aware. Still, something traumatic like that, seeing her daddy killed, that's gotta stick in there." Wingo said, leaning back even further in his chair.

Farley gazed at the chair. One of the legs was split, maybe it would break if Wingo leaned back far enough. It sure as hell would if he sat in it, but he was nearly three bills to Wingo's lean frame.

"Yeah, well, why don't you go and see her for yourself," Farley snapped, adopting a facade of false bravado. About the last thing in the world, he wanted to do was go anywhere near Jess Aaronson's place and risk getting fingered by the girl. But he also had no interest in having a little girl killed so he'd made his peace with it and figured it was worth the risk. As winter had slid into spring and there had been no rumors or accusations, he'd breathed easier. Trust Wingo to dig it all up.

"Maybe I will." Wingo responded, his tone cool, coated in steel.

"Well, you do that." Farley snapped, wishing, as he had done all the rest of the winter and spring, that he had never had anything to do with James Wingo in the first place. "If there isn't anything else, I'll be going. I've a town to run."

He turned and headed for the door, his heavy frame caused the old wood underneath to groan loudly, bowing beneath the weight. The damn place was falling apart. As his foot crossed the threshold down to the step below, he could hear Wingo speak. What he said was low, deliberate, and insidious.

"There will come a time of reckoning, Farley. It might be tomorrow, next month, or in five years. But these things have a price. Eventually the bill will come due."

Jonathan Farley said nothing in return as he walked away. He said nothing to his son, other than instructing him to stay away from Wingo, and he felt a wash of relief a few months later when Wingo was shot in some deal gone wrong.

A child that small? She won't remember. Who would expect her to? He thought to himself. Nevertheless, he gave Jess Aaronson's small family a wide berth in the months and years that followed.

Author's Note

Thank you for reading *War's End*. I hope you enjoyed it. If you have not read it yet, I highly recommend you check out the *Gliese 581g* series. There are a total of five books in the series, and it is set around fifty years after the last of the *War's End* stories. The books are as follows:

G581: The Departure

G581: Mars

G581: Earth

G581: Plague Tales

G581: Zarmina's World

Thanks again for reading *War's End*. Please leave a review so that others will be interested in taking a chance on this post-apocalyptic fiction!

Don't miss out!

Visit the website below and you can sign up to receive emails whenever Christine D. Shuck publishes a new book. There's no charge and no obligation.

https://books2read.com/r/B-A-BOLF-BQTTB

BOOKS 2 READ

Connecting independent readers to independent writers.

Also by Christine D. Shuck

Benton Security Services
Hired Gun
Smoke and Steel
Broken Code
Benton Security Services Omnibus #1 - Books 1-3

Chronicles of Liv Rowan
Fate's Highway

Gliese 581g
G581: The Departure
G581: Mars
G581: Earth
G581 Plague Tales
G581: Zarmina's World

War's End
War's End: The Storm
War's End: A Brave New World
Tales of the Collapse
War's End Omnibus - Books 1-3

Standalone

The War on Drugs: An Old Wives Tale

Get Organized, Stay Organized

Winter's Child

Short-Term Rental Success

Watch for more at christineshuck.com.

About the Author

Fueled by homemade coffee ice cream, a lifelong love of words, and armed with strong female (and male) characters I cross genres like the Ghostbusters crossed the streams in pursuit of the question.

"What is the question?" you ask.

The question is simple. It asks, "What would you do, if..."

What would you do if you were fifteen years old and the world as you knew it fell apart? Would you run? Would you fight? Would you survive? – Meet Jess and her brother Chris in the *War's End* series.

What would you do if you had a chance to live your life over? Not just once, but twice? – Meet Dean Edmonds in *Fate's Highway*

What would you do if everyone you loved was lost to a terrible virus and you faced the real possibility of the extinction of the human race in the dark void of space? – Meet Daniel Medry in *G581: The Departure*

What would you do if hitmen were after you and you had no idea why? – Meet Lila and Shane in *Hired Gun*

If I don't keep you turning pages late into the night, desperate to know what happens next, then I have failed at my job. I'm a Taurus and born in Missouri. That makes me bull-headed and stubborn to boot.

I don't believe in failure or mistakes, only learning opportunities and clever conversation. There's not much I won't do to make you burn the midnight oil reading my words while you suffer sleep-deprivation the following day. It's my secret superpower.

Born in flyover country, I've also lived in Arizona and northern California. I am an eclectic mix of snark and oddball humor. My colorful metaphors would make a fishwife blush. I'm an incompetent gardener, a dreamer and doer, in love with old houses and shooting pool, and chief organizer of all thing's household and financial. Feed me tiramisu and I'm yours forever.

Find me on all major platforms by visiting Linktree: https://linktr.ee/christinedshuck

Read more at christineshuck.com.

www.ingramcontent.com/pod-product-compliance
Lightning Source LLC
Chambersburg PA
CBHW030346310726
48979CB00001B/207

* 9 7 8 1 9 5 5 1 5 0 5 3 8 *